# "The Adventures of Mr Hawkins"
# The Golden Secret

# "The Adventures of Mr Hawkins"
## The Golden Secret

20. 3. 14

To Niki

Welcome to Crowthers Hill!

Very best wishes

*Simon Gilmore*

Simon Gilmore

© Simon Gilmore, 2013

Published by Windwhistle Publishing
www.windwhistlepublishing.co.uk

A CIP catalogue record for this book is available from the British Library.

ISBN 978-0-9576194-0-1

Book design by Clare Brayshaw

Cover design by Pascal M. Mindlin www.interlane.co.uk

Prepared and printed by:

York Publishing Services Ltd
64 Hallfield Road
Layerthorpe
York YO31 7ZQ

Tel: 01904 431213

Website: www.yps-publishing.co.uk

# Contents

# Note from the Author

This story is for people with young and adventurous minds, who love the spirit of adventure and who seek to explore the challenges and wonders of discovery.

Life is really – essentially – about one thing: experience.

The more we venture and seek to discover and the more we experience, the richer we become.

Here you will discover a world you never knew existed.

Nothing is ever as it seems.
I hope you enjoy this adventure.

**Simon Gilmore**

# Part 01

# Chapter 1 – The Beginning

The sun was warm on his face, but the south-west wind was blowing hard, slowing his pace as he ran up the high path and through the long grass into the steep sloping meadow that rolled down to the cliffs far below. It was a beautiful day.

When he reached the top of the path, he paused at the small wooden gate to catch his breath. Then he climbed up onto it and sat astride the top bar. He smelt the freshness of the air and the wild flowers growing all across the meadow. He jumped down from the gate and walked the short distance to the top of the hill. He stopped for a brief moment and smiled as he turned towards the steep downward slopes and saw the mass of gulls circling over the cliff edge. He listened to their loud chatter and high pitched screeches crying out in the distance. The wind carried their echoing voices way out across the bay, over the fields and below the cliffs.

Beyond the cliffs lay the English Channel. From where he stood, the sea was a calmy blue and looked inviting. He saw some sails far out in the distance and small fishing boats bobbing on the waves. Some were heading west for their night's work and others were moving back east and home towards Rivermouth, his home town.

The wind blew his long blond hair, curling it back behind his head. He held out his arms as if to gather in this glorious scene before him. He let the wind fill the sleeves of his shirt. His fingers pointed out and up towards the sky. His smile was wide and his heart beat fast with the feeling of freedom and excitement. The spirit inside wanted to be free and, despite the trouble he knew he would be in, this was his moment.

After a short while he lowered his arms and stepped forward. One first step down, then another and slowly he moved down the steep, sloping meadow towards the cliffs.

He began to walk and then his walk became a quick stride, which became a run and then, at a fast pace, he was charging down the hill. He gathered speed. His legs moved faster and faster and then they took over from under him. He could not help himself now and, as he ran, he began to chuckle. Then, breaking into laughter, he raced uncontrollably towards the cliffs. He laughed as the sea came closer and the size of the gulls grew bigger, the sounds of their shrieks becoming louder. He was moving so fast and now he could not stop. He closed in on the cliffs with every leap and bound. The edge was close, so close that he could smell the sea, two hundred feet below. His head whirled, his face was red with running and his heart beat fast with the thrill.

The edge was just a few paces away. Could he stop now? He had run the gauntlet before and never missed. Suddenly there was the edge and in an instant he threw himself to the right, his arms outstretched and legs wide apart. His chest hit the ground first, then his knees. His hands grabbed wildly at the long grass. He dug the toes of his shoes to act as brakes, deep into the ground, churning up the earth as he slid frantically towards the edge. *Anchors now!* he said to himself, as he dug in deep with his feet and hands feeling out for anything he could hold on to. His whole body ripped through the long, sharp blades of grass. The edge was too close. Was he going to make it this time? He continued to dig in hard using his whole body, pushing himself further into the ground to slow down. It was all a whirl and his chest ached. He felt his shirt rip from under him and the buttons tearing away as he tumbled. His knees were cracking as they thrashed into the hard red soil. He felt every rut and bump as stones rasped through the thin cloth of his trousers. He was too close.

Desperately he grabbed at the earth, his fingers and nails black and raw from the hard soil; but still he clung to anything he could until, at last, he began to slow. He saw a rock to his right and was just able to get a hold. For a second it held but then gave way and rolled over the cliff edge. It was just enough to slow him further still.

*One more big dig* he thought to himself and dug in again for a final attempt to stop. There was no more space; the edge was there, right in front of him. Suddenly his right shoulder smashed into a rock at the very edge and he stopped. He was exhausted and bruised.

Sweat rolled down his muddied face. His hands were raw and his chest felt like he had been kicked by a heavy horse. His knees hurt and he ached all over. His face was buried into the ground. He was still, but his heart beat fast. Then the heat came to his face as he lay panting. His body shook. *That was crazy* he thought, still trying to breathe properly.

After a while he lifted his head. Below him he saw the rocks and the mighty sea crashing into them. The sound from the waves bellowed up towards him as he peered over the grey cliff face. It was as if they were calling to him: *You were lucky this time.*

He was still panting and the sweat stuck to his face, but he began to laugh. *That was close* he said to himself. *Never got that close before.*

This was a game of "chicken" played by the boys in the town. It was a foolish way of proving your bravery and manliness. They all knew it was madness and dangerous, but for young bucks like Thomas Parker it was simply the thrill of the challenge as to who would dare to go nearest the edge. He had needed to go there today to prove to himself he could do it one more time. He had never been that close before.

His breathing began to ease and he regained his thoughts and composure. It was then that he felt the pain. His chest ached and his knees were throbbing. He looked back at his legs and saw that he had ripped his trousers below one knee and his leg was bleeding. "Ouch," he cried as he tried to lift himself up. His head was hanging over the cliff edge. One shoulder had struck a small rock and the pain went right through him. It was probably the rock which had prevented his certain death fall.

He bent his elbows outwards and pushed himself up onto his hands and was just able to turn himself over onto his back. He saw the seagulls circling above him. There were hundreds of them. To Tom it appeared as if they were laughing at him as if they were saying, *You fool Thomas Parker. When will you learn?* As he looked up, he saw the clouds drifting over him and they made him dizzy. He lay on his back watching them as his head swirled around and around.

There were so many gulls and the noise was deafening. He thought they were particularly restless and their flight was most exaggerated as they made short, sharp turns up and down the cliff face. He noticed one suddenly snap up in front of him and then disappear in an instant below the ridge. It went out of sight, then immediately it was back and bleating into his face. Its shrill cries grew louder and there was a strange sense of excitement in its behaviour.

He noticed the pitch and chatter and the cries from the birds had changed and the wind carried their shrieks away over him to the east and then to the west. Suddenly the sound took a different tone: it was one he did not recognise and, then again, it was familiar.

He sat up and looked around him. *What is it?* he asked himself. There it was again, to his right in the distance; no, now it was coming from somewhere else, or was it coming from the rocks below? He tilted his head to try to hear more clearly, but the wind was blowing the sound away and then back again.

One gull came so close it touched his back and then bounced away; its claws had snagged his shirt. "Hey you gull, watch it!" he shouted. The gull just shrieked back and flew frantically away down the cliffs and out of sight.

He heard the sound again. It sounded like a long scream. This was not the noise that gulls make. It seemed to be coming from the west cliff. He pulled himself up onto his feet. Although he was in pain, he was now more interested in this strange sound that had distracted him. As he stood, he heard it again. It was a high pitched cry that seemed far away in the distance. This was not a bird, it was a human.

Someone was down the cliffs. He tried to run along the cliff's edge but it was not easy, his legs and chest ached terribly. He limped on and heard it again. Now it was much nearer. He ran on. Somebody was in trouble.

After a few yards he stopped and peered carefully over the edge. He had never seen so many gulls swarming in such a mass. Something was agitating them.

Something was terribly wrong.

He frowned as his view was hampered by the mass of birds. He could see little else than flapping white wings and yellow beaks. There were so many of them.

He ran slowly forward and with every twenty paces he paused to look over the edge. The cries were closer and clearer. Someone was shouting: "Help!"

Suddenly there was a short moment when the mass of birds broke away over a small ledge on the cliff face about thirty feet down. Then he saw it. Someone was lying face down on a narrow ledge. He ran as fast as he could and came to a crevice where the ground had fallen away into the larger rocks below. The earth was loose and crumbling. Lying on the ground was someone's jacket. A long wooden pole was lying beside it. The pole had a net fixed to one end.

Carefully he crawled to the edge but his footing gave way and he slipped. He scrambled to find something to hold on to and, just in time, caught hold of a root protruding from under a rock, which brought him to a halt. He would have fallen to almost certain death and went pale at the thought of what might have happened. He must be more careful.

"Who's there?" he called down. A cry came back, "Help me. Help!"

Tom was uncertain what to do; he could not get closer without falling himself. He saw a small rock and managed to get hold of it with one hand and, by grabbing the pole with the other hand he could support his weight to prevent him from sliding further. Now he could see over the edge. The gulls were everywhere, swooping over the body on the cliff. Some came so close they tore at his shirt and then quickly swooped away out of reach. The gulls were attacking the body below. It was a small boy. He was lying face down but trying to fight off the attacking birds with one arm. He was pinned down and crying. His left leg was buckled under him but had also twisted outwards. Tom thought the leg would likely be broken.

"Hey, can you hear me?" Tom called down.

"Help me; they're hurting me," came the reply. The voice was familiar to Tom but he was unsure. "I don't know how to get you, I need a rope and some help." Tom called. "It's too steep."

He looked back over his shoulder to see if anyone was around. His shoulder was aching badly from his earlier antics and he now regretted playing the gauntlet game. Nobody was in sight and he turned back to see seagulls everywhere, darting, striking and shrieking loudly at him. Some again came too close and they scraped his hair with their claws. "Ouch, back off!" Tom shouted and waved his arm at them.

When he looked back down he noticed a bag lying beside the boy on the ledge. The bag had gulls' eggs in it. *The fool was stealing their eggs* Tom thought, and knew now why the birds were so distressed. Just then he noticed a rope. Half of it was trapped under the boy and the remaining part was hanging down over the cliff and waving around in the wind.

"Hey, can you hear me?" Tom called again through the din of the gulls.

"Yes," came a weak reply.

"Can you get the rope?"

"No, I can't move." The boy began to cry again. Tom recognised the voice at last. It was Daniel Corby.

"Danny, its Tom, stop crying and try to help. I need that rope," shouted Tom.

The small boy tried to turn over and lifted himself up a few inches but he was lying on the broken leg. The pain hurt so much, he screamed and the yell cut right through the shriek of the gulls. Then he went still.

"Danny," Tom called in despair. There was no answer.

*What was he doing stealing those eggs?* Tom wondered. He knew Daniel Corby well. This was not the sort of thing he would do. Daniel would never do anything as dangerous as this. Not on his own. Tom had often been to his rescue when the bigger boys had bullied him. Tom was normal in height for his age, but with a strong frame. Little Danny, as he was known, was smaller in every way and was often fair game for the bullies at school and in the town. His pretty, almost feminine looks were a constant problem to him. He was considered a sissy although he was as normal as any other boy. His small figure made him an easy target for others. He had often relied on Tom for support. This time, Tom thought, they had gone too far.

"Danny, get the rope before it slips off," Tom called down, but there was no reply. Little Daniel had passed out with the pain and now the gulls were darting around him and shrieking angrily at the little body lying still on the ledge below.

Tom was frantically trying to see a way down. He crawled back up to the top to see if anyone was near, but there was nobody in sight.

He felt helpless; he wanted to help his little friend but could do nothing. He thought hard. All he needed was a rope. There was a large boulder behind him a short way back from the cliff top. He could tie a rope round it and then lower himself down to get the other end round Daniel. He knew, though, that it was going to be impossible on his own and then frustration began to get a hold of him.

He started to get cross and paced up and down. Then he began to shake with rage. He had never felt this way, so helpless and angry.

Then, instinctively, he held out his arms. His fists were clenched tight. He had no idea why he did this. It was as if he were being been taken over by some force, a strange power from within. His eyes went wide and wild. He opened his mouth and screamed: "Lord help me! I don't know what to do. If you hear me, help me now!"

Still holding out his arms with fists clenched tight he looked up to the swirling skies.

Suddenly a shadow came over him. Everything went dark. For a second it was as if he were blinded and then the swarming gulls disappeared. Everything went quiet. There was not a sound, save the wind, which was now a gentle breeze. Then he heard another sound, a heavy thud from down below the cliffs, but he could not see clearly from where he was standing. He lowered his arms and moved carefully to the edge, holding onto the small rock in front of him and peered over. It was an uneasy feeling. There was a flapping sound from lower down and then, suddenly, he could not believe what he was seeing. His eyes and mouth were wide open. What was this? Hovering over the small boy, who had remained still, was the most enormous seagull. It had wings bigger than he had ever seen. Its whole body was bigger than any other. Then, as he dared to look again, he saw that the gull had picked up one end of the rope in its beak and was bringing it up to him. With its large powerful wings outstretched, it lifted itself up onto the cliff top. Tom immediately fell backwards. He wanted to run but he couldn't. It was as if his feet were glued to the ground. He tripped over onto his hands and knees and tried to scramble away as the gull, with its wings still spread, holding itself against the breeze and with the rope still in its beak, stepped forward towards him. Tom was shaking with fear. He had never seen such an unbelievable thing. Could this be a dream? Where did it come from?

The sea below splashed against the rocks and the breeze blew gently but all else was still. There were no more seagulls around, save this one large bird standing before him. Its bright yellow eyes were wide and staring at him. Its head did not move. The feathers rippled through the tips of its wings, which were still stretched out as it came nearer to him.

Tom froze, transfixed as if he were cast in stone. The bird came closer, then it stepped passed him and walked towards the large rock behind Tom. It turned to look at him, then lowered its wings and dropped the rope beside the rock. Tom was in awe of this wondrous sight. Where did this bird come from?

As the seagull stood watching Tom, the rope began to move on its own and slid back to the cliff's edge. Tom quickly got up and ran back to the edge. Perhaps Daniel had come round and was pulling the rope to climb up. When he saw over the edge that the boy was still lying on the ridge, he looked back and grabbed the rope before it slipped over the top.

Holding the rope firmly in both hands he turned again to look back, but the bird had disappeared. It was the most peculiar thing he had ever seen. Had he really seen this? Was that really a seagull and did it actually bring him the rope?

He looked all around but there was no sign of the seagull. He quickly ran back to the large rock and tied the rope around it. His father had shown him how to tie good knots like the bowline, the strongest sailors' knot and the safest. He tugged at it to make sure it was firm and then walked back to the cliff edge, both hands firmly gripping the rope. He made a turn with the rope round his waist. He paused again to look for the seagull. It had gone. How could he ever explain this to anyone, nobody would ever believe him. Where had it gone so suddenly?

Then he brought his mind back to the matter of saving little Danny.

He knew that he would be capable of swinging down on the rope to get to his little friend. A few gulls were circling around him above but none was as big as the one he had just seen. Although he was still pondering on his odd predicament, he knew he must continue with the rescue.

He leaned out with his back to the sea and began his descent. He pushed himself out away from the cliff so as not to trample on any seagulls' nests that would be lodged into the rocks.

Eventually he landed on the ledge where Daniel was laying very still. "Danny, wake up," he called and tried to shake the boy. There was no movement. Tom tried to turn him over but it was difficult and he was worried about losing his footing.

After a short struggle he managed to put three turns of the rope around Daniel and tied a secure knot. This would stop him from slipping out of the rope when he pulled him up. Then he felt Danny's pulse and was relieved that there was still life in him. "I'll get you up now Danny, don't you worry." He knew Daniel was still unconscious which was just as well in one way, but really he could do with his help.

Just before he started to climb back up, he noticed the eggs in the bag and then saw some empty nests, which had been set into the cliff face by the seagulls.

Tom had often been unpopular for not agreeing that gulls should be culled and did not like the way the boys had made a sport of killing them. Some of the fishermen had encouraged the boys to cull the gulls as they were seen as a threat to fishing and the environment and some people wanted to keep their numbers from growing too fast. Tom believed that there was enough in this world for both man and beast and the sea belonged to the seagulls as much as it did to humans. He put the eggs back into the empty nests and hoped he had done the right thing. He managed to climb back up the cliff. When he reached the top he flopped down to catch his breath. He was tired and ached all over.

As soon as he had regained enough strength he began to try to pull Daniel up. Although Danny was a lightweight he felt like a lead weight and Tom was straining. Every muscle in his body ached as he heaved hard on the rope. But he could not move him and was now worried that he would cause some harm to Daniel if he slipped or if he were to be scraped across the sharp rock face.

As he sat trying to work out a better way, he heard a noise and looked around to see what it was. The sound came from behind and when he listened again, he heard someone shout. Then there were other voices. Tom had dug his heels into the ground and had a firm grip on the rope but turned his head to see where the sound was coming from. He saw that up on the high sloping hill some people were moving quickly in his direction. There were several of them now, running down the slopes of the meadow. As they came closer, he realised they were boys from Rivermouth. They were carrying culling poles like the one that lay near the crevice where Daniel had fallen. The poles had nets attached at the end to catch the young seagulls and the eggs from their nests. Two of the boys carried a large rope between them.

"Hey," one of them called down as they ran closer. Tom instantly recognised the tallest boy; it was Johnny Benson. Tom disliked Benson: they were enemies. The five boys came up short when they saw Tom. They were panting and had a wild look of excitement upon their faces. "Hey, Parker, what you doin' 'ere?" called Johnny.

"Where's Danny Corby?" they asked.

"He's down the cliff, over the edge. He's fallen and I'm trying to get him up. He's broken a leg but I think he's alive," replied Tom still hanging onto the rope. "Don't just stand there, help me," Tom shouted.

Two of the boys ran to the edge to see. "Oh my God, he's right down there. Looks like he's stuck," exclaimed one of them.

"What were you all up to, Benson?" Tom asked, knowing full well what they had with them.

Until now Johnny Benson had looked sharply at Tom and was full of his usual brashness, but now he was quiet and grabbed the rope, trying to pull it with Tom.

"You were trying to kill the gulls, weren't you Benson?" Tom spat the words at Johnny. He detested their killing game. Johnny ignored the remark and was still trying to heave on the rope.

"It's likely as stuck, give us a hand, you two," Johnny shouted at the others.

Tom told one of the boys to use the pole as a lever to free the rope from catching in the cracks on the rocks. "When he comes up, push him out with that pole to keep him away from the rock," ordered Tom. But the boy was scared of getting too close and did not have the strength to push the rope out with his pole.

"I can't, it's not easy," called back Billy Prior. Billy was Benson's shadow and did anything Johnny told him. Tom disliked him too. He was a coward and a creep. "Get back 'ere, Billy, I'll take your end. You lot help pull him up," said Johnny with his orders to his gang of followers. They all obeyed.

All the boys heaved together. "He's coming up!" shouted Johnny and they made another huge effort to heave on the rope. Johnny had relief in his eyes but it was apparent to Tom that he was nervous of what the repercussions might be.

Tom and Johnny Benson were of even height but Johnny was a few pounds heavier. The two of them had often scrapped over disagreements at school and when they had fought, Benson had often won because he had cheated by calling on his other bully followers to hinder his opponent by tripping Tom up or pushing him over in the fighting circle. Johnny knew, however, that one day Tom would catch him alone and then it would be different. Tom waited for the day he could get even. Johnny would then have to face the truth. Who was the stronger?

They all pulled again, groaning with the strain. Suddenly Daniel's head appeared, then his chest – and finally he was up and over the edge.

"Keep his leg away from the rock, and mind his head, Billy you fool," shouted Tom. "Mind your business, Parker, and we'll mind ours," Johnny hissed back arrogantly and with one last tug Daniel was up on the grass slope, lying still on his back.

Tom quickly ran to Daniel, then Johnny, followed by his fat friend Billy. The others stood back, uneasy at what they had done and what may have happened to little Danny. The small boy was still motionless and looked like a baby asleep.

Tom moved his ear up to Daniel's mouth and then his nose to listen for breathing.

"Well, is he breathing?" asked Johnny Benson nervously.

There was a pause for a moment and then Tom looked up, but not at Benson. Then feeling Daniel's broken leg, he said: "Lucky for you Benson, he's alive."

"What d'you mean, it weren't my fault, I wasn't 'ere, was I?" Benson replied angrily.

"How did it happen then? Oh yes, let me see, you made him go down to do your dirty work and steal the eggs, didn't you? Then he fell, 'cos he's not strong enough to hold on and you ran off and left him – didn't you? That's what happened isn't it?" Tom was angry and his eyes glared into Johnny's. Tom hated bullies, especially Benson and his cowardly friends. When he looked at the others, they turned away sheepishly.

"None of you have the guts to do your own dirty work, so you used Danny didn't you?" Tom was about to continue his accusation when Johnny sprang to his feet and, with one leg, kicked Tom full in the side. Tom had been kneeling over Daniel and as the kick hit him, he reeled over, losing his balance. But he broke his fall by putting out a hand to stop himself crushing little Danny. Tom was now astride Daniel balancing on one hand.

"Who d'you think you are, Nosey Parker, and what were you doing up 'ere then, eh?" jeered back Benson. "I bet you wanted them eggs for yerself," he continued and turned to look to his friends for their approval. He stood with his hands on his hips grinning down at Tom. The others all laughed and jeered at Tom, gloating at Johnny's victory.

Tom was furious and needed to do something fast. His temper would not hold; he was going to boil. Then he saw one of the poles with the attached net lying next to Daniel.

The poles were six feet long. That was length enough to snatch the eggs from the high nests on the rocks and swipe at young baby gulls that were still weak on their wings. Johnny, Tom quickly calculated, was about the same distance away as the length of the pole. He planned his move quickly and then, with the speed of lightning, Tom skipped across Daniel and, in one complete movement, picked up the pole and swung it round at Johnny so fast that there was not time for him to duck. Tom thrust the net over Johnny's head and twisted it round his face. The others stopped their jeering instantly and went to make a move towards Tom.

"Don't even think about it," Tom snarled back at them "or I'll break his neck." He pulled the pole downwards still twisting the net. Johnny could only try to grip the rim of the net with both hands as it was now tight around him and, as Tom pulled down harder still, Johnny fell to his knees. Tom stood over him. "Stop it – you're strangling me," Johnny cried.

"Now you know how those gulls feel, Benson. You are a coward." Tom was enjoying his moment but he knew it could not last. They heard a groaning noise from the ground. Daniel was coming round and was in severe pain and Tom knew they would have to get him home. He needed treatment quickly.

"Leave Johnny alone, Parker," Billy called. He was looking for a way to show his support to Johnny. Up until now he had kept his distance. Now he could do something without getting into trouble with Tom but at the same time win favour from Johnny. He knew too that Daniel needed attention and their squabble must stop.

"All right, Benson, you've had your lesson. We've got to get Danny home." Still twisting the net around Johnny's head to keep him down, he turned to the others "You lot, use the rope and the poles to make a stretcher, twist the rope, like a weave, round the poles" Tom ordered. They were amazed at Tom's directness and, although they would not admit it, had to agree that he was quick thinking. Tom had learnt at an early age from his father, an experienced sailor, how to use ropes to their best effect.

They immediately began to construct a stretcher.

Tom looked to Benson who was moaning on the ground with his hands still gripping the net wrapped around his neck. "I'm going to let you loose, Benson, but I want you to promise you'll not come up here again, got it?"

Benson hated to be at a disadvantage but needed to concede quickly and get free. "Only if you don't say nothin' to no-one about this and – I'll agree," he conceded.

"Promise, Benson, promise!" Tom held fast.

"All right, all right, let go now." Johnny was aching to get free.

"Say it," demanded Tom. "Say it."

"I promise," he mumbled.

"Louder!"

"Promise." Johnny Benson's agreement finally came for all to hear.

"Right then." Tom untwisted the net and lifted it from Johnny's head. He quickly stood back and waited for the retaliation from Benson or one of the others.

Benson immediately jumped up and made a move towards Tom but Tom had the pole in both hands holding it over his shoulder ready to strike. He was ready for any of them.

"You promised Benson; you help them get Danny home. Remember, I make no promises to you, except if you make another move I'll break your neck for good and tell everyone in Rivermouth what you did to Danny."

In any other situation, Johnny would have gone for Tom regardless but he knew this time Tom had him beaten fair and square and he went to help the others who were moving quickly to build the stretcher. They had made a reasonable rig and when it was completed they helped Daniel onto it. Daniel had come around and was starting to cry from the pain.

The boys were anxious to get away.

Finally they had Daniel on the stretcher on his back and, between them, lifted it up and began to walk up the steep hill. Johnny followed at the rear. None of them turned to look back. Tom called to Daniel: "Don't worry Danny, you'll be all right."

He stood there for a while and watched them climb up the hill. Johnny Benson had not bothered to look back; instead he was planning how he would report the incident and how he could win favour for returning Daniel safe after his accident. He also began to fuel his hatred for Tom and planned how he could get back at him for this humiliation.

Tom thought about the giant seagull and wondered if any of the other boys had considered how he had managed to retrieve the rope from the cliff. Surely they must have thought about it?

He walked to the edge of the cliffs and threw the remaining pole over the top and watched it fall the two hundred feet into the sea and rocks below. *They won't need that again* he said to himself with some satisfaction.

He stood alone for a short while and watched a few gulls soaring high up in the sky and then gracefully sweeping down to the sea below the foot of the cliffs. He smiled and was about to turn to climb up the hill when the shadow came back over him and that peculiar feeling he had before came upon him. He looked up and saw, just a few feet above his head, the seagull had returned. It glided round and round above him; its wings did not move as it circled. Tom stared at it in awe of its power and skill in flight. "Amazing," he whispered to himself as he stared. He thought the gull looked older than the others and seemed to have a knowing look in its eyes. Its head held proud, it looked noble and elegant. The bird seemed to be watching him as it circled above. Tom was not so scared now; he felt easy, and knew somehow that this seagull was a friend. He wanted to wave but somehow he couldn't. Instead, he just smiled. For a second, he sensed that the seagull had smiled back.

The bird circled once more and then was between Tom and the last of the afternoon sun. Tom blinked and held up his hand to his eyes so he could see better and squinted into the sun. The seagull had disappeared again. Quickly Tom turned around to look in every direction. *Where is it?* he wondered. But it was nowhere to be seen.

On his way back up to the footpath at the top of the meadow, he kept looking back but there was no sign of the bird. Eventually he reached the top and then his mind turned to other things. He was due home to help his mother in the kitchen.

Tom's parents owned the Windwhistle inn by the waterfront in Rivermouth. The inn had a restaurant and was well known for its seafood.

His mother ran the restaurant and the general day to day matters of the inn. Tom always helped out on weekdays after school, but only after he had finished his homework, which on this day, he had not done. He knew he was late and was struggling to think of excuses why he should have been home so late. Then he looked at his clothes, which were torn and dirty. He could never tell anyone about the seagull. Who would ever believe him?

Johnny Benson was lapping up the praise and attention he was receiving for masterminding the rescue of little Daniel Corby. The whole town had learned of his courage in saving the boy. Mr and Mrs Benson, who had lived in Rivermouth all their lives and had hardly ever been further than Plymouth, were also enjoying the prestige and were so proud of their son. Even the Mayor and the police had visited them to convey their approval and commendations.

Daniel's parents, usually timid and unassuming people, had arrived at the Benson's house with gifts for Johnny and a bottle of red wine for Mr and Mrs Benson to celebrate the saving of their precious little boy. They thanked Johnny over and over again for his bravery and courage.

As Johnny and his four friends had carried little Danny back home on the stretcher, Johnny made all of them swear to keep quiet about the truth. They would be the heroes and none would face prosecution or have any trouble with their parents. They all agreed that it would be stupid to let Thomas Parker receive any praise for the rescue. They shook hands on the deal and had convinced Daniel that it was they who ran back to get ropes, climbed down the cliffs to rescue him and made a stretcher to take him home. Daniel had been so scared; his broken leg and the whole ordeal were too much for him. The fact that they were carrying him safely home was good enough for him. He was simply pleased to be alive.

Tom ran home as fast as he could along the path from the hilltop, through the overhanging trees, down into the edge of Rivermouth and at last arrived at the little church at the estuary. The church was where his ancestors had all been buried and it always caused him to pause in reverence at the thought of it. It was also where he would sometimes go on Sundays, with his mother and father. He ran down the track to the small bridge at the creek. He paused to catch his breath for a moment and then saw his father's boat swinging gracefully on her mooring. The sweat poured down his face as he stopped to admire the vessel. The *Firefly* was holding nicely on her anchorage as the fiercely strong falling tide swept past.

Tom loved to sail with his father and the crew aboard the *Firefly*. She was a fine old ketch rigger, seventy feet long, who had seen many nautical miles but because of the love, devotion and constant maintenance his father had given her, she lay beautifully on her mooring as if she had just arrived from the builder's yard. Her white wooden hull shone brilliantly in the evening sunlight, her polished topsides and teak decks were a beautiful sight and the chrome winches and cleats sparkled from the polishing they had recently received. Tom dreamt for the day when he would be old enough to sail her across the oceans to adventures in some far and distant lands.

He shook himself from his day dreaming and hurried on into town.

Maggie Parker had just arrived back at the inn from her monthly shopping trip to Plymouth. She dropped her bags in the hall and went straight into the kitchen. She had hurried back to meet her new chef who had just arrived from London. The chef was keen to make a good impression with his new employer and had arrived earlier than expected. The cleaner had shown him into the kitchen to wait for her.

She was also keen to make a good start with the new chef. Good chefs were hard to find, she would always say, and her lateness, due to delays on the road back from Plymouth, had sent her into a fluster. She hated to be late for anything.

The last chef had been with them for thirteen years but his liver had finally given up due to his excessive and incurable drinking of hard liquor. After too many mishaps in the kitchen and his regular tantrums, which could be heard by all the customers in the restaurant, Maggie had finally let him go.

Bernard, his replacement, had been busy taking note of the layout of his new place of work. He began to imagine what it would be like here. This was where he would create the most exquisite and delicious dishes to impress his customers from all points of the compass. He checked the knives, pans, crockery and every piece of equipment he could find. As he moved round the kitchen, he muttered to himself, sometimes in approval of what he had discovered, sometimes in disapproval. He chatted away to himself in a world of his own and had not seen Maggie come through the door. She brushed her dress straight with both hands, flicked a hand through her hair and composed herself.

Bernard, who was originally from Switzerland, had spent his last six years working in a top London restaurant. He was fifty-five years old now and wanted to spend his time in quieter surroundings. He was a heavily built man but was not fat. He was full in the face with red cheeks and a large nose. He was smartly dressed, wearing a green sports jacket and well pressed tan coloured trousers, brown shoes and a white cotton shirt.

Maggie Parker was known to be a very calm lady with a passion for perfection. She was always immaculately dressed and expected the rest of her family to be the same. She believed in punctuality and good manners. Although she set high standards, she was a charming and very popular lady with many friends, and was well connected in Rivermouth.

Maggie was delighted when she saw him. It was important, she believed, that her staff looked professional and smart. She so wanted her new chef to be different from the last one and she was pleased that this man was well turned out. He looked like a gentleman, which was also important. He looked "continental", too which was important and she immediately imagined him in his chef's uniform talking to her guests and receiving compliments for their excellent meals. Yes, he looked just fine; she smiled and clapped her hands together. "Oh, marvellous," she said finally and suddenly out loud.

Bernard, at this moment, had his head inside a large cupboard; he had not noticed Maggie standing at the door observing him. When she spoke, it took him completely by surprise and as he jumped, he cracked his nose on the edge of a shelf. "Ahhh, non!" he cried and, holding his nose in his hand, turned quickly to see who it was. "Oh, I am sorry. I didn't mean to startle you. You must be Bernard," Maggie apologised, though she thought it was quite amusing. "I am so sorry for keeping you waiting. I'm afraid the traffic can be quite bad at this time of the year," she continued and then went to shake his hand.

Bernard was deeply embarrassed and, while still holding his nose, thrust the other free hand out to shake the hand of his new employer. As he did so, his arm caught the rim of a plate, which was protruding from the table in the centre of the kitchen. The plate flipped up and took flight over the corner of the table and down onto the tiled floor. It crashed loudly and shattered into pieces, sending splinters of white china scattering across the newly polished floor. The sound of the plate smashing could have been an earthquake to Bernard and it seemed to last forever. When finally the last piece of china had come to rest, he stood motionless, stunned by his own clumsiness.

Maggie looked in astonishment and for a few painful moments the two of them were speechless and just stared at each other without speaking a word.

At last, Bernard stepped across the debris and held out his hand again to shake her hand. "Madame, I..."

"How do you do?" The two of them spoke simultaneously which now added to the confusion and complicated a first meeting that could have been so simple.

"Oh, er..." Maggie was about to speak again but was interrupted by Bernard. "Madame, I offer my sincere apologies. I did not see you there. I am sorry about the plate." He looked down at the floor. His look was slightly pathetic, but he was feeling very awkward. He spoke good English but his French accent was obvious.

But Maggie just smiled and her face was kind and welcoming. "Please, Bernard, it's fine, I am really sorry I startled you." She held out her hand again. I am Maggie Parker. It is nice to meet you; we have been looking forward to your arrival."

She was amused but tried not to let it show. He seemed to be a kindly man and would have been even more embarrassed if she had shown her amusement. She could tell that he was nervous and, being of a good-hearted nature, would not wish to see him suffer any more.

Maggie never had a bad word to say about anyone. Although she ran her restaurant in a ship-shape fashion and required her staff to work hard, she paid them well and was fair and always pleasant. She had earned great respect from her staff and her customers.

The Windwhistle inn was very popular and never empty. In addition, the inn had five rooms for bed and breakfast, which were always let to various travellers and visitors to Rivermouth.

"Please don't worry about the plate. Now, how was your journey?" she enquired, immediately changing the mood of the conversation and trying to get to know her new chef.

"Ah Madame, you are indeed most gracious. I had a very comfortable journey, merci. The train took me through some charming English countryside and along the beautiful coast. I was even able to take luncheon at midday." As he spoke he trod in the pile of broken china and looked up. "I do apologise, Madame."

"Please, it really does not matter." Maggie needed to get her evening menus planned and prepare the kitchen as the staff would be arriving at any minute. She needed to make Bernard feel at home and ready for work. She had a feeling tonight was going to be a long one.

"Let me show you to your room, then we'll have a cup of tea in the kitchen and I'll go through everything. Tomorrow morning I'll show you around Rivermouth." Maggie was now happy to get things under way.

"We open at seven in the evening and last orders are at nine-thirty. In the high season, we do last orders later at the weekends. The high season starts next month. You have come just at the right time, Bernard, and I am certain you are going to like Rivermouth."

"Yes Madame, I am sure I will." He was now smiling and happy. He liked Maggie already.

As they were talking, Tom, who had just arrived at the back door puffing frantically for air after his long run from the cliffs, then along the creek and through Rivermouth, came hurrying through the door. He had not noticed the shopping bags left in the hall by his mother and ran straight into them. He tripped over one bag catching his shoe through the handle, which brought him to an immediate halt, landing him face down on the hall floor.

Maggie and Bernard heard the crash as they were speaking and turned to see what it was. The kitchen door was open and Tom had landed immediately in front of the doorway.

"Tom!" exclaimed Maggie, "What in God's name are you doing there?" she said. Then seeing that he had tripped over her shopping, said: "Oh I'm sorry dear; I completely forgot to move the bags, are you all right?"

Tom was shaken but he quickly realised that his predicament had given him the opportunity to distract his mother's attention from his lateness and the state of his clothing. He looked up quickly, and replied, "Hello Mum, I'm sorry I'm late. Oh is this our new chef?" Tom had picked himself up onto his knees and was stuffing things back into the shopping bags quickly, whilst looking directly at Bernard.

"Oh yes," replied Maggie. "Bernard, may I introduce you to my son, Tom."

"Hello Tom, I am pleased to meet you. Have you broken anything?"

"I may have smashed an egg or two," Tom replied, realising, of course, that the chef was actually referring to Tom's welfare and not to the contents of the shopping bags.

"I hope nothing else is broken, Mum, I really didn't see the bags there." Tom was putting on a grand performance of distraction and gaining sympathy. This is an art that only children know how to carry out to perfection. Bernard, however, could see through this and had noticed the state of Tom's clothing. He smiled privately to himself and made a subtle wink of the eye in Tom's direction. Tom did catch it, but pretended not to. "Well, I had better get upstairs, I have some things to do, but I'll be back down soon. What do you want me to do first, Mum?" Tom asked politely.

"Oh yes Tom, you could get the tables laid first; I am going to show Bernard around and then we'll be back in the kitchen in a little while. Don't be long now," Maggie added.

"Er, Madame," interrupted Bernard, "You have your shopping to attend to. Perhaps Master Tom could show me to my room and the rest of the place, oui?"

Bernard noticed Tom's exasperated look and found it greatly amusing. Tom was hoping for some time alone to change and clean up without anyone noticing and was now suddenly faced with the task of having to entertain this very large, red faced, foreign gentleman.

"That is an excellent idea. Thank-you, Bernard. Yes, Tom would you mind darling?" She smiled at her son, "I do have a great deal to do before we open and it would be nice for you and Bernard to get acquainted." Tom had now picked himself up but managed to hide his torn trouser leg behind the chair that stood in the corridor. He felt that this stranger appeared to know that he was attempting to hide something. "All right," he replied with reluctance. "Would you like to follow me, Bernard?"

"Mais oui Monsieur," smiled Bernard, picking up his two suitcases from the corner of the kitchen and walking into the hallway. "Please, Tom, after you," said Bernard with a broad smile.

Tom quickly left the chair and walked to the end of the hall trying to keep his back to his mother to hide the tear in his trousers. Bernard knew exactly what Tom was up to and he recalled his own childhood and remembered the times he had learned the art of hiding trouble from his parents. He sympathised with the boy, but was equally amused by his actions.

"I'll see you both in a while," Maggie called back, as she watched them walk towards the stairs.

"We will be back to begin our work, Madame," Bernard called back over his shoulder, as he and Tom headed up the stairs. At the landing on the first floor, Tom stopped and watched as Bernard climbed the next few steps with his bags. "Are you from France?" he asked as he waited.

"Uh? oh, non, I am from Geneva in Switzerland," Bernard replied trying to keep his composure from the climb up the stairs. His bags were heavy.

"I am French Swiss. My father was from Paris and my mother from Geneva. My accent is French, as is the case with most people from Geneva."

"Were your parents cooks?" Tom enquired as he turned to continue the journey along the first floor corridor.

Bernard followed, still out of breath, and was struggling to keep up. "You must remember that I am not as young as you, Tom." He paused before continuing, "These stairs are indeed steep. No, to answer your question, my father was an engineer and my mother was a singer and entertainer." Tom paused at the foot of the next stairway.

"Just a few more steps and we will be there," Tom advised. "Would you like some help with your bags?"

"Oh thank-you, Tom, do you think you could manage this one?" Bernard passed over one of his bags to Tom.

"Boy, what have you got in here, rocks?" Tom asked as he dragged the bag up three steps and paused again.

"Oh no, that is treasure from my last crusade," Bernard replied with a wry smile, and then said, "It looks like you have been on a crusade yourself, my friend, eh?" Bernard's eye had a glint and sparkle of fun and Tom looked at him carefully. "What do you mean?"

"I mean it looks like you have been out there on some adventure and perhaps had some misfortune, oui?" Now Bernard was smiling to the point of nearly laughing. The two of them, still halfway up the stairs, had not moved on any further but now seemed to have found, in each other, some amusement. Tom smiled back.

"Misfortune? No way," Tom replied immediately and was about to give him the whole story but then paused again. "I, er... I had a fall climbing a tree with some friends and had to run back here fast in case I was late. I always help in the kitchen after my home..." He stopped and suddenly remembered that he had not done his homework.

Bernard was quick to ease the situation, "Ah yes, the trees, there are many, no doubt, in this area. I used to love to climb trees when I was your age," he continued, at the same time looking up and down the corridor. "Which is my room? I expect you have much to do before we return to the kitchen for tonight's work?" He paused, smiled and then went on, "Like a wash, and a change, and some homework perhaps? Learning is such a great art. Ah, the enjoyment of discovery. The eighth wonder of the world, do you not agree Tom?"

"Er, yes I suppose..." Tom was stuck for words. Bernard was a most unusual character.

"Good then, I take it that these are my quarters?" Bernard interrupted, deliberately pointing to the door that stood ahead of them.

"Yes, that's it, right here. The keys are in the door."

"Thank-you my friend, I shall make myself accustomed to my room and look forward to starting my work downstairs. I will see you, Tom, thank-you for your assistance and your company."

"I'll see you around, probably later, if you wish?" Tom said, being grateful of the time Bernard had afforded him. The two shook hands and walked their separate ways.

Bernard stood still for a moment to take a breath, then stepped through the door and closed it behind him. The evening light shone through the large window into the room. He was instantly delighted. There was more than one room. Where he stood was a small lounge area with a leather sofa and an armchair. In front of the chairs was a low mahogany coffee table with a shelf underneath. There were some books stacked neatly. On top of the table was a glass vase with some yellow roses, recently cut. He leant over to take in their sweet scent. He was charmed by their fragrance.

In one corner was a wooden cabinet. On top of it was a large model sailing ship. The detail was incredible and he studied it with great interest. Directly ahead of him was a highly polished oak table with two chairs.

There was an archway to one side of the room. This led into a small kitchen. To the left of the lounge area was a door, which opened into his bedroom where there was an old but well sprung oak framed bed, a very large oak wardrobe, a dressing table and a wash basin. Leading off from the bedroom was a small bathroom which was old but in perfect condition. His bedroom had a window that looked out over a few rooftops and across the river, where he could see the harbour and people going about their business. There were ships unloading their cargo and others tying up on their anchorages. Small vessels were sailing up and down the river.

He listened to the wailing sound of the seagulls and opened the window to breathe in the sea air and smiled again. Everything was perfect. Bernard was a happy man. He walked around his rooms, smiling and thinking to himself how he would make himself comfortable in his new home. He was delighted with this place and the people he had met so far seemed very pleasant. Rivermouth could well be what he had been searching for. It was a breath of fresh air for him to be away from the hustle and bustle of London. He walked into the lounge and sat in the old armchair and smiled. Just as he was about to drift away and close his eyes for a while, to savour the moment, he was startled by a shadow, which suddenly blocked the light that had beamed through the window. It was just for a moment, and then the light returned.

He thought for one ridiculous moment that someone was watching him. He was unsure of what it was and walked to the window. Suddenly he stopped. Outside the window, on the flat roof, sat a very large seagull. It was staring directly at him. The shock of this sight made him jump backwards and he bumped into the back of the leather sofa and almost toppled over.

"Mon Dieu!" he exclaimed aloud and almost stopped breathing with the suddenness of the moment. The large seagull just sat and stared at him. Bernard stood still, staring back, his eyes wide, his mouth open and his hands clutching the back of the chair tightly.

Then, the gull blinked. Its large yellow eye flashed like a camera lens as the lid shut over it and then flashed open again. The gull suddenly opened its wings and in one single movement, it was gone.

Bernard stood for a while trying to take in what he had just seen and then shrugged it off.

"Stupid bird," he whispered to himself as he stepped back to his armchair. "It is just a large seagull. Well now, let me see if I can rest before my work begins." He sighed and flopped down into the old chair, put his feet up onto the small table in front of him and drifted off.

Tom had gone to his room, washed himself and changed his dirty clothes for a fresh pair of trousers and a clean shirt. He sat for a while on his bed looking at a school book and made notes on a pad, which he had placed, beside the book. The book he was reading was on geography, which was his favourite subject. He loved to discover the wonders of the world – the mountains and the oceans, the forests, the jungles and deserts. There were so many wondrous things and places he wanted to see and he dreamed of exploring the world and seeing all it had to offer. However, his mind was on other things. The encounter with the seagull on the cliffs had left him confused and he wanted to find a way to make it all explainable, but he couldn't.

He closed his books and stood up to look out of the window. He could see the estuary from his room and watched the comings and goings of the sailing vessels on the river. He saw *The Eagle* sailing up river to the quay. The cutter's tall masts were unmistakable and she looked beautiful as she sailed into Rivermouth in the evening light. He wanted to get a better look and quickly turned and went to the door. He pulled it open and ran through the old oak doorway at the end of the hall and up a stone stairway. The stairs led immediately onto the roof of the building, a well laid-out patio where his mother grew her herbs in large stone pots. There was always a strong and pleasant smell of basil, chives, dill, mint and lemon grass, which grew in abundance.

He ran over to the wall, where he had an excellent view of the whole of Rivermouth. He could see across the river to Kingsport and also the main channel out to the estuary and finally to the English Channel.

*The Eagle* was almost ready to come alongside the quay where a number of onlookers were watching. Some were waiting to catch the heavy mooring ropes from the crew on board and some were simply watching the Master of the vessel expertly slip her long hull alongside the harbour wall with the ease and grace of a true professional. Tom knew the Captain who was a friend of his father. He was Jacob Morgan who had sailed more miles than most sea going captains in England and had encountered many challenges and adventures in his time. Tom loved to listen to them talk about their travels and experiences. Often, when they had been away for a long time, they would bring back gifts and they always brought something back for him. On this occasion though, Tom knew that *The Eagle* had only been gone for a few days and therefore there would be no need to run down to the quayside. Then he saw his father, a tall and sturdy man, stepping out from the crowd on the quay. He shouted something to the crewman at the bow who then threw a heavy rope over the side of *The Eagle* straight into his hands. He fastened the line to the quayside and waved over to Jacob who was standing at the bridge. Tom could just hear their exchange as the wind carried their voices. The two men were laughing and exchanging pleasant conversation. Tom smiled down on the scene. He loved his father and enjoyed watching him. Jack Parker was one of the most well respected men in Rivermouth. He had many friends and was known for his good nature and wit. He was also a highly respected mariner and he never found trouble in recruiting crews for his voyages.

Jack Parker and Maggie owned the Windwhistle inn jointly, but Maggie was really the one who ran the place as Jack was usually away at sea taking people across to France or on fishing trips along the Devon coast to Cornwall. Sometimes he would be away for many weeks at a time when he sailed to the West Indies or the Middle East to buy fruit, sugar, spices, fine cloth and all manner of wonderful things.

Tom had often been to sea with his father but not for any great length of time. They had a good relationship and spent many hours aboard *Firefly* out in the English Channel but Tom had never been any further. They often brought back fish for the restaurant. They would catch plaice, sea bass, mullet, eel and occasionally some fine lobster.

Jack Parker had never coped easily with the modern world and loved to do things as his ancestors had done. Sailing ships were more appealing to him than modern powered boats. "It may take longer, but that is the way I like it," he would say.

He was tall with broad shoulders, his face was tanned and weathered by the sea and his gold and greying hair waved in the evening breeze. He stood on the quayside and shook hands with his friend Jacob as he stepped ashore. Then they walked away talking. Tom watched for a while until they were out of sight.

The patio was Tom's favourite place where he would spend many hours day dreaming and planning the adventures that he would have one day. It was quiet here and he could see everything going on in Rivermouth, unseen by others.

This was his special place. He stood quietly watching the evening draw in over Rivermouth.

*I wonder if I'll ever see that bird again* he said to himself. Then, aloud, "How could little Danny ever know that it was a seagull that had saved his life and what would he say anyway?"

"He could begin by thanking me," came a voice suddenly from behind.

Tom was startled and turned round quickly. His heart stopped, he could not breathe. His eyes were wide open. The large seagull had returned and was perched on a table behind him.

"Wh-what was that?" Tom was asking the question but did not understand why. "Who said that?" He was trembling and confused. "Who's there?" he called again but he was looking straight at the seagull.

"No need to be afraid, Tom Parker." *The words seemed to be coming from the seagull!* Tom refused to believe this and called out again, "Stop this. Who's there?" But he was still staring at the bird.

This time he saw the beak of the seagull move. "I said, you have no need to be concerned." The seagull really had spoken the words and Tom was stunned and shaken. Was this a dream? He shook his head and wiped his eyes with his hands.

"Why do you do that, Tom Parker?" asked the seagull.

"You're talking!" Tom had to swallow; his mouth had gone dry. His head was whirling around in confusion and amazement.

"This is true; can you see anyone else here?" asked the seagull again.

"N-no, I can't," Tom answered very quietly.

"Exactly, therefore it must be you, to whom I am addressing. Is this not so?"

"Yes, I mean, I..."

The bird jumped up onto the wall where Tom was leaning and Tom stepped away quickly, shaking and still confused. For a second there was no sound from the bird and Tom stood very still. The two of them stared at each other. Then suddenly the bird cocked its head to one side and blinked. "You are a good boy, Tom Parker. I am sorry to have scared you. I am sure it was a shock for you."

Tom had not moved but was just staring. His eyes were wider than ever as if he had seen a ghost.

"Oh come now, I will not harm you, what could a simple old seagull do?" said the bird.

"Who...? What...?I mean, I don't know what to say, you're scaring me. I mean – birds don't talk." Tom was feeling very strange. Was he really speaking to a bird?

"Of course birds don't talk, everybody knows that. Except – I do. I have been able to for a very long time but have never had the opportunity to do so, until now." The seagull settled on the wall next to Tom.

Tom looked closely at this huge bird who seemed friendly and now he felt a little easier. "You will have to understand that this is very strange, I mean if anyone saw me talking to you they would probably say I was mad," said Tom, who was now standing with his arms folded. "And if anyone saw me speaking to you, they would probably put me in a cage in a circus," replied the seagull. "How do you know about circuses?" asked Tom. "I know a great deal Tom Par..." Tom interrupted again. "And how do you know my name?"

"Well that is very easy really. I have been watching you and I saw how you saved your young friend and how you showed care for my friends on the cliffs. Those other boys – I do not like and they will have no friendship in me. I know your name because I heard them call it out."

"Do you mean – your friends, the seagulls?"

"Well of course, who else?"

"Then how come you can talk like a human, you're just a bird?"

"Just a bird! Why do you say, just a bird, Tom Parker? Can you fly, do you have wings?"

"No, sorry, that's not what I meant. I mean nobody has ever known of a speaking animal. Even parrots don't speak like you can. How come you can?"

The seagull spoke like a man in a deep, soft unusual voice but Tom thought he could detect a very slight hint of a Devonshire accent.

"That is a very long story, Tom Parker."

"Tell me, I promise not to tell anyone," said Tom, who was now very excited and still completely amazed.

"I have watched you, young Tom, and I am aware of your integrity and your word of honour."

The seagull paused, then stood up and stretched its wings, which startled Tom.

Then the seagull stared into Tom's eyes. The stare mesmerised Tom. It was hypnotic; the eyes of the bird widened and Tom looked into one eye and saw a golden moon set deep in the darkness, as black as night. Tom was still and then whispered, "Thank-you for saving little Danny."

The seagull spoke, this time very slowly and deeply, "Thomas Parker, I believe we are to be friends for a very long time. I need to know that you will not tell anyone about this meeting between us and of our conversation. Our relationship will always be our secret, do you agree?"

"I agree," replied Tom who was still stunned by what was happening.

"Good, then it is done." The seagull lowered itself again on the wall and tilted its head to look at the boy. Tom was first to speak. "Are we friends now?"

"We most certainly are." The bird almost seemed to be smiling and Tom remembered the look he had been given earlier when they were on the cliffs. "I couldn't tell anyone, they wouldn't believe me anyway," Tom said.

"You don't like the other boys, do you?" asked the bird.

"Oh, some of them are all right, but Johnny Benson is a creep" Tom answered and leant back against the wall, putting his hands deep into his pockets and thought about the other boys.

"If you know who I am, then who are you?" asked Tom, suddenly shaking off his thoughts about the other boys. "My name is Hawkins. Mr Hawkins to you, Tom." The seagull stood as tall as he could as he called out his name. "Mr Hawkins!" Tom grinned at the seagull and then said, "I'm pleased to meet you Mr Hawkins."

"And I am delighted to meet you, Tom Parker." The two of them looked at each other and then Tom held out a hand nervously and felt rather stupid as he did, but then the seagull pushed forward its large wing like a hand and let Tom hold the end of it. Very carefully, Tom shook the wing, like a handshake.

Tom smiled widely. He could not believe what was happening and hoped that it was not a dream. "You still haven't told me how you are able to speak," Tom said suddenly.

"And I said that it was a very long story and you do not have time to know all this now," said the seagull.

"Oh my goodness, I completely forgot, I'm supposed to be helping in the kitchen. I've got to go." Tom went to run away, then stopped and turned to the seagull. "Will you come back later so we can talk again?"

"I will be back my friend," replied the bird. "Go before they discover you up here." Tom waved to the seagull and walked quickly but just before Tom reached the stairs, the seagull called to him: "Tom!"

"Yes, Mr Hawkins?"

"Remember, this is our secret."

"Our secret, I swear."

# Chapter 2 – The First Meeting

Jack Parker was deep in conversation with his friend Jacob Morgan. The inn was full of people chatting together. Occasionally some raucous laughter would drown the conversations and some would look up to see where it had come from. Groups of seamen gathered round the wooden tables drinking and there were town folk and visitors to Rivermouth standing at the bar. Everyone was drinking and exchanging conversation and the whole place was alive with a vibrant atmosphere.

Outside, it was starting to rain and it began to beat against the windows.

Jack and Jacob were sitting at a corner table by one of the inn's front windows.

"Well one thing is certain, Jacob," said Jack as he wiped the condensation away from the window behind him and peered out. "What's that?" replied Jacob.

"We will never understand the weather."

"Oh yes, the rain, it wasn't forecast today, it's been as clear as my compass glass, but it must be coming in from the west. It was starting to blow up a good'n last night when we were off the Northern Brittany coast," said Jacob. He too was now peering through the steamy window. "Can't see much out there now my friend, just as well we got in when we did," Jacob continued.

"Tell me more about that ship you saw – where were you?" Jack had now forgotten about the rain and was looking directly at his friend.

Jacob took another sip from his beer and thought for a moment. "It was forty eight degrees, forty-seven minutes north, and four degrees, forty-nine west, by my account." He thought again and continued, "Yes, that would be right, our compass head was steering 042 degrees at the time we took sight of her. We were on our way back to Rivermouth. I tell you Jack, and make no mistake on this, there were somethin' right unnatural about the way she were laying."

"What do you mean?" Jack enquired. He was now showing some interest. Earlier Jacob had mentioned that they had sighted a strange vessel on their return to England, but Jack had thought little of it. "How was she laying?"

"Well, for a start, she was not like the type of boat we get in these parts. She was very low in the water and seemed to have taken a lean on the port side, but strangely, she was making way at a fair pace. Must have been doing nine or ten knots. Trouble is, we couldn't make out her type. We saw her sails full set for a short time but then she just disappeared in the night."

"How do you mean, disappeared?"

"Just as I say, she just went out of sight. Ol' Mat Flynn said he saw three masts on her but they were not square rig, nor gaff, not even sloop. Like I said, I don't know of any vessel in these parts with any unusual rig and as you know I have been sailing in these waters all my life."

"Could have been up from the Brittany coast maybe or anywhere for that matter. She may have been in distress. Did you try to make contact?"

"There wasn't time. Like I said, we saw her for a few minutes, then she popped right out of sight."

Jacob finished his beer and cupped his glass in both hands, putting it back on the table and looking thoughtful. "It was almost like she were a ghost," he whispered into his glass.

"Oh come now Jacob, it's not like you to be drawn into the world of gremlins. You're always telling your boys that there is no such thing as demons at sea," Jack laughed and patted Jacob on the back. "Come on my friend, I'm sure there's a simple explanation to all this; let me buy you another drink – you look like you could do with one."

Jack left the table and picked his way through the crowd to the bar.

There was uproar from one end of the room as one of the seamen had managed to drink a pint of beer while balancing another on his head. The crowd around him cheered.

Jack was amused at the antics of the seamen and then looked through the crowd at his friend. Jacob was staring out of the window. He was in a world of his own, completely detached from the crowd around him. Jack stopped laughing and watched his friend with interest. He had not seen him look like this since he lost his son at sea some years before. There was definitely something troubling Jacob.

Jack was concerned for his friend; they had grown up together and as young boys they had shared their thoughts and secrets and had always been close. He thought about what Jacob had told him of this strange vessel and thought he should enquire further. He took the two re-filled glasses back to the table and sat down. Jacob was still looking out through the window but the rain was beating against the glass so hard it was impossible to see out. The sky was black and a storm was threatening.

"Penny for your thoughts, old friend?"

Jacob quickly looked away from his gaze and returned his attention to Jack. "Ahh, nothing like a pot of good ale to clear the salt, thank-you," said Jacob trying to hide his troubles.

"If you don't mind me saying, Jacob, you do appear to have something worrying you," Jack insisted, finally.

"Not at all, I er... well, there are a couple of things. I'm puzzled by that ship we saw. I never thought I'd hear me say this, but I have a funny feeling that maybe what we saw was nothing. On the other hand..." He paused.

"Yes, what?" Jack persisted.

"Well, it's what Flynn said, really."

"What did he say?"

"He said that he was sure there was nobody on board."

"How could he tell that?"

Jacob raised his hands above his head and then opened his eyes wide and leaned across the table to reply. "Well, you know Flynn, he has the eyes of a hawk, even at night." When he had finished demonstrating the appearance of a hawk, he sat back in his chair and smiled at his friend.

Jack was persistent and ignored Jacob's melodramatics. "Didn't you or anyone else see?"

Jacob nodded negatively, "I was, for most of the night, on the helm, it was a rough night, blowing a gale. It came from nowhere. The rest of the crew saw the ship, we all did, but we were working hard to keep our heading, but..."

"But what?"

"I have to admit, now I have been doing some thinking on it, that ship did seem to be unmanned. It was most strange, Jack, but I can't put my finger on it. She looked like she was deserted, yet..." Jacob paused again.

"Oh, come on Jacob, the suspense is killing me. What's bothering you?"

"Well, just think about it. How could a sailing vessel, of any size, be sailing at nine to ten knots into the wind in weather like that with all sails set?" He paused and then continued. "And with no-one on board?"

Jack thought about what Jacob had said: "You have a point, my friend, yet you did say she was leaning to port. It could be she had hit something, the crew could have been overboard. God help them."

"Aye, indeed. It's all very well what you say and I know what you are implying Jack, but remember, by the time we had realised that things weren't right, the next time we looked, she had vanished. You know as well as I do, Jack, that even in the worse situation, a boat of her size would take several minutes to go down. In her position, there were no rocks or anything that would sink her so fast. No Jack, she vanished." Jacob sat back in his chair with a sigh and looked deep into his glass.

"And the other thing?" said Jack, breaking the sudden silence.

"Mmm?" Jacob lifted his head.

"The other thing. You said there were a couple of things worrying you."

Jacob put down his glass and looked out through the window at the rain bashing against the glass. "Ah yes, the other thing. What tides are we having right now?"

"What are you talking about?" asked Jack, now leaning forward to hear his friend speak softly.

"I'm talking about the moon, Jack."

"What. Are you sure you are all right, you aren't making much sense?"

"Aye, of course I'm all right, I'm trying to tell you that the tides are at springs just now, aren't they?" Jack shook his head and answered, "Yes they are but so what?"

"And we should be having a full moon tonight." Again Jack nodded but was still unsure where this was leading. "Yes, that's right," he replied, cautiously.

"Have you seen the moon, tonight?" Jacob nodded towards the window for Jack to see.

Jack wiped the condensation from the dripping glass and peered out, tilting his head to see into the black sky. Suddenly he saw it flicker in and out of the darkness and his eyes widened in disbelief. He saw the blackness of the stormy night and way up in the black night sky was the moon, but it was not a full moon: he saw it clearly as if it were a still summer's night. He saw only a crescent moon. It shone brilliantly down over Rivermouth. "It can't be!" Jack said in disbelief and turned to his friend. "It's a crescent moon, and it should be a full moon, I'm certain it should." He was puzzled and sat back down and looked at Jacob. I don't understand," he said and Jacob leaned forward so as not to be heard.

"I'm telling you Jack, something is very strange here. That crescent moon has been as bold as brass since the time we saw that ship. I swear the moon was much closer to being a full moon just before we saw that strange ship. I just don't know what to think."

"I say we sleep on it Jacob. What say you, we get back to *The Eagle?*"

"Good idea, Jack, good idea."

Tom had just finished laying the tables in the restaurant. It had taken him nearly twice the usual time and Maggie had needed to call over to him several times to get a move on.

Tom's mind was on other matters: he had just made the most amazing discovery and a new friend. A bird that could talk. He was so excited and very keen to finish his chores so he could get back to the roof quickly, but yet his day dreaming about his encounter had slowed him down almost to a halt. On two occasions, Maggie had caught him standing in the middle of the room staring blankly with his arms hung down his sides, his hands firmly gripping the knives and forks that he was supposed to be laying on the table.

"Tom, what are you doing?" Maggie shouted.

She was puzzled by Tom's vagueness but also disappointed that Bernard had arrived back to the kitchen late. In fact he would not have arrived at all if she hadn't woken him up: he had drifted off to sleep in the armchair and was only woken by Maggie banging on the door. He was highly embarrassed by this, especially as he had not made a very good impression since he had arrived. Maggie had accepted that he was probably weary after his journey but was also hoping that this was not going to be a regular occurrence.

Finally she had everyone at work and was happy now that they were almost ready to open.

Bernard and Maggie had discussed the menu together, checked the pantry and the stores.

Bernard was impressed how well Maggie had everything organised and complimented her on what he called her "exquisite taste and professionalism". Maggie was grateful for the praise and forgot about his falling asleep earlier.

By seven o'clock they were ready in the kitchen. They had agreed on a new system of ordering, this was something that Bernard had brought with him. An expert's knowledge of top restaurant operations was what Maggie had hoped for and was keen to listen to Bernard's experiences. When they had finished talking, they went into the dining room and were horrified to find that the tables were a mess. The cutlery was all over the place, there were no napkins and only some of the tables had glasses. Tom was rushing here and there but not appearing to be doing much. "Tom, good grief, where is your head this evening?"

"Er, I..."

"Well?"

"I am sorry Mum, I really don't feel very well, I think I am a little tired."

"Whatever is the matter, darling? I don't think I've ever seen you look so pale."

"I'm not really sure; would you mind if I went to my room?"

"No, not at all, you go straight up and I'll be up to see you shortly. If you are not feeling any better later I'll have to call Doctor Crowther."

"Thanks, I'm sure I'll feel better after some sleep," Tom replied gratefully and immediately left the room. His heart was pounding and he was wondering how he was going to be able to find his friend. His mother was sure to be keeping her eye on him. He had to get back up on the roof to Mr Hawkins.

Jack Parker and Jacob left the inn and walked back through the rain to the quayside. They had to row across half the width of the river to get to where *The Eagle* was anchored. Jacob had ordered his first mate to move her off the harbour wall and onto her mooring for the night. She would be safer there than by the quay in the strong winds that were coming. "Got a strong tide tonight, Jacob; better see that she's well tied. This wind is kicking up."

"Aye, I reckon you're right Jack. All the crew have gone back to their homes tonight. I gave 'em a couple of nights off. We have been away a lot the past few weeks and I'll be the devil in black if I don't let the wives have their men home." The two men looked up to see the strange crescent moon still shining down on them.

Jacob climbed aboard *The Eagle*. He looked up at the mast and checked the rigging. "Give me a hand, will you, Jack. I need to tie her down tight. Those sheets are going to fly loose." The wind had become much stronger and the rain was beating horizontally from the estuary and up the river into the heart of Rivermouth.

The two men began lashing down all the lines and ropes. They had to hold on tight as they worked.

They had not noticed the large seagull sitting on one of the spreaders on the mast, high above the deck. The bird looked down upon them and watched them moving about below. Its eyes followed them with every move they made.

Finally the two men fixed all the lines and made *The Eagle* safe for the night.

"Thanks for your help, Jack. How about a dram before you go?"

Below decks, *The Eagle* was beautifully structured with teak wooden furnishings from the Indies. The main stateroom was a large open area with a centre table and seats that were fitted around.

*The Eagle* had been built by one of the best English boat yards many years ago. But although she was a well built and very seaworthy vessel, she needed some attention. Some of her paintwork and varnished woodwork was looking tired and needed some loving care.

Jack loved these old sailing ships. He had restored his own boat, *Firefly*. It had taken him many years of hard work. There was always much work to do on wooden sailing vessels like these. It took a lot of time, money and devotion.

Jack looked around the ship for a while as Jacob rustled around in the galley for some glasses. At the stern of *The Eagle* were two large cabins for the crew. There was a store room for food and supplies and also the aft "heads" (the washroom and toilets). On the port side, just forward of the main saloon, was the Captain's cabin and this was where Jacob lived for most of his life. It was a handsome room, panelled in teak with matching cupboards and shelves. There were many books on navigation and old sea charts rolled up in leather tubes scattered around the cabin. Jacob had no family; his wife left him fifteen years previously and he never re-married. When his son died in an accident at sea, Jacob lost all interest in family life and used *The Eagle* as his home. Although he had a house in Rivermouth, it was often left empty.

Jack Parker was at sea with Jacob when Jacob's son, Harry, died. Jack had helped Jacob through his grief and it developed a strong bond of friendship between them. Neither of them would ever forget that dreadful day. Jack was always careful not to touch the subject and Jacob was grateful of it.

"That wind is going to rip right through this place tonight, Jack an' I'll sleep like a log after that last dram." Jacob had finished nearly half the bottle of whisky he had found in the galley but Jack had restrained himself from joining him in the drink. He knew there was something troubling Jacob. The sight of that strange sailing ship was surely a mystery. *What could it have been?* he thought to himself. He looked over to his friend and smiled. Jacob had fallen asleep in his chair by the chart table, his head lay over the table and his hand was still holding the empty glass.

Jack managed to lever Jacob away from the chair and get him into his cabin. He hauled him onto the bunk bed and pulled a blanket over him. "Sleep well old friend and may the spirit of the ocean look well upon you." He spoke the words quietly as he looked down on Jacob and pulled the blanket over him.

Jack closed the cabin door quietly and looked around the saloon. There were pictures on the walls of sailing vessels and sea captains from the past. There were also pictures of old maps of regions where Jacob had sailed. These would have been places where others had rarely ventured. He looked carefully at one of the charts in particular. It was the western coast of France. He remembered the latitude and longitude that Jacob had told him where he had seen the strange ship. He paused and stared at it for a while and then took the picture down off the wall and laid it upon the chart table. He took out a pencil and a sliding rule from a drawer and plotted the position that Jacob had given him.

Unbeknown to Jack, two eyes were peering through the large porthole above him over the chart table. The eyes were dark, with a crescent moon set deep in the centre. The seagull had flown down from the mast where he had been observing the two men earlier. He could see quite clearly through the porthole and onto the chart table where Jack Parker was sitting.

Jack was puzzled by this strange sailing ship that Jacob had seen and was determined to get to the bottom of it. There was also the moon; had something gone wrong, or were they wrong? "There's something very odd here," he whispered to himself. "I can't make it out. How can a boat just disappear without trace? Why would she be sailing with a full set of sails in gale-force winds? Why did it look like no-one was aboard and why was she leaning to port?"

Jacob had also mentioned the strange rig of the sailing vessel. It was not like the type normally seen in these parts, he had said. So where did it come from, and where did it go?

The wind was rattling through the boat and the rain beat hard against the roof. *The Eagle* rolled dramatically from side to side. There were ropes and halyards thrashing against the mast and booms and thunder cracked through the air like a loud cannon. Jack looked up at the porthole to see the rain pounding hard on the glass. As he did so, he noticed a yellow streak flash past. It was very quick. He looked up and wondered for a second what it was. *Must be a ship's light reflecting off the glass* he thought and cast his eyes back onto the chart table. *What kind of ship would the mystery vessel be?* He recalled Jacob's description of the strange sails. *Three large masts, each rigged in full sail. Not gaff rig, nor Bermudan sloop or square rigged. It must be some vessel from more distant lands.* Jack let his thoughts wander and pulled some paper out from under the table and picked up the pencil. He began to sketch a rough drawing of a sailing ship with three masts. The sails were shaped like triangles and the line of the hull was arched, the lowest part of its hull dipped in the centre. He leant back to consider his drawing with a smile. *Mmm, not bad for an amateur.*

The eye had re-appeared at the porthole; it was open wide and staring right at the drawing.

Although Jack had impressed himself with his crude idea of an old fashioned sailing ship he knew full well that it was incorrect and frowned and tried to think of how it was when Jacob and his crew saw it. *I shall have to wait until Jacob wakes and I'll ask his crew when I see them* he decided. He scratched his head and sighed. *There is something very peculiar about all this.* He walked across to the galley to pour himself a drink. The wooden slatted doors at the top of four steps, leading to the deck, were being blown inwards and they thrashed on their hinges. He knew he would be unable to row ashore in the small tender, which they had hauled on board earlier in case it was cast adrift by the storm. He knew also that Maggie would be busy in the restaurant and with some luck the weather would ease later so he could get ashore. She would be worried if he did not get back tonight. But, for now, he was trapped on board *The Eagle*. As he poured a drink into his glass, he listened to the snores coming from Jacob who was sleeping deeply on his bunk. Jack knew he would be here for some time and decided to take a look around. He pulled out two large leather bound books on sailing ships from the shelf over the saloon table and sat down and opened one.

He was still unaware of the eye watching him from the porthole. It was switching its gaze from the book to the drawing that Jack had left on the chart table. Jack continued flicking through the pages of the large book; the eye watched and blinked with every turn of the pages.

The eye was very similar to a crescent moon.

Jack came to the end of the first book, pushed it aside and opened the second one. After several pages had been turned, he finally paused at one. This was a large but faded colour print that had been taken from an old oil painting of a sailing ship from another land and a time from long ago. As Jack studied it, there was suddenly a crash from above. He looked up to see where it had come from and missed the eye at the window by a second, but again he saw the yellow light flash past. "What was that?" he whispered and got to his feet. He tried looking out of the window but he could see nothing through the beating rain. The wind was shaking *The Eagle* from side to side. He put on his jacket and climbed the stairs to the slatted doors, which were still rattling in and out. He pulled up his collar and launched himself onto the deck. The wind knocked him back as he attempted to walk over to the wheelhouse and he was thrown against the frame of the doorway. He managed to hold onto a large cleat and pull himself over to the side of the cockpit. He looked back towards the porthole where he had seen the yellow light flashing, but saw nothing. He looked to the stern but the rain driving right into his face blinded his vision. It was as if he was being sprayed with tiny stones, the rain was so hard. He looked aloft but could only see the masthead light swaying with the roll of the ship. A shadow of light flickered over him and around the deck.

Suddenly a brilliant light appeared from overhead. It was so bright he had to cover his eyes. As he let go of the cleat the wind pulled him immediately backwards and tossed him onto his back and sent him sliding across the cockpit deck. As *The Eagle* pitched over on a sudden wave, he slid further; this time he had no control and was sent crashing into the wooden sides of a hatch cover. His head hit the side and the blow knocked him unconscious.

From below decks a bright glow appeared. It was as though a fire had been started in the saloon. Down below on the chart table the picture that Jack had been attempting to draw was changing. The paper around the picture was blackening as though it was burning, but there was no fire. A beam of bright light was streaming through the porthole right out of the eye with the crescent moon. The seagull was sending this ray of light onto the paper and turning Jack's drawing into a detailed picture of an old sailing ship from long ago. Suddenly the beam of light turned gold and a cloud of gold dust emerged from the picture. Then suddenly it was gone. The light had disappeared, the seagull had gone and a groan came from the deck. Jack was waking up. His head hurt and he was wet through from the rain and the spray of the sea water that had come over the sides.

*The Eagle* still thrashed on her mooring but it seemed as if the wind was finally dying down. He slowly got onto his feet and staggered to the hand-rail over the coach roof of the main saloon.

He rubbed his head, which was aching, and saw he was bleeding slightly. He stumbled down through the companionway and into the saloon. He was still dazed and missed one step. This sent him flying down three steps and crashing onto the saloon floor. Jack was still dazed from the blow to his head and was lying face down on the floor of the saloon. The sudden noise woke Jacob. "W-what's that, who's there?" he called and crawled from his bunk.

"Jacob!" Jack called back. "Give me a hand." Jacob saw his friend lying on the floor and went to pull him to his feet. "You should go easy on that whisky, Jack, it's strong stuff. Damn it, you woke me an'..." Jacob suddenly stopped talking as his eye caught sight of the picture on the chart table. "What the...?"

He had almost pulled Jack to his feet and then let go of him when he saw the picture. His jaw dropped and his heart began to thump hard.

"Ouch, what are you doing man?" cried Jack as he hit the floor again. "I thought you were helping!"

Jack stopped speaking too and looked at his friend. "What are you staring at? What's the matter, Jacob?"

Jacob paused before he spoke. "Unless my eyes are misguiding me, I am looking at something I don't reckon I want to see."

"What? What are you going on about?" Jack pulled himself up and joined Jacob at the chart table. "I think it's you that should watch that whisky. You just dropped me on the floor. There's been a right old storm out here tonight and..." Jack stopped talking. He too saw the chart table and the drawing. "Where did that come from?" He looked closer at the picture. The two men gazed down onto the table.

There was a charred piece of paper in the place of Jack's drawing. On the paper was a beautifully etched drawing of an old sailing ship with three masts with sails set full. Painted on the sails were two red crossed swords and a crescent moon. The sails were triangular in shape and the superstructure around the ship was finely decorated with gold patterns. Around the top of the hull were shields with different colours and shapes painted on them. At the bow, carved in gold, was the head of a bird. It hung boldly over the bows, with carved wings in gold, folded back down the sides of the hull. It was, indeed, the most elegantly decorated vessel.

"The Lord be...!" exclaimed Jacob. "That's it!"

"Jacob, I drew a sketch of a sailing ship on that piece of paper while you were asleep. That is not it." Jack looked as puzzled as his friend.

He continued to try to describe what had happened while Jacob had been asleep, but was finding it hard to do. Nothing seemed clear. He thought about the flashing yellow light he had seen from the porthole, but it was not worth discussing; it could have been anything. Then he looked over at the saloon table and studied the books he had been looking at.

"This is very strange Jacob. I did a sketch of a different type of boat; I am no artist and you know I can't draw like that." They both looked again at the picture. Then Jacob spoke.

"Jack, this is it. It's the ship we saw. I'm certain of it."

"What?" Jack was completely confused and went to look up the picture he had seen in the leather volume of sailing ships. He was astonished when he came to the page where he had found it earlier. "It's gone!"

"What's gone?" Now Jacob was confused.

"There was a picture in this book that I was looking at. I thought it resembled the one you were describing, the one you saw last night."

Jacob shook his head "No, no Jack, don't you see? This is it." He pointed at the drawing on the chart table "This one. This is the ship we saw, I'm as sure as I'm alive."

The two men stared back at the chart table. Not a word was said for some while. They were so puzzled and yet there was some excitement between them. Then Jack finally broke the silence. "Jacob, let's take this slowly. You say this picture resembles the strange ship you saw at sea, the one that disappeared?"

"Yes, I am certain."

"Then where is the drawing I did? This is a work of art, and it looks very old."

"I don't know what you are talking about, Jack – this is the only picture here, ain't it?"

"I'm telling you, I drew a sketch of a ship. It has similar shaped sails and a low cut to her hull shape, but this is not it. Something is very odd." He looked a little closer. "Wait a minute. What have we here?" Jack stared down at the picture and ran his finger over the gold paintwork of the picture. The gold came off and stuck to his finger. He held it up to his nose. "That's odd. I don't smell paint or anything."

"What do you expect, it's old. You tore this from the book didn't you? The only trouble is that knock on your head has given your memory a knock too." Jacob patted his friend on the shoulder. "No matter, though, Jack, this is her. This is the ship we saw and, like I said, she's not from these parts."

"No you're right Jacob; she's like an Arab dhow!" They looked at each other and thought the same thing. *Why would an Arab dhow be sailing in these parts?*

"Not only is she a dhow, but this is a very large one, probably belonging to someone of great wealth or nobility."

"Jacob, two things. First, I did not tear the picture from the book and second, I did not draw this picture. Mine must be around somewhere." They started to look around but found nothing.

"Third," said Jacob suddenly.

"What?"

"Third. That gold paint would not come off on a print. This is a painting or something. Let's have a look at the gold." Jacob drew a desk lamp over to the chart table and produced a large magnifying glass from a drawer. "Hold your finger under the light, Jack." He pulled the lamp closer and it shone over the finger with the gold paint. "See, it comes away easy. Hold on a minute." Jacob found a small glass plate and took a razor blade out from a bag. He held the glass plate under Jack's finger and began to gently scrape the gold paint from the finger onto the plate.

Then he held the plate under the light and held the magnifying glass up to his eyes.

He looked carefully at it for a while and then turned to Jack.

"This is not paint, it's gold," Jacob said.

"You are kidding me?" Jack replied, astonished.

"It's gold dust to be exact. I don't understand how or why or who put it here but this is a picture of the ship we saw and this, my friend, is real gold."

"This is all a little crazy Jacob. First you fall asleep and then I go outside and get knocked out. Somehow, my picture gets changed for this and a picture from your book vanishes. Then you tell me it's gold! The whole thing is madness."

Behind them, an eye appeared at the porthole, then vanished.

It felt like an eternity, for Tom. He had been sitting in his room watching from the window all through the night. He watched the storm blow through Rivermouth and wondered where his new friend had gone.

"Where are you Mr Hawkins, where are you?" Tom whispered into the glass of the window from his bedroom.

He had managed get onto the roof for a short while but when the seagull had not appeared, Tom decided to return to his room for fear of being discovered by his mother who was worrying about him.

He lay on his bed for hours. Sometimes he wished he could have fallen asleep and not woken up until morning. But he could not stop thinking about Mr Hawkins.

The hours slipped by and finally Tom did fall asleep. He fell onto his bed and drifted gently away into a wonderful world of dreams. He dreamed of flying across the ocean and of strange lands. Then suddenly he saw the seagull flying beside him. They were smiling at each other as they flew across a huge blue ocean. There was soft music and the air was warm. It was a sweet dream and Tom lay blissfully on his bed.

The wind was calmer and the clattering sound from the slatted tiles on the roof outside his window had ceased. The air was still and a gentle fall of rain tapped lightly on the window panes. Tom was fast asleep, curled up on top of his bed.

There was a creak from the floorboards outside his room and slowly his bedroom door opened. A shadow appeared at the door and the light from the hall outside cast a glow over his room and across his bed. His mother stood silently in her dressing gown and smiled. Although it was very late, she had woken up to check up on Tom. She slowly walked across the floor and over to his bed. She pulled the blanket over him and tucked him in very gently. Then she kissed him softly on his head, turned and left the room, closing the door so quietly no-one would have heard.

No-one, that is, except the seagull at the window. It blinked quickly and then its eye cast a beam of light across the room onto Tom's bed.

Tom was still dreaming; he was floating down through the sky with the seagull. They were landing on a huge haystack in a lush green field.

"You must wake my friend. Wake." Tom was restless but remained asleep, although a voice had come into his dream. He had not moved. Still he floated down towards the field and the voice came to him again.

"Thomas Parker, you must wake. Wake my friend. Wake."

Tom was restless and turned in his bed. The seagull was sitting on the windowsill outside his room and again it sent in a beam of light. This time the light went directly to Tom's head, and a round circle of light pinpointed on his forehead. Tom again heard the voice and was troubled. He rolled around in his sleep and finally began to stir. The voice became louder as he turned in his bed until the voice in his dream had stopped. He was not dreaming any more, he was awake and still he heard the voice.

He rubbed his eyes and shook his head to wake himself up. Then he heard what he thought was the tapping rain on his window and looked over to it. There, to his surprise, he saw the seagull tapping his beak on the glass. Tom's face lit up and his heart beat with excitement. "Mr Hawkins!" he called out, but softly so as not to wake anyone.

He threw back the blanket and scrambled over to the window and opened it carefully. The large bird stepped back when it opened and then returned gracefully to the sill of the open window. "Well, my young friend, we are going to have to sharpen up your senses before we begin to understand each other."

"What do you mean, senses?" Tom asked, scratching his head and rubbing his eyes.

"I mean that I have been calling you for some time and it took you quite a while to wake up and respond to my message."

"Your message?" Tom asked again.

"I think we had better make a clean start of this, young friend. I have something to tell you that is of very great importance. We must meet tomorrow in a place where only you and I can be."

The seagull stepped forward and turned his head to give Tom that look, the look that seemed like a smile. The bird's eye blinked again.

"How did you wake me up, was it the tapping on the window?" Tom asked.

"Good heavens no," the seagull replied. "I can reach you without words or sound. I will tell you all about it tomorrow." The bird opened its wings "I am sorry to have woken you Tom, but we have great things to discuss; they will not wait any longer and I have a feeling I can trust you."

"You most certainly can, Mr Hawkins," Tom assured the bird. "Where shall we meet and when?"

"The cliffs, but over towards the west bay. There is a path covered by bracken. No-one knows about it except me. Follow the path down until it goes no further, then look to your right. You will see a small opening.

You will be able to crawl through. You will find that it opens into a large cavern. Make sure you keep to the ledge against the cliff wall. Then you will see some rocks that have been cut away to form steps. They were made by smugglers many years ago. The steps lead down into a larger cave. I will meet you there."

Tom was wide awake now and excited. "Why can't we talk now?" he asked.

"Because you will wake the whole house. I saw your mother look in on you and she may be back." The bird then hopped to one side. "Besides, I have much to tell you and you need to be fully awake. So sleep tight, Tom Parker. Until tomorrow." The bird jumped up to take flight and Tom leaned out of the window. "Wait, what time shall we meet?" he called out.

"Be there at four o'clock of your afternoon," the bird replied as it flew away into the night.

Jack Parker had managed to row against the tide and the wind to get to the harbour wall. He could not stop thinking about what had happened on board *The Eagle*. He finally made it to the quayside and tied the small rowing boat to the pontoon.

He was cold and soaking wet and was glad to shed his clothes as he walked into the warm kitchen of the Windwhistle inn.

Maggie Parker was upstairs in bed when she heard him. "Thank the Lord," she said quietly and looked at the clock by her bed. It was two-thirty in the morning.

As Jack came up the stairs, Maggie was waiting for him. "Thank heavens, Jack, I was so worried about you. Is everything all right?"

"Yes, it's all fine my dear, but I've got some very interesting news to tell you." Jack was tired, but keen to tell his wife everything.

"Is Tom OK?" Jack asked.

"He's asleep. He's been acting very strangely. I think he's coming down with something. He was late home and his clothes were in shreds when I found them lying on the floor of his room."

"Oh, he was probably mucking around with his friends after school. I'll go and look in on him quickly."

Tom was pretending to be fast asleep when his father opened the door and quietly tip-toed over to him.

He looked down at Tom and smiled to himself. Jack loved his son and whenever he had been away, even for one day, he would always go and see him before going to bed.

He whispered very softly to Tom. "One day soon my lad you will be coming with me to sea."

Jack leaned over and kissed Tom gently on his head. The boy did not stir when his father quietly slipped out through the door, but he smiled and closed his eyes.

Just after the end of lunch break the school bell rang and everybody walked quickly back to their classrooms. Tom was sitting alone on a bench at the far end of the courtyard.

"Come on now, Parker, get yourself back into class," called over Mr Ambrose, the history teacher. "Yes Sir," Tom replied looking up at him from a deep thought.

"Why, you look like you have the worries of a man heading for the rope, Parker, what's the matter?" the teacher asked. Mr Ambrose was a decent man who loved his work and enjoyed the company of his brighter pupils. He was not bothered about those who had no taste for knowledge. He knew, though, that Tom was keen to learn and encouraged him and treated him like an adult to give him confidence.

"Oh, nothing Sir I..." Tom stopped and looked up at the sky to see a large seagull flying past.

He smiled and then nearly laughed when the bird suddenly went into a dive and turned a complete circle. "Mr Hawkins," he whispered and then grinned.

"What was that Tom?" asked Mr Ambrose again. "Nothing Sir – really it's nothing." Tom stood up suddenly and rushed back to the class.

Mr Ambrose stood and looked up at the sky and saw nothing but clouds. He shook his head and muttered to himself, "Sometimes I really wonder about these kids." Then he stopped trying to work out what Tom had said and walked back to the classroom.

For most of the afternoon Tom sat at his desk looking out of the window, only looking down at his books when he thought he was being watched or pretending to be attentive when he had to. He nodded at the right times and frowned sometimes to look like he was thinking about something that had been said. All the time, his thoughts were on his walk to the cliffs. He must not be seen by anyone. This was such an important secret.

At last, at three-thirty, the final bell rang. Tom frantically collected up his books and dropped two on the floor in his eagerness to get away.

"Well, Parker, looks like you 'ave a right old strut on. Off to do the dishes are we?" Johnny Benson was leering over at him and had seen him drop his books. "Who's a clumsy boy then?"

Johnny continued his jeering to the keen amusement of some of the other boys who were left in the room. Tom chose to ignore the insults and the temptation to retaliate. As he collected his things and walked to the classroom door, Benson stood in the way with his arms folded. He was still sneering. Tom knew there was going to be trouble and he did not want to be late for his meeting.

"Come on Benson, I have to get home, let me past," he said trying to shrug off an inevitable situation.

"Oh dear, will Mummy be cross with little Tommy if you're late?" Benson replied, trying to provoke Tom into a fight.

"Leave it out, Benson, you're making a fool of yourself," Tom said as he looked at the other boys. He realised that they were with Johnny and knew, of course, that this was only because they were afraid of him. He was on his own. "Ha, looks like it's you an' me, Tommy boy," Johnny said suddenly and kicked out with one leg and sent Tom's schoolbooks flying across the floor. As Johnny went forward to grab Tom, a sudden bright light beamed through the classroom window straight into Johnny's eyes and he faltered for a brief second. Tom instantly saw his chance and launched a fist straight at Johnny's face. The blow landed in the middle of Johnny's face causing him to let out a yell and drop to his knees holding a bleeding nose.

Tom grabbed his books and ran out of the room. The other boys watched in amazement but did nothing to stop him as he sped from the classroom and along the corridor.

He ran and ran as fast as he could to the sheds where the boys kept their bicycles. Tom's bike was old but trusty and had a small bag behind the seat for his books. He peddled quickly along the main road back to Rivermouth and finally, just before the top of the hill, which led down into the town, he turned right along the footpath to the west cliffs.

   While he was supposed to have been listening to his teacher during the class he had been working out where he could hide his bike. The thick bushes were a perfect place. It would be safe here while he climbed the rest of the way up the track to the top of the cliffs and down through the steep grass meadow to the edge. He kept looking back to see if anyone had seen him and was relieved when he saw no-one.

   He was thinking hard about the seagull's instructions and as he walked down the steep slopes, he began to look around for the hidden path covered with bracken. He stood at the top of the cliffs looking over to the west bay. He looked all around for the break in the bracken where the path should be. There had been some rain over the last few days and the footing underneath was wet and the bushes were thick with sharp thorns growing all around the bracken, which made his search even harder. He found a stick and pushed the bracken carefully away to find the path. He did not want to disturb the bushes too much in case he revealed the path to anyone else. Suddenly he found it. There was a narrow path a few feet beyond some thick bushes. It looked like no-one had been here for a long time. The path was well covered. Carefully he picked his way through the bracken, pushing back the bushes behind him as he went. After a short while the path became easier to navigate and he continued until it went no further. He recalled the seagull's instructions and looked around for an opening in the hill. He noticed a small hole in the bank, almost at the edge of the cliff. It did not look safe and seemed too small to climb through, so he continued searching but saw nothing else that resembled an opening. He turned back to the small hole again. *I wonder* he thought and approached it warily. With his stick he pushed back some loose soil and weeds growing around the small entrance. The entrance was just about big enough to squeeze into. Although he was very nervous and extremely cautious, he decided to try to look through the hole. First he poked his stick through the hole and found no contact on the inside. He decided that it was quite deep. He leant down and slowly lowered his head to try to see inside. He managed to get his face right up to the opening and suddenly he heard something; he jumped back quickly and a rabbit burst out of the hole and ran straight past him. His heart pumped with the shock. He sat down beside the hole to regain his composure. Then, when he was ready, he moved closer to the hole. This time he made the entrance bigger by scraping away some of the earth around it. He fumbled around in his jacket and found his pocket torch and wondered why he hadn't used it in the first place. Again he got his head inside the hole and shone the torch. Sure enough, there was a large cavern beyond the entrance. He quickly squeezed his head through, then his chest, and finally his whole body slipped through the narrow entrance and eventually fell down onto a ledge inside. He managed to rest against a rock and take note of the strange underground surroundings he had found himself in. He remembered that he had to keep close to the wall of the ledge and shone his torch over the edge. There was a sheer drop. He knew if he fell down there he would never get out and now realised that he was taking a terrible risk.

The ledge slipped away down to some rocks and as his torchlight found them, he noticed the rocky steps, which Mr Hawkins had said were made by smugglers many years before. He began to think of the ghosts of men and pirates and quickly tried to shrug off these thoughts. He could not pretend not to be scared, because he was.

Very carefully, he edged his way down to the rocky steps. They were wet and slippery. The rocky ceiling above him became higher and he realised that he could stand up quite easily. He shone his torch around and sensed that he was in the right place. Although he was still uncertain of what was happening, he was sure this was the large cavern that Mr Hawkins had told him about. He was very nervous and thought about escaping as fast as he could run. He looked back, shining the torch upwards towards the entrance. He knew how to escape if he needed to. Although it was damp and each step echoed around him, there was a strange warmth, which did not seem right. He pointed the torchlight ahead and called out.

"Mr Hawkins, are you there?"

Suddenly he saw a glow of light appear from the other side of a larger wall. Slowly Tom crept closer and with his back to the wall, peered around the corner. There was a bright light, a golden glow, coming from an even larger cavern on the other side. He turned off the torch and again moved closer. A voice suddenly sounded in his ears; it was loud and made him jump with fright.

"Is that you, Tom?" The voice echoed all around him.

"Mr Hawkins? Yes, it's Tom, you're scaring me."

"Walk ahead Tom, there is no need to be alarmed."

As Tom approached, he was stunned again by the bright light. When he focused his eyes upon the area where he had heard the voice, he suddenly saw the most remarkable sight.

In the centre of the chamber was a large square rock. On the top was a nest of thick straw and reeds, held tightly together with thin sticks. The sticks were bound around the nest, which was the biggest he had ever seen. From the centre of the nest came the source of the golden glow. Standing in the centre of the nest was the seagull. It was the most peculiar sight. There was a beam of light streaming right through the large bird and out of his eyes, rays of light danced around the cavern.

"Welcome, my friend," the voice echoed, "I am indeed impressed with your tenacity and bravery to come here to my home and meet with me." The seagull spoke clearly and in a majestic tone.

Tom stared with his mouth wide open. What was he seeing? Surely this was not all a dream?

"What are you... doing?" Tom choked out the question.

"I have asked you here as I trust you and know you will keep this and what I am about to tell you in utmost secrecy." Mr Hawkins stepped forward, out of the glowing light. His eyes immediately went back to their proper appearance and apart from his size he looked like a normal seagull again.

"My my, you do look so worried. Come and take a seat." The bird pointed with its wing to a small rock, which had been carved like a chair. Tom sat down obediently.

"What was that light in your eyes Mr Hawkins, and what is that beam of gold light? How does it shine like that?" Tom asked curiously.

"Ho, so many questions – and indeed they do deserve answers. Are you comfortable, Tom?"

"Yes – thank-you."

"Good, now I have much to tell you. Are you a believer in mystery, Tom, and do you understand that there is sometimes more to things than at first it seems?"

"Well yes, I suppose." Tom was not certain where this was leading but he knew he was about to discover something extraordinary. He nodded frantically and swallowed hard. There was a large lump in his throat. *What was going to happen now?* he wondered.

"Well then this is indeed good, for what I am about to tell you will change your life for ever."

As the seagull stood tall on the edge of the large grey rock in the centre of the cavern, Tom sat silently waiting to hear what mysteries were about to be unfolded.

The seagull stood very still and looked down at Tom with that smile he had come to know. Then he settled down on the edge of the rock and quietly hummed to himself. He suddenly stopped and closed one eye, but with the other, he stared at Tom.

In a soft voice he said: "Look into my eye, Tom, and say after me, these words.

"I Tom Parker..."

Tom repeated: "I... Tom Parker..."

The seagull continued with Tom repeating after every few words.

"Do swear by the Sword of Isis that my fate has been blessed and as I am to discover the Golden Secret of the Temple of Serapis, I will not reveal any part or expose to any other living soul, my fate and the fortunes that lie within."

Tom repeated the words slowly and carefully. Although he had no idea of what he was promising or swearing to, or even why he was saying it, he obeyed and listened.

"Excellent, excellent," the seagull replied and then stood up and walked up and down the edge of his rock. "There was a time many, many years ago Tom when I was a man."

Tom swallowed again and was stunned. "A man?" he asked cautiously.

"Yes, Tom, I was once a man. In fact I was a leader of men. I was captain of a large merchant ship."

"But how, what happened?"

"I shall tell you now. We were sailing in uncharted waters. In those times there were only very primitive charts and most of the time we mariners sailed blindly in places we had no knowledge of." The seagull was about to continue when he looked down at Tom and saw the confusion in his face. He realised that this was all very strange and unbelievable to him. He turned his head to one side and blinked.

"I can see that this is not easy for you to comprehend, Tom, but you must believe me when I say that everything I am telling you is true. I was a gentleman in my days as a human. I was well respected as a mariner and captain aboard one of the fastest and largest sailing ships of our time. My men loved me and I loved them. We were as close to being a family as ever you could have.

My ship was called *The Glaros*. She was given to me by a King from a foreign land. I will tell you more of this later." The seagull paused and then continued.

"We had been at sea for many days. First we were becalmed and the sun scorched down upon us relentlessly. I lost some of my men to the fever and they were given an honourable burial at sea.

Then, some days on, the storm came. It was the worst storm I had ever seen. Waves a hundred feet tall. Lightning that lit the sky like firecrackers and winds that ripped our masts right out from the bottom of the ship. We lost twelve good men. The storm raged for three-and-a-half days.

It was on the noon of the third day that we sighted land. Eventually the storm passed and the sea became calm again. We had no knowledge of where we were or where our destiny lay. *The Glaros* was badly damaged and needed much work to make her seaworthy again. We were only able to sail her with one mast and a steady sail but we did make it to land.

We salvaged four of the eight small boats that we had on board and prepared them to get us ashore once we found a safe anchorage.

There were many rocks ahead, and a good friend, who I have missed these many years, Mr Joseph Trelawney, was able to call down from the crow's-nest of the only mast still standing and give us our heading. He could see the reefs and where the shallows were. I could steer *The Glaros* through the rocks by his instruction. We were a fine team, Tom, and for many years we had sailed from one adventure to another. But somehow we had an uneasy feeling about this place and we were wary as we picked our way between the rocks. It was a dangerous moment, Tom, but finally we sighted a gap between two reefs. Beyond was a bay. As we neared the reef we headed into the opening. We were lucky, with only inches between our fragile wooden hull and the treacherous coral reefs around us. Finally we made it through.

We all cheered as we sailed our ship slowly into a large lagoon.

It was the most beautiful place I had ever cast my eyes upon. The water was as blue as a sapphire and as clear as glass. All around the lagoon were white sandy beaches with palm trees and lush green forests behind them. We had not seen land in many days so you can imagine, this was a welcome sight."

Tom had been listening with his mouth wide open, imagining the beautiful lagoon. "Did you go ashore, Mr Hawkins?" he asked.

"Aye we did. When the anchor splashed into the clear water, it echoed all around us. We saw birds leap from the trees. These were birds of the most wonderful colours. The noise from the forests was incredible. It was as if we had woken the whole place and the shrieks and sounds that cried out were the strangest we had ever heard."

Mr Hawkins jumped across from his rock onto a ledge. He flapped his wings and let out a shriek, the sound that a seagull would make, and it made Tom jump. Then the seagull stood still and lowered his head. The echo from his shrieks died and then Tom noticed that his new friend looked sad. The dripping sound of water and the distant rumble from the sea from the outer walls of the cave returned to him, echoing from below.

Tom thought quickly and tried to say something to get the seagull talking again. "How far from the cliffs are we?" he asked.

The bird slowly lifted his head and looked up at the ceiling of the cave and then over to Tom.

"You can see the ocean from my window just down there," Mr Hawkins pointed with his wing towards an opening and Tom could see there was a faint glow of light. There was a narrow passage, which led away from the opening. "Is it safe for me to go down there? It looks very steep." Tom stood up to take a closer look.

"No," cried the seagull. "It isn't safe, it falls away very steeply and it is very slippery. It is safe for me because..." He paused and then continued, "Because I am a bird. This place is my home while I am here and I know every passage and crevice of this cliff. You must never try to climb around in here. Not without my assistance. Now sit down, Tom, I have much more to tell you."

Tom, of course, realised that he was in strange surroundings and the seagull was right. He also knew there was great sadness with his friend and he should wait and listen. This was no ordinary bird and he knew he was about to discover a whole new world. It was all so very strange and quite unbelievable.

Mr Hawkins continued. "I could never begin to tell you how strange it felt to be standing on the deck of my ship and to witness this sight. We knew not whether we had found an island or some coastal region of a new country. Our charts were primitive and the storm had cost us dearly. We had lost most of our supplies and were indeed lucky to be alive. We stood in amazement as we looked all around us and saw beautiful birds, incredible plants and trees growing in abundance. We had never seen the likes of anything such as this. There must have been a hundred different types of birds alone."

The seagull was about to continue when he noticed Tom staring at the nest on the large rock in the centre of the cave. He was staring at the golden glow of light which beamed out from the centre and shone up towards the roof of the cave.

"I see you are curious of the light, my friend. I will tell you about this." The bird flew down from the ledge and landed back on the nest. He disappeared for a moment and Tom wondered what was happening. He was scared to get too close in case he offended the seagull. Suddenly, the glow became much brighter and then a pillar of gold light appeared. Tom cried out: "What's happening?" It was like some kind of magic and it unnerved him.

The seagull re-appeared through the bright light. Now he was holding something in his beak. It was a gold chain and hanging from it was what appeared to be a large shining stone. Then Tom looked closer so see that it looked like a huge diamond. Suddenly, shadows danced all around the cave, caused by the strange light. It was so bright that Tom had to hold a hand over his eyes. "Wow! What is that, how did you do that?" Tom had so many questions. First the story of the beautiful, strange lagoon and now this. He was confused yet so excited. It was all so incredible.

The seagull held up the glowing stone and it swung from his beak. Slowly he laid it down on the rock beside the nest. "This chain holds the Stone of Isis. Look Tom, look at the Stone."

Tom squinted into the light. "Is it a diamond?" he asked and held his hands up to his face. "Upon my word, I have never seen anything so beautiful. It must be the biggest diamond in the world." He stood up to take a closer look. "May I?" he asked.

"Yes, come and see, Tom, but be careful, the light that shines from this stone is very powerful. Do not touch it. It has powers that are beyond anything you have ever dreamed of."

Tom was hesitant and walked warily towards the centre of the cave to the rock where the large stone lay.

The seagull continued. "This stone has shone like this for over two thousand years. It originally was set into the Sword of Isis, which came from the Temple of Serapis. This was the ancient temple of dreams. Unfortunately the stone was separated from the sword. I shall tell you about this later. The stone, when it is reunited with the sword, will have powers beyond your wildest imagination.

In the time of the third century, a secret order of Greek monks, who had devoted themselves to keeping peace on earth and to bring all people together, discovered that the temple was the home of the Sword of Isis. This came from the Egyptian Goddess Isis, who was supposed to represent kindliness, peace, harmony and healing. The monks made a long and treacherous journey by sea to the Temple of Serapis, where they discovered that the pagans and Christians were in bitter rivalry. The Christians wanted to bring down the temple and destroy all within it. The Greek monks, unhappy at the violence and hypocrisy of all the religious fighting, sneaked into the temple, found the sword and escaped with it back to a secret island. For over two hundred years the monks had the Sword of Isis safely hidden on the island. The secret was handed down, monk to monk, all through the years. The Temple of Serapis was razed to the ground and many people were killed – all in the name of Christianity. It is a strange tale, Tom. It will take a very long time for us to debate this part of history, so I will not discuss this further for now.

On one of my voyages to the East, hundreds of years ago, we were caught up in a battle between two sides from different regions. The Greeks and the Arab King were allies and finally the battle was won by the great King who stood for freedom and peace in the world. He married a Greek princess called Dorothea and they had a daughter. This brought together the two worlds of the East and the West. They discarded their differences in the belief that the world was now a better place. The monks, delighted that finally a great King had brought peace to the world, decided that the

Sword of Isis should be given to him as a gesture and symbol of his great worthiness.

Many years later, the sword was given to me by the King; his name is King Hafidh Al Kadi, for saving the life of his daughter, Princess Tasia. It was to be the future symbol of freedom and harmony. I was greatly honoured to be its keeper. The sword proved most valuable to me in later events.

For many years, harmony prevailed and all was well. Then, sadly, an evil man rose out from the desert with one aim – to destroy the peace and rule the world."

Tom was truly in awe of his friend and yet puzzled. How could anyone be that old?

"How is it that you have been alive so long? I don't understand."

The seagull answered: "I will come to tell you all these things in good time, Tom, but you must be patient and listen. You will have to learn everything before we make our journey."

"Our journey?" Tom asked in surprise.

"Yes, we shall be engaging on a journey that will take us into great adventure. A journey where you will find the secrets of a world that you never knew existed. This is a world within a world. Lost in time, but never died and has never changed. A time that man has forgotten. No one in your world knows the truth and the reality of what I can tell you."

"But how can you know so much? How can you be so... old?"

"Aha! My word, Tom, you have put your mark well on the chart. Yes, my dear friend, I am as old as time itself. At least that's how it appears. I have made journeys through time and seen more than most." Tom struggled with this. None of it made any sense.

"I don't understand – what do you mean a world within a world?"

The seagull gave a little chuckle and nodded his head up and down as if he knew that an easy explanation was necessary. "Let me put it this way, Tom. You will have no doubt learned in your school about black holes?"

Tom nodded and said "Well, yes, a bit, but they are in space – in the universe and anyway no one really knows much about them".

"Exactly, Tom, no one knows anything about them – how right you are. But you will have heard that your scientists say that it is possible to travel through black holes into a different time. You see there are two worlds. One world is here, now – where you live – this is your world. But there is another world and only I know how to get there".

Tom scratched his head and frowned. "But you talked about Greece and Egyptians – they are in THIS world"

"Aye, Tom, indeed I did and these places are also in the other world – but they are also different – and in another time".

Tom was so confused. He put his chin in both hands and looked down at the floor.

The seagull knew full well that this was indeed going to be a difficult task and sighed. "Forgive me, Tom. You are so young and I know this is indeed hard for you to understand. I do, however, admire your reserve. Let us return to the story I was in the process of unfolding. Give me time, Tom, and I will get to where you want us to be. You must have the full story before we move forward."

Tom tried to take it all in. It was the most incredible story, and he agreed to sit back down and listen.

The seagull continued. "From the lagoon, we were able to take some provisions ashore but most of our food and water had gone in the storm. We knew that although we had appeared to have found a peaceful haven and shelter for ourselves and a place where we could repair the damage to *The Glaros*, we would need to find fresh food and water and build a shelter to accommodate ourselves ashore.

I ordered a party of my men to secure the long boats in a small inlet on the shore where it would be easy for us to slip in and out of the bay, unnoticed if need be. We could escape quickly should we fall into danger. We did not know what we would find in this strange land, nor did we know if we were alone. I asked Joseph Trelawney to stay with four men and guard the boats and took the rest of my men into the forest to search the region. I had with me an Arab by the name of Braheim. He was an old and trusted friend and was an excellent scout and tracker from the desert. There was also Trouseau, a Frenchman. He was once a thief but I rescued him from a hanging and he too became a loyal friend. He was a master swordsman and taught me a great deal about the art of sword fighting.

We were armed with swords and long bows. I carried with me the Sword of Isis and, with it, I defeated any foe that came at me in anger. I had been told of its great powers by the King when he presented it to me but I had not understood fully the truth of this power until much later.

We hacked our way through thick bush and blades of grass taller than a man and as sharp as knives. All the while we were followed by monkeys of many types and birds with voices we had never heard before. These were birds of all colours. There was no chance of us being able to march quietly and I began to worry that we would bring attention to ourselves. I ordered my men to stand still and make no sound, not to make even the wink of an eye. After a few moments the shrieks and cries of the forest died down and then there was no sign of any life at all. The forest fell silent. It was strange and we were uneasy with this. For some time we stood there making no movement or sound. Nothing could be heard or seen, not even a flicker from the tree tops or an insect crawling on the grass. I whispered to my men: 'Softly lads, this forest knows we are here and we must continue slowly and without a sound.'

As we continued, I gave my orders by hand signs. Our journey was much harder, now, as we were not able to hack down the razor sharp grass. We were cut from head to toe. Our visibility was no more than a few feet ahead because of the thick bush all around us. We felt the creatures of the forest were watching us. I could sense their eyes all around. Somehow they did not cry out or scream like before. It was as if they were welcoming us and now they knew we were there, they were happy to watch us. After all, we must have looked very strange to them. Slowly we continued, with difficulty and in silence.

After a long trek, a clearing in the bush appeared. It was very hot and although we were in the thickest of forests, the heat of the sun beat down on us relentlessly. We desperately needed water and to get out of the sun. I told the men to rest for a while and find shade if possible. It appeared that the forest life had woken again, but this time there was no panic and the sounds we heard were more like the typical noises you would hear in any forest or jungle.

Braheim, who had gone on ahead to scout the area, came running back. 'Sahib, come quickly!' he shouted. I could see he was excited and eager for us to follow him instantly. 'What is it Braheim?' I called. He just nodded in the other direction for us to follow. Jumping over rocks and fallen timber, we chased after him through the long grass. Suddenly the ground beneath us began to tremble and a rumbling sound gradually became a thunderous roar as we ran into a huge open area where the noise became deafening. This was a terrifying sound and now there was a dampness in the air and the noise was like the sound of continuous cannon fire. Braheim was standing on a large rock waving his arms at us. I could not believe my eyes when we reached him and looked down from the rock. We were hundreds of feet above a vast ravine, which dropped down into a lake. On the far side of this giant ravine was a massive waterfall, which rolled down the sides of the cliffs and finally poured into the lake below. In the distance, on the other side of the ravine, there was a river with white water smashing against rocks and pushing itself over the edge to become the waterfall and then falling down hundreds of feet into the lake. It was the most impressive and powerful sight. It was clear that nothing would survive the strength of such a torrent.

Suddenly one of the men shouted, 'Captain, look over there, I see some movement.' He was pointing toward an area of the bank on the far side of the lake at the bottom of the ravine. Then I saw it too. There were some very small buildings dotted beside the lake. There were people moving around. Then we saw a horse and rider galloping along the side of the lake. He appeared to be waving something. It was too far off to make out who or what these people were. I was sure they could not see us so far up the ravine. We were at least a mile away, but the light was good despite the haze from the sun over the waterfall. We needed to get water but had to be careful not to be seen, until we knew more about these people.

I sent Braheim to look for a way down the side of the ravine and ordered the men to cover up anything that would shine or reflect in the sunlight. It was important that we were not seen or made any announcement of our presence.

Cautiously we walked in single file along the ridge until finally Braheim found a place for us to climb down. The rock was firm beneath us for a while and then became very treacherous. One wrong move and we would move any loose rocks under our feet, which would fall away and down the ravine, drawing attention to ourselves and this we did not need. Carefully, we continued. Suddenly we heard some voices. Someone was shouting and then someone called back. They spoke in a language unknown to us.

'Down!' I whispered the order. We all hit the ground quickly. The voices were nearer this time. Braheim tugged my arm and pointed to a rock directly above us. We were lying close to the cliff face, which made it hard to see past the overhanging rock above us. I could not see who was there or exactly where they were. It was a tense moment. Then, we heard the galloping of horses and more shouting. There was another sound that was even more disturbing: the men were drawing their swords. We were in no place to make a stand and fight. I needed to think fast and signalled to Trouseau to move further up to try and get closer to where the voices came from. He was light on his feet and made no sound as he climbed up the rock.

All we could do was wait in silence, staying close to the rock face. There was much activity above us and a great deal of shouting. We heard orders being given. Suddenly there was a fierce crack of a whip and then a scream. The crack was followed by another and then another. The screams were terrible, people were suffering and we could not see what was happening. Then there was some kind of commotion, a man shouted and another cried out as if he was pleading for mercy. Some earth fell over our heads and as we pushed back further against the cliff wall, a pile of small rocks fell over us. Then another scream and a body fell past us. The screams died away as the body fell to the rocks hundreds of feet below. All was quiet for a few moments until the crack of the whip resounded again and then more shouting. After a while it appeared that the sound of the voices was drifting away. The snorting of horses and thud of their hooves faded.

As we wondered what was happening, Trouseau reappeared. Quietly he gave his report. 'Mon Capitaine, these are not friendly people. They have slaves in heavy iron chains. The soldiers are of dark skin. They wear white robes and the pointed steel helmet. Their faces are covered. I think these are bad people. They threw a man to his death. We should leave this place now'

"I held a finger to my lips to quieten the men. I needed to be certain that the soldiers above us had gone. There were no more voices and the sound of horses faded into the distance.

I made the decision that we should continue down to the lake: we needed to find water and food and return to Joseph and the others on the beach. This beautiful place no longer had the feeling of paradise.

Finally we arrived at the lake. It was very wide and the water was aqua blue. Had it not been for our encounter with the slaves, we would have enjoyed a swim in this beautiful place and washed our clothes, but we were uneasy. I was uncertain of what lay ahead and began to consider Joseph and the others on the beach. I hoped that they would lie low until we returned. I also thought about *The Glaros* and wondered if we would manage to repair the terrible damage she had suffered.

I did not feel good. On one hand this was a place of great beauty and on the other I sensed terrible dangers that lay ahead of us if we were to remain here.

The men filled their leather flasks with the clear fresh water from small streams that came down from the mountain and poured into the lake. They took some rest under a tree while I surveyed the area. Earlier I had forbidden the men from swimming in the lake for fear of being seen, but now I saw no immediate dangers and let them go into the water, insisting that they stayed close to the rocks by the shore. There was a flat rock, which we laid upon to let the sun dry our clothes. We put the flasks in the water to keep them cool. After a while, the men began to relax and feel good. A joke or two had everyone laughing. Trouseau, often the entertainer in our crew, was demonstrating the dance of the women of the city of Kadistaar; this is a wonderful place, famous for its entertainment and arts. One day I will return there. In fact you and I will take a journey to Kadidtaar soon"

Tom looked up at the seagull in complete awe and also with some hesitation.

"Where is Kadistaar, how could we ever go there?"

"Time is on our side, my friend. I have the Stone of Isis, which will help us on our journey. When we find the sword which holds the stone, the full power of Isis will be ours, but mark my words, Tom; we shall need to be careful."

Tom suddenly thought about time and realised that he had been there for quite a while. "Oh no, I'm going to be in trouble now, it's getting late. I should be getting home." Then he looked at his watch. The time indicated that he had only just left the school. "My watch has stopped, I can't believe it," he exclaimed. "It'll be getting dark soon, I'm sorry, Mr Hawkins, Sir, but if I'm late home I'll be in trouble, then my parents will be watching me.

It will be really difficult to get out here again." He was about to stand up and search for his torch when the seagull stopped him.

"Wait a minute, Tom. Look at your watch. You see the second hand still moves but yet the other hands are not moving. You see, time is standing still."

"Yes – that's odd. Maybe something's wrong with my watch." Tom started shaking his arm to get the watch going again.

"Hold on, Tom, there is no problem with your watch. It is working fine. It is time that has stopped." The seagull stretched his wings and gave them a little flap. He then continued, "Tom do you hear me? It is as if you have never been here. The power of this stone has enabled us to have our meeting without the interference of time. You see, you can stay much longer, the day is still young. You are not late and you will get home in time for your duties. Trust me."

Tom was astonished. "You're kidding! You mean to say that you have frozen time so we could have this meeting?"

"Exactly! That is correct, Tom. We are in a place where there is no time. The Stone of Isis has powers that no mortal will ever understand. This must be a total secret, Tom. Do not let anyone know of this." The seagull paused to look at Tom and then continued. "You have nothing to fear, young friend, there is no evil or harm done here."

Tom looked at his watch again. "So, how long have I been here?" he asked.

"No time at all – I promise – you will not return home late. Now I must continue with the story. You need to know everything." The seagull jumped back up onto his rock and looked at Tom. "Ready?" he asked.

"Ready," replied Tom and he sat back down.

"Kadistaar is a big country and its city the most wonderful place. It was built at the delta of a large river so many, many years ago." The seagull gave a little laugh to himself and continued. "This was a place where people came from all the lands to trade in peace and friendship. There were often great feasts with music and dancing from the many regions of the Arabians, Egyptians, Greeks and other visiting countries. The nobles would parade in their rafts along the canals. There would be laughter and merriment all around. In the evenings, people would go to the great temple to thank their God for their good fortune. Although it was all so different, life was just beginning; it was a time of great peace. Sadly, though, it was not to last." Mr Hawkins paused again and seemed to be in deep thought. Tom looked at him closely and saw the sadness return.

"What's making you sad, Mr Hawkins?" Tom asked.

The seagull looked up and stretched his neck up high as if to retain his dignity. "All in good time young friend. Now – back to my story. I must finish this before you return to your home as there is much to be done."

The seagull looked down affectionately upon Tom and then stretched his neck out and threw his wings wide. With a quick step, he lifted himself up and hovered over the rock and the stone, which still glowed around the cave. Finally, he settled back down and shook his feathers.

"As I was saying." He paused and then continued. "We all loved to listen to Trouseau's tales and jokes and we laughed and applauded when he recited and sang, telling his stories. It was a beautiful day, the sun was warm but we were beneath the shade of a huge tree. We were clean and had tasted the clear, fresh water. But then we heard something. We did not know what it was. At first it sounded like thunder, then it seemed like a huge herd of elephants was nearby. This, added to the noise of the waterfall, startled us. We were quick to gather up our things and moved to a safer position. The sound was moving closer and was becoming louder. Then we heard the scariest sound and immediately we knew what it was. It was the sound of trumpets and horns. There was also the beating of a heavy drum. The beat was for the rhythm of oarsmen. We heard the splash and movement of the oars in the water. In the distance, we heard shouts of men giving orders. Again this was a language we did not know but one thing was certain, we should not remain here. We climbed up through the rocky hillside to get as high as we could. It was hard going as the soft ground and flaky rock crumbled under our feet. Eventually I put up my hand, a sign to halt. We all cowered down behind a boulder which hung out from the hillside. There was very little space to stand as the ledge was narrow and we were trapped against the rocky wall with just a few boulders and pine bushes to use as cover. The sound of the horns and drums came closer. It was so close now that we could hear the panting of breath from the oarsmen. Then without any further warning, a huge ship with many oars appeared from around the corner of the lake. The ship had two tall masts and a third smaller mast set behind her helm. There were no sails hoisted; she was being rowed very quickly by at least a hundred men. These were not crewmen, they were slaves. They rowed to the beat of the huge wooden drum, which was mounted upon the quarterdeck and was being beaten by a huge dark skinned man in white robes which matched those of the other soldiers around him. Some of these soldiers were carrying whips and unleashed their anger on any slaves who flagged and were too weary to row further. There were shouts of commands and cries of pain and misery. This was a deathly sight and I wondered where the ship was heading on this giant lake. I scanned the ship looking for someone who could be her captain. Then I saw him – a tall, thin man standing alone at the stern of the ship. He was dressed in black with a gold belt which hung diagonally from his shoulder to his waist. The belt was hung with a long curved sabre. The man wore a long black and gold braided cape over his shoulders and a head-dress also in black and gold. He had a beard, which was pitch black and pointed beneath his chin. His skin was dark brown, his eyes were deep set and dark, his nose was long, hooked and sharp. He looked Arabian, but I couldn't be sure. It was unmistakable; he had to be the leader of these men in white robes. I could not take my eyes off this man as he stood taller than most of the others, his hands on his hips and legs placed firmly apart upon the deck of his ship. He was a leader; he looked like a man who should be feared. Occasionally he snapped an order at one of his men and the order was passed quickly along the line. No-one delayed, the order was carried out swiftly, quietly and efficiently.

We watched the ship move along the lake and eventually it passed right by us. The tops of the tall masts were almost level with our ledge. Braheim nudged my arm as the tall masts moved slowly along right in front of our eyes. 'Sahib, see the top of the mast, a man is looking out.'

Sure enough, there was a man up in the crow's-nest. He was looking all around. If he saw us, we would be in big trouble. 'Keep low', I whispered along to my men. We could not make a sound or any movement. If we were seen it would not take long for them to form a shore party and search us out. We were badly outnumbered and although my men were brave and skilled in combat, we knew it would take a miracle for us to win against so many.

The drumming and the trumpets and cries of men passed below us as we clung desperately to branches or rocks. The look-out on the ship did not see us and eventually the ship slipped away and disappeared beyond the peninsular of rocky headland beyond us. We remained pinned down until I was certain there were no more boats following. 'Come on men, we must return to our own. Go, as fast as you can,' I then ordered. It did not take us long to climb to the top of the hill. Trouseau went over the top first to make certain it was clear. When we heard his whistle, we moved quickly and, one by one, we climbed over the top and ran across the open space, where the thunder of the waterfall rumbled below, and back into the thick forest.

Once we had all made it safely, we moved swiftly, in single file through the bush back to where we knew Joseph and the others were waiting. The return journey took longer than we had hoped, as the heat was unbearable and we were worried about waking the forest again and alerting any potential trouble.

Finally we came to the edge of the forest and we could feel the sea air and heard the sound of the waves on the beach. I looked round at the men behind me and saw the smiles on their faces as we all realised that we were near to our base and friends.

When we reached the beach, I knew immediately that we had reappeared in a different place and for a moment I thought we were miles off. Then I noticed the cove where we had left the boats and where Joseph would be waiting. Although we saw no sign of the others, we guessed that they had taken cover from the scorching sun and would see us as we approached.

There was no time to waste. We hurried along the beach keeping close to the trees in case we needed to take cover. But, there seemed to be no sign of our friends and I became worried. Joseph should have known by now that we were there. I was not happy with this and my heart began to sink with the fear that something had gone wrong. I turned to the men and saw their concern. They, too, had sensed that this was not right.

'To arms, men', I ordered over my shoulder and the slicing sound of steel instantly came from behind. Every man had drawn his sword. We moved in closer to the palm trees, which lined the border between the forest and the beach. It was hard running along the hot, soft sand. We were already tired from the trek back from the lake and the possibility of a fight weighed heavily upon me, as I knew the men were weary. It was times like this when good lives were lost unnecessarily.

As we approached the cove, where our long boats were hidden, we heard no sound nor saw any sign of the others. I cannot tell you how my heart felt at that time, but I will tell you that I felt cold inside. I knew that we were in danger and I was worried about what might have happened to Joseph and the rest of the crew. There was no sign of them as we rounded the corner from a clump of trees and stepped cautiously onto the beach. 'Spread out', I called to the men. They immediately fell into a single line either side of me. Slowly we approached the top of the sand dune and peered over. Horror hit me as I saw the long boats. They had been smashed to pieces and their timbers lay all around the cove. There was no sign of the other men. I fell to my knees and prayed that no harm had come to our friends. I thought of Joseph, my long and trusted friend, where was he? Where were the others, all good men and loyal friends?

Trouseau and my comrade Malik, from the North lands of the great desert, came over to where I knelt in the sand. Malik spoke first. 'Sir, the ship has gone, we are thinking that it could be that Master Joseph and the men have taken *The Glaros* away.'

'What?' I called and quickly ran further over to the ridge of the cove. Sure enough, our ship gone. A thought then came to me. Had Joseph guessed that trouble was lurking and decided to hide the ship? Although she was badly beaten by the storm, she could still sail with her temporary rig. Sadly, this thought was quickly shattered when suddenly we heard one of the men call out. 'Sir, come quickly.' I ran over the ridge and down onto the beach by the wrecked long boats. 'Where are you, man?' I called back in frustration, as I could not see him. One of the men came running out of a small cave waving his arms at me. 'Here Sir, in here.' I ran over and ducked down into the small cave and then I saw a man lying in the corner. Braheim had found him and sent the others to get me. I ran over and knelt down. It was Gordon, the youngest of our crew. He was pale and shaking. 'What happened, lad?' I asked. He tried to speak but all he could do was mumble. His eyes had the look of terror in them and he shook badly. Then I saw his side. There was much bleeding. He had been badly wounded. I could not get any sense out of him. He was a young boy and had not seen any combat or danger before. His wound was very bad. We did not have the necessary medicines to heal him and I feared the worst.

'Listen lad, I know you are in pain but you must tell me what happened here; I will do everything I can for you, I promise. Can you tell me?' I asked him softly.

For a moment he kept shaking then he grabbed my arm. There were tears in his eyes. We all felt so helpless and sorry for him. He was close to death. Then he tried again to speak. He was shaking. 'S-so many of them. Like ghosts, everywhere, took everyone, I hid, scared, s-sorry, Sir.' The lad had hold of my arm very tightly and I tried to pull it away. As I pulled, his arm hit the top of the handle of my sword and he grabbed it. I tried to pull his hand away from it but his grip was like steel. Suddenly and without any warning a bright light burst out of the sword and we jumped back in surprise. We covered our eyes. The boy was clutching onto the sword and was now glowing with a golden light. Then he began shaking even more. Suddenly his eyes turned bright yellow and he threw his hands away and leapt up off the ground. We all looked up in amazement. The boy was standing completely normally but now he was swaying. Finally, the glow left him and he began to fall to the ground. We managed to grab him before he fell and sat him down. This was the strangest thing, but he fell into a deep sleep. His wound had completely vanished. There was no blood and he looked peaceful in his sleep and his breathing was normal. He was healed from his fatal wound and was now sound asleep.

Braheim ran out of the cave, waving his arms and shouting in his Arabic tongue. The others were all scared and stood well away from the boy. I was simply stunned and fell back against the cave wall. I took the sword from its scabbard and saw a faint glow coming from the jewel on the handle. I had no idea what was happening and then thought back to what had once been said to me when I was given the sword by King Hafidh. I remembered his words:

'I give you this sword as a token of my deepest gratitude. You rescued and returned to me my most precious of all jewels, my daughter. You must use it well and learn of its strength and power. In time this sword, the Sword of Isis, will be more valuable than life itself.'

At the time these words had meant little to me, save the honour of receiving it from such a noble and wonderful man. King Hafidh was the ruler of a vast empire; the land of Kadistaar. He ruled the deserts, the mountains and the oceans. He had great armies and built beautiful cities.

He strived for peace and he married the daughter of a great Greek King to bring harmony between the Arabians and the Greeks so that trade would flourish and people would prosper. He and his wife produced a beautiful daughter called Tasia."

For a moment Mr Hawkins paused and Tom noticed that the seagull's eyes looked tearful. There was a long pause but Tom dared not interfere. He waited until his friend was ready to continue.

There was a long sigh from the seagull and then he let out one of his shrieks. The sound echoed all around the cave and Tom held his hands over his ears. Eventually, the sound died down.

Tom looked up to see his friend standing over the stone. He stretched up his head and shook his long neck and then looked back at Tom.

"This Stone, Tom, belongs to that sword and they must be reunited. You see, it was the sword that healed the boy, Gordon. By some miraculous power, the boy was able to live. After a short while he woke and walked out of the cave. Although slightly shaky, he was well. We all ran over to him delighted that he was alive but equally stunned to see that he had no trace of any wound. He had been completely healed. It was the Sword of Isis. We realised then that there were strange powers in the sword and I told the men not to be scared. The King gave me this sword to protect us against dangers. The men gave Gordon water from one of the flasks and then sat down on the sand to learn of the boy's story. We needed to know everything.

He recalled a terrible attack by ghosts in white robes who appeared from every direction. They threw huge nets over the crew and captured all of them except him. Although our men had put up a great fight and had killed some of them, the battle was short and soon they were prisoners. The figures in white gathered up those who had fallen and carried them away with their prisoners. They captured *The Glaros* too and towed her away with one of their own ships. We all sat in silence as the boy revealed his tale to us. When he finished, I walked to the sea and watched the waves roll up onto the beach and then fall away out to sea. I wondered about Joseph and the others and prayed for their safety. I thought about *The Glaros* and needed to know what had happened to her. We had to find the men and take back our ship. Then I looked at my sword and pulled it out of the scabbard and held it up to the sunlight, which now was dwindling. A red sunset was rising out from the horizon across the ocean. The sword cast a long beam of light across the sea. I knew not what I was saying but as I held up the sword I made a vow that wherever they were, I would find those who took my friends and by the power of the Sword of Isis I would destroy all evil that came our way. As I made this promise, the sword shook in my hand and glowed. The beam of light fixed on the top of a cliff far away in the distance. As it did, I could swear that I saw a glimmer of light return. It was like a sign."

"What sign, Mr Hawkins, what was it?" Tom asked eagerly.

"At the time I was unsure, but it was not long before we were to discover the answer," replied the bird. He continued.

"As I held out the sword I was uncertain of what was happening. The light from the cliff faded away and the beam from the sword also faded. I looked at this strange thing in my hands and wondered. I thought again about the words that King Hafidh had said. I must have been standing there for quite some time when a voice called to me.

'Sir, we must find shelter, for the night will close in on us before long. Come, Sir.'

It was Sam Little. He ran over to me as he called. As I turned to him I sensed that we were about to encounter something most powerful. Whatever it was, I knew that we must be very cautious from this moment on.

I followed Sam back to the others. They had been able to find some fruit in the forest and we ate and prepared to move on. We had to find Joseph and the others. If they were captives, we needed to find them quickly.

As we walked into the forest, I turned to look over my shoulder. The glow that I had seen from the cliffs in the distance had gone and the night had come."

# Chapter 3 – The Land of Fire

"After finding a suitable place to make camp, we set out our blankets in a close circle. We did not want to be seen or heard by anyone, so I gave orders for a four-hour watch, which meant that everybody had four hours to sleep and four hours on watch. If there was the slightest sound or hint of trouble, the person on watch was to wake all of us. Everyone understood the order and we went about our business. I was aware that the men had been through several days without rest, but I made it quite clear to them that our comrades had been through more than us and therefore we needed our strength to be able to go to their rescue. All night long, we kept alert. I was proud of the men; they had been through a great deal, but still they remained keen and willing to carry out their tasks.

As morning came upon us, we heard the sounds of the forest awake and we felt the freshness of the air quickly turn into a sweltering hot day. The humidity was quite intense and became a burning heat almost immediately. We took small sips of water from the flasks. I was concerned that it might be some time before we were able to replenish our water bottles and told the men to take it easy until we found more water. I gave the order to break camp and move on. I decided that we should head towards the area where I had seen the light from the cliffs. It was, I thought, a simple journey along the edge of the forest.

We cleared our camp, leaving it as if nobody had been there and moved out.

Keeping a single file, we moved swiftly through the forest. I was keen to keep as close to the beach as possible. If there was any sign of trouble we could, at least, run to the rocks by the sea and take cover. I told the men that if trouble came we should split up into small groups and hide amongst the rocks and cliffs. It would be hard for our enemy to find us as there were so many places along the coast to hide. We would be able to disappear amongst the cliffs without trace.

As we marched forward, we saw huge coloured birds swarm above us in circles. We kept close to the trees along the coastline as far as we could until eventually an inlet of a river appeared ahead of us. To our right was the sea. We would be noticed if we headed in that direction now. To our left were the forest and the treacherous cliffs. The river seemed to wind its way through the rocks into the forest but I noticed a small creek just a short way ahead. The rock face was several hundred feet high and would be difficult to climb to the top. I decided that as we did not know what lay up there, it seemed more sensible to remain below, out of sight and unnoticed.

I called back to the men: 'We'll take the creek up ahead and see what that has to offer. Trouseau, you and Blake can go on, but not too far and keep within calling distance, do you hear?'

'Oui, mon Capitaine, we will do as you ask. Come my friend,' he called to Blake and the two men quickly ran on ahead, slipping through the trees and out of sight. I prayed that they would not come to any harm and hoped that they would keep to my orders. Trouseau and Blake had been with me for many years and I trusted them implicitly.

The rest of us crossed the creek, knee high in water. The water was salty which meant we were still close to the sea. As we crossed over I noticed a huge gap between the massive rocks of the cliff face.

Braheim called to me, 'Sahib, I would be very careful about venturing in there, we do not know this strange place – the men are becoming worried. They are thinking that this is a bad place.' As Braheim spoke, I saw the fear in his eyes. He was talking for himself; the others seemed reasonably happy for the moment.

'Why, Braheim, do I detect a slight of concern in your heart?' I asked him playfully

'Sahib I am only thinking of your safety and also of ours; this place does not give me a feeling of ease and we have seen enough to make us cautious. Perhaps we should be a little careful about where we go?'

I did agree with him. 'You are right my friend', I said, 'We should take good care not to make our presence noticed. However I am interested in that gap between the rocks ahead. It looks like a door that has been unopened'.

Braheim was in the mood for an argument. 'Sahib, with respect, does this door really need opening? Could it not be that on this occasion we could pass by and the door remains closed?'

I replied: 'Braheim, my dear friend, we have been through so many interesting times together. Does a small crack in a rock deter us from our mission? Remember that we do have to find our comrades and it will take whatever we have in our power to do this. We do not know what lies ahead and this is a strange place, but we must stand by our word as brothers. Is this not so?'

I knew that Braheim would be unable to argue this point but I did, for a minute, hope that what we were doing was wise. All I could think of was finding our friends and getting away as fast as possible. I did not wish any harm or danger upon my men. They were my friends and closer to me than anyone I had ever known.

I turned back to the others who had caught up with us and were shaking out the water from their clothes.

'Well what do you say, men? We have an adventure ahead of us. We do not know this place or what it offers. It may be safe or it may not be. Whatever lies ahead should not stop us from rescuing our brothers. We have seen the swiftness of our foe. They have captured the others and we must get them back. Let us not fool ourselves in thinking we will be safe or our mission easy. We do not know this place and there is no way out until we find the door. We have the ability to fight and the skill to win, we have seen these times before. We are family, I look to you all as brothers but our family has become incomplete. We must rescue the others quickly. Do we go forward?'

There was a resounding cheer and the men all held up their weapons and shouted 'Forward!' They all cheered. Trouseau and Blake returned. Blake spoke first. 'What did you think we would do Captain? We would never desert our brothers, so we go on until we can all go home.'

I was very proud of the men and smiled back. 'I know we are brothers in all ways. Come, let us go and gather our family.'

We moved closer to the giant wall of rocks ahead. Eventually it was clear to see that one part of the cliff face was smooth. The huge crack down the centre was now more apparent than before. I called out quietly to the men: 'Perhaps there is a way through here. I have a feeling about this place.' I had a strange feeling that we were not alone and sensed another presence, apart from ours. The crack in the rock face was only just wide enough to get a hand through and we began looking for another way to get in. There was something bothering me and I was not sure why. No-one else could be seen, we had not been followed and there seemed to be no sign of trouble.

As we looked around for a way ahead, I continued searching for signs of either our enemy or a clue to get us out of this area and a way through the vast rock wall.

Each of us searched the foot of the vast cliff for an entrance. I scrambled over a few loose rocks and with my sword I hacked away at some reeds and tree roots. I found a small opening but again it looked too narrow to pass through. What happened next will always remain a mystery to me for I do not know why I did what I did. I took the sword and probed the crack that was nearly twenty feet high but just a foot across at its widest point. I ran the sword up and down the crack, pushing it just a short way at first, then deeper inside until the whole blade had penetrated. I was foolishly thinking that I could prise open this huge rock so we could get inside. As I thought this and sliced the sword up and down the crack, a bright light shone from the sword and it began to shake in my hand. I had to hold onto it with all my strength.

Just a few seconds later the whole mountain began to shake. Everyone fell back as the ground beneath us trembled and moved like an earthquake. I was still holding the sword as I fell onto my back. Small rocks fell upon us like rain from above. Then the great mountain began to open in front of us and the ground shook violently. The roar of moving rock was deafening and huge clouds of dust choked us. My sword was still glowing with the bright light and the stone, which sat deep in the handle of the sword, also glowed. I was shaken by this strange and frightening power. The men all gathered around me. I was pleased to see that we were all present, no-one was hurt but we were all stirred by this incident and looked in amazement at the sword. This was the second time it had performed strange powers. I held it carefully and said to the men that I could not say how this had happened. I was just trying to find a way through as I placed the sword inside the crack. Before I could do anything, the rock was opening before our eyes. We were dumbstruck by this strange event and, for a few moments, we stood in silence and in awe of this strange happening. Then the dust began to settle and we could see that we could pass through the crack with ease. I was about to give the order to the men to follow me inside, when from nowhere hundreds of arrows rained down on us. We held up our shields and ran towards the opening in the rock. Then we heard the sound of loud trumpets with drums beating. We heard men shouting. The sun was so bright in our eyes we could not see them and still the arrows came down on us. One struck Maris, the ship's carpenter, in the side and he fell. Trouseau and Braheim helped him. He cried out in pain, but was still able to keep up with us.

We all ran as fast as we could. The shouting from above increased, as did the attack of arrows and then spears. Fortunately we made it to the entrance of the great rock and slipped through. Maris was dragging behind but was just able to escape the assault.

Braheim called out, 'Where do they come from, I could not see them?' He tried to look out through the entrance. The daylight from outside was too bright and we realised very quickly that we did not have time to wait. We had to run as fast as we could. I looked around the inside of the great opening that we had run into. It was a huge cave but it had been built by man. The walls were smooth and there were great engravings of strange faces and tall pillars with snakes woven around them, carved in stone.

Braheim cried, 'What is this place?' 'I have no idea my friend', I told him, 'but we do not have time to find out, we must hurry, come everyone, run like the wind.' The men followed me further inside the great cavern. It was an eerie place and we sensed great danger ahead.

I did not know where we were heading, but just ran towards a vast archway with huge vines growing around it which hung down to the ground. There were strange stone faces like masks of the devil himself carved into the arch. We all looked above us with caution as we passed through.

I turned back to check that we were all there. Maris was still with us but straggling behind with Trouseau helping him. I called out, 'keep up with us Trouseau, I don't want to lose you both, somebody else lend them a hand.' Blake and Gordon fell back to help. I was pleased to see that young Gordon was back in good health and then looked to my sword and laid a hand upon it. I was grateful for the strange and mysterious power that it had shown us. Had it not been for the sword, we would have fallen to these strange people and to a certain death.

We ran on through corridors of tall grey walls, which must have been at least thirty feet in height. Then we heard the sound of many feet running behind us. The echo of men chasing and the sound of steel rattling was enough for us to gather more speed and we ran even faster.

We came to a bend and found there were two more corridors. We stopped and quickly made a decision about which way to go. 'To the right', I called out loudly and then quickly signalled the men to go left. I hoped that our decoy would buy us some time. We could hear our pursuers close behind.

Braheim was panting. 'They run fast, Sahib. I think they have wings.'

'I hope you are wrong my friend', I called back. I too was scared, but I knew we should keep up a fast pace.

Trouseau suddenly cried, 'Capitaine!'

'What is it?' I asked.

'Look up there. I can see a place we can go.'

I saw where he was pointing. There was a narrow stairway, which led to a small arch. There seemed to be light coming from beyond it.

'Lord give me strength', I said – 'I hope this is a sound idea, Trouseau'. I looked at him and saw the urgency in his eyes and then the others. They too looked for me to decide. The others were nodding urgently.

'Right', I told the men, 'that way it is, let us go quickly, not a sound. Muffle your weapons and do not slip'.

I was concerned about Maris; he was slowing down and we had to make sure he was not dripping blood on the ground for our followers to trace. I whispered: 'Get Maris up there first, let's go!'

The men moved swiftly up the steep steps. We had no idea where we were going or what lay ahead. I looked behind and suddenly saw the glow of hundreds of fire torches moving closer. Then we heard much shouting, voices of a tongue we did not understand. There were many of them. Then we saw they were armed with long spears and swords. As they came closer we saw their white tunics well lit by the fire torches. It would not be long before we could see their eyes, I thought, as we climbed up the steps.

We were finally at the top and now hidden in the darkness. Our foe would not see us as long as they did not know which route we had taken. I whispered again: 'Hold still. We'll wait here. We don't know what lies beyond that archway. It could be a trap.' I gave the signal to take cover.

We all pressed up hard against the wall and stood still in the dark shadows of the rock. They would be unable to see us from below, but were now assembling in masses beneath us. Their fire torches lit up the whole area of the vast cavern and the strange faces, some with horns and others like snake heads, danced across the huge walls like ghosts. This was an evil place for certain and we could be in deep peril. Again, I thought about our friends and feared for them at the hands of these people. The hoard came to a halt and then a command was called and suddenly they produced bows and tipped their arrows into the fire torches. A command was given again and a massive glow of fire flew across the vast cavern lighting up the high areas. We all pressed up as hard as we could against the wall. But the light was growing brighter with the fire arrows flying like search lights. Our pursuers ran past and onwards through the corridor. 'That was close', I whispered. 'We shall continue into the next chamber, it's our only chance'. I went first this time with Braheim. We held Maris between us. He was becoming weaker. There was another short passage with a narrow gap. We all grouped up close inside the small passage and I peered through the gap. The light was very bright beyond the chamber and I had to squeeze through carefully.

My first glance caused me to pull back and cover my eyes. The sudden brightness of what lay beyond had almost blinded me. I shaded my eyes and again looked through. I was suddenly taken breathless. I could not believe what I was looking at. A room, a huge chamber, hundreds of feet wide and higher than the cavern we had left behind us, built in solid gold. The light was blinding and we were forced to protect our eyes.

Gordon exclaimed: 'Upon my word, Sir, it's gold!'

'Aye Gordon', I replied, 'I think you are right, I have no idea what this place is but look over there, to the far side, see a huge entrance? Look at those statues on each side of the entrance, what do you make of that?' We all carefully stepped out of the darkness onto a balcony, which overlooked this huge chamber of gold.

On the far side was what appeared to be an enormous gold door. It must have been a hundred feet high and at least forty feet wide. It had giant carvings of figures dressed in robes, their hands crossed over their chests. Each held the head of the snake, which coiled around their bodies. On their heads were strange headdresses, like war helmets. They were pointed at the top and had narrow slits where the eyes should be. The helmets were long at the back – to protect the neck in battle, I thought.

The figures were not identical but I could not decide what the difference was, until suddenly I saw it. Some were the figures of men, the others women.

I continued to look around and saw that in the centre of the floor was a large circle. It appeared to be made of something like onyx or black marble. Inside the circle was a pattern of crossed triangles. All around the outside of the circle were short stone columns identical in size, no more than three feet high. It was a fantastic place of elaborate carvings decorated in gold and black. Then Braheim noticed the ceiling and pointed for us to look up. It was dome shaped and in the centre was a circle, which looked like glass, but there was no light beyond it. The whole place was lit by hundreds of fire torches. After a while our eyes became used to the brightness.

Gordon whispered: 'What is this place, Captain?'

'It appears to be some kind of temple or meeting place, but I cannot say for sure', I replied and was about to suggest that we should find a way down to the floor from the balcony, when suddenly a loud gong sound rang out and the huge doors with the giant gold figures opened.

Within seconds, swarms of figures dressed in the white cloth robes ran into the great room. There was a sense of urgency about them as they entered. They immediately formed into some sort of rank and file system and in a very short time had formed a human circle around the black circle in the centre. After about a hundred or so of these people had appeared, a small party of older looking, dark skinned men walked slowly through the doors. These people were less hurried than the figures in white. They were dressed in long gold garments with black patterns woven into the cloth of their robes. It was clear to us that these men were more important than the figures in white. They took their places in front of each of the stone columns around the black circle. We all crouched down low so as not be seen. I was glad that we had stayed in our place. We could see everything.

When the older men took up position at each of the columns, they just stood still. Then, the large gong sounded again. A few moments later eight very tall, black men walked through the doors. They were scantily dressed in white and gold cloth with nothing above the waist. They were armed with long curved swords, which hung from their waist belts. Each of these men had shaven heads. They were immense in size. They walked in perfect step, very close together. Then I saw him. He was there, right in the centre of these black giants. It was the captain of the ship we had seen earlier. The one in black who stood still and silent as the night. The one with the narrow face and dark eyes. Although he was very tall, he was dwarfed by his eight guards. Suddenly the eight men peeled away and now we could see him clearly. The bodyguards formed a half circle around him as he stepped slowly towards the edge of the columns surrounding the black circle on the floor. The whole room fell silent; not a sound could be heard, not even a heartbeat. He was clearly the leader, the one to be most feared. I could feel the hair rise on the back of my neck and I looked to my colleagues to see that not a sound would come from any of us.

Again the gong sounded and, as the tone died away, the man raised his hands high up towards the dome ceiling. Suddenly there was a rumble from above us. Then we saw the circle on the ceiling open. As it did, a bright beam of light flashed down directly into the centre of the dark circle on the floor. All the figures in white robes fell to their knees and began to mutter words that we did not understand. Then the middle of the circle on the floor began to glow. We could feel a noticeable increase in temperature. The whole room began to heat up. The beam of very bright light was beginning to sparkle and then suddenly it turned into a flame. There were bolts of fire, like lightning, shooting onto the circle on the floor, which continued to glow brighter. And then it started to melt, becoming a pool of liquid gold. Suddenly from all around the walls of the great room, small doors opened and more figures appeared. These men were again wrapped in white robes. As they entered the room we could see that they were being pushed. Some fell and began to wail and protest. Some pleaded as if to some invisible God with their hands clasped together and fell to their knees. As this pathetic sight of crawling, begging figures continued, some different figures appeared. They looked like warriors, heavily armed with swords and long knives. They were dressed in battle style dress with oval shaped shields strapped on their backs. They also wore armoured breastplates, and helmets which covered their faces. In one hand, each of them carried a long spear and in the other they wielded whips. With the whips they terrorised the crawling figures in white, lashing out at them and urging them towards the circle of people gathered around the pool of liquid gold. The screams of these terrified people were most distressing and we felt helpless, not being able to do anything. The other consideration was, of course, the fact that we were considerably outnumbered. It would have been an impossible battle. I looked at my mysterious sword and thought that even with the strange power that it appeared to have, it would be of little value in such a fight. We were just a few men against so many. There was no telling how many others would be waiting behind the solid gold walls and doors of this strange place.

The leader stepped forward and four figures in white appeared with a platform for him to stand upon. He shouted some words and clapped his hands. The whole room stood still. Then he pointed to the terrified people who were huddled in a group on the floor and surrounded by the warriors. He called again, this time his words were slow and deep. The low, eerie tone in his voice sent shivers down my spine. Three warriors grabbed two of the group and dragged them to the side of the circle of gold, which lay still, like liquid silk. My men and I sensed something evil was about to happen. In one natural movement, we all laid a hand on our swords.

A command was given and the two helpless figures were taken to the edge of the pool of gold. Now they were quiet but trembling. It was as if they had realised that their time had come: it would be useless to resist. The gold beam from the ceiling had turned into a ray of massed gold dust. It was very strange how this beam of light, still shining down from the top of the ceiling from this temple, changed shape and twisted and moved, all the time glowing and pulsating as if it were a living thing.

The tall man drew his sword, which glistened from the reflections of the gold all around the room. He called out to the two, who were being held by their necks by the soldiers. His deep voice echoed around the great room. The words dragged and moaned. The figures in white began to chant. The chanting was almost hypnotic and then they began to sway as they chanted. Then the man, this strange, terrible man, began to speed up his fearful words. Although they were unknown to us, I listened carefully. Once he called out a word that, somewhere in the back of my mind, I felt I knew but I could not be sure. The word was Saharadeen. When he said this word everyone let out a sigh of reverence. I looked back to Braheim with a finger on my lips to show I wanted to speak without being heard by others. He slipped past the men and came up next to me. I put my mouth to his ear. 'What was this word, Saharadeen?' I asked.

Braheim returned his answer in the same way. 'I cannot say, Sahib. It may be something to do with the great desert, the ocean of sand, but mostly, I have no answer to this.'

I was about to reply again but a loud scream stopped me. One of the figures was being stripped of his robes. He was revealed as a thin, dark skinned individual who looked like he had been starved and beaten. He was now only wearing a cloth around his middle. He screamed as he was thrown into the pool of gold. As he hit the liquid, he vanished instantly. No further sound was heard. The other man was given the same treatment and as he entered the pool, he disappeared too. Then, all those in the great room dropped to their knees, even the warriors and the giant guards. The only one standing was the tall man in black who held out his arms to the beam of gold and called out some more words. He used the word Saharadeen again and another outburst came from all those kneeling. Then, from the golden pool we noticed some disturbance. It began to move. Then sparks shot out like stars. This was followed by a blinding flash spurting out from the heart of the pool. There was an explosion of light and from this appeared a fountain of fire and gold. There was a loud roar as the fountain appeared. Everyone in the room started to bow up and down in worship of this fantastic spectacle. The golden beam had become a fountain of fire. Sparks were flicking around like fireflies and the colours were incredible.

From beyond the great room we heard trumpets and chimes playing. The sounds came nearer and then more people came into the room, soldiers dressed in fantastic costumes, again gold and black. The trumpets were long and were played by soldiers as they marched forward. *What now?* I asked myself.

Suddenly, to our horror, we saw our friends, my own good men. They were being led in chains into the room. I saw Joseph, immediately. He walked with dignity but it was clear he was scared.

From the centre of the hall, the huge fountain of fire was spurting up and sparks flickered out over some of the people. The tall man in the centre turned to look at his captives. He stood still. His arms hung down by his sides. There was an evil smile upon his thin face. He raised his head to look up to the ceiling where the beam of golden light was coming from. Then he turned to the fountain of fire and bowed to it, as if it were some King. Our friends were taken to the edge of the ring of guards. I signalled immediately to my men. They gathered quickly. I whispered but with urgency in my voice: 'We cannot let them down. I need quick answers from you. Who will be the decoy?' There was a quick pause then Gordon said, 'Me Sir.' For a second I nearly denied him – he was so young – but there was no time to argue. 'This is dangerous', I told him, 'take good care, we will look out for you'. He recognised the trust I was placing in him and saw my acceptance as a great honour. The decoy was most important. He would have to let the enemy discover him and lead them after him. He would also have to be able to take out any leaders or officers. This would cause panic among those who would follow them.

'Trouseau?' I called quickly. He immediately answered, 'Oui Monsieur?'

'You are Point, find your position now. I'll expect you back with us when you have done your work'. Trouseau smiled – he knew what he must do. It was work that he had much experience in. He left us immediately.

I gave more orders. 'Those of you who have bows prepare to load and fire, the rest of you stay with me'. I looked back over the balcony to see what was happening. Our colleagues had been bundled together by soldiers who had their swords drawn. It was as if they were waiting for something. All the people around were chanting and then again, that word – Saharadeen, Saharadeen, Saharadeen. They repeated this chant over and over. Then I realised what it was. It was the name of the tall dark man who was their leader. He was the Saharadeen.

There was another fanfare from the trumpet players and everyone turned to look up at a space high up. I could not make out what they were looking for. I wanted to get a sign or signal to Joseph but he would be unable to see me from where he was, unless he looked up in our direction.

He and the others probably had us for dead or gone and would not expect that we were here with them and were about to attempt their rescue. My real problem was our escape route. I could not see anywhere for us to go. This was going to be tough and I knew that we were as good as dead unless a miracle happened. I needed Joseph's help. He would have to know of our presence and cause some kind of a disturbance to give us a chance to make our move without being seen. I had a firm grip on the handle of my sword and as I was thinking through my plan I felt a warm glow; the sword was telling me something. I could hear something, but I knew not what it was; it seemed that as I thought, the sword thought too. I looked over at my friends on the floor, who were in great peril. As I glanced down at Joseph, I thought *Please look up Joseph, see your friends are here to help you, we must work together, Look up!* Suddenly, Joseph moved his head upwards, he seemed to be searching around, looking for something and then he spotted me. He saw my head just above the balcony wall. Somehow I knew now that he could hear me. All the time my hand was upon the handle of the sword. This truly was the magic of the Sword of Isis. I was now convinced about its powers. When, at last, Joseph's eyes found mine, he grinned but very quickly and without the notice of those around him. 'I shall save you Joseph,' I whispered. *I hear you* came a faint voice in my head. Of course I knew it was Joseph. The power of the sword was with us. We were speaking without words!

Then I remembered that we had a wounded man with us. When I last saw him, Maris had been bleeding badly from the arrow wound in his side. As I turned to look at him now I could not believe my eyes. He was smiling and looking back. Then he crept towards me. 'Sir, I am ready to do my duty. Thank-you for healing me. I am in your debt.'

I was amazed and overwhelmed. I was seeing Maris as though nothing had ever happened to him. But there was no time to sit and wonder as the fanfare had come to its peak and the chanting had reached a point where everyone on the floor in the great room had thrown themselves into a frenzied state. Even the master of this evil place, the Saharadeen himself, was chanting with them. The noise grew louder and louder, everyone began to look up to a small opening halfway up the great wall on the far side of the temple. Suddenly, the walls began to move and all the people on the floor began to sway in time with each other. Our friends and the other frail and frightened captives were forced by the guards to kneel on the ground with their heads touching the floor.

As the wall above moved, it became clear that another door or window was opening. The music from the trumpets grew louder and the chanting more intense.

The wall behind a gallery parted and from it appeared a woman wearing a tall, golden head-dress. Three other women, who looked like servants, accompanied her. She, like the Saharadeen, was dressed in gold robes with the black marks of the serpent. She paused at the balcony and looked down upon the frenzy of bowing and crying figures who looked up at her in awe. She turned to the Saharadeen and smiled with a bow of respect. He lowered his head in return. Then she looked over to the captives and lifted one arm and pointed to them. Our friends were singled out by her gesture and a great roar came from all those around them. I could see the fear in the eyes of Joseph and the others. We needed to act fast.

Suddenly Joseph tried to pull away from one of the guards but was knocked back. As he fell to the floor he grabbed the ankle of the Saharadeen. 'Please save us, help!' he pleaded. I could see this was his attempt to cause a disturbance. The Saharadeen kicked him off and called to the guards to take him. But Joseph would not let go. Three guards grabbed Joseph and finally forced him to his feet. Then I heard his voice in my head: *Make your move, Captain, go now!* Suddenly Joseph let fly with his free arm and punched one of the guards. Then he wrapped his other chained arm around the guard's neck pulling him onto the floor. Joseph was a strong and very powerful man and the guard was felled with ease. Immediately, chaos followed. The Saharadeen tried to push through the crowd of guards who were trying to get to Joseph, who now had taken the guard's dagger and held it to his throat. Two of Joseph's men were jumped upon by several guards. The other three attempted to start a fight by swinging their chains. They tried to do as Joseph had done, but met with strong resistance. As this was happening, Gordon made his move. He leapt across the balcony and shouted at the crowd below. 'Hey you pretty fools, look at me,' he called. The Saharadeen turned quickly and saw Gordon. He called to his guards. Within seconds, they were in pursuit of Gordon. Meanwhile Joseph had been subdued, and so had his colleagues. I was about to order those still with me to fire, when suddenly an arrow felled the guard who was standing next to the Saharadeen. The crowd whirled around to see where it had come from. As they did so, we fired our arrows. There were five of us; five arrows struck and five guards fell. This caused even more chaos. The Saharadeen charged through the crowd with four of his giant guards close to him to cover him from being hit. An arrow hit one of the giants in the back and he fell. Trouseau was doing his work. The woman who had appeared at the balcony had quickly retreated with her servants. Swords were drawn and every soldier was charging towards Gordon. But he was high up on a balcony and the guards could not reach him. Gordon kept his calm and drew his bow, firing one shot directly at one of the soldiers who had been leading a section of men towards him. They now had ladders and were attempting to climb up to get Gordon.

The soldier fell as the arrow struck him. The Saharadeen was furiously screaming at his men as we maintained our volleys of arrows upon them. I could see Joseph and the others had been completely pinned down. Trouseau was trying to take out the guards holding them, but for every guard he hit, another took his place. It was looking hopeless. I could see no way through. Gordon started running along the wall high above his pursuers. The wall ran all around the great room and he skipped with great ease along the narrow ledge. Then more soldiers came through the great doors. They had fire arrows and began firing them at Gordon immediately they entered.

'To arms men, our battle is down there, not up here', I shouted. As I stood up, I grabbed my sword and pulled it from my belt. Suddenly an incredible force came over me. The sword was light in my hand. 'I want that one', I called and pointed my sword directly at the Saharadeen. As I cried out the Saharadeen turned and saw me. The others jumped out and began to climb down the stepped columns, which led from the floor up to the ceiling.

With both hands firmly gripping my sword, I leapt up onto the small wall. I had the sword pointing at the Saharadeen and suddenly my thought became reality and a bolt of fire shot from the sword and struck three of his guards, sending them quickly to the floor. Panic ran through the enemy soldiers and the men in white robes retreated against the wall. The elders in the elaborate tunics were amazed and looked to the Saharadeen for an answer. Maris and the other three had reached the floor and, with swords drawn, they charged towards the centre of the room. They were encouraged by the retreating groups of confused soldiers, whose leader was unable to command them. The Saharadeen was frozen still staring at me and at my sword.

I shouted at the Saharadeen. There was fire in my voice. 'Release my men or I swear you will perish. By the Sword of Isis, I command you!' I thrust the sword again towards some of the soldiers who were making a move on Gordon. Again came a shot of fire and four more of the Saharadeen's men fell. The rest of them stopped instantly and fell back.

Suddenly the room was still. Not a word was said. I could hear the beating of heavy hearts and felt the fire inside me boil. I shouted again: 'Release them now!'

The Saharadeen was clearly dismayed. He was the all-powerful, yet I was in control. I heard his thoughts and could sense him making decisions on what he should do.

I decided to help him. 'Do not dwell on this, Saharadeen', I said. 'I know your mind and will strike before you have finished your thoughts. You will die if you do not release my men now'.

He was furious, I could feel it. But he knew, for now, he must do as I say or he would lose all his men by this stranger with the powerful sword.

I was stunned by what happened next: the Saharadeen spoke to me in English. 'I speak your tongue. Who are you?' he said. I gathered myself together quickly and replied: 'No matter who I am. I have no time for talk. I want my men released from the chains'.

The Saharadeen turned to the guards holding Joseph and the others and nodded. The guards unlocked the large iron clamps, which fell onto the floor. Joseph and the others quickly armed themselves with swords from the guards. I called all my men together and climbed down onto the floor of the great room. I was now at the same level as the Saharadeen and could see how tall he was. He stood perfectly still and studied me as I approached. I noticed his eyes had turned to my sword. I held the sword firmly in my hands. He looked deeply at it, his eyes staring without blinking. It was not I that he was considering, but the sword. He spoke again: 'You have taken much liberty in your intrusion into my land. Why do you interfere, what is your purpose?' The Saharadeen asked the question in deep slow words. His Arabic accent was prominent but he spoke English well. He was, without doubt, an educated man but clearly most evil and powerful.

I told him that we had been drawn there by a storm and needed shelter. 'You took our ship', I said to him, 'and destroyed our longboats while we were looking for water and food. Then you took my men captive and from what we have witnessed, you were about to send them to the same evil fate as those other poor wretches'. I did not know why I was bothering to talk with this man. I just wanted to take my men and leave.

The Saharadeen replied. 'What do you know of this, who are you to judge before the facts are told?'

'What you do here is of no interest to me', I told him, 'save my distaste for your lust for cruelty. In my country you would hang like a pig for this'. I spat the words out at him, but the Saharadeen laughed and threw up his hands. 'You are nothing but a small fish just waiting to be eaten by the jaws of a larger one. Take your men. You will not last long. You are in my world. You have nowhere to go.'

'You have my ship, Saharadeen. I wish it returned to me so we can make repairs and leave. You have my word that we will take no further interest in your affairs if you leave us alone to go about our work'.

The Saharadeen stepped down from the column and approached me. He was surrounded by his guards and all those in the white tunics moved forward with him. As he came nearer, now I could see his face better. His hooked nose and narrow jaw line gave him the appearance of a vulture. His skin was silky and of dark tanned complexion and his hair was jet black and hung down to his shoulders. He was immaculate: even his thin pointed beard was trimmed to perfection. He had one hand on the handle of his sword, the other hung still by his side. Now he was close, just a few feet away. I saw the deepness and evil in his dark brown eyes. One eye was slightly closed and I wondered what caused it. There is always a moment of strangeness when you look your enemy in the eye, but this man was different. This was the strangest of all.

"Come no nearer, Saharadeen. I can only stand the smell from a distance. My men laughed, forming a tight group around me. Trouseau was still nowhere to be seen but I knew he would be watching, hidden, ready to strike.

The Saharadeen paused and immediately all those around him stopped; some bumped into others as they suddenly came to a halt. 'You take great courage in that sword; without it you would be nothing. I would give a fortune to see how much of a man you really are. What is your name, where do you come from?' I could tell he was prying, trying to unsettle me with his bold questioning, although, in my heart I could not disagree, the sword had given me great strength and had helped us to rescue our friends. Now we were surrounded by hundreds of soldiers. He was right, without the sword, we would be helpless.

'My name is of no interest to you, nor is the purpose of our journey; one more step and I will show you the true force of my power'. I lifted up the sword and prepared to strike again.

There was a shriek of awe from the men all around us who were very nervous of what powers I could muster.

The Saharadeen paused before replying: 'Your ship has been taken away to our own port; you will not be permitted to go there.' 'What is this place', I retorted, 'where on God's earth are we?'

The Saharadeen seemed amused at this question. 'Not on your God's earth. This is my kingdom.' He raised his arms and pointed all around. 'And that of the Queen of Saharadeen. This, in your language, means the flame of all power. This is the Land of Fire. Nobody ever comes here without my notice and nobody leaves here alive. This is your final destination; your final hours of life are mine.' He laughed loudly and raucously and it echoed all around the great temple.

I had heard enough and began to step backwards. I pointed my sword at the Saharadeen and said, 'I shall find our ship anyway'. I signalled to the others and we headed for the doors. I felt that it would be impolite to leave without making a final gesture. Once more I swung my sword through the air. My thoughts were to make our foe retreat far enough back to give us a head start through the doors. Then, I knew, we would have to run for it.

The sword worked its magic, shooting out bolts of fire and a strange light so bright that it caused the mob to fall to their knees and cover their eyes. Even the Saharadeen cowered. Several of his men were caught and died instantly. With the fireballs came a terrible screeching sound. I turned to my men who were amazed by this power. 'Come my friends – it is time for us to leave, make for the doors but keep your eyes peeled, for these vermin will strike at any moment'.

The Saharadeen was covering his eyes with one hand but now he had his sword drawn and tried to run at me. I thrust my sword towards him and flames flew from it, knocking him over. He screamed like a madman but was not hurt as he managed to escape the strike.

We all moved closer to the great doors. Hundreds of Saharadeen men were standing by, hoping to strike out with their spears but were too terrified of the damage I could bring on them with the Sword of Isis.

We ran through the doors into a huge hall with giant pillars and corridors leading off in many different directions. We had no idea which direction to go, but instinct told me to go towards the vast archway ahead of us. Saharadeen's men were in pursuit. Their leader was screaming out his orders.

'Where is Trouseau?' I demanded, as we ran.

Gordon replied, 'I saw him briefly when he was picking off the guards. He was hiding high up near the roof. I am certain he was not spotted Sir.'

'Good, but I want him here now, we must not get separated. Come, we must run, but look out for him, everyone'.

There were several arches leading off to the left and right but we continued straight ahead at a fast pace. Eventually we saw another large archway, which looked more like a gate. Suddenly the arrows of fire came at us from behind and they were getting very close again. I shouted to the men to use their shields on their backs and keep running. Some arrows struck the shields but bounced off. More and more came at us like raining fire. It would be a miracle, I thought, if we made it out alive. As I thought this, an arrow struck Malik clean through the neck. He fell instantly. I ran back to see to him but he was gone. It was too late, even for the sword to do its work. Sadly there was not time to carry him and give him a decent burial. We had to leave him. We could only be grateful he died quickly, so the enemy could do no more harm to him.

'Go on!' I shouted to my men, and we continued. I could feel the sorrow in their hearts as they ran.

We approached the gates ahead and were immediately greeted by more soldiers, heavily armed and with huge nets. I called a halt and everyone stopped. I pulled out the sword and thought hard. *Burn those nets* I thought and pointed the sword at the enemy ahead of us. Suddenly the nets burst into flames. The soldiers fled, shaking away the burning nets. We ran on and confronted yet more enemy: 'Have at 'em men', I shouted. We ran right into them, swords swinging and shields ready. Some of the soldiers ran into attack and were quickly taken by Maris and Mababe, who was a giant of a man, and then Blake charged into them. They were all excellent swordsmen. I took three out and was ready to do more when suddenly for no apparent reason, our enemy retreated. There were so many of them, yet they were not pressing. We edged forward towards the gateway where we could see daylight. Were we really going to escape this place? Just as we reached the entrance, a huge solid iron cage came crashing down, surrounding us all completely. We were captured."

Tom sat mesmerised as he listened to this fantastic tale and stared wide-eyed at the seagull, who stood tall in front of him on the rock as he told his story.

It seemed to Tom that he had been sitting there for ages but when he finally managed to take a quick glance at his watch, he saw that the time had not moved since he last looked.

"Am I losing your attention, Tom?"

"Oh, n-no. Definitely not, Mr Hawkins, I just wanted to see what the time was. I can't believe that the time hasn't changed. It seems like hours. Please carry on. I really want to know how you escaped."

The seagull dropped his head and looked down at the shining stone, "Yes, quite so, the escape. Not perhaps what you will be expecting." Mr Hawkins stretched his wings on each side and curled his neck as if to relieve it from an ache. He was about to continue, but as he raised his head to speak he was startled by Tom, who was suddenly standing over him.

Tom had walked over to the seagull. He held out a hand and rested it gently on the seagull's neck and slowly began to rub it. "How's that feel, Mr Hawkins?"

The bird glanced up nervously with one sharp eye and then blinked that little smile that Tom had come to recognise as a sign of affection and friendship. "That feels just fine, Tom," he replied, and then, "Oh yes, yes, oh... yes." Tom's hand felt warm on his aching neck. Nobody had ever done this for him. Not in hundreds of years.

"Thank-you, Tom. That will do now. I think you have fixed the little ache in my neck. I feel much better now," said Mr Hawkins. Tom laughed a little to himself. He knew he had embarrassed the bird and also felt good that they were getting along so well. This was truly the most incredible relationship. Nobody would ever believe it possible.

"That's all right, Mr Hawkins. Can you continue the story? I really want to know everything."

"Of course, Tom, but take care that you do understand one thing," replied the bird suddenly quite seriously.

"Yes?"

"Yes, Tom. This story is true, everything I am telling you actually happened. The outcome is not what you will wish to hear and you will understand soon that I wish too that it could have been so different." Mr Hawkins nodded his head towards the flat rock, where Tom had been sitting and Tom returned to it obediently and sat down again.

"Good, now where was I? Oh yes." The bird stood very still for a brief moment and then raised his long neck up towards the ceiling of the cave and a small glimmer of light, which had found its way through the rocks, caught the bird's eye and reflected a bright beam, which darted upwards and then, in a flash, was gone. Tom was startled a little, but then he noticed the bird's eye. It was dark and deep. The centre of his eye was the shape of a gold crescent moon; all around the crescent was blackness, just like the night.

Although Tom wanted to say something, he didn't. Instead he sat and watched and waited.

There was suddenly a chill in the air, the atmosphere in the cave had changed and somewhere, far away in the distance, Tom could hear something. He couldn't quite make out what it was but for some strange reason, he thought he could hear the beat of a drum. It was a deep thudding sound, like a war drum. But then it was gone. The chill in the air had gone too and Mr Hawkins continued his tale.

"In all my years, I never needed our God so badly. We were completely cut off and surrounded. Then, to my horror I saw that Gordon had been captured too. He had been outside the range of the cage as it crashed down upon us, but now the evil, black-robed soldiers had him. One of them held a knife to his throat. He was trembling with fear. I screamed at them to let him go, but they laughed.

The cage was made of thick iron bars, too strong to bend open and too heavy to lift up from the floor. We were in a desperate situation, huddled closely together in the centre of the cage trying to avoid the stabbing spears of the black-robed soldiers, who had now returned and were swarming all over the cage. They cheered and chanted. It was an evil tongue. Their dark skinned faces peered into the cage and their yellow eyes stared wildly towards us. One of them, who had climbed onto the top of the cage, had no teeth but his mouth was red, like blood, and his screams cast a chill through us like a knife. In his hands he held a curved sword and he shook it at me in an evil gesture of defiance and hatred. There were so many of them chanting and waving their weapons. Then I thought – the sword, I could use it to break open the cage and escape. I went to grab it from my belt. It was not there. Desperation came over me: where was it? My comrades all realised what had happened and immediately looked around. 'Sahib! Quickly, there, look.' Braheim saw it lying in the corner of the cage, right beside the bars. Like lightning he dived across the floor of the cage and grabbed the blade, but as he did so, a hand came through the bars and took hold of the handle. The soldier tried to pull it away but I could see Braheim holding onto the blade, which was cutting into his hand.

"I kicked the hand of the soldier and he let go. Braheim quickly pulled the Sword back and handed it to me. His hand was almost severed in two. Without hesitation, I placed the bleeding hand onto the stone on the sword. Instantly, the bleeding stopped and the hand was completely healed. It was a miracle.

"There was a sudden silence. All around us the wild screams, hissing, jeering and chanting had stopped. Our enemies had witnessed again the wonders of the sword and were silenced by its powers.

"I took advantage of this and held the sword up. I warned them: 'By the power of the Sword of Isis I shall destroy all who dare to stand in our way. Open this cage or you shall perish.' I shouted my order slowly, loud and clearly.

"The soldiers did not understand and just stared blankly back at us. I thought to myself, *If only I spoke in their tongue.* Within an instant something came over me and I was up at the bars of the cage, holding the sword over my head, speaking words that were not mine.

I spoke in their language and now they understood and cowered back. I could see they were frightened. My men were completely astonished and looked at me with open mouths in disbelief and amazement. The enemy soldiers began to mutter to themselves. Those who held Gordon were unsure what they should do. Gordon tried to struggle from their grip. Suddenly, a voice called out from behind us. 'Do not listen to this infidel, he is our enemy and his powers are not as strong as mine.' I could understand their language now. The voice called the soldiers to order. The guards reinforced their hold on Gordon and the dagger was again held to his throat. The voice was deep and cold. It was the Saharadeen. He appeared from the darkness between two large pillars and was followed by a few of the large bald warriors who we had seen before in the temple of gold. They carried some kind of statue on a wooden frame but it was hard to see what it was.

The Saharadeen continued: 'Captain, I see you have found the language of our land. Use it carefully; it will not help you beyond this place. But I must tell you, there is nowhere for you to go. You are all now under my command.'

'I care not for what you say, Saharadeen. You fill my heart with contempt and I shall take pride in your downfall. Release us from this cage this very instant or you will all perish'. I believed my voice to be powerful enough and my message clear.

The Saharadeen paused for a moment. 'You are bold with that sword. I am aware of this Temple of the Isis that you speak of and also of the land in which it stands. I had heard of the sword and I can see that it has great powers.' He seemed to laugh to himself and then stepped boldly from the pillars.

He went on: 'So, you captain of humble men. Surely you cannot believe that I would release you so easily. First I must show you my gift. Although I have a feeling that you will not share my pleasure.'

He clapped his hands twice and instantly all around us came light from the fire torches, which were held high by the hundreds of men who looked dangerously upon us. Then the statue, carried by the guards, was rolled into our view. We saw that it was covered by a cloth, which bore the gold and black markings of the Saharadeen – the twisted serpents and crossed swords.

My men and I stood together in the centre of the cage. I was about to release the power of the sword again when we all suddenly stepped back in horror at what we saw. The statue was revealed. It was Trouseau. He had been turned into gold. His face had the expression of pain and fear. 'You see, your friend here has become more valuable than he ever could have dreamed of. He is now mine. This is a golden victory to the God of Fire who has the power of all powers and the wealth of a thousand worlds. I will have him melted down perhaps, or turn him into something more pleasing to my eyes.' The Saharadeen laughed and then continued, 'I can also have him returned to human form. The power is within me and the Temple of Fire.'

'Why do you do this?' I cried out. 'We did not come to your land to harm anyone and yet you seek to destroy us. Why?'

The Saharadeen did not bother to reply and called for Gordon to be brought to him. The men dragged Gordon across the vast stone hall and threw him at the feet of the Saharadeen. Gordon was frightened and remained on his knees, forced by the spears of several of Saharadeen's men.

'Wait!' I called. One more move and I shall cast the power of this sword upon you.

His reply was immediate. 'I do not think you would be so foolish. I shall have the boy killed before you make your move, Captain. You release the sword, pass it out of the cage and I shall have the boy released. If you do not, he will die.' The Saharadeen drew a gold dagger from his belt and held Gordon firmly in his grip.

I turned to my men, and then looked to poor Trouseau's figure, now helplessly turned into gold. I could not believe such a thing was possible. If I did not give up the sword and made an attack, Gordon would die and there would be no chance of Trouseau ever being returned to us. These were my friends. They were loyal to me and I could not betray them.

'If I give you the sword, you must return Trouseau and Gordon to me in good health', I demanded.

The Saharadeen replied, 'Very well, I shall agree to this, but first the sword.' This was a shrewd attempt to discover my weakness and the loyalty of my men.

'No, no Saharadeen, you give me my men first', I insisted.

He shot back: 'You must think me to be a fool, Captain. I shall return one man to you first; the other shall be returned after I have the sword but you shall stay in the cage. You are my prisoners and shall be sent to the mines as my slaves.' I now understood what this was leading to and his intentions.

I turned again to my men. 'This is a hard decision; we can risk our friends and fight, or we surrender and take our chances in the mines and find a way to escape once we are all together again. What do you think?' Joseph was the first to speak. 'We have been through many dangers together, seen more hard times than most men in twenty lifetimes. We can fight another day. I say let's have our friends back and regroup to fight again.'

I looked to the others. 'We do not have much time; what do you all say?'

Maris, Braheim and Blake all agreed. Mababe was too confused to give comment and simply said he was with me in whatever I decided to do. The others agreed with him. I could tell that in their hearts they would have preferred to stand and fight but we were all as one, and as brothers, we should take our chances together. Joseph and Mababe both finally nodded their agreement in silence.

'It is decided then', I said solemnly, and turned to the Saharadeen.

'Release Trouseau from his state and do no harm to the boy and I shall give you the sword. I want your word that no harm will come to my men'. I waited for his reply. It was a grim moment.

The Saharadeen ordered the statue of Trouseau to be brought forward. 'Very well,' the Saharadeen called back. 'It is agreed.' He clapped his hands again and suddenly the cage was hoisted just enough for two large iron rods to be pushed under the lowest rails of the cage. At the outer ends, chains were fixed and then slung over four wooden beams. Then some slaves were hustled into the hall and forced to take up the beams across their shoulders. Then they began to walk, moving the whole cage. We had to keep up inside the cage, moving with it. We saw that we were going back towards the Temple of Fire.

Eventually we arrived back in the great hall. There were so many soldiers scurrying around us and the noise of frantic chattering and slapping of feet on the stone floor was deafening as they ran around us, whooping and yelping and prodding at us with their spears and swords.

I held my sword firmly with both hands, knowing that to surrender it would lead to disaster, but I knew of no other way out of this trap we were in. It was obvious that as soon as I made a move, Gordon and Trouseau would be taken from us. There seemed no other way that I could save our friends. A thousand thoughts passed through my head in those dreadful moments. Finally we came to a stop and my attention returned to what was happening around us. The cage was slowly lifted from above our heads and instantly a wall of soldiers closed in on all four sides. They must have been ten men deep, forming a perfect square around us. There would be no escape once I had relinquished the sword into the hands of this evil man.

The Saharadeen and four guards appeared. They had Gordon, who was being tormented by the white-robed soldiers as he was pulled towards us by the guards. He was terribly frightened. Then the gold statue of Trouseau was hoisted into the air by chains, which were hooked onto four corners of a heavy wooden platform on which his statue stood. The tops of the chains were attached to a long and very thick timber arm. This came out of a gap in the solid gold walls. It was then swung across the vast hall and held over the pool of liquid gold. This was clearly a purpose built construction and had been used many times before.

Then the loud, heavy drumming stopped. The Saharadeen spoke. 'Captain, I give you the boy after you hand me the sword. When you have done this I shall restore your other friend to a man again.' He pointed up towards Trouseau's figure hanging helplessly from the chains.

'You will be witness to my powers and behold...' I interrupted, 'How can you do these things? I do not believe in magic. None of what you say will happen.'.

The Saharadeen replied angrily. 'All these things are possible in my kingdom, Captain. The Land of Fire is mine and so are its secrets. I have been honest with you. You know that you will not leave this land. Although I will let you live, your fate is to become my slaves in the mines. I swear by the Temple of Fire that this will be.' He seemed almost in a trance when he spoke. Then he broke off and clapped his hands. The sound of many trumpets blasted all around us. The mass of soldiers separated one part of their square that surrounded us. We could see now, at the back of the hall, two vast doors. They suddenly opened and some guards ran into the hall, rolling out a long silk carpet. It was woven with black and gold braid markings. It stopped at our feet. The soldiers then drew their curved sabres and stood still, staring menacingly at us.

My men and I were bunched in a tight group. Joseph and Braheim stood on either side of me. Two guards brought Gordon up. The fanfare of trumpets and drums continued and then we heard a different sound. It was the sound of many chanting voices. The chanting was quite eerie and came from beyond the large doors from where the carpet had been rolled out.

Finally some men appeared, clad in gold robes and head-dresses. In the centre of the group was a figure wearing a long gown, which reached the floor and slid along the ground as it moved towards us and a headdress which covered the face. Those around this figure carried long black poles, at the top of which were black feathered fans. The men waved them slowly back and forth as they approached us. The masked figure in the centre seemed to glide across the carpet as if it were floating. It was an unnerving experience. The chanting continued I could not see any face behind the gold, masked figure.

At last this strange spectacle stopped right in front of our group. The fanfare and chanting also stopped. At this moment the Saharadeen walked over to join the masked figure and together they turned to us. The Saharadeen nodded to the guards holding Gordon and they instantly released him. Quickly he ran over to us, grateful and yet deeply shaken. He was trying hard not to show his fear but I could see a tear in his eye and saw how he shook and sweated. I held his arm tight and whispered in his ear. 'It will be all right boy, hold fast now. We are all in this together'. Joseph put one of his huge hands on his shoulder and drew him into our group.

Then the Saharadeen spoke, almost politely, in English: 'The sword, Captain, please.'

The masked figure held out its arms for me to hand over the sword. Its hands were gloved in gold satin. I noticed that there was an eye embroidered in the palm of each glove.

My heart pounded and so many thoughts were whirling around in my head. It was all a haze. From somewhere, words came. 'This is the Sword of Isis', I said. 'It can only belong to one worthy of its power. It is the defender of good and the destroyer of evil'. I looked at the masked figure in front of me. 'Show me your worthiness. Speak with your own mind and reveal your face so that I can see into your eyes'. These words were not mine but somehow I was speaking them. Then I said again, 'Remove the mask'.

I was speaking in the tongue of these people. The Saharadeen was surprised. There was silence.

Finally he said, 'Captain, you are untrue to your word. Our agreement was to...' Again I cut him short. 'Our agreement was for a fair exchange for my men. I was not informed of any intervention by a masked figure who has no tongue and no face. How can I trust someone who does not show their face?'

I held the sword firm and braced myself, asking, 'Who is this whose eyes cannot be seen?' Some of the soldiers became restless and took up arms but the Saharadeen held up a hand to halt them.

Then, without a further word, the arms that were held out to me moved; the hands clasped the mask and lifted it slowly. Just then, I could feel my skin tingle and my nerves were unsteady. I will admit that I was scared of what was about to be unfolded before us. The mysterious figure was about to show its identity. As the mask lifted, I could see a face behind a thin silk veil. The mask was handed over to a guard and then one hand pushed the veil away.

I was stunned. I was standing before the figure of a woman. Her face was beautiful. It was perfect, almost too perfect. Her pale, olive skin was smooth and shining. She had piercing, deep green eyes. Her slender figure moved towards me. I looked quickly behind me at my men who stood transfixed. Then she spoke. 'Captain, you must accept your fate, for no man other than the great Saharadeen himself shall know me. It is written this way. You will hand me the sword as a matter of honour.' She spoke softly. Each word seemed to pierce my soul and her eyes were hypnotic and searching. I looked at all the soldiers around us and saw that every one of them had their heads bowed to the floor. I truly believed that if any of them saw the face of this extraordinary creature, they would surely perish.

My head was like mist and my thoughts were clouded. It was as if I had been caught in a dream. I had to shake this away and realised that I was being taken in by this strangely beautiful female. Although it was not easy, I forced my eyes away from her gaze and my sword gave me strength.

'No, you cannot fool me with your sorcery. You will never have this sword', I finally called out, still shaking.

The voice spoke again, but this time in a sharp, spitting tone. 'Give me the Sword! I am the Queen of the Land of Fire and of the Saharadeen, you will obey me!'

The Saharadeen made a move and grabbed his dagger. His sharp blade struck across my hand, cutting right through a vein. Instantly deep red blood spilled out and rolled down my hand onto the handle of the sword. Before I knew what was happening, the sword began to glow and moved without my control. I was compelled to work with it and I fended off the next attack from the Saharadeen. The sword deflected his lunge and knocked the dagger from his hand; in the same movement the tip of my blade sliced the side of his face. The wound instantly opened and he let out a terrible cry and fell to the floor holding his face, screaming. Instantly the Queen pulled a long gold dagger with a jagged blade from her sleeve. My sword seemed to sense her attack before she made her move and, with my left arm, I lunged.

What happened next was even more incredible. The blade of my sword pierced her. There was a deafening scream and then she burst into a blaze of light. Golden fiery sparks flew out from her. They sent flashes of light and fire, like meteors, across the vast temple hall. Then there was another flash of light. This time it was so bright that we had to cover our eyes. The guards and soldiers began to flee. Some fell to their knees. The explosions and fireballs caught some of them and they were gone instantly. It was a most spectacular, yet terrifying moment.

I stood still, the sword still held firm in my hands with my arms outstretched in readiness for another attack. The Saharadeen was reeling in pain on the floor, holding his wounded face.

Joseph and the men were quick to move and grabbed swords, lances, shields and huge curved sabres, which the soldiers had dropped as they fled. Everywhere there was confusion. People were running and screaming. Some of the slaves were aimlessly running about shouting with their arms held high as if some great God or spirit were about to take them. Those who chose to fall to their knees seemed to be praying. The floor shook and we felt that disaster was about to descend upon us. As the dust settled and the light dimmed, we saw a cloud of golden dust slowly fall to the floor.

Then, as I looked over to see the body of the woman, I realised I was looking at something ugly. The perfect face of the olive-skinned Queen had changed to that of a haggard and pitted old woman. Her jaw bones almost split her grey, paper-thin skin. Her once beautiful, piercing green eyes were now empty holes. The body lay motionless on the floor, partly covered by her golden gown. Then I saw the worst of it all. The hand that still clutched the golden dagger was covered in a green scaled skin. I was horrified, as were my men. The Saharadeen still lay on the floor squirming with the pain from the wound that I had inflicted upon him. Then he looked over to his Queen and lifted himself to his knees. I saw his face: my sword had made a terrible wound, causing a deep, bloody gash down one side of his face that had taken out his right eye. It was almost impossible to comprehend the speed of the attack and the damage I had done. The Saharadeen crawled moaning on his hands and knees to see his Queen. He reached the gown which covered her and pulled it away. The Queen's beautiful olive, silk skin had changed. It was now scaled, wrinkled and slippery. Her whole body was now covered in the skin of the snake.

We stood motionless at this deathly and vile sight. Suddenly the silence was broken by the dreadful cry of the Saharadeen. He let out a loud and piercing scream. The sound travelled across the temple and beyond. Suddenly the withered and rotting face of the Queen crumbled into grey dust before our eyes but the skin of the serpent remained quivering on the floor.

We had no time to lose. I had caused complete devastation and we needed to escape while we had a chance. Just as I turned to speak to my men, a voice called out from above us.

We all looked up to where the voice came from and, with mouths open in astonishment, we saw, swinging down from the chains above the pool of liquid, gold was Trouseau. 'Alors mes amis, wait for me,' he called and finally jumped down in front of us with a huge smile on his face.

'May God preserve us, you are alive! I exclaimed. 'Good to have you back with us, you rogue'. I laughed and then all the others laughed, patting him on his back and giving him welcome handshakes and embraces. I could only be thankful that once again the sword had saved us. I guessed the spell on Trouseau was broken when the Queen died, although I could not really say for certain how it happened.

There was no time to waste. 'Quickly men, we must go. Head for the big doors. Be armed and prepared', I ordered.

We met little opposition from the Saharadeen or his army. They were in complete chaos and mourning the loss of their Queen. We ran through corridors with gold statues over huge doorways and arches ornately carved with strange symbols and masked faces. There were more chambers, beautifully decorated in marble, gold and onyx and with coloured rugs hung from the high walls and across the marbled floors, as we passed from one chamber to the next.

We saw women with their servants, young children, slaves and soldiers dashing this way and that, not knowing where to go or what to do. It seemed as though everyone knew of the death of the Queen and now their lives were worthless and had no guidance or purpose. The whole place was in disarray. When we faced any of Saharadeen's soldiers, we simply took them fair and square. Braheim wielded a huge two-handed sword with a wide, curved blade, as he ran through the crowds. Nothing and no-one hindered his pace. Trouseau was like a mad fiend, furious from being captured, tortured and cast into a statue. He was on his own mission of vengeance. For one brief moment in his life, his personal value had become incalculable as a gold statue. In his mother country he had a price on his head, for he was, after all, a thief. He was in no mood for friendship with these people. Nothing survived that came within the length of his sword.

Trouseau, Maris and Mababe swooped through a room with long tables laden with plates of food and pots of milk and water. There were also great flagons of wine. They cut down a Persian rug from one wall and laid it on the floor. Then they scooped as much food and jugs of water as they could onto it. Maris pulled a long staff from the hands of a solid gold statue and tied the rug, full of their plunder, to the staff. They picked up the bundle and carried it over their shoulders. They moved so fast that their actions did not hinder our pace by much and I saw no reason to stop them. After all we would need food and water to stay alive.

Although we were running fast and fighting off attacks by the guards, we were well grouped and together we made a fearsome force. Joseph, a giant of a man, took on four or five at a time. His wild engagement in combat was really something to behold. Mababe, another giant, took no prisoners as he too wielded his sword at the oncoming enemy.

It had not taken long for the Saharadeen army to compose itself and they now wanted our blood. The chase was on and we needed to find a way out of the maze of corridors and chambers and to get outside the walls where we would have a better chance of escape.

We had a fair start on his army and could sense that there was some distance between us, but not that much.

Finally we came into a wide open area. It was a large courtyard, with grapevines hanging from many arches and trellises. The floor was patterned in mosaic and in the centre there was a large pool of clear blue water. Around it were beautiful flowers in crimson and pink and white. This was a paradise, a haven of tranquillity. We shattered the silence as we charged into the square.

There were women and children with their slave servants, who could not have known about the Queen. The children had been playing in the grounds and the women swimming in the pool. I wondered what these women and children were to the Saharadeen. When they saw us they panicked and began to flee. The women screamed and the children cried in fear of who we were. The slaves were so taken aback that they knew not whether to run or stand and fight to defend their mistresses. When they saw Joseph, Braheim, Mababe and Gordon approach them, they dropped their weapons and fled.

Suddenly we heard the sounds of horns and drums. There were many behind us and they were getting closer. 'I think that was their battle sound again, Sir,' Sam Little called as he ran up soaked in sweat and panting hard. The sun beat down on us and it was then that we realised that we were, at last, out in the open.

Knowing this, we all looked frantically for some way over the wall as an escape route. We had to get away from the clutches of this evil place. I looked to my sword and was thankful that we had saved it. I was about to consider calling on it for a sign when suddenly I heard a voice.

It was Gordon. 'Sir, look there!' He pointed to an arch with a gate, which was partially hidden by a vine. We ran towards it, but the bolts were rusted into the ironwork on the gate. Joseph took the handle of his sword and hit the bolt hard but it would not move. Wait, I said, and reached for my sword.

'By the help of this Sword of Isis', I whispered, and laid the blade on the top bolt. Instantly the bolt turned white and melted. It was all we needed. One hard shove and the other bolts gave way and the gate swung open.

We had entered a vast orchard of date palms. It looked beautiful and, at last, we tasted freedom. There was no telling which way we should go. I was still holding the sword and again it glowed. In the distance I heard a faint sound but it was not clear; then, instantly, I knew. Something or someone was telling me which way to go.

'The high ground, men. Look, up that way, there's a path'.

None of the men argued and we ran as fast as we could. We could tell that the path was beginning to take us higher. Although it was rough underfoot we were able to maintain a fast pace. None of us paused or needed rest. Considering the plight we had been through and the lack of food and water in the heat, we were making a good speed. As we ran, I saw the stone in the sword still glowing. It was as if the sword had given us strength and the stamina to run at such a pace without rest. I knew that whatever I thought, the sword heard me. We were running with the power of the Sword of Isis. It was as well, for we needed to keep ahead of our enemy. We could hear them gathering behind us.

At last we came to the summit of a hill and paused to see from where we had come. We could not believe the distance we had travelled and the speed at which we had reached this place.

We saw the orchard of palm trees fall away below us and away in the distance the vast mountain with its grey rock face rising up over the trees and up into the clouds. This was the evil kingdom of the Saharadeen and we were free of it.

We took water from the leather casks that Trouseau and Maris had found and felt the dust clear from our throats. Way down the hill, in the distance, we saw a cloud of dust rise up over the trees.

'Horses!' I exclaimed. 'Now they have horses'.

Words were not needed and we gathered up our things and turned to pick up our pace. I looked back occasionally to see our foe closing in on us.

We ran over rocks and hacked our way through long, razor sharp blades of grass. It would not take much of a scout to track us. We were the hunted. I felt like a rabbit being chased by mad dogs.

After a while we began to see that the surroundings were changing. The air was slightly cooler and there was dampness in the air. Then the ground seemed to rumble under our feet.

I knew what lay ahead. Soon there was that familiar sound, one we had heard before. It was the thunder of a thousand elephants and the ground beneath us trembled. A cloud came over and surrounded us.

We were near the falls. I warned everyone not to go close to the crumbly rocks. I had to shout to be heard amidst the thundering rolls of the great falls.

As we approached the falls, the rocky ground quaked violently underfoot and the noise grew even louder. We had to cover our ears as we edged in uneasy steps slowly towards the giant ravine. Soon we were standing upon a vast rock and saw that we had reached the highest point over the falls, on the other side of the lake from where we had first seen this place. The cliff face was steeper and we could clearly see the rapids of the wild river running down into the massive crater and into the jaws of the lake below. Nothing would ever survive the pull of this tremendous force. To cross here would be impossible. We had to find another way and time was not on our side. We heard the sound of Saharadeen's army gaining on us. Even through the din of the falls we could hear their battle cries and the thunder of hundreds of horses approaching.

I ordered the men: 'Come, let's go. The only way is up river'. We hacked down anything in our way as the jungle became thicker and much closer to the river's edge. There were giant twines and huge trees hanging across the sandy banks. It was hard to run fast but we were able to keep moving rapidly. We ran in single file, Joseph and I at the front, followed by Trouseau and Maris who still carried the staff with the food wrapped in the carpet they had plundered. The others followed closely behind, with Braheim taking up the rear. He had a large palm leaf and was brushing away our tracks in the sand as he ran. This was a standard practice for us in these circumstances. We had been on many adventures before and were able to work like a team without a single order from me. No-one ever complained, they just did what they had to do.

It seemed for a while that we had a good lead over our pursuers but we did not let up. They were not far away and with horses they would catch us soon.

"The power of the sword was still with us and although we had reduced our pace to conserve our energy we still moved quickly along the sand and over the rocks.

We had been moving for a while, looking for a likely safe place to cross, but found no opportunity. Suddenly there was a roar. This was not that of the wild river or the falls. This was a loathsome sound and one we knew well.

Out from the jungle leapt a huge lion. It ran straight for Braheim. He had no time to defend himself, and was sent crashing into the sand. He struggled desperately beneath the huge beast: it was a horrible sight. His screams were pitiful and it was clear that he was being badly mauled. Joseph boldly charged straight at the lion screaming at it in a fearsome tone. He took up the spear that Braheim had dropped and hurled it from close quarters. The lion was unable to move quick enough to fend off the attack and let out a dreadful moan as the tip of the spear tore into its side. It fell, dead, upon Braheim. They both lay still. Joseph fell to his knees. We all stood in silence. 'I was too slow,' Joseph's voice was quiet, his head bowed low.

I too felt the pain of sorrow upon me, as did all the others. 'You did well my friend. No-one could have tried harder', I told Joseph.

Said Mababe solemnly, 'We must give him an honourable burial.' He had never forgotten the day that he had been rescued from a slave market by Braheim some years before. I too recalled the event and also the many years we had spent together. I had known Braheim as a younger man, when he was with my father. We were all terribly saddened by this tragedy and approached the beast to pull it away from our friend.

Suddenly there was a moan and then a grunt. Then a foot moved. There was a cough and another grunt. 'I will give a thousand gold pieces to the man who rids me of this filthy beast,' croaked Braheim, who was now struggling to crawl from under the lion. We all burst into laughter and rushed to haul the beast away and help our friend. As he lay there in the sand, although badly scarred and wounded, covered in dirt and blood, he had his long Arab dagger in his hand. This had done its work. It had the lion's blood on it. He had struck the beast clean through the neck. Joseph's spear had merely finished the job. It was a shame that such a beautiful beast should die, but we so very pleased to see Braheim was alive.

We helped Braheim to his feet and Trouseau immediately attended to the shoulder wound with the water from one of the leather casks. He wrapped a torn sleeve around the wound and tied it tight. I was never so grateful. The loss of Braheim would have been so hard to bear.

We had temporarily forgotten our situation but were soon brought back to it when we heard the sound of the Saharadeen's army. They were very near. 'His scouts will be upon us soon, Sahib,' said Braheim. 'We must move quickly; waste no more time on me, you can see that I am well,' he said with a brave smile.

The situation was again serious. 'Can you run?' I asked him. 'Like the wind, Sahib,' he replied.

The heat was burning through our clothes as we set off. There was no let up from the sun in this dangerous and unfriendly country.

As we hurried along the bank of the river, we saw it bend. Now there were many more rocks in the river and the water thrashed over them like charging horses with white caps. The noise was deafening and we could not hear our own voices when we paused to consider our next move.

Mababe, who was once an African tribal chief, had much knowledge of the jungle and surroundings such as this. He came over and shouted in my ear. 'I think we can cross in this place, Captain. As the river bends, it also narrows, see there, up a way.' I could see he was right, but the river was moving too fast and we would be sent like driftwood, down into the jaws of the deadly falls if we tried to cross. I relayed my thoughts to him and he nodded in agreement. Then he pointed to the long, thick vines which hung from the huge trees above our heads. 'These are the ropes of the jungle, Captain. Allow me to show you.' Placing a long knife in his teeth, Mababe disappeared up one of the tall trees. The tree was so high that we could not see its top. He climbed up so fast that it made me think of what he would have been like in his own country, living in the jungle, completely at home in a place such as this, had he not been captured by Arabs and sold as a slave in the markets of his homeland.

After a short while there was a shout from above. 'Take care below' Mababe called down. Then came a thrashing of leaves and suddenly a huge vine dropped out of the thick leaves above us and we moved quickly to get out of its way. It crashed to the ground. Within a few moments came the smiling face of Mababe. 'This is our bridge, Captain. It will take us to the other side.'

It did not take us long to agree what should be done and we ran swiftly to the river's bend.

Sure enough the river was much narrower here and there were more rocks in the water.

One end of the thick vine was tied to a tree and then we discussed who should go in first and cross the river. I volunteered but Joseph butted in. 'Excuse me, Captain, Sir. I have the height to reach the branches on the far side and you need to be here to give orders, beggin' your pardon, Sir,' he smiled. I knew there would be no point in arguing with him and, in a way, he was right. There was no time anyway. Saharadeen's army were too close.

Joseph tied the end of the vine around his waist and plunged into the river. Although he was strong, the river was stronger and he had to swim with all his might against the tremendous pull of the current. I called out to him, 'Take good care my friend and mind the rocks, use them to help your crossing'. 'Aye, Sir,' came a faint call as his arms pushed hard into the fast moving water.

At first the rapids seemed to have the better of him and he was dragged under. Then he reappeared and we sighed with relief when his arms came up and we saw him swimming. Then he was thrown against a rock. It was a dreadful blow but still he kept going. He picked his way from one rock to the next. We all cheered him on as we watched him fight against the force of the river. A few times he completely vanished, then came up again in defiance of the river's strength. We all shouted to give him encouragement but it was unlikely that he could hear us against the raging torrents.

Suddenly came that familiar sound again. It was Saharadeen and his army. Now they were really close. Quick men, take arms and prepare to fight, I said. Some watched after Joseph in the water, while instantly the others took up positions.

Mababe called out, 'We can make a sling, Captain. We can fill it with rocks and send it to them with our blessings.'

'How so?' I asked. Mababe explained his plan. Wasting no time, he cut down two lengths of vine and tied them to two small trees. As he pulled tight, the trees bent over. He secured the centres of the vines to a rock.

'We must put in small rocks here,' he said, pointing to the wide leaves that he had fixed in the centre of the vines. 'When the enemy come, we will let this go. It will send them a message from us.' He held up a rock. 'This will be our message,' he said. We all smiled at his smart design and set to work. We continued to keep our eyes on Joseph and could see that he was nearing the far side. 'By the light, he's almost done it', I exclaimed. We all looked across to see him make one final dive from a rock into the water to reach the bank.

The enemy were now so near I felt uneasy. This was going to be close. We had to get across before they got to us.

When we had finally prepared the sling, I had Trouseau and Maris climb a tree with their bows. They could pick off the scouts before the full army was upon us. I did not wish, at this time, for another engagement with the Saharadeen, although I dearly wanted to have him for myself. But it would be in my time and that was not now.

The sling was ready and so were we. I glanced across to check Joseph's progress. He was almost there. If Saharadeen attacked now, we would be seriously outnumbered. I doubted that even the sword could help us then.

I heard a faint shout and looked over to see, with great delight, that Joseph had made it across. He waved his arms to tell us that he had secured the vine. In no time, Blake, Gordon, Little and Braheim were in the water. I watched them as they slipped along the vine through the rapids. They were quick to move. Even Braheim, with his wounded shoulder, was able to hold on.

Suddenly there was a cry and out of the jungle came several screaming soldiers with spears.

Mababe waited until they were near enough and then cut the sling. It released the bended trees and the vines released the pile rocks straight at them. The rocks cut the soldiers down like skittles. Those lucky enough to escape the rocks fled back into the bush.

Then came a second attack. The arrows fired by Trouseau and Maris struck with deathly accuracy and once again our foes retreated.

This gave us the time we needed. We hurried into the water clinging onto the vine to cross the river. It was hard to hold on against the power of the water rushing past us.

Gordon and Little made it clear, safely reaching the other side to Joseph. I saw them help Braheim who was struggling. The rest of us did not look back and kept on going. Then we saw arrows piercing the water around us. I gave a quick glance back and, to my horror, saw hundreds of Saharadeen's men charging into the river behind us. Some of them were stupid enough to try to swim and were immediately swept away. Their screams disappeared as they were tossed towards the rapids and then they were gone.

Finally we all made it to the other side but there were many soldiers climbing along the vine after us. Arrows were being fired with deadly closeness. One struck a tree just a few inches from my head. We were all out of breath and soaking wet. Trouseau and Maris had only just made it before a mass of arrows hit the dirt where they had just been standing.

Once we were all across, Joseph cut the vine. It whipped away and within seconds the Saharadeen soldiers who had been clinging to it were washed away down the river. Then I saw the Saharadeen himself on his horse on the far side. He looked desperate and furious. He let out his fury on his men and more arrows were fired, but we were now just out of range.

'Come, let's get out of here', I shouted and we all ran into the jungle, hacking our way frantically.

We marched through thick bush for hours. We couldn't assume that the Saharadeen was going to let us get away with this and he knew the terrain well. We, on the other hand, had no idea where we were. I had no compass to give us a heading and I longed to get back to our ship and away from this Land of Fire.

We had lost our food and water when we crossed the river, and we needed water now, more than anything.

The jungle seemed endless. There were strange and deadly creatures all around us. We came across a huge snake, which could eat a man whole, and avoided it very carefully. Giant spiders fell on us out of trees. One, which landed on Gordon's neck, was as big as a man's hand and coloured in black and red stripes. Mababe flicked it away with his sword. 'You were lucky, my friend, one bite would have killed you,' he said.

We tried to keep moving parallel to the river in the hope that it would lead us to the lake. I had remembered the lake was where we saw the Saharadeen's ship. It would have sailed in from the sea. If we could find the river that connects the lake to the sea, this could be where our ship would be. All I wanted now was to be back on board *The Glaros* and away from this place.

I put my hand on the sword and thought carefully about our situation. There had to be a way out of here and we needed to find it fast. I needed all my men fit and able. Just as I was considering Braheim's wounds, we heard a hearty cry. 'Allah be praised!' It was Braheim, who was sitting on a huge fallen tree. We all turned to see him stand up on the tree with his hands on his hips, looking down upon us. 'Sahib, I am as strong as an elephant, see my wound is gone. Your mighty powers have cured me and now I can fight as well as any man here.' He was smiling so widely and we all laughed and were again thankful for our good fortune to have the Sword of Isis with us.

It was unbelievable that a man, who had just been so badly mauled by a ferocious lion, showed no sign of ever being touched.

'Come, Braheim, throw away your stick and join us,' I called. 'Now we can move faster and let's hope that soon we will be back on board *The Glaros.*' He jumped down and ran over to us, throwing away the stick that he had used to help him walk.

We were all back in fit shape and again running with great stealth through the jungle.We could still hear the distant sound of the wild river to our left and knew that it was likely that the Saharadeen and his army were on the other side and moving in the same direction. He would have realised that our plan would be to make for the ship. Somehow we would need to find a way to throw him off our scent.

The jungle was thick and the burning heat hindered our progress as we cut our path through the dense undergrowth. Screeching birds, flying monkeys, dangerous snakes and spiders were all about us. We were grateful to have Mababe with us. He knew the names of most of the creatures and strange plants. Some of the most beautiful seemed to be the most treacherous. One plant with enormous, wide, dark green leaves had a beautiful and ornate flower in its centre. But the flower was an evil decoy. The giant leaves would suddenly snap together and envelope any inquisitive passer-by, dragging its prey into its jaws, which were hidden behind the flower. The plant could kill a full-size man.

Blake poked his head inside one of these plants to get a closer look at the wonderful flower. 'Do not go near,' yelled Mababe. Too late, Blake was lifted up by four huge leaves and dragged into the centre of the plant. Braheim and Trouseau got hold of his legs and tried to pull him out. The plant's leaves were very strong. 'Help! Get me out,' cried Blake, who was almost completely engulfed by the giant plant. 'Wait,' called Mababe. 'You will not free him like that. The more you pull him, the stronger the jaws will hold him.' Then he climbed up on top of the plant and thrust his spear deep into the top of the main stem. Almost instantly the leaves burst open and a long yellow tongue, like a spring, flew from the centre of the flower sending Blake flying through the air. Trouseau and Braheim also fell backwards as the immense power of the plant tossed all three of them onto the ground. 'My word, what was that?' exclaimed Blake and then jumped up yelling 'Ugh, oh no, I'm covered in... what is this? Ugh, help me Mababe, get this off.' Mababe just laughed. 'That is what we call the *Mangulp* plant and you have been covered in its sap juice. Its sticky texture glues its prey to the walls of the leaves inside. You will start to smell badly soon unless we get you into water and wash you down.' We all laughed. 'That will teach you to be so inquisitive, Blake,' I joked. 'Come, let's find us some water before the smell becomes too bad'.

Already, Blake was beginning to smell like rotting vegetables. It was not helped by the fact that the sun was at its hottest and he was now looking quite sick.

As we ran on through the jungle, I felt the strength was with us, thanks to the power of the sword, but we did need water badly. Our lips were cracking from the lack of moisture.

Luckily, my wishes were soon met and we could smell the dampness in the air again. It must be the lake, or water at least, I thought.

Sure enough, soon after a further mile of hacking through the bush, we came to the edge of a small lake. Long bending trees hung over the crystal blue water, shading it from the furnace of the scorching sun. We could see right to the bottom of the lake. The water was so clear and looked cool and inviting.

Suddenly something moved in the water.

# Chapter 4 – The Escape

A ripple formed a ring on the surface of the lake and some bubbles appeared. Beneath the ring, a dark shape moved and then it was gone. 'What is it, mon Capitaine?' asked Trouseau. 'I have no idea', I replied, 'but I think we should take a closer look before we jump in'.

Braheim pointed to another part of the lake. 'Sahib, look there. See – there are more shapes in the water'. He moved closer to the edge of the lake, drawing his huge sword and holding his shield as if he were about to be attacked.

Blake, Mababe, Maris and Little followed him and prepared to defend themselves. Gordon and Trouseau walked around to the other side of the lake. Gordon had seen something and convinced Trouseau that it should be investigated. Joseph and I watched the centre of the lake and saw more bubbles appear on the surface.

Sam Little made his way right to the edge of the water and was lying, chest down, on a large flat rock peering into the blue water. I could only see his back and legs as he had now stretched down with his shoulders hanging over the edge. I heard his voice echo back to us over the rocky rim around the deep water. 'I can't see anything here Sir, I think it's safe to go in. Reckon it was just some fish.' Then, without any warning he slipped over the edge but we heard no splash. I called out, 'Little don't be so hasty'. Then I rushed over. There was no sound from him and then I noticed Trouseau and Gordon, who were standing on the far side of the lake. They were very still and staring at the water.

Everyone ran to see what they were staring at. 'What is it?' I called. They did not move except for Gordon who pointed to the area beneath the rock where Sam Little had been lying. I could not see what he was looking at until I finally arrived at the edge. The others had arrived at the same place too and were all staring at something. I looked over the edge and saw what had caught their attention. Little had not slipped into the water at all. He had stepped down onto what he thought was another rock and, to his utter amazement, had found himself on the back of a giant turtle. He couldn't speak, he was so shocked. The huge head of the turtle had turned to look back at him and, with a slow and gentle nod, it then swam gracefully into the centre of the lake. Little was sitting on its back and had the biggest grin across his face. He was nervous and didn't wish to startle the huge creature.

I was about to speak, when suddenly three more turtles popped their heads up out of the water. Their backs were like enormous leather shields. The smallest of them was at least four feet across. One of them swam up to the turtle with Sam Little on its back and nodded to it. Then it looked at Sam, stretching its long neck further out of its giant leather back. Sam, still grinning, held out his hand very slowly. The turtle let him stroke its head and then pulled it back quickly. It startled Sam and as he pulled his arm away, he lost his balance on the turtle's back and slid off into the water. We all ran to assist. He let out a very nervous yell as he slipped into the water and disappeared, but only for an instant. He reappeared splashing around, his legs kicking away underneath. 'Help, help, I can't see them, where are they?' he called. We all burst into laughter as he suddenly came up face to face with one of the turtles. Its head was just a finger's length away from his face and curiously looking at him. 'Hold still Sam', I called. 'It's trying to see what you are. I reckon it thinks you're mighty strange'. We were all laughing and then suddenly Sam rose right out of the water. One of the turtles had moved under him and lifted him up. I told the men we should be safe enough here and instructed Blake to take himself over to a waterfall on the far side of the pool and wash away the foul smell. Everyone laughed and ran into the water, but carefully, so as not to upset our new friends. The turtles seemed quite happy to have us join them in the lake and swam around us. Occasionally one would stick its head up out of the water and look curiously at one of us.

The turtles had gentle faces and were harmless. Although such large and cumbersome creatures when on land, they moved with much grace and ease through the water.

We all washed and drank the cool fresh water from the waterfall, which fell through the trees down into this beautiful lake. It was good to feel that fresh water on my face and to drink again. I felt the sting of it as it touched my cracking lips.

Blake yelled out loud with great delight as he washed the smelly slime from his skin and clothes. 'Oh aye, this feels good,' he called out happily.

Trouseau started singing, as he always did when he was happy. The others sang along with him whenever they could remember the words, which were generally in French.

Joseph and I sat smiling at the men enjoying this happy moment and discussed our situation. We knew we could not stay here for long and needed to find a way out of the jungle. We did not know where we were, although by the position of the sun, which I had been watching through the day, I had a good idea where north was. The only problem was to find where we had landed three days ago. It was strange to think that we had seen two suns, but with the strength and power of the sword we had not rested, moving through night and day. However it was now growing darker and the sun was going down fast. I shall not forget that sunset, which glowed over the lake turning the crystal blue water into a purple shine. The turtles' backs also glowed in the sunset and we watched them disappear under the waterfall. This was one of the most beautiful places I have ever known.

Joseph made an observation about the turtles' large leather backs. 'See how thick and strong those shells are Sir', he said, and then pointed out that they resembled the shape of our shields. He said, 'No arrow or spear would have any effect on them. That is a truly good piece of their defence, don't you think?'

'Aye Joseph', I replied. 'They do look just like shields and very strong. I hope that the Saharadeen does not kill them for that very reason. These creatures are friends of man and should be respected so'.

Joseph agreed and smiled as he watched the last turtle drop out of sight under the waterfall.

I looked up to the sky. The sun had been replaced by a bright moon, which cast a glorious glow over the jungle. I listened to the waterfall pouring into the lake against a background of noises from the animals and birds of the jungle. Crickets clicked loudly, birds let out their evening chorus, and monkeys called out way up in the tops of the tall trees. They were so high up that they could not be seen. Sometimes we saw the shape of one jump from one tree to another and heard the rustle of branches as it landed. The whole place was alive and yet, even though there were so many different sounds around us, there was a strange peace about it. It was a tranquillity that calmed us. I had to shake myself and return my thoughts to our position. We needed to escape and find our ship. Even though she was badly damaged by the storm, we could make repairs. Maris was a fine carpenter, as was Joseph. Together they would find timbers and materials to do their handy work. The men were all keen to see *The Glaros* set sail again. But none of them more so than I.

Eventually the singing and chatter died down and the men found places to sleep. We had agreed who keep watch and that we would remain in twos when on guard. Joseph and I agreed to take the first watch. Mababe and Maris had taken it upon themselves to find food earlier that day and had returned with some strange looking plants and fruit. There was a bright red flower, which could be eaten, but was very sweet. According to Mababe, it would give us energy. The fruit was star shaped and gold in colour. It was delicious and there was plenty. They had also found coconuts, which gave me hope that perhaps we were near the coast. The most interesting thing we ate was a large brown snake, which was six feet long and had a wide girth. Mababe had caught it with his spear and skinned it. After starting a fire by rubbing two pieces of wood together, he cooked the snake. It did not take us long to eat it all. It tasted good, and we were grateful Mababe was with us.

The men were soon snoring. It was good to see them rested and well. I looked at the sword, pulling it from my belt. It reflected the light from the moon sending a flash skipping across the lake, which was now a dark purple with sparkles of light bouncing here and there across the water.

Joseph said softly, 'You have a true friend in that sword. May it take us all home safely.'

I agreed. 'Aye, my friend', I said, 'see how it shines. It is as if it is talking, showing a sign. I am amazed by its power and yet I have no knowledge of why it is so'.

Joseph wanted to know more. 'How say you, Captain?' he enquired.

I reminded him that it had been given to me by a great King. 'As you well know', I said, 'he wished to thank me for saving his daughter from pirates. He told me at the time of its great strength and power, but I had no idea how true this was'. As I spoke, the blade caught the light of the moon and sent a beam across the lake. For a brief moment, the light stopped at the edge of the falls, where the turtles had disappeared. The light held fast for a short while and then went out. It was as if it were another sign.

Joseph and I looked at each other, realising how strange that was. Something made me want to take a closer look at the falls, where the beam of light had made its mark. Joseph was of the same mind and followed me. We made sure that we did not wake the men and also kept a lookout on the surrounding area. 'We must keep a sharp eye open, Joseph', I said. 'The Saharadeen and his army may be close. We must not take any chances tonight'. Joseph agreed.

Quietly, we picked our way around the small lake. The moon cast a friendly light around us and we could still see the men sleeping peacefully beside the water's edge.

The falls sparkled in the light of the moon as we tried to find a way behind where the rock face hung. It was slippery underfoot but we were able to hold onto some overhanging vines. I grabbed one and swung it to see how far it would travel and where it would end.

'Joseph', I said, 'I think I can swing on this to get behind the falls'. He looked concerned. 'Captain, you do not know what lies beyond. There may be no place to land if you get past the falls.' 'True', I replied, 'but unless I try, we shall never know'. Joseph knew that once I had set my mind on something, nothing would deter me.

I took hold of the vine tightly, took a few steps back and ran forward, finally jumping off the rock and swinging straight into the cascading falls. I passed straight through swiftly. The water was cold and the power of it falling over me nearly made me lose my grip. There was a flat surface under my feet and quickly I let go of the vine. I landed cleanly. Falling to my knees I was able to grab hold of a smaller rock to keep my balance. I was delighted that I had achieved my aim on the first attempt. The sound of the falls behind me was loud and the water falling into a deep pool splashed noisily. To my astonishment, I was inside a vast cave, which glowed from the phosphorus in the water. I wished I had more light to see where the cave led and how far it went. There seemed no point in venturing further that night, but there was something telling me that this was our way to freedom. Perhaps there was a way through, I thought: what was on the other side? I had faith in the sword. After all, it had shown me a sign that this was the way. The light reflected from the moon had also been a sign. It had pointed me to this cave. This must be the way. But where, and how?

I looked around for a while and decided that this was a good place to hide. Then I noticed a gap between some rocks to one side of the mouth of the cave. Now that I could see a little better, as my eyes had become accustomed to the darkness, I ventured to see where it led. I could see through the silver screen of water and out into the small lake. I saw the silhouette of Joseph standing on a rock trying to look to where I was and smiled when I realised he could not see me. I saw his tall figure clearly with the sparkling light of the moon dancing upon the water. It was a truly memorable sight. To this day I still hold that picture in my mind of my dear and trusty friend.

I was interested to find that the crack between the rocks led me back outside the cave behind the falls. I suddenly found myself back by the lake. The narrow entrance was hidden behind some smaller rocks and a tall bush. I realised that I could have passed behind the falls without having to swing through them, getting very wet in the process. No-one would think of this small gap in the rock as being a way to get into the caves. I made a note of where the entrance was as I backtracked my way over to where Joseph stood. He was still peering through the falls, trying to find me. He had not seen me slip through the rocks. I tried not to laugh as I crept closer.

I was able to get just a few feet from him. He had his back to me. I suddenly pounced up and tapped him on the shoulder. 'You appear to be looking the wrong way my friend', I said and he spun round in total shock, grabbing his sword as he turned. His sword whipped through the air and would have removed my head, had I not ducked in time. 'By the love of Mary!" he exclaimed Who goes th...?'

"Ho, take it easy, I shouted.' 'Tis only me!'

"Joseph was taken aback. 'Upon my word, I could have killed you, man. Where did you come from?' The poor fellow was shaking with the thought that he had nearly removed my head. It was my fault: I should have realised that a prank like that was foolhardy. But after a few moments, we both laughed and I told him where I found the crack through the rocks and possibly our escape route. The others were quickly woken by the noise we made and came running across to us. 'What is it?' asked Braheim.

'We are all still safe – I am sorry to have startled you. Come – now that you are all awake, let me show you what I have found'. I beckoned them over to where the cave's entrance was hidden. 'See here, we have a way through to the other side of the falls and I am certain that there is a way to take us deeper into the caves and through to the other side of these hills that surround us. If the Saharadeen comes, we will at very least be able to hide in safety until they are gone. However, I do believe there is a way out of here. As beautiful as this lake is, this jungle is full of dangers and our enemy is on our back. They will not rest until they have us and we should not rest until we are back aboard *The Glaros* and setting our sails to freedom. Agreed?'

'Agreed!' Came a resounding reply.

We collected our weapons and provisions. The few water bottles we still had were refilled and then we made our way through the rocks and into the cave beyond the falls. Once we had all found a dry place to lie, we fell into a deep sleep. It felt so good to be able to rest and my eyes felt heavy for the first time in many days.

The sound of the water pouring over the rocks woke me and I had to hide my eyes from the brightness of the sun's rays as they burst through the occasional gaps in the falling water, casting bright beams all around the cave. It was like the dance of a million candles. But it was not the sound of the water or the bright light of the sun that had caused me to wake. I could hear something different. There was a change in the tone of the water rolling over the rocks.

I took myself up onto a higher ledge inside the cave to see if I could get sight of the lake outside. It was hard to see through as the bright sun light was blurring my vision.

Maris called: 'Captain, Captain, come quick.', He had been back outside through the hidden entrance. He too had heard the new sound and by the look on his face, he had discovered the source of the sound.

I jumped back down onto the lower platform of rocks, where the men had now woken and taken up their belongings.

'What news, Maris?' I called as he ran up to us.

He replied nervously: 'They are here. The Saharadeen and his army. They surround the lake.' Maris was panting and out of breath. 'I heard the sound and could not see through the falls, so I went back outside, through the rocks. There are so many soldiers. I have sealed up the entrance Sir, but I hope the dogs will not find it.'

'Dogs?' I asked.

He stretched out his long thin arms. 'Oh yes, Sir, and very big they are.' Blake drew his long Arab knife, 'We should do something about them, Sir.'

'Aye my friend, but one knife will not help us, no matter how sharp', I replied and started looking around. 'We must look for a way now we have light. Come with me,' I said and immediately we began searching the cave for a way to escape.

Suddenly there was a snorting sound and a spray of water came out of the pool. 'What was that?' I called and we went to investigate. At first, nothing appeared and then suddenly it happened again, but this time we saw what it was. One of the giant turtles had returned. It appeared to be playing with us by snorting water at us from its mouth and then dropping back into the water and out of sight. It happened a few times. Then, Sam Little, who had his shield strapped to his back bent over and looked into the pool to see where the turtle had gone. It was then that I had an idea.

'Quickly everybody, come over here. I do believe this creature is trying to tell us something'. They joined me at the pool. The giant turtle had climbed up out of the pool and grunted at us.

'See how Sam looks like a turtle with his shield on his back. I wonder if this turtle thinks the same.' They agreed that there was a close resemblance between Sam and the turtle.

Suddenly more turtles appeared. Before long there were many of them. They climbed out of the pool and sat beside the edge of the water. There was one very large turtle who looked much more worn and battered than the rest. 'He must be their leader', I noted. 'He appears so much older and scarred than all the others; I would bet a hefty penny that he is as old and wise as the ocean itself', I said, and looked closely at the huge turtle who had now come right up close to me. Its neck was protruding out from the huge shell on its back and its head was nodding up and down. Was it trying to tell me something? It turned its large head towards the pool, which now was full of turtles bobbing up and down in the waves that they were making, as they swam up and down, climbed out and then slipped back in. There was a great deal of commotion between the turtles as they thrashed about in the water. They began making an odd grunting sound, which echoed all around the cave. Then they became more anxious. Suddenly the old leader took the edge of Trouseau's round shield in its jaws and shook it. 'The crazy beast is trying to pull me into the water, Monsieur,' he called.

'I think I have it!' They want us to join them in the water. 'It could not be more plain. Let us go with it – we have nothing to lose. Our enemy is just beyond that waterfall and getting closer. If they discover us in here, we will be finished, for certain'.

I grabbed the handle of my sword and again that strange feeling came over me. It was as if something was telling me to put all my trust in this. It told me that we all should follow the turtles into the water. I wondered – was this the way, or am I imagining it. Where would this lead us now?

'Quickly, men. Put your shields across your backs, do as Sam has done; we shall disguise ourselves as turtles'.

As soon as I had given this order, we heard a shout and a babbling of manic voices from outside. Our enemy was almost upon us. They were near the waterfall, outside, and then more shouting came from the rocks. 'They have discovered the secret entrance, Sahib,' Braheim said, looking very anxious.

'Quickly, now we must go,' I ordered again. We heard the growling of the dogs outside.

We strapped our shields to our backs and together we dived into the pool. Instantly all the turtles slid back into the water and were heading for the far side of the pool. They dived under the water and we followed them. As we did this, I could hear the echo of voices above us. The Saharadeen's soldiers were looking down into the water. They could only see turtles down in the depths of the pool. Our disguise was working well.

The next few moments were like a dream as I found myself swimming with the turtles. We were all as one. Now the bright blue water was turning darker and I could only just see the shapes of my friends swimming with me. We followed the turtles further on into the depths of the underwater cavern. I took another quick look up above and saw strange dancing shadows of figures, their voices were distant but their echoing shouts were still calling out. As we dived further down, it became even darker and then it was black. I could no longer see or hear the sounds of my friends. It was as if we were drowning, falling into a deep silent sleep. The faint gurgle of something in front was unnerving. Then it was gone. All was silent. Was I alone, and where were my men: had this been a terrible mistake?

But then, I realised that I was still awake. I was alive. All my senses were with me and I was still breathing. It was strange. I was still breathing – after all this time under water and in the dark depths. It seemed an endless dream. I felt like stopping and wanted to go up. For a moment I faltered and stopped swimming but suddenly something pushed me from behind. I was shocked and tried to look back to see what it was and then – another shove. It almost winded me. As I turned I saw the huge dark shape of the giant turtle swimming straight for me. I just managed to move to one side before it rammed into me again. It stopped and looked at me and opened its mouth. An eruption of bubbles came out from its mouth, followed by a moaning sound. Its head turned to the right and nodded. I understood, turned away and continued to swim on.

"How long had I been under water? Where was this leading? Where was I? All these questions were rushing through my head. Still I could see nothing. The dream went on. It all moved in slow motion and the wailing of strange noises came back to me, like something calling.

After a while, I began to see a glimmer of light ahead of me. At first it looked like a shadow dancing. The dream became brighter and then I saw the water was changing colour to a lighter blue and green. Beneath me I saw a white floor. It was pure white sand. Now the water tasted different. It was salt! We were in the sea.

The water became a brilliant crystal blue and I was able to see around me. There were glorious fishes of many colours, shapes and sizes. I saw what I thought were three huge turtles and then another, which looked unusual until I realised it was Joseph. He looked just like the giant turtle as his arms and legs pushed out and then in again. It was unbelievable and truly wonderful. I found myself drifting upwards and, as I looked up,

I could see the bright reflection of light as it danced across the water's surface. I was coming up. The air was near. It felt warm. The sun was streaming through the water.

I burst through the surface. The brightness and the sounds around me were violent and I screamed with relief as I breathed in the clean, fresh air and cried as the air filled my lungs.

The waves splashed over me and for a while I drifted and bobbed up and down in the sea. I heard sea birds shrieking and men's voices shouting. Finally I turned and saw my friends standing on a white sandy beach waving frantically at me. They were calling and whooping, jumping up and down and smiling at me. The dreaming was over; we had landed.

A giant turtle came up and passed close to my side. I was so delighted that I hugged and kissed its leather back and then flopped across it and let it pull me to the shore.

Panting and aching though I was, I was so delighted to see that all my men were there. Again I cried with delight and choked some water out of my lungs as I saw three smiling faces looking down upon me.

Gordon was laughing as he asked: 'Captain, are you all right?' Maris had a water bottle and held my head up to take a sip. I thanked him as I drank the clean fresh water and delighted as I felt it flow through me as if new life were being poured into me.

I looked along the beach and saw the turtles slowly crawling towards some rocks. I nodded over to where they were assembling. 'We have much to thank them for. I cannot understand why they did this, but I am truly grateful. They are such wonderful creatures, and should be protected from the dangers of man.' I said.

Joseph, who was covered in seaweed, said, 'Aye Sir, we are truly grateful to them. 'Tis not as if we can thank them so easily'.

'By the stars', I laughed, 'you look like Neptune himself, Joseph'. Everyone saw his amusing appearance. He was covered in seaweed from his head down and everyone joined in the laughter. We were all so pleased to have escaped from the jungle and our enemy.

I saw the wise old leader of the turtles wading out of the sea. He moved awkwardly across the sand towards his family and I walked over to study him closer. I knelt down in front of him and he stopped. I held out a careful hand and he let me touch his head. 'Thank-you old friend, I shall never forget you', I said, 'I wish you could talk. You would probably know where our ship is and even a way out of here. If I could speak the language of the turtle, I would say to you and your kind that as long as I live, you will have nothing to fear from us. We are your friends'. I felt strange speaking to the creature but I felt I should. The turtle looked up and I saw into his eyes. They were dark and wise. There was a friendliness about them. They almost smiled. The turtle then looked at the sword, which still hung from my belt. It seemed to stare at it for some time, turning his head from side to side.

I pondered for a moment and then spoke to him again. 'Do you know this?' I asked, holding out the sword. 'Do you understand it?' I asked again.

The huge turtle just looked up at me and gazed right into my eyes. His stare was quite alarming. Then he nodded to me. This time the nod was like a bow. It was graceful and slow. Then he let out a howl and all the others, which had assembled by the rock under the shade of a vast tree, began to whoop and howl too. It was the oddest sound. The turtle gave a last, quick glance towards me, nodded again and slowly moved away towards his family.

'Goodbye old friend', I whispered. 'Thank-you'.

We found a place under some trees, just away from the sun-scorched beach. The shade was welcome but the heat was relentless as it fired down on us from the cloudless sky. There was no wind and we cut down palm leaves to fan ourselves as we rested and drank small sips of water so as not to exhaust our short supply. We only had two bottles left – enough for another day, perhaps a day-and-a-half if we were careful.

Blake asked the question that must have been on all their minds. 'What do we do now, Captain?'

'We rest until darkness, when it will be cooler, then we move out'. My suggestion was quite direct. It seemed the right thing to do. No-one disagreed.

At last the night came and a small breeze picked up, cooling the air. It was a welcome relief from the heat of the sun. The moon lit up the beach and cast its silvery light over the bay. The tall palm trees bayed gently with the breeze and their long hanging branches rustled in the fresh evening air.

The sea rolled up and down over the sand and for the first time in days, I felt at ease. All appeared to be well. When darkness fell, we collected our things and moved out. I had no idea which direction we should take, I just followed my instincts.

I gave orders to my comrades. 'We must stay close and keep to the shore. Make no sound as you march. This time we must find our way home. Now we are all together, there will be no need to venture further into this strange land'. I spoke quietly and with this, we walked on.

We walked for several hours keeping close to the trees along the shore. Occasionally we had to climb over rocky ledges and at one point we climbed a small cliff, only to climb back down onto another beach. We lost one of the water bottles as it ripped from Blake's shoulder when he tripped over a sharp rock. Now we just had one bottle left. We needed to find our ship and supplies before daylight.

We came to a small bay, where a rough grassy bank rose up over a hill. It was agreed that we should climb up as there was no other way around the bay. The rocky cliff on the other side was too steep and it would be impossible to climb without ropes.

As we climbed the hill, we heard a sound. The sound grew louder as we neared the top.

'Easy, men, we must not be seen', I whispered.

We crawled the last few feet on our fronts and finally arrived at the top and saw to our astonishment that we had come to the top of a hill overlooking a harbour.

Joseph whispered excitedly: 'Will the good Lord love me? Look over there. 'Tis *The Glaros*. She's been newly rigged.'

'Well I'll be...! You are right', I replied, 'it is our ship, with new masts. But it had been rigged in the Arabic style.' Her booms leaned awkwardly across her masts. The golden figurehead remained intact. Her sides were lined with shields in many colours and shapes. Now she was lying at anchor in this unknown harbour. To see her without her old masts and square rig was most strange and I was furious that our ship had been altered in this way. But I was amazed how quickly the alterations had been carried out. She looked just like the three other ships in the bay, except she was so much larger. The only thing that gave her away was her hull, which unmistakably was *The Glaros*. It was clear that the Saharadeen needed her as his war ship.

Trouseau had a nose for danger and could smell trouble a mile away. 'I do not like the feel of this, mon Capitaine. I can feel we may find trouble here. Look down there.' He pointed to a cluster of small buildings where a fire was burning. There were only a few men standing around talking together, but very little else was going on. 'For a harbour, it looks very quiet, mon Capitaine,' he whispered and then indicated to a hill far over to the other side of the harbour. There was a castle. Its fortress walls looked unmanned. There were a few lights burning but it all seemed too quiet. 'I think you follow my thoughts, Capitaine. Where is everybody?'

'That is indeed a very good question', I said. 'Look to the three ships, can you see anyone on board?'

'Non, Monsieur, there is only one guard on *The Glaros* and I see only one man on that other ship to the left. It is too quiet, oui?'

'Aye, my friend. I have a feeling they are expecting us. I would bet a king's ransom that they have laid a trap'.

I was wondering what our next move should be when Maris and Mababe crawled up to us through the long grass. Maris whispered: 'Captain, we have sighted soldiers over on the far hill. They are laying low. I would not have seen them but Mababe has the eyes of the eagle.'

'What did you see?' I asked.

Mababe's eyes were bright against his dark face. 'I saw their shadows beneath the trees. The moon shines brightly again tonight and it cast its light on them for a moment. Then I saw them. I think there are many.' He was certain of what he had seen and I had no reason to doubt him. We had noticed that the harbour was just a simple bay and easy for us to swim across. We could get to *The Glaros* without being seen by the soldiers on the far side as the shadow from the tall ships would hide us in the darkness. It was clear that they were expecting us to make our way to the far side of the bay where there were some long boats tied up to a stone wall. They assumed that we would take one of the boats and row out to the ship. The Saharadeen had deliberately left the boats there for us. They would have attacked us as we tried to board them.

'We must move now, before they realise that we have arrived', I said. 'We should swim out and climb up the anchor cable. The tide has turned and now our ship points towards us. See how the bow is hidden from the far side. They will not see us'.

We agreed to slip back down the grassy hill and pick our way over the rocks to the water's edge. Finally we made it to the bottom of the hill and began to climb across the slippery rocks towards the edge of the small harbour. We tied our shields onto our backs, as we had done before and made sure that our swords, and anything else that would shine and reflect the light, were hidden from the brightness of the full moon.

'Make no ripple in the water. Not a sound. Is that understood?' I whispered to the men. They nodded. Trouseau was the first into the water. He slipped in without a single ripple or splash. Then, without any effort, he went under the water and began to swim towards our ship. It would not be easy for us to swim like this with our weapons and shields, but it had to be done. We had no choice.

'Watch Trouseau. That is how we shall all go. Come, let us board our ship'. I spoke very quietly and we all slipped into the water.

I kept an eye on the shore to watch for any movement. There was none from the small camp and nothing moved on the castle walls. I could not see if anything moved on the far side, where our enemy waited.

The water was as black as ebony and as still and flat as glass. The surface had a silvery grey glint and I wondered if the moon would show us up. I signalled to the men to keep their faces under the water whenever possible. Although, Maris, Mababe and Braheim were dark skinned, their eyes were as bright as lights and would easily be seen from a distance.

Eventually we made it to the anchor cable. Trouseau was first to scuttle up. Not a sound could be heard and he moved so quickly. He truly was a valuable member of our small family.

When he finally slipped out of sight and over the wooden rails, we waited anxiously. There was a sound: a thud and a quiet moan, then, suddenly, a gentle splash in the water. It was too dark to see what it was, but it did not arouse the enemy on the shore. A rope appeared above us. Trouseau had fixed another line for us to climb up. We just saw his head in the darkness and he signalled that it was safe to go up. I said nothing but pointed to the others in the water to go. We were all experts in climbing ropes and within a very short time we were all, at last, back on board *The Glaros*. It felt good to stand on her decks again. She was, after all, our home. Although we could see the changes that the Saharadeen had made to her, she was still *The Glaros* and it would not take long for us to have her under way and for us to be clear of the Land of Fire and its evil leader. But it was not going to be easy for us to sail her off her anchorage as the wind had dropped to nothing.

We could only hope to use the current, which was, for our good fortune, heading out to sea.

My plan was to cut the anchor rope and let *The Glaros* drift out to sea with the current. It was dark and even though the enemy still waited, hidden on the banks of the far side of the harbour, it would take them a while to notice the ship was free and moving away.

I made certain that we were alone on board with no unexpected company. I beckoned Trouseau over. 'What was that noise when you got aboard?' I asked.

He replied with a glint in his eye. 'Let me say that we will not have any guests for dinner, Monsieur.'

I sent Joseph, Little and Blake to search below decks for any further signs of enemy aboard. After a short while they reappeared smiling. Joseph came over to me as I stood by the helm looking at the new wheel that had been built. It was clear that the Saharadeen had every intention of using our ship for his treacherous attacks on other ships and victims. He had done a fine job of fixing her broken timber masts and replacing the torn sails with his own. We could not see the full extent of the new sails as they were rolled up around the cross-booms. But I looked forward to seeing them dropped and full set with the wind in them and taking us out to the great ocean that waited for us.

Joseph had a look of delight in his eyes. He whispered into my ear. 'They have stocked her full, Captain. There's food in plenty and fresh water in the barrels. There be no evil aboard either, Sir.' I smiled and whispered back. 'Good, let us make way. Quietly now and keep your eyes on that shore. One wrong move and we'll be back in the arms of the devil'.

Joseph quickly moved across the deck to where Gordon and Mababe were waiting for instructions. There were no words, only signals and quick actions. The anchor rope fell quietly into the water. I looked down at my sword and whispered to it: *Help us now in this moment of truth.*

The jewel in the handle of the sword glowed dimly under its leather cover. I smiled and held the handle firm. Were we finally free of this terrible place? It was an anxious moment for all of us.

We began to drift slowly out to sea. I signalled to my men to stand by to set the sails and then looked up to the sky. I could see the blackness of the waiting ocean. It was an uneasy feeling, but the lights on the shore were glimmering and grew distant as we drifted away. Still there was no movement from our enemy. How could it be, I thought, that they did not see us drifting and why was all this so easy? There were so many questions swirling around in my head. The men looked anxious. There was something wrong. It was too simple.

As we approached the edge of the harbour, the ship began to roll, slowly at first and then gradually it pitched up and down on the waves that rolled into the estuary.

Joseph ran up to me; he looked concerned. 'Captain, this don't seem right, there is no reason for a swell like this; we have no wind with us, the tide is weak beneath us and yet we list like an ailing bird.' He was right; there was no reason for this, I agreed.

There was a cry from Braheim. 'What do you see, Braheim?' I called back.

He returned: 'Look to the ocean and above to the skies'.

I looked to where he pointed. The sea beyond was as black as the night and the dark sky had lost the moon. It was as if we were headed for a vast black hole and the sea was becoming rougher by the second. I looked behind and suddenly there were lights on the shore and fires were burning. We saw thousands of figures assembling on the beach and around the harbour. Then came the sound of war drums from the shore.

As we pitched and rolled towards the ocean, the wind began to pick up. 'Make ready the main sail', I shouted. 'We are in for a rough ride. Make reefs in the main as they roll and take care. Keep all eyes ahead and aft', I ordered.

Suddenly huge waves came upon us. The first washed over the bows and *The Glaros* heeled to port, and the next rolled us to starboard. We had dropped the main sail halfway to give us steerage and I felt the helm take control, but it was only for a short moment. It was then we noticed that the sign of the Saharadeen had been painted on the sail. It was the twin headed serpent.

Without warning an even bigger wave, higher than the tops of the masts, came upon us and smashed the ship over onto its side. Then a bright light filled the sky and turned into a mountainous fire. The men all ran to join me at the stern. *The Glaros* rolled back onto its keel and we headed towards a wall of fire. The ocean was ablaze and as I looked into the centre of the mountain of flames, I saw a dark shape appear. At first it was small but it grew larger and larger. Then we saw the shape of a giant figure coming quickly towards us through the waves of fire.

We were trapped in a huge wall of flames. None of us could speak for we were too scared to say a word. There was a dreadful rumbling sound and *The Glaros* hove to, right in the midst of this evil fiery sea. The black figure drew closer and closer. It was the shape of evil in a hooded veil. There was no face and its arms engulfed the whole area around us. The walls of flames were on all sides and it was as if the arms of this figure were pushing us and the wall of fire back to the harbour. The giant head of the demon was right above us and then we saw its eyes. They were blood red but there was no face. There was a frightening sound. It was the sound of screaming men. The eyes beamed down onto the ship and we all ran for cover. I drew my sword and held it up towards the demon towering above us. Suddenly the flames caught the sail and in seconds the ship was alight. Run for it, men, abandon ship, I called. I saw Little, Gordon and Mababe dive into the sea. There was fire everywhere and I prayed that they would survive this terrible thing, this monster from the deep, black ocean. This was the work of the devil himself. It had to be the Saharadeen working his evil powers.

The black cloaked arms of the demon moved closer. The face of darkness was now right above me. I tried to hold onto the mast and swiped with my sword to fend it off. I looked to the stone which shone and spoke to it. 'Help us now – rid us of this evil thing.' The sword glowed. I heard Joseph speak to me. 'Captain, jump, you must jump overboard.' I looked around but could not see him. 'Where are you Joseph?' I called. 'Captain I...' His voice was replaced by another. 'Sahib, you are in terrible trouble, jump, for the sake of Allah. May peace be with you' Then his voice disappeared too. I heard calls from the others. Trouseau called, 'Mon ami, mon ami, come with us now, you must jump.'

Where were they? I could see nothing but the fire around me and the huge, dark figure, which towered menacingly over the ship.

Suddenly the mast burst into flames and I could see it was going to fall and destroy the ship. I thrust out with the sword and to my astonishment it cut clean through the mast, sending it overboard into the fiery sea. I could not believe that a sword could cut through such a huge mast so cleanly. If I had not seen it with my own eyes, I would not have believed it possible, but it saved *The Glaros*.

Then I saw the arms of the demon move closer to me. I swung my sword at the black, veiled arm and as I struck, it let out a terrible scream. A noise, so evil, rang out across the sea. The arm whirled away quickly and then burst into flames. The hooded head of the demon figure tossed up into the sky and suddenly a face of terror looked down on me. It was the head of a giant serpent. Its eyes were gold and its skin was silken in green scales and slithering liquid gold which ran down the skin to the arm that I had struck. Suddenly, from out of its arm, a huge gold spear appeared. It rose up and then was hurled towards me.

There was a terrifying explosion of fire and the sound of a million screams rang out.

I do not recall what happened next. It was all a dream. In the distance I heard voices of my men calling me. I heard the screams of others. Explosions, dark hooded figures were floating all around me. There was fire everywhere and then – the worst thing – the face of evil was looking down. It was the moment before death and I was to be taken by the devil himself.

I cannot say what happened in those dreadful moments after I struck the demon, but nothing could compare to the terror that struck me when I awoke in chains in a dungeon of darkness.

I was alone and stripped to my waist. The dungeon stank of death and the dampness in the air made me choke."

# Chapter 5 – My Destiny

"It was dark, and as the dripping water from above fell to the floor, it echoed loudly. I tried to move, but the chains, clanking loudly as they dragged across the wet floor, tore into my flesh.

I was trapped in a pit of darkness. Then I felt something moving across me but it was so dark I could not see. Then there were two red eyes staring at me out of the darkness, and something flicked over my feet. I kicked out and there was a shriek. Then I saw something run over my legs and away across the floor into the dark. It had bitten me and my foot was sore. I could not reach it, as my hands were chained up to the walls of the pit.

It seemed like hours had passed into days and I was weak. I had seen no-one and had received no food or water. I was a prisoner who had been left to die in hell.

I fell into a dream. I saw faces of the ghosts of men who had died. I saw Joseph and the others fighting against a huge monster. Then a beautiful woman came to me in a dress of sapphire and silver. Her long dark hair fell over her smooth olive-skinned shoulders. It was Princess Tasia. Then to my horror she disappeared and was replaced by the face of evil. The Saharadeen laughed in my face and a giant serpent swirled around his feet and spat its venom at me. There were sighs and screams in the distance and, again, the face of darkness. A hooded figure in black with eyes of gold staring, staring...

Suddenly I was being shaken and water was thrown into my face. I awoke to find myself surrounded by soldiers. This was all a dream, I thought. Then I was being picked up. My chains were unlocked from the wall, but were still clamped tight around my ankles. Someone hit me in the back and I fell to the floor. I heard words of evil hatred and a gibberish babbling around the room. I was picked up and dragged. There was a loud crash of steel and a huge door opened in front of me. I put up my hands to my eyes, as an explosion of bright light hit me full in the face.

I realised then, that I was awake. This was real. I was in a huge corridor lined with soldiers and people chanting, slamming spears and rattling swords against their shields. Their black faces and white robes brought it all back to me. I looked up and saw the walls of gold and giant statues of serpents and demons. Huge eyes were carved into the golden walls of the high arched corridors. I was back in the Temple of Fire.

They dragged me along the lines of the soldiers and sneered and tormented me with every step I made. I was surely about to die a terrible death.

My eyes bled and my vision was blurred. My legs ached from the weight of the chains and I was weak from hunger, but I was walking. I tried to hold up my head and maintain some form of dignity and thought of the things I loved. I thought of my home that I had not seen in years. My friends and comrades, where were they now? I thought of Princess Tasia and I tried to imagine her pretty face when we were last together. They were happy times. I hung onto whatever I could that was good in my memories.

Two huge doors opened before me. Beyond was another crowd of people. These were the servants of the devil himself. All dressed in gold and black, they formed a single line around me. Their faces were motionless; their piercing eyes stared into me. It was as if they were not human.

Then *he* was there. In front was an altar covered in a gold cloth and upon it was the Sword of Isis. The Saharadeen waited as I stumbled towards him. He was standing tall with arms folded. His smile was burning into me. My heart felt heavy and what little blood was still in me, boiled with anger. Suddenly I was pulled to a halt by three bald-headed guards.

The Saharadeen spoke, staring into my eyes, 'Your time has arrived, Captain Hawkins. You are mine and I shall deliver you to my kingdom for ever.' I saw the scar that I had given him. It ran from the top of his missing eye, down below his jaw. It was ugly and I felt pleased that I had given it to him. The hole with the missing eye was now covered with a gold patch, which amused me.

The Saharadeen lifted my sword in both hands and spoke again. 'It was your destiny that you should deliver this to me. It belongs to one more powerful than you. You are an infidel and I am now the ruler of the earth. With this sword I shall live forever and all who stand in my way shall perish.' His words were those of a madman. Then I noticed something wrong about the sword and then realised what it was. There was no glow. The stone had gone from the handle.

The Saharadeen suddenly cried out, 'Take him!'

I was pulled back and turned to face the place I knew was to be my end. It was the pool of gold and fire. Hundreds of people had gathered around. I tried to look for my men but could not see them. This time I knew there would be no escape. The chanting had begun and the horns blew and drums began to beat slowly. With every beat, the room rumbled and the ground trembled. The noise was dreadful. I tried to release myself from the grip of the guards but I could not. They were giants and I suddenly felt very small as I approached my fate.

This was to be my destiny.

The Saharadeen followed, walking behind his guards and, as they turned me with my back to the pool of liquid gold, he came up and grabbed both my arms. He was tall and his hooked nose hung like the beak of a giant hawk between his two dark evil eyes.

He called out some words that I did not understand. All the crowds around sighed and moaned. Suddenly the pool of liquid turned into a pit of fire and a fountain of sparks and flames blew out and up from the centre. I turned my head and saw the fountain reach up to the dome at the top of the ceiling of the temple. There was another explosion and the flames turned into a bright beam of gold light. I looked into the pool. It was as if there was no bottom to it. It was a mysterious liquid of gold and light. As I stared into the pool, I saw my life flash past and then it died away. I cannot explain what happened next. I turned to face the Saharadeen who held me. I saw a gold chain fall from out of his robe and there, on the end, hung the stone from the sword. My eyes fixed on the stone. I tried to think but I was in a daze.

The Saharadeen screamed: 'You will go into your next life as my servant. You came here on a ship called *The Glaros, The Seagull,* and you shall therefore go as you came. I shall turn you into the bird that you are.

He laughed and the crowd roared with approval. 'Your ship will be mine. It will serve me well.' He laughed in my face and I despised him, but I could do nothing.

The fountain of gold was like a pillar beaming up to the skies. There was no heat but I began to tremble with weakness. The Saharadeen held me further over into the fountain of gold. 'Go now!' he called and pushed me backwards. As I fell back into the fountain, I grabbed at his throat and caught the chain. All I remember was pulling back my arms over my head as I fell.

There was a blinding flash and I knew no more.

I can only recall bright lights in my eyes and I heard those terrible screams. I felt immense pain and then nothing. I felt as if I were being lifted up. It was as if my body had become lighter. I felt different. I was floating in the air.

Then horror struck me and the realisation of what I had become was too much to bear. I wanted to die now. It could not be so..."

There was a long pause. Tom walked over to the seagull.

"Are you all right Mr Hawkins, Sir?"

"Mmmm, er, yes thank-you, Tom. Just give me a moment."

Tom stood silently looking at his friend. His head was full of thoughts and he wondered about the feeling that Mr Hawkins must have had. This was truly the most incredible story. He was honoured to have been told it and his head swirled with thoughts about what he had just learned.

"Mr Hawkins, that is the most amazing thing I have ever heard. What happened next? And how...?"

The seagull looked up at Tom and his eye blinked. Then Tom looked at the stone, which glowed from the rock beside them. "How... ? Tom wanted to ask the obvious questions but Mr Hawkins interrupted.

"The Stone, Tom? How did I manage to get it?"

"Yes, you said you had hold of the Saharadeen's throat and grabbed the chain – what happened then?"

"My arms came over my head as I fell back into the fountain. The chain must have fallen around my neck by chance. Then, when I felt that feeling of being lifted up, I realised that I had..., I had become... as I am now. The chain was still around my neck as I floated up. Then I knew that I was flying up towards the dome in the centre of the temple. They fired arrows at me and then instinct took over. I quickly found my wings and I dodged the arrows. I found myself swerving in and out and up and down to avoid being hit. But a part of me wanted them to strike, a part of me wanted to die, but somehow I managed to escape. I knew that they were trying to get the stone from me. The Saharadeen will not have the power until the sword is reunited with this stone. However, the stone has its own powers. It has helped me these many years."

"Wow," said Tom. "That's fantastic, so what happened then, where did you go?" Tom wanted to know everything.

"Tom, Tom. Do you not think you have taken in enough for one day?" The seagull looked to his friend. He knew he had to tell the boy everything. Soon it would be right for them to make their first journey together and Tom would need to be prepared in every way.

Tom looked at his watch. He just could not believe that time had barely passed. It was true − the stone did have magical powers. It could make time stand still. It was so exciting and Tom needed to know it all.

"Mr Hawkins, or shall I call you Captain Hawkins?" asked Tom as he stood over the stone, peering into it with wide eyes.

"I am no longer a captain, Tom. It was so long ago that I was Master of a ship." The seagull stood squarely opposite Tom and picked the stone up in his beak and placed it back in the centre of the nest of straw. "We must take great care of this, Tom. It will be our guiding light for whatever awaits us. You and I will need to trust each other Tom, there are going to be times when the real test of friendship will be placed upon us. This stone will give us hope when there appears to be none and new life when it seems that all is lost. It will be our voice when we are apart." Tom looked at the seagull. "How do you mean, our voice?"

"You recall me telling you how I was able to speak without words when we were in the Temple of Fire?"

"Yes, I do."

"You now have this power, Tom."

"Me? How?"

"How does not matter, but you will be able to hear me and talk to me without speaking. All you need to do is think what you want to say and wherever you are and wherever I am, we will have the power of speech but without talking." The seagull looked at Tom and could see that it was a little hard for him to understand, but he knew it would not take long for Tom to catch on and soon he would be ready.

"I can talk to you when I'm at school or at home, or...?" Tom paused and then smiled. "I understand Mr Hawkins. You don't have to worry. I won't tell a living soul."

"Oh, I know that Tom; why do you think I chose you in the first place?"

They both looked at each other and then, after a short pause, they both laughed. Their laughter echoed all around the cave. They laughed and laughed and for the first time in so many, many years the seagull was happy and felt certain he had made the right choice in Tom. For so many years, the seagull had been alone and he hoped that, one day, he would find a companion that he could trust and who would join him with his search for the Sword of Isis.

After Tom had stopped laughing and after running all around the cave, jumping from rock to rock and ledge to ledge, skipping and throwing his arms out in total elation, he stopped and stood still in the centre of the cave, looking at this most amazing bird, who was mysterious and magical in every way. But best of all – he was his best friend.

"Mr Hawkins, I really want to know where you went to after your escape and how you came here to Rivermouth. What happened to your friends and...?"

"Yes, I know Tom, there is still much to tell you, but all in good time. My flight from the Land of Fire was a strange and frightening journey. Along the way, though, I made new friends and I also saw old ones. I can tell you that there really is magic and there will be strange and very wonderful things to see and there are some things we shall need to be fearful of. Soon you will discover all these things.

My dear friends, Joseph, Braheim, Trouseau and the others are still trapped in the Land of Fire. They were sent to the mines as slaves. I would dearly like to help them escape. They are not like me and will soon perish if I do not save them. The Saharadeen is very much still alive and will not rest until he has this stone. He has many evil powers of his own and we will need to be wary of him as we make our journey". He paused and looked into Tom's eyes.

"You will note that you have been in this place for just a blink in time – yet we have spent much time together. This is the power of the stone. One second of your time is equal to one day in the other world."

"The other world?" Tom looked confused again.

"Yes, as I told you earlier. This is a time – in another world that we will travel to – One that your world knows nothing about. It is in a different time, but within your time as you know it.

It will be hard for you to understand, but soon you will – when we start. So we will speak no more of this now. As you can see, there is plenty of time."

The seagull stretched out his neck and shook his head. "This is my destiny, Tom. I believe I will have this body for ever. I shall never get old and unless I am slain, I shall never die. However, there is something I must do and the time is now.

You are a good boy, Tom, and together we will do great things. Trust me and you will not regret it. Together we will have the greatest of all adventures."

The thought of adventures with Mr Hawkins was so exciting. Tom had a big lump in his throat when he thought of what it must be like, to be trapped in the body of a bird. It was surely so hard to bear. He was proud to have been chosen to be Mr Hawkins's friend.

"I do trust you, Mr Hawkins, and I shall help you in any way I can." Tom stood proudly and then smiled at the seagull.

The seagull blinked and suddenly Tom heard words in his head.

*You should take your leave now Tom. I have much to do and you have much to think on. Keep your head, my friend.*

Tom replied also without words. *Thank-you, Mr Hawkins, thank-you.*

*No, Tom, it is for me to thank you.*

# Chapter 6 – Bazellgoose and Rumpitter

"Tom, Tom. Time to wake up now." The voice in his head whirled round and round and Tom rolled into a tight ball beneath his bedclothes. "Tom!" the voice echoed and then he felt that he was being pushed, was it the cliff, was it...? "Ugh, no, don't, don't, Mr Hawk..."

"Tom !"

"Whaaaaat?" Suddenly Tom opened his eyes and then sat straight up on his bed. "What?" He called out again.

"Tom, it's only me, are you all right?" He saw his mother looking down at him. Her friendly face was smiling. "My, my you have had a nasty nightmare or something. Look at the state of you," she said brushing his hair down with her hand. "You look like you've been pulled through a hedge and then tossed back again," she laughed. "What were you dreaming about, something about a hawk, or some name – what was it?"

Tom rubbed his eyes and quickly regained some composure. "Oh, it was nothing Mum, just a dream or something. You made me jump."

"I'm sorry I startled you, Tom. Now come on, you have school to go to, so up you get, my darling. You've got clean clothes on the chair." She drew back the curtains. A bright light burst through the window like a golden ray. Tom quickly crawled over his bed to the window, but saw that it was just the morning sun shining through.

"It certainly is a lovely morning, looks like summer is finally on its way," his mother said as she stood beside him at the window. Then she turned to the bedroom door. "Right then, Tom, let's be having you!" Maggie threw a towel at Tom. "And get in the bathroom." Then she left the room.

Tom scratched his head and gazed around. He had been dreaming all right. It was the strangest dream and now he sat on the end of his bed thinking and remembering all the things Mr Hawkins had told him. He had nearly called his name out when his mum woke him. That was close.

*Yes Tom that was close. Good morning my friend, did you sleep well?* Mr Hawkins' voice was soft but startled Tom.

"Mr Hawkins!" he called out and ran to the window but was confused when no-one was there.

Then he remembered: speak without words.

Tom did not speak with his mouth but concentrated hard. *Good morning to you too, Mr Hawkins. I had a very strange dream and then my mother woke me. She heard me nearly say your name.*

*It matters not Tom. You said nothing to cause concern, but you will have to watch that.*

*Yes, I'm sorry.* Tom was annoyed with himself for his mistake. *It won't happen again, I promise.*

*As I said, my young friend, it does not matter. Now you have your school today and I have much to do. Study well, Tom, we shall speak later.* The voice had gone. Tom was so excited about his new friend and, as he washed and dressed, he thought constantly about everything he had learned and about all the things that were about to unfold.

Mr Ambrose was in full swing, giving a hearty rendition of the Romans and Julius Caesar's last moments as he fell at the hands of his assassins in the great Senate building in Rome. The whole class sat in silence as he delivered the famous words from Shakespeare: *Et tu, Brute?*

*Then fall Caesar!* replied Marcus Brutus, and then he raised his dagger. *Liberty! Freedom! Tyranny is dead!*

As Mr Ambrose continued, Tom sat silently staring out of the window. He thought of how Mr Hawkins wanted to slay the Saharadeen and free his own men. He wondered what sort of man the Saharadeen was. Why was he so bad? *One day I shall help him do it* he thought.

*That day will come soon, Tom, but are you not listening to your teacher? He really is very good* came the familiar voice.

Tom looked out of the classroom window and smiled. *Mr Hawkins where are you? Did you hear me thinking?*

*Of course I did. To be honest I was listening to your teacher. He is a fair actor, but he has not quite got the text right.*

*Why, how do you mean?*

*Well, it was Marcus Brutus who was the last to strike Caesar but it was a Senator by the name of Cinna who called out liberty and freedom and set about telling Rome that Caesar was dead.*

*Oh boy, poor Mr Ambrose, he hates it if he gets things wrong.* Tom looked across the classroom to watch his teacher delivering his final speech.

*Well in that case, Tom, perhaps we should just let him be."* Tom agreed and they chuckled.


Johnny Benson had been attentively watching the teacher but also took a moment to look over at Tom and saw him smiling at something. Benson immediately thought Tom was being smug or was finding something amusing and glared menacingly at Tom.

*Oh dear, Tom, your enemy has seen you. We really are going to have to do something about that boy.* Mr Hawkins had known somehow that Benson was watching Tom.

Tom quickly glanced over at Benson staring at him.

Benson mouthed something at Tom in an unfriendly way but Tom was not ruffled by him and pulled a face at him. Unfortunately Tom had not noticed Mr Ambrose watching them.

"Is there something you two boys would like to share with all of us?" he asked. Both Tom and Johnny Benson turned to look at the teacher. "Oh, er, no Sir," replied Benson.

"And what about you, Parker?" Mr Ambrose called over. He was standing by his desk with his hands on his hips. "Am I to assume that your knowledge of history is so great that you no longer require the services of a teacher?" All the class laughed at Mr Ambrose's little joke and Tom was embarrassed and also annoyed that he had been spotted.

"No, not at all Sir, I..."

"Good, then perhaps you might like to repeat what I have just been talking about," the teacher interrupted and walked to the middle of the classroom, now with his arms folded, and waited for Tom's reply. The whole class turned to watch and Johnny Benson sniggered smugly at him.

"Well Sir, I was just thinking about what you were saying about Caesar's death."

"Really and what was that?" enquired the teacher.

"Well Sir, you said that Marcus Brutus called out the news that Caesar was dead and shouted for liberty and freedom..."

"Indeed, that is so, and what of it, Tom?"

"Well, Sir... it was..." Tom was nervous about his reply. He knew Mr Ambrose was not going to like it. "Yes – well come on, out with it," Mr Ambrose persisted.

"Sir, it was not him who said that." Tom bit his bottom lip as he said it and waited for the response.

"What are you talking about Tom? I asked you to repeat what I had been saying."

"Yes Sir, I know and that is what I was thinking about when you asked me." Tom was beginning to hope that this confusion might soon come to an end.

"Tom I am very certain that you were not listening to my rendition of Shakespeare's *Julius Caesar* and I am also displeased that you seem to have completely ignored my question." *Ooops* Tom heard Mr Hawkins say. *This could be tricky, Tom.*

"No Sir I didn't. I was trying to say that Marcus Brutus did not say..." He was interrupted again by Mr Ambrose. "Right, that's enough, Tom, you will stay behind after school and write a four page essay on the final hours of Caesar's life." Benson was smiling widely at Tom and looked even more pleased that he had got Tom into trouble. "The same applies to you, Benson," Ambrose demanded. "Sir? Why me Sir? I..." Johnny Benson couldn't believe he had been pulled up too.

"You were also talking behind my back Benson and therefore you can write the same essay."

Benson tried to wriggle out of it and protested that he was not talking.

"Quiet, that's enough, you can both stay behind and that's final."

Tom looked at Benson and thought that at least there was some justice.

*Did you hear that, Mr Hawkins – I've been grounded?*
*Not to worry Tom, I have a plan.*

*A plan?*

*Yes, just wait and see.*

All the class sat attentively throughout the remainder of the lesson. No-one else wanted detention.

Finally the bell rang and all the class jumped up and began closing their books. "NOT SO FAST!" shouted Mr Ambrose. "Before you all go rushing off you will need to know what homework I have prepared for you. So you can all sit down and wait until I have finished."

There was a moan of protest from everyone and then, just as they were all about to sit down again, there was a terrifying scream from the far side of the classroom. Suddenly all the class started jumping up on their seats. There were more screams from some of the girls and then a yell from one boy. "Sir, Sir, it's a..."

"What are you all doing? Sit down everybody, at once," shouted Mr Ambrose.

Suddenly Johnny Benson leapt up onto his chair and then cried out "aaagh" and screamed, "Help, help!" There was so much commotion going on, Tom had no idea what was happening and could not see why they were all standing on their chairs, although the sight of Benson standing on his chair crying for help amused Tom immensely.

Mr Ambrose was turning bright red in the face as he screamed at them all to sit down.

"Get down Benson, immediately," he shouted again. Then there was more chaos. Some chairs fell over on their own and desks started moving across the floor. The whole class was in disarray and Benson was still pleading for help. Suddenly Tom jumped back in total shock, his eyes wide open and in total disbelief. Standing on his desk was a huge black crow, looking straight at him.

No-one else had noticed the bird as they were all running around screaming and standing on chairs. Some were tugging at the door to escape, but it would not open. Then Mr Ambrose let out a deathly cry. "A rat!" he yelled. "It's a rat. Who brought it in here?" he called and then he too jumped up on his chair. The rat, almost as big as a small dog, was charging around the floor, knocking over anything that got in its way. It had also jumped up at Benson and snarled at him, showing its large, yellow teeth. Benson was beside himself with terror. Tom thought it was all very funny and laughed when he saw the whole class in a complete mess.

As all this confusion was going on Tom was still confronted by the huge crow. Then suddenly the crow opened its mouth. "Hello, don't be alarmed. My name is Bazellgoose. I'm a friend."

Tom was completely stunned and looked quickly at the chaos going on in the classroom. The bird turned around too and looked at the desks and chairs being turned over and dragged across the floor. "The rat is Rumpitter, he's a friend too. He gets a little carried away sometimes. Takes his work far too seriously," said the crow. Tom was amazed and began to chuckle and then stopped. He stared in disbelief at the crow, who picked up Tom's pen in his beak and started writing something in his schoolbook. The crow was writing at an incredible speed.

"Wow! What are you doing?" Tom asked the bird.

The bird stopped writing and tipped his head to one side to look at his work. "There, that should do it."

"Do what?" Tom asked. "It's your homework, *The last days of Julius Caesar*. I have written it for you. Not bad eh?" replied the crow and tipped his head to admire his work.

"Not bad, it's brilliant!" Tom looked at the writing. "It's in my handwriting!"

"Oh yes, that's one of my specialities. Personalised writing – no extra charge. Well, nice to meet you Tom, but I better be going. Now where's that stupid rat?" The crow turned and lifted up into the air and let out a loud croak. "Haaaaark," it cried and suddenly the whole class screamed even louder when they saw the huge crow fly over their heads.

Tom saw the rat running across the floor. The whole class, including Mr Ambrose, were ducking down and then leaping out of the way as the crow and the rat completely wrecked the classroom. Mr Ambrose had passed out on his desk and some of the girls had tried to jump out of the window but that too was stuck. Benson was standing on his desk, trembling like a jelly.

Suddenly there was no sound or movement. The whole class stood still and stared at each other in total silence. They were still standing on chairs and desks. One boy had even climbed into the book cupboard. Paper drifted down from the air from books that had been thrown in terror at the rat. There was just one large black feather, which floated down onto Tom's desk.

"Have they gone?" asked one girl who was still shaking with fright.

"I think so," said someone.

"Oh no look at Mr Ambrose, he's dead!"

Little Daniel ran over to Mr Ambrose, who was slumped motionless over his desk.

"I think he's had a heart attack," said Daniel, softly. One of the girls broke into tears and ran to the door. To her surprise, it opened. She ran out and down the corridor shouting for help. She was followed by three others.

Tom quickly collected his books and ran over to see to Mr Ambrose. "He isn't dead, he's fainted," said Tom and he picked up Mr Ambrose's jug and poured water over the teacher's head. "Sir, wake up, Sir." He shook the teacher's arm as he tried to stir him.

Then, there was a grunt from Mr Ambrose and he moved. "Ugh, where am I? What happened?" he said as he tried to pick himself up. Tom and Daniel helped him to sit up. The others all watched on. Most of them were still in shock.

Then Tom looked at Benson and laughed. "Look at Benson. Not so tough now, eh Benson?" he called mockingly. All the class laughed. Benson was still standing on his chair. "Where's that... thing?" he asked, still trembling.

"Oh, my head. What are you all staring at?" Mr Ambrose spoke suddenly. He seemed a little strange and looked completely dazed.

Tom said, "Are you all right Sir? I think you had a bit of a fright." The others chuckled. They were all feeling braver now.

"Who... who are you?" Mr Ambrose asked. "Sir?" Tom was certain that the teacher must be very dazed. "It's Tom Parker, Sir."

"Who?"

"Tom, Sir."

The teacher was just staring blankly at the children. "What are you all looking at – who are you anyway?"

"I think Sir has amnesia, he doesn't even know who we are," said one of the boys.

At that moment the door opened and Mrs Buckles came running in.

"What's going on here. Will someone explain, please?" she asked sternly.

No-one really knew what to say. It was, after all, very odd.

"Mr Ambrose has bumped his head," said Tom.

"How... what happened," she asked and waved her hand in front of Mr Ambrose's eyes.

"Don't know. He must have slipped or something," said Tom and then looked around at the others for support. They all looked back and shrugged their shoulders. No-one could explain the very strange thing that had happened. After all, who would believe it? Where did those creatures come from anyway?

Mrs Buckles looked at the state of the classroom and then saw Johnny Benson still standing on his chair holding a heavy book. He was staring blankly, almost like he had been hypnotised.

"Benson!" Mrs Buckles called. "I might have known. This was all your doing wasn't it?" She stood looking at him with her arms folded. Mrs Buckles was the headmistress. She was a very large, round woman and was fearsome when she was angry.

"Sorry, Mrs Buckles, what do you mean?" Benson whispered back. "I didn't do anything, honest."

Mr Ambrose mumbled something. He had his head in his hands and was sitting on the edge of his desk. "No, no it was that rat. He did it," he said.

Mrs Buckles looked at him, shaking her head.

"Indeed, Mr Ambrose. Benson is a little rat sometimes and this will not go unpunished." She had convinced herself that all this was Benson's doing. Benson was well known for being a bully and a troublemaker. So with her mind made up she demanded that Benson report to her study immediately.

"I want this classroom cleaned up before any of you go home. Oh, and Mr Ambrose, will you come with me please, I would like a word with you?" She went towards the door. "Oh, and Tom Parker?" she said, turning her head back to the classroom. "Yes, Miss?" replied Tom wondering what she was going to say to him. "Well done for helping Mr Ambrose. I am sure he will thank you himself, when he has fully recovered." "That's OK Miss." he replied and then said, "Oh, Miss?" He had remembered his homework detention that Ambrose had given him, but then he thought again. This would only complicate things and he could use the completed essay to buy himself a favour another day.

"Yes Tom?" Mrs Buckles smiled back. "Nothing Miss, it's OK," said Tom.

"Very well," said Mrs Buckles and then led Mr Ambrose and Johnny Benson out of the room.

Outside, Bazellgoose was sitting on a branch of a tree stretching his large wings. The sun made them shine and he picked a few loose feathers from his chest with his strong beak. He was the largest, blackest crow and was also the oldest and wisest.

Rumpitter sat below in the fallen leaves under the tree. He rolled around in the leaves trying to get rid of an itch on his back, which had been annoying him. When that failed he rubbed his thick, brown fur coat against the trunk of the tree. It took quite some rubbing to get rid of the itch. Finally he was happy and sat down in the grass and looked up at the crow.

"Quite a fair day's work, don't you think, Bazellgoose?"

"Yes, quite." Bazellgoose swooped up into the air, turned and then settled back down onto a large branch, which had fallen on the ground.

The two companions looked down from the clump of trees at the top of the meadow, behind the school and chatted about their latest event.

"I must say, Rumpitter, you did get a little carried away. You weren't supposed to scare the living daylights out of them."

Rumpitter chuckled to himself and rolled over in the leaves again. His long, thick tail twisted around in the air. "Well, yes I suppose," he chuckled again and continued, "Did you see the old fella, he completely passed out?"

Bazellgoose shared his friend's amusement and also began to laugh. "I know. Poor chap. I hope he'll be all right." Then he stopped laughing and flew up into the tree again and looked down at the school. "He seems a nice enough boy, that Tom."

"Yes indeed," replied Rumpitter, "although I didn't get much chance to meet him properly. I was a little busy."

Bazellgoose looked down on the large rat, who was still lying on his back. "Mmmm, well I am sure you will get the chance sooner or later. Mr

Hawkins assures me of his integrity." The crow spoke with great respect when saying *Mr Hawkins.*

"Well if he says so, that's fine with me. Mr Hawkins is always right," agreed Rumpitter.

Bazellgoose stretched out his wings and then folded them back by his sides. "I did a jolly good job on his homework, you know."

"Good, good," replied Rumpitter, who had found a nice sunny spot and was lying on his back with his front paws over his head. "I think we sorted out that other boy. You know, the one Mr Hawkins said was Tom's enemy."

"Indeed we did," replied Bazellgoose, who then took a slow breath of the fresh afternoon air and continued, "Yes, a good day's work, indeed."

They sat quietly together enjoying the warm sun.

The Windwhistle inn had just seen the last of the lunchtime guests leave. The only people still in the dining room were Jack Parker and Jacob. The table was covered in sea charts, books and drawings. Jacob had hardly touched his food and his plate had been pushed aside and replaced by a glass of beer and the strange picture of the sailing ship that they had discovered aboard *The Eagle* the previous night.

"You haven't touched your food Jacob. Not to your liking?" Jack asked, just as he had cleaned his plate and complimented Maggie on finding such an excellent new chef.

"I have to say that was the best salmon I have had in a long time. Shame you haven't tried it," he continued and tried to persuade his friend to eat.

"I am not hungry, Jack. Not until I find out where this came from." He tapped the picture with his rough finger. "There's some very strange goings on, mark my word." He looked seriously at his friend and pondered over the charts again. He was completely absorbed by this mysterious picture and the ship they saw at sea in the storm.

As the two men chatted, a pair of deep and watchful eyes observed them. Mr Hawkins had found a position in a tree outside from where he could watch without being noticed.

He was, however, having great difficulty concentrating on listening to their conversation because his attention had been drawn to the uneaten plate of delicious salmon. He watched carefully and even though he would dearly love to get at the fish, he was listening to every word they said.

"Well then, there's only one thing for it," Jack said suddenly.

"What would that be?"

"We shall have to sail out to the position you found that ghost ship of yours and settle this once and for all." Jack slapped his hand down on the table as he said it and smiled at Jacob.

"Yes Jacob, my friend, I feel a little fishing trip coming on."

The pair of eyes watching from the tree widened and moved in on Jack.

"I reckon you are right, Jack. Mind you, the chance of seeing that ship again is pretty unlikely," he continued.

"Well we'll go and see shall we?" Jack said and then thought for a moment, rubbing his chin.

"Do you think you can round up your crew in the next couple of days? We could be a few days out and we'll need some good hands on board, with sharp eyes. You could start with Mat Flynn."

"Aye, you're right, I don't reckon it should be too hard, you leave them to me. Only one thing we haven't got though," replied Jacob as he thought about it all.

"Oh, what's that?"

"We lost our cook. He had trouble with seasickness on the last trip and then the crew got a little concerned," said Jacob with a wry look on his face.

Jack looked at his friend and thought for a moment. "Mmm, I understand. Leave that to me, I have an idea." Jack had a crafty look on his face and then, just as the two men were about to continue, Bernard, the new chef, walked into the restaurant. The men looked back at each other again and Jacob immediately understood his friend's thoughts. He smiled as Jack quickly winked at him.

Bernard was anxious to please Jack Parker. He was enjoying his work at the Windwhistle inn and hoped he was being appreciated. He walked across to the table.

"Excuse me gentlemen, have you enjoyed your luncheon?" He stood tall but in a humble manner with his hands folded at his waist and bowed to the two men. Then he began collecting up their plates.

Jack leaned back in his chair and folded his arms. Jacob lit his long pipe with the candle from the table. He knew his friend well and was about to enjoy watching him handle the chef.

"Bernard that was the best salmon I have had in ages and the sauce was delicious. Thank-you for asking". He looked quickly over at Jacob and continued, "My friend was not hungry, please take no offence by his poor appetite."

Bernard looked at Jacob for his opinion anyway. "Oh yes, that's right. I er... have seemed to have lost my appetite, but what I did eat was really good, er, yes, well done Bernard, very good indeed."

Jacob was a little awkward with his words. He was not accustomed to small talk and etiquette.

"Thank-you Monsieur, you are very kind." Bernard smiled with delight, nodded again to both the men and started to turn back to the kitchen. "Bernard, just a moment," Jack called suddenly and Bernard stopped and turned with an even more extended smile. "Oui Monsieur?"

"How long have you been with us now?" Jack asked.

"Oh, just three days Monsieur," Bernard replied with a nod.

"Excellent, excellent. I am pleased you have settled in well. You seem to have a way with the fish."

"Monsieur?"

"I mean your seafood is very good," Jack said with a more assertive tone.

"Oh thank-you again, Monsieur, I always like working with fish, there are so many ways to make a simple creature from the ocean become a star on the table, oui?" Bernard smiled widely.

"Indeed, that is quite so," Jack replied and then, just as Bernard was turning to walk back to the kitchen, he said, "Bernard, have you ever caught your own fish, I mean fresh out of the sea?"

Bernard stopped dead in his tracks. "Monsieur, I have not had this opportunity for many years. I am not a very good fisherman but I have much respect for those who are."

Jack replied with a broad smile, "Aah yes, it is not just the fishing I agree, but surely as a creator of fine cuisine such as this, isn't the art only complete by actually fishing the subject of your creation straight from the heart of the ocean?"

Bernard stood and pondered this thought for a moment and then replied, "You are very right Monsieur, I have not thought of this in such a way. I admire your understanding of the art."

Then Bernard continued, "I have always loved the sea, it has so many mysteries. What lies beneath is another world completely."

Jack was enjoying this conversation. "Come, Bernard bring another bottle of that wine we had earlier and join us."

"Oh thank-you but I have much to do in the kitchen before I finish for the afternoon."

"Nonsense Bernard, there's plenty of time for that and I have something that may be of interest to you," said Jack as he pulled out a chair from their table.

"Oh well, perhaps for a few minutes, I shall fetch the wine." Bernard was secretly delighted to be invited to join Jack Parker at the table. He had not been in town long enough to make many friends and Jack was, after all, the husband of his employer. It was indeed an honour, especially as he knew how highly the people of Rivermouth respected Jack Parker.

He hurried out with the plates and brought back the wine.

"Well done, Bernard. My wife tells me that you have selected the new wines here and I must say they complement the fish brilliantly."

Bernard sat down with the two men and poured the wine. "It is a simple thing Monsieur but wine plays an important role with the meal. If you do not have this appreciation, you cannot enjoy the food at its best, non?"

"Oh absolutely," said Jacob, who was trying not to show his amusement and sucked at his pipe to hide his smile.

"Bernard, I have something to ask you."

Suddenly Bernard looked seriously at Jack. "Oh oui Monsieur, is there a problem?"

"Good heavens no, what I was going to ask is that I know you have not been here very long, but you have already made such a great impression here and our customers are telling everyone about how good the food is. I, er, simply wanted to show my appreciation in my own way."

Bernard was delighted and showed his thanks by vigorously shaking Jack's hand and nodding with delight. "Oh thank-you so much, Monsieur, thank-you. You know, I am very happy here in Rivermouth, your dear wife and all the people I have met so far have been so kind."

"Well that's great Bernard, but I have not told you what I had in mind."

"Oh, yes Monsieur, I am sorry, what did you want to ask?"

Jack put his hand on Bernard's shoulder and looked at him kindly and nodded. "Bernard, I am going to ask Maggie if she wouldn't mind you spending a couple of days with my good friend here and me for a spot of fishing. It would be good for us to get better acquainted and you can try your hand at catching something really special. What do you say?"

Bernard wasn't quite sure what to say. Part of him was uneasy, as he was not a very good sailor but didn't have the heart to admit this to Jack. The other part of him was pleased to have been asked.

Finally he replied. "It would be a pleasure, I am not an experienced sailor but I am certain I am in good hands, oui?" he said, nodding and smiling. Jack and Jacob both laughed with him and Jacob leaned across the table to shake Bernard's hand. Just then Bernard seemed to have thought of something and said, "Er, gentlemen, do you have a... how do you say – ah oui, a ship's cook?"

Jack looked instantly at Jacob with wide eyes, as if to say, *we did it!* He quickly turned back to Bernard and said, "Oh, you may have a good point Bernard, er, would you...?"

"It would be a pleasure and an excellent experience," Bernard said with a huge smile.

The three men laughed and celebrated their decision with more wine and continued chatting. Jacob looked at Jack and smiled to himself about how smoothly Jack had manipulated the situation and had convinced the chef that he should join them. He looked at Bernard and thought that he did actually like the man and therefore all was well.

The seagull had disappeared from the tree.

Bernard was scratching his head as he stood in the kitchen looking at the plate on the table. He was certain that there had been a large piece of salmon on it. Jacob had hardly touched the fish but now it was not there, only some potatoes, a few French beans and the delicious sauce. He had enjoyed taking wine with his new friends in the restaurant but was sure he had not had so much wine that he would lose his memory. *That is strange* he said to himself, *I know it was here.* He looked in the bin to see if he had thrown it away. It was not there. He had not noticed anyone go through the doors and the back kitchen door was locked so no-one could have got into the kitchen from outside, unless... "The window!" he whispered to himself and walked towards the open window. There was nobody there. Then he saw something. "What is this?" he whispered to himself again. He looked into the sink and saw a very large white feather.

It was the feather of a large seagull. "Scavengers!" he said and looked out and into the sky. The sun was so bright in his eyes that he could not see clearly. "Those seagulls, I might have guessed, but how would one get in here?" He scratched his head again and made a note. In future he would keep the window shut.

Mr Hawkins was beside himself with joy. He was in heaven. He had not eaten food like this for many, many years. He sat up in the tall tree and enjoyed the salmon. Although he did regret that he had actually stolen the fish, he also realised that it was only going to be thrown away by the chef. What a waste that would be. He smiled inwardly, content with this thought and recalled the days when he was a man and when he had eaten delicious food served on silver plates and when servants had poured fine wine into golden goblets. He remembered the days when he and his men would catch fish when they were at sea and the ship's cook would serve a hearty meal for them all. Then afterwards they would sing songs and laugh and tell jokes and stories. They were wonderful days and although it was so long ago, he knew he would never ever forget them.

Then he pondered on the latest meeting with Jack and Jacob. He thought of Tom and wondered how he could arrange it for Jack to allow Tom to go on *The Eagle* with them. The adventure was about to begin but still there was much to do. He slapped his beak across a leaf after finishing the last piece of salmon and blinked his large eyes. *Delicious* he said to himself.

*Tom, Tom, where are you?* Tom was walking back home from a very strange day at school. He had been thinking about the rat and the crow.

He heard the voice in his head. Then without speaking he replied, *I'm on the old North Road, walking home, Mr Hawkins. I've got to tell you what a day I have had. I met your friends Bazellgoose and Rumpitter. It was amazing. The crow wrote all my homework and...*

*Yes, yes, I know Tom. I arranged it all. But never mind that for now. I need to talk with you in person. Let's meet on the roof at the Windwhistle inn.* Mr Hawkins spoke with urgency in his voice.

*Right, I'll be there as soon as I can* replied Tom and he gave out a little joyful yell of excitement and started to run along the lane as fast as he could.

It was not long before Tom arrived home. He dumped his school bag in his room and ran straight up to the roof.

There had been so many times when he had stood alone in this quiet place, with the fragrance of the potted herbs around the balcony, looking over the beautiful harbour of Rivermouth. His mother had a great deal of style in everything she did. The roof garden was one of her best works of art and the beautiful array of potted plants and herbs placed around the balcony was truly the work of an artist. There was a round mosaic table with white iron chairs placed neatly around it. Lanterns hung from the whitewashed walls and, when lit, they cast a soft glow around the garden. There was a rustic tiled floor, which gave the roof garden a Continental feel. Quite often Maggie and Jack Parker would entertain their friends here and Maggie would serve dinner in the warm summer evenings.

Tom loved this place, it was peaceful and he always felt happy here. It was easy to drift away and dream of adventures and all kinds of wonderful things. Never, though, did he really expect any of his day dreams to actually come true. Now here he was waiting for his new friend – a seagull who could talk, who was hundreds of years old, who had seen so much and had so many tales to tell. And now, more than all this, there was a real adventure brewing but he was not quite certain what it would be. Life for Tom was about to take a very different course.

Suddenly a shadow appeared across the sky, then it disappeared and Tom arched his back and looked over his shoulder to see where Mr Hawkins was. There was nothing and then, without noticing, because his back was turned away from the light, the bird landed directly behind him. Tom turned around quickly. The shock of seeing the seagull appear so fast made him trip over and he fell onto the floor between two large pots.

"Oh, wow!" he exclaimed. "You made me jump. Where did you come from?" Tom asked, as he picked himself up and walked towards Mr

Hawkins, who was now settled upon the edge of the stone wall. Tom had a wide smile and his eyes were bright with expectation.

"Aha, the element of surprise, Tom. Did I scare you?" Mr Hawkins replied with a slight chuckle.

"Oh, no, not really, I just didn't see you," Tom said, rather embarrassed.

"Never mind my young friend, I shall have to teach you about that someday."

"I wish I could fly, it must be fantastic," Tom continued.

"Well, it does have some advantages, I must admit," replied the bird. He looked carefully at his young friend. "There will come a time soon when matters like flying will become less of a miracle, but more of a necessity," Mr Hawkins said as he gave his neck a little stretch and a twist.

"What do you mean?" asked Tom, slightly confused again.

Mr Hawkins looked at Tom with that affectionate sparkle in one eye. Tom knew this was his way of smiling and he smiled back.

"I must say, Mr Hawkins, there are times when I just think I'm dreaming all this. I mean, what about your friends Bazellgoose and Rumpitter, where did they come from? You didn't tell me about them."

Mr Hawkins gave a little squawk, which was, in his way, a laugh. "Come now, Tom, if I told you everything all at once we would get little done and your head would explode with too much information. A little at a time Tom, that's the answer and then eventually you will pick up all the pieces and begin to understand. You are still young and there is much for you to learn. It would be impossible for you to learn it all now." He paused and then continued. "Bazellgoose and Rumpitter are very loyal friends. I asked them to assist you at school today because you need to be rid of anything that might steer you off our course."

Tom looked confused again.

"That boy, Benson. He will not bother you for a while and you have your homework completed for you. But don't you fear, Tom, you have also learned and digested everything that Bazellgoose wrote in that essay."

"What do you mean, learned?"

"I mean that it would not do to simply cheat and do your homework for you. So you have already absorbed the facts and learned about Julius Caesar and the great changes to the Roman Empire."

"I have?" Tom gulped. "You mean I know all about it?" He began to think about this.

"Indeed you have. But come, we must not dwell on this now. I have much to tell you and we have things to do."

Then Mr Hawkins hopped onto the table. "Hmmm, this is a nice table, it reminds me of something," said Mr Hawkins as he looked across the pieces of mosaic, which had been artistically set into the circular top.

"What does it remind you of, Mr Hawkins?" Tom asked as he sat on a chair opposite the seagull.

"The Aegean Isles. The Greek isles to be precise." The bird tilted his head from side to side as he looked at the table and his eye gave a blink. Tom noticed the look and asked, "What bothers you about the table?"

Mr Hawkins looked up at Tom quickly and Tom saw the slight glaze in the eye. Just for a second, he thought he saw a tear. The seagull opened his beak and paused for a moment before speaking. "I do believe Tom, in this very short time we have known each other you are beginning to know me well." His voice was quiet and soft as he continued. "The table reminds me of a time, long ago; in a place where peace reigned and the land was kissed fairly by the sun. I lived for many years in Greece. It was a beautiful place and my home was blessed by the touch of the most beautiful woman I have ever known. Princess Tasia would visit me sometimes for several days when her father was in the region. One day she brought me a beautiful mosaic table, which sat on the terrace overlooking the sea. This was my home and, just for a moment, this table reminded me of it."

"It must be hard for you to remember your life all those years ago," Tom said sympathetically and then tried to cheer things up. "Who knows, maybe you will have a place like that again?"

The seagull again looked at Tom and suddenly his eyes lit up. "Yes, yes exactly my point Tom. This is why I need to talk to you. Somehow we got distracted. Now where was I? Ah yes."

Mr Hawkins straightened himself up before continuing and then his mood changed a little. This time he was very direct and began to sound like a captain talking to his crew.

"Tom, we are about to embark on our first journey, there is much to do and we require the assistance of your father and his friend Jacob." Mr Hawkins paced up and down the wall as he spoke to Tom.

"Father and Jacob Morgan? Why do you need their help?" Tom asked.

"We need *The Eagle* and Jacob and your father to sail her. That is why. We are going to sea.

"Great, but why them, I don't understand?" Tom scratched his head as he asked the question.

"They have discovered something that they have no understanding of and yet, have taken it upon themselves to look into it. However, they do not realise the danger they may be in."

"Danger!" Tom exclaimed. "What danger?"

Mr Hawkins could see the concern in Tom's face. "They have discovered something by accident. What they have discovered is quite remarkable but they have no idea what they are letting themselves in for."

"Then I should tell them," said Tom in a determined voice.

"And what will you tell them Tom?" asked the seagull.

"I... er... that is... we should tell..." Tom realised that he did not know what he was talking about.

"What is it that they have found, Mr Hawkins?" he asked after some thought.

"I wondered when you would ask," said Mr Hawkins and then he lowered his voice and stepped closer to Tom.

"Tom, listen to me carefully. We are about to take our first journey together. However there will be some danger. I can protect you and me, but I can make no assurances for anyone else. You see, a couple of nights ago, when Jacob Morgan and his crew were out at sea, they saw something very strange. When Jacob sailed into Rivermouth the other evening, he told your father what they had seen. I heard them talking and realised then that this was important. Then, that night, when the storm blew up I followed them out to *The Eagle* to try to discover more about this. It was your father, who I must say is a very astute man, who discovered the true identity of what Jacob and his crew had actually discovered."

"What was it?" asked Tom anxiously.

"Jacob had reported the sighting of a strange sailing ship while they fought against the gales that had suddenly blown up from nowhere." Mr Hawkins paused for a moment. "This ship, Tom, was no ordinary ship, she comes from no ordinary place and she brings with her much danger.

If your father ventures back to look for this ship and they actually find it, I will fear for their lives." Tom was again very confused. "What do you mean?"

"What your Father and Jacob have accidentally discovered is the real identity of the strange sailing ship. But to be honest I did help them a little. Your father was struggling with a drawing of the ship from a picture he had found. I knew exactly what it was and where it came from. I needed to buy some time and then, as the storm was blowing hard outside, I created a reason for your father to go up on deck. When he returned, he found that the picture he had been drawing had changed. This I had done because I needed to be sure that the ship Jacob had seen was mine.

"Yours?"

"Yes, but never mind that for now. Tom, we are going back to the Land of Fire!"

"What?" Tom leapt up off out of the chair and ran to the edge of the roof garden and looked out to the estuary of Rivermouth. Then he turned to Mr Hawkins. "The Land of Fire? How do you know, why...?"

Mr Hawkins hopped up onto the wall next to Tom.

"There are still many things to tell you and I know you are uneasy about this, but believe me, Tom. Trust me. You will not be sorry. We are going to take our first adventure. We only need *The Eagle* to get us to the actual mark on the chart where our journey will begin. There should be no reason for the others to get involved, if we are careful. They will come to no harm if we do this right. Anyway, I have a plan that will keep them away from trouble. Tom, I have been waiting for this for a long time. The time is now and I am going to share with you some of the most unbelievable secrets. These are the Golden Secrets that no living human has seen or even heard – except you, Tom."

Mr Hawkins leaned over to Tom, who was staring out to sea.

The seagull's eye was as deep as night and the golden crescent moon appeared again in the black centre of the eye. It blinked and Tom turned back to speak.

"Please don't let any harm come to my father," he whispered.

Mr Hawkins smiled at Tom, tipped his head and said, "I promise, Tom. All we need them to do is to sail out to where they sighted the ship. Then you and I can begin our journey"

The following morning Jack Parker had been speaking to the captain of a visiting French boat and then after welcoming him to Rivermouth he rowed back across the harbour to meet Jacob and his crew aboard *The Eagle.*

It was a sunny day and the gulls were swarming around the fishing boats as they returned home with their catch. He loved the early mornings and smiled as he looked up towards the lush, green hills, which surrounded the town. The houses, all built closely together and painted in different colours, looked a pretty picture and he could smell the pine from the tall cedar trees which grew high up on top of the hills in large clumps. The wind was gently blowing from the North and brought with it the scent of the flowers growing amongst the gardens of the houses in Rivermouth and from the little park in the centre of the town, which was the pride of the townsfolk. It was a lovely day.

"Morning, Flynn, take my line would you?" Jack called as he approached *The Eagle.*

Mat Flynn was standing waiting for him to arrive. Old Flynn, as the locals called him, was a tall, quiet man of few words. His face was wrinkled by the sea and his deep brown eyes told the tale of both hardship and wisdom. He was loyal to Jacob and was a hardy sailor. In his time he had sailed to many places and seen many things. He would often be found telling his tales in the inns of Rivermouth. Sometimes though, his tales would wander and a story may not always be the same if repeated. No-one ever really knew if they were true – except of course, Old Flynn.

"Morning, Jack, a fair one she is too," Flynn replied as he caught Jack's line and secured the small rowing boat to the high deck.

"The boss is down below, checking the charts. We don't have a full crew yet and the boss hasn't told us where we're headed." He helped Jack on board and together they went down the companionway into the saloon.

"Ah Jack, good morning," said Jacob with a smile. He was always in a good mood when a new trip was being planned. This time though, it was to be unusual. They were off to find something that might not even exist.

"So, Jacob, do you reckon this ship is still going to be there?"

Jacob looked at Jack and nodded to Flynn.

Flynn had not been fully briefed on what was happening.

"What's this about, a ship, what ship?" Flynn asked as he leaned his hefty head across the chart table. Then he stopped. "Oh, wait up, I reckon I know. You mean that strange vessel we sighted the other night, don't you?"

"That's the one Flynn. Jack and me have been looking into it and there is something very unusual about it. She may be just a ghost or something we imagined, but it's all about the drawing we found on board the other night," Jacob replied.

Flynn shook his head and his straggled black hair hung over his eyes. "Don't talk to me about ghosts. I saw her out there, that's for certain." Flynn paused and rubbed his thick bearded chin. "Whether she'll still be there now, who knows?"

"Exactly, which is why we must go and see. It's a good day's sail to the point where you sighted her." Jack tapped the area on the chart, with a finger as he spoke. "It could all be a complete waste of time, but unless we go and see, we'll never know. If there is nothing, we still have the fishing. It's a good area and we even have a chef aboard." They all laughed. And Jacob said, "And let's not forget the gold dust."

"Gold dust, what gold?" Flynn's eyes lit up.

Jacob pulled out of a drawer the picture of the ship. "This," he said and put it in front of Flynn. The three men studied the picture of the sailing ship and wondered what it really was.

The picture was covered in a thin layer of gold dust. It was the most incredible thing that Flynn had seen. The picture was drawn in perfect detail. There was, however, something very odd about it.

"This is truly unusual boss, it looks like she was built out of gold." He rubbed his finger along the sides of the drawing and observed the dust at the end of his finger.

"You see Flynn, this is why we must investigate. It could be something or nothing," Jack said. He stood firmly with his arms folded and continued. "We can't let this get out. Not a word to the rest of the crew or anyone else, is that clear?" He looked at Flynn.

"Oh aye, very clear. Wouldn't want to let this cat out of the cradle, no Sir," Flynn said and they all laughed. The eye was again at the porthole.

\*\*\*

All morning the whole school could talk of nothing else but the strange attack on Mr Ambrose by a huge crow and a giant rat. The story had become more exaggerated as the day went on.

However, Mr Ambrose had made a miraculous recovery from his severe state of shock.

Mrs Buckles had given him the rest of the week off but as next week was the start of the school holidays that seemed pointless to him so he returned as usual the next morning.

Tom had returned his homework early to an astonished Mrs Buckles who had told Mr Ambrose to personally congratulate Tom on a brilliant piece of work. All the teachers had seen the homework and were astonished that one of their students had actually studied and learned the facts about Julius Caesar with absolute perfection.

"Tom, this is really a very good piece of work, well done lad, we are all delighted. You have captured all the facts and delivered some excellent work. I hope you'll keep this up next term."

"Oh yes Sir, I'll do my best," replied Tom who was surrounded by the school's teachers. They were all standing in the Head's study, and Tom just happened to look over at the window.

Sitting on the windowsill outside was a large rat and an even larger crow. The pair were sitting very still, watching. Tom suddenly heard a voice in his head. *Well, Tom, looks like all's well then.*

Tom replied without speaking. *Who's that?*

*It's me, Bazellgoose, of course.*

*Sorry, I didn't recognise your voice. Thanks for your help yesterday.*

*Absolutely no problem at all. You won't have any trouble for a while from the others either.*

Rumpitter added, *All in a day's work, Tom.* Tom didn't recognise Rumpitter's voice either. It was thin, in a slightly higher pitch. More befitting to a rat, he thought. He smiled quickly at them and said *Thanks for everything, I hope we can meet sometime soon.*

*We will, we will,* replied the rat and the two disappeared.

School went quickly and soon Tom was back at home. He had been asked to help Bernard in the kitchen as his mother was preparing the tables in the restaurant.

Bernard was singing quietly to himself in some indistinguishable tone as he carefully prepared a large lobster.

Tom was washing the dishes and generally getting in the way. But Bernard was an unusually patient man for a chef and did not really mind. After all, Tom was just a boy.

"So, Tom, what are you going to do with your holidays?" Bernard asked him.

"I'm not sure yet."

"Did you know that your father has asked me to join him and his friends on a fishing trip?"

"No, when is that going to be?" Tom asked.

"I think they are planning to go quite soon. He has to ask your mother. Do you think she will object?"

Tom paused, thinking that this must be the same trip that Mr Hawkins was planning. "Well, I suppose she won't mind. I don't know."

"Oh, of course, she is a fine woman and most gracious. It is only because I have not been here long and I wondered..."

"I think it's an excellent idea, Bernard," Came the voice of Maggie Parker, who had been listening at the door.

Bernard and Tom swung round together in surprise. They had no idea that she had been listening to them.

"Madame, are you sure?" asked Bernard, who was slightly embarrassed by the intrusion.

"Oh, yes of course. Goodness me it's only for a couple of days and if we prepare ahead, I can take care of everything here. Jack has already discussed it with me and I shall look forward to you bringing some nice fresh fish home. I would be grateful if you could manage that," she said with a wide smile and then looked at Tom. "Oh, and Tom, I suggested to your father that you should go with them too. It would be good for you and as you have worked hard at school this term, I think you deserve it. Mr Ambrose told me about your wonderful essay. Apparently the whole school is talking about it. I'm very proud of you, darling."

Tom's eyes lit up and he turned and smiled at Bernard who was also delighted. "Thanks Mum, that's brilliant! Where's Dad?"

"He's gone over to meet up with Jacob. I don't know, those two are thick as thieves when they get together." She was joking as she said this and had one of her radiant smiles when she spoke.

Maggie was well aware of the long lasting friendship between the two men. "I expect he'll be back soon because he said he'd stock up the cellar and do a few jobs before you sail." She paused and then said, "Oh, and Tom, your father is really pleased that you are going with him."

Maggie looked at Bernard seriously for a moment and said, "Bernard, can I ask you to look after my two men, they are very special to me?" As she said this, she put an arm around Tom and hugged him. Tom tried to shrug off the embarrassment by wriggling away and pretended to do something with some plates, which were piled on the kitchen table.

Bernard smiled affectionately and was quick to reply. "Madame, you have a very special family, I can see that. It would be my honour and I am grateful to be asked. You can rely on me to assist." He gave one of his rosy cheek smiles and placed his hand on Tom's head. "And Tom, you'll have to teach me all about sailing, oui?" Tom smiled. "Oui, Monsieur, ces't mon pleasure," he said, in an attempt to speak French. They all laughed together.

As the evening closed in over the estuary of Rivermouth a thick mist, like a grey velvet cloak covered the cliffs, and silence fell. High up in a cave in the rocks, an important meeting was being held. The three companions sat in a circle around the stone.

"It's not going to be so easy this time, you know," said Rumpitter, who was cleaning one of his ears with a paw.

"We must stay on course and everything will be just fine," replied Mr Hawkins and then said to the crow: "Bazellgoose, you did a fine job with Tom. In fact you both did. Well done. Thank-you both." "Tom is a fine boy – it's a shame other humans can't be like him. I know that we shall all be great friends. I cannot afford for any harm to come to him or his family. I am depending on you both for your support." He looked seriously at the crow and the rat who were sitting obediently listening, for they had great respect for Mr Hawkins.

Bazellgoose replied, "Well, you know you can rely on us. It is a long time since you ventured back there and we wish you well on your journey."

"Oh, yes," said Rumpitter, quickly. "You can count on us."

"And we both wish you God's speed and a safe return," said Bazellgoose, who flapped his wings and hopped up and down on his rock. "Yes, a safe return," agreed Rumpitter.

"Well thank-you. By the way, Rumpitter, you are coming too."

"I am?"

At ten-thirty the next morning, Mat Flynn finally arrived back on board *The Eagle* with two new crewmen. Tom was really excited and ran up and down the deck trying to lend a hand with anything that needed doing. He took great delight in showing Bernard around the ship. He also helped Flynn tie the tender to the davits at the stern of *The Eagle* and then rolled out the sail bags.

Bernard was enjoying watching the crew go about their work, preparing the ship for their voyage.

"Well Tom, I can see you have learned well from your father about boats and I think I can say that I am now able to tie the bowline and the round turn and hitches thanks to you, oui?" Tom laughed and replied, "Yes that's it Bernard, I think you've got it." He watched Bernard finally tie the knot properly around a cleat. "Well done Bernard!"

Bernard congratulated himself on completing the task and then said, "So, Tom, now we must see to the kitchen. Where is it?"

Tom shook his head. "No, no Bernard, it's not the kitchen, it's the galley. We call the kitchen a galley, on a boat."

Bernard remembered and said, "Oh yes, of course, so, where is the galley?"

"Follow me," said Tom rushing off along the deck.

Bernard followed as he saw Tom jump down some steps and disappear below.

The day had turned into a beautiful one. The sun was shining. Down below decks, it was very warm indeed and Tom opened some portholes and hatches to let the breeze through into the cabins and saloon area. Bernard explored the galley and was impressed to see that, despite its small size, it was very compact and well equipped. He looked through the cupboards and checked the crockery and cutlery. Everything looked fine. He was just starting to unload a bag of supplies that he had asked to be taken on board, when a voice came from above.

"Morning, Bernard, I hope all's well with you down there?" Bernard jumped, dropping a large saucepan on his foot. He looked surprised when he saw Jacob's hairy face looking down at him through a porthole. "You startled me, Captain," replied Bernard a little embarrassed.

Jacob laughed at the Frenchman, who amused him. "I hope you have everything you need?"

"Oh yes, I think we shall be just fine down here; I have an expert assistant to show me the ropes." Bernard was referring to Tom, who was still keeping himself busy by sorting out which bag was whose and in which cabin it belonged. Then he came over and saw Jacob's face at the porthole. "I've put Bernard's and my gear in the starboard cabins – is that all right, Jacob?" Tom asked. "Aye, lad, that'll do fine. Well, must get on. We're sailing in one hour. Let me know if you need anything Bernard." "I certainly will do that," replied Bernard who was enjoying the thought of being the ship's cook. Jacob looked at Tom and smiled. "All right Tom?" he asked with a wide smile. He was pleased to have the boy with them and was very fond of him. He could often see his own son in Tom and said that if he had still been alive, he and Tom would have been great friends. "Just like me an' your dad," he would say. He smiled again through his wiry beard and said to Tom, "Good to have you with us Tom; we'll be in for a fine sail this morning. You can take the wheel when we go past the rock if you like." Tom was delighted with the invitation and took it as a great honour. He also knew the other reason; the rock he referred to was well known by everybody as "Jacob's rock". It was situated just off the eastern approach to the estuary of Rivermouth. This was the place where Jacob had lost his son in a storm several years before. It had become a tradition for Jacob that every time he sailed past the rock he would stand alone at the bow of *The Eagle* and raise his hat in memory of his son. This was one of the few times when he showed any emotion. "Thank-you Jacob, I'd like that very much," said Tom.

"Good, good, that's agreed then. See you later," said Jacob. His face disappeared from the porthole and for a moment Tom and Bernard stood quietly. "He has great respect for you, Tom and it's good to see," smiled Bernard and patted Tom on the head.

The previous evening, Jacob and Flynn had brought *The Eagle* alongside the town quay to load supplies and make the ship ready for their journey. Some of the crew laid out the sails on deck, while others were up in the masts arranging the rigging and generally preparing the old ship to set sail. Mat Flynn was standing on the quayside talking to one of the townsfolk.

"Where are you off to this time, Flynn?" asked the man. "Oh just a spot of fishing. Jacob and Jack have found a good spot and reckon to be bringing a good catch home." Flynn was careful not to disclose their true reason for the trip. He was just thinking about the journey ahead and whether it was going to come to anything, when suddenly he felt a tap on his shoulder. "Good morning Mat," said Maggie Parker. Flynn turned quickly. "Oh hello, Maam, and don't you look a sight for sore eyes on this sunny morning," replied Flynn, with a wide and toothless grin. Flynn had few teeth left in his mouth, save a couple of gold ones, which, he often joked, were for a rainy day.

"An' what do we owe the pleasure of your lovely presence, Maggie?" He had a sparkle in his eye, when he asked. He, like many others in Rivermouth, had the utmost respect for her. After all, she was a handsome woman as well as bright and charming. There were many men in Rivermouth who envied Jack Parker for having such a lovely wife but, equally, had great respect for them as a couple.

"I've just popped down with some goodies for your trip," she said holding up a bag and swinging it. Flynn smiled again. "We always look forward to your goodie bag, Maggie – what 'ave you in there this time?" he asked trying to look into the bag. Maggie laughed and pulled the bag away from him. "You'll just have to wait and see, won't you?" she teased. She liked it that the men enjoyed her bag of surprises, which were usually home-made cakes and biscuits; sometimes she would put in some of her own fudge. "I put in a few extras this time," she smiled. "Ah, would that be because of a certain young gentleman being on board?" laughed Flynn, who was referring to Tom.

"It certainly might be that. Shall we...?" Flynn laughed again and took Maggie's arm to escort her down the gangway and onto *The Eagle*.

Just as they were about to step on board an enormous rat ran right under their feet, over the gangway and onto the boat. Its legs were running as fast as they could. Maggie let out a shriek as it pushed past at such speed, almost tripping her up. The rat was being chased by a large black cat. The two animals paid no attention to the humans as they dashed past them and Flynn shouted at the cat.

"Go get 'im Bibs," he yelled. But Bibs, in hot pursuit of the rat, had no time to listen. "My goodness," exclaimed Maggie, "what was that horrible thing?"

Flynn composed himself and scratched his head. "That is the biggest rat I've ever seen, I 'ope that cat gets 'im before we sail. Will you excuse me, Maam, I think I'd better find that cat an' see if we can't catch us a rat?"

"Oh, yes, quite. It wouldn't do to have that thing on board, it's huge," she said, shaking down her dress and picking up the bag. Flynn ran off after the cat and Maggie made her own way on board and looked around for Tom and Jack and then smiled when she saw them standing together in the cockpit by the ship's wheel, chatting to each other.

"Jack," she called and Jack and Tom turned to see her walking towards them.

"Hello my love, are you all right? You look like you've just seen a ghost."

Tom smiled when he saw his parents kiss and embrace. He walked over and joined them. "Hello Tom, are you enjoying yourself?" asked Maggie with a smile. Tom replied, "Oh yes, I can't wait to get going."

Jack laughed, "So what was all that commotion about just then? Are you OK?" he asked Maggie. "I'm all right, but you have a very unwanted passenger on board."

"What do you mean?" Jack asked.

"A rat. You have a huge rat on board. It ran right under my legs and down below. Flynn and the cat are looking for it."

Tom was curious. "What rat, Mum, what do you mean by – huge?"

"It's huge. I've never seen anything like it. It was almost the size of a small dog!"

Tom suddenly became concerned. Could it be Rumpitter? If so, he'd have a hell of a fight on his hands. Bibs was a very large cat who lived on *The Eagle*. She was also well known as being the meanest cat, an expert mouser and rat catcher.

Tom needed to find out and quickly started to run off. "Wait Tom, I've got some goodies for you," called Maggie.

"Thanks Mum, you're the best. I'm going to help Flynn. See you when we get back, bye," Tom called, as he chased off, very worried that Bibs would get to Rumpitter before him.

"Oh," said Maggie, "I just wanted to give him a hug. Do take care of him, darling." Jack looked at his wife and smiled, "He's just a boy, Maggie, he'll be full of his tales of adventures when we get home, you'll see. I won't let him out of my sight. You know he loves you very much and, by the way, so do I." Jack kissed her full on the lips. They stood there for a short while talking.

"Are you going to be all right at the inn?" Jack asked, returning to other matters.

"Yes, yes, I've got Jessie and Rosemary coming to help out." She paused and smiled, "You might want to tell your son that he has an admirer."

"Hmm, who's that then?"

"Jessie. She is always asking about Tom and was quite disappointed when she found out that he was not going to be there this week."

Jack laughed, "Oh, is that a fact? Maybe I'll tell him at an appropriate time then." They both laughed again. Jessie was a lovely, bright young girl from Tom's school. Many of the boys admired her, but it appeared that she only had eyes for Tom, but Tom, being a typical boy, was completely oblivious to the fact.

They were just about to say goodbye, when the cat, followed in hot pursuit by a bumbling Mat Flynn, pushed past them. "'Scuse us, we'll get that rat, before we sail, never fear," shouted Flynn as he puffed his way after the cat.

By now the other crewmen had become aware of the rat-chase and assembled around the bridge deck, where Maggie and Jack stood. They all laughed at Flynn as he chased after the cat. There was no sign of the rat anywhere.

Bernard appeared on deck. "I appear to have missed a joke, oui?" he said.

"We have a stowaway rat on board," laughed one of the crew.

"A rat! Mon dieu, this is terrible, what shall we do?" asked Bernard who was concerned about his galley and the provisions. Rats are well known for eating their way through an entire ship's rations unless they are caught.

"Don't you worry, I am sure Flynn and that cat of his will soon find it," laughed Jack. He turned back to Maggie and they exchanged a few quiet words before she passed Bernard the bag of goodies and said, "Well then Bernard, remember what I asked you, and take this bag for me. It's my little treat to you all." She paused and tried to look for Tom but he was nowhere to be seen. "Well, have a great trip and I'll see you all when you get back." She waved to all the ship's crew and they all called back together, "Goodbye Maam." Jack escorted her ashore and gave her one final kiss before she departed up the quay and away into the town.

Jack came swiftly back on board. He was ready and happy that all was well. "Right then Jacob, my good friend – when do we go?"

"About fifteen minutes. Flynn is still trying to catch that damned rat," said Jacob.

"I expect the rat has done a bunk, if it knows we have Flynn's cat on board." Jack looked around the deck. "Where's Tom?" he asked. "I saw him down below somewhere," replied Henry Higgins, the young deck hand.

"Well, can someone ask him to come up on deck, please?" said Jack.

Bernard took the bag of goodies and began whistling a little tune to himself. He disappeared down the steps into the galley.

Tom was scurrying around below decks, looking for the cat or Rumpitter, but had little success in finding either of them.

Bernard found him crawling under some boxes in the stores. "What are you looking for Tom?" he asked, puzzled.

Tom quickly jumped up. "Oh nothing. I was just looking for something," he said awkwardly.

"Your father is asking for you. I think he needs you on deck," said Bernard. He felt that there was something odd about the way Tom was behaving. "Is everything all right Tom?" he asked. "Oh yes, everything is fine, Bernard," Tom replied.

"Hmm, well you had better get up above then, mon ami."

Tom gave up his search and quickly returned to the deck where his father was waiting.

"Ah, there you are Tom," said Jack, "come over and give a hand. You'll need to get used to the helm if you are going to take this old lady out to sea."

Everything was now ready aboard *The Eagle*. Bibs had not given up her search for the rat and was crawling through the lower decks and squeezing into places where no person could go.

Flynn arrived back on deck looking a little flustered and embarrassed that his cat had not found the intruder. "Oh there you are, Flynn," laughed Jacob "Seeing as you and that cat have wasted enough time looking for that rat, you'd better get your men to work. So let's be away and to sea." Jacob was often joking with Flynn and Flynn was used to it. "Aye Cap'n," replied Flynn and then he turned to the crewmen. "Well then you lot. What you standing around for? Let's get her movin', shall we?"

The crew all leapt into their jobs. Young Henry Higgins went ashore to untie the large ropes and feed them back to the men on board. The sheets were rolled out and ready to hoist the large sails. Jacob stood still by the helm with Jack and an eager Tom, who was excited about being allowed to steer *The Eagle* out of Rivermouth. "If it's all right with you Tom, I'll take her off the quay and you can have her once we're sailing out," Jacob said to Tom with a little smile. "Yes, that's fine by me, Jacob." Tom knew well that leaving port was always the Captain's responsibility and sailing a large boat like *The Eagle* off her mooring, was definitely a job for an expert.

Tom walked along the deck watching the people on the quayside. A large crowd had gathered to watch the beautiful old sailing ship set sail. He was standing next to one of the large wooden mooring posts, which held the last spring rope for *The Eagle*. This rope would be gradually paid out as the ship slipped her mooring. Tom had not realised that Bazellgoose was sitting on top of the post, watching him. *Hello Tom* he said. Tom heard the words in his head but he answered out loud in his surprise. "Bazellgoose!" he said. *Shhhh, Tom. Remember; speak without words* said the crow, looking down at Tom from upon the post. *Sorry, I forgot, how are you?*

*That's better. I'm very well, thank-you. Now listen. Rumpitter is on board.*

*Yes, I know, I can't find him anywhere* Tom replied.

*Don't worry, he'll be hiding somewhere, but you have got to get that cat off his back. Rumpitter has an important job to do and the cat will spoil everything.* Bazellgoose was staring at Tom with his black eyes.

Tom looked around to see if anyone was watching, *How can I find him?*

*Wait until you are sailing and then call for him in your head. You'll need to sort that cat out. Rumpitter won't cause any trouble but he's going with you and...* The crow paused and lifted his head upward to the tops of the masts.

Tom looked up too and saw the seagull sitting way up on the highest point of the main mast. Tom spoke again without words.

*Mr Hawkins, I was wondering where you were.*

The seagull looked down at them and his eye blinked at Tom. *Hello Tom; well this is it, our first adventure together. Are you ready?*

*I most certainly am, Mr Hawkins, and Bazellgoose tells me that Rumpitter is going with us.*

*That's right. How do you feel now my friend?*

*I'm really excited; where are we going?* Tom was keen to know more. After all, it was all still a mystery. *When will I know?*

*Don't you worry about that, Tom. You will know sure enough, when the time comes.*

The seagull flapped his wings and took off up into the clear blue sky and circled around the ship. Tom watched, turning on his heels as he saw him glide gracefully around and then settle back on top of the mast.

Bazellgoose gave a squawk and then turned to Tom. *"Have a nice adventure, Tom, and I'll see you when you return."* He nodded his head at Tom, who smiled back. The crow gave another squawk and lifted himself off the post and flew up to the mast to join Mr Hawkins.

*I wish I could fly like them* Tom said to himself and then heard his father's voice calling.

"Over here Tom, we're moving off now."

Tom ran back and jumped aboard.

The last of the heavy ropes slipped away from the old wooden post and were pulled quickly on board by the crew. One of the jibs was hoisted and the wind filled the sail, turning the bow of *The Eagle* away from the quayside. Two men pushed the bow out from the quay and Jacob pulled hard over on the wheel. The crowd on the quayside cheered as they watched the ship's master sail *The Eagle* majestically away from the harbour wall. Then another sail unfurled to give them more speed. The ropes rattled through the large wooden blocks as the crew heaved together and the next of the sails rolled up the second mast.

"A pretty sight, don't you think Tom?" said his father, as they all watched the crew work to set the sails. "It's fantastic," replied Tom with the biggest smile.

*The Eagle* sailed gracefully down the river, passing smaller boats and the cable ferry, which took passengers from Rivermouth across the harbour to Kingsport. This was the village on the eastern shore. People were waving at them from the ferry and Tom laughed with excitement.

The sun was warm and there was a pleasant, gentle breeze filling the sails as they cut with ease through the sparkling water casting a reflection of blue sky on the white, wooden hull of *The Eagle*. It was such a wonderful feeling and a moment that Tom would never forget for all his life. This was it, his first adventure. The time had finally come.

# Chapter 7 – The Golden Secret

As *The Eagle* sailed gently down the river towards the estuary, the crew were kept busy sorting out the ropes and halyards in readiness for hoisting the larger main sails once they were past the estuary and into the English Channel.

"Have you said anything to the crew yet?" Jack asked Jacob. "No – saw no reason to. As far as they know, this is a fishing trip and there's no need for them to know anything else for the moment. There may be nothing out there – if you get my point?"

"For the moment, nothing out there, Jacob?" asked Jack with a wry smile. "Don't tell me you have doubts now?" he continued.

"I know you think I'm going crazy but I'm not and I do have a feeling about this. I know it was not all imagined," said Jacob as he steered *The Eagle* further down river, towards the open sea.

"I don't think you're going crazy Jacob but you have to admit, it is all a little odd."

"The night we saw that strange ship there was a bright glow from the moon, even though it was a stormy night with black clouds in the sky and all. For a short while, just as we sighted her, the sky was lit by this bright glow from the moon."

"Well, that's not completely unusual you know. So what was wrong?" Jack was confused a little by this thought.

"I'll tell you what was wrong – or at least, not right. You know as well as I do that you don't get much light from a crescent moon. Not in those conditions any rate."

"So, I know but..."

"But, what you have overlooked, Jack, is that we have had that same crescent moon up there in the sky ever since we saw that ship. It has not changed in days. We've had these really strange gales coming out of nowhere, but yet there's been this bright glow of light from the moon over the Channel for the past four days. Old Mike told me last night, when he got back to Rivermouth in his trawler, that they too saw the moon and couldn't understand it. What's more, several of the skippers in the harbour office were talking about it. Nobody can work it out. It's just unnatural, that's what it is, Jack – unnatural."

Jack thought about it carefully. Jacob was right. The French captain he had met earlier had commented on it as well. There was something very odd about the whole affair. Perhaps there was more to this than he thought. Maybe there was some freak weather pattern coming from somewhere in the Atlantic. He just could not work it out.

Meanwhile, down in the deepest part of the ship, where the cargo was stowed, Bibs the cat had found a gap between two thick wooden beams and had managed to squeeze through into an opening which lead to the main hold at the bottom of the ship. She could hear the sloshing of the sea against the heavy wooden hull but it did not bother her; she had been the ship's cat all her life and was used to any sudden noise or movement.

However, Rumpitter was not. He was feeling very odd indeed and really was fed up with this game of hide and seek. He had a job to do and somehow, by hook or by crook, he was going to carry out his task. He was curled tightly in a corner with his tail wrapped around an iron bracket to stop him from sliding out of his hiding place. Up above Jacob had called out to the crew that they were nearing the castle at the estuary and then had to pull over to port on the wheel as they picked up the wind. *The Eagle* heeled to one side.

Down below Rumpitter had temporarily relaxed and let go with his tail. This was not a good idea and he suddenly flopped out of his corner and rolled out along the lower deck of the hold.

Bibs turned and saw the giant rat tumble across the deck. She sprang into action and got into the pounce position and eyed her prey before the deadly attack.

"Ouch!" called out Rumpitter, as he rolled along the floor. He went crashing into a large tin container. It made a terrible clang as he knocked it over and watched stupidly, as it rolled towards a dark shadow. He wiped his aching head with his tail and gripped the deck with his claws to stop him sliding into the shadow. Then, he saw something move, very slightly.

*What's that?* he said to himself and tried to focus his eyes into the dark. Suddenly his eyes caught sight of something glowing. Then the something became two things. Then he froze.

*Oh no* he said to himself again.

From out of the darkness two green eyes slowly moved closer. The cat had not blinked and was staring directly at her prey. Bibs had found her rat. She would wait for ages until the time came to strike. Her skill in catching rats had made her famous and very popular with the seamen. She knew exactly what do – and when to do it.

However, Rumpitter, although big and often clumsy, was a clever old rat and had been through a great many scrapes with cats, dogs and people – and he had one very special secret, a friendly seagull who could come to his rescue. The problem he had this time was that the seagull was unable to get down below decks. The voice in his head was telling him to use his brain and be smart. Rats are well known for their cleverness. *You must deal with this on your own, Rumpitter. Perhaps the cat has not realised just how big you are* said Mr Hawkins, in his head.

The rat and the cat stared at each other without a single blink of an eye or any movement at all.

It seemed ages until Rumpitter saw a trickle of light come through one of the beams. He noticed how it made a long shadow across the deck. He realised that if he could get between the light and the cat, his shadow would stretch all the way along the deck. It would make him look even bigger than he was. It could just scare away the cat.

He waited for the slightest move from Bibs and then the moment came. *The Eagle* had rolled to one side again as she tacked for her final stretch to the open sea. The crew above were all busy and almost all the sails had been hoisted. She was now leaning well over as she sailed towards the castle. At the same moment the cat moved her head, just for a second. But it was all Rumpitter needed to spring out into the light. He made his move swiftly and was delighted to see his shadow enlarge quite dramatically. He tuned to the cat and let out a growl, showing his terrible sharp, yellow teeth and then thumped his heavy, long tail on the floor as he glared at the cat.

Bibs was taken back, and hissed at the rat. She was horrified to see how big this intruder was. *He really is big* she thought as she glared back at the growling monster in front of her.

"You – you don't scare me, rat. Better take care, I'm going to get you," she hissed in a sleazy cat-like way. She was trying to out-fool the rat, hoping that this would work.

"Oh really, cat, perhaps you haven't seen just how big I am. I could eat you for breakfast," Rumpitter growled back and then lashed out his huge tail. A cloud of dust flew up as it hit the floor with a heavy thud.

This was not good. Now Bibs was not sure what to do. How long could she stare this rat out before she tired and he pounced on her?

Being eaten by a rat was not the way she had planned on ending her days. Retirement with a soft and kind hearted human in a cosy cottage with a nice open fireplace where she could curl up and sleep was what cats like her needed and she, more than any other, was overdue for her retirement. She had never had trouble like this before and although she was annoyed that she was in an awkward situation, she was not about to spoil things.

Just as she was about to try something, although she didn't know quite what, the rat spoke again.

"Look cat, I know what's on your mind. You think we could be here all day and then the first one to fall asleep gets it – right?" Rumpitter licked his jaw with his red tongue and showed his teeth again. Just for good measure, he thumped his tail again on the floor. The cat looked at the tail. It was long and much thicker than others she had chewed. In fact the thought of chewing this one almost repulsed her.

"How do you know what I'm thinking?" she replied cautiously.

"I know more than you would give me credit for, cat, and what's more, if you want that easy life in a nice little farmhouse somewhere, you would do well to listen to me." Rumpitter knew what the cat was thinking.

"So – what brilliant idea could you possibly have?" Bibs asked. She didn't like it that the rat knew her thoughts.

Rumpitter chose his words carefully before speaking. This had to be good and it needed to work.

"Look, I don't have any need for anything on this boat. In fact I can't wait to get off it. However, there is something I have to do and if you and I can call a truce for a few days, I'll be gone and no-one will be any the wiser. You could go back up on deck and lick your lips, clean your paws and all those things you cats do after a meal and perhaps the humans will think you've had me. I don't care as long as you and I can agree that there will be no more trouble between us." Rumpitter paused for a moment then said, "So, what do you say?"

Bibs was confused. She didn't like compromises – why should she? She was a cat after all and cats don't like losing. However, this was no ordinary rat, it was very large. It could be that she had met one rat too many. After all, she had won so many battles and hunts in her life, what was one like this going to prove. The best thing of all was that her humans could not see this and would have no idea that she was about to back down from a fight.

"All right," she said finally. "So what do we do now, shake paws and go for milk?"

"Not quite what I had in mind, cat. How about you just backing off? Go and get some fresh air and I shall make myself scarce." Rumpitter paused and then, just for a touch of dramatic measure, he said, "Or we fight to the death" and smashed his tail again very hard on the floor and ground his yellow teeth.

The cat moved her back legs underneath from the pounce position. "If you promise to stay well away and don't let anyone see you, I suppose I can agree. You look a little on the leathery side for my stomach anyway," she replied, trying to keep her dignity in some kind of order.

"Right then – it's a deal. You walk away now and we call a truce," said Rumpitter.

Bibs slowly, but very carefully, crawled backwards along the floor. She moved back into the shadow and when she felt safe, she trotted quickly out from the ship's hold, back through the hole and finally back into the human's accommodation area. She needed something to eat so that she could lick her lips and clean up in front of everyone. She moved her way into the galley. Bernard was rattling around in some cupboards.

The cat was not stupid and rubbed herself affectionately round Bernard's ankles.

"Ah, and where have you been?" he said, looking down at her. "And have you found that rat?" He could see that the cat was hungry and laughed at her. "Ah ha, you have not found it. I think this one was too much for you eh? How would you like a little snack? Oh, OK, how about this?" Bernard leaned down and gave Bibs a piece of raw fish, which she grabbed and swallowed very quickly. Then she looked up with glazed eyes as if to say, "I like this human, he understands what cats like." She purred and gulped down more of the fish until it was all eaten up.

Back up on deck, Tom was now holding the helm. He was delighted to feel the wind in his face, standing with his father and watching the old castle at the estuary slowly move behind them as they sailed past.

"Tom, we'll be going past Jacob's rock in a short while." Tom looked ahead to the east and out to sea. The rock was now visible and he looked at Jacob who was coiling a rope. Everyone knew to leave him alone at this time.

Jack whispered into Tom's ear, "It's Jacob's time now Tom, hold her steady." Tom looked at his father and nodded, then he saw Jacob walk up to the bow of the ship. The tall man stood silently and alone. Tom was keen to keep *The Eagle* sailing smoothly and held the great wooden wheel firmly in both hands, concentrating on his important job. The sea was bigger now as they sailed out into the English Channel and the chopping waves tried hard to knock Tom off his course. "Easy does it son," Jack said quietly and then nodded to Flynn, who, in turn, gave a silent order by a subtle hand movement to the crew who were responsible for trimming the sails. They knew what to do and quickly let out the large booms to spill the wind out of the sails and slow *The Eagle* down just as they approached Jacob's rock.

The large grey rock loomed above them on the port side. Seabirds swirled around its sharp and rugged peaks and heavy waves thrashed against it, bursting up into the air like wild, white, prancing horses.

Jacob had been standing with his arms down by his sides. As they slowly sailed past the rock, he removed his hat with one hand and held it up to the rock. This was his salute to his son. It was a solemn moment and, as always, the ship's crew stood in silence to show their respect.

The moment they had cleared the rock, the crew hauled back the booms, which instantly brought *The Eagle* back up to speed. The wind filled the sails again. The ship leaned to port and began to smash through the waves. They were sailing fast again. "Eight knots," called out one of the crew.

Jacob returned to the bridge and smiled at Tom, "Fine sailing lad, we'll make a skipper out of you yet." He tapped Tom on the head and went down below decks. Tom smiled widely at his father who looked proudly at his son and, with one hand on Tom's shoulder, looked up to the mast tops, smiling to himself.

A voice came to Tom. *Nice work. I know your father is proud of you. Enjoy this moment – it will stay with you forever.* Tom replied without words, *Where are you now, Mr Hawkins?*

*I am still here Tom, I am always here.* Tom smiled with strange feelings. He was enjoying this moment at sea with his father and Jacob and the crew and yet he still had no idea where he was really heading to and what adventures lay ahead.

*Tom, I know you are worried. Trust me. No harm will come to anyone. I give you my word.*

*If you say so, Mr Hawkins.*

*Indeed I do, lad, indeed I do.* There was not another word from the seagull and Tom looked up every now and then to see if he was there at the top of the main mast, but it was not easy to tell.

The breeze was stiffening and *The Eagle* glided smoothly through the sea.

Bernard had already prepared lunch for everyone and Bibs the cat followed him everywhere.

"I reckon you've found a friend there, Bernard," laughed Jack as he saw the cat curling around Bernard's feet as he tried to walk along the deck with a deep tray full of food for the crew. "She is a persistent thing indeed," replied Bernard as he almost tripped. One of the crew managed to stop him falling flat on his face and grabbed the tray of bowls with steaming hot stew. "This smells very good Bernard, what have we here?" enquired Jacob, who reappeared on deck at the smell of food. "It is a simple fish stew, with some fresh herbs and garlic. I also have some fresh baked bread from Mrs Parker."

Jack smiled, "Good old Maggie, we can always count on her fresh bread."

"Aye Jack, you've a good'n there, that's for sure," agreed Flynn. They all sat around on deck and enjoyed their lunch.

Tom had given the helm over to one of the crew and, after gulping down his food, he went below. The cat watched Tom intently as he disappeared down the steps into the main saloon.

From the saloon, Tom began searching the cabins and every space that he knew of. Finally he crept down into the hold where all the supplies were kept.

*Rumpitter, where are you* he thought as he climbed over boxes, sacks and sail bags.

*"Tom, Tom, I'm over here, behind the ropes."* Tom looked along the hull and saw a large coiled rope in the corner. He looked behind him to see if anyone was looking or had followed him. It was clear. He slowly crawled along until; at last, he reached the rope. "Rumpitter?" he whispered.

*"Hello Tom."* Suddenly two large red eyes were staring at him. It made him jump.

*"Oh sorry, did I scare you? That confounded cat has been tailing me everywhere. I had to make a deal with it. But you can never trust a cat you know."*

Tom regained his composure. "Are you all right down here?"

*"Speak without words, Tom, in case someone hears you. No I'm not alright. I hate boats and can't wait to get off and out of this damp, nasty place. I am also starving hungry but there's no chance of me getting anything to eat until dark, I suppose. Then we'll be off anyway."*

"*Off*, what do you mean?" Tom asked. He was desperate to know what was going to happen and what Mr Hawkins had in store for them.

*"Of course, you don't think we are staying here, do you? I would never have agreed to come on this trip if it meant staying here. I get seasick anyway."*

"Well, where are we going?"

*"Hasn't Mr Hawkins told you? Oh dear. Well, I suppose he has his reasons."*

"Oh come on Rumpitter, you can tell me, we're friends aren't we?" Said Tom now speaking without words.

Suddenly a voice came to both of them. *I knew you two would finally get together. Now you must listen carefully. The reason why I have not told you anything is because this is a delicate operation. We need to be in a certain position at a certain time. If we are not, then we miss our chance. I am relying on the skilled navigation of your Captain, who I place great trust in. He and the others, of course, have no idea of what lies ahead. But before you get worried Tom, no harm will come to them, we just need this ship to be in a particular place tonight.*

*Where Mr Hawkins, where?* Asked Tom.

*I'm afraid I cannot tell you because if we miss the chance there will have been no point. However, once I am certain of our chance, I shall give further instructions. I am sorry if this bothers you Tom, but as I have said, all will be revealed very soon.*

Tom looked at Rumpitter, who cocked his head as he looked back at the boy and then twitched his nose which made his long, grey whiskers flicker up and down. *"It's going to be all just dandy, Tom. Don't you worry yourself about a thing. Now if you can get me something to eat, I would be most grateful."*

Tom scratched his head in confusion. *"What do you eat?"*

*"Absolutely anything. Except salad stuff, I hate greens."*

*"I'll see what I can do,"* Tom replied and then crawled back into the main accommodation area of the ship. He could feel the ship leaning over and rising up on each wave, then rolling back down with a sudden thud as the ship's bow smashed into the belly of each wave. Tom thought about Rumpitter and felt sorry for him, knowing how he hated the sea and was probably now feeling very ill.

Nevertheless he was going to find something for the rat to eat; at least some food would make him feel better, he thought.

Tom was delighted to discover that there was nobody in the galley. He quickly began opening cupboard doors, looking for something suitable for his friend to eat. He found an oval tin on a shelf and pulled it down. His face lit up when he opened the lid. There was a large piece of cheese, wrapped in a cloth. The best thing was that it had already been cut, so he could take a piece without anyone noticing. He found a knife in a drawer and cut out a good size chunk, then replaced the cloth over the cheese and returned the tin to the shelf. He remembered to clean the knife and put it back in the drawer. After checking that he had not left any traces behind he returned to the hold.

Rumpitter was not in the best of moods. "Are you OK?" Tom asked, knowing that no one could hear him.

"No, I'm not, I feel ghastly. In fact I really wish I hadn't offered to do this. The ship is rolling all over the place. Can't you tell the driver to be more careful?" Tom giggled.

"We can't help the weather, Rumpitter, and it's just the way these boats are." He opened up his hands to show Rumpitter the cheese. "Here I've got you something nice to eat."

Rumpitter's nose twitched as the scent of the cheese was quite strong. Then his eyes rolled in their sockets. "Th-thanks Tom, I really would, in normal circumstances appreciate this, but I..." Suddenly Rumpitter lurched away to a dark corner. There was a horrible sound.

Tom, realising what it was, tried not to laugh. Instead he left the cheese on the floor by the coiled rope and left his friend alone to recover.

It did not take Tom long to return to the deck and as soon as he felt the fresh sea air blowing into his face and saw the waves splashing past, he felt pleased to back on deck and immediately started looking for jobs to do.

Flynn came over to him. "Hello Tom, you look like you're enjoying this. Have you seen that old cat of ours? She's gone missin' again."

Tom looked to his left then to his right. "Oh, no Mat, I haven't, but don't worry, I'm sure she's around somewhere." He knew only too well that Bibs was lying low so she wouldn't have to meet up with Rumpitter again. The cat was certain that the rat would show himself again and then the crew would blame her for not catching it.

Several hours passed and *The Eagle* continued on her course. Every couple of hours Jacob would check their position and set the charts, at which time he would give the order to his crew to alter course to a new compass heading. On this occasion Jack Parker took over the helm from Henry Higgins. "You go for a mug of tea Henry and bring me one up when you can."

"Right oh, Jack, here's the wheel then. There's nothing to report, seen nothing, heard nothing, but the light is fading. I'll have the lights put on."

Tom watched the helm change-over and saw his father looking out to sea. He noticed that the sun was going down and although it had been a beautiful day, the warmth was now easing away. There was the making of a fabulous sunset building up over to the west. It was beginning to get a little chilly so he went below and put on his jacket.

Tom wanted to get back on deck to watch the sun setting, but as he climbed the last step at the top of the companionway he heard his father and Jacob Morgan talking. He waited for a moment and hid behind the coach roof of the main saloon hatch and then listened.

"See – I told you that moon was not right. Look at it," he heard Jacob say.

Tom looked up and saw the crescent moon shining brightly down over them. For a very brief moment he swore he was looking into a giant eye – an eye he had seen somewhere before. Then suddenly he realised. It was the eye of the seagull: the blackness as dark as the night surrounding the golden crescent in the centre. "Mr Hawkins!" he exclaimed in a whisper. For a second he thought he was looking into the seagull's mysterious eye. But then it changed back to the crescent moon. However, he did realise what Jacob had meant. The light from this moon was as bright as a full moon. This was definitely most odd. It was so bright.

"Yes Jacob, you're right. Have you set a course to where you saw the ship?" Jack asked.

"Aye, I reckon we are right on course, Jack," Jacob replied and then paused, "That's if she's there at all.".

"Like I said Jacob, there's only one way to find out. But even if what you saw was really there, it does not mean that it's going to be there now. After all, what ship would be sailing around aimlessly doing nothing and going nowhere?"

"Mmmm, I have considered that Jack. I guess we'll just have to catch us some fish then won't we?" The two men laughed. Then Jacob said, " You OK out here on the wheel for a little longer – the crew are having their supper early, just in case we need all hands later, if you follow me?"

"Yes, my friend, I follow you. You could ask Bernard if he could bring me up something though."

"That I can do, Jack, I'll go and ask him." Jacob left Jack at the wheel and slipped below decks.

Tom had not been noticed by them or the two crewmen up at the bow who were leaning over the rail and chatting together. Flynn, Higgins, Bernard and the others were all enjoying a rest and a hearty meal around the oval mahogany table in the ship's saloon.

It was a very clear and crisp evening and Tom could see just about every star in the sky. He found a cosy place to sit by a couple of large canvas sail bags and some neatly coiled ropes. He lay back and admired the beautiful starry night. For a while he was happy just looking up and listening to the waves splashing along the hull. Then, he began thinking. He realised that soon he was going to hear from Mr Hawkins and their adventure was going to begin.

He knew that Mr Hawkins had made some preparations, but he did not know what. He was very excited, but also nervous. *What was this, where was he going, what would happen?* Then he thought about his father and leaned round the coach roof to look at him standing at the wheel. *Was his father going to be safe, would he get into trouble, was this all a strange dream?* There were so many questions going around in his head. He sat back and lifted his eyes up and stared into space. Suddenly he saw something move. The sky was quite black now. Night had come upon them quickly. What was that? Something definitely moved. He kept staring up to see if he could find it, whatever it was. Then without warning came a bright yellow light. It appeared out of the sky and suddenly came very close, skimming over *The Eagle*. It was like a small comet or a shooting star.

*Wow, what was that?* He asked himself. He jumped up to see where it had gone. It disappeared into the night. He wanted to run over and tell his father and was confused as to what to do. He was just about to call out, when Bernard appeared from the hatchway holding a bowl with a cloth over it. "Ah, my young friend, I was wondering where you were. Are you hungry? You have not eaten. Come, I'll find you something in the galley."

"Oh, I'm not hungry, but thanks. Maybe later. I'd like to look at the stars for a while."

"OK, Tom but don't get cold and don't fall asleep without food inside you. You will be starving in the middle of the night." Bernard then walked over to greet Jack at the wheel with some of his fine stew and a mug of hot tea.

Tom wondered. What was that strange light, why didn't anyone else see it?

Then he heard that familiar voice in his head. *Tom, it's me. Don't worry any more about your father and his friends. They will be perfectly safe. You must trust me. But now you must get ready. We are nearly there. I have spoken to Rumpitter who is on his way up. I must say, I would have preferred him to be a little more with it.*

Tom giggled, *Poor Rumpitter, he really doesn't like the sea does he?*

*I'm afraid not. I would have thought he was used to it by now. Never mind. Now, Tom, I shall call you soon. Be ready for me when I call you.*

*Please Mr Hawkins, tell me what's happening, where are we going and...*

*Hush now. There's plenty of time for your answers later. Relax, I will be back* came the quick reply.

Suddenly, again there was that bright yellow flash high up over the mast head. Tom looked up and saw the eye amongst the stars in the darkness. The eye with the gold crescent moon was looking down at them. Suddenly it blinked and reappeared. The yellow light flew across the stars, and the eye with the crescent moon disappeared within the bright light. "Wow!" exclaimed Tom. It was almost like a private firework show – a show all for him. It was truly amazing.

Bernard had been talking to Jack over at the helm and then returned just as Tom was staring blankly up at the sky. Bernard was about to say something when his toe got caught under the end of a loose rope and he tripped over. "Ooooh, aaaah," he cried as he lunged forward, past Tom and down the five steps of the companionway into the saloon. There was a terrible crash down below and Tom rushed to see if he was all right. Flynn and Higgins immediately jumped up from the table to help Bernard. When Tom reached the top of the stairs and looked down he had to laugh.

Bernard had fallen, flat onto the saloon floor and, as he fell down the steps, he had startled the cat, who thought she had found a quiet hiding place under the top of the stairs. Bibs screamed and leapt up into the air and landed on Bernard's back. She dug her claws into his shirt as she landed. Her loud meowing and Bernard's groaning alerted the whole ship's crew and everyone rushed to see what had happened. The sight of Bernard lying, face down with the cat on his back and the dreadful noise they were making between them, was hilarious. Flynn called to his cat. "You stupid old cat, you're supposed to be on rat duty." Then he took hold of Bernard's arms and lifted him to his feet. "You all right? Thought you'd come a real cropper then," he laughed.

In fact everyone was rolling around laughing. Everyone that is, except poor old Bernard, who was aching from head to foot. Although he was only a little bruised, the main damage was to his pride. Tom was chuckling away as he saw the chef try to regain some composure. As they were all laughing the cat darted away into another part of the ship and suddenly there was a cry from above.

Tom quickly turned to look over his shoulder, "Hush everyone, I heard something."

Jacob was the first to respond. "What lad? What did you hear?" Then there was another sound. It was a loud swirling noise, like a rocket. Immediately everyone stopped their laughter and looked up towards the saloon door. Tom had gone and the ship's crew ran up on deck.

Tom ran to the helm where his father was staring up to the sky. "Look Tom, everybody, look up there!" They all looked up to see the sky full of shooting stars and rockets, like fire balls shooting around above them. Tom was trembling with excitement and grabbed his father's arm.

"What on earth is this?" Jack called out. "I've never seen anything like it."

Everyone stared in amazement at the fire-lit sky. "Good heavens Sir, it's just like a Christmas tree," exclaimed Henry Higgins. "Never seen a Christmas tree like that, Henry," returned Flynn, who was completely stunned by the whole picture above him. "It's unbelievable, that's what it is."

Rockets of fire and shooting stars were swooping above them. Gradually more and more appeared. The stars became bolts of fire and sent ashes of gold dust drifting down. *The Eagle* was being completely covered in gold dust.

Tom looked further out to sea and saw the whole ocean light up. It was incredible. Then he saw the moon. It had turned again into a giant eye. *Was this more magic from Mr Hawkins?* He wondered. Gold rays of light shot out from the crescent in the centre of the eye. More fireballs appeared. They came lower and lower. Then they came so close that they were swooping just over the heads of the men on deck. One came so close that it missed Jacob's head by inches and he dropped to the deck to avoid being hit. It was becoming dangerous, Tom thought. Someone was going to get hurt. He looked over at Flynn, who had fallen over. "Flynn!" Tom yelled. But there was no response. He looked to the others and they too started falling down. The sky was so bright and full of the strange golden dust. The dust was now turning into a golden mist. But there were no more fireballs or shooting stars. Everything was covered in gold. "What's happening to everyone?" Tom called out and then turned to his father. He had fallen asleep and had flopped over the ship's wheel. Then, strangely, there was no wind. It was as if they had sailed right into a thick bank of golden mist. The mist had swamped the ship. He could not see further than the ship's rail and realised then that everyone had fallen down. They were all asleep. "Dad!" he shouted and tugged at his father's arm. It was no use. Jack Parker was in a deep sleep. Tom looked around, but it was now impossible to see anything and suddenly he felt very alone in a very strange place. The sea was as flat as glass, without a puff of wind.

Then a voice came to him. *No fear, Tom, all is well. We have arrived at the Gateway. Our journey now begins.* It was Mr Hawkins. His voice sounded calm and reassuring. *They only sleep Tom, no harm will come to them, I promise. Now come, we must make our move. Walk carefully to the side of the ship and watch.* Tom stumbled over two sleeping crewmen and saw Bernard lying across the top of the steps of the saloon hatchway. He hadn't quite made it to the deck before the dust had arrived. It had knocked the whole ship's crew out and sent them all into a deep sleep. Some of them were actually snoring.

Suddenly there was a crash, which made Tom jump. "What's that, who's there?" he called, trembling. Then, through the thick dust he saw a rope move and then a sail ruffled on the deck. The rope wasn't a rope at all. It was Rumpitter's tail. The rat crawled out from underneath a folded sail, darted up onto the rail, ran along the top towards Tom and stood up on his hind legs to sniff the air and twitch his whiskers. He was a friendly sight and Tom was relieved to see him. "Ah ha. At last, we are here. Thought we'd never do it. Come, Tom, no time to waste. We must get there before we're back," said Rumpitter and then stopped to give some thought to what he had just said. He continued, "Or should I say, leave before we go. No, I mean, so we can get back before we left." He paused. "Yes, that's it — back before we left. Come on."

Tom was completely stunned and speechless. "What are you talking about? Can't you see what's happened? Everyone has passed out! Look at my Dad!" Tom was worried about his father and was unhappy about leaving him there.

"Yes, absolutely Tom, they've all gone to sleep and when they wake they won't know a thing about it and we will be back and all returned to normal. We must get a move on. No time to lose. Now get up onto the rail and when I say jump – jump."

"Wait! I can't. My father, I can't leave him here." Tom was really worried.

"Tom, I know you find this hard to believe, but I mean it when I say they will be safe. We will be back before they wake. I promise." Rumpitter was still standing on his hind legs but he had his front paws held out in front of him in a sort of pleading gesture. He looked Tom right in the eye and gently touched Tom's nose with his own. "Trust me," he whispered.

"Promise?" asked Tom. "I promise," replied the rat in a soft voice. Then he twitched his nose and then in a much louder voice, said, "Now come on, let's GO!"

"What do I do?" Tom asked quickly. "Climb up onto the rail," said the rat and he moved over to one side to let Tom up.

"Any minute now we are going to jump. You must remember to do exactly as I say. If you miss the landing, you'll, you'll..."

"I'll what?" asked Tom, shaking his head in confusion. "You'll get wet," said the rat finally.

A gentle breeze picked up and then gradually the gold mist started moving around, like smoke being blown away. Then *The Eagle* began bobbing up and down and Tom looked over the side into the water. The sea had turned completely gold, but now small waves were forming. Then there was a ruffling sound like sails flapping. He looked up at the masts and noticed the sails were not moving. He couldn't work out what it was. Then, like a ghost, looming out of the thick golden haze he saw the most incredible sight. A huge golden bird with large round eyes appeared through the mist. Then he saw that it was the bows of an old sailing ship. The golden bird was the figurehead with its wings spread from the bows, down the sides of the hull. Tom gasped for breath as it drew nearer.

Clouds of gold dispersed around as the vessel cut slowly through the water. All along the wooden hull were round shields painted in bright colours.

Three huge sails puffed through the mist and then Tom saw they were painted with red and gold crossed swords and a crescent moon. "It can't be!" he called out. His mouth was wide open in disbelief.

Rumpitter quickly shook Tom by his trouser leg. "Here, grab this rope. We are going to jump and swing over to it. Got it?" Tom took the rope and held it tight in both hands. "Got it," Tom replied nervously. The huge galleon came closer. It was a fantastic sight. No-one would ever have believed such a thing existed. It was so big and so old – a strange ghost ship from a thousand years ago was moving right towards him. It came alongside *The Eagle*. Tom stared up in astonishment at the fantastic sight. The rigging creaked and groaned, but there was no-one on board.

"Ready?"

"Yes."

"Jump!" shouted Rumpitter. Together the two of them jumped up and swung on the ropes. As they approached the galleon, Rumpitter shouted, "Let go!" They both let go of their ropes and fell. Tom felt as if it were an age before he hit the wooden deck of the strange galleon. He landed with a heavy thud. The rat, being much lighter than Tom, went sliding off across to the far side of the deck and crashed into a barrel. "Ouch!" he called out.

For a moment Tom couldn't get up. It was as if he were glued to the deck. He knew this was because he was absolutely terrified. He really was still very uncertain about what was happening, but after a few moments he was able to lift himself off the deck and crawl over to the side of the ship to look for *The Eagle*.

To his horror, the ship had vanished. "Wh-where's *The Eagle*, what's happened to her? Where is everybody?"

Quickly he turned to look for Rumpitter. He was not there. "Rumpitter!" he shouted in a very loud voice and then again, this time even louder, "Rumpitter, where are you?" There was no reply. Suddenly something appeared through the haze. At first it looked like a black dot and then it came closer and grew bigger. It was making a noise, which became louder as it approached. Tom ducked and the rat went screaming past over his head. "Aaaagh," cried Rumpitter. He was clinging onto a rope, swinging down from above at great speed. The rat flew through the air and crashed straight into the foot of the thick wooden mast. Tom covered his eyes and waited for the bump. It sounded awful when he heard Rumpitter's cry as he collided with the mast. Tom quickly ran over. "Rumpitter, are you all right?" he asked. There was a dreadful moan. "Rumpitter?" Tom was beside himself with concern as he called out his friend's name again. "Rumpitter!"

The rat lay very still, stretched out on the deck. Tom bent down and stroked the rat across his long grey back. "Oh no, what am I going to do now? Rumpitter." Tom wanted to shake him to wake him up.

One eye slowly opened and the rat moved a foot. "Ugh. It, it's all right Tom, just give me a moment to recover." Tom's face quickly lit up and gave a wide smile when he heard the rat speak. "Rumpitter. Phew – thank heavens. I thought you were dead."

The rat slowly regained consciousness. "Maybe I am. I ache all over." The rat rolled onto his side and panted heavily and moaned in agony, "Ow, ow, ow – that hurt – a lot."

"What on earth were you doing?" asked Tom, now much happier that Rumpitter was alive.

"I climbed up the mast to see if I could see anything. Then I saw you walking towards the ship's side. I thought you were going to try to jump, so I grabbed a rope thinking I could slide down it, but it came loose. It went so fast that I couldn't stop. It's a very high mast, you know."

"I know," said Tom, "I can't even see the top from here. How are you feeling now?" The rat picked himself up. "I'll be all right – we rats are quite hardy animals you know."

"Yes, I can see that. Also pretty crazy too." Tom laughed and then thought again about *The Eagle*. He stopped laughing and looked out to sea. "Rumpitter, *The Eagle* isn't there, I can't see her, what's happened?"

The rat was about to say something when... "Shh, don't speak."

"Why, what's happening now?" whispered Tom.

"He's coming."

"Who?" Tom whispered again and then looked around him. The mist was clearing quite rapidly and stars were beginning to reappear in the sky. The sea had turned dark again and all the gold mist had gone. A stiff wind was blowing up and they felt the galleon begin to move in the water and then the sails began to fill. Ropes creaked and the wooden cross booms started to swing in the direction of the wind. The whole ship began to creak and roll. Now they were sailing quite quickly through the water. Tom couldn't understand how the ship could sail without anyone on board. Was it indeed a ghost ship?

"What now, Rumpitter, what's happening?" Tom asked. He felt the ship heel over to one side. "Have we got to sail this thing on our own? Where are the crew?"

"Shh, not so loud," Rumpitter said, holding his front paw to his mouth. Then he said, "Look, look up Tom, what do you see?"

Tom arched his head up towards the masts. For a moment he couldn't see anything other than the sails and the sky, which was now brightly lit by the millions of shining stars. The wind was becoming stronger. "I can't see anything."

"Yes you can, look again," said the rat confidently. Almost instantly the starry night sky turned to day and the sky turned bright blue. Tom was dazzled and amazed. His smile returned and he laughed and then ran to the side of the ship to look up into the blue sky where he saw a seagull gliding high up and moving towards them. The bird circled above them and gradually descended. "Mr Hawkins!" he cried out and waved. Tom turned back to Rumpitter. "It's Mr Hawkins!" The rat seemed to smile too and hopped over to join Tom at the rail. "Indeed it is my friend, indeed it is." They both watched as the seagull flew closer and closer.

Finally Mr Hawkins landed on the rail, settling beside the two of them. Tom noticed that there was a thin leather strap hanging from the bird's neck. The strap seemed to be attached to something hiding under Mr Hawkins' large wing.

"Hello my good friends." He turned to Tom. "How do you do, Tom," he said with a sparkle in his eye.

"It certainly is good to see you Mr Hawkins," replied Tom, "but where are we? What has happened to *The Eagle* and...?"

The seagull interrupted. "It can all be explained right now, Tom. First of all, *The Eagle* is still out there, nothing has happened and all on board are perfectly safe. Your father is in no danger. They are all safe."

Tom scratched his head and was confused again. "But where, I can't see them?"

"No, you can't Tom. From where we are, aboard this ship, you can't see anything but the place we are now in. *The Eagle* is just over there but we are now in a different time. A different world. This ship is the Gateway — the link, if you like, between your world and mine. If the crew on board *The Eagle* were awake they would have seen us and this ship. It would have been too much for them to comprehend. For their own peace of mind and safety, I left them to sleep." Tom looked out across the sea and saw nothing but water. "Can you see them?" he asked the bird. "Ah ha, I knew you would ask that," said the rat, who was standing beside Tom. "Bright boy, very good question, Mr Hawkins," said the rat to the bird.

Mr Hawkins laughed and then answered the question. "Yes Tom, I can and I can see them all sleeping like babies safely on deck. When we return to them, they will not have any knowledge of this and it will be just a few seconds in their time. Where we are going now is many hundreds of years in the past. We have gone back in time and to a different world. I know it is all very strange to you. This is why I could not begin to tell you everything before. You would never have understood or even believed me."

Tom felt slightly better, knowing that his father and friends were safe but now needed to know more. "So where are we now and where are we going?"

We are aboard *The Glaros*, Tom. This is my old ship. It has had a few changes made to it, but it is my ship. If you can recall my tale of how I lost it to the Saharadeen you will remember that we tried to sail her away during our escape, which was unfortunately scuppered by that evil man?"

Tom replied, "How could I forget that, but I thought you lost the ship when you were caught?"

"Yes, that is right, but as you can see, I have her back now, but I can only use her to cross between your world and mine when the crescent moon is directly in line with the same moon in this world." Mr Hawkins could see the confused look on Tom's face. "I have many unusual powers, Tom." Mr Hawkins lifted his left wing to reveal a small leather pouch.

"You have the stone?"

"Indeed I do." He looked up towards the sky and then back to his two friends who were waiting patiently for further explanation. "We are going to return the stone to its rightful place – back together with the Sword of Isis in the temple from whence it came originally."

"Is this our mission? Is that why we are here?" asked Tom excitedly. "Yes Tom, that is our quest and in doing so we will try to free my friends who have been the slaves of the Saharadeen these past three years."

At this point Tom went quiet and thought for a moment. The rat and the seagull looked at each other with a wry smile from Rumpitter. Then Tom spoke. "Just a minute, I thought you said we are going back hundreds of years?" Mr Hawkins flapped the free wing without the leather pouch and chuckled. "I did indeed but I forgot to mention that because of the mysterious time difference, we can travel back hundreds of years in time, but with no difference to us when we arrive in the other world, which we are not quite in yet."

Tom's confused expression was an amusing picture for the bird and the rat. Rumpitter began to giggle a little and then looked at the seagull, "May I?" he asked. "Please do," replied Mr Hawkins. "You see Tom, while you live in your world, and ours when we are in it, there is still another world which happens to have been left behind in history somewhere. A hundred years in the other world is only a short time in yours. This moment that we are in now is a drifting place, a special, frozen time, if you like, between the two worlds. That is why we can use this Gateway to move from your world to ours without affecting anything. This is also why, when we return to *The Eagle*, it will only have been a mere flash in time. A few seconds perhaps. Are you following me?" Tom had an odd glazed expression but replied, "I think I am, but what about this ship, how can you use it, how...?"

"Oh, that's far too complicated and really only on a need to know basis. To be honest, do you really need to know all that?" asked Mr Hawkins, again interrupting Tom's questioning.

"Well, I suppose not."

"Good – then now we are all clear on this, I think it's time we were under way. Now Tom, this next stage is going to get a little hairy, you'll need to tie yourself down." Mr Hawkins jumped off the rail and flew over the deck to the tall wooden main mast. "Over here Tom, my boy. Take this rope and tie yourself to the mast. We're going for a little ride."

The rat also jumped down from the rail and stood by the mast. "Can you help tie me up, Tom, I hate this bit?" Tom laughed, "You hate every bit, Rumpitter. OK then." Tom sat down on the deck at the foot of the mast and coiled the rope around his waist and then found a slightly smaller rope to tie around the rat. Once they were both tied up and Mr Hawkins had checked the ropes were secure, he then flew up to the crow's-nest high up the mast. "Are you two ready?" he called down.

"Yes we are," they both replied together. Tom was wild with excitement, Rumpitter went very still and clenched the rope tightly with both paws and shut his eyes. Tom looked up to see Mr Hawkins standing on the edge of the platform with his wings outstretched.

Suddenly the wind began to blow harder, the sea grew bigger and *The Glaros* pitched right over to one side. The clouds started turning grey and then went black. They were now sailing at a fast speed. The wind whistled, and the ship creaked and groaned all around them. Then a flash of lightning came from the black sky followed by a loud crack of thunder. The waves pitched high over the sides of *The Glaros*, spraying Tom and Rumpitter. Tom licked the salt from his lips. His whole body shook with fear. Then, without any warning, the ship began to lift out of the sea. They were travelling at great speed. Tom's long blond hair curled back across his forehead. Rumpitter screamed with his eyes shut and called out in a long drawn out cry, "Hold on!"

The wind blew the ship right up into the sky. Tom cried out but his voice was lost in the wind and the crashing waves beneath. The ship began to lift higher and higher until they were actually flying through the air. The sails filled with the wind blasting through them.

Tom hung on tight. He couldn't even move his head. He was pinned to the mast by the speed of the ship and the wind. *The Glaros* was flying through the air and now soaring high up into the black clouds. Tom's eyes were popping out of his head with excitement and he yelled out, "Wow!" Rumpitter still had his paws clenched tight to the rope with his eyes shut.

"Aaaaaaagh!" they both cried as they flew into the blackness. The ship shook wildly. Everything on board that was not tied down flew off the ship and down into the sea beneath.

The flying ship rattled and whistled on and on, higher and higher, until soon they were deep into the clouds. It became cold and damp and streams of water poured off the sides of *The Glaros*. Tom and Rumpitter were soaked to the skin. Tom's teeth chattered together with the cold. They clung tightly to the ropes, pinned to the mast. Finally, after a while, the ship began to level out and fly straight. Eventually it slowed down and, for a short while, they just floated high above the clouds. Tom looked around and saw blue sky. He could not see below because he was tied to the mast. "That was scary! I can't believe this is really happening," he said, panting with relief as everything began to calm down. He stuttered his words because his lips were cold and he was trembling with the shock of being shot through the sky on a flying ship. Rumpitter opened one eye and looked at Tom.

"Don't you go thinking it's over yet. The next bit is worse."

"What?" said Tom, and before he could say anything more, they saw the head of the golden bird at the bows begin to tilt downwards. Then, without any warning, *The Glaros* just fell out of the sky. It picked up speed again instantly and now they were falling down and down. The rat and the boy started screaming again as they were thrust forward. Almost at ninety degrees they fell out of the sky. Down and down they went. Tom felt the ropes pinching him tightly as he was thrown forward. He tried to put his arms behind him, around the mast, but the mast was so thick he couldn't get them all the way round. He thought he was going to slip right out of the rope. His fingers went white from gripping on so tightly and his arms began to ache. Rumpitter was hanging on for his life but suddenly he started to slip free from his rope. "Oh no, I'm going," he cried.

The rope loosened. Rumpitter was about to fly right out of the ship and fall to his death, but Tom managed to get one hand free and, just in time, he caught Rumpitter by his tail.

The ship kept on falling, twisting and turning as it swooped down and down. Tom was still hanging onto the mast with one arm and had the end of Rumpitter's tail in his free hand. "Help, don't let go Tom, I'm going to fall. Aaaagh," screamed the rat.

Tom, still gripping Rumpitter's tail, struggled to hold onto the mast. His fingers were slipping and his arms ached. Now it would be down to the rope to hold them. He prayed that the rope would hold. The speed with which they were dropping was terrifying. Then, below them they could see the ground. There were trees and open spaces. He saw the sea and then more land and trees. The ship began to twist and shake violently. *Hold on, you two*, came a voice. *We are almost there.* Mr Hawkins's voice was reassuring to Tom but still he couldn't see him.

"I don't think I can hold on any longer," Tom called. "Please do Tom, please do!" cried Rumpitter, who was now just dangling by his tail in Tom's hand.

Suddenly *The Glaros* levelled off. They saw the bows come back into sight and then turn upright and level to the ground, which had now gone out of sight again. They were flying parallel to the tops of trees, passing by them very quickly. The ship descended a little more. There was a hefty thump and a loud crash. Water splashed up into the air and then washed over both sides of the ship. Finally *The Glaros* settled and began to wallow up and down in the water. They had landed back in the sea, but it was clear to Tom that this was a different place. There was a different smell in the air. The sea was aqua blue and there were unusual sounds. Then he realised how hot it was. The sun was burning down on the deck.

At last, *The Glaros* finally came to rest on the water. Mr Hawkins swooped down from above, landing on the deck in front of the two shaken friends.

Rumpitter was so relieved to have survived the dreadful journey, and was beside himself with joy that he was still alive. "Oh thank-you, thank-you, Tom. You saved my life. I'll not forget that as long as I live."

"That's all right, Rumpitter, I thought I'd lost you forever," Tom replied. He too was shaken up.

"Are you two all right?" asked Mr Hawkins. "In future we must find a safer way to do this. I'm sorry if we scared you, Tom." The seagull pecked at the rope with his strong beak and the rope fell free from around Tom's waist. Tom tried to stand up. His legs were weak and his chest ached from the tight rope. He walked in a wobbly fashion to the side of the ship and saw the most amazing sight. They were in a beautiful lagoon of calm aqua blue water, and a beach with pure white sand was just a few yards away from the ship. There were millions of beautiful birds flying all around. At first the noise they made was almost deafening but after a while the screeching became quieter and then the birds just circled the ship, some dived into the water and others flew over the trees beyond the beach. It was a fantastic sight of colour and birds of all types and sizes. The sun beat down from the bright blue sky.

Tom checked his shirt, which had been torn by the rope and covered in salt from the sea spray during their dreadful journey.

Rumpitter made a speedy recovery and wobbled over to join Tom. Then Mr Hawkins flew up and circled the bay. He made a few circuits above them and then returned to the deck, landing beside the two recovering passengers. "Everyone feeling better now?" he asked. The two nodded. Tom was speechless and in complete awe of the scenery surrounding them.

"What is this place, Mr Hawkins, where are we?"

"This is a very special place; we are quite safe here. I call this place Heaven's Bay, because the first time I clapped my eyes on it I thought I had made it to heaven."

"Well, I for one am very pleased to be here at last. I really don't like travelling and especially like that," said Rumpitter in a rather grumpy tone of voice. Tom laughed at the rat as he wobbled around trying to get his legs back.

Tom turned to look all around him again and asked, "So – where are we then?"

"On a small island in the middle of the great ocean that divides your world from the Land of Fire," replied Mr Hawkins in a more serious tone. It was almost as if he were expecting to hear Tom complain when he said it.

"Oh boy, that means we are near that Saharadeen – I'm not sure I like the sound of this."

Rumpitter, now recovered, jumped up onto the rail where Tom was leaning over and looking across the bay to the shore. "Actually, Tom, the island is invisible to anyone from anywhere. That's why no-one can find it and that means no-one can find us," said Rumpitter.

"Aye, that is correct, Rumpitter, and this island has never been charted," said Mr Hawkins.

"So how come you found it and we can see it?" persisted Tom.

"Aha! You and your questions. It is no wonder you are a bright lad. You keep on asking questions and if you get good answers, you will learn much," laughed the seagull and then continued. "Let us just say that we can see it and I can find it because I knew about it in the first place, many years ago. I found this island quite by mistake when I was fleeing from the Saharadeen. Then I realised that it only can be seen if you have the power. It is all very strange Tom and, to be honest, even I do not really understand it. But I discovered that I can use this as the transit location between our worlds. You can see it because you have some of the powers that I have."

"I do?"

"Yes, you will learn much about all this in time, Tom. I have chosen you because of your integrity. You are a good person and I like you. Tom, you are about to learn the Golden Secret."

"I am?"

"Aye, but for now you must get out of the sun and into some fresh clothes, more befitting to where you are going. We will leave your own clothes somewhere safe for your return. We will also find you something to eat. In the middle of the day the sun is at its hottest so it is not safe to be out in it for long. The sun here is far hotter than in your world, so take care," said Mr Hawkins, again in one of his more serious voices.

Tom looked up into the bright blue sky and saw the sun blazing down. Then he saw something very strange. "Hold on a minute!" he said, still looking up. "There are stars in the sky, thousands of them."

"I wondered when you'd notice," replied Mr Hawkins.

"But stars don't shine in the day time."

"They do here. In this place, the stars shine both day and night. We call them the Navigator stars. They are particularly bright at night but useful in the day as there is always a yellow haze across the sea. This way the stars help us to navigate and find our way across the great ocean."

"Why is there a yellow haze?"

"It comes from the mountains of the Land of Fire. The Saharadeen has vast gold mines inside the great mountain. He rules the whole area. It is his evil kingdom. He never ventures to the islands because they cannot be seen from the land. Although he has many powers, he has not understood the real purpose of the stars. It was thanks to these stars that I was able to escape from the Land of Fire. It was, however, by sheer chance that I ventured into your time aboard *The Glaros.*"

"How did you get *The Glaros* after you had been turned into a seagull?" Tom asked curiously.

"I stole her back."

"But how could you if you are a bird..."

"A bird, you say? Yes, I am a bird, Tom, but not just any bird, eh? Oh, and this ship is not any old ship either." Captain Hawkins gave a little chuckle.

"That's incredible!" exclaimed Tom. He was about to carry on with his questions when he turned and saw Mr Hawkins fly along the deck towards the ship's stern and to an arched doorway. Then he paused to let Rumpitter catch up with him.

"Come, Tom, this way," called the seagull.

Tom jumped down from the rail and ran along the deck. As soon as his feet hit the wooden planking, he leapt up and then started hopping from one foot to the other. "Ouch, the deck's burning hot!" he called. There was no answer and he saw the seagull and the rat pass through the door. "Wait for me," called Tom as he hopped along the deck after them. He had lost both his shoes and it was a long hop to the rear of the ship. As he approached the door, he noticed how elegantly the entrance was decorated.

It had wooden carved arches painted in gold leaf. At the centre of the arch, above the doorway, there was a man's face, which had been beautifully carved in wood and again painted in gold. For a moment Tom studied the face. It looked kindly and had an important look about it. Tom decided that the carved face looked like an Arabian. He had seen faces like this in his history books. He looked up in awe at the noble face and then, as he started to walk through the doorway, the eyes on the face seemed to follow him and, for a moment, it looked like the face was smiling. Tom passed through the door and came to a stairway with rails on either side running down the stairs. They were carved in wood to look like thick rope. The rails were attached to the walls by gold brackets. These were large, golden bird's heads. The rails passed through the thick, hooked beaks of the birds all the way down to the bottom of the staircase. Tom had never in his life seen a sailing ship like this. The corridor at the bottom of the stairs was brightly lit by candle lamps, glowing from hanging crystal glass lanterns on either side of the fine polished teak-panelled walls. The ceiling was a beautiful mural painting of blue sky with white fluffy clouds. There were seagulls flying through the clouds. Tom smiled when he saw this and thought that Mr Hawkins might have had a hand in this.

As he looked around him in total wonder, he suddenly noticed that some of the panels in the walls were actually doors. They had small gold buttons in the shape of the crescent moon. He put his finger very gently on one of them and it immediately popped out on the end of a thin gold rod. Tom wasn't sure if he should have touched it but curiosity took the better of him and he turned the moon shaped door knob.

There was a click, which made him jump, and he quickly looked left then right to see if anyone was around. As soon as the handle clicked, the door began to open. Slowly he tried to stretch his neck around the door to see what was on the other side. At first he couldn't see anything but, as the door opened wider, he saw a light glowing from a room on the other side. He was nervous and wondered if he had done something wrong. Then he peered into the room. As he looked down he saw a fine red carpet with an array of patterns and shapes woven into it. Finally the door was now wide open and Tom carefully ventured in.

To his complete surprise he saw a fine wooden table with six elegant chairs placed around it. There was a warm glow from a beautiful candle-lit chandelier, which hung from the hand of a cherub, which had a gold chain attached from its back to the ceiling. There were twelve candles burning. Each one glowed from its own crystal glass bowl. He was completely stunned by the elegance of this room. The walls surrounding the room were beautifully carved mahogany panels; highly polished and supporting rows of shelves packed with leather bound books of various sizes and colours. He noticed a large red leather armchair. It was facing some drawn, red velvet curtains, which hung down to the floor. The back of the chair was facing Tom so he could not see it properly. He walked around the table in the centre of the room, skimming his fingers across the highly polished top. He walked over towards the curtains to see what was beyond them. Suddenly the large red leather chair swung around. Tom jumped out of his skin and then almost instantly sighed with relief when he saw Rumpitter sitting in the centre of the chair, wiping his whiskers with a paw.

"Ah there you are, I was wondering when you'd arrive. Well done, you found the library. We wondered which room you'd find first. Mr Hawkins was right. He said you'd come in here first. I wonder how he knew?"

"Rumpitter, you made me jump, I nearly had a heart attack!"

"Oh no, I don't think so Tom. I just surprised you that's all." Rumpitter stood up in the chair.

"This is amazing! Who does this ship really belong to?" Tom asked. Now he was feeling a little more relaxed.

"This is definitely *The Glaros* and it belongs to Mr Hawkins. Although, between you and me, he is really Captain Hawkins," said Rumpitter. He spoke with great respect for the seagull.

Rumpitter decided to change position from the chair and jumped up onto the table. As he did this he slid all the way along the table to the other side. He would have fallen off the end but managed to hold onto the edge with his claws and pulled himself back up. Tom couldn't control his laughter.

"I suppose you thought that was funny," said Rumpitter after composing himself.

"Oh Rumpitter, you do make me laugh." "Eh? Oh well, never mind. Now you get yourself over to that chest and open it." Rumpitter walked carefully back across the table and pointed with his nose.

Tom saw the large wooden chest and looked nervously at it. "Why, what's in it?" he asked.

He opened it slowly and then peered in. Inside the chest were some clothes. He pulled out a shirt. It was unlike any shirt he'd seen before. It was long, had a short, cut-off collar and wide floppy sleeves.

"Very good, now put it on and when you have done that, put on the trousers," said Rumpitter.

Tom did as he was asked and then pulled out the trousers. At first he thought they looked too short but after putting them on he found they fitted rather well. "It looks like I'm wearing pyjamas," Tom joked.

He saw a mirror set in a very thick, wooden frame hanging on the wall by the door and looked at himself. He giggled when he saw himself dressed in the strange clothes and wondered if these were clothes from many years ago. He tugged at the collar disapprovingly and Rumpitter chuckled as he watched Tom tie the trousers up at the front.

"Oh well, I suppose you'll get used to them eventually. OK, you'll do. Now put some shoes on and come with me," ordered the rat and then started towards the door.

"What shoes?" called Tom. "In the chest, oh and get the headscarf, you'll need that too," came the rat's answer. Rumpitter then disappeared through the door. Tom hurried to catch up. He leant into the chest and grabbed some strange leather shoes and an odd looking scarf, which had tassels on the end, and hopped after the rat, trying to put the shoes on as he ran. "Oh no, not again," he whispered to himself as he saw that the shoes also had straps which had to be tied. Then he looked even more puzzled when he saw the scarf. It was really large when he unfolded it. "I'm going to look ridiculous," he called out, as he ran through the door. He was just in time to see Rumpitter's tail disappear round another door at the end of the corridor.

"Rumpitter wait!" he called out and followed quickly, making it to the door just before it slammed shut. He put out his hand and pushed the door open. "Rumpitter, what are you..?" He paused and then stood in amazement with his mouth wide open.

"Oh my goodness!" he exclaimed. His eyes lit up when, to his utter astonishment, he saw the most fantastic sight. Right there before him was a beautiful table completely covered in food. There was just about everything there. A huge spread of roast chicken, great silver plates of fruit, cakes and buns of various colours, shapes and flavours, jugs of juices and a huge pink salmon dressed with citrus fruits and salads. There were biscuits and a huge wooden board full of different cheeses. He smiled when he saw Rumpitter sniffing over the cheese and then realised why the rat had been in such a hurry and laughed. At the head of the table Mr Hawkins was sitting on the back of another large red leather chair. The room was even more beautiful than the library. The ceiling was carved in fantastic patterns. In the centre of the ceiling hung another chandelier, but this one was gold and even bigger than the last. It had at least twenty candles burning from crystal glass holders. The light cast a sparkle all round the room and reflected shadows, which danced across the pictures of ancient faces of old sea captains on old oil paintings hanging from the panelled walls. There was also a fine teak sideboard with crystal glass decanters full of different drinks. Each drink was a different colour. Behind Mr Hawkins was a large window, which looked out across the lagoon, and the afternoon sunlight cast a bright light through the window and silhouetted the seagull. The whole picture was truly fantastic. Tom almost wept with joy. It wasn't until then that he realised how hungry he was. If this was just a dream, he thought, he never wanted it to end.

"Well Tom, lad, you look much more comfortable in those clothes," laughed the seagull and Rumpitter chuckled. "He'll get used to them Captain. Especially when he realises how useful they are where we are going," said the rat. They laughed and Tom began to drool at the sight of the spread on the table.

"Come Tom, take a seat. I know you are hungry and we thought you deserved a hearty meal before we begin our journey."

"Yes, yes, take a chair Tom," continued Rumpitter.

Tom walked round the great table and pulled out one of the dining chairs. It was a heavy framed solid oak chair with the two crossed swords carved into the back. All the chairs were identical and each arm had the head of a bird carved into the hand-rest at the end. Tom was careful not to pull the white linen tablecloth as he pulled out the chair. Rumpitter took a folded white linen napkin with his front paws and tied it round his neck. Tom couldn't believe his eyes. "How did you manage that?" he asked.

"Well, we must dress properly for dinner, mustn't we Captain?" Tom thought Rumpitter looked as though he was wearing a tent and laughed.

"Yes quite. Napkin, Tom?" Mr Hawkins pointed with his beak at the folded napkin on the table in front of Tom's empty silver plate.

Tom looked totally bemused. "Oh, yes. Right," he replied and unfolded the napkin and placed it under his chin. "Good, well let's say grace and get started, shall we?" Tom nodded although he wasn't sure what to do now. He just wanted to get stuck into the delicious food in front of him

Suddenly Mr Hawkins lifted his long neck up high and coughed. He then raised his wings and spoke: "May the good Lord make us forever grateful for what we have and keep us strong together." He spoke in a quiet tone. For a short moment all was quiet and then he said, "Right, let battle commence!" They all laughed and began to eat.

Tom didn't know where to begin but he started with two very large chicken drumsticks and poured himself a glass of ice cold lemon juice. "Oh boy, this is the greatest. No, Mr Hawkins, you're the greatest" he said in a loud voice and a mouth full of chicken and, again, they all laughed again.

The three companions ate, drank and were very merry for the rest of the afternoon. They talked about all sorts of things and occasionally Rumpitter and Mr Hawkins would speak quietly together and then continue eating and nodding happily at Tom, who just ate and ate. Every now and then he rested and looked around the room. He noticed the four giant oriental vases, one in each corner of the room. They were also made of gold and had red dragons painted on them. The paintings on the walls were exquisite and surrounded in carved gold-leaf frames. There was a beautiful brass sextant sitting on the windowsill and next to a shelf filled with books was a huge globe, which was fixed to a mahogany frame. There were long royal blue velvet curtains draped down to the floor on either side of the window. He had never seen a ship like this before. He thought of his father and wondered what he would think of this. *He would be amazed* Tom thought to himself.

"Indeed he would Tom." Mr Hawkins had heard Tom's thoughts. Tom looked surprised.

"Can you hear everything, Mr Hawkins?" he asked. "Well, there is not much I miss. Let's put it that way," the seagull replied.

Tom looked at Mr Hawkins in astonishment as the seagull picked a large slice of salmon from the long silver platter with his beak and placed it neatly on the plate in front of him. Then he took a piece of lime from the side of the platter and, with his beak, squeezed the lime over the slice of fish. When he had completed this, he took the fish up and swallowed it whole. Tom sat with his mouth wide open as the large lump in the seagull's neck gradually slithered down until it vanished.

"Ah – my absolute favourite," said Mr Hawkins with a sigh of pleasure.

"How do you do that? Doesn't it hurt?" asked Tom.

"Of course not! I enjoyed this meal when I was a man and I love it even more now," laughed the seagull.

"And a good thing too, it's just about the only thing you do eat, Captain," said Rumpitter with a huge piece of cheese in his mouth. The three laughed again.

Tom ate as much as he could and his stomach ached from all the food he had stuffed into it. He eventually began to feel very sleepy.

Mr Hawkins and Rumpitter looked affectionately at the boy as he slowly slid back in his chair and began to nod off. As his eyes fell shut, his head hit the back of his chair and the scarf, which Tom had hung on the back of the chair, fell over his head and covered his eyes. He fell into a deep sleep.

The seagull and the rat slipped quietly out of the room leaving Tom to rest. It was going to be a long night and he needed all the sleep he could get. They left him alone for several hours.

In another room, the seagull spoke quietly and looked out of the porthole, while the rat curled up on a chair and listened.

"We must make our way to the caves before dark," said Mr Hawkins.

"Yes, I agree, will you call our friend?"

"Aye, I shall do just that." Then the seagull looked up into the sky and opened his crescent eye to the moon. There was a long moment of silence until he spoke again. "Well, that should do it," said the seagull as he turned to look at Rumpitter, who had dozed off.

*Hmm* thought Mr Hawkins. He decided to leave him for a while. There was no point in waking him just yet. Mr Hawkins looked out again through the round cabin window and watched as the sun slowly fell down behind the hills beyond the bay. It left a beautiful red sunset, which turned the trees on the western shore into a deep purple and red colour. It was magnificent. He sighed as he watched the sunset.

All the life and sounds from the jungle had died away, leaving a quiet stillness in the air. Nothing moved. There was not a breath of wind. It was going to be a very warm night – in more ways than one.

Mr Hawkins pushed open the window and hopped out onto a ledge, then gave a flap and lifted up into the still red sky. He flew up high above the masts of *The Glaros*, circling around and around. The blue water of the lagoon had turned into a midnight black; nothing moved anywhere. Nothing – except a long dark shadow moving under the surface of the water, very slowly towards the ship. It circled around for a while and then came close to the hull.

Suddenly there was a hefty crashing sound and the ship rolled to one side. The ship's booms swung from side to side. Chairs slid across the deck, and a gold candlestick fell over onto the floor waking Rumpitter very abruptly. "What on earth...?" Then he quickly ran out of the cabin, along the corridor, hopped up the stairs and finally onto the deck. *Oh my goodness, he's here already* he said to himself and then quickly ran back down the stairs and into the dining room.

The ship took another huge thump from the side and rolled again, even more violently than the first time. This time Tom was shaken from his deep sleep and his chair fell over.

Just as he tried to pull himself up out of the fallen chair, the door swung open and Rumpitter ran in. The ship was rolling heavily from one side to the next and all the plates, food, bottles of drink, candles and cups slid off the table and were sent crashing to the floor. The noise was deafening. Tom was still only half awake. It was a terrifying noise and made even worse by the sudden appearance of a huge wave which washed right up to the window and poured into the room. The salty water rolled across the floor up to Tom' knees. Rumpitter jumped up onto the table to avoid the wash and the table slid across the floor. "Tom, watch out – the table!" he cried. Tom looked up sleepily and saw the huge table sliding towards him. He leapt out of the way just in time and the table crashed into the wall.

"Rumpitter, where are you?"

"Over here Tom, quick we must go – look out!" Another chair was sliding rapidly towards him in the wash from the sea water, which was slopping around in the room. This time Tom wasn't so quick and the chair crashed into him and trapped him into the corner. Tom pushed the chair away and crawled towards the door. Rumpitter was hanging onto the table top, swinging from his front paws. Tom saw him. "What's happening, are we sinking?"

"I hope not. We just left the window open," replied the rat, who had managed to escape the next wash of water by jumping from the table onto Tom's back. "Come on Tom, let's get out of here." Tom splashed through the door and up onto the deck. He saw that the day was now night and looked at the dying sunset. "Wow, look at that sunset!"

"Yes, yes, it's lovely – now come on over to the rails. Look, there's Mr Hawkins."

Mr Hawkins was standing on the ship's rail looking down into the water.

Tom, with the rat on his shoulder, ran over and joined the seagull. "Aha there you are.

Well rested, I trust, Tom?"

"Er, yes thanks, but what's happening?"

"Look down there." Mr Hawkins pointed with his beak towards the water and Tom leaned over. What he saw made him jump back in complete astonishment.

"What's that?" he asked as he stood well away from the rails.

"That, my friend, is Kahuluna. He has come a long way and is very excited about seeing me again. He's an old friend, but I'm afraid he gets a bit excited and sometimes clumsy."

"But that is a very large and, if you don't mind me saying, strange-looking fish."

"Oh yes, you will not have seen anything like this in your world Tom but then you will see many things you will not have seen before. Don't worry; Kahuluna is harmless, just a little excitable sometimes."

"Excited? He nearly sank *The Glaros*!" replied Rumpitter.

Tom walked slowly back to the rail and peered over carefully. Kahuluna was as big as the ship and at least half as wide. It had a huge head, nothing like any ordinary fish, with great big eyes, which peered up at Tom. The eyes were a watery grey and followed Tom's head as he looked up and down the length of the giant fish. It had two huge fins rising up out of its back, each at least six feet high. At the rear end, its tail fin was like a whale's and was splashing up and down in the water. It was this that had caused the ship to heave and roll from side to side.

After a while Tom looked back at Mr Hawkins. "What kind of fish is this, Mr Hawkins; I've never seen anything like it?"

"As I said, Tom, you will not have seen anything like Kahuluna. He actually comes from another region, thousands of miles away, but he can swim as fast as lightening and with great skill. Kahuluna is to be our transport for the next part of our journey."

Rumpitter was looking anxious and ran up and down the rail. The seagull hovered above them and called down, "Come, we have no time to lose, climb down the rope, Tom, and hold onto the fin. You will be quite safe. He is an old friend and is very friendly"

Tom obediently followed instructions. He grabbed hold of the rope and slid down onto the back of the large fish. As he landed, the fish gently bobbed down and then up again. Tom found a place to sit astride its rough leathery back. He wrapped his large scarf around his head and then grabbed hold of the huge fin, folding both his arms around it. "Come on, I'll catch you," he called, looking up at the rat, who was still prancing back and forth along the rail. "Jump Rumpitter, you have done this before. Tom will catch you this time," called Mr Hawkins. Suddenly the rat leapt off the rail. He landed right on Tom's lap and was about to slide off into the water when Tom caught him by the tail and pulled him up. "Got you!" said Tom with a smile.

Rumpitter looked up at Tom. "Thanks, that was a good catch, but please don't hold my tail, I hate that." The rat then quickly ducked under Tom's shirt and re-appeared with his head sticking out of the top. "Hey, you're scratching me," shouted Tom. "Careful!"

"Sorry. Do you mind if I stay here?" asked Rumpitter.

"OK, but just keep still. You've got very sharp nails."

The seagull laughed at the two companions struggling to stay still on the fish's back. Then when he could see they were settled he whisked over their heads and settled on Kahuluna's head.

"Right, my good friend, it is time to go," he ordered. Without any further ado, the fish lurched forward causing Tom and Rumpitter to jolt backwards. Tom hung onto the huge fin as they began to move through the water. In no time at all, they were rapidly moving across the water with a wash of salty spray spreading out from both sides.

"Wow!" Tom called out. "This is great."

They travelled through the water at an incredible speed and soon *The Glaros* was out of sight.

As they sped through the water, tiny sparkles of phosphorous glittered over the sea. The giant fish ploughed with ease through every wave they met. It was the oddest thing, thought Tom, to be riding on the back of a giant fish with a seagull and a rat who was keeping dry inside his shirt. The oddest thing indeed. Rumpitter would occasionally slip down Tom's shirt and then scramble up his chest again to peer out from the top, his eyes wide open. Then he would look up at Tom for reassurance. Tom would laugh and say, "You're so brave, Rumpitter, what would I do without you?"

"Very funny," replied the rat.

They moved on through the water and occasionally Mr Hawkins would fly up into the night sky to see where they were and then swoop back down. Eventually he called back to Tom and Rumpitter, "Nearly there, soon we will be at the caves, you must prepare yourself, Rumpitter."

"Yes boss," replied the rat.

They had been riding on the back of Kahuluna for nearly an hour when eventually Tom could see a shape ahead of them on the horizon and called to Mr Hawkins. "What's that over there?"

"Our landing place, Tom," replied the seagull. "We will be ashore any minute now."

The caves came closer and closer and Tom could now make out the jagged rock formations along the coast. There was no beach, just high cliffs and rocks. It looked a formidable place. He also noticed how warm it was even though it was late at night and they were at sea.

The giant fish began to slow down as they approached some sharp black rocks ahead of them. This was an eerie place and Tom felt uneasy. They moved quietly and slowly through the water. None of the companions said a single word as they passed under jagged rocks above, into the mouth of a great cavern. The wash of the waves splashing against the rocks echoed around them as they entered. It was dark at first but they quickly became accustomed to it and saw strange markings on the walls of the huge cave. Tom was the first to speak, but only in a whisper, "Where are we now Mr Hawkins?"

*Shh, Tom, we must remain silent until we are through.* Mr Hawkins spoke without words, which reminded Tom that if he needed to speak, it should be only this way. Tom nodded back to show he understood. Rumpitter just peered out from the top of Tom's shirt, his dark brown eyes staring up at the strange green flashes of light dancing across the roof of the cave.

Tom spoke again, but this time without words. *Look at those faces on the ceiling. What are they?*

Mr Hawkins hopped along Kahuluna's back, towards Tom. *They are carvings made thousands of years ago. No-one really knows what they mean but some say that they are the ghosts of doomed sailors who dared to enter this place and have been trapped here for all eternity.* He saw Tom was worried. *Do not worry yourself, Tom; we will be safe, you will soon see.*

Tom didn't reply but just stared all around him and held on tight to Kahuluna's fin as they continued deep into the cave.

After a short while the giant fish slowed down and drifted towards a ledge, which lay just a few inches above the water. Suddenly, without any warning, Rumpitter scrambled out from under Tom's shirt and jumped onto the ledge. He shook himself and then hopped up onto a low wall and then disappeared. Tom asked, *Where is he going?*

*To call our friends* replied Mr Hawkins. *What friends?* Tom asked again.

*You will see. Now, my young friend, it is time to leave Kahuluna and continue our journey on foot.*

Tom looked into the huge eyes of the giant fish and then at Mr Hawkins, who seemed to be whispering to the fish. Then the bird hopped up onto the ledge and instructed Tom to do the same.

Tom looked at the fish's eyes again and whispered, "Thank-you Kahuluna." The fish bowed his giant head into the water and waved with one of his huge fins. The fish slowly turned around and swam back out towards the entrance of the cave. Tom stood watching as Kahuluna disappeared into the night.

Mr Hawkins was standing on a small rock above Tom and whispered, *follow me Tom.*

Tom followed as the seagull hopped from rock to rock along a slippery passage of smooth, grey rock. *Watch your step Tom it's going to be a little slippery for a while* said Mr Hawkins without words. Tom ran along behind. Strangely, he did not feel tired or scared or even gave another thought about this strange place, but just kept on following his friend. After a while the ground became less treacherous and eventually they were running along a flat, dry floor of smooth stone. Mr Hawkins flew just a foot above the floor, darting from left to right at every bend in the passage, and Tom thought how wonderful it must be to be able to do that.

The passage grew wider and wider. It appeared to be getting lighter and eventually Tom could see quite well. He noticed that there were many passages leading off from left to right, but still they continued straight ahead. Suddenly Mr Hawkins stopped and settled on a shelf. *Wait now Tom, come a little closer, but easy now.* He turned to see if Tom was with him. Tom stopped running and crept up slowly and carefully beside the seagull. *Look down there, Tom.*

They peered over the ledge in front of them and saw a glow of light. Tom looked down towards the light. At first he couldn't see anything and then he saw a vast opening, several feet below. There was another huge cavern and a glow of light shone down from above. Something below didn't look right. It looked as though the floor was moving. Tom rubbed his eyes and looked again.

Then, when he saw what it was, he jumped back in shock. "Oh no!" he wanted to shout but knew he couldn't.

*Rats!* he whispered to himself in horror. *Mr Hawkins, there are millions of them!*

*Aye Tom, and look over there on that ledge, who can you see?* Again Tom peered over and then saw Rumpitter high above the mass of rats, which covered the entire floor of the huge cave below. It was an impressive sight. Rumpitter was standing alone on a single rock. He was so much larger than all the others and was looking down upon the sea of rats.

Rumpitter was hopping up and down and it appeared that he was communicating in some way to all the others. They were all listening and then, as if by some invisible command, in an instant, all of them stopped moving. Then they grouped together in straight lines, one row behind another until, there were literally thousands of rats standing in files, like military columns. This was an enormous army of rats. Rumpitter was their leader and they were listening to him. Although no words were spoken, it seemed that they knew what he was saying. Then, Rumpitter hopped up onto a much higher ledge of rock and with his head he pointed up to where Mr Hawkins and Tom were standing. The vast army of rats all turned together and looked up at the seagull and the boy. *Oh no, they've seen us, let's get out of here* Tom thought. Mr Hawkins hopped down in front of him. *No Tom, don't worry, they are on our side. Come and see.* Mr Hawkins jumped off the rock, glided down and hovered above the vast army of rats and then circled around them, finally settling down beside Rumpitter. Tom heard Mr Hawkins' voice. *Come down Tom, there is nothing to fear, I assure you.*

Tom was uneasy about this but carefully put one foot before the other and gingerly picked his way down into the huge cavern below. The massive army of rats stood perfectly still in silence and watched him slowly walk towards them. As Tom drew nearer, there was a sudden shuffle and a whole column of the rats moved simultaneously to one side to let him pass. Tom kept his eyes firmly on them. Their heads all turned to follow him as he moved through the columns towards the rock where Rumpitter and the seagull waited. The walk seemed like an eternity to Tom, but finally he arrived at the rock and then very quickly scrambled up onto it to stand with his two companions. It wasn't until then that he could see just how many there were. There were millions of them! It was horrifying, and yet, in its way, quite impressive.

Rumpitter jumped up onto another ledge just above them and gave a short, sharp squeak and stood on his hind legs as he did so. Then Tom heard Mr Hawkins's words in his head again. This time he was addressing the great rat army.

*Friends, 'tis good we meet again.* There was a pause and then thousands of rats nodded their heads up and down in approval and agreement. *This is Tom Parker, he is my friend. He is here to help us in our mission. Rumpitter has given you all your instructions. Follow him. Do as we have agreed and we shall be victorious.* There was more movement from the army below. They looked impatient and were ready to move as soon as the order was given. *Our friends, my comrades, are captives of the Saharadeen. We must rescue them from the caves of the Temple of Fire. They will be locked in the dark cells down in the deepest parts of the mountain. If possible, the Saharadeen himself must be brought to me. I have waited many years for this time. We must succeed!*

There was a chorus of raucous shrieks and squeals from the rats and then Rumpitter stood upon his hind legs again to give an order and instantly the rats fell silent. Tom was stunned and amazed. Mr Hawkins looked to Tom, *Come closer Tom, take this and put it around your neck. It will keep you safe for now. You must guard it closely. You know how important it is.* Tom nodded and took the small bag from around the seagull's neck and hung it around his own. *Don't worry Mr Hawkins, I'll look after it.*

The seagull nodded his head. *Good, now let us make way. Follow Rumpitter, Tom.*

*Right* Tom replied eagerly, although he was really not sure exactly what he was supposed to do. Suddenly Rumpitter ran through Tom's feet and down into the army of rats. *Come on Tom, follow me. Keep up now, do you hear?* Rumpitter had almost disappeared into the mass of rats but then they parted just enough for Tom to see Rumpitter galloping through them towards what looked like a small gap in the cave wall. *Wait!* Tom called out as he chased after him, trying not to step on the rats, who obediently stood still just long enough to let him through. As soon as Tom had passed, the rats turned and followed on. Tom caught up with Rumpitter, who had paused to wait for him. As they approached the gap in the wall, the rats were suddenly given another order from Rumpitter and they darted through thousands of tiny holes in the cave wall. Tom hadn't even noticed the holes. As Tom and Rumpitter slipped through the gap, literally thousands of rats suddenly appeared, running along ledges above them and beside them on the left and the right. They moved at great speed but without a sound. Tom was now running right behind Rumpitter and side by side with the rats. He tried to look back to find Mr Hawkins but he couldn't see him. The gap they had passed through was now out of sight and all he could see were thousands of rats darting up and down and along ledges. He just kept on running after Rumpitter. He did not feel tired or out of breath and felt a strange sense of power in him, as if he could run at this fast speed forever. He called Rumpitter without words, *Where's Mr Hawkins?*

*Don't worry about him, he'll show up soon, you'll see. Come Tom, we must hurry.*

*What's the rush for?* Tom called back.

*We must get to the Temple of Fire before the sun comes up.*

*Why?*

*Because the Saharadeen sends the prisoners then to the mines and we must find our friends before they go. It would be hard to find them in the mines and the Saharadeen's soldiers will be everywhere.*

*Soldiers! But what about the Saharadeen?* Asked Tom, still running closely behind.

*I don't know.* Rumpitter replied.

*Oh, great!* Said Tom.

Tom tried to recall the story Mr Hawkins had told him about the Saharadeen and the temple and how he and his men had been caught by his evil powers. He was not sure how this was going to end now they were actually here. He looked down at the small bag hanging around his neck and saw it was glowing. He touched it and the glow grew brighter.

They ran and ran through one passage after another. It seemed endless and then, just as he thought this, he noticed Rumpitter was slowing down and so too were all the rats. Eventually they stopped. He could see a light shining from ahead and stepped closer to Rumpitter.

"Are we there?" he whispered. "Yes," replied Rumpitter. "Now we must move carefully, not a sound now." The army of rats moved as a mass, in silence, towards the opening before them.

Tom saw a tall arch with a huge iron gate. There were several dark figures, dressed in long black robes. Their heads were completely bald. They appeared to be standing to attention by the gate. Then he saw their weapons. They held tall lances with long jagged blades at the end. Long, curved swords hung from their leather belts. The men were at least seven feet tall. They looked frighteningly dangerous.

Without words, Tom asked, *what do we do now?*

*Don't look* replied Rumpitter.

Rumpitter nodded to a group of about a hundred or so of the rats which had formed just above them on a ledge. Suddenly, without any further need of an order, the rats charged in complete silence at the guards at the gate. They scrambled through the bars and, in a deadly attack, swarmed over the soldiers and brought them down. It was all so quick and carried out with great efficiency. It was a deathly moment. Tom couldn't bear to watch and covered his eyes. When he finally uncovered them, the soldiers had vanished. *What happened?* Tom asked Rumpitter, who was standing still and completely unmoved. *Don't ask* he replied.

Then, one of the rats came back to them. In his mouth was a large key. He dropped it on the ground in front of Tom. *Pick up the key, Tom, and open the gate* said Rumpitter.

Tom did as he was instructed. It was hard to turn the heavy lock, but finally, after two attempts, he managed it and the huge gate swung open. Immediately, the army of rats charged through. They formed into different groups. Three groups formed a cover around Tom as he walked through. *They will be your bodyguard, Tom. They won't let you out of their sight* said Rumpitter reassuringly. *You must guard the Stone with your life, Tom. It is the key to our success.*

*I'll keep it safe, I promise* Tom replied and looked around him. Running on the ground and along the walls were his own personal guard.

Rumpitter spoke without words. *We are now in one of the main corridors leading to the cells. There will be more soldiers, so take care. Keep close. Right, let's go.*

Again the sea of rats surged through the corridor. As they came to a bend, they were met by another group of soldiers, who were completely taken unawares by the vast army of rats. Before they could let out a cry of help or sound an alarm, they were swept off their feet and dragged away. *Keep moving Tom, we will soon be there.* Tom saw a sword lying on the floor and picked it up. It seemed heavy at first but then, oddly, it felt like nothing in his hand. As they ran through the corridor he swung it around. He caught it against the wall and it bounced away and just missed Rumpitter.

*Hey, careful with that, I'm on your side, remember?*

*Sorry.*

They came to a wide room with wooden chairs on either side against the walls. There were more soldiers asleep on the floor on straw mats. Their weapons lay beside them. They were completely oblivious to the huge army of rats that was passing through.

Along the walls there were wooden doors with small barred windows. The rats darted up into the windows and then came back. Some found a way in under the doors and then reappeared through a crack or a hole.

*What are they doing now?* Tom asked.

*Looking for our friends. They must be here somewhere. I do hope they are alive.*

*If they have been locked up here for three years… how would we know?* Tom said, looking through the gap in an old doorway.

*We must remain positive Tom, but this is a dreadful place; not many men survive the perils of  the mines or the evil of  the Saharadeen. Three years in this place is like an eternity.*

Tom felt a lump in his throat and swallowed at the thought of it. There was an odd smell. Was it something burning? He could not tell. There was also a musty odour, like something rotting. Fire torches hung from the walls and the smoke from them hung in the air like a low cloud. It was a very unpleasant place indeed.

Tom was surprised to note that his feet were hardly touching the floor as he ran. He was running without any sound at all. He was beginning to feel like a warrior himself, leading his army. His confidence grew stronger by the second.

Rumpitter lead them on through passage after passage until eventually they came to a great hall with carved arches and further corridors leading off  in every direction. Rumpitter gave the order and they all paused and then waited.

# Chapter 8 – City of Fire

High above the vast dome of the Temple of Fire, up in the darkness of the blackest of nights, a seagull circled round and round, then dropped out of the night, swooping down onto the top of the dome. He darted from window to window, then down to the high stone walls, hovering at every window and door. He flew up high again and then dived further down into the very heart of the City of Fire.

Tall, dark buildings with pointed arches and enormous wooden doors and windows covered in carvings of snakes and faces of demons lined every street. The seagull settled on a roof high above the city square. He watched every movement and studied his surroundings carefully.

The city was alive with soldiers and people massing together. There were horsemen galloping through the streets, dressed in dark robes, waving their swords in the air. Then great columns of foot soldiers marched through the wide streets of the city, dressed in tribal costumes, some in black and some in white. Their gold head-dresses and the crossed serpents on their shields showed the mark of the Saharadeen army. Women danced around the fires which lined the streets and squares, dressed in black robes with veils covering their faces. They wailed and swayed, waving their arms above their heads to the rhythm of tribal drummers who pounded on their huge drums as they marched into the main square. The vibrations shook the whole city.

This was the City of Fire, the home of the Saharadeen and his evil army.

Mr Hawkins knew something was about to happen. The chanting and deafening roar of the massive army was enough for him to realise this was no ordinary time. Something was about to happen. What had he missed since he had been away? What was happening? The soldiers who were not marching were lining the wide streets, pushing people back against the stone walls. They appeared to be clearing a path for someone or something to pass.

The chanting and swaying of thousands of people and soldiers to the rhythm of the drum beat thundered across the entire city. The huge army of the Saharadeen was massing together before his very eyes. He saw the great pillars of the Temple of Fire. They towered above the square and over the whole city. Tall poles with fire torches flickered all around. The shadows from the flames flickered and danced on the high, stone grey walls surrounding the city. The smell of burning embers was choking the city.

The darkness from outside the city was no longer visible as the fires prevented sight beyond the city walls. He knew that in a short while, something would happen. The city was alive and something terrible and evil was about to take place.

He thought for a moment about his friends. Had they reached the lower gates? He needed to locate the gates of the dungeon and find the holder of the keys. The seagull swirled around, flying from corner to corner, street to street, building to building. He darted, hovered and swooped in and out of the lights. No-one saw him. He was fast and stealthy. He needed to find the key-holder to the dungeons fast and get to his friends before it was too late. Suddenly there was a loud blast of horns and the crowds in the streets began to move into straight lines, leaving a clear, wide space in the centre. The chanting and swaying of the wailing women grew louder and more intense. Suddenly the huge gates of the temple began to open and four chariots, driven by soldiers dressed in white and gold, appeared from the opening and charged into the square. The chariot drivers lashed out with their whips at anyone who got in their way.

Then another fanfare of horns blasted out across the city and the huge crowd drew back in awe as a large chariot, cast in gold and driven by three giant warriors of the Saharadeen army, appeared between the huge gates and entered the city square. In the centre of the chariot, standing tall and proud, dressed in his famous gold and black robes, was the Saharadeen himself. The crowds were beside themselves, chanting and praising him and swaying to the rhythm of the drummers, as the four black horses pulled his chariot past the columns of soldiers and through the crowds surrounding the square. Instantly, Mr Hawkins saw the Sword of Isis hanging by the Saharadeen's side and his blood began to boil. He wanted that sword. He wanted the man who was wearing it!

Within a few moments another column of Saharadeen foot soldiers ran in straight lines behind the chariot. They were followed by the Saharadeen's special guard. They were the fiercest of all his soldiers. They were called the Dark Army, known for their deathly attacks at night; moving in silence, unseen and unheard, they could destroy a whole city without a trace.

They charged into the huge square riding their black Arab horses. There were hundreds of them pouring through the gates. Soon the massive Saharadeen army was assembling in front of Mr Hawkins's eyes. He couldn't believe what he was seeing. What was happening? Why was such an army assembling like this? His thoughts were mixed and he was confused. But he had to focus on why they were there. Rescue the men, get the sword and get away. That was the mission and he hoped that Tom, Rumpitter and their friends would be able to carry out their task amongst such formidable odds. The army was enormous. Even more soldiers poured through the gates into the huge square. There were thousands of them.

It was not going to be easy with such a massive enemy around to get the men out of the dungeons. He worried about Tom and hoped that Rumpitter would keep a safe eye on him until he returned. He had not planned for what was unfolding before his eyes.

Mr Hawkins trained his sharp eyes on the matter at hand and searched the scene from his position high on the battlements. He scanned the streets and alleys. He looked deep into the crowds, through doorways and windows of tall buildings until he could find something that would lead him to what he needed. Tom, Rumpitter and the other rats would not remain unseen for long. The Saharadeen's army was growing, as more and more soldiers from every part of the desert charged though the huge city gates. They were massing together to hear the great Saharadeen, the thief of the world and the ruler of evil; speak for the first time in three years. They were preparing for war. But with whom?

Suddenly, Mr Hawkins turned as he heard a sound somewhere in the distance and swooped down amongst the rooftops to find where it came from.

His unique hearing had alerted him to the sound of clanking chains and the hammer of metal against metal. Then he heard voices; he settled on a roof and listened. His head tilted down to the street below and the voices came nearer. They were the city guards of the Saharadeen. He instantly knew their strange language. As they appeared out of the shadow of a large door, he immediately recognised two of the men. They were the head jailers, and one of them had keys hanging from his belt, and they would be the keys to the dark pits where he was once imprisoned. He thought of his old comrades. *They must be beyond that door* he thought to himself. *I must get those keys.*

He spoke to Rumpitter without words. *Rumpitter, are you all assembled? Yes, we are all ready.*

*Good, I have located the entrance to the dungeons, but beware there are many soldiers. The whole city is alive with Saharadeen's army. Something terrible is about to happen. I do believe they mean to start a war but I am uncertain why or who with. We must move fast. This is a very dangerous place to be. But I have a plan. You must stay there and keep silent. Do not be seen by anyone, do you understand?*

*Perfectly* replied Rumpitter who carefully turned his eye to Tom who was looking very bold with the sword he'd picked up. The stone around his neck was working and its power had given Tom great courage. Rumpitter knew this could be disastrous unless great care was taken. He was just a boy in a very strange world where bad and dangerous things happen.

*Rumpitter, I will make my move then you must take Tom and find our friends. Look for my signal. What is unfolding here has been expected, but I just hope we have made it back in time to rescue our comrades. I fear we may be too late, but we must continue – do you understand?*

*I understand, Captain Hawkins.* Replied Rumpitter.

Mr Hawkins watched as the soldiers walked out of the shadows into a courtyard. He could see more clearly now as the men stood under the light of a large torch. The men grouped around the fire and were laughing and babbling away to each other in their strange tongue. At the far end of the courtyard was a large, round, wooden building with a straw roof. Light flickered from some of the windows. He listened and heard more voices. The soldiers in the courtyard were now walking towards the round building. Suddenly a door burst open and a soldier appeared. There was a loud blast of noise from within the building as he opened the door. He shouted something to the soldiers walking towards him. There was a reply from the tall guard with the keys and they continued towards the doorway, which was now wide open. Now Mr Hawkins could see through the doorway. There were many soldiers inside, sitting on wooden benches. He heard the loud chatter and bustle and then he smelt something. He realised what this building was. This was the soldiers' eating quarters. He could smell their spicy food and the foul wine that they were drinking. As the soldiers in the square approached the door, they exchanged greetings with the guard and went inside. Mr Hawkins watched. Then he smiled to himself. They had left the door wide open and he now had a clear view of everything going on inside. He found a lower position on a pillar just above the building and observed for a short while. He must not lose sight of the man with the keys. He swooped down lower and settled by a window. The crescent moon eye blinked and he focused on the keys dangling from the belt. Then on a bench with several others, the key-holder hammered on the table with the hilt of his dagger and shouted something. Within seconds a lowly figure came scuttling up to the table with his head bowed. He brought them plates of food and drinks on a metal tray. The head soldier smacked the small man over his head with a fist and the wretched servant scurried away backwards, bowing as he went.

The soldiers took off their weapon belts and laid their swords upon the table. Mr Hawkins fixed his crescent eyes on the keys and then, as if by some miracle, the soldier took them off his belt and laid them on the table. Mr Hawkins smiled again. *Excellent!* he thought.

His eyes scanned the room, which was bright with fire-lights and candles.

He focused one crescent eye on a lantern, which hung just below the straw roof from an old wooden beam. A ray of gold light shone from the crescent moon eye directly to the hanging lamp. The candle inside flickered and then the lamp began to swing, as if being blown by the wind.

The lamp swung higher and higher over the men seated around the tables. The candle drew closer and closer to the straw roof just above it. Mr Hawkins continued to focus his eye on the lamp and his eye grew brighter. A strange breeze swirled just around the lamp. Still no-one noticed. Then, finally, it happened. The flame from the candle caught the straw hanging from the ceiling. At first, just a little, but then eventually it caught properly and the flame ate into the straw. After only a few seconds the ceiling was alight. It would only be moments before the soldiers realised. Mr Hawkins prepared himself and took up his position on the window ledge just inside the room.

The flames lapped away for a few moments and then smoke began to billow and suddenly the ceiling was ablaze. A shout came from one of the guards. Then a babbled cry from another and instantly soldiers were running towards the fire, which had now covered the whole roof. The building was ablaze. The head soldier jumped up screaming at the others to do something. He picked up his cup of wine and threw it towards the ceiling as if this was going to stop the blaze, which was now engulfing the room in smoke. The soldier turned away from the table for a split second. There was a flash of gold light and suddenly the keys had gone. The soldiers were falling over themselves to escape from the building. They poured out into the courtyard and more soldiers appeared from doorways and passages all around the city. The head man turned to the table and let out a scream of fury. He raised his fists and shouted in anger. The keys had gone. He turned to escape and as he tried to jump over the lowly servant, a huge wooden beam, covered in flames, fell from the ceiling and sent him crashing to the floor. He was trapped; no-one tried to help him.

Meanwhile, as Tom and the rats waited in silence in the great hall, Rumpitter was giving his instructions. He described the men they were to rescue in detail allowing for the fact that they may be thin and weak. After three years as slaves in this place, they would have changed considerably.

Tom was told that most of the slaves would have been from African and Asian regions. It was unlikely that there would be many white faces here. But they were to free all the slaves while freeing Mr Hawkins' comrades. Tom was told to look up to the ceiling of the dome, where a number of small windows opened out to the sky. "Keep your eyes firmly up there, Tom. Look to the top of the dome, he will come. This I promise."

"OK Rumpitter, I'll be watching," Tom replied.

The seagull swooped in and out of the shadows, darting from roof to roof. Finally, he settled on top of a huge domed roof above the great hall. He had the bunch of keys in his beak.

He spoke without words. *Rumpitter, are you ready?*

*Yes Captain, ready* he replied and turned to Tom. "Tom, get ready to catch the keys, they will drop from up there."

Tom looked up again and then saw something moving. It was Mr Hawkins. Suddenly one of the small windows in the dome flipped open and something dropped down. He ran underneath the falling keys. He had to catch them before they hit the floor. If he didn't catch the keys, the noise of them hitting the stone floor would alert the Saharadeen's men. The keys fell quickly. Tom stumbled as he darted to get underneath, but somehow kept his footing. He dived with both hands stretched out as far as they would reach. The keys came down into his hands just an inch from the floor. *Great catch!* Tom whispered to himself, the sweat pouring from his brow. *Phew, that was close.*

Rumpitter ran to Tom. *Well done, come on, let's get going. Follow me.*

The huge army of rats moved in silence across the floor to follow Rumpitter and Tom towards the wooden doors.

Meanwhile, Mr Hawkins was trying to find out what was going on outside. He was also keeping his eyes open for the jailers. It wouldn't be long before they realised the guard with the keys was missing.

Tom and Rumpitter were the first to reach the massive doors to the dungeons.

*Now Tom, let's not waste any time, open the doors, but quietly now"* said Rumpitter, twitching his nose from side to side.

Tom sorted out the keys: there were four of them and not knowing which one was the right one, he systematically tried them all. Finally he slipped in the fourth key. The key clanked inside the lock and one of the doors moved. "It's opened!" Tom whispered.

"Good," replied Rumpitter, "now push on, Tom. There's no time to lose."

Tom put one shoulder to the door but it was too heavy. Instantly all the rats realised he was struggling and ran up to it and put all their weight against it. Some of the rats fell over each other as they scrambled to push the door. Gradually the door began to move again and then more rats joined in. Finally it opened just enough to see inside.

Before Tom could say a word, hundreds of the rats charged through, some still pushing the door to open it further.

Tom nearly trod on a few as they slipped under his feet and scuttled past into the chamber beyond.

Tom managed to step through the door and into the chamber. He was about to run on with the rats when Rumpitter called him without speaking, *Tom, take the key out of the lock.*

*Oh, yes, of course, sorry.*

At last they were all inside. Tom and some of the rats slowly pushed the door shut again.

In front of them was a huge chamber with a high vaulted ceiling. There were corridors leading off in different directions with doors on both sides. It was an unpleasant, dark and damp place. Tom wondered who, in their right mind, would enjoy being here.

"Where now, Rumpitter?" Tom asked, looking from left and right.

"Straight on, follow me." Rumpitter ran on quickly ahead with Tom and the army of rats following. They moved quietly. Tom was full of excitement and courage. He clasped the stone around his neck and smiled as he ran. This was a real adventure, he thought.

Eventually they came to another chamber. This was a square room and much darker. The light was dim and the atmosphere was damp and stale. Then Tom realised that they had been running down hill as the stone floor sloped away ahead of them.

We must be far below ground, he thought as he looked around at the dark grey walls.

"Tom, start opening these doors," whispered Rumpitter.

Tom fumbled with the keys and walked up to one of the thick, wooden doors. He put a key in the lock and turned. It worked!

The door opened and suddenly there was a terrible smell. He unhooked a fire torch that was hanging on the wall and held it up carefully as he stepped through the door. He had to throw his scarf over his face as the smell was so bad. The rancid scent of rotting flesh in the midst of a place where there was no air was unbearable. The stone walls dripped with condensation from the rising heat and the damp floors. Steam rose from cracks in the stone slabs on the floor. This was, Tom thought, just like hell would be.

The rats had already scattered around the hall and inside the room. It seemed they were not bothered by the smell. Tom peered through the doorway holding the torch. Then he saw a terrible sight. There were people lying all around the room. Some were huddled together in groups, some were curled up in corners, but they were all chained to the walls, which dripped with slime and rotting mould.

Rumpitter scurried around looking at all the people. Some were dead and others were barely alive, choking and coughing.

Tom started calling out names: "Joseph, Blake, Little, Mababe, Braheim, Gordon, Trouseau, Maris."

Rumpitter ran over one body as it lay in a pool of stale water. There was no movement as he hopped over it and darted across to another group of people who were huddled in the centre of the room. They were draped in tattered rags. Some had terrible scars and bruises on their faces, others looked thin and dying. There was a faint cry from someone who must have seen a large rat and then saw all the others. However the rats ignored them as they continued their search. This was a desolate place. No mercy had been shown to these poor individuals and now their lives were virtually at an end. Tom kept his face covered as the smell grew even stronger. He ran from chamber to chamber looking for Mr Hawkins's men.

This was a deathly and miserable place. Nobody could survive here, he thought, and wondered if they would ever find the men they were searching for. Would they still be alive?

Tom thought carefully and then, without words, he called Mr Hawkins.

At first there came no reply. He called again. *Mr Hawkins, I need your help, where are you?*

*Tom, I hear you, you must keep looking. They will be in one of the cells, probably the smallest. The Saharadeen would have spared no mercy on them. He is full of hatred, especially as he knows we have the stone and our friends are his slaves until we try to free them. He knows that one day I will return. Our only advantage is that he does not know when. This is our time, Tom, it is the only time. We cannot fail. We must find them.*

*Yes, I know, but I can't see them or anyone who looks like them.*

*Keep moving through the chambers, Tom. They must be in there* replied the seagull.

Tom searched all around the first cell. He saw a small group of men. They were scared and thin, their clothes torn and ragged, kneeling and holding up their arms. They looked ill and weary. One of them tried to speak but it was clear he could hardly do so. He beckoned to Tom in a language he did not understand but he felt that he knew what the man was trying to say. The man pointed to the heavy chain, which was attached around their ankles and bolted to the wall.

Tom quickly ran to the chain and fumbled with the keys. He found the one which unlocked the chain and as soon as he had pulled the chain through the iron clamps, the men scrambled to free themselves. Tom held up his finger to his lips to tell them to keep quiet. The men understood and nodded at him to show their thanks.

Rumpitter ran over to Tom and the men jumped back in fear as they saw the huge rat. Tom held up his hand to them. "It's all right," he whispered. "He's friendly," he said quietly and then stroked Rumpitter on the back to show them there was nothing to be concerned about. Although the men thought it odd, they were so very grateful for Tom's appearance and quickly continued freeing themselves from the chains.

"Come Tom, the next cell, let's move!" said Rumpitter impatiently.

"You did say we were to free all the captives," Tom whispered.

"Yes, I know. Well done, now let's get going."

They came to another door and found the key to open it. This was another dark, damp cell and the smell was no better. They heard the men from the first cell chatting in their strange tongue and then some ran into the chamber where Tom was holding up the fire torch to light the way. One of the men tapped Tom on the shoulder. It made Tom jump and he turned quickly around. The man was black and skinny, most of his teeth had disappeared. His hands were dirty and he had cuts and scabs all over him. Then Tom noticed the other slaves had now joined them.

Tom signalled to the men to be quiet and wait in the hall outside the cell.

He whispered, "I am a friend, we have come to save you, but first I need to find some men." He plucked his cheek, "Some are white men like me. Do you know where they are?"

The old man didn't understand and still looked very nervous, especially as all the rats had assembled in the hall outside the cell and just sat watching them. "They are my friends," Tom said again. This time he put his hand to his heart and pointed at the rats as he spoke. "My friends, it's all right," he repeated, trying to reassure the old man.

The man appeared to understand and half smiled. It was a toothless smile, but Tom could see he was beginning to catch on, although still very unsure.

Tom waved the torch around the cell. There were even more people lying around the floor. Some coughed and groaned, some tried to cry out. Just then, the old man hobbled past Tom and held out his hands to all the prisoners, who were now getting very excited. He began talking to them in their native tongue and pointed to Tom and the rats. Tom could see they were all now beginning to realise that they were being freed. He was grateful for the old man's assistance. "I must find my friends," he said again to the man. They still didn't really understand and Tom was getting very anxious. Suddenly he heard Mr Hawkins's voice. *Hold the Stone, Tom, and speak to them.* Tom looked down at the stone hanging from his neck and grabbed it.

He looked up at the old man and then, by a strange miracle, he spoke words he didn't even understand himself. The old man suddenly stood back in astonishment and then there was a complete change in him. Tom had spoken to him in his own language. He threw up his arms and then dropped to his knees and began kissing Tom's feet. "What are you doing?" Tom whispered, this time in English. The man jumped up and begged Tom to follow him. He took the key from Tom and threw it to another prisoner, who immediately began to unlock all the chains that bound the prisoners in the cell. There was a great commotion and Tom could see the relief among them. They were being rescued by a boy and an army of rats. It was strange indeed, but they did not complain and suddenly they all began working in total silence to help each other. They knew that they must not arouse the Saharadeen's soldiers. The old man grabbed Tom's arm and summoned Tom to follow him. *He wants me to go this way Rumpitter. I think he knows who we are looking for,* Tom spoke without words.

*Good, then let him take us, but be careful, this place is a labyrinth of passages and tunnels,* Rumpitter replied. Before following Tom, he quickly turned to the army of rats. He leapt up onto a stone slab, high enough for all the rats to see him. Immediately the rats turned towards Rumpitter and listened obediently. Rumpitter enjoyed his status as their leader and gave them their orders. All the rats had remained in the hall but now, after Rumpitter's orders, they turned into a complete military column and turned to face the main doors. Their job would be to attack anyone coming through the entrance to the cells. They would act as a decoy to hold off Saharadeen's soldiers, should they appear. The rats were fearless and Rumpitter was proud to be their leader. After giving his orders, he hopped off the stone slab and scuttled after Tom.

The old man hobbled along the hall to some stairs leading down into a dark pit. He took another torch off the wall and waved to Tom to follow him and then disappeared down the stairs.

*Come on Rumpitter, I think he's going to lead us to our friends.*

*Keep going Tom, I'm right behind you.*

They carefully descended the stairs, holding the torch to see where they were going. It was very dark. Tom ran his hand along the wall as he went. Some of the stairs were uneven and he tripped and nearly fell but the old man was suddenly there and stopped him from falling. The old man whispered something, shaking his head. He held Tom firmly by the shoulders and told him to be careful. Tom understood. Their footsteps echoed as they walked but they tried to keep as quiet as they could.

Finally they came to a small chamber. There was a wooden bench and a table. On the table Tom saw a long wooden lance with a curved blade at one end. It was a formidable looking weapon. Then he saw blood stains on the floor and then, hanging from the stone ceiling, a cage. Inside it was a monkey. It eyes were bright red and it suddenly shrieked when it saw them. The shriek was so loud it rang out all around the room. Tom held his hands to his ears. The monkey was jumping up and down in its cage, shrieking and showing its horrid yellow teeth at them. Its eyes were wild as it banged violently against the cage. It shook the bars and the cage swung from side to side. The ape had clearly been trapped here for a long time and its claws were long and curled at the end. It had hardly any fur left on its back and it was covered in scars. Tom almost felt sorry for it. *I think it's gone mad*, whispered Tom, backing away from the cage.

*Clearly so, and it's going to alert everyone around. We must do something to keep it quiet*, said Rumpitter.

Before Tom could even think what to do, the old man grabbed the lance from the table and speared the monkey. It died instantly. The old man looked at Tom and said something which, Tom thought, was something about his good aim.

*Well, that solved that problem,* said Rumpitter, very relieved. *The monkey was an alarm. I hope no-one heard it.*

*Me too,* agreed Tom.

As they were speaking the old man had found a small door. There was a key hanging from a hook on the wall and he showed it to Tom, indicating he should open the door with it.

The key slipped into the lock easily and, as Tom turned it, the door opened. He peered nervously inside, holding up the torch again to see what lay beyond. There were some figures huddled together at the far end of the room. The light from the torch flickered and cast shadows around the ceiling and walls. The old man said something and then called the name "Mababe".

Tom cleared his throat and he too called out the names. "Joseph, Little, Gordon, Braheim, Trouseau, Blake," he said. "My name is Tom, I am a friend of Mr... Captain Hawkins, and we have come to rescue you. Are any of you here?"

There was a shuffle on the floor and one of the figures appeared slowly out of the darkness.

At first it was a grunt, then a halting phrase, "Who are you?"

"My name is Tom Parker, are you who I am calling for?" The question seemed a little silly but Tom was scared and didn't know what else to say.

"I am Joseph Trelawney. Am I dreaming?" He tried to move but his chain pulled him over and he fell to the floor.

*Oh my goodness, we've found them – we've found them!* Tom called out to Rumpitter.

*Thank the stars!* Tom heard Mr Hawkins say.

Rumpitter ran into the room. *Unlock the chains. Tom, let's get them out of here,* said Rumpitter, *and you had better tell them I'm on your side.*

Tom and the old man quickly ran over to the huddled group. Joseph was a tall, strong-looking man but looked as though he had suffered greatly. As Tom unlocked the chains he looked at the men. They were a sorry sight, with terrible wounds, and looked pale and thin just like all the other prisoners. They saw the huge rat and Tom quickly said, "He's with me, he's friendly, don't worry about him, he's quite safe."

"You have strange friends, boy," said Joseph. The youngest, Gordon, backed away when he saw the rat. "We have seen so many of them, but not as big as this one. I hope he keeps his distance."

One of the men began to cry and held Tom's arm. "Thank-you boy. Thank-you."

"Who are you?" asked Tom. "My name is Blake. Thank-you." He turned to look over his shoulder. "You must help him." Blake pointed to a small figure lying huddled in the corner. "He is very sick and needs help quickly."

"Who is he?" Tom asked as he and the old man unlocked the clamps from the chain. "His name is Trouseau. He has been badly treated. We fear for his life."

"I'll do my best for him, but you are all going to need your strength to get out of here. We haven't a moment to lose," said Tom who was now sweating from the stale and rancid heat, but also very worried about being caught by the Saharadeen soldiers. He hoped the monkey had not alerted them.

A huge black man touched Tom on his shoulder and smiled at him. "You, I do not know, I am Mababe, but you say you are friend of the Captain. Is he here?"

Tom didn't know what to say. "Yes, well, sort of... look let's just get away from here and we can talk about it later. I don't like this place at all." Tom was shaking and Mababe could see the boy was scared. Mababe nodded and helped Tom with the chains.

The last of the iron clamps came off the ankle of a tall Arab man. "Oh thank-you a million times, you are a gift from Allah. We were thinking it was our last night before we die. Thank- you, boy."

Tom smiled at the Arab. "You must be Braheim?" Tom asked. "You know of me? asked the Arab in bewilderment. "Captain Hawkins has told me a great deal about all of you."

The old man and Mababe seemed to know each other and exchanged greetings. Between them they freed the others and helped them to their feet.

One by one they all made it to the door. Tom held the fire torch high enough for them to see. It was clear that they had spent so much time, cramped up in darkness, that the light was hurting their eyes.

Sam Little and Blake helped Trouseau to his feet and carried him to the door between them.

When they were all assembled in the chamber outside the cell, Tom spoke without words to Mr Hawkins. *Mr Hawkins, Captain, we have them all, what do we do now?*

There was a pause.

*I know, Tom, you have done very well. I am so happy. Thank-you. You must get back to the entrance of the dungeons and find your way back to the caves where we started. Rumpitter and the rats will lead you. Please take care; I fear that the Saharadeen's men will soon discover that the prisoners have fled.*

Tom turned to the old man and said, "Will you lead us out of here?' Then to the others: "You must all stay together and keep up. The rats will help us – don't be afraid of them, they are on our side. Follow us, quickly."

They all moved off as fast as was possible. Tom could see the men were weak, but a little strength was returning to them now they could smell the sweet scent of freedom.

At last they returned to the higher chamber where all the other prisoners had assembled. They armed themselves with long knives, swords and lances, which they had found stacked in one of the smaller chambers. Some had found bread and jugs of water and were sharing it out with the others.

Joseph, Maris and Braheim also helped themselves to the bread and water and passed it around their comrades.

Finally, they were all ready to go. Rumpitter ran ahead of the huge column of rats.

He jumped up, giving his signal.

As one, the rats moved forward ahead of all the prisoners. "Follow the rats," Tom called out. He clutched the stone around his neck and prayed they would be successful. He found the sword that he had obtained earlier and held it in both hands.

Braheim turned to his comrades, "This is no ordinary boy. He has great courage. He is a friend of the Captain. We should trust him." The others all nodded in agreement.

The rats led the way in silence, moving as one massive army. The prisoners could hardly believe what they were seeing. How could it be that, by some fantastic miracle, a young boy and an army of rats would help them escape? Was it all a dream?

It did not take long for them to reach the huge doors. On the other side was their chance of freedom. Just a few more yards and Rumpitter would lead them into the caves and out into the fresh air and freedom. The atmosphere was tense. Sweat ran down Tom's forehead as they stood before the doors.

Rumpitter was at the front and Tom made his way through the prisoners, stepping over the rats, which only moved just enough for him to find his footing on the floor as he picked his way through. "The key, Tom, quickly," whispered Rumpitter.

"It's here Rumpitter, I have it," he replied. The two of them looked at each other for a few seconds, each of them thinking the same thing, and then Tom lifted the key to the lock.

# Part 02

# Chapter 9 – The Long Journey

The mighty Saharadeen army massed in great columns, forming huge squares of soldiers and horsemen. They were now gathering outside the city gates amidst the cheering crowds. Horses pulling war chariots roared into position, pulling up in neat rows.

Thousands of soldiers marched into the arena and formed perfect lines. As soon as the dust settled another huge column of men would arrive and again the dust would blow up into the sky like a thick red cloud. The brightly lit moon flickered through the hot dust reflecting a red glow from the shields and armour of the marching soldiers.

The chanting from the on looking crowds continued and drums beat louder and louder. The earth seemed to tremble and the air was thick with red dust.

Mr Hawkins watched in silence from his vantage point, high above the city walls. He could sense the impending danger ahead and the dust and smoke from the ground was drifting as high as the tallest castle turrets.

He noticed a rider galloping through the crowds, picking his way through the massing columns of soldiers. His horse swerved left and right, its neck thick with sweat. It tossed its head as the rider pushed it harder and faster into the crowds. Horses snorted and kicked their hooves into the dust as the rider charged past. He was forging a way through the ranks, towards the Saharadeen's war chariot. There was a sense of desperate urgency in the rider's face as he charged through: he spared no thought to anyone or anything in his way. One soldier tried desperately to hold onto his horse as it reared up and then lurched to one side, kicking out with its hind legs. He was unable to hold on and fell hard on the ground.

This caused a number of other horses to rear up and the unseated soldier was trampled by another stamping horse. His life ended even before he went into battle. There was chaos in the ranks as the lone rider charged on. Soldiers shouted and cursed as they tried to control their horses. Foot soldiers jeered and shook their lances at him and then quickly reformed into their columns under the curses and whips of their leaders.

At last the rider was through and approached the group of soldiers who surrounded the Saharadeen's chariot. He shouted something to one of the guards. As he spoke, he turned on his mount and pointed back to the castle gates. The guard quickly realised that the rider's message was important and turned his horse and galloped towards the Saharadeen with a message of utmost urgency.

Mr Hawkins knew this meant trouble and swooped down into the hot, red dusty air below to get a closer look. By now he hoped, his friends would be preparing their escape. *It can't be long now* he thought, *they must leave, now!*

As he flew over the heads of the soldiers, he saw an even larger cloud of dust, which seemed to be heading towards him. He banked to the right and flew up a little higher to get a better view and then, to his horror, he saw hundreds of soldiers charging back towards the city gates. *They've been discovered* he thought. Then he heard the horns bellowing in the distance.

Mr Hawkins watched as the Saharadeen ordered a section of men back to the City of Fire. He screamed at the leader of the guards, "No one escapes, kill them all!" His eyes were wild and red with rage. He furiously shook his arms at the guards and immediately ordered his chariot to be turned around and head back to the city gates.

Mr Hawkins watched carefully as the Saharadeen shouted at his men and wrestled with the reins of his chariot. The Saharadeen was seething with anger, his snarled and badly scarred face twisted with rage.

Mr Hawkins looked again at the sword he wanted still hanging from the Saharadeen's waist.

In a flash, the seagull dropped out of the sky; he stretched out his claws and flipped back his wings so he could drop faster. Just as he was about to fall into the charging horsemen, he gave a quick flap of his wings and lifted up, just high enough so he could still see the Saharadeen. He angled his attack directly. A gust of air lifted him inches above the Saharadeen's head and he struck out quickly with both claws. One claw struck the Saharadeen completely by surprise, tearing at his shoulder and ripping a piece of his cloak. The Saharadeen ducked in utter astonishment and twisted to one side. He swerved and thrust out with his arm and then looked up in horror – he knew this bird. The Saharadeen's blood red eyes glared up at the seagull swirling above him.

He felt the scar on his face and grimaced as the throbbing pain wrenched at his cheekbone. The Saharadeen knew, only too well, who this was. The seagull... the Englishman had returned!

He would make sure this time, there would be no mercy, there would be no prisoners. He would kill them all.

The Saharadeen looked up at the sky and watched again. He saw the seagull drifting high above, darting down and then swooping upwards. It was tormenting him, willing him to follow. Then the Saharadeen heard a voice in his head. He grabbed the sword and held it up, shaking it violently at the seagull. The voice in his head was clear...

*I have returned, Saharadeen – you know who I am. I am your worst enemy, I will destroy you!*

The Saharadeen shook with rage. He could not believe the seagull had returned after so long. It was impossible. The messenger had told him there were men escaping and he had alerted some of his soldiers to kill the prisoners. The Saharadeen was about to wage a war on his enemy and nothing would get in his way.

"Kill all the prisoners!" he shouted again. Then he looked up into the black sky. "Kill that bird, shoot, shoot!" He waved at one of his archers and shouted, "Shoot that bird." The soldier was confused and hesitated, not really understanding the order. The Saharadeen pulled his chariot up next to the soldier and lashed out at him with a leather whip. The soldier fell to the ground screaming in pain and cowered to his master as he was beaten. "Do as I say, or I will see you burn in the Temple of Fire," screamed the Saharadeen.

The archer picked himself up and trembled as he tried to draw an arrow through his bow. "Give me that," growled the Saharadeen and snatched the bow and aimed up into the air, looking for the bird. But it had disappeared. The Saharadeen desperately searched but could not find his target.

Suddenly, – Mr Hawkins swooped in from nowhere and, with both claws outstretched, struck a hefty blow, tearing the head-dress from the Saharadeen's head. Then he screeched as he ripped past and flew high into the sky. One of the horses pulling the chariot reared in fright at the noise. The other three horses were spooked too and the chariot went out of control and fell on its side. The Saharadeen and his guard tumbled to the ground. The guard was crushed by the chariot, but the Saharadeen escaped. The horses broke loose and ran wildly through the crowds. Mr Hawkins saw the disruption he had caused and hoped that this would buy his comrades some more time. He spoke to them, *Tom, Rumpitter, you must get away now, the whole army has been alerted and they will be upon you very soon. Go now!*

Both Tom and Rumpitter heard the seagull's words.

Rumpitter gave the nod to Tom. The army of rats prepared themselves and reared up their hind legs in readiness to charge. Tom turned the key and slowly the huge doors opened. The rats ran at the doors. Suddenly there was a roar from the other side. Bright lights of fire poured in through the opening. The Saharadeen army were on the other side. "Oh, no!" Tom cried out, "We won't make it!"

"Yes we will," shouted Mababe and he and the other comrades took up their weapons.

"Let the rats through," Mababe called. The prisoners all stood to the side. The doors were now half open and the rat army poured through in a huge mass. They charged straight at the Saharadeen soldiers, jumping up at their faces and biting into them. Tom covered his eyes. It was a terrible sight. The rats showed no mercy. Within seconds, thousands of rats were swarming like flies over the soldiers, bringing them to their knees. Some soldiers dropped their weapons to cover their faces, others threw their flame torches into the crowd, but instead of hitting the escaping prisoners they set light to their own men. There were terrible screams of pain and agony. It was a dreadful sight.

Joseph, Mababe and Braheim gathered their courage and hurled themselves at the struggling soldiers. Little and Blake helped Trouseau to his feet and guided him through as the prisoners did their best to fight off the attacking army. Some of the weaker men fell under the crush. Maris, finding strength, joined the prisoners bringing up the rear.

Mababe and Joseph battled against the front line and Braheim wielded a huge iron bar over his head, taking out several soldiers. This allowed just enough time for the comrades to slip through the doors, and the swarming rats to forge on and do their deadly work.

There were more and more soldiers appearing from the back of the great hall. The Saharadeen had ordered reinforcements into the chambers to stop the escaping prisoners.

Mababe turned to Tom with desperation in his eyes. "There are too many for us – we must find another way." Rumpitter heard this and instantly raced ahead, leading a large column of his rats away from the main group and towards an opening in the wall, just ahead of them.

Tom saw this and called to Mababe and the others. "Follow the big rat everyone!" He pointed to where Rumpitter had gathered the rats by the opening and were blocking off any attackers.

There was commotion everywhere. The rat army was fending off the soldiers, but slowly the enemy's numbers were mounting and it would only be a short while until even the rats would be unable hold them off.

Trouseau was desperately slow on his feet, but his comrades carried him boldly through the mayhem while some of the rats formed a circle around them to prevent the soldiers getting to them. Fire torches were thrown and the whole place was ablaze. The great hall was now a mass of screaming soldiers with huge flames ripping through the woollen wall hangings and the timbers on each side. Eventually they broke away from the wall and fell down onto the soldiers. The rats continued their onslaught relentlessly to give time for the comrades and prisoners to get to the opening, where Rumpitter had now formed a back-up group and was waiting for the comrades and prisoners to reach them.

Outside, the Saharadeen had recovered from his fall and ordered three divisions of his army back inside the castle to seal off all escape routes. "No one survives, kill them all!" he screamed again.

He was wild with rage and wanted revenge so badly. He now regretted not having the English captain killed when he had had him in his grasp. He was angry that although he had turned him into a bird in the pool of fire, he had made a big mistake and now the seagull still had the powers of the Golden Secret.

The Saharadeen mounted his black stallion, which had been brought to him, but the dust cloud raised by the battle made it impossible to see clearly.

Mr Hawkins had managed to slip out of sight, having narrowly escaped being struck by an arrow. He had to move fast. He flew up over the castle walls and over the fortress battlements. No-one noticed the bird as he swooped in and out of passages and through groups of riders charging through the streets. Then he saw some smoke floating out of a large window and flew towards it. He couldn't get close because the smoke was so thick and black, but he heard the screaming and shouting from below of the battle taking place. Then he saw the flames.

He spoke without words. *Where are you Tom? What is happening?*

*We are surrounded by soldiers, the rats are holding them back but we need to get out and back to the caves. Can you help?* Tom looked up towards the highest opening and, for a second, he saw the flicker of a white wing. *I think I just saw you, Mr Hawkins – can you see us?*

*No Tom, I can't, but I know where you are. I fear the Saharadeen will block all the entrances and gates. Your only escape is through the caves. I will try to get help but you must get through. Do you hear me Tom?*

*Yes, I hear you. We will try.*

*Good lad, hold onto that stone, Tom, you will need it to give you strength. We will also need it as soon as I have the sword. Then we'll finish the Saharadeen for ever!*

Rumpitter also heard their conversation and called Tom. *Quickly Tom get everyone together over here!* Rumpitter was standing on a high ledge so Tom could see him. Just below the ledge was the opening. It was just a small passage through the wall. But Tom thought they might just be able to get through.

Suddenly Rumpitter stood high on his back legs and called out to the army of rats. It was a high pitched eerie shriek and so loud that it cut through the great hall and brought everyone to a halt. It changed everything.

The soldiers fell on their knees with their hands over their ears. Tom's ears rang and he too had to cover his ears, as did everyone. But it was not the noise that stunned Tom so much as the amazing sight before his eyes.

All the rats had instantly formed a wall around the comrades and prisoners. They stood on each other's backs, shoulder to shoulder, and snarled and screeched loudly displaying their sharp yellow teeth at the soldiers. The wall they had formed was so high it almost reached the ceiling of the great hall. The escaping comrades were safely blocked behind the wall of rats.

*Quickly, Tom go now!* ordered Rumpitter. The comrades and struggling prisoners immediately slipped past the rats and through the opening.

Almost as soon as the last prisoner was through the gap, the huge wall of rats collapsed and lunged again at the soldiers who were scrambling to their feet. It was a ghastly sight.

The comrades had managed to get through the opening and followed Rumpitter and a small battalion of his rats into the passage. Sadly, a few of the weaker prisoners had not made it and fell to the mercy of the soldiers.

Meanwhile, Mr Hawkins was hatching a plan.

Hundreds of horsemen and foot soldiers were chasing through the city streets and into the outer perimeters of the castle. The shouting and beating drums grew louder and chaos continued to reign across the City of Fire.

The seagull saw a dozen riders trying to control their mounts as their horses reared and snorted in fright. One rider was dismounted and another two horses collided into each other.

Mr Hawkins saw his chance and once again swooped down low, circling just above the rearing horses. He dived on top of one rider's head and dragged him out of his saddle, then hopped onto the neck of his horse and screeched loudly. The horse came to an immediate halt and three riders who were galloping right behind were thrown forward into the dust as their horses collided. The seagull stared deep into the eyes of the leading horse. The crescent moon opened, and a beam of gold light shone into the horse's eye. He whispered something in its ear and suddenly the horse turned and stomped his front hooves in the dust. The horse gave a heavy snort and nodded his head to the other horses. All together, they turned in the dust, reared up and threw all their riders. As soon as they had shaken off their mounts, they began to gallop back through the crowds. They followed the seagull through the streets, leaping over anything in their way, twisting and turning as the seagull flew just a few feet above the ground. They charged on, throwing anyone in their way to the side. They were unstoppable. They charged to a wooden gate where some guards tried to grab their reins but the horses reared up again and, with their front hooves, beat the guards back down.

Mr Hawkins flew over the gate and turned to the horses. Again the golden beam of light shone from his eye. The lead horse turned around and with his back legs began to kick the gate. The other horses joined in. It did not take long for them to kick the gates open and they all charged out into the desert. The guards were helpless and blinded by the cloud of dust kicked up by the horses. They were unable to see that they had escaped out into the desert beyond the city walls. By the time they had realised what had happened, the horses had disappeared.

The seagull led them out into the desert. They followed him, galloping over the dunes and through scattered palm trees, leaving nothing but a cloud of dust behind them.

Rumpitter led the companions through the dark, damp passages. The fire torches that they had retrieved from the soldiers lit their way. Some of the elderly prisoners tripped and moaned as they tried to follow but, although some were helped, there was not enough time to help all of them.

The comrades pushed on in great haste. Tom clung to the stone around his neck and although he was scared, he regained the courage to run as fast as his legs could carry him.

Joseph and Mababe, who were the biggest and strongest of the men, stayed as far back as they dared to help the few remaining prisoners who were alone in the dark passages. The Comrades and the prisoners ran for their lives. Their footsteps and heavy breathing echoed as they ran. The passage was narrow and sharp rock ledges stuck out from the walls, occasionally cutting the arm or leg of some of them. But still they ran on, never stopping. They could smell freedom. Nothing would stop them now.

Rumpitter ordered the rats to split into two lines, left and right, just ahead of the comrades.

On and on they ran. Eventually they came to a large iron grill and stopped. There was nowhere to go.

The prisoners were exhausted, panting and breathing heavily. Sweating and groaning with aching legs and bones, they desperately tried to find another exit.

The iron grill was set deep into the rock. Nothing would move it. They were trapped, and just beyond the grill was daylight and freedom. Mababe used every grain of strength to heave the heavy grill from the rock, but it was impossible.

"It is no good. I cannot move it," he panted, wiping the sweat from his face.

"What are we going to do?" said Tom, leaning against the wall breathing heavily.

Rumpitter had sent some of the rats through the grill to investigate. One of them returned and uttered a shrill squeak to Rumpitter, who immediately ran through the grill and disappeared.

"Rumpitter, wait. Where are you going?" called Tom.

Braheim grabbed the iron bars to try and see beyond. He looked defeated. "Perhaps they have all gone, left us to die in this hell. They are rats after all. They have left the sinking ship." He slumped to the floor with his head in his hands. The others also looked defeated. "I knew we would never escape," said Blake, who was nearly in tears. "We are doomed," said Sam Little.

Joseph looked at Maris and Gordon who were tending to Trouseau and sighed. "We will find a way, we must." He tried to sound convincing.

Just as he had spoken, the ground began to tremble.

Tom suddenly leapt to his feet. "Wait a minute..." he said and his eyes grew bright again.

Suddenly he laughed out loud and then he heard a high-pitched squeak. Tom turned back to the others with a wide grin as Rumpitter appeared through the gate, followed by two other rats, all looking very excited. They fell over each other and rolled along the floor squeaking with excitement.

Rumpitter jumped up into the air at Tom. *Quickly, Tom, tell them all to stand back, help is on its way.* He jumped up and down in excitement. The other two rats did the same.

"What is this boy, what is happening?" Joseph asked, looking at the odd behaviour of the rats, still unsure of them.

"We have to stand back away from the bars. Quickly, we must do as he says." The companions all looked strangely at him. "What are you talking about? What is going to happen, lad, why are you saying this?" Joseph asked again.

"Just do it!" Tom shouted and stepped back against the wall. *Yes, Tom, that's right, just do it,* Rumpitter said, then ran up to the grill and then quickly back again to Tom, *NOW!*

Tom repeated the order to everyone. "Stand back – NOW!" he shouted again. The rumbling grew louder and the ground shook violently under them. Everyone fell back against the far side of the passage. Mababe turned and called out. "Not good! Soldiers coming, many of them – I can hear them," he said and drew his sword up as if to take them all on single-handed.

Then they heard the shouting and footsteps of many soldiers moving closer along the passage, getting nearer, very quickly.

Tom was very anxious and stared at the grill.

"Look!" he suddenly called out and everybody turned. A huge cloud of dust billowed towards the iron bars from outside and there was a thunderous noise. Suddenly, looming out through the cloud of red dust appeared the head of a large black horse. His eyes were bright and steam snorted from his nostrils. He looked at the trapped men and his eyes found Tom. The horse let out a loud neigh and a heavy snort and then turned back into the dust.

Seconds later it reappeared, this time with the seagull standing on its back, and the seagull had a rope in his beak. Tom was stunned and then called out. "Mr Hawkins!"

The comrades looked on in total astonishment. The seagull dropped the rope through the bars.

*Tie the rope to the bars, Tom, quickly,* said Mr Hawkins.

Mababe was amazed at what he was seeing but also concerned about the closeness of the Saharadeen soldiers. Joseph was the first to speak. "Hawkins... what are you saying, lad?" he asked.

The seagull stared momentarily at the men. He had waited so long for this moment and wanted so much to speak to them. Tom caught his eye and understood. "No time now, we must tie this rope to the bars," said Tom.

Braheim ran up to the grill. The horse had pushed up close to the bars and he realised that he should also tie the other end of the rope to the saddle. He managed to slip his arms through and tie the rope around the wooden pummel at the front of the saddle and then the other end to the bars. Then another horse appeared through the dust. The second horse managed to get under the rope so it was also looped around its neck.

The seagull let out a shriek and suddenly the two large horses began to walk away and the rope tightened on the bars. *Stand away from the bars, Tom*, Mr Hawkins ordered. Tom quickly stepped back telling the others to do the same. Three other horses came up to the grill, walking backwards. Then they began to kick with their hind legs at the rock which held the bars in place, splintering the wall as the two pulling horses heaved on the rope.

But the bars were not moving.

Mababe called out urgently, "They are so close. I can hear them." Then they all heard shouting coming from behind them and the pounding of feet and ironware along the passageway. The enemy were almost upon them.

Joseph called to the others to push the bars from their side. "There is no time, we must push"

All the men ran up and heaved at the bars from inside. Some pushed with their backs against them and others used all the strength in their arms to push. The horses heaved and kicked, the men pushed as hard as they could.

Suddenly, there was a flicker of light from behind.

"Torches!" shouted Mababe. Everyone turned to look in desperation. Then Mababe saw the bars slowly bending and quickly ran to help. He was the tallest and strongest of all of them, with huge muscles. The veins in his arms almost burst through his skin as he heaved with every ounce of his strength. Suddenly there was a crack in the rock wall at one side.

"It's moving!" exclaimed Tom. Again everyone gave their last breath to push the bars. The horses gave an even harder tug and snorted and groaned in their effort.

A loud resounding bang rang out. Then a roaring, thunderous noise from above and a huge rock began to fall from the roof.

"Get back, everyone – back!" called Joseph and suddenly the grill broke free and ripped away from the wall. The ceiling collapsed with tons of rubble and rocks descending on them. They all leapt to escape the falling rocks. *RUN!* shouted Rumpitter.

Tom repeated the command and everyone charged over the collapsed grill; some fell and were picked up. Maris and Blake helped Trouseau across and eventually they were all free. The horses continued pounding the rock wall from the outside to loosen more rocks and cause more dust. Braheim cut the rope from the horses. His hands were shaking as he did so.

At last they were all clear and out into the hot sun of the desert. They saw more horses standing by.

The seagull was still on the back of the large horse.

*Quickly, Tom, get everyone onto a horse. Double up if necessary, but get going!*

Tom called out to everyone to mount a horse and then, with Rumpitter, climbed up onto the large black horse.

The men stared in amazement. They could not believe that this young boy and two strange animals were actually leading them to safety.

"Come on!" Tom shouted at them, "Let's get moving."

Mababe was the last to mount. He had to run after his horse as it began to gallop away, and as he ran there was a deafening roar of falling rocks behind them and then cries of men being trampled by the wall collapsing onto them. The Saharadeen soldiers had fallen under the tumbling rocks just seconds before the companions had managed to gallop away.

Some of the horses had three men on their backs. Regardless of this they galloped swiftly with the others across the desert and away from the City of Fire.

Tom hugged the seagull. *Thank-you Mr Hawkins. You saved us!*

*Good to have you all back Tom, you did well lad,* he replied. He tried to sound unmoved by the whole occasion, but in his heart he was so delighted. He looked at his men. *They're free at last* he thought, delighted.

Rumpitter hung on for dear life as the horse galloped at great speed across the hot sand of the desert. Some of the prisoners had not seen daylight in years and covered their eyes from the pain of the bright light and the hot sun beating down upon them.

The horses charged on and on without stopping. Joseph came up alongside Tom and the seagull. He couldn't find the words to thank them. He was still very confused, but he smiled at Tom as they galloped side by side. He couldn't take his eyes off the seagull.

Mr Hawkins looked at his friend and cocked his head to one side and his eye caught Joseph's. There was a sparkle in the seagull's eye and Joseph saw something he thought he had once seen before. *Can it be?* he thought to himself.

The prisoners were tired and thirsty as they galloped across the dusty terrain, up into the hills of the desert. Some were looking on at the boy and the seagull ahead of them. They were overjoyed to be free from the Saharadeen but nevertheless quite bewildered. Who was this boy and his animal friends?

Not all of them were good riders and some found it very hard to stay on. They clung to the necks and mains of their mounts. Occasionally, one of the men who could ride would grab a leg or arm of one about to fall from his horse.

Blake rode with Trouseau in front of him. Little and Gordon rode either side of Blake's horse to be close at hand if Trouseau should fall. This way they could keep up the fast pace with the others. Mababe and Maris helped some of the prisoners keep up at the back.

Tom was holding on as best he could. He was amazed that he was able to sit firmly in the saddle without falling off. He had never ridden a horse quite like this before. He looked at the stone still hanging around his neck. *This is incredible, Mr Hawkins. I feel like I could ride this horse for ever!* Mr Hawkins was still clasped onto the front of Tom's saddle with his claws, and Rumpitter had found a place to sit right behind him. He bounced up and down, sometimes with his back legs being thrown up into the air. *Well good for you, Tom, but I am really struggling to hold on back here — oooooh,* he cried.

The seagull and Tom chuckled at Rumpitter. Mr Hawkins replied to Tom without words, *It is the power from that stone Tom. When we retrieve the sword and place the stone back into its rightful place, we will be able to finish the evil Saharadeen for ever. He was foolish with his greed. He did not realise that the sword is only truly powerful when it is united with the stone.*

Tom replied, *How are we going to do that? The Saharadeen has the sword and we are running away from him.*

*We will find a way Tom. But for now, we can rejoice that we have our friends back safely.*

*Yes, that's something else we need to discuss. When do we tell them about... er, well, I mean how do we tell them?*

*You mean tell them about me?*

*Yes, that's what I mean.*

*I think they already suspect something, Tom,* replied Mr Hawkins with a sigh. *There will be a right time to talk, but, for now, we must keep going.*

The comrades continued on into the desert mountains.

Maris suddenly shouted from the back, "Look behind, look!"

Everyone turned. They saw a long dust cloud. It was moving towards them at great speed. Then they saw shimmering lights from within the cloud. As they slowed down their horses to see what it was, they saw the bright flash of lights again. "Horse soldiers!" Mababe called out.

The bright sunlight was reflecting from the shields and weapons. The long cloud of dust stretched over the hill. There was a massive army moving ever closer towards them.

Joseph was the first to speak. "There must be thousands of them!"

Mr Hawkins flew up out of the saddle and hovered above Tom. *Keep going Tom. Let the horses lead you, they know where to go. You must ride now as fast as you can. I have an idea.*

Tom didn't discuss this any further and called to the others. "Come on, keep going, let the horses take us." He gently kicked his horse and it immediately powered forward into another gallop. He clung on for all his worth. Rumpitter held on tightly to the back of the saddle. *Ooooooooh, here we go again,* he said as his ears flipped back in the wind.

Mr Hawkins flew high into the air and disappeared in the haze of the sun.

The comrades galloped on, letting their horses take them higher into the mountains. The ground changed from sand to small rocks, which made their progress slower and the horses' hooves sometimes slipped over a loose rock and riders would almost topple from their mounts. The going was becoming harder, but still they rode on, higher and higher into the peaks.

Joseph shouted: "They will see the dust we are making and follow our tracks easily." Everyone knew this, but there was nothing they could do except keep going in the hope that they were faster than their enemy.

Mr Hawkins swirled up high and could see the whole desert below him. He saw the small group of comrades high up on the trail into the mountains and then turned to see the enormous army in a massive dust cloud, like a huge wave, charging on behind. They were not far away. He flew up higher so he could see beyond the cloud and as he drifted up he could see over the hill from where they were approaching. To his horror, he saw a huge army moving up in ranks. He calculated that there must be at least four thousand soldiers in each column. There were chariots, and battle towers being pulled by huge elephants. Thousands of foot soldiers in full battle dress were walking at a quick pace in the centre of the main group. There was another vast column of mounted soldiers on camels charging on behind the first and an even larger column of horsemen beyond them. Carts and carriages, probably with supplies, followed from the rear. The battle flags of the Saharadeen waved in the wind. This was a war machine moving at a great speed.

How could the Saharadeen have assembled such a massive army? he wondered. He swooped down to get a closer look. Then he saw the Saharadeen standing on his war chariot. He was urging his army forward, shouting out orders. The Sword of Isis hung from his belt. His face was scarred and twisted. There was evil in his eyes.

His guards cracked their whips over the soldiers' heads to move them onwards.

Mr Hawkins turned quickly to the left and glided back towards the mountains and then soared even higher into the sky. In the distance he saw the snow-capped mountains. He needed to act fast before the Saharadeen caught up with his freinds.

The comrades charged on and on, never stopping, never looking back and keeping close to each other. As they climbed, the rugged pass grew narrower and they grouped tighter together.

The hot dusty air from the desert had now changed to a cooler temperature, which was more bearable. Eventually the pass into the mountain became very narrow. They could only ride in single file. One behind the other they rode, higher on up the pass. Rocks crumbled under the hooves and disappeared over the edge, rolling down hundreds of feet below. Some of the men were becoming very weary and they had to lean low with both arms around the neck of their horses.

Suddenly, out of the mountain, came an eerie screeching sound that echoed through the great ravines and steep mountain walls. They looked around to see where it was coming from. Tom clung to his horse as it reared up at the high pitched noise echoing all around them. He almost fell out of his saddle. Braheim grabbed his reins and pulled Tom's horse to a halt.

"What was that?" Joseph shouted. He had also stopped on the narrow trail and craned his neck to see where the sound had come from.

"I don't know, but let's keep going," Tom called back. He looked at Rumpitter and leaned forward in his saddle. *What was that, Rumpitter?* Tom asked.

*Look. Up there*, Rumpitter said, jumping up onto the saddle on his hind legs.

They all looked up into the sky and saw black dots swirling high around the mountain peaks.

The dots seemed to be falling and then grew larger and larger. Gradually, they changed shape.

"They're birds?" shouted Joseph.

"There are hundreds of them. Look!" Tom pointed up at the sky at the black shapes, which were swirling high over the peaks of the mountains and were multiplying in numbers. Soon, the birds were filling the sky, all soaring around the mountain.

They swooped down in one enormous mass, all moving at the same time and in the same direction. Suddenly one bird moved one way and the whole mass moved with it. Their numbers grew by the second. The sides of the mountains were now covered in black shapes – swirling, darting and gliding upwards.

Now they could see them more clearly.

"Eagles!" exclaimed Braheim.

"By Jove man, you are right, they are enormous!" replied Joseph.

Tom sat in his saddle and stared up into the sky in amazement. "Where did they come from?"

Now everyone had stopped to see the incredible sight. Thousands of large black eagles were swirling above them and all around the mountain. At first it looked as if they were flying around in a circle. Then, as more and more eagles joined the huge swarm, they began to move in another direction. The swarm of birds danced from one direction and then another as their numbers grew. Eventually they formed a giant circle in the sky, like a massive wheel spinning through the air.

Even Trouseau, who was very weak, looked up to see the birds. His watery eyes opened as wide as they could to watch the spectacle. Everyone was in awe of the whole scene developing above them.

The eagles began to screech and wail in the wind. It was an eerie sound. The noise grew louder and louder and it echoed off the high sides of the canyons. More and more eagles appeared from the sides of the mountain, through small caves and ledges, hundreds of feet up on the steep sides of the canyon walls.

The enormous mass of eagles created a circle around an empty hole in the sky. No-one could understand why the birds were flying like this. They formed a wheel spinning around the circle and it grew larger. The companions covered their ears from the noise. The screeching became deafening. The horses became restless and reared and snorted, frightened by the sound.

Suddenly, from nowhere, a single white bird flew right through the centre of the wheel of eagles, like a dart through a target. Its flight was straight and fast and as it soared through the hole. The circle of eagles closed in and, like a giant arrowhead, the black eagles followed the white bird in a straight line and at great speed.

Tom stood up in his stirrups and pointed up. "It's Mr Hawkins!" he shouted, to the utter confusion of his companions.

Tom was right. Mr Hawkins had called for the assistance of the ancient black eagles of the Kharamun mountains. These eagles were incredibly large, with a wingspan of twelve feet, able to carry a fully grown man up into the highest mountains and devour him. They only lived in the Kharamun mountains, named after a giant eagle that once ruled the skies many hundreds of years ago. Rumpitter explained this to Tom, who relayed the tale to the comrades.

Mr Hawkins and the eagles were heading directly for the Saharadeen army.

The comrades all turned to look at Tom.

"What did you say, lad?" asked Joseph. Braheim also looked at the boy with a questioning look in his face. The others all went quiet.

Tom looked down at Rumpitter. Without words, Tom asked *what should I say, Rumpitter?*

Before Rumpitter could reply another voice came into Tom's head. *It's all right Tom, you should tell them soon. I can hear your thoughts. First you must climb to the top of the mountain; when you get there it will be clear to you what you should do. Then, when you are all together, tell them everything. I know you will find the right words. Rumpitter is there to help you. I and the eagles are going to cause a little problem for Saharadeen. This will buy you more time. Get to the top of the trail, take good care and be brave, Tom. Now go!*

Tom and Rumpitter looked at each other in the eye and then Rumpitter winked. *Shall we go, Tom?* he asked. Tom smiled at the rat and nodded.

Tom turned to the men, who were all waiting keenly for him to answer Joseph's question.

"I have a lot to tell you, but first we must reach the top of the mountain where we will be safe. Trouseau needs help. We all need to rest. Meet me at the top of the trail." On his last word, Tom dug his heels into the stirrups and his horse immediately galloped on up the path. Joseph was stunned. He was about to call back to Tom but it was useless. Tom was already a hundred yards away. He looked back at the others.

"Come men, we will follow the boy. I have a few questions for him – and I want answers."

"I would say we all have," agreed Gordon, and the others all grunted and nodded and then reined in their horses and charged on, following Tom up the steep path.

It was a treacherous ride. One wrong move and any one of them could topple over the edge and fall to their death. The bottom of the ravine was a thousand feet below.

Mr Hawkins led four thousand giant black eagles in a huge spiral through the sky, like a spinning arrow, towards the evil army.

The Saharadeen army was charging over rocky and dusty ground. Horsemen choked the foot soldiers in the dust they kicked up as they raced ahead of them. The war chariots bumped and toppled as they rolled over the rough desert ground. They were approaching the narrow trail to the mountain peak.

One of the horsemen happened to look up into the blistering hot sun, high above them. For a second he thought he saw something, but then all he saw were the high peaks of the mountain ahead. He did not see the giant black arrow in the sky swirling at great speed from out of the sun directly towards them. The eagles were swift in their attack and not until they were just a few hundred yards away did the Saharadeen see them.

Several soldiers suddenly looked up and then screamed out, pointing into the sky. In no time at all, the whole army saw it.

The Saharadeen couldn't believe his eyes. "What is this treachery?" he called.

He commanded his men to take cover under their shields. The horsemen suddenly changed direction swerving to take cover under the overhanging rocks. They were too late. The black arrow of four thousand eagles suddenly began to spiral faster and faster. As they spun through the sky they caused a huge sandstorm. The ear piercing screech from the eagles deafened the whole army. The Saharadeen was helpless. Eagles swirled over his chariots and knocked horse soldiers from their mounts. Everyone drew swords to try to fend off the birds but the sandstorm became too much. Soon the whole army was choking in a huge dust cloud.

They were blinded and lost in the storm. Men charged into each other, horses reared and lost their riders. Chariots ran into rocks and turned over. The whole army was in chaos. The Saharadeen himself was struggling to find a way through the dust storm and was forced to hide behind a large rock and cover himself over with his cape.

The eagles whirled and whirled above the sandstorm, causing complete disarray to the Saharadeen ranks. They kept on swirling above them until there were no soldiers standing. The whole army had taken cover behind rocks or were buried in the sand under their cloaks.

Mr Hawkins watched from a rocky peak above the scene of chaos. He was pleased with the attack.

*That should buy my friends some time* he thought to himself. Once he was satisfied that the eagles had done their work, he called to them in a high pitch tone. One very large, black eagle hovered above him with its wings outstretched into the wind. "Our work is done, my friend. Now we shall return to the mountain."

Mr Hawkins looked up at the eagle. "Thank-you, I will not forget this." The seagull gave a blink of his eye and a golden glow of light appeared. The eagle also blinked with his large yellow and brown eye and nodded proudly down to the seagull. "Until we meet again," he said and then lifted up his great wings and floated up into the sky. The eagle let out a loud screech, which hung in the air for a long time. All the other eagles heard the call and replied in the same sound. One by one they flew above the seagull and looked down on him as they passed by, then turned to ascend back up into the mountains of Kharamun. They vanished as quickly as they had appeared.

When the last eagle had flown past, Mr Hawkins took off to survey the desert area. He still could not see anything below as the dust from the sandstorm was still thick in the air.

The desert storm lasted for a long time and the Saharadeen army was forced to stay under cover until the dust finally settled, many hours later.

The comrades continued along the narrow, rocky trail. Steep cliffs shaded them from the sun. As they rode higher into the mountain pass, the air became still and cooler. After a while they reached a wide ridge and looked at the wonderful view over the great ravine and saw the most spectacular scene of the desert below and the surrounding mountains. The landscape was an array of wonderful colours. It was truly a wonderful sight. The desert was a blanket of red and gold. For as far as they could see the canyons and ravines were shades of copper, yellow and red. The whole area was under a roof of clear blue sky.

They kept up a steady pace, riding in single file, round each of the treacherous winding corners. Eventually they could see they were near the summit. They stopped in stunned silence when they saw, above them, a huge rock in the shape of an eagle's head. It was magnificent. As they approached, the sun burst out over the head. The bright, golden light shone into their eyes and they covered their faces from the light. Carefully they moved towards the enormous eagle's head rock. The pass was now slightly wider. Joseph and Mababe drew their horses up beside Tom.

*Tom, it's time to start explaining things, I think.* said Rumpitter without words.

Tom heard Rumpitter but his attention was on the huge eagle's head, carved into the mountain peak. Then he noticed that the beak of the eagle was an opening. *Look Rumpitter. The eagle's mouth. It's open. It looks like a cave.*

Joseph was now up close to Tom and took hold of the reins of Tom's horse and drew his horse to a halt. "We must talk lad, there are things I..." Tom was still staring up at the eagle's head and interrupted him. "Wait, Joseph, look up there, I can see an opening. This pass leads straight to the eagle's mouth – look." Tom pointed up towards the eagle's head. Then he turned to Joseph and the others. They were all staring at him as if waiting for him to address them. Tom noticed Blake and Sam Little tending to Trouseau, who was fading fast.

"Your friend, Trouseau, needs help. We must get him into a safe place and find water. I know you all want to know what's happening and I can tell you, but first we must take shelter and find food and water." Tom knew they needed an explanation, but now was not the time.

Joseph nodded in agreement. The others also agreed and they continued towards the peak.

Finally they came up to the huge gaping mouth of the eagle's head. It had been beautifully carved into the rock and looked so very real. Its eyes seemed to be looking at them, which disconcerted the comrades.

Mababe jumped down from his horse and strode up to the huge mouth of the eagle. He drew his sword and, as he took one single step forward, the mouth slowly opened wider. He hesitated and turned to the others, who nervously stepped forward to join him. Mababe walked in bravely with his sword held high as if he were about to attack something or someone.

"Oh no you don't, my friend, I am coming with you," said Joseph. Then all the others jumped off their horses and followed. Mababe turned to see his comrades standing beside him and smiled.

"Just like old times eh?" Joseph said quietly. Tom stayed on his horse with Blake who was caring for Trouseau. Braheim tied all the horses together and slowly followed on.

They were now all dismounted with the exception of Trouseau. They walked the horses into the eagle's mouth. Soon they were all standing inside the head of the eagle. They were in a large cavernous area. Strangely, the floor was smooth and quite slippery. The cavern led them deeper into the eagle's head. As they went deeper, they realised they were climbing upwards. The ceiling and walls were made of what appeared to be thousands of thick ivory coloured arched poles, and the sound of the horses panting and snorting echoed very loudly around the cavern. It was the strangest place. Tom looked down at the stone hanging around his neck and held it tight. He was nervous, but the courage came back to him as he saw the others moving forward. Some were looking through gaps in the walls to see if there were any other doors or openings. The path became narrower and eventually the floor turned into a soft, soggy footpath. The floor seemed like a rubbery substance and was very hard to walk across.

The horses slipped on the floor and their legs buckled because they couldn't keep upright. Eventually everyone, except Trouseau, was walking on foot, leading the horses by hand. It was odd, thought Tom, that the air seemed warm and yet they had walked deep into the mountain, where it should have been cooler. It was not until he looked more closely at the walls of the cavern on each side of the pathway that something caught his eye.

"Hold on a minute," he called and his voice echoed everywhere.

"What is it lad?" asked Joseph.

"Does anyone have anything we can make a light with?" Tom asked, as he dug his finger into the cavern wall.

"Why, what is it boy?" asked Mababe.

"I was wondering if we could have a little more light."

A few of the men came up to see what Tom was looking at. He was staring into the wall.

Gordon was looking over Tom's shoulder. "What do you see?" Gordon was straining his eyes to see what Tom was looking at.

Tom reached through the wall of ribbed ivory poles and, with his fingers; he touched the surface of the wall behind. It suddenly moved and Tom pulled his hand a way quickly and jumped back. "Oh my goodness!" he exclaimed.

Joseph came up beside Tom, "What is it, lad?" he asked, trying to see where Tom had put his hand.

"It moved!" cried out Gordon, "the wall – it, it moved."

Joseph carefully touched the wall beyond the ivory coloured poles and very gently pressed his hand flat against the wall. It moved in and out, making his hand rock slowly back and forth. Then he whispered: "The Lord protect us," and quickly pulled his hand away and turned to the others.

"Get out! We must get out of here. Everyone, come on, let's go!" he shouted.

"What are you doing Joseph?" Tom called, but then he saw the others were trying to get back to the eagle's mouth to escape. He closed his eyes and held onto the stone tightly and thought hard.

Without words he said *Mr Hawkins, where are you? What is this place you have sent us to?*

The voice came back to him. *Hold on tight Tom. Don't let the others leave, it's too dangerous. Stop them.*

Suddenly, just as Tom was about to shout to the men, there was a loud screeching sound. It pierced their ears and echoed all around them. The sound echoed through the cavern. It was so loud they all fell to their knees and covered their ears. The horses were very frightened and reared up kicking their legs into the air. The men struggled to hold them still. Then a violent gust of wind blasted through, knocking over anyone still standing. The deafening, screeching sound came again. They all fell to the floor and the horses began to panic, neighing and whining and jumping.

They kicked out with their hind legs and one just missed Tom and he rolled over across the slippery floor and grabbed onto one of the ivory coloured poles. Then the floor moved like a snake with every gust of wind and screech.

"The door!" shouted Joseph. "It's closing!"

Some of them tried to reach the mouth, but it was too late and suddenly they were in darkness.

Tom heard screams of terror from the men and horses as they struggled to stop themselves being trampled and thrown in all directions. Tom heard the voice again. *Tom, hold tight, call the men to take hold of the walls and calm down. All will be well, just hold on and wait.* Mr Hawkins's voice was clear and firm. Tom called out to the others in the darkness and chaos.

"Everything will be all right, just hold onto the walls. Tie the horses down and hold tight," he called out. But against the loud eerie sound from all around them and the noise of desperate horses and men yelling, his voice was drowned. No one heard him.

Suddenly there was a terrible roar. The floor beneath them began to move violently and everything trembled and shook. Tom thought they were in an earthquake. He held onto one of the ribbed walls and Rumpitter dived into Tom's shirt and clung on with his claws.

The Saharadeen and his army were finally out of the sandstorm and had reassembled and were marching up the mountain. He had sent a phalanx of his army in a different direction and, in a cloud of dust, thousands of horsemen charged off into the desert. They were ordered to follow a wider track around the foot of the mountain. The rest of his army of horsemen, chariot drivers and foot soldiers followed the tracks up the steep path towards the peak of the mountain.

They were moving rapidly towards the top. Then the Saharadeen saw the head of the eagle carved into the huge mountain rock.

He paused and looked up at the eagle's head carved into the mountain. *Kharamun* he said to *himself. I hope he sleeps.*

He turned to his men and, with the Sword in his hand, waved them on. The army climbed higher and higher until they were near the peak. The whole mountain path was now lined with the Saharadeen's army. They were being shouted at by their leaders to carry on marching. Any soldier who dared to stop for breath or pause to peer over the cliff into the great abyss, was whipped or beaten with a lance.

Suddenly there was a terrible roar from all around the mountain and then the mountain began to shake. Rocks fell from above the soldiers and some of the path gave way and toppled thousands of feet down the side of the mountain. The soldiers scrambled to clutch onto a rock or a branch in the side of the cliffs to stop themselves being thrown over.

The rumble grew more and more violent and then huge boulders from around the eagle's head began to roll away and went crashing down the mountainside.

The Saharadeen pulled his horse up and shouted at his generals to halt the army. His eyes were wild and red as he screamed at his men. "Get back, get back! Tell them to keep to the cliff walls or we will be doomed."

The giant head of the eagle began to crack and a deafening noise drowned out the roar of the trembling mountain. More rocks fell away and then the Saharadeen soldiers looked up in terror as they saw the most frightening sight.

The eagle's head was beginning to move. From behind the huge eagle, more rocks fell away. The sound was deafening. Rocks and giant boulders flew through the air as if there had been a huge explosion. The loud screeching sound continued. The head of a giant eagle was moving. The whole mountain was moving. Suddenly a giant eagle was rising up out of the mountain. The noise echoed all around the mountain and the ground trembled even more violently.

The soldiers were terrified as they looked up in horror. The eagle's head moved as it rose up. Its eyes rolled and a giant wing tore out of the rocks. Then the other wing appeared. The wings were gigantic and they burst through the rock, tearing up the mountain as the whole massive body of an eagle appeared through the flying rocks and debris, sending more boulders rolling away down the side of the mountain. The ground shook as if the world was being torn apart.

The whole body of the giant eagle rose up into the air through the cloud of dust and flying rocks. The soldiers cried out in fear that they would be destroyed by the monster.

The eagle screamed out a thunderous shriek and threw away the remaining rocks from its body. It lifted up and its head rolled from side to side. The wings flapped up and down sending a powerful gust of wind across the great ravine below it. The strength of the wind was so strong that some of the soldiers were unable to hold on and they were sent flying through the air and over the cliff. Their screams were heard drifting away down the mountain.

The Saharadeen shouted orders to his generals and in response they called their men to retreat back down the pass.

The eagle stared down at the tiny figures scurrying away and lifted up one giant claw which smashed through the rocks and settled back down on top of the mountain pass. Then the other leg lifted out of the rocks and the giant eagle let out another terrifying screech which shook the whole mountain.

One claw grabbed a huge boulder the size of a house and dropped it onto the pass beneath.

The boulder hit the ground and began rolling down towards the Saharadeen's soldiers. They tried to scramble away, but in vain. The boulder crushed hundreds of them as it gathered momentum, before it bounced and rolled over the cliff and far away down into the canyon, taking with it chariots and horse soldiers.

The Saharadeen and some of his men managed to ride away from the charging boulder and galloped back down the pass. They did not stop to save anyone who got in their way.

The eagle lifted high up into the air. The terrible sound shook the ground beneath and the great mountain of Kharamun shook violently.

The comrades, now trapped inside the giant eagle, were still struggling to hold onto anything they could.

Then something changed. The screeching sound stopped. The rolling and rumbling stopped. The movement inside the eagle became smoother.

Tom called out, "We're flying! We're inside the eagle, it must be real."

"Heaven save us," called out Gordon who was clinging to one of the ivory ribs with one hand and holding the reins of his terrified horse with the other. "We have been eaten alive."

Then Mababe called out, "We are doomed – prepare to face your Gods."

All the prisoners and the comrades crossed themselves and prayed.

"No, wait, it's all right, really!" Tom called out again. "Mr Hawkins has ordered this, we will be all right." The others all looked at Tom with confused and questioning looks.

Finally Joseph spoke. "Are you mad, boy? What crazy talk is this?"

"Mr Hawkins, your captain and friend is with us... but not exactly... well, he's looking after us. Let's put it that way." Tom was struggling to explain himself. It was all very odd indeed, but having to tell them was so difficult. He also realised how strange it must be to them.

He had to try to explain things. "The Captain – Captain Hawkins, escaped from the Saharadeen. He was trying to free you all from being slaves, but..." Tom was about to tell the story when there was a sudden movement and the eagle turned in the sky and they all rolled into a heap on one side and then back again to the other side. Rumpitter lost his grip and was tossed like a feather and then bounced along the length of the red, rubbery floor.

Suddenly a bright flash of light burst inside and a strong gust of wind blew them all over again. Rumpitter was still rolling along on the rubbery surface, which was bouncing up and down like a wave. Then they could see the sky and clouds and the warm air burst into their faces.

Again they had to cling onto the sides to save themselves from tumbling out of the opening. Tom saw Rumpitter tumbling towards the opening.

"No!" Tom screamed, "Rumpitter, Oh no! We must stop him." Tom let go of his grip and crawled towards the opening. He realised now that this was the eagle's mouth and it was open. He could see the giant top beak moving up and down. "Rumpitter," he called again, "grab something." Joseph had a rope around his shoulder and pulled it over his head.

"Here lad, take hold of this. I will take the strain." Tom took the rope and looped it around his shoulders and then continued crawling towards the eagle's mouth. The others were helpless to assist with fear of falling out of the eagle and to certain death.

Rumpitter rolled head over heels landing into the eagle's beak. Tom could see his little legs scrambling to try and find a foothold and something to grab onto, but it was hopeless.

"Rumpitter – no, Oh God, no, please!" He saw the rat tip over the edge of the eagle's lower beak.

By now Tom had crawled right into the giant beak and could see the sky stretching far above. He crawled to the very edge of the beak and looked down. "No!" he cried as he saw the rat falling through the sky towards the ground. Suddenly there was a hefty jolt and then he was thrown right out of the beak and flipped out into the air. Joseph held onto the rope and some of the others also took the strain.

"The boy has gone over!" shouted Braheim. Then they were all tossed forward as the eagle seemed to being diving down. Tom was hanging from the rope, which had been caught around the lip of the eagle's beak. He was swinging in the air like a spider on a web. The eagle dived down and down. Tom was desperately holding onto the rope. Then he looked down and realised the eagle was flying towards Rumpitter. They were catching up fast. The small figure of the rat became larger as they grew nearer. Tom called again, "Rumpitter!"

He could now hear the screaming from the falling rat getting louder and louder. The eagle swooped down and scooped the rat up in its beak and, with a flick of its tongue, threw Rumpitter through the air and straight inside. Rumpitter screamed out as he flew past the men and landed in a heap, rolling backwards as the eagle lifted its head and began to soar upwards again. Joseph quickly pulled onto the rope. There was a sigh of relief as they saw a hand grab onto the lower beak and then another. Tom's head appeared over the lip.

With a final tug, Tom tumbled over and fell back inside. He slid along the floor towards the men and settled with a bump right beside a very relieved Rumpitter.

*Oh my,* said the rat, *that was close. Thought I was gone for certain that time.*

Tom was out of breath and clung onto the stone which, miraculously, was still hanging around his neck. *You're not kidding, I thought I'd had it that time too!*

The men were pleased to see the boy safe and began to cheer. "Welcome back lad," said Joseph with a big smile. Tom smiled back to the men. "Thanks."

"I can see you are very fond of your rat friend. You risked your life for it," said Mababe, scratching his head. He really didn't understand why anyone would want to save a rat.

Tom looked at a very shaken Rumpitter and smiled. "He'd do the same for me," said Tom.

"We are flying inside the mouth of a giant eagle. This is madness, such madness. What will become of us? Allah save us," Braheim said as he held his arms upwards as if he were talking to someone above.

They all looked towards the eagle's beak and saw the blue sky whistling past them.

Then the eagle let out another screech and again the horses reared up, snorting and kicking out.

"Hold them fast men," Joseph called. Then he looked at Tom. "I do believe we are in safe hands. You have some explaining to do lad, but I think it can wait."

No sooner had he spoken, the eagle began to dip his head again. "Hold tight, men," Joseph called out and they all looked out from the eagle's mouth.

Suddenly the tip of a sandy hilltop appeared, then another, and then another. "We're going down!" Tom called out. "It looks like we are landing."

The eagle was floating slowly down. As it glided past a hill of soft golden sand, it turned and lifted slowly upwards. Then it opened its mouth a little further.

Suddenly Tom saw a shape of something fly past. "Mr Hawkins!" he said softly. Rumpitter looked up at Tom and said quietly, "He has saved us Tom, he is always with us."

Tom told the men to look out of the eagle's beak and pointed. "See, there, a bird."

The men all looked out into the sky as they floated past hill after hill of soft sand. "A bird?" asked Gordon.

"Well actually, he's a seagull," Tom turned to the others. "In fact, that's Mr Hawkins..." Tom looked at the reaction from the men. But his words were drowned out by the wind.

They all stared out of the eagle's mouth. The seagull was leading the eagle towards a hill-top. They saw a plateau coming towards them as they gradually came closer to the ground.

The eagle raised its wings and stretched out both its giant legs. Its claws opened out like huge elephant tusks.

It landed gently onto the soft sandy surface and finally came to a halt. Slowly it lowered its head to the ground and dug its lower beak into the sand.

*Quick Tom, get everyone out* he heard Mr Hawkins say.

Tom turned to the others, "Come on, let's go!"

Quickly, the men scrambled to their feet and, dragging the horses with them, they walked towards the eagle's mouth and out onto the sandy ground. Immediately they all looked back at the giant eagle. Its eyes were watching them, flickering and rolling in their huge sockets.

As soon as the last man was out, the eagle closed its mouth and lifted up its massive head.

The seagull glided over and settled on Kharamun's head. Mr Hawkins looked like a pinhead against the giant eagle, towering above the men on the ground. They looked up and saw the seagull tilt his head and a glint of gold light flicked out from his eye into the eye of the eagle. The giant eagle lowered and raised its head slowly, as if it were bowing to the men. Then the seagull lifted up into the air and swooped to one side, settling on a mound of rock. The eagle raised its huge wings and lifted off the ground. The downward flap caused the sand to rise up like a cloud from the desert floor. They had to dive for cover to protect themselves as the sand cloud moved towards them. They coughed and choked as the dust flew around them like a whirlwind.

After a while the dust began to settle and, as they crawled out from their covers, they saw the eagle had vanished.

Mr Hawkins swooped down low over them. *Tom, quickly get them to the top of that hill ahead of you. You must tend to Trouseau before he weakens further.*

Tom picked himself up and brushed the sand out of his hair. He called out, "Rumpitter, where are you?" There was a rustle from a sand dune to the left of him and then he saw a few stones roll down the slope, followed by a very dusty, large rat, who rolled down and landed at Tom's feet. Tom laughed at the sight of him. "Are you all right?" The rat coughed and spat out the gritty sand from his teeth. "Ugh, I've got sand all over me," he complained.

Tom saw the others all picking themselves up and grouping together. It had been a terrifying experience for all of them. But at least they were safe. For now.

Joseph walked over to Tom and looked down at the boy with careful but appreciative eyes.

"We owe you much boy. You have freed us from hell. I don't know who you are and I don't understand how you came here, but I have a feeling we are soon to discover the meaning of all this."

"There is a lot to tell you, Joseph, and I hope you will be able to understand it. It's very difficult for me, but all I can say now is that we are in good hands. Mr Hawkins, er... I mean Captain Haw..." Tom was cut short.

"Hawkins! You know the Captain? Where is he? We thought he had died by the hand of the Saharadeen."

"No he didn't die, well not really. He..." Tom was again about to try to explain everything when he heard a voice in his head. *Tom, not now. Trouseau needs help. All the men need rest and you must get them up the hill and then follow my instructions. There will be time for explanations later.*

Tom stopped talking when he was listening to Mr Hawkins and Joseph thought it odd that the boy had suddenly gone quiet.

"Are you all right boy? You have gone silent. Are you ailing?" Joseph asked.

"No – no I'm fine. I think we should get away from here, out of the sun. Mr Trouseau needs help and we need to find water. We have to keep going. We must carry on. I will tell you everything very soon, I promise."

Joseph nodded and some of the others who had been listening agreed that finding shelter from the heat and food and water were most important.

They gathered themselves up and helped each other up the steep sand dune.

*Tom,* called Mr Hawkins, *Well done, lad, now keep going and get Trouseau out of the sun as soon as possible.*

*OK Mr Hawkins, I hope we find water soon.*

*You will Tom, don't worry.*

It was a struggle for the men to climb the hill. The sand was very soft underfoot and it took twice the effort and energy to make the climb. Some of the men crawled on hands and knees and some were so weak they rolled or slid back down the thick red sandy hill. The stronger men went back down to help others climb up.

The horses snorted and grunted as they were pulled up by their handlers. It was a long and arduous climb but finally they made it to the top. No one was lost.

Mababe was first to reach the top. He stood tall and, despite the terrible time he had suffered in the caves as a prisoner and a slave, he was still strong. He knelt down on one knee and stared across the vast desert plains before them. At first he could not see anything but desert. There were mountains to the right, but they were many miles away. A narrow gorge ran from the hill and cut through the desert, far into the distance. At one time, he thought, there would have been a river running here but now it was dry. He saw no signs of any water.

He glanced his eyes towards the direction of the sun, which was burning bright and made focusing in its direction very difficult. He held a hand over his eyes to see into the sun. There was a flash of light and then it disappeared. He looked again trying to protect his eyes from the bright sunlight. The others had all grouped together and Joseph saw Mababe staring into the sun.

"Careful, my friend. The sun will blind you. What do you see?" Tom heard Joseph talking and went over to the two men.

Mababe was silent, still staring into the sun with his hand shading his eyes. "I thought I saw something, a light," he replied to Joseph.

"The sun can tell lies, Mababe. It could be a reflection from a rock or anything," Joseph said trying to look in the same direction.

Tom was also dazzled by the bright sun. He cast his eyes up towards the blue sky and away from the sun. He saw a small black dot high above and he rubbed his eyes to correct his sight. He looked again and the dot grew larger. It appeared to be heading towards them. Then, he knew. He spoke without words *Is that you Mr Hawkins?*

*Yes, Tom, head towards the sun, follow the gorge. It leads you to safety.*

*Are you sure?* Tom asked. *Positive, Tom. Go quickly. I fear the enemy will not rest and you must find cover.*

Tom quickly turned to the men and pointed towards the gorge. "We must follow that gorge towards the sun. Quickly, let's keep moving."

Mababe turned to speak to the men. "I think the boy is right, we should go that way. There is something down there, although I cannot see what it is."

Everyone agreed and followed. It was an easier climb down the slope to the gorge although some of the weaker men tripped and slid. The horses stumbled but were able to navigate their way with the lead of their handlers. It took almost an hour to reach the gorge but once they were finally down in the valley they could keep going without the sun being so bright as it was occasionally shadowed by the mountain peaks.

The sun would soon fall behind the mountains and it would be dark. The floor of the gorge was flat which made it easier underfoot.

As they continued along the path of the gorge, to their astonishment they saw some trees at the top of a short slope. Then, very strangely, the horses became excited and kicked at the dust and snorted, tossing their heads. Maris and Blake were doing their best to stop Trouseau from being thrown from his horse. It took both of them to hold the horse steady and lead it on up the slope towards the trees.

Mababe sensed something in the air. He knelt down and took up some soil in his hand and sniffed it. He rolled some sand around in his hands, then he smiled and looked up to the others. "I know why the horses are so *excited.*" He smiled again. "They can smell water!" The others became excited too. "Water?" called out Gordon, who was parched from the hot sun. His mouth was dry and cracked around his lips. Some of the weaker prisoners seemed to understand and looked over in bewilderment. Water, could it be so?

"I knew it!" Tom cried out and ran on up the gorge. The others all seemed to find some hidden strength; a last spurt of energy would get them to water and everyone moved on with more purpose.

As they approached the rise, they could see that there were more trees. The horses picked up speed and the men had trouble holding them steady. They didn't want to lose the horses in the desert. They would need them later.

Tom had one hand firmly clasped around the stone hanging from his neck as he reached the top first with Rumpitter scampering along between his feet. Joseph and Mababe were now running close behind. "The boy has great strength, Joseph," Mababe panted as he ran. "Aye, he is young indeed but I agree he has courage and speed." The two men were exhausted as they came up to Tom, who was staring ahead with a wide smile on his face. He turned to the men.

"We've done it!" he exclaimed proudly. "Look!" He pointed ahead and then ran towards the trees and disappeared.

Mababe called back to the others. "Come, keep up. Follow us." The others followed on through the trees. When they pushed their way through they found Tom standing by a large pool.

"It's an oasis!" Joseph whispered. "He has saved us," he said, looking at the men pushing through the trees. "The boy has found water, just as he promised." The men ran straight towards the pool and fell into the water. Some were crying with joy. Others who were weak just sighed with relief. Even Rumpitter jumped into the water with his legs pumping up and down to stay afloat.

Tom looked up at the sky and said, without words, *Thank-you Mr Hawkins, thank-you.*

Then he saw the seagull sitting on a rock on the far side of the pool. *Well done Tom, you found it. The trees hide the pool from the desert and the hills and trees cast a shadow over the water, keeping it cool. This is a secret water hole; not many know of it. There is an underground spring that comes from those mountains over there. Only the animals and nomads who live in the desert know of it.*

"It's amazing!" Tom called out. He was so happy and ran into the water with a big splash. He saw all the other men and horses splashing and drinking, all so happy to be alive. One of the horses was rolling in the water and snorting with delight. Blake and Maris helped Trouseau by pulling his horse slowly down into the water and let the horse lean over as it entered the pool. Trouseau slipped easily from the saddle and into the clear cool water. "Hold his head up," Sam Little called and ran over to help. "We should clean his wounds and give him a little water at first or he will be sick." They washed Trouseau and then pulled him under a tree to see to his wounds. Mr Hawkins gently drifted above to watch them help Trouseau. He was pleased to see his friend safe in the hands of his comrades.

Braheim walked across and watched Tom jumping up and down in the water. Then he looked at the rat who had found a rock and was pruning himself, nibbling at his fur and rolling on a rock to dry himself. He smiled, shaking his head in disbelief. *A strange boy and a rat have saved us from death and yet we know nothing of him* he thought to himself.

Just as he was thinking this, he saw the seagull fly overhead and swoop over Tom's head.

He saw the boy looking at the bird and, for a moment, he could swear he saw the boy speak to the bird. He shook his head again and ran his fingers through his beard. A seagull in a place like this was not normal, he thought, and wondered. He found a place to sit and consider this strange thing. *The young boy, a rat and possibly a seagull are together? This cannot be.* Braheim was a wise and thoughtful man who considered most things carefully. "I am much confused," he whispered to himself. He turned as he sensed someone behind him. It was Joseph. "You seem as confused as I, my friend," Joseph said as he stabbed his sword into the sand and knelt next to Braheim. "This is no ordinary boy, Joseph," Braheim said quietly. "There is more to this than we know, just watch." The two looked at Tom laughing and playing in the water, talking to Rumpitter like the rat was a human, and the seagull hovering over his head.

It was not long before some of the others had joined Braheim and Joseph and they all sat in silence as they watched the boy, the rat and the bird as if they were embraced in some strange dance. Tom was dancing along the water's edge, the rat was bouncing around between his feet and hopping up and down. The large seagull hovered and swooped over Tom's head, occasionally flipping upside down as if in some kind of aeronautical display. It was the strangest sight for the men to witness. They had never seen anything like this. Finally everyone was sitting in silence – watching. Not a word was said.

Tom was dancing up and down on his toes, skipping along the water's edge. *We did it Mr Hawkins, we did it. We saved them. You are such a clever bird.* He laughed and Mr Hawkins was also delighted and laughed back. Rumpitter was skipping around Tom's feet, singing a little rhyme.

*We three friends of different worlds*
*Saved the men so brave and bold*
*Led them to water from a terrible fate*
*And home soon we go for a feast on a plate*

*Away from here, the Land of Fire, away from here the Land of Fire...*Rumpitter repeated the rhyme over and over. "That's a fine song, my dear friend. Do you not know any other lines?" laughed Mr Hawkins. The three laughed and laughed.

Rumpitter was about to continue the song for a sixth time, when he happened to look over and saw all the men sitting staring at them in silence.

*We three friends...*

"Oh." He stopped. "Er, Tom, Mr Hawkins, I think we should stop." Rumpitter stood looking in the direction of the men sitting by the trees. "Oh come on, Rumpitter, what's the matter?" said Tom, still skipping along. Then Mr Hawkins stopped flipping around in the air and hovered very still above Tom, lifting himself up a little higher. Tom looked up at the seagull and then at Rumpitter. "Come on, what's the matter?" He paused and looked in the direction to where Rumpitter was looking.

He, too, saw all the men watching them and stopped. Now he felt very awkward. He had not realised that they were all staring and it didn't take him long to work out why. Tom's laughter quickly reduced to a smile and then he had a more serious face. "Oh," he said quietly. He looked at the seagull hovering still in the air above. "Mr Hawk..."

"Yes, Tom," the bird interrupted quickly. "It's time, Tom. You have to tell them."

Tom looked at the seagull. *Can't you?* this time without words.

*No, Tom, only you and Rumpitter can speak to me or hear me. You must tell them — they will have many questions.* As the bird said this he began drifting a little higher.

Tom noticed. *Where are you going, don't leave me alone. I may need you.*

*I can't be here when you tell them Tom, it's too upsetting and may be worse for them. Not until they have become accustomed to me. You'll be fine Tom, they are good people. Rumpitter is with you.* The rat looked up and blinked at the bird and turned to Tom. *It is time, Tom,* he said in a serious tone and nodded towards the men.

Tom stood for a moment and thought quietly to himself. He looked over to Joseph and bit his lip. This was not going to be easy.

Joseph sensed Tom's mood and slowly stood up and walked down to him. He nodded to the boy with a gentle and kind smile. "I have a feeling you have much to tell, lad, but you need have no fear, we are grateful for your help and we are in your debt." Tom looked up nervously at Joseph. He was a very tall, rugged and strong man, but his eyes were kind. Joseph put a hand on Tom's shoulder.

"Come," Joseph said quietly. Tom nodded and walked with Joseph towards the group of men sitting patiently by the trees. Rumpitter hopped along, close behind. Tom turned to look back. The seagull had disappeared.

The sun was slipping away behind the mountains, the sky turned red and the air was still.

As they approached, the men began to stand up and, as if by some unmentioned command, formed a circle around Tom and Joseph.

Joseph decided to be the first to speak. "Men, we have come far. We owe much to this boy and although we all have many questions, I must ask you to hold still and let the boy have his say. We are free of the Saharadeen, but we do not know where we are and how far behind our enemy is. Soon we will have to move on and find cover and food. It is well that Trouseau has rested but he will need medicines and we have none." He looked down at Tom with another friendly smile, his hand still on the boy's shoulder. "Tom has much to tell us and we should listen to him. "Come lad, speak to us." He said.

Tom braced himself and looked around at all the men who stood still, patiently waiting for him to speak. He cleared his throat and began.

"My name is Tom Parker, well, you all know that anyway. I don't come from this land. It's a little tricky to try to explain this, but my home is a long way from here. In fact I come from a different world. Some of you probably know where England is" Tom scratched his head. He wasn't really sure about the two worlds and if he was going to make any sense. "That is, if you know the same England as I do. In fact I'm not really sure how I can get back home. Only Mr Hawkins will know that." He was about to continue when he was interrupted by shouts and calls to explain. "Where is the Captain?" shouted Gordon, and then Blake interrupted, "Why are you saying 'Mr Hawkins' what do you mean, boy?" Immediately they were all shouting at once, calling for explanations. Tom didn't know where to look first or who to answer. "Silence!" shouted Braheim. "Let the boy speak. There will be time for questions later. Come Tom, tell us," he said in a quieter voice.

"I'm sorry," said Tom quickly. "I know this all sounds strange to you. Mr Hawkins, your captain and your friend..." He had to pause to think what to say. "... was captured by the Saharadeen in the Temple of Fire. You were all taken prisoners and locked up in those dungeons. The Saharadeen played a terrible trick on your captain. But he did escape – but then something happened." There was a lot of chatter and mumbling amongst the men and, before they could start to shout out again, Joseph put up his hand for silence and Braheim and Mababe stepped into the ring and stood by Tom for support. Tom continued. "Your Captain Hawkins, who I call Mr Hawkins and who is my friend too, found a way out. He was unable to come to your rescue and, well, he found his way to England. He lived for a long time there and then, one day, we met and became friends. He told me of his adventures with you and about the Land of Fire. His only wish was to return here to save you. He has kept his promise and I am here to help too. Me and my friend, Rumpitter." Tom pointed to the rat sitting very still on the sand by his feet. Rumpitter looked up at Tom and, without words said, *Keep going Tom, you're doing just fine.*

Tom swallowed again and continued. "It's a very long story and we know what dangers are out there. The Saharadeen is after us. He wants this stone." Tom pulled the stone from under his shirt and held up the pouch. The men began nodding and talking to each other again. Tom was suddenly gaining more courage and held up the stone to show them all and walked around the circle of men holding the stone in the air. Then he put it safely back inside his shirt. "The stone must be reunited with the Sword of Isis that once belonged to... Captain Hawkins. The Saharadeen has the sword and if he gets this stone as well, he'll be indestructible. No one will be able to defeat him. He will conquer every land under the sun and kill everyone. Mr Hawkins is my friend and yours, he is alive and you have seen him. He has saved you and now together we must finish the task. We must defeat the Saharadeen and get the sword back in safe hands."

"You say we have seen Captain Hawkins. How do you mean, lad?" asked Joseph. The others all nodded at Tom.

This was the hard part, thought Tom, and looked to Rumpitter for reassurance. The rat looked at Tom and nodded. *Go on*, he whispered.

Tom continued. "When Mr Hawkins was caught by the Saharadeen, he was sent into the pool of fire to an eternal doom, a curse made from the Saharadeen's vile magic. But the Saharadeen had not counted on Mr Hawkins grabbing this stone as he fell. The stone is magic and has great powers. The Captain – did not die, but he returned in a different form." There was uncontrolled shouting and questions being thrown at Tom. He couldn't answer all these questions at once so he shouted even louder than them. "PLEASE BE QUIET!"

Silence fell again. "Thank-you. Mr Hawkins, as I call him, or the Captain as you know him, are the same, but... he is not human. He was turned into... a bird."

There was a deathly hush. Nobody said a word. Tom looked up into the sunset and, without words, said something. Only his lips moved, but without sound.

"Mr Hawkins now lives an eternal life. He will never die. Neither will he ever be the same man as you knew him. But he is here with us. You have seen him already and you saw him just now, with me, by the water over there." Joseph jumped away from Tom. "What madness is this boy? What are you telling us? Captain Hawkins is a bird? I cannot believe it!" Joseph was suddenly startled by something and out of the deep red sky came a shape. The shape had wings and swooped down over them. The large seagull flew over their heads. At first in a wide circle, then he began moving slowly downwards towards them. There was suddenly a flicker from his eye and a beam of bright light shone from the eye onto Joseph's head. Joseph was mesmerised by the light and stood perfectly still, staring up into the sky.

Tom looked up and called out to the bird. "Mr Hawkins, who is Braheim?"

The light moved from Joseph to Braheim, who was so taken aback that he fell to his knees. Tom called out again and suddenly Mababe was touched by the light.

One by one all the comrades were shown the light of Mr Hawkins. They could not speak and were deeply touched by a strange feeling of peace and compassion for their dear friend and leader.

"Gentlemen, I give you your captain – Mr Hawkins!" Tom exclaimed proudly, but strangely, for he could see such mixed feelings of emotions from the men. Feelings of both joy and sadness showed in their eyes and some had tears running down their faces. Gordon could not control himself. Even the very weak Trouseau looked up when the light reached him and had great sorrow in his eyes.

Tom held out one arm firmly and, very slowly, the large seagull settled onto it. The men were stunned and some took a step back. "Mr Hawkins is here. He pledged an oath to save you from the Saharadeen and take back the sword, which has saved so many of you. The Sword of Isis must be returned to its rightful place, now that Mr Hawkins cannot keep it. He can talk to you through me and, together, I mean with your help, we can do this. Do it for your friend, do it for freedom, do it for justice and peace and hopefully we can all get out of here."

Tom was proud of his great speech and Rumpitter looked up at him again, *Mmm, not bad.* Mr Hawkins looked Tom straight in the eye. He nodded at Tom: *Thank-you Tom. You did well.* The bird looked around at all the men. He let out a squawk and flapped his large wings, nearly toppling Tom over.

"You see. This is Mr Hawkins. He's our friend and he has great powers. He will lead us to safety. You have nothing to fear, trust me," said Tom again boldly.

The seagull lifted up his long neck and tilted his head proudly.

The sun had set into a deep, fiery glow over the desert. The palm trees surrounding the edge of the oasis were silhouetted against its red blanket and all was peaceful.

One by one, the comrades all came up to Mr Hawkins to pay their respects. The large seagull had settled on a rock and allowed the men to touch him. Some stroked his head and others were less bold and simply bowed their heads in respect.

Mr Hawkins could see Trouseau lying on the ground under a tree with his comrades, Blake and Sam Little. The bird jumped up and landed in front of the three men. He blinked his eye and the beam of light settled on Trouseau. Then he walked closer and tapped Trouseau's hand with his beak and tilted his head to one side. Although Trouseau was so ill and weak, he managed to lift his head slightly and look into the seagull's eye.

He smiled, then looked up at Blake who was sitting on the sand next to him. Trouseau was so sick and weary and could hardly speak, but he found just enough strength to force a smile and quietly say in a croaky voice, "Mon ami, I know this is my captain, I see it in his eyes."

Blake and Little were immediately stunned by Trouseau's words. He had not spoken for many days. They both looked at the seagull and then knelt down and bowed their heads in respect.

Tom was sitting with Rumpitter on the rock watching as all the men formed a circle around the seagull and Trouseau. They knelt down and bowed. Their leader and comrade had returned.

Mr Hawkins nodded his head up and down to all the men around him and then looked across to Tom. He spoke without words. *We have not reached our destination yet Tom. Now they are rested we must move on. Night will soon be upon us and we have much to do.*

Tom jumped down form the rock and, as he did so, Joseph, Mababe and Braheim approached him.

"So Tom, it seems we are in your hands," said Joseph. "Where do you take us now?"

Tom looked surprised at their immediate understanding of the situation and replied, "Well, I'm not certain, I shall have to ask Mr Hawkins." The seagull heard this and quickly intervened.

*This is good Tom, they will follow you. You must move on to the west. Wait one hour until it is dark and then march. You will need the horses later so keep them well and watered. The men will need food; you will find it at the crest of that hill.* He hopped up into the air and then landed back on the ground. *Move quietly and with stealth. I fear the enemy are not far away and we must not allow them to see or hear us. We must not be discovered by the Saharadeen.*

Tom explained the next move to the men in a quiet voice. "Pass the word to all the men," he whispered. He was feeling hungry but somehow he knew Mr Hawkins would not let them down. It would not be long before they would find food. It was easier now that the air was cooler. He watched the huge red sun slowly fall behind the mountain until it finally disappeared in the west.

Tom looked around as the men quietly prepared for the next march. The horses were kept on a tight rein and gradually everyone was assembled and ready to go. He could not see Mr Hawkins anywhere, so, without words he asked, *Where are you Mr Hawkins?*

*Don't worry, Tom, I am not far away. I have gone on ahead but I will return soon. The desert is a dangerous place at night and you could easily get lost out here. You must head exactly in the direction I have told you. Do not look back and neither must you step to the left or to the right. In a while look up to the sky and you will see my sign* replied the voice in Tom's head. Tom smiled and felt reassured. He looked down at Rumpitter who was sitting patiently on the rock. "Come on Rumpitter, let's get going," he whispered. The rat jumped down and scampered towards the boy. He too had heard the voice. "Ready when you are," he said.

Tom smiled and walked to the front of the line of men. He nodded at Joseph who, in turn, nodded to the men. Everyone began to walk in silence.

Although they were hungry, the rest by the oasis had given strength to the comrades. They were able to walk quite quickly. There was a new sense of purpose. They did not know where their path took them but they put great trust in the boy and the seagull.

These were strange times, thought Joseph, but he knew they must carry on. There would come a time when there would be peace and all would be well. This was firmly in his mind as he marched through the night towards the hill to the west. It looked like a dark shadow in the distance.

Two long hours passed and gradually some of the men began to tire and stumble. Joseph signalled to his comrades to help the weaker men onto the horses, quietly but quickly. They did so in total silence.

Rumpitter had jumped up onto one horse and sat behind Trouseau, who had been propped up in his saddle. Blake and Gordon walked either side of Trouseau's horse. Gordon smiled when he noticed the rat sitting on the rump of the horse. Although it was odd indeed, now he knew that the rat was the boy's friend, it seemed quite natural.

Another hour passed when Tom came to an abrupt halt. He stared directly ahead of him. His eyes opened wide and, with a great big smile, he looked back at the men and pointed ahead. "Look!" he whispered. "Up there. It's Mr Hawkins. He's showing us his sign."

Mababe came up beside the boy and looked ahead. "Where boy? I see only the moon above the dark hill." Joseph and Maris were with them. "Aye, it is just the moon."

Tom nodded, "No, no – look again," he insisted.

They looked up at the crescent moon, which hung over the peak of the hill, and then realised what Tom meant.

They all saw the same thing.

The moon was bright against the black sky but something moved. They all stopped in their tracks and stared.

The moon suddenly dipped just like the blink of an eye and then something moved across the moon. It was silhouetted against its light.

"Upon my word," exclaimed Joseph in a whisper. "Did I just see a bird?"

"You most certainly did Joseph. It's Mr Hawkins and he's showing us the way." He looked back at the shadow of men behind him and signalled to them to keep walking. Joseph and Mababe also urged them forward.

"Mababe, pass the word for them to follow the moon and tell them to make haste," said Joseph quietly.

Mababe nodded and ran to the back of the line of men. The horses were pulled along. The soft sand under their hooves meant they could move faster without making any sound.

They were always on the look-out for the Saharadeen. For now, all was well.

As they climbed the slopes of the hill, the moon appeared to grow larger.

The darkness became slightly lighter and now they could see much better. The desert behind them was so vast. They knew that without the guiding light of the moon, the help of the boy and Mr Hawkins, they would most certainly have become lost and perished in this place.

At last they assembled at the peak of the hill. The moon hung brightly and majestically in the sky before them. Its bright glow was so bold with the blackness of the night sky behind it. Its upturned shining arch was shaped like an old sailing ship with the two ends, front and back, tipped sharply towards the sky. Sitting in the centre was the silhouette of a bird.

Tom smiled again at the men. They were in awe of this fantastic sight.

Then Tom saw something ahead. He looked lower below the moon and noticed on the ground, further ahead, a small flicker of light.

He tugged at Joseph's arm and pointed. "Down there," he whispered. Joseph saw it too and nodded. He signalled to the others and held a finger to his lips for them to stay silent.

Braheim walked over and looked down at Tom. His deep brown eyes sparkled under the reflection of the moon. "I believe I know what this is," he said. "If we are to go that way, we must be cautious." The others agreed and together they slowly stepped forward towards the flickering lights.

# Chapter 10 – The Al Kadi

Tom could sense the tension amongst the men as they picked their way slowly towards the lights.

Soon it was clear that the lights were bundles of small fires flickering in and out of shadows and then they could see dark shapes of large tents. The moon still shone over them and gradually the scene before them became clear. They saw hundreds of tents. Dark shapes and shadows of people moved around like ghosts amongst the fires and tents.

They smelt the scent of fires and then the smell of cooking. The figures moving around grew larger, the smells grew stronger. They heard strange sounds. It suddenly became obvious that what they were hearing was Arabic music. It drifted hauntingly through the night air.

Braheim was the first to speak. "This is a large Bedouin camp. It may not be safe. We do not know who they are."

Joseph agreed with a nod. Tom heard them and whispered, "Wait. Something is coming this way." He pointed ahead.

A dark flickering shape was moving towards them out of the flames of the encampment. Then there were more shapes quickly moving behind. They were black, slim, swirling shapes, which seemed to form into a line as they came closer. The men were nervous and began to prepare themselves for a fight. They drew their weapons. Gordon and Maris drew their horses up beside Trouseau. All the others formed a united group and braced themselves. Rumpitter jumped off the horse and hopped over to Tom. *We have been spotted.*

Tom looked ahead. *You're right, they're riders. Look, it's men on horses.*

Tom was right and almost instantly they saw several horsemen galloping towards them. Then they heard a snort from a horse and the ground thumped underfoot from the beat of hooves.

The dark shapes of the horsemen became taller and were now close. Tom heard the soft clatter and slapping of steel against leather and again the heavy breath of galloping horses.

Quickly the men formed a circle and with swords drawn, stood ready to fight.

The horse riders approached very quickly and within a few short moments they had formed a circle around the comrades. The horsemen were dressed in black robes with head-dresses like turbans with a red band around their heads. Their faces were covered by black veils. Only their dark eyes could be seen through narrow slits in their veils.

The comrades were ready in case they attacked. They were uncertain. Mababe and Joseph stood in front of Tom to protect him. Joseph held his sword firmly in both hands and looked down at Tom. "Stay with me boy, we will not let them get you."

Tom shook his head, "No, I think they are friendly, let's ask them" The horsemen just stood still; their restless horses snorted and nodded their heads up and down. Their front hooves stabbed the ground as if they were about to charge. Some of the prisoners who had escaped from the dungeons of the Saharadeen had grabbed long lances as they fled through the corridors. They now had them pointed forward towards the riders, ready to spear them if they attacked. There was silence – nothing happened and nothing was spoken.

Finally, one rider gave his horse a gentle kick and it made two steps towards the comrades. He did not draw his sword, but looked into the group of men. He bowed his head towards them and then spoke in a firm and deep voice. "We have been waiting for you. You are welcome here. Now, please, come with us."

The men all looked surprised and turned to each other in confusion. What was this? Why hadn't they attacked?

Braheim stepped forward and spoke in his native Arabic tongue. The rider seemed to understand him and replied in Braheim's language. He bowed his head and raised his right hand to his brow in a salute. Braheim replied by bowing his head to the rider.

Braheim turned to his comrades and raised both his hands into the air. "Allah be praised," he said loudly with a wide smile. "Everything is good. These men are friends. They ask us to go to the camp with them. They have been expecting us. They will tend to the sick and give us food."

The comrades instantly relaxed. Gordon let out a cry of thanks and everyone started nodding to each other. For the first time in such a long time, they laughed and thanked their Gods for this relief.

The leader of the horsemen waved his arm in the air in a gesture for the comrades to follow. All the other horsemen turned their horses around and walked along beside the men, now all weary and relieved. Were they finally safe, could they at last sleep? Tom wondered. They were hungry and Trouseau and some of the others badly needed rest and caring for.

Tom looked cautiously at the horsemen. They looked tall and proud in their dark robes. Their black leather saddles were beautifully decorated and the raised pommels on the front of the saddles were studded with small silver coins. Each of the riders carried a long curved sword, hanging from a black leather belt. They wore red cloth sash belts, too, with a curved Arab dagger tucked inside. Tom noticed the dagger on the leader's belt. The curved handle was noticeably more elaborate than those of the other horsemen. It was ivory and beautifully decorated in what looked like jewels, possibly rubies and diamonds, thought Tom. As he was staring, the tall horseman turned to look at Tom. This made Tom nervous and he quickly looked away, pretending that he had not been looking at the man. The rider continued to stare at Tom. Finally, Tom plucked up the courage to turn back his head and look at him again. All Tom could see of the man's face were his deep brown eyes surrounded by two bright white corneas, which sparkled in the moonlight. They did not blink. Tom tried to show he was not scared by almost arrogantly looking the tall man up and down. The rider suddenly lowered his head and saw the leather pouch around Tom's neck, which held the stone. He looked at it carefully for a moment and said something in soft Arabic words that Tom could not properly hear. "Pardon?" Tom said quickly, trying to understand the rider's words. The rider replied by saying nothing but bowed his head and saluted Tom in the Arabic way, with a quick wave of his hand from his forehead. He turned his head away, shouted something loudly at his horse, and with a gentle kick of his heels the large horse suddenly launched into a gallop and sped away in a cloud of dust. The other riders moved out of his way to let him pass. He headed right into the heart of the camp and vanished.

Braheim was watching and came up beside Tom. "What did he say to me Braheim? Did I upset him?" Braheim laughed, "No, no Tom, he said 'I am your servant' – that is what he said."

"Really?"

"Really!" Braheim smiled at the boy. "It seems we are most fortunate to have you amongst us. He is a chief and he has honoured you."

"He has?"

"Oh yes, indeed he has."

Tom looked at Rumpitter who was tucked under his shirt. *Did you hear that Rumpitter?* he said without words. Rumpitter looked up into Tom's eyes and replied *Yes, indeed and so does Mr Hawkins, Tom. You know that he is always near. He brought us to this place.*

They now approached the outskirts of the camp. There were noises of many kinds coming from the tents. Fires were burning everywhere. There were thousands of men in long robes, carrying swords. Some had large, round shields strapped to their backs. They lined the path either side of the group as the procession passed through and into the heart of the camp. It was a village of tents. There were corrals which held goats within wooden frames, larger pens with beautiful horses unsaddled and trotting around, tossing their heads and neighing. Interesting smells of all kinds wafted around the camp and smoke billowed from cooking fires on every corner.

The horsemen led the way through the streets of tents. All were different in shape and size. There were women dressed in traditional long black robes, wearing black head-dresses and veils over their faces. Only their eyes could be seen. They stared at the group of men in silence showing no reaction to the outsiders as they were led through the streets.

One woman noticed Tom and stared at him carefully. She ran along following him until he went out of sight around a corner. Tom arched his head back as far as he could until she too went out of sight. Then there were other women in fine, brightly coloured robes and head scarves, but their faces were not covered. Nearly all of them had jewels and rings studded in their noses and ears. These women were quite vocal, calling out strange words, wailing and waving as they passed along the sandy street. One very pretty young girl with bright brown eyes and olive skin ran up close to Tom and followed his horse by running alongside. She was calling out something to him, but he did not understand what she was saying. Then she held out her hand. Tom looked down at her and slowed his horse. Suddenly there were hundreds of similar young women and girls all appearing from out of nowhere, all laughing and giggling and calling to him. Some had small bells and miniature cymbals on the ends of their fingers and they clinked them together to attract his attention. Tom had no idea what this was about.

There was a loud shout from behind. It was the deep tone of a man's voice and then a horseman charged his horse towards the crowd of girls and women. He waved his arm at them shouting something. One of the women fell over but then Tom saw her pick herself up out of the dust and scamper away back into a tent.

The rider came up alongside Tom's horse and grabbed the reins. He led the horse away, back into the group. He said something firmly to Tom, but it did not seem unpleasant. Tom got the impression that the horseman meant him to stay with the group and not stray off. Tom just nodded back. Braheim had kept along with them as did Maris, the Tunisian. The two of them were laughing their heads off and pointing at Tom. Some of the other comrades began laughing too. Rumpitter did too, but only Tom could hear him. "What are you all laughing at? What's so funny?"

Maris answered. His wide smiling face showed off all his yellow teeth, but his eyes were bright and his face showed him to be a good man. "They have never seen a boy with golden hair, Tom. They think you are handsome. The girls would all offer themselves to be your wife." He was laughing uncontrollably and teasing Tom by waving his hands around in the air.

Braheim was trying not to fall off his horse with laughter. "Imagine, Tom. You could have all the wives in the world and never have to go outside.".

Rumpitter was giggling in his rat-like way. "Oh Tom, you could have been in so much trouble back there."

Tom was very embarrassed and said, "Well, I don't think that's funny at all." For a moment he remembered Jessie back in Rivermouth. He imagined her standing at the quayside, her long blonde hair floating in the breeze and her bright blue eyes full of life and excitement. She was waving to him. Home, he thought. Where was home? So far away. In another world, another time. When would he see Rivermouth again? He remembered *The Eagle* and his father and Jacob and all the crew asleep on the deck, frozen in time. He had to get back to them soon. He shook his head and suddenly he was back in the noisy Arab camp being hustled along by the horsemen.

Joseph had been listening to the men teasing Tom and he and Mababe had a little chuckle to themselves. However their main concern was the situation at hand and where were they being taken. They were less jovial.

They continued twisting and turning through the streets of tents passing by large numbers of Arab men, some on horseback, some on foot. One thing was certain: These men were soldiers of war, armed and fierce.

After a while they entered the main encampment. There were now fewer tents and fires. There were hundreds of tethered horses tied in long lines to ropes fixed between thick wooden stakes, which had been driven into the ground. At each end of each line of horses was an armed guard. Then they came past a group of camels lying on the ground. The camels groaned and snorted. Soldiers shouted and moved them into tighter groups to keep them in order as the horsemen and the companions passed through.

Ahead of them, it was darker, for there were fewer fires and tents. Further on they came to a clump of trees. They had arrived at an oasis. The light from the moon cast shadows, which danced over the water. It seemed peaceful.

The noise and smells from the main camp were behind them. Up on a small hill there were three very large tents. Four guards stood outside the entrance to each one. Light glowed from within them. There were hundreds of soldiers all standing still watching the group as they approached.

One of the horsemen turned to Joseph and said something. It was an order, but Joseph had no idea what he was saying. The Arab repeated the order and then indicated that they should dismount. Braheim called over to the horsemen and spoke to one of the guards and pointed at Trouseau, who was still on his mount and looking very pale. The Arab acknowledged Braheim and nodded in an agreeable way. Braheim said, "Trouseau can stay on his horse." Blake and Little stayed with Trouseau. All the other horses were led away by the Arab soldiers. As they walked to the top of the rise, it was clear that they had arrived at their destination. There were many guards standing outside the largest tent. All these guards were dressed in exactly the same dress as the horsemen. There were piles of lances stacked up in neat rows. Beautiful Arab horses were tethered to ropes. Their saddles were laid on rugs on the ground. They were clean, polished and sparkled in the moonlight. Everything was in order, everywhere. This was without a doubt a place of great importance. Tom's eyes darted here and there. He looked on in awe at the splendour of this incredible scene.

The horseman called to them to stand still and wait. They did so.

They were standing just a few yards away from the largest tent and were being carefully watched by the guards outside. A large brightly coloured rug had been placed outside the entrance. On each corner of the tent was a line of tall lanterns. The glow from the lanterns danced in the gentle warm breeze casting flickering shadows across the ground.

They were all tired and hungry. Tom looked at the men and felt sorry for them. He put a hand on the stone inside the leather pouch and thought of Mr Hawkins.

Suddenly a tall Arab emerged from the great tent. He walked quickly and boldly up to the comrades. His hands hung down each side. He was a man of great confidence. He lifted one hand up to his veil and let it fall away. His face was lean and dark skinned. His piercing eyes shone like jewels. He had a neatly trimmed beard, which covered only the area around his mouth. He opened his mouth to speak and his perfect white teeth sparkled in the flickering torch-light. His voice was deep and soft; he spoke with an enchanting mixed accent of Arabic and English, but his words were spoken in a velvet tongue, soft and clear but yet with purpose.

"I am Bassar, first son of King Al Kadi. We have been expecting you. Your enemy is our enemy. We had news of your escape." He paused for a moment to look at the comrades and prisoners from the mines. There was sympathy in his eyes. "You must go with these men." He gestured a hand towards the soldiers obediently waiting beside him. "They will tend to your sick and give you food and drink. You will rest and in the morning we will meet." He took a long look at the mixed assembly of men and at the boy with the rat. He shook his head very slightly and then asked, "Who is your leader?" The comrades all looked at each other. They had not considered this, as they had all escaped together. It had all happened so quickly, but had it not been for the strange boy … Joseph and Mababe looked to each other and turned to the Arab. Mababe was about to speak when Braheim spoke out quickly. "HE is our leader." He pointed at Tom, who was holding onto the stone in one hand with Rumpitter well tucked inside his shirt. Tom looked around at the others. "No," he said defiantly. "Joseph, you're the leader, you were always Mr Hawkins' right hand man." Joseph smiled at Tom and said, "We were all the Captain's right hand men."

Braheim agreed and then said, "The boy and this man, they lead us." Bassar looked cautiously at the boy and then stepped forward and smiled down to him. "A boy is your leader? Then this boy must be very special. I would like to know – where do you come from?" He smiled and waited for Tom to reply. Tom didn't have a proper answer.

"You wouldn't believe me if I told you," was all he could think of. Then he heard a voice.

*Tom it's me. You are in good hands here, trust me. Tell him you come as a messenger from Captain Hawkins.*

Tom replied without words, *Captain? You're a captain again?*

*This is what they will understand; you will come to no harm. I know these people.*

*What?* Tom thought hard and remembered back to when Mr Hawkins told him the story of a King and his daughter. He was an Arab and she was from another land. Yes, that was it. His daughter had a Greek mother. Mr Hawkins had saved her life many years ago, when he was a man, a captain.

*I will explain. But you must go with Bassar. He's a very important man. Go with him now.*

Bassar tilted his head to one side and looked puzzled, unsure of what the boy had meant.

Tom quickly continued. "I am a messenger, for Mr – Captain Hawkins."

Immediately all the comrades started nodding their heads agreeing to what Tom had said. "Yes, yes, the Captain," they all said.

Bassar took a step back as if he was surprised. "Indeed so?" he said with a smile. Then he pointed to Joseph. "You and the boy, please come with me. The rest of you, please go with these men."

Joseph nodded to Mababe and the others, "It will be all right. We will see you soon. Get some rest and food. See that Trouseau is tended."

Bassar stepped backwards, not taking his eyes off Tom for a second.

"Come with me please," he said quietly and ushered Joseph and Tom towards the great tent.

As Bassar stepped towards the torch-lit glow of the entrance to the tent, the guards bowed very low in respect. The one nearest the entrance waved his arm towards the tent canopy covering the doorway. He pulled his arm back to draw the cover and Bassar entered inside. For a moment he disappeared behind a screen to what appeared to be an inner chamber. This was protected by four very tall guards who stood in front of the opening with their arms folded and legs apart. They looked fearsome in their black tunics and covered faces. They also wore the red cloth bands supporting very large curved swords. Their stance was very unapproachable and made it clear that any effort to continue forward would be costly. Tom and Joseph just waited.

Joseph put his hand on Tom's shoulder and stared at the guards proudly.

A shadow cast over the light in the doorway and Bassar reappeared.

"Come," he said and gestured with one hand towards the opened flap, now held open by the guard. They both walked forward warily. All the time Joseph had a hand on Tom's shoulder.

Tom had his hand on the stone and as, he clasped it tightly, looking all around him as he stepped forward, he noticed that Rumpitter was not with him. He stopped and turned, looking to see where he was.

*Rumpitter!* He called without words. There was no answer.

"Come!" he heard again and Bassar was looking strangely at him, calling him into the tent.

They entered the inner part of the entrance. Three more guards stood obediently inside. Each held a tall black lance. At the end of each lance there was a large curved blade with a red cloth ribbon tied at the hilt. Bassar spoke just one word and the guards stepped aside to let them pass.

They stepped through a thin veil of silk cloth covering another entrance. The light was much brighter now and at last they were inside a vast tented chamber. The top of the tent flapped very gently inwards and outwards from the outside breeze. There was a strong scent of musk drifting around the room. The floor was completely covered by richly coloured woven rugs. There were cushions of all sizes and shapes covered in coloured silks with an array of different patterns. These were spread out in a huge circle in the centre of the room. They surrounded a large intricately carved oval wooden table. The top was so highly polished it looked like glass.

Bassar gestured towards the cushions. "Please, sit," he said. Although it was polite, it was an order.

Tom and Joseph did as they were asked. Joseph found sitting on the deep soft cushions very difficult. He had spent three years, which seemed like a lifetime, in a damp and rotting dungeon, digging gold out of the mountain for the Saharadeen. Such luxury, such soft seats were inconceivable for someone who had been through what he had suffered. For Tom it was also hard to sit straight and he kept subsiding into the deep soft padded silk. Joseph nearly laughed when he saw Tom disappear and held out a hand and pulled him back up. He half smiled at the boy, "Maybe you should sit on the edge." Bassar clapped his hands and in an instant a parade of women entered, dressed in fine coloured fabrics with jewel-studded headscarves and carrying large round trays on their heads. Each of the women was young and beautiful. Their smooth, olive-skinned faces radiated in the light of hundreds of flickering torches around the chamber.

They swiftly, but silently, glided across the carpeted floor and placed the trays on the table. Joseph and Tom could hardly believe their eyes. The trays were laden with all kinds of interesting food like couscous with meat and fruit and odd looking cakes. Two large jugs of water and one small jug, which one of the serving women placed deliberately in front of Joseph, were set on the table. Tom immediately gulped down a cup of water, followed by another and another. Joseph did so too. They were so thirsty. It had been a long and dusty walk through the desert and even at night the temperature was very warm.

"Eat and enjoy your meal. I will come for you in a while," Bassar said, then turned and walked through another opening, disappearing behind some hanging rugs.

The serving women, having laid the table and bowed to the two hungry visitors, stepped backwards a few paces and then knelt on the carpeted floor and simply watched them tuck into their food.

Tom's mouth was full as he spoke. "It's a bit odd, those women just staring at us like that. They haven't even blinked." He picked up another jug of water to wash down the food.

Joseph nodded, "Aye lad, I have no idea what this is but it tastes very fine." He saw the small jug in front of him, picked it up, sniffed it, shrugged his shoulders and took a large gulp. No sooner had he swallowed, he suddenly gasped for breath, his eyes went red and he grabbed his chest and coughed, nearly spewing his contents over the table. His face went purple and he fell on the floor. "Oh my God!" he screamed with blood red eyes bulging out of their sockets.

Tom quickly stood up over Joseph and tried to pat him on the back. The serving women seemed to find it amusing and two of them quickly trotted over to help Joseph to his feet.

"What's the matter Joseph, are you all right?" Tom asked anxiously.

"Good heavens!" Joseph cried out again. Two of the serving women helped him back onto the cushions and offered him cold water. When he finally began to regain his composure he picked up the small jug and looked more carefully at it. He looked at one of the young women who was giggling to another.

"Hey, you woman, what is so funny? What in God's name is this stuff? It nearly killed me!" he exclaimed.

One of the women was kneeling beside him and tried to explain. "Pashuk, Pashuk," she said, pointing at the jug and nodding.

Joseph did not understand. "Pashuk? What is that?" he asked, still rubbing his chest for relief.

The women picked a strange looking fruit from a bowl and held it up to Joseph. "Pashuk," she indicated and then began to hold the fruit in both hands and demonstrate a squeezing motion with her hands. The fruit was a large round object with a brown skin. The woman took a knife and cut the fruit in half. The centre was bright red and had a very strong aroma. She held the fruit to Joseph's nose and he sniffed. He immediately pulled his face away, "Ugh, that is the most disgusting thing I have ever smelt." He recoiled from the woman. Suddenly he felt really strange and light-headed. He tried to stand up and immediately fell back into the cushions.

He tried to speak but he made no sense at all. He slurred and spluttered utter rubbish. Tom saw the other women laughing and it made him laugh too. Joseph had suddenly become completely intoxicated. Now all the women were giggling quite loudly. Tom was looking at his friend and thought it was very amusing to see Joseph drunk and unable to speak sensibly.

Tom picked up the jug and moved it towards his nose to smell it for himself. Suddenly the women all shouted something and two of them rushed to grab the jug before he got it to his mouth. They pulled the jug from his hand. One of the women was shaking her head as if to say, "Oh no you don't!" She smiled a bright and friendly smile. "Pashuk," she said and shook her head again this time waving her hand over the jug.

"I only wanted to see what it was like," Tom said, but she didn't understand him and carried on smiling and nodding at him.

Joseph had suddenly fallen into a deep sleep and began to snore loudly. Again this made the women laugh. Tom sat down again and finished his food, making sure to avoid the Pashuk fruit drink.

Meanwhile, in another tent, the comrades had also been given a feast of food and drink. The Pashuk had completely knocked them out and all of them had fallen into a deep sleep.

Trouseau had been taken to another tent, where he was receiving medical attention from the physician, a fat Arab man with a very large black beard, who worked with all types of strange potions. Two assistants moved Trouseau onto a low bed of soft white linen and silk-covered pillows.

Once the physician was satisfied he had done his good work, he ordered his assistants to watch over Trouseau, keeping him cool with damp linen cloths to cover all over him and giving him drops of liquid at regular intervals. The room was filled with a strong smelling odour from bowls of boiling herbs. It was not a pleasant smell but Trouseau was too weak to care.

Tom was the only one awake. He had filled his stomach to the brim and could not eat another thing. He fell back into the cushions and sighed. It was not long before he too was fast asleep.

The women all smiled and nodded to each other and then one of them stood up and walked towards him. She was quickly followed by three others. The other women cleared the table and carried the trays away. The four women standing over Tom had produced a large board covered in soft silks with a long silk cushion at one end. They carefully lifted Tom onto it as if it were a stretcher and carried him out of the room. Not a word was said.

Rumpitter had been watching from a corner of the tent, being careful not to be seen in case he was mistaken for a desert rodent and probably killed. This was the main problem for rats, especially large rats like him: no one liked them.

He was disappointed that the serving women had cleared the table and not left a single scrap, but at least he had been able to grab some food from a plate when one of the Arab soldiers hadn't been looking. When the Arab returned to his meal, he immediately blamed another soldier for stealing the food from his plate and an argument broke out between them. Rumpitter didn't wait to find out the outcome but hurried away to find Tom.

He saw the women taking the sleeping boy away and silently followed behind, making sure he didn't lose sight of Tom. He was relieved to see the women place Tom onto a raised bed and slip away quietly without waking him. The stone was still in its leather pouch hanging around Tom's neck.

The women had left a tray of food and a jug of water by Tom's bed. Rumpitter noticed the cheese and could not believe his eyes. His nose twitched frantically and his large tail swished in the air. "Oh heaven, this is a miracle, oh thank-you, Mr Hawkins. Thank-you." He said to himself and grabbed a large piece of yellow cheese from the plate and quickly jumped down onto the floor and hid under the bed, tucking into his cheese.

*Ah Rumpitter, I see all is well then?* He heard that familiar voice and raised his head from under the bed to see if he could see anyone. No one was there. Rumpitter was not sure if Mr Hawkins was referring to the fact that he had found a very large piece of cheese or that the men were all safe. He looked at his prize cheese and then shrugged, taking another look to see if anyone was there. Without words he replied, *Oh, Mr Hawkins, thank goodness you are back and thank-you for getting us here into this safe haven. As you probably already know, all is well. Tom is sound asleep, the stone is still with him, the men are also sleeping and that French chap is being well cared for by the physician.* Rumpitter continued as he nibbled away at the cheese.

*They have had a tough time. Some have suffered more than others and they need to rest. I knew they would be well cared for. HE has never forgotten.* Mr Hawkins paused. *Tomorrow will be a long day and we are by no means finished. We must complete our mission. I have seen a bad moon over the mountains, Rumpitter, and there is trouble afoot. However we are amongst good friends. We will need to keep to our plan and Tom has much to do.*

Rumpitter wiped his whiskers. *Yes Sir, I am right on it and keeping a watchful eye on T...* The seagull interrupted: *Yes Rumpitter, I can see you are extremely busy right now and when you have finished feasting perhaps you would keep a look out and let me know if anything happens. HE will be here soon and HE will want to see the boy.*

*Oh yes, absolutely, I'm right onto it* Rumpitter quickly reiterated.

*Good, then we will meet soon when all have rested.*

Rumpitter quickly gobbled the cheese down, licked his lips and cleaned himself before hopping up onto a shelf above the bed. He crouched down and focused his beady red eyes on the boy. He was fast asleep.

That night seemed endless and the warm breeze drifted across the camp. The night sky was covered in stars and the bright moon floated in and out of the slowly passing clouds.

Soldiers changed guard at regular intervals, fire lights flickered around the tents and groups of resting soldiers. All was quiet.

In the early hours of the morning, as the final embers of the camp-fires dwindled, a rider galloped over the hill and into the camp. The horse's hooves pounded across the ground, stirring the tethered horses and camels as he wound his way around the tents and fires up towards the great tent.

The rider was covered in dust, and sweat ran down the shining coat of his horse. He stopped by the entrance and instantly dismounted. As his feet touched the ground, the rider threw the reins to a waiting guard and ran into the entrance of the great tent. He tore his scarf from his face and the guard instantly saw urgency in the rider's eyes.

A few quick words were exchanged and the rider waited patiently. A guard offered him a leather water bottle. The rider took it and swallowed several long gulps of water, then poured some over his head and nodded his appreciation to the guard.

A few moments later Bassar appeared. He was dressed in a light robe and his head was uncovered. He had been woken urgently from his sleep. They also exchanged a few words. The rider was out of breath but managed to deliver his important message.

Bassar thanked the rider and ran back inside the tent. As he passed the guards, he gave them an order and immediately two men ran in the direction of the smaller tent where the comrades had been resting.

Bassar shook Joseph's arm to wake him. Joseph had slept well on the soft cushions. He was drowsy and disoriented as he woke so suddenly. "What the...?" he said and tried to doze off again. He was again shaken by the arm. Bassar was in no mood for politeness. "Wake up, we must speak now. Please hurry and come with me," he said sternly.

Joseph looked up at Bassar and could see he looked serious. Then he noticed Tom was not there.

"Where is the boy?" he asked quickly. "What have you done with him?"

"He is sleeping but we must wake him and your friends now. I am sorry, it is urgent. We have grave news and must move fast."

Joseph had no idea what was really going on but managed to get up and shake his head to wake himself up.

"Quickly, follow me," Bassar ordered.

They stepped outside and Joseph saw that the orange glow of the sun was slowly appearing over the hill. It was a beautiful sight, but he realised that there was no time to stare and gaze. There was much activity going on all around him. Masses of soldiers were assembling. Horses were being saddled and camels led from their tethers and being prepared. Men were running everywhere as orders were being given by officers.

He looked down the slope to the main encampment and saw a scene of great activity unfolding before him. Tents were being taken down and people were running here and there. Fires were being kicked out and women were rolling up rugs and filling sacks with bottles, pots, food and all number of things. He noticed the hustle and bustle of activity was extremely well organised and controlled. These people had moved fast like this before, he thought. He followed Bassar into the next tent.

He was met by Mababe and Gordon. "What is happening?" asked Mababe. "I have no idea. One minute I am sleeping like a lamb, the next thing I know I am being woken by all this."

Bassar turned to them. "We have had news that the Saharadeen is nearby with his great army. They have captured some of my outriders and scouts. We had warning they were on their way but did not realise how close they were. We must take action now. We are breaking camp and moving to higher ground."

He beckoned all the comrades to follow him.

Tom had been in a deep sleep. He had been dreaming of strange men in robes charging on black horses through the dessert. The seagull was hovering above them and Tom was calling to him.

Then he heard voices. "Mr Hawkins, where are we, what shall we do?" he shouted out aloud and then suddenly sat up in the bed, gasping for breath. Then he heard different voices. These were not from Mr Hawkins. "Tom, lad, wake up, wake up," the voice kept saying. Tom shouted again, "Mr Hawkins!" Suddenly he opened his eyes and saw several men staring down at him. At first he tried to crawl back and escape from the bed. He was in shock and still half asleep. "Tom, lad, it is me, Joseph."

"Joseph?" Tom replied, still confused and slightly delirious. "Aye, lad, it is me."

Tom finally opened his eyes wide and shook his head. He saw Joseph and Bassar with Mababe, leaning over him. Then he saw the others. They were all standing around him. He saw people running around in the background. "What's happening, Joseph, where's Mr Hawkins?"

Rumpitter quickly jumped down from the ledge and said: *Tom, we have to get going. It's all right.* Some of the guards, and Bassar, jumped back when they saw the giant rat. One guard drew a large knife and was about to strike, when Bassar grabbed his arm. He said something to the guard and shook his head. The guard drew back and replaced the knife in his belt, shaking his head in disbelief as he saw the boy stroking the large rat.

Rumpitter jumped onto Tom's chest and looked at him in the eye. Without words he said, *It seems that we have a matter of urgency Tom, we have to get going, you had better get up now.*

Just then, the seagull flew over the top of the tent and let out a high pitched squawk. He saw someone he had not seen for many years. HE was walking quickly towards the tent. HE was surrounded by twenty guards all with swords drawn. They marched straight into the tent.

Tom was now on his feet and Bassar was trying to explain what was happening and why they needed to move fast. Suddenly there was a loud deep voice.

"So – this is our young hero and his worthy fighters." Everyone turned around. Bassar and the guards stepped back and lowered their heads in respect.

A large man, dressed in fine Arab clothes, was standing in front of them with his guards. He had his hands on his hips and stood sturdily with his feet apart.

He was tall and extremely well built. He had a thick moustache and a small trim beard on his chin. His deep brown eyes were bright as they stared towards the group of men. He was also dressed in a long white and gold tunic. His sword hung from a polished brown leather belt, which had jewels studded into it. His head-scarf was a black and white Keffiyeh, an Arabian scarf, with gold bands around his head. The scarf was thrown across his shoulder to expose his face. He had a proud and honourable appearance. His dark face, although weathered by the sun, showed wisdom and strength, but also kindness.

He clapped his hands and the guards formed a line behind him and stood to attention. Bassar was the only one not to move. He stood perfectly still with his head lowered.

"My lord," Bassar said and then raised his head. "Permit me to introduce our new friends."

Suddenly there was a gust of wind and Mr Hawkins swooped into the tent and settled on Tom's shoulder. Tom looked at his feathered friend. *I was wondering where you were* Tom said without words. Mr Hawkins cocked his head to one side and blinked his eye and a glint of golden light shone across the room to the tall Arab in front of them.

The man gave a wide smile and showed an array of perfectly formed white teeth and one gold tooth.

"You are Tom, I know this because we share the same good friend." He bowed to the seagull.

It was clear that this man never bowed to anyone unless he deemed them of the utmost importance.

"I am the King of the Al Kadi. I hope you have been well treated by my son". He spoke in English so most of them could understand him. He stepped closer and held the boy's chin up and stared into his eyes. "Mmm – the Captain was right. You are an honourable young man. I can see it in your eyes. Tom, you and your friends are welcome here." He smiled all the time he was speaking and then looked to the others. "I would like to have had more time to be better acquainted with you. Unfortunately it seems our enemies are rattling their sabres for a fight. So, we have much to do."

He turned to the seagull and nodded. He seemed uncertain and awkward as he acknowledged the seagull. "It is good to see you again. We have missed you. I am saddened by the things that have passed." He spoke directly to the seagull.

Then he turned back to the comrades.

"I have spoken to – Captain Hawkins." He very slightly lowered his head as he mentioned the seagull's name. For a second there was a hint of sadness in his eyes, but he was quick not to show it. "Captain Hawkins and I have known each other for many years. We are great friends. I will always be in his debt for what he has done for me. Now it seems I am again in need of his help. He has told me everything." He smiled again and put his hand on Tom's head. "I believe you are his assistant." He looked around at the others. He nodded at Joseph and Braheim and then to Mababe. "You are our brothers – I welcome you." He looked at every man as he spoke, leaving no one out. They all lowered their heads in respect.

"We do not have time now to discuss the tragedy which fell on our dear friend, but I tell you all now – the secret will stay with me." Again he turned back to look at Mr Hawkins. The seagull lowered his head and nodded up and down twice.

The King looked again at Tom and whispered in his ear, "I too have the Golden Secret."

Tom looked at him carefully and then at the seagull. The voice spoke. *Tom, I told you about this man. He is the great King of all lands north and south. He is King Hafidh Al Kadi. When he gave me the Sword many years ago, before it was taken from me by the Saharadeen, he had the ability to speak without words. This is the Golden Secret.*

Tom looked up at his friend and then back to the King. The big man smiled at Tom and nodded, "I too can speak without words."

Tom was amazed. Now, at last, their journey had not been wasted and the plan that Mr Hawkins had told him was about to unfold.

"The King looked at the leather pouch hanging around Tom's neck. "You have carried that a very long way, Tom. Thank-you. It will soon be reunited with the Sword of Isis and once again peace will reign over our lands." He paused and then continued. "We knew you were coming, the Captain told me. But unfortunately we have little time. Our enemy is massing his army on the other side of these hills. My army is now preparing for war. We have come here to stand against the Saharadeen who threatens to take our lands and destroy everything we hold so dear. He must be stopped and now is our time. His army is greater than ours in numbers. But I will wager one of my men to every ten of his." He waved his hands at some of his guards standing behind him as he said this.

"You have the Stone, he has the Sword, and now we must take back the Sword and destroy him and his evil, for ever!"

Joseph stepped forward. "We will do whatever we can to help, my Lord," he said proudly and turned to look at his comrades. They all stepped forward. "Aye, for peace, for you and for the Captain," they all agreed. Tom looked at Mr Hawkins and whispered, "We are all with you, Mr Hawkins." The seagull lifted his head and spiralled his neck upwards shaking his wings. He nearly knocked Tom over with one of his large wings. Rumpitter jumped up onto Tom's other shoulder. This startled the King, who stepped back. Everyone laughed. "So now we have a rat in our group," the King exclaimed. "It's all right, he's our friend," Tom explained as Rumpitter wobbled on Tom's shoulder. It was a funny sight for all the men to see but, for some strange reason, it was also now all quite acceptable.

The King laughed again and so did everyone else. Suddenly he stopped when he noticed Bassar looking a little anxious. He nodded to his son.

Now the King looked more serious and turned to his guards and then back at the comrades.

"So – back to business." He put his hand on the handle of his sword.

"Those of you who are fit and willing to fight can go with these guards. They will find you everything you need. I know some of you have suffered. I will understand if you are not able to join us. You will be looked after by my reserve guard. We have physicians here who will aid the sick ones. The choice is yours."

Suddenly there was a shuffle from behind and someone was shouting words in French. Two guards jumped out of the way and a small man stepped forward. "If it is a fight, then you will need me in order to win."

Everyone suddenly roared in laughter and cheered as Trouseau stepped up to King Al Kadi.

He looked thin and weak but he was certainly feeling better. He had been through so much, but he was a tough little man with a big heart.

Joseph had a wide grin on his face and was so pleased to see the Frenchman back on his feet.

"Ha, Trouseau, will nothing ever stop you, my friend?" Joseph turned to the King. "This is Trouseau. He has been with the Captain and I for many years. He can match any one of your men by his cunning alone," he laughed. Trouseau stood proudly smiling at his comrades and winked at Tom, who laughed. Tom could hear Mr Hawkins laughing in his head.

The King raised his arms up high. "So, it is written. We shall win today," he shouted and everyone cheered.

All except for a few of the older prisoners who had escaped from the dungeons, agreed to fight. Some of them had nothing left in their lives and sought revenge. Others wanted to join the great King Al Kadi who was legendry and respected by so many. They were honoured to fight for him and for a better world. For freedom.

The comrades had now accepted that their captain was no longer a man but a seagull. They too wanted revenge and to destroy the evil Saharadeen. They had seen what had become of so many good men and remembered when Trouseau had been turned into a gold statue, how they were so badly treated by the Saharadeen and how their captain had been cruelly turned from a man to a seagull. There was no doubt; they would fight for their captain and for good to win over evil.

They followed King Hafidh outside the tent.

The sun had now risen above the hills and the deep orange glow across the desert sands was turning into a golden hue.

They stepped out into the daylight to a deafening cheer from the army.

They were astonished to see the whole camp had packed up and was ready to march.

The Al Kadi army was now assembled in long lines. There were endless columns of horse soldiers, camel riders and foot soldiers. Swords and long lances were held high and being waved frantically in the air. Soldiers banged on their shields which created a thunderous, terrifying roar. Women were standing in lines, wailing high pitch chants from the sides of the columns to support their brave men and sons. They rocked from one side to the other in slow motion as they chanted. It was an unbelievable sight for Tom and the comrades to witness.

A white Arab horse was being held by a guard. It reared up on its hind legs and its handler struggled to control it. The beautiful horse was saddled and ready for war in an ornately decorated harness and bridle coloured in white and gold, the colours of Kadistaar.

The King walked up to his horse and mounted. Instantly the wild horse calmed down. The King was now in control. Again the massive crowd roared and cheered. He waved his long sword into the air and again his white steed reared up on its hind legs. The King sat firm in the saddle wielding his sword in circles in the air. It sent the crowd of thousands into a frenzy.

A group of his personal guard rode up and surrounded him. They galloped off up the hill into the sun. It was a glorious sight. Tom was in awe of the whole spectacle.

"Wow, Mr Hawkins, this is amazing!" Tom exclaimed

"He is truly a legend, Tom. He is the life and soul of millions of people who will follow him to defend what is right and just."

Bassar walked up to them. "Come my friends, we have work to do, yes?"

"Oh yes, indeed," Joseph replied. He turned to his comrades. Mababe, Sam Little, Braheim, Trouseau, Maris, Blake and Gordon. They were all together. "Well then?" he asked them.

"Justice and honour!" they all called and followed Bassar down to the waiting soldiers.

They were given weapons, head-dresses, shields and horses. Tom, Mr Hawkins and Rumpitter were given a camel with a very good Arab handler who rode beside them on his own camel. He had only one tooth at the bottom of his mouth. His eyes were dark and wild and he looked mean, but he was good at his job. Tom was wary of him, but said nothing. The handler strapped one of the large round shields to the side of the camel and placed a sword behind it. He shouted something to Tom and pointed at the sword. "He said you might need this and you should not be afraid to use it," said Mr Hawkins.

Rumpitter chirped up. "Yes, but I think it might be best if we stay on the hill with the Al Kadi guards, Tom. This is going to be a dreadful battle, many will die today." Rumpitter was very glum when he said it. Tom then realised quickly this was not so much an adventure now. He was in the middle of a war.

He put his hand on the stone and felt a strange wave of dizziness come over him. He nearly fell off the camel. His ears started ringing and his head felt heavy and drowsy.

*TOM!* Came the voice from Mr Hawkins. *STEADY!* Tom quickly came round and a brown wrinkled hand grabbed his arm. It was the camel handler. He pulled Tom back into the saddle.

"Wow, what happened?"

Without words, Mr Hawkins replied. *The Saharadeen knows we are near and he knows you have the stone. He needs that stone as badly as we need the Sword of Isis. You must take great care now Tom, do not allow yourself to dream. Stay awake, keep your mind focused and stay with the guards.* The seagull looked down at Rumpitter. *We stay together Rumpitter, keep him always in your sight.*

*I certainly will, Sir* replied the rat, who was perched on top of the wooden pommel on the front of Tom's saddle.

Joseph and his comrades were ready and all agreed to ride with Bassar. They embraced each other as brothers and agreed that they would keep together. No man would be left alone and stranded. "We are in this together, Bassar, we are all with you!" Joseph said.

Bassar shook him warmly by the hand and said, "My father is a wise man. He knows he has great men with him and so do I." He smiled at the comrades and they all agreed the feeling was mutual.

Bassar stood up high in his stirrups and looked back at his army. Thousands of soldiers had assembled behind him. He drew his sword and it glistened in the now fully risen sun.

"The Al Kadi is the ONE King; he will lead us to victory. Today is our day to win the glory of honour, for freedom, for our women and children, our homes and farms, for the glory of our kingdom and for Kadistaar!" The last two words rang out loud from Bassar's lips and the huge army called back, "Al Kadi, Al Kadi, Al Kadi". They repeated the words over and over.

Bassar wielded his sword high in the air and then thrust it forward, kicked his horse and suddenly the whole army was in a flat-out gallop towards the hills, where their King was waiting and preparing for war.

Tom jolted backwards as the camel suddenly lurched forward and took off with the charging army. A huge dust cloud reared up from behind the thousands of charging horses. On both sides of them were thousands of foot soldiers and the Arab caravans moving at a slower pace but, nevertheless, in haste. They were all heading towards the hill, which overlooked the great plains.

The heat began to rise from the ground. As they climbed up the hill, Tom saw the tents flickering in the heat haze.

The camel snorted as it carried them up the hill. Tom looked behind to see the vast army of soldiers forming into rectangular shapes as they approached the ridge around the hilltop. Each group had a leader out in front who held a lance up as a signal to his battalion to keep moving forward. Almost instantly the cheering and wailing had stopped. The only sound was the huge army assembling for battle. They moved silently into flanks all along the slopes of the valley, overlooking the plains.

There was an eerie silence. No one spoke but everyone knew what to do. This was a day they had been preparing for. The time had come.

Finally Tom and the others had reached the top. They saw the King sitting proudly on his horse looking out towards the desert plains. His officers stood obediently next to him and waited.

The King turned to see Bassar, Joseph and the comrades riding up towards him. He smiled and bowed his head.

The great army was still assembling on the lower banks and forming into long ranks of both foot soldiers and horsemen. As each battalion moved into position, their commanders turned to look up the hill at their King and waved the flag of their rank to confirm they were ready. It took no longer than a half hour for all the ranks to complete their moves. The Al Kadi army was almost ready.

Tom whispered to Mr Hawkins. "What will happen now?"

"We wait, Tom. Soon we will see what we are about to confront. The Saharadeen and his army will show themselves. I fear we have much to contend with." He paused and stretched his neck upwards. "This will be a bloody fight, Tom. You must stay up here. Promise me you will stay back here with Rumpitter."

Tom swallowed hard and now he was worried. "But what if we lose, what will happen?"

"We cannot afford to lose today, Tom. This day has been due for a very long time. The King has been preparing to rid this world of the evil of the Saharadeen for many years. We have to get back the Sword of Isis and reunite it with that stone you have around your neck. This is why you must stay out of harm's way. Keep back here. You will be safe as long as you stay out of sight of the Saharadeen."

Tom looked into Mr Hawkins's eyes and felt uneasy. He could see darkness in the seagull's eyes. The brightness had gone; something was not right, but he could not understand what it was or why he had these thoughts. "Will you stay with us too? I don't want to lose you either." He reached over and stroked the seagull's long neck.

The seagull tilted his head slightly and looked at Tom. "There are some things I must do, Tom. I must try to help in any way I can. However, I promise you I won't be far away."

"Why do they have to have this war? Can't they just discuss it round a table?" Tom asked.

Mr Hawkins thought for a moment and then answered. "It seems Tom, that throughout history there has been and always will be someone who wants more. There are always people who are obsessed with power and, to get what they want, they turn to evil. Even in your world, Tom, there have been, and will continue to be, evil people who use excuses for their greed, hatred and their incurable appetite for power. Whatever reason people have for their lust for blood, be it greed or all kinds of madness, it always comes down to one thing in the end."

"What's that?"

"That good must always win over bad. This is worth fighting for. There is only one reason for war and that is when you must defend your home and save your people from people like the Saharadeen. To seek power is not the right reason".

Tom thought on this and then asked, "So, if the Saharadeen didn't exist there would be no reason for this war?"

"Yes, Tom, that is right"

Suddenly there was a strange sound. Then a rumble and the ground shook. It came from far away in the distance. Everyone stopped to look across the desert sands across the plain. The sand beneath their feet moved for just a second and then stopped.

"What was that?" Tom asked and he tried to stand up in his saddle to peer over the heads of the men in front of him. Joseph turned back to Tom and gave a nervous smile. "Don't you worry now, lad." He gave a quick glance at Bassar and they nodded to each other.

Bassar pulled his horse back and trotted across to the group of guards behind them. He spoke a few words and pointed at Tom and the comrades. The head guard nodded. He had understood his orders and then turned to his men and called out an order. Immediately the guards rode up and surrounded Tom and his friends. Bassar rode over and spoke firmly, but quietly, to them.

"Tom, you have something most precious to all of us. We must not let you come to any harm. These soldiers are our King's personal guards. They are the best of the best. They will stay by you and protect you should the need arise" Then he turned to the comrades. "You must understand that this battle is ours, not yours. We have been preparing for this moment for many years. The Saharadeen has been out of our grasp for too long, but now he has come out of hiding. Now is the time we must finish this and rid our world of his evil. I know, and I am honoured, that you offer to stand with us and fight. By this, you have proved your loyalty and we salute you."

Joseph immediately spoke out. "Now wait a minute, Bassar, we told you that we are with you. This does not mean that we will sit and watch you and do nothing. We told you that we are on your side and, besides, we have no other place to go today." He put his hand on his sword and with a wide smile across his face he turned to his friends, knowing they were all with him. "I am sorry, Bassar, but we are riding with you and you cannot stop us."

Bassar sat still in his saddle for a brief moment and then nodded. He put a hand on Joseph's shoulder and smiled. "You know, my friend, I had a bad feeling that you would say that."

He nodded again, pursing his lips. He looked deep into Joseph's eyes and said finally, "You are good men indeed and I have a feeling that to stop you from charging down that hill will be impossible. I will have to keep an eye on you."

They all laughed and gave a haughty cheer. Bassar said, "So, let us go and catch ourselves a thief, what do you say?"

The men all cheered. "We will catch him and hang him up," shouted Mababe, who immediately kicked his stirrups into the side of his horse and galloped off down the hill to join the army.

Bassar turned to one of his own men. "Keep your eyes on them." The soldier nodded. "Yes my Lord."

Mababe was cut off by several of Bassar's riders. One of them grabbed the reins of his horse and pulled him to a halt. He shouted something in Arabic. Mababe had no idea of the words but knew what he meant. He looked back at the others riding down the steep hill of soft desert sand. As he looked across the hill he saw the massive army now all assembled in long ranks. Swords and shields sparkled in the sunlight. The array of colour from the soldiers' head-dresses and flowing tunics was magnificent. At the head of the columns of horsemen, leaders sat motionless and proud, waiting to face the enemy. In their hands they held long lances with the flag of the Al Kadi flapping gently in the hot breeze – the white flag with two red crossed swords and a red crescent moon in the centre.

An eerie wind blew gently across the desert plains.

Other than commands being called out and the stamping of hooves from the impatient horses along the lines of their battalions, not a word was said. Eventually there was silence. The Al Kadi army was ready.

Tom looked at Mr Hawkins. "When will they come?" he whispered.

"Soon, Tom, very soon." The seagull popped his head up as if he could smell something in the air and then turned round to look at Tom. "Promise me, Tom. You will stay here. Do not go anywhere." Tom paused and then spoke without words. *I promise.*

"Good. Now I have work to do." The seagull flapped his wings and lifted into the air.

Tom watched him fly over the long lines of the army positioned along the slopes of the dunes. He soared high up and into the sun. Suddenly he was gone.

The King was sitting motionless as he listened to Bassar speaking. When Bassar had finished, the King nodded and held up his hand. There was a loud cheer from his army and the sound echoed across the hills.

Tom watched the foot soldiers with their huge round shields walking slowly down the slopes. He noticed that they held something inside the shields.

He looked down at the shield resting on the side of his saddle and noticed the handle. He put his hand on it and noticed a small clip on the top of the handle. He flicked it with his thumb. There was a click and suddenly a sharp spike, the shape of a spear head, flicked out from the outside centre of the shield. Tom jumped when the blade flew out. The toothless Arab guard, who was beside him, laughed and muttered something in Arabic and wagged his finger at Tom, then he put his hand back inside the shield and turned the handle. The blade flicked back inside, safely. "These are not toys, be careful!" Joseph trotted over to Tom. "That shield looks a little big for you lad, but it will, at least, cover you should you need it. You must stay out of harm's way, just as Captain Hawkins has asked. You understand lad?"

"Yes Joseph, I do understand and you'd better be careful too, all of you. Mr Hawkins will keep his eye on all of us."

Joseph nodded and looked into the sky. "Aye, lad. That he will."

They rode to the crest of the dune to join the others and looked down upon the vast desert plains and into the horizon. The heat haze was all they could see. There was an eerie silence.

Then, without any warning the ground began to tremble again, but this time it was stronger. The sand started to blow across the ground and a warm dust cloud blew through the stifling hot air. The ground started to move more dramatically and made the horses restless. Some reared and jumped. Others stamped their hooves in an attempt to run away, but their riders held them steady. The foot soldiers of the Al Kadi tried with difficulty to stand firm. The ground was shaking and the sound of thunder grew louder and louder and then, in the distance, they saw something dark and ghostly floating through the heat haze. The dark shape grew larger and seemed to be moving nearer. They could hear battle drums and horns. The drumming was a constant thud and the ground vibrated with every beat.

The Al Kadi army stood firm. Although they were scared, they would not flinch.

Bassar turned to the comrades. "They come," he said and nodded his head in the direction of the moving shapes.

The beat of the drums became even heavier and louder.

"Stand firm men. We will not be threatened by this. Let us wait to see what this brings," Bassar called out to his chiefs. The message was repeated along the ranks of horsemen and foot soldiers.

The King just sat motionless on his white stallion. Tom saw great pride and wisdom in his old face and could not help but stare at the great King.

"He doesn't seem at all worried, Rumpitter," Tom whispered to the rat, who was standing on his hind legs trying to get a glimpse of where the drumming was coming from.

"Indeed, Tom. He is a great leader. If he shows no fear, then his men will take courage. This is the way of a great King in battle."

"We will win, won't we?" Tom asked with a slight tremble in his voice.

Rumpitter turned his head round at Tom and his little brown eyes looked into Tom's. He smiled and nodded but said nothing.

The thunderous noise of the oncoming enemy was constant and beginning to unnerve Tom. He clasped the stone in his hand and thought carefully about everything. He remembered his teachers at school telling him stories of the Zulus in Africa and how they would beat on their shields to scare their enemy and how the Scottish soldiers used bagpipes in battle to drive the enemy mad. This was probably nothing more than that and he realised he should just get used to it and not worry so much. At least not for now. The enemy were approaching but were still obscured by the dust and haze of the desert heat.

The sun was high and burned down over the dunes.

The Al Kadi army still stood firm and the chiefs all looked to their King for an order.

Bassar remained beside his father.

Tom was trying to find Mr Hawkins, but the haze was too much and he couldn't look into the sun without it blurring his vision.

The plains were surrounded on three sides by the high dunes, the highest being where the Al Kadi army waited. Tom could see the lowest of the dunes to his right and just for a second he thought he saw something, but when he looked again, there was nothing.

Still the beating drums kept up their thunderous rumble and the battle horns of the Saharadeen grew nearer.

The dark shape in the distance danced in the haze and through the dust something approached them. It looked like a sea of ants. They knew this was the Saharadeen army coming slowly into focus.

Tom wiped his eyes to see if he could make out anything over on the lower dunes. He was sure he saw something. He stood up on his saddle to try to get a better view.

Bassar noticed Tom peering over to the right with a hand over his eyes to guard his vision from the bright sunlight.

He called over to Tom. "You have good eyes boy, what can you see?"

"I-I'm not sure. I thought I saw something moving over on the top of that hill, but all I can see now is the sand blowing over the crest."

Bassar pulled a telescope from under his tunic, pulled it open and held one end against his eye and focused in the direction of the lower dunes.

Sure enough he could see the sand being whipped up by something, but there was no strong wind this morning. He looked again.

"Riders," he said quietly and then to his father, "Riders, father, look over there!" This time he spoke louder and some of the others heard him.

Tom heard the men discussing the situation.

Rumpitter was standing on his back legs sniffing the air. "The Captain will know what to do Tom, you wait and see."

Bassar ordered a small group of horsemen to ride across the higher level of the hill to survey their movement. As they galloped away, Mr Hawkins appeared above them. "Look," called Tom, "it's Mr Hawkins." Tom heard his friend's voice. *Tom, tell Bassar to call his men back immediately – they will be outnumbered. There is a large battalion of bowmen on horses. The Saharadeen has ordered them to create a decoy.* Tom quickly turned to Bassar. "Call them back, Bassar, the Captain has seen what they are, it's a trick."

Bassar looked at Tom and immediately turned to see his riders charging along the top of the dunes. Then he saw the Saharadeen's riders more clearly. They were indeed a much larger group.

He nodded to one of his men, who knew what to do. He produced a small glass disc and held it up to reflect the sunlight on it. He then turned the disc and moved it up and down to create a flashing light. This was a signal. He was sending a message to his riders.

Very quickly the riders saw the flashing light and drew to an immediate halt. They spotted the large group of enemy horsemen and noticed they were armed with bows. Immediately they turned their horses around and began to retreat as fast as they could. The enemy riders saw them turn back and gave chase. Suddenly the sky above the fleeing riders was a thick cloud of falling arrows. The enemy had fired at them from a full gallop. The arrows began to fall down towards their targets.

It was too late for the fleeing riders. They had no time to escape the enemy arrows and within seconds nearly all the riders had fallen.

Finally, only two of them escaped. One of the riders pulled his comrade up by his arms, hauled him up onto his horse and galloped away from the attacking soldiers.

Tom could see the anger and sadness in Bassar's eyes as he watched his men fall to the enemy.

Everyone watched speechlessly as the two riders on one horse galloped away from the falling arrows.

Finally the Saharadeen's men halted. They had no instructions to chase them and turned back to their original standpoint on the far side of the hill. The two had escaped and finally appeared over the summit and pulled the horse to a halt as they approached the King and Bassar.

Bassar immediately rode up to them and put his hand on the shoulder of the man who had rescued his comrade. The King saluted them with respect and the men were told to go to the camp to rest.

Bassar was angry that he had allowed himself to be tricked into sending his men to their death. It would not happen again. He turned the head of his horse towards the waiting columns of soldiers on the lower slopes and shouted an order. One of the chiefs acknowledged the order and immediately called out just two words to his waiting men. Instantly the huge column of soldiers formed into one long line and began to move slowly forward. These men all had long bows tied to their backs with leather quivers full of arrows. They also carried the long, curved swords strapped to their saddles. The round shields hung from the other side of their mounts, ready to be snatched up quickly. They were ready to fight and proud to be fighting for their King.

Mr Hawkins hovered over the heads of Bassar and the King. The King held out his arm and the seagull settled onto it. Tom could see they were discussing something but couldn't make out what was being said. Tom noticed that the Saharadeen riders who had killed Bassar's horsemen had now come to a halt in a long line along the ridge. They just seemed to be waiting and did not move.

Then, again came a blast of horns, followed by the heavy beating of drums. It was an eerie sound and very unnerving. The ground began to shake again and the black shadow of the enormous Saharadeen army moved further towards them. They could now see smoke floating in the air and then a hideous smell of something burning. The cloud of smoke grew thicker and the smell stronger as the enemy came nearer.

Tom couldn't believe his eyes. "There are millions of them!" he exclaimed. He looked down at the Al Kadi army standing proud and ready, waiting for their next order. When he looked again over towards the blackness of the enemy army gradually unfolding before him, he realised how terribly outnumbered the Al Kadi army was.

The horsemen on the far hill had still not moved.

Again he looked into the centre of the evil army gathering and moving towards them. He saw something tall and dark flicker through the smoke. Then it appeared and then another and another. They were tall towers and it was from these that the black smoke billowed.

"What are those things?" Tom asked to anyone who was listening.

"Fire towers," answered Joseph solemnly. He then turned to Bassar who was still in conversation with the King and the seagull.

With every minute the enemy came closer. It was a frightening sight. The noise from the beating drums was now so loud that it was hard to hear anything else. The smell from the fire towers was so strong. Tom could now just about see the faces of the first line of enemy soldiers.

It was about two hundred yards long and ten men deep. It moved ever closer.

These men were stripped from the waist up and carried nothing more than long lances with very long blades. The lances were held forward and they came closer and closer.

Behind these men was a massive column of horse soldiers who were heavily armed with lances, long swords and shields. They were dressed in black from head to foot. Their faces were covered.

Beyond this were even more columns of horse soldiers. There were thousands of them walking slowly forward. They had come to destroy the Al Kadi. They looked fearsome and ghostly, riding amongst the tall fire towers with smoke drifting in the air, blackening the sky from the sunlight. Still the drums beat and the horns blew.

Back in the ranks of the Al Kadi army, horses grunted impatiently and stamped their front hooves into the sand. Their riders, however, remained unmoved. The rumbling of the oncoming army and hammering of the drums continued to beat louder and louder.

Now they could see the massive wooden towers of fire. There were ten of them, each over a hundred feet tall. Each tower was pulled by six huge elephants harnessed in black leather bridles and chains. Around the huge elephants were thousands of foot soldiers carrying shields and heavy swords. They also wore black tunics and pointed leather helmets. Their faces were covered by veils. The faceless dark enemy had arrived.

The smoke now became so dense that it was impossible to see what lay beyond the approaching enemy.

Tom was still trying to hear Mr Hawkins, who was sitting majestically on the pommel of the King's saddle. Finally, Tom asked, "What's happening? They are getting so close, there's so many of them." He clutched the bag with the stone inside. "Surely if we can just get the Sword back from the Saharadeen and set the stone to it, we can beat them. We'll have the power with the Sword of Isis and we can stop this."

The King looked at Tom and smiled. "You are a clever boy and what you say is correct. However, first we have to execute our plan. The man we want is hiding somewhere over there. He will not expose himself, so we must find a way to bring him out so that we can capture the Sword."

*That's right, Tom, and I was unable to find him when I flew over, The smoke was too thick. We are still uncertain as to what lies beyond the towers of fire.* Mr Hawkins spoke this without words.

Suddenly there was a high pitch sound, different from the blasting horns and it rang out across the desert for a long time. Everyone covered their ears from the dreadful noise.

Bassar's horse reared and he pulled on his reins to control it. He looked to his King and nodded. The King recognised the nod and acknowledged him with a salute by waving his hand from his forehead to his heart and then held the hand up in the air.

Mr Hawkins lifted up from the King's saddle and spoke again to Tom without words.

*Tom, you must stay here with the King and promise me you will not go anywhere.* His words were serious and Tom replied, *I promise.*

*Good, this is not going to be an easy job, Tom, and now the battle is about to begin. But we do have a plan and we will need to know where you are and that has to be up here on the hill and nowhere else, do you understand?*

*Yes I do* Tom replied.

*The King has a guard of two hundred of the finest men – look behind you.*

Tom turned to see two hundred horsemen in fantastic tunics with the long swords by their sides and lances with the flag of the Al Kadi. They stood at the crest of the hill in a long straight line and slowly drew up right behind the King.

King Hafidh called to Tom, "Come boy and join us, we will watch everything from here."

Tom nudged his camel in the side and, with the help of his Arab handler; he came up beside the great King.

The Al Kadi army was now all ready to go and they waited for the orders amidst the thunder and rumble of the enemy drums and blasts of horns blowing sharply across the desert.

The chiefs of each group looked to their King, waiting for his sign. The enemy rolled forward, closer and closer.

Joseph and the comrades waited. Mababe looked over to one of the ranks of foot soldiers and saw the slaves who had escaped with them from the Saharadeen's dungeons. He nodded to an old man who smiled back with a toothless grin holding his sword and shield proudly. Mababe turned to Joseph and his friends. "I would not wish to be in the way of those men from the dungeons. Their eyes are filled with revenge and their hearts are proud to fight. I pity anyone who gets in their way." The others all laughed.

A horn from the Al Kadi guard sounded out across the hillside and everyone turned in anticipation. The sound echoed across the plains.

The great King stepped forward on his white Stallion and looked down with admiration at his army and nodded to Bassar who was ready with his horsemen. Bassar returned the nod with the salute of respect.

The King raised his sword in the air and there was a huge roar of cheers from his army of twenty thousand men. They cheered and thrashed their weapons against their shields. Horns blasted out and flags flew from their lances. The sound from both sides was deafening.

The battle was about to begin.

After his salute to his King, Bassar turned to his army and rode proudly to the front row of his first column. As he passed by Joseph and his comrades, he saw the smiles on their faces and, although he thought they were all a little crazy, he had to admire their courage and loyalty to their captain, this very clever and magical seagull who had come to help his father. He smiled as he rode past.

Mr Hawkins settled back on Tom's camel with Rumpitter, who was not at all happy with any of this and was keeping very quiet.

"Tom, I have much to do. You and Rumpitter must stay here with the guard. If you need me, you know what to do. That goes for you too my friend," he said, looking now to Rumpitter.

Tom agreed and then saw Joseph and the others looking back at them.

Joseph called over. "Don't you worry lad, we will be back with you soon. We just have a little business here, don't we, men?" They all laughed and cheered and then waved to Tom and Mr Hawkins.

"They are good men," Mr Hawkins said quietly to Tom. "They're all crazy, more like," replied Tom.

Bassar rode along the whole line of his horse soldiers. He said nothing but smiled and bowed his head to his men. The soldiers in the front row all held out their lances and Bassar rattled his sword along the line of lances as he galloped by. His men all cheered as he did so.

As this was happening, there was another sudden crash of drums and a different blast from the enemy horns. Without any warning, the whole front column of enemy foot soldiers charged. With their lances held forward they started to run towards Bassar and his men.

Bassar held up his sword straight into the air. This was a sign to hold fast. He looked into the charging infantry and studied them carefully. Then he looked to his archers. He called out "Hold! These are the slaves of the Saharadeen mines. He shows us he has no mercy and holds no value in their lives. He is testing our strength and skill. These men know they are doomed so they charge without care. They will try to get past us. They will die anyway if they do not. Look to the hill to see their archers." The Saharadeen's horsemen who had assembled on the hill were aiming their bows straight down into the valley of soldiers. They were to strike them down if the slaves did not charge.

Bassar called to his archers. "Bowmen, take these poor souls out of their misery and may Allah spare their souls."

At this command, the archers rode forward a few paces and drew their arrows. The head archer held up a hand to hold his men until the enemy were almost on top of them. He looked up at the Saharadeen's horsemen who just sat, watching. Then he dropped his hand and thousands of arrows took flight straight into the attacking Saharadeen column of slaves. They struck well and almost all of them fell. It was instant. For the few who had not been hit, they just picked themselves up and just stood still. The charge had been halted.

Bassar was not sure what to make of this, but then he looked up at the Saharadeen horsemen on the hill. They now aimed their bows down into the valley. But they were not aiming at Bassar's army; they aimed at their own slaves. Bassar shook his head in disbelief, "What madness is this?" he whispered to himself.

Suddenly the Saharadeen archers let their arrows fly and every slave still standing was struck. All that was left was a pile of bodies amidst the dust and heat.

Joseph was stunned. "The fools are killing their own men!"

Bassar was quiet for a moment and then said, "The Saharadeen wants us to know he has no care for life and his army will do whatever he commands. He wants us to see his power over his army. He does not care that we think him mad or evil. He laughs in the face of death. This is, of course, madness but he tells us he will destroy everything to win this war." He turned to his army and shouted to them "This is a madman. He will falter, for his madness has many weaknesses. We will not be moved and we will show them that courage and honour are our way and our way will stay here until the end." His army cheered again, this time even louder than before.

The drums continued beating and the enemy marched forward.

The seagull hovered above Tom's head. He lowered his head and took a look at the boy and the rat, blinked an eye and then swooped up into the air and over the great Al Kadi army, turned and flew away over the dunes and into the sun. In an instant he had vanished.

The drumming continued and the blowing smoke from the approaching towers grew thicker and stronger. Now the faces of the enemy were in view and Tom looked down upon this terrifying sight before him. Black smoke floated high into the sky and just for a moment he thought he saw a small dot fly into the smoke. Then it disappeared.

The Al Kadi generals were calling instructions to their men and the columns changed position into long thin lines. Then a horseshoe shape was formed. The long lines covered the entrances to the horseshoe positions.

To Tom it looked all very difficult to understand what was going on but it seemed to all flow like magic. Foot soldiers moved into position and horsemen changed their lines continually.

It seemed to be taking an effect because Tom could sense the uncertainty of the oncoming army as they moved forward. They seemed hesitant as their targets seemed to be changing shape all the time.

Behind their defences was the Al Kadi kingdom of Kadistaar and the great and beautiful city and the home of the Al Kadi people. At whatever cost, Kadistaar must not fall to the Saharadeen. It would be the end of hundreds of years of peace and a land much treasured by its people.

The Saharadeen was determined to capture the city of Kadistaar. It would be his last and most needed conquest before he could completely rule the world. The Land of Fire would be complete and he would be all powerful with no one able to ever challenge him again. He would conquer all and his evil hand would reign for eternity.

Kadistaar was a large city, surrounded by vast fortress walls. The city lay on the coast of the great sea, which stretched far away many miles to the north and many distant lands. If the Saharadeen was to capture Kadistaar, he would easily be able to continue his march of evil to all other lands. There would be no end to his madness. No one would survive his evil. The world would never be the same again. It would become a world of darkness and fire.

Inside the Royal palace of Kadistaar was Princess Tasia, who was guarded by an elite regiment of one thousand soldiers. They were the final line of defence against the enemy. But even they would not be able to hold off the Saharadeen for long, should the Al Kadi army be defeated.

Princess Tasia was once Captain Hawkins's love. They had vowed to be married, but she had no idea of what had become of him and was unaware that he was back in her world. She knew nothing of the curse placed upon Captain Hawkins.

Bassar galloped along the lines of his ranks, all now in place and ready for battle. The flags of the Al Kadi waved gently in the light breeze.

The thunder of the enemy drums kept up a deafening beat. The ground moved underfoot as the two armies finally drew to a halt, just four hundred yards apart.

Suddenly the drums stopped and the air was thick with smoke. There was a long blast of trumpets from behind the enemy ranks. The very second it stopped, there was a deafening cry from the front lines of the enemy and, without warning, they charged towards the Al Kadi front lines.

Two long columns of Al Kadi horsemen moved forward to meet the oncoming enemy. As they did this, another rank of Al Kadi horsemen positioned themselves immediately where the first group had been. Four hundred horsemen charged into the enemy foot soldiers, led by one of Bassar's most loyal officers. Their lances were held low in the striking position and their horses galloped forward. They tore right into the heart of the enemy and within seconds half the enemy column was wiped out. The enemy foot soldiers tried to regroup into another line, but as they did so the Al Kadi horsemen had turned around and struck them from behind, just before the next wave of enemy soldiers could get close enough to cut them off. The horsemen ripped through the first wave of enemy and annihilated them.

As the second wave of enemy thought they had reached the front line, the first Al Kadi horsemen retired to the back of their lines only to be replaced by the next column of riders. Lances pointed low and shields to cover them they charged right through the second enemy group and tore them to pieces. The enemy were in disarray and some of them turned to look back at their leaders for support. For a moment it looked like no help was coming. The second group of Al Kadi riders had turned back to finish off the remaining enemy foot soldiers. Then suddenly from right between the massive ranks of the enemy army, a horrendous scream rang out.

It took the Al Kadi riders by surprise and they quickly turned back to face the main enemy army to see what was happening. Dark shapes appeared through the thick smoke, the ground trembled and the riders struggled to hold their horses from rearing and dismounting them.

Through the smoke, the massive column of Saharadeen horsemen appeared, followed closely by the elephants pulling the fire towers. They were supported by at least three thousand horsemen dressed in their black tunics and holding enormous curved swords. The enemy screamed wildly as they charged.

The Al Kadi riders were too close and quickly made an attempt to retreat. Just as they started to turn, thousands of arrows ripped down from the hill where the Saharadeen's archers were still positioned.

Bassar called urgently to his riders to retreat, but it was too late; they had been demolished in just a few seconds. A loud cheer rang out from the Saharadeen army and the drums started beating again, but this time much faster. From behind the smoke screen of the approaching towers of fire came a loud roar. The ground shook.

Bassar's eyes stared in disbelief at the approaching disaster in front of them. Then his eyes turned to steel.

He called over to the leader of a column of his mounted archers. "Move to the hill, take a position and wait for my order." The commander nodded and, without a single word, they turned quickly and galloped up to the higher ground.

Bassar waved his hand up to the hilltop on the left bank and, high up on the hill, there appeared a single rider.

He galloped over to the main column of foot soldiers and spoke to their commanders.

"We will make a double wave of attack. Our plan is in place. The very minute you see the signal, you must charge into the heart of the enemy. You have the skills and the heart for this. Do not disappoint our king. He knows you have it in you to do this. Go with honour." The commanders saluted and returned to their ranks.

Tom and Rumpitter were watching from the highest point. They could see Bassar's soldiers moving rapidly into new positions.

The Saharadeen army continued moving forward.

Instantly Bassar's horsemen attacked in single file. Suddenly from behind there was a flash of light and a flare soared up into the sky.

By now thousands of Saharadeen foot soldiers had moved forward. They were closing in rapidly on the oncoming Al Kadi horsemen. Both the Al Kadi and Saharadeen armies shouted war cries as they approached each other.

The lone rider up on the hilltop yelled at the top of his voice. His words were indistinguishable but were carried by the wind and heard from all below. He held his lance upwards and then pointed it towards the enemy below.

Suddenly from behind the rider, over the hilltop, something appeared. It was a dark shape. It looked like a large round ball. Then there was another and then another and within seconds there were many of them. The dark round shapes lined the hilltop.

Tom could see them but he couldn't make out what they were. He could see at least fifty of the strange dark round shapes all positioned in a long line along the crest of the hill.

The single rider shouted something and immediately the dark shapes moved. They rolled down the hill picking up speed. Sand flew out from under them. As they descended they rolled faster and faster. They were heading directly towards the centre of the oncoming enemy.

The enemy looked quickly to their right and saw them rolling down towards them. One of the Saharadeen leaders turned his horse and looked strangely at them. He called to his troops to alert them, but it was too late. The large round balls had pitched straight into the heart of the enemy.

Bassar immediately called his men to halt, just a short way from the front lines of the charging Saharadeen horsemen.

The large round balls crashed over the soft desert sand knocking down Saharadeen soldiers as they charged.

The Saharadeen soldiers fell over each other. They were being taken down like skittles. Total confusion struck their ranks. The leaders held up their swords to halt their regiments and change their attack.

The enemy came to a grounding halt. The leaders shouted orders to charge. They did so, but in total confusion. The balls were all exactly the same size, eight feet in diameter with a hard outer surface in dimpled sections. To Tom they looked like giant fir cones.

Two Saharadeen leaders urged their soldiers to fall back into line. But it was too late.

Instantly the sides of the balls moved. Razor sharp blades struck out from all sides, slicing into the enemy as they ran past. There were cries of agony and many fell to the ground. They were surprised and helpless.

Suddenly the balls burst open. Men leapt out with huge swords, wielding them, and cutting down hundreds of Saharadeen soldiers in their path.

The round shapes were Al Kadi soldiers who had formed a tight ball, each with ten men. They used the round shields to form a ball. By interlocking with each other into a tight ball, using their shields as an outer core, they had rolled at great speed straight into the heart of the enemy. Not only did the element of surprise fool the Saharadeen soldiers but the Al Kadi soldiers could get into the middle of them without losing a single man.

The blades were triggered from inside the shields. These were used to slice into the enemy before the soldiers opened up and attacked with their swords.

The Al Kadi soldiers struck hard, wielding their swords, cutting down hundreds of Saharadeen. The enemy were stunned and caught completely off their guard. The large horseshoe shape of Al Kadi foot soldiers formed a position with the opening of the horseshoe to allow the Saharadeen soldiers to enter. They were trapped and now unable to charge forward towards the Al Kadi horsemen and were left with no choice but to stand and fight.

Within an instant, Bassar shouted something and his horsemen charged at a full gallop outside the horseshoe and straight towards the enemy. Their lances struck the heart of the Saharadeen soldiers. There was no escape. The tactic had worked.

A huge cloud of dust and sand blew over the battlefield and no one could really see what was happening. Cries and shouts from officers and the clashing of steel and horses neighing wildly were heard.

The Saharadeen himself was way back behind the attacking lines. He stood on his chariot, surrounded by his guards. He was quickly informed by a retreating rider that something strange had happened. The rider tried to explain about the round shapes that had smashed through their ranks. The Al Kadi had broken through and now the Saharadeen infantry was in complete disarray. They had been surprised and were now being destroyed, trapped within the Al Kadi front lines.

"What is this?" he shouted furiously. "Attack them. Don't be fooled by their trickery. Attack now or I will hang you all." He was wild with rage. He cursed the rider and, with the flash of his hand, lashed out at him with his whip. The rider screamed in pain, turned away and returned to his command.

The Saharadeen ordered more men forward and then shouted to his commander. "Bring up the riders. Attack now!"

Bassar and his horsemen were in the midst of the bloody battle, lashing out at their enemy and striking with deadly accuracy, bringing their foes down all around them.

A loud burst of horns rang out across the plain and Bassar turned to see where it came from.

Within moments the Saharadeen foot soldiers were thinning out. There was a sea of blood and bodies all over the ground. Mostly they were Saharadeen soldiers who had fallen.

Just as he thought they had done their work, Bassar looked behind him from where he heard galloping horses. To his horror he saw the biggest charge of horsemen he had ever seen.

Thousands and thousands of horses with riders were charging towards them. They too had long bladed lances lowered in the striking position. The Saharadeen riders were covered in black tunics, their heads protected by steel-pointed helmets with iron visors covering their faces. It looked like the devil had unleashed terror on them.

Bassar's horse rose up on its hind legs and he wielded his sword to the men on the hill. Trumpets sounded and from over the hill came more Al Kadi riders. They charged down the dunes towards the battlefield to form a left flank attack. Their numbers were not as great as the Saharadeen horsemen but they galloped at great speed and with purpose.

He reformed his own brigade back into a long line. Their horses sweated and panted, kicking up the sand with their front hooves and breathed heavily from the charge and the hot sun.

Bassar's men, who had rolled down the banks in balls made with their shields, had regrouped into another battle formation. This time they formed into tight squares, each square with ten men inside. They were protected completely by the round shields, which formed a hard wall around and above them. The squares positioned themselves into groups of three. They were backed up from each side and behind by the wide horseshoe shape of another two thousand foot soldiers. Behind this was another battalion of horse soldiers. In this group were Joseph and the comrades.

This clever formation meant the enemy had no choice but to charge into the opening and around the squares. By doing this, the tight grouping of Saharadeen horsemen would be broken up.

The Al Kadi army moved forward as one massive shape towards the oncoming enemy.

Dead Saharadeen soldiers lay all over the ground around them.

Another trumpet sounded from the Al Kadi defences up on the hill. Instantly Bassar and his horse soldiers moved to the left and right flanks of the horseshoe and into the oncoming enemy.

From high up on the hill the King watched from his white stallion. His officers waited on their horses beside him.

Tom could see more clearly as the dust from the initial attack was settling. He saw Bassar and his army charging forward. Trumpets sounded out, giving instructions to different brigades and regiments. From behind Bassar's battalion, Tom saw another group of horse soldiers. With this group were Joseph and the comrades. They were waiting to be called to attack in a following wave. He smiled to see his friends looking so proud but also worried for their safety and then looked up to the sky to search for Mr Hawkins. There was no sign of him.

In front of them he saw a long line of foot soldiers, ten rows deep. He also noticed the old man from the dungeons and some of the other prisoners, standing in the first row.

Then he looked towards the Saharadeen army and, with horror, he saw the attacking horses with their dark riders. There were so many of them, he couldn't see where the last row was.

"Oh my God, there are millions of them!" Tom shouted.

The King heard Tom, but pretended he had not.

Clearly his army was terribly outnumbered. Would they be beaten and have to fall back?

He thought about Kadistaar and the beautiful country he ruled. Would hundreds of years of peace and happiness in his lands now come to an end? Would the Saharadeen actually win and destroy everything he had achieved? These thoughts were going through his mind.

He noticed that the Saharadeen archers on the far hill had not moved. He signalled to his own archers to change position and prepare a second wave attack on the Saharadeen bowmen.

As if they were a wave of leaves, three thousand horse soldiers peeled to the right and in one movement they charged to the other side of the valley.

There was much activity going on in the rear ranks. Soldiers were changing position, riders were moving back and forth. To Tom, it all looked so complicated.

And still the dark riders of the Saharadeen charged forward.

Bassar's men had formed a wide defence outside the horseshoe of infantrymen. Their swords were drawn and they were going straight towards the Saharadeen army.

The terrifying sound of enemy drums beating and the smell from the thick black smoke bellowing from behind the Saharadeen army from the fire towers was frightening but still the King was unmoved. Tom watched him giving orders to his guards and discussing the whole situation to his officers from his mount. He was in a good position to see clearly the whole picture before him.

Suddenly there was a loud cry from both charging armies. The Saharadeen horses had charged right into the open mouth of the horseshoe. They wielded their swords as the charged though.

The rows of squares formed by the foot soldiers protected by their shields seemed to be working as the enemy horses were forced to break away from a tight group and weave around the squares.

There were now thousands of Saharadeen horse soldiers inside the horseshoe. They charged at the squares to try to smash them. As soon as they were upon them, the squares suddenly burst open and the blades from the shields struck out at the enemy as they galloped through. The Al Kadi foot soldiers broke open and attacked the charging horsemen bringing many of them down. When their riders fell they were finished. The Al Kadi soldiers struck with deadly effect, then immediately reformed into tight squares again and continued moving forward.

At least two thousand enemy horse soldiers were trapped inside the horseshoe. The entrance had been closed and now the enemy were completely surrounded by the Al Kadi. Bassar's men then charged into the enemy horses outside the horseshoe.

The war cries of the two emerging armies were deafening.

The enemy within the horseshoe formation had been completely destroyed. The horseshoe reopened and moved forward again. Bassar's men were now in full hand-to-hand combat with the dark riders of the Saharadeen. It was a terrible battle and many from both sides were falling. Swords clashed and lances struck. Horses neighed loudly in terror as the smoke and dust covered the battlefield amidst the clash of the two armies.

The three thousand Al Kadi horsemen ordered to attack the Saharadeen bowmen on the hill were now very close. But a sudden trumpet sounded from behind the enemy and in an instant, thousands of arrows filled the sky and flew directly into the charging Al Kadi horses. Then they charged down the hill to meet the Al Kadi. There were two battles going on and it was hard to see clearly through the dust and smoke.

The ground moved again and the terrifying and evil sound from the enemy echoed across the valley. The sky turned red and, through the thick smoke, bursting huge balls of fire, cutting through the sky, headed directly towards the hill where Tom and the King were positioned.

The balls of fire whistled fiercely as they flew through the air. The first one fell nearby and exploded as it struck the ground. The soldiers closest were blown to pieces.

More fire balls came and this time they were aiming higher. Suddenly the tent behind Tom was hit and it burst into flames.

The King turned to see the tent engulfed in flames.

"They shoot well. We must take out the towers now before they come any closer," he called out to one officer.

Soldiers tried to put out the fire with rags and water but it was too late. The tent had burned to the ground and in minutes there was nothing left.

More fire balls came at them, exploding as they hit the ground.

A horn from an Al Kadi signaller blew out across the plain.

Down in the valley Bassar and his men were fighting hard. It seemed like an endless battle. Each time they cut down the dark riders and thought they had made an impact, more came at them.

Bassar yelled to one of his officers to regroup the ranks. Just as he turned his horse to re-join his men, a giant elephant burst through the black smoke, then another and another. They pulled the fire towers and were surrounded by hundreds more Saharadeen soldiers.

They were so many.

Bassar heard the signal from the hill and, in response, signalled to his men in the field.

The squares of Al Kadi foot soldiers ran forward towards the elephants but it was no use: they were trampled down.

"Move back, move back!" Bassar called out. He saw, standing on top of one of the towers, a man wielding a flag. Then he realised this was a signal and without any warning a fire ball burst through the smoke and over his head. The fire ball cut right through his men, killing many of them.

Thousands of enemy soldiers kept coming at them. Nothing could stop the fire towers moving forward. The Al Kadi did not have anything that could topple the elephants and stop them moving forward. If they could not stop them, they would keep marching on until they reached Kadistaar. Bassar turned his horse one way and then the next, searching for a break in the oncoming invaders. Everywhere he turned, he saw his men being overwhelmed, desperately trying to hold back the Saharadeen.

Arrows continued to fill the skies from both armies. Fire balls continued to strike at the Al Kadi army. Already many tents on the defences had been burned down.

It was hopeless to try to put out the fires and the force from the striking fire balls was too strong. It seemed that nothing was going to stop this enemy. The King had shown his strategic skills in the battle, but with an enemy army as large as this, he was unable to make any impact.

Bassar looked helplessly around him as he saw his brave soldiers struggling to survive the onslaught. He signalled a retreat. The horseshoe had been sliced in half by the enemy and quickly the Al Kadi soldiers began retreating. They fought hard as they tried to retreat without turning their backs on the enemy. They regrouped into tight formations and the remaining squares reformed also, although now they were fewer they could not have such a strong impact on their enemy.

The Al Kadi horse soldiers reformed quickly into long columns. Bassar looked towards his enemy in desperation. He was weary from the battle. Blood ran down the side of his face. The leather armour on one shoulder was torn, showing a bad gash from the cut of an enemy sword. "You must have that healed Sire," called one of his officers. Bassar looked at the cut and then to the soldier. "There is no time for that," he snapped. "Look!" They saw the enemy were also regrouping. Bassar's army had done well against such a vast foe, but he knew in his heart that the next attack would be the last one.

The elephants had disappeared into the smoke and the Saharadeen army was re-assembling.

They were still almost untouched in numbers and their lines of ranks of foot soldiers and horsemen rolled back through the smoke into the distance.

The King looked down at the desperate scene before him. His army had done well and there were many fallen enemy on the ground. They had managed to take out most of the enemy bowmen who had inflicted much damage to his army, but against such overpowering odds from such a huge enemy force and the giant fire towers moving through his army so easily, he could see no victory. He called to his officers. "We must regroup and change our position. All we can do now is defend and hold. We cannot let the enemy get through; they will take Kadistaar if we fall."

Tom heard this clearly and was now very worried. He clutched the stone from under his shirt.

"Rumpitter, what can we do? The Saharadeen wants this stone and he'll stop at nothing until he gets it. Then he'll take Kadistaar and we'll all be killed."

"We must not let him have it, Tom. We must get that Sword of Isis. If we can somehow reunite it with that stone, we will be able to stop this." Rumpitter jumped up onto his hind legs and looked up at Tom. He put his front two paws on Tom's chest and looked into Tom's eyes. "Listen to me. The Al Kadi can only defend this position for a short while. It won't take long for the Saharadeen to get through. We must contact Mr Hawkins. He will know what to do."

The two companions looked up into the black smoke filled sky. There was no sign of the seagull.

Way back behind the enemy lines a vast camp had been set up with large tents and fires.

One large tent marked in black and gold colours sat in the centre. This was the tent, surrounded by guards, of the Saharadeen himself. His personal chariot stood outside the entrance.

Carts full of oil-covered iron balls were being carried forward to the fire towers.

Columns of soldiers were standing patiently waiting for orders to join the next attack. Fresh horses were tethered to long ropes. Blacksmiths tended their fires and smashed their hammers onto steel, repairing weapons and making new blades.

This was the scene of a well prepared army, so large in size that no matter who their opponent was, it would be smashed.

The Saharadeen stood by the entrance of his tent and smiled. He was pleased with himself for creating such an undefeatable army, so big that he could take over the world without any effort. He smiled at the thought of taking the Al Kadi and winning Kadistaar.

He walked inside his tent to where his officers stood obediently waiting for instructions.

In the centre of the room was a large wooden table with a map laid across it. He threw his knife at the centre of the map. It landed with the tip of its blade right on the spot where the city of Kadistaar stood.

He looked around the table at his officers and grinned.

"Tomorrow I will have Kadistaar in my hands. I want the Al Kadi King for myself. I want his son who dares to defy my army. They shall perish at my hands alone. I will own their lands and take their world. They are weak now. It will not take long to finish what we started."

He turned to his soldiers. His eyes searched into them and his twisted face had the look of evil. His scared eye twitched with pain and he rubbed a finger along the scar. He thought of the Captain who had given him this and snarled at the thought. He had turned him into a seagull, but he should have killed him instead. He growled to himself at his mistake.

"That seagull," he spat. "That small bird who tries to defy me, he is somewhere nearby. He has the bright stone which belongs to this sword." He drew the Sword of Isis from its sheath and laid it on the table.

"This sword is mine and I want that stone. Then I will have the ultimate power."

He paused to look at the hole in the handle which was missing the stone. "Kill them all and bring me the stone. Whoever brings it to me will be richer than you can possibly imagine." His soldiers looked at each other grinning and nodding with the thought of such wealth.

The Saharadeen picked up the sword and held it up above his head. "Go now. Take the Al Kadi King and his son and bring them to me. Bring me that stone. Bring me victory!" he shouted. For a second his soldiers looked nervously and hesitated. "Go!" he shouted again and immediately they disappeared from the tent.

The Saharadeen held the sword in both hands and again thrust it into the air. "The world is mine," he whispered to himself.

From a small opening on the roof of the tent, a pair of eyes blinked.

The seagull had heard everything.

The Al Kadi King watched his army regrouping and forming into new columns. He saw the fallen soldiers who had fought so bravely and he sighed. He looked into the distance and saw the enemy preparing to charge again.

He had captured the hill with his own archers, having successfully taken the Saharadeen bowmen and held their position. This was a good move, he thought, but he knew it was a small victory and, even now, this would not win the battle. The enemy had reformed into a massive force. It would take a miracle to stop their invasion.

Tom had moved back to join the King's guards on top of the hill. This was the last post between the Saharadeen and Kadistaar, which was just two days' ride behind them.

The comrades were still mounted in ranks with the remaining Al Kadi horsemen. From the hill, Tom could see the Saharadeen forces reassembling and gathering more and more soldiers. They had formed endless rows. He saw one row after another of horse soldiers and infantry forming together with the towers of fire and, behind them, even more soldiers. It looked hopeless.

The Saharadeen walked calmly to his chariot. He shouted to his soldiers, "Soon Kadistaar will be ours!" Instantly they roared, cheering and screaming loudly. The giant elephants were whipped into motion. The fire towers glowed, armed with new ammunition, and were jolted forward by their drivers.

This time the Al Kadi army stood motionless and waited. The archers drew their bows and waited for orders. The horse soldiers also sat still and waited. The squares of foot soldiers waited patiently in position. The ground thundered and the sky became black with smoke again.

Once more the enemy looked like a black cloud slowly moving towards them.

Tom was searching the sky for a sign. He called without words to his friend. *Mr Hawkins, we need you. Where are you?*

Bassar was sitting on his mount in front of his army. He turned to look at his King. *Would this be the last time?* He thought to himself. The King looked down on his son with pride and honour. Their eyes met but there was no expression. Tom saw the connection between the father and son.

He thought about his own father and his friends in Rivermouth. Would he ever see them again?

He looked at his friends waiting in the ranks. Trouseau was wielding his sword around in his hand. He was a master swordsman, that was for sure, but his skills would not make much difference to the huge numbers of enemy that were about to charge into them. The others sat still on their mounts and just waited. Horses kicked the dirt with their front hooves and snorted. The heat of the burning sun melted into their hearts.

The Al Kadi army had encountered great losses from the last attack. What they had left would not hold back this vast foe before them.

Tom continued searching the sky. He tried calling again without words. *Mr Hawkins, where are you?*

A horn sounded from way back in the distance, then another, this time nearer, then another and in a few seconds, hundreds of trumpets blew out across the desert.

There came a loud roar from the enemy ranks and instantly they charged forward.

The fire balls whistled through the air and landed in front of the Al Kadi army, exploding into flames as they struck the ground. One after another they came thundering across the valley.

The Saharadeen horse soldiers charged. The Al Kadi army waited – motionless.

Foot soldiers appeared from the back of the Al Kadi ranks. They carried long wooden spikes and stuck them into the ground behind the lines of horse soldiers. There was nothing between them and King Hafidh and his guard of loyal soldiers. Behind them was Kadistaar.

The thunder of the approaching enemy tore into the hearts of the Al Kadi soldiers, but still they stood firm.

Tom turned to the Al Kadi King. "There must be something we can do!" he exclaimed.

The King looked at Tom, "In every world and every lifetime, Tom, there will be someone who has a way to force their evil power over people. So much that they can do almost anything. This man, the Saharadeen, is like many others who have stained the world with blood. He only understands his own desires. He has no interest in anything you or I believe. There is no good in his heart and he will stop at nothing. I even believe he does not know why he does this himself. We have to stop this, Tom. We have to stop his evil. I do not know any other way we can do this but to stand and fight for what we believe." He looked at the leather pouch hanging from Tom's neck. "That stone is the only answer. The Saharadeen must never have it. Kadistaar must never fall to him." He turned his head up towards the sky. "Allah will show us the way. The way to defeat evil. The Saharadeen is just a man. A mortal just like you and me. But he is driven by hatred and power and has no interest in anything else. We must stop him!"

Tom looked carefully at the King and whispered to Rumpitter. "Well, Rumpitter, it looks like it's down to you and me, then."

Tom turned his camel's head around and kicked his heels into the camel's side. The beast protested with a moan and then lurched forward.

A loud horn sounded and Tom turned to look down the hill at Bassar and his army. Bassar held his sword up high and shouted something through the noise of the oncoming enemy. Instantly his whole army charged forward to meet their foe.

Tom saw Joseph and his friends cheering as they galloped in line with Bassar's men. Shoulder to shoulder they rode into the dust and smoke.

Way back behind the enemy, Tom could see a group of gold and black flags waving in the breeze.

Beyond this he could see the tops of tents and fires flickering.

Suddenly a fire ball burst through the air, missing Tom and some of the guards by a few feet. It crashed into the side of the hill and exploded, causing a great commotion amongst the Al Kadi rear guard. Horses leapt up and their riders struggled to hold them steady. The King himself tugged at the reins of his horse to hold it still. Flames leapt from the explosion and caught one of the tents. People ran from within the tent screaming. The Al Kadi flag almost toppled to the ground, but one man got to it just in time to hold it up again. Then another fire ball whistled through the air. This one hit a small group of horse soldiers and burst into flames. Their screams were terrible. Tom was scared, but there was a strange strength within him that made him believe he could do something. He tugged at his camel's reins to make a run for it. His toothless handler came up close and grabbed the strap around the camel's chin. He kicked his own camel and together they galloped further up the hill for cover. As they raced, another fire ball smashed through the cloud of smoke from a previous blast. It struck the ground close to them. The impact of the blast from the fire ball threw the camel handler from his mount. The smoke was too thick for Tom to see where he had landed. He had to keep going for cover.

There were some large rocks just a few yards away. He decided to head for them. Rumpitter held on tightly to Tom's shirt.

The King was shouting orders to his soldiers. There was chaos and men were running for cover and trying to regroup into their defence lines. Horns sounded and men shouted. There was no time for them to notice that Tom had disappeared.

The two charging armies met, head on, in the valley. The thick smoke from the fire balls and the dust rising up from the desert made it impossible to see what was happening.

Bassar and his army charged right into the heart of the attacking dark riders of the Saharadeen.

He called orders to his men as they charged forward. "Take the elephants, bring them down!" Men rushed forward carrying ropes with a weight at one end. The elephants came closer but they were protected by the Saharadeen dark riders. Bassar had to create enough damage to the enemy horse soldiers to enable his men with the rope lassoes to get close enough to swing their ropes at the feet of the elephants.

The clash of the two armies was terrifying. Horses and men screamed either in anger or agony as they crashed into each other. Swords clashed and lances struck. Horses and men fell from deadly blows. Bassar was in the middle of the frenzy, completely surrounded by his foe attacking from all directions.

The elephants charged into the fray, crushing men beneath their giant feet. The noise from the charging elephants was deafening. Al Kadi riders charged forward with rope lassoes. They wielded the lassoes at the feet of the elephants, but some soldiers were crushed as they got too close.

The elephants charged on. Each elephant had a man sitting on top wielding a long whip and holding a net. Bassar was struggling to fight off his attackers, striking to the left and right, turning his horse one way and then another, rising in his saddle to either dodge a lance or sword or to thrust down at his foe. Thousands of men were now engaged in the bloodiest of all battles. It was hard to determine which way to turn.

Bassar charged his horse right between the legs of one of the elephants, taking out several of the enemy as he dodged in and out. Suddenly a net fell from the top of the elephant, landing on top of Bassar and four of his men. The elephant's rider cheered as he successfully trapped his target.

Bassar and his men struggled to free themselves from the net, but became more tangled. Suddenly they were torn from their horses and crashed to the ground. Three enemy riders appeared out of the smoke, took up the net with long hooks and dragged it along the ground back behind the enemy lines. There was nothing Bassar could do as he and his men were pulled, rolling and tumbling through the dust.

Meanwhile the Al Kadi riders with the lassoes were still trying to topple the elephants. One of the lassoes finally caught around the leg of one of the beasts. The rider quickly galloped forward and pulled the rope towards him and tied it to the pommel on his saddle. Another Al Kadi rider took aim with his lasso and successfully caught his rope around another leg. The two ends were tied together and then the riders went as fast as they could to one side. The ropes were now tightening, pulling the elephant forward. The men struggled against the strength of the enormous animal. Their horses breathed heavily as they were urged on. More Al Kadi soldiers saw what was happening and threw ropes at the other elephants. Joseph and his comrades joined the Al Kadis, throwing more ropes and charging into Saharadeen soldiers, swords wielded and striking at their foe. One of the elephant riders took an arrow in the chest and fell to the ground. Saharadeen soldiers on two of the fire towers looked down in horror as they saw their elephants were unable to move. Hundreds of Al Kadi arrows struck the men in the fire towers and many fell to the ground.

Hope suddenly came to the Al Kadi army. "Bring down the elephants, topple the towers." Joseph shouted.

The riders with the rope lassoes drove their horses to their limits. It seemed as if they would never manage it as their horses strained and heaved. But then it happened!

One of the elephants tripped. Its front legs were tangled by the rope, making it unable to move. The huge beast lost balance and fell forward. The elephant behind it then stumbled, causing others to falter and lose their balance. This caused a chain reaction and all the elephants pulling the fire tower finally fell to the ground. Their sheer weight on the towing ropes caused the fire tower to lean over. The large wooden wheels creaked and groaned under the strain of the toppling tower. Finally one of the wheels snapped.

On the ground, soldiers from both sides ran to escape being crushed by the falling tower or burned as boiling oil poured down on them from the top of the tower, catching fire as it touched the flame fuses. Suddenly there was a loud explosion and the first fire tower fell. Men were thrown through the air. The fire ripped into the wooden frames, catching the fire balls and blowing them to shreds.

The Al Kadi soldiers cheered wildly as they saw, at last, the damage they were causing. Inspired by this, other Al Kadi soldiers lassoed another elephant.

Chaos ran throughout the battlefield. Men were caught in hand-to-hand combat. Horses charged and fell, Al Kadi soldiers desperately tried to lasso more elephants while others battled to hold back the onslaught of the Saharadeen army.

Joseph looked at his brave comrades battling against their foe. He saw Braheim wielding his huge sword round in circles, and then crashing it down into the enemy. Trouseau was now dismounted but fighting off attackers, cutting them down two by two. But Joseph could see that even Trouseau, the master swordsman, could not keep this strength up for much longer. For a second everything seemed like a whirlwind in Joseph's eyes. The screams and cries of the battle echoed all around him. He saw men fall and die. Horses gasped for a single breath in the heat of the battle. The noise of steel against steel and the thudding of hooves echoed all around him. He shook his head and kicked his heels into the sides of his horse and urged it forward.

Arrows of fire soared across the sky from both directions. Fire balls from the Saharadeen towers that had not been tumbled continued to smash into the Al Kadi ranks. The sky was black with smoke and the air had the smell of death.

Bassar and his men were finally hauled to a halt. They choked from the dust. They were dragged to the entrance of the Saharadeen's tent.

When the Saharadeen heard news of the captured Prince, he roared with joy. "Bring him to me," he shouted at his men.

Bassar was badly wounded and blood streamed down his face. He lay bedraggled and beaten, tangled in the net.

The Saharadeen looked down on the beaten son of the Al Kadi King and grinned. "You are finished Bassar, and now you are mine." He laughed out loudly, then clapped his hands and turned to one of his soldiers. "Take them to the cages," he ordered.

The defenceless prisoners were dragged away, tormented by the faceless men in black robes shaking their swords at them, screaming and yelping with glee. They were thrown into a cage with iron bars, heavily guarded by Saharadeen soldiers.

Bassar maintained his dignity and did not show his fear to these people. But then he saw a long line of his own soldiers, tied by ropes and being dragged across the sand, urged on by the black veiled horsemen with long whips lashing down on them. He grabbed the bars of the cage and screamed out "NO!..."

It was too much for him to bear to see his own men being handled like this. They had become prisoners of the Saharadeen. His eyes welled with tears. Hundreds of his soldiers were being led away. They looked bedraggled and beaten. It was as if life itself had been sucked from their hearts.

When they saw their beloved leader caught in the cage, their heads dropped and the fire in their hearts died.

The battle raged on. The King was still positioned on the hilltop, riding back and forth on his white stallion, calling out instructions to his chiefs.

More elephants had been toppled and their fire towers crumbled to the ground. However, the two armies were still fighting hard and although the Al Kadi were seriously outnumbered, they proved to be a far more organised and skilful army. But the overwhelming odds against them were their main threat and it was now apparent that a new plan would need to be made to save them from defeat and Kadistaar falling into the hands of the Saharadeen.

Fire balls continued their assault on the hilltop. They were causing great damage to both the Al Kadi ranks and their defensive point, which was now severely under siege.

Tents were hit and men were scattered. Every time they regrouped, they were forced to run for cover as the next wave of enemy arrows and fire balls struck with deadly effect upon them.

A rider galloped up to the King and broke the news that his son Bassar had been captured together with many of his soldiers. They had suffered great losses in the last wave of attack, but with Bassar gone, what should they do?

The King was distraught by the news. He turned on his horse and lowered his head in sorrow. His hand gripped the handle of his dagger and he lowered his eyes. A guard approached him and spoke softly. "Sire, we are so very sorry." He coughed the dust from his throat and continued carefully, "My King... we must retreat. The Saharadeen army are too many, we..." He was interrupted by the King, "Yes, I know," he snapped abruptly at the guard.

"My Lord, I am sorry."

The King took a deep breath and replied, "No – I am sorry." He nodded to his guard.

"Order a retreat of the left and right flanks. Enclose the gap of the centre. The main columns must hold. Do you understand?" His words were firm, but it was clear he was deeply saddened.

The guard nodded and saluted. "It will be done." He bowed and immediately galloped away with two other soldiers.

In the bombardment of the last wave of fire balls, several tents were smashed and the whole defence group on the hill had been disassembled. Soldiers ran to escape the explosions and horses stampeded all around them.

Tom and Rumpitter managed to take cover behind a large rock higher up the hill and quite some way behind the Al Kadi viewpoint. They could hear the raging battle below but, for now, they were out of sight.

Tom was breathing heavily with sweat pouring down his face. "What do we do now, Rumpitter?" he said, looking at his friend who was still hiding under his shirt.

Rumpitter peeked out and smelt the bad air. "The battle is not going well for us, Tom. We need a new plan. Have you called Mr Hawkins?"

"Yes, but he's not answering me. I hope he's all right." *How are we going to get out of this?* Tom asked himself.

Suddenly there was a voice in his head. *Tom, are you all right?* Tom looked up to the sky and then stood up to see where the voice had come from. *Mr Hawkins! Where are you, where have you been?*

Rumpitter jumped up. "Keep your head down!" He too could hear the words of their friend.

*I am well, but the Saharadeen has captured Bassar and many of his soldiers. If we don't stop the Saharadeen now, the battle will be lost. Everything will be lost!*

Tom scratched his head to try to think of something. "What can we do?" he called aloud. "It's all gone mad down there, we had to escape."

*Shhh, Tom. Speak without words. Yes, you have managed to escape and this is good, but now you must stay unseen and unheard. Things have changed. We have to make a new plan and we must act quickly.*

*What do you suggest?* Rumpitter asked cautiously.

*The smoke from the fires has covered the whole valley. You must take the path to the east and get close to the Saharadeen camp. I have been observing the enemy and I think I have found a way for you to get inside...*

Tom interrupted. *Are you kidding? There's millions of them. We'll be caught. No way!*

*Tom, you must hear me out. I know you are worried. I know what you are thinking, but you must trust me. We must take the Saharadeen himself, it's the only way.* He paused and then continued. *You have the only answer to this Tom, you have the 'Stone'. We must get the Sword from the Saharadeen and reunite it with the stone. This is our only chance. I will be your eyes. I can get you into the enemy camp and out again. Trust me Tom, this must work.*

Tom held his head in his hands and then took hold of the stone. "This stupid thing is all madness. It's all stupid," he said again and then tears ran down his face. Rumpitter crawled up and curled his body closely around Tom's chest and looked into his eyes.

"Tom," he said softly. "None of this makes any sense. We all know this, but Mr Hawkins won't let you come to any harm. I am certain of that." He touched his nose against Tom's cheek.

"You have the stone to guide you. If we can get the Sword of Isis away from the Saharadeen, we will have everything we need to finish this and save the Al Kadi and the world will be rid of all evil. Mr Hawkins needs you but he won't let you come to any harm. I promise."

Tom looked into Rumpitter's bright brown eyes and fell back against the rock to look up at the black smoke wafting across the sky. He heard the thunder of the battle below in the valley, the war drums beating and horns blowing. In the distance he heard the cries and screams of men fighting.

The sun had been covered by a cloud of black smoke. He peered over the top of the rock and saw they were quite some distance from the main battle. In the chaos no one had seen them escape.

Then he looked east and saw the sand dunes of the desert. Nothing was there. Both sides had thrown everything they had into one massive attack. Everything was now centred in the valley. The Saharadeen archers had been drawn into the heart of the valley leaving the eastern hill deserted. It could be possible, he thought, to pass along the dunes, just below the hill-top, without being noticed. He knew that they would have to move quickly and stay unseen.

"All right, we'll do it." He wiped his nose, grabbed the reins of the camel and mounted.

He heard Mr Hawkins's voice again. *That's my boy* the seagull said. *I will be with you all the way, Tom. Go to the far side of the hills and then wait until dark. Then I will tell you what to do.*

*What about the King? He'll wonder where we are.* Tom asked as he tugged on the reins and turned the camel's head.

*He already knows.*

Tom looked up into the sky with a wry smile and shook his head. *You crafty devil, Mr Hawkins.*

Rumpitter jumped up onto the saddle and clamped his front paws around the pommel and said, "Hold on tight, Tom. These camels are so clumsy. Keep a firm hold on him and don't let go."

"OK, Rumpitter, I've got it – let's go," Tom replied, holding onto the reins very tightly.

He gave a gentle kick, the camel lurched forward and they started across the desert.

They stayed out of sight, keeping below the top level of the dunes so the dust from the camel could not be seen. They could hear the battle raging below on the other side of the hill.

Tom kept looking behind as they galloped across the sand in case the enemy spotted them.

They headed straight for a cluster of rocks on the edge of a steep dune. The camel snorted in protest at being made to run so fast. Rumpitter leaned forward and stuck his nose into the camel's ear. *Just do as you have been instructed, camel, and all will be well. Don't even think of trying anything funny* he said without words. The camel seemed to understand, tilted its head round to look at Tom, snorted and then stopped moaning and trotted to a group of tall boulders in the distance. After a while they found themselves under an overhanging rock.

Tom searched the area again to see if they had been spotted. It seemed safe enough. He lifted a leather water jug from the side of the saddle and took a long gulp of the fresh water. Then he tilted it into his cupped hand. "Here, Rumpitter, drink this," he said, and the rat lapped at the water.

Tom looked around him. "I think we will be safe here for a while. I wish I knew what Mr Hawkins was planning. I don't feel easy with any of this and I'm scared" he said quietly to his friend. Rumpitter was lapping up the water and didn't answer.

A few small stones fell from the top of the overhanging rock. It startled Tom and instantly he grabbed his sword. He was about to pull the sword from its sheath, when he saw a shadow move above them. Then there was a flicker of light. Rumpitter looked up, standing on his back legs.

*Shh, Rumpitter, someone's up there* Tom said without words.

"Hello Tom, it's me", Came a familiar voice. Tom immediately smiled when he saw the seagull standing on the rock before them.

Tom was overjoyed to see his friend and ordered the camel to kneel low so he could dismount.

As he jumped out of the saddle, the seagull swooped down to join them.

"Am I glad to see you!" Tom exclaimed with a wide smile.

Rumpitter jumped up and down on the camel's saddle. "Oh thank goodness you're back."

"Well done to you both for getting here," Mr Hawkins said, flapping his wings. Then he hopped up onto another rock. "Come up here Tom. Come and see."

Tom and Rumpitter ran to join him. Tom stroked his hand across the seagull's back.

The seagull arched his neck as Tom stroked him.

*Thank you, Tom, that's very nice. From now on we must speak without words.* He said and then turned his head in the other direction. *I am afraid things haven't gone exactly as I had hoped. Look down there.*

The three friends peered carefully over the top of the rock and Tom gasped at the sight below them.

The Saharadeen camp had been well organised. Ranks of fresh soldiers were standing ready to join the battle. There were thousands of them. Tom looked to his left to try and see where the Al Kadi army was, but the thick smoke obscured his vision.

Mr Hawkins nudged Tom's arm and pointed with his beak. They saw Bassar chained inside a cage. There were four others with him. All around the cage were Bassar's soldiers tied up with ropes. They sat helplessly on the ground in groups. They were the prisoners of the Saharadeen.

*Oh my God!* Tom exclaimed without words. *What are we going to do now?*

The seagull turned his head toward Tom and looked him right in the eye. *We're going to free them.*

*What? Are you crazy? There are millions of guards, we'll be caught. Then what?* Tom replied. *Tom, when I say I have a plan, I mean I have a plan.*

He turned to Rumpitter. *You, my friend, have a very important job to do.*

*I do?* Rumpitter asked hesitantly.

*Yes. You have to get down there and chew through those ropes and free the soldiers. With any luck they will cause enough of a distraction so we can get inside that tent.*

*What? Which tent?* Tom asked again staring into the enemy camp.

*That one.* The seagull pointed again with his beak.

Amidst the smoke, on the far side of the camp, Tom saw the large black tent with a gold symbol on top, a serpent's head curled around a sword. Standing outside the entrance were Saharadeen guards with long curved swords. Their faces were covered by black veils.

*Is that the Saharadeen's tent?* He asked.

*Yes it is and that is where we will end this battle*, replied Mr Hawkins.

*You sound very sure – are you sure?* Tom asked again nervously.

*Yes Tom, you'll see. But first we must wait until dusk.*

Tom thought for a moment and then asked, *OK, but what about the King, what's he going to do?*

Mr Hawkins gave a little chuckle. *Let us just say that he is going to have a little surprise for the Saharadeen while we distract him.*

The three companions watched helplessly as the battle raged on. The Al Kadi army were putting up a brave defence against such overwhelming odds.

Finally the sun slowly disappeared below the hills to the west.

The noise of battle gradually died down and finally the Saharadeen ranks withdrew to their camp. When the sun rose up again they would charge towards Kadistaar.

Fires flickered through the evening. They could just see the Al Kadi army camp-fires up on the hill in the distance. Long dark lines of soldiers lined the rim of the dunes. They were watching – and waiting.

When finally darkness fell over the desert they could no longer see the Al Kadi army.

It was clear to see now from the size of their enemy that in the morning, the Al Kadi would be defending their homeland, Kadistaar. This would be the final stand. They would not be able to attack such an opposition. However, for now, there was time for them to rest, for a while at least.

Tom hoped the King would be able to hold them back, and whatever Mr Hawkins had planned, it had better work.

Mr Hawkins looked sadly into the distance and sighed. He lowered his long neck on Tom's shoulder.

*They have fought well, Tom. Every breath they have left is only now to save their homeland. All that is good in this world lies just north beyond their lines. I fear that if our plan does not succeed, the Saharadeen will storm Kadistaar and destroy everyone who gets in the way.*

*This world will not be worth living in. Everything and everyone will die."* The three companions looked towards the north. Beyond the dark hills was Kadistaar.

*Will I ever get home, Mr Hawkins?* Tom whispered.

The seagull turned to Tom and gently rested the end of his long beak on Tom's forehead.

Without words he replied *Tom, I will see to it that you do. Remember that time in this world is but a blink of an eye in yours. I promised your safety and I always keep my word.*

Tom clasped one hand around the stone and felt a warm glow from inside the leather pouch.

He looked into the seagull's eyes. They looked back at him. There was a faint sparkle of light deep within his eyes. Then the seagull blinked one eye and Tom suddenly jumped back.

*Wow!* He exclaimed. *What was that?*

Mr Hawkins tipped his head back and looked up at the dark sky. A bright glow shone around him. *Tom, we have everything we need to finish this. Hold onto that stone, we are going to need it very soon.*

The seagull looked down at Rumpitter. *Are you ready?*

*Yes Sir,* replied the rat. Then the seagull and the rat looked at Tom, *And how about you Tom?*

*I'm ready Mr Hawkins,* said Tom.

*Good. I am going to disappear for a little while. You stay here until you here my call. Do you understand?*

*Yes,* Tom replied nervously.

*When you hear me, you and Rumpitter must get to those rocks down there. Do you see them?*

There was a small clump of rocks on the edge of the camp and not so far from a group of tents. *Soon it will be as dark as it can get. The night will be ours and we will use it well,* the seagull continued.

Tom nodded in agreement. *OK, I can see it. I just hope no one sees us.*

*Think well of how you will get down there. Perhaps you can use that shield?* Mr Hawkins said, turning his head towards the camel.

Tom turned away to look at the large round shield hanging from the side of the camel. He observed it carefully. When he turned back to answer Mr Hawkins, he had vanished.

*He has gone Tom,* Rumpitter said. *We must get ready and wait for his call.*

The seagull glided silently across the fires of the Saharadeen army. He watched them preparing for the night. Most of the soldiers were squatted around their fires, eating and talking quietly. He circled over the large black tent and then swooped lower over the cage which stood outside. One of the guards was leaning against the iron bars at one corner of the cage staring aimlessly into the night fires. The guard felt a gentle breeze of air blow over his head and then a shadow in the air above. He quickly turned his head around and then up at the dark night sky. He saw nothing. There was another whoosh of air behind him and his helmet was knocked off his head. He was startled and jumped away, one hand grabbing his head-scarf. When he pulled his hand away he saw blood on his fingers and quickly called to the other guard. They whispered in confusion to each other. The first guard showed his bloodied hand to the other. Nervously they searched all around the cage and into the night, but found nothing.

When they looked into the cage they saw Bassar lying on his back next to the bars. "He sleeps," one guard said. "Maybe it was a bat. Don't worry, it's nothing." The guard waved his hand and slumped back to the other end of the cage. The first guard looked around again, wiped the top of his head, looked around him again then shrugged his shoulders and went back to his post.

Bassar opened an eye and smiled slightly. *The captain has given us a sign, he thought to himself.*

Up in the night sky the seagull circled around. He turned and headed north towards the Al Kadi. Tom was lying on his front, peering over the top of the dune, down into the Saharadeen camp. Rumpitter sat beside him. *Do you have any idea what Mr Hawkins is up to, Rumpitter?*

*I have a good idea, but whatever it is, we must do exactly as he asks.* The rat looked at Tom and sniffed. *Let's look at it this way, Tom. The Saharadeen has the sword, you have the stone. All we have to do is get the sword and the stone back together. What could be more simple?"* His eyes sparkled and he winked at Tom.

The boy shook his head and rested his chin on his hands. The two friends sat together silently watching and waiting.

It seemed like hours had passed and Tom was beginning to nod off.

He was suddenly startled by something scratching on his arm. "What...?"

*Shhhh, Tom.* Came a voice. It was Rumpitter, tapping Tom's arm. *"Don't fall asleep now, we have work to do."*

"Oh, sorry, I just..."

*Yes, yes, I know. We must speak without words Tom. Promise me from now on you'll...*

He was cut off when a familiar voice came to them. *Tom, Rumpitter. It's time* came the words they had been waiting for. *Rumpitter you know what to do. Tom, are you ready?*

Tom looked around him and realised the seagull was not there. *Yes, I'm ready.*

*Good, now go. Let's do it!*

Earlier Tom had unhooked the large round shield from the camel and set it up on the edge of the sand dune.

*Rumpitter, get on.* Rumpitter jumped onto the shield. Tom grabbed the sides of the shield and pushed it so it was just balancing over the edge of the dune. He leant over the top to take a final glance down the hill and eyed his target. He gently pushed the shield and jumped on. The two companions disappeared over the edge. They started to slide down the soft, sandy slope. Rumpitter was hanging onto the handle in the centre and quickly turned to see Tom was on board. Tom still had both hands firmly clasped to the sides. The shield acted like a sledge and took off down the hill, picking up speed as it went. They slid silently, skimming across the soft sand. The shield bumped and twisted as they flew down the slope of the dune.

*Whoa* cried Rumpitter.

*Hold on tight Rumpitter.* Tom tried to steer the shield by leaning to one side and then the next. They slipped easily over soft sand. He remembered the fun he had with his sleigh back home in the winter snow on the hills near his school.

The shield cut through the sand and jumped up into the air, then bounced back down. At every landing Tom had to lean one way or another to counterbalance the shield to prevent it from turning upside down. It was a fast and bumpy ride as they slid down through the darkness towards the Saharadeen camp.

Although it was very dark, the glow from the Saharadeen camp-fires gave them light to steer by. They finally landed in a soft lump of sand at the bottom of the dune. Tom quickly jumped off and pulled the shield down in case it could be seen. His heart was beating fast and he looked at Rumpitter who looked oddly very calm and somehow almost distant. The large rat had jumped off and was now peering over the top, eyeing the camp carefully. His little brown eyes peered intently at their target.

They were now very close to the enemy camp. They could smell the Saharadeen camp fires and heard the crackle of wood burning. They heard the strange voices of men. They could smell cooking fires and camels, horses and the rancid scent of something burning. The two crouched down and waited.

Tom thought carefully about what was to come.

He put one hand on the stone, still concealed in its pouch hanging from its leather strap around his neck. He felt the stone pulse. It was like a heartbeat. He felt a strange warmth flowing through him.

Rumpitter was staring at him. His brown eyes sparkled and stared widely at Tom.

*Tom, you understand what all this is about don't you?* Came Rumpitter's voice in his head.

*I think so. I feel the stone knows we are near to the Sword of Isis. I think it can sense it.*

*That's right, Tom. Trust in your feelings, let nothing distract you. You will know when it is time to act and you must do as your heart tells you without hesitation.* Rumpitter was still staring at Tom as he continued. *The stone knows it is close. It knows that is where it belongs, so we must make sure that what we do now, is for the best. We cannot falter. The stone will guide you, Tom.*

Tom listened to his friend and at the same time he thought about where they were and what was happening. He realised how wise Mr Hawkins was, not to reveal more than was needed. One step at a time. Make sure everyone is ready. Get everything in its place and then – strike.

Tom had no idea what he was supposed to do next, nor did he know what Mr Hawkins had up his sleeve, but he did feel suddenly very sure that whatever Mr Hawkins had planned, it was going to be right. But of course, he realised how serious this was. Whatever he was about to do must go exactly according to plan.

For the first time in ages there was no moon. The night was very black. There were no stars tonight.

Tom began to think.

Here they were in the midst of a war. A terrible battle had taken place between two armies and yet, it was strange that, as night had fallen, the battling had ceased. Both sides had retreated to their camps. It was almost like a game, but it was a game of death and destruction. Why? Who decides the fate of men? Who decides when the game starts and ends? He thought about his history lessons at school and about what he had learned of the great wars and historic battles of his world. Men had become heroes and demons all in one time. How odd it was that bad people decided to change good things simply because they hated so much someone else's ideas. It was like a dream that never ends, just changing from one person to the next. One king, one leader and a flock to follow him, one madman or one God. Who decides? The only sure thing was to believe in what was right. Good must conquer bad.

They waited in silence, crouching low behind the dune.

Suddenly Tom heard a sound from behind. It was a quiet sound, almost like grains of sand blowing across the ground. He turned to look behind him. At first he saw nothing, but then there was a dark shape descending towards them.

*Rumpitter! Something is coming down there.* He pointed up the dune. *Oh – I can't see it now, has it gone? No, wait – there it is.*

Rumpitter turned quickly and he nodded his head up and down. Another dark shape moved silently towards them. There was a gentle rush of wind and then more shapes appeared, moving rapidly closer.

Tom clasped his hand firmly over the stone and then drew his sword.

*No, wait!* Rumpitter's brown eyes sparkled and his whiskers twitched from side to side. Tom ducked down and stared into the night.

Out of the darkness a large dark shape appeared. Then it turned into a figure of a person sliding down the hill on a shield. Then another came and another. More of them came closer. Then Tom saw them.

It was Braheim and Trouseau. They slid straight towards them and bumped silently into the soft sand to a halt right beside Tom and Rumpitter. Trouseau rolled off his shield then dropped down onto his front next to Tom. "Hello mon ami," he whispered. His eyes were wild with excitement as he smiled at Tom. Braheim was next. He brushed the sand off his tunic and adjusted his Arab head-scarf. His smile was a picture. "Did you think we would let you have all the fun my friend?" he whispered with a wry smile. Tom grinned. He wanted to shout out loud and laugh but instead he just smiled widely at them.

Within a few moments Joseph, Mababe, Gordon, Little, Maris and Blake were all rolling over the sand, crawling towards them. The comrades all looked at Tom and Rumpitter nodding with wide smiles. Tom was overjoyed to see them but he did not shout out or make a sound. He simply smiled the biggest smile and nodded back to the comrades. Rumpitter jumped up and down on his front legs with excitement.

Joseph nudged Tom's arm and whispered. "There's been a change of plan."

"I'm very pleased to see you, Joseph, but what's going on?" Tom whispered back. *You'll see,* came Rumpitter's little voice. Tom quickly turned back again to his other side. *What? You knew they were coming too?*

*Of course,* Rumpitter replied. *It's all arranged, don't you worry about a thing my boy. Mr Hawkins has it all in hand.* Joseph whispered, "The King has new instructions from the Captain." Joseph was, of course, referring to Mr Hawkins. "So what have we got to do?" Tom asked.

Joseph pointed towards the Saharadeen camp. We are to rescue Bassar and seize the Saharadeen himself."

Tom was quiet for a moment. "But there are so many Saharadeen soldiers. They're everywhere. Look!" The comrades all peered carefully over the dune. The Saharadeen camp was bustling with soldiers. There were even more fire towers lined up ready for the second attack. Giant elephants were tethered near them. All around the Saharadeen's own tent, guards patrolled with huge dogs on chains. A few of the dogs howled and growled as passers-by carefully circled around them. Camp fires burned all around the rows of tents. Joseph replied: "The element of surprise can work wonders, Tom. Just you see."

Tom looked at the comrades, shrugged his shoulders and thought to himself. *What are you up to now Mr Hawkins?*

Rumpitter heard Tom's thoughts and hopped up to him. *Fear nothing Tom. Let the Stone guide you. Trust in your heart. We are all in this together. We have come so far together and now we will finish what we started. Agreed?*

Tom looked at his friend and nodded. *Agreed.*

In his majestic tent, surrounded by his generals, the Saharadeen stood at the end of a long table.

His officers stood patiently around the table listening to their leader speak. On the table was a large map. He used a long curved gold dagger, studded with jewels, to point to positions on the map as he spoke. He was giving orders for the final attack.

"Take this position with the horses and move quickly to the right side. The dunes will be to our advantage tomorrow." He paused for a moment, then his next words were more of a menacing tone and he spoke slowly. "We will kill every one of them. There will be no prisoners. I want Kadistaar in my hands tomorrow and the whole world the next day." His scarred face scanned around the table and he looked into the eyes of his generals.

He continued. The tone of his voice was cold. "This is my destiny. I will conquer and destroy all who do not follow. Tomorrow we march north.

Kadistaar has but a few men to guard it. The Al Kadi King has placed his entire army in this valley. We outnumber them one hundred to one at least. They have been weakened by our strength in numbers. Do not falter. Kill them all!" His deep, rough voice echoed around the table and all the generals nodded obediently in approval.

Scattered around the room, large black dogs lay on colourful rugs which covered the floor. They growled as they gnawed on huge bones of meat.

Slave women in black robes, with their faces covered by veils, kneeled around the sides of the tent with trays of food and wine, waiting to quickly jump up and serve the men.

The Saharadeen snapped his fingers at one of the women and she ran quickly to the table with her head bowed low. She never looked up, keeping her head bowed down all the time as the men grabbed at the food on her tray. They hardly noticed her. When the tray had been cleared, one of the generals swiped her across the head with the back of his hand. She didn't make a sound and retreated to her position at the side with the other slaves. The other women didn't look at her. They just stared at the floor.

The generals scoffed at the food and drank the wine while they listened obediently to their leader.

"They wait for us up on that hill, believing their faith will help them. They believe the Al Kadi will live for ever and their God will save them. They are fools!" The Saharadeen laughed and all his men laughed loudly with him. Then he stopped and the generals immediately fell silent to wait for his next words.

The Saharadeen enjoyed their subservience. "I want the Al Kadi King. I want his heart in my hand."

As he said this, he squeezed his hands tightly around an orange and some of the fruit oozed through his fingers.

"No one will deny me my destiny." He threw the half crushed orange onto the map and threw his dagger at it. It sliced right into the heart of the fruit, skewering it to the table.

"Tomorrow I will own the world. No one will dare to oppose me again." He drew the great Sword of Isis in both hands, raised it in the air and shouted, "SA-HARA-DEEN!" Again his men cheered in a wild frenzy, drawing their swords and shaking them in the air.

The Sword of Isis began to tremble violently in his hands. It was as if he were in a trance. His whole body began to shake. The veins in his neck stood proud from his stretched, rugged brown skin. His eyes turned red and evil.

The generals watched nervously. They watched the Saharadeen in awe but also in fear of this man who had so much power over them. He could send them to their deaths at the snap of his fingers or the crack of a whip. He could control everyone.

The sword began to shake in his hands. It became almost too hard for him to hold, even with both hands. His body started shaking as the sword vibrated. Then it whipped to the left and then to the right. It slashed through the air, almost cutting one of the generals, who jumped back out of the way just in time, knocking one of the others backwards onto the ground. The others all stepped back nervously. They were confused and scared of what was suddenly happening before their eyes.

It was all the Saharadeen could do to stop the sword from flying out of his hands. Again it lashed out, one way and then the next. Even the dogs retreated, whimpering into the corners of the tent. The women servants ran away.

The Saharadeen was now unable to control its strength, but still he hung on. The power of the Sword of Isis was too much for him and, on the next thrust, it threw the Saharadeen onto his back, sending him across the table. He slid along the full length, tearing the map as he rolled over and landed on the floor at the far end.

The generals desperately tried to help the Saharadeen onto his feet. But he screamed at them in an uncontrollable rage. They were completely confused, looking at each other wondering what to do.

As he tried to get onto his feet a high screeching sound came from out of nowhere. He had just got back onto his feet when the Sword of Isis suddenly leapt out of his hands and flew through the air, landing on the floor.

"What is this madness?" screamed the Saharadeen. He tried to regain his composure and threw himself over the table to grab the dagger.

The loud screeching sound came again. It echoed all around them.

The Saharadeen looked up at the sky through the small gap in the top of the tent.

"It is him!" he screamed again. "It is him," he repeated. Then he turned to his generals.

"Get him, get him!" he yelled. "Prepare the army. Fetch my horse!"

High up in the night sky, an eerie sound wailed through the air.

Tom and the comrades heard the sound too and looked up. Suddenly they saw a bright flash of light shoot across the night sky. For a second it lit the whole area then it vanished in an instant.

Tom felt inside his shirt and he noticed the stone was vibrating against his chest. He peered into the leather pouch. It was glowing brightly.

*Cover it up Tom, the light will be seen,* whispered Rumpitter. Tom quickly covered it up and shoved it back inside his tunic.

Then Tom heard the voice they had been waiting for.

*Tom, do you hear me?* Came the voice.

*Yes I do* he replied without words.

*Good, tell the comrades to go with you to the small rocks behind the great tent. Look above, what do you see?*

Tom looked into the camp and towards the Saharadeen's tent. Right above it he saw a light in the sky. *Is that you, Mr Hawkins?*

*Yes Tom, this is your mark. Get here now.* There was a pause – and then, *Rumpitter, you know what to do.*

*Indeed I do Sir* replied the rat.

Rumpitter immediately jumped up and ran down the slope.

*Rumpitter!* Tom called without words. *Where are you going?*

*Follow your heart Tom.* Came the reply and the rat disappeared into the enemy camp.

Tom turned to the comrades who were looking at him for an answer.

"Let's go!" he whispered and together they slipped down the slope in silence following Tom. They darted in and out of the shadows of the tents making sure they were not seen.

The Saharadeen ran to the door of his tent. His generals followed.

Suddenly the ground began to tremble. The floor seemed to be moving beneath his feet. It was hard to stand firm as the ground rumbled beneath him. The tethered horses were stirred and began stamping their hooves, neighing in fright. Some reared up on their hind legs, ripping the posts that they were tied to right out of the ground. Hundreds of horses began to scatter smashing into anything in their way. Saharadeen soldiers tried desperately to control them, but it was useless. Their horses were stampeding and out of control.

Then, far worse, the trembling ground became even more violent and the elephants ripped from their posts and started to run. They crushed men, carts, chariots, tents and all that was in their way. They charged through the camp and into the night, leaving behind them a field of destruction. The Saharadeen army was in complete disarray.

The Saharadeen looked around him desperately trying to gather his senses and screamed out orders to his men to gather themselves together.

His generals ran round the camp rallying their men to arms. Horses without riders were stampeding all over the camp.

Then the Saharadeen heard another sound. He looked ahead through the chaos of his army trying to bring itself together. He saw a faint dark shape at the far end of the camp. It looked like a long dark shadow. The shadow was moving. It was moving towards his camp.

Instantly he knew what this was. He screamed like a madman at his soldiers to form ranks. Then he looked down at his belt and realised the Sword was still on the floor in the tent.

As he turned towards the tent, he looked again into the night to see the dark shadow moving closer and closer. Then he heard them. He heard the thunder of horses and then the war cries of men and horses approaching at great speed.

He looked up into the sky and saw a bright flash of light whirl around high above and then it vanished. A faint, high pitched sound cut the air. Instantly he knew what it was and shook his clenched fists at the sky and screamed out. His eyes were wild with rage as he ran back inside the tent.

The Al Kadi army was charging through the darkness of the night towards the unprepared Saharadeen army. They came as swift as the wind and looked like ghosts charging through the darkness. Within moments they reached the camp. The Saharadeen soldiers were amazed as they saw their enemy charging out of the night mist towards them. They scattered, running away to escape. But they were surrounded. There was nowhere to run. The Al Kadi army had taken the night.

Rumpitter managed to run, unseen, through the enemy camp. He darted in and out of the shadows until he finally found Bassar. He looked wounded, but he was alive.

Rumpitter scrambled over to the cage and hopped through the bars. Bassar had managed to pull himself over to the side of the cage to see what was happening. There was no time to waste. The rat ran quickly towards Bassar and immediately started gnawing with his sharp teeth at the rope around his feet. Bassar looked amazed as the rat nibbled easily through it. No sooner had he bitten through the rope around Bassar's feet, he then started on the rope tied around his hands.

Bassar was stunned. He looked over his shoulder to see his own army charging into the surprised Saharadeen army and watched in awe as they tore through the camp, destroying their foe.

He watched his own men being released from their ties by his soldiers.

The Saharadeen soldiers, who had been guarding the prisoners, suddenly did not care anymore. The surprise attack from the Al Kadi army was too much and they began to flee.

The whole Al Kadi army charged through the heart of the Saharadeen camp. No sooner had the shambled Saharadeen army reformed their ranks, they were immediately crushed by the charging Al Kadis.

Saharadeen generals screamed out orders to their men to keep in file, but it was hopeless.

Rumpitter bit through the last of the rope and looked up at Bassar, twitching his whiskers.

Bassar smiled at the large rat. "You are a very smart rat, my friend. I thank you." He found the strength to get to his feet and hobbled to the door of the cage.

It was locked. Rumpitter, realising this, instantly darted through the bars and ran straight towards the soldier who had the key. The guard was running to join his comrades with his sword drawn, ready to fight off the attacking army.

Rumpitter ran like lightning and darted straight between the guard's legs and then bit into his ankle. The guard yelled in pain and tripped. He fell flat on his face. Rumpitter bit hard into his hand and the guard screamed out. As the guard rolled over on the ground, Rumpitter grabbed the keys in his teeth ripping them away from his belt. The guard had not even noticed as he reeled in pain.

Bassar saw the rat running back towards him with the keys in his mouth. He was stunned by the cleverness of the animal and swore he would never look at rats in the same way again.

Rumpitter dropped the keys at Bassar's feet. He fumbled with them, but finally unlocked the cage and jumped free onto the ground. "Thank-you my friend," he said to the rat, who just looked at him with bright brown eyes.

Bassar ran to his men.

The Saharadeen soldiers saw the prisoners escaping and turned to attack. Bassar picked up a rock and hurled it at one of the enemy. The rock hit him square on the head and he fell instantly to the ground.

He picked up the soldier's sword and lunged at another, punching out with his strong fist at another, sending him to the ground. His own men ran into the soldiers with fists flying. After a few moments of hand-to-hand combat, they had overwhelmed the Saharadeen soldiers and armed themselves.

Bassar felt good to be back in control again. Despite his wound, he felt his strength returning. "Come my brothers, let us finish this," he yelled and they ran towards another group of Saharadeen soldiers who were trying to mount their horses.

They caught up with the riders and brought them all down. He looked around the Saharadeen camp to see hundreds of enemy soldiers being rounded up and taken prisoner by his own army. He smiled at the scene before him. Through the smoke and screams of the battle, he saw more and more Al Kadis emerging. Horses were being rounded up and tents were burned to the ground. The fire towers were also burning and toppling into the dust beneath them.

All the elephants has escaped into the night.

Although there were still thousands of Saharadeen soldiers trying to reassemble themselves and fight back, the surprise attack was working.

*Perhaps today will be a good day after all* he thought to himself.

The Saharadeen, surrounded by forty of his own loyal guards, ran back inside the tent.

He stared in utter disbelief when he saw, standing in front of him, a young boy holding the Sword of Isis.

The boy just stood still. He held the great sword in both hands. It had a magnificently engraved guard and a silver framed handle with fine leather binding wound between the silver framework. The long blade had strange markings all down each side.

Strangely Tom felt great courage as he held the sword in his hands. The sword, although it was big, seemed quite light and he was able to hold it up easily.

The Saharadeen guards formed a half circle behind their leader. Their large curved swords with jagged blades were drawn. They walked slowly towards Tom.

Tom could not see their faces, as they were covered by black veils, but he stared straight into the eyes of the Saharadeen.

The guards were about to attack but the Saharadeen held up a hand, "Wait!" he ordered and then turned towards Tom. He had a sly and evil stare. Tom could not believe that he was so close to the evil ruler and tightened his grip on the sword.

"You would not even know what to do with that sword, boy." His rough croaking voice had a menacing tone. It was almost like a deep whisper, but loud enough to be heard from ten feet away.

Tom swallowed the lump in his throat.

"Give me the sword, boy, and you can go free."

Tom stood firm. Suddenly he felt great courage. The stone was still hanging from under his tunic. He felt its pulse beating against his chest.

The Saharadeen saw a faint glow from under Tom's clothing and smiled to himself. He knew what the glow was.

He held out his hand. "Give it to me, boy. See around you. You will not escape from my soldiers. It is best you give the sword and that stone to me – for your own sake." He gestured again with his outstretched hand for Tom to pass over the sword.

"NO!" Tom replied. He made certain that his voice was clear and loud and did not tremble.

"This sword does not belong to you. It belongs to the King and I am going to give it to him.".

The Saharadeen's slanted eyes stared into Tom's.

"I will not ask you again. Give it to me now." He almost spat the words.

"NO! Tom shouted back. "You will never get this," and with his last word Tom lifted the Sword higher.

The Saharadeen turned quickly to his men and nodded. Instantly they started moving towards Tom to attack.

"Get back!" Tom screamed. Suddenly, from the shadows of the tent the comrades charged in from behind the Saharadeen and his guards. "Leave the boy alone!" shouted Joseph.

The surprised guards turned to see their attackers. Mababe stormed into them with his huge curved sword. He immediately killed three of them. He was followed by the others and a vicious battle began.

The Saharadeen focused on Tom who was still standing on his own. He knew time was running out. He needed the sword now. He drew his dagger and hurled it at Tom who managed to dodge it by an inch. Tom stepped back, still pointing the sword at the Saharadeen. "Keep back!" Tom shouted, raising the sword again.

The comrades had taken down several of the guards but they were tangled in a tough fight. Trouseau, the master swordsman, had disarmed two of the guards and was standing on the table fighting off another two. He kicked a stone jug at one guard and jumped into the air, over the head of the other. As he jumped past, he slashed the guard in the face. The guard fell instantly screaming in pain.

Braheim also had two guards against him, but he was wielding two swords at the same time.

The others were all busily engaged in fearsome combat.

Tom noticed the empty hole in the handle of the Sword and instantly realised what it was. He stepped back and fumbled inside his tunic. For just a second he took his eye off the Saharadeen. The Saharadeen saw his opportunity and pounced.

Tom now had the stone in his hand and, as the Saharadeen grabbed his tunic, he dropped the stone.

The Saharadeen shoved Tom backwards, snatching the sword from his grip. As Tom stumbled back he saw the stone on the floor and kicked it away.

Joseph saw the Saharadeen standing over Tom with the sword held up to strike him. He immediately charged forward but the guards blocked him from getting through.

The Saharadeen slashed down at Tom, but somehow Tom managed to avoid the attack as the blade of the sword cut into the rug on the floor, just and inch from his head. Tom yelled and tried to roll away. His hand grabbed out for the stone but the blade of the sword whistled through the air again. Tom rolled back the other way, again dodging the blade by an inch.

The comrades were struggling to break through the guards. Joseph couldn't see Tom and called out for him. "Tom, Tom, are you all right? Where are you?" Then he saw the Saharadeen wielding the sword in the air. Joseph was desperate and he screamed out "NO!" All he could see was the sword being sliced downwards and then he heard Tom's yell. "Tom!" he cried again.

Joseph looked over to Trouseau. "Can you see anything?" he called to his friend. Trouseau was in mid battle with two guards but shook his head. Joseph could see the look of concern on his face.

"Mababe?" he called. "No – I cannot see him," came the reply.

"Anyone?" he called out in desperation. "Nothing Joseph," came several replies.

The Saharadeen seized his moment and skipped over the boy to grab the stone from the floor.

Tom was right underneath the evil ruler. The Saharadeen clenched the stone in his hand and cast an evil grin down on the helpless boy. He put one foot on Tom's chest so he couldn't move.

He hissed the words, "I have what I came for." He lifted the Sword of Isis up in one hand and the Stone in the other.

Tom was shaking with fear. He tried to wriggle away, but the Saharadeen's foot was holding him tight to the floor.

The Saharadeen lowered the stone down towards the handle of the sword.

Tom screamed again: "NO!" He tried to push the Saharadeen's boot off his chest but the boot pushed down harder.

Joseph heard Tom's scream. "He's there, I heard him!"

Suddenly a deafening high pitch shriek ripped through the air and a blinding ray of light burst through an opening in the roof of the tent and Mr Hawkins swooped down, straight across the fighting soldiers and comrades.

The Saharadeen turned to see a ball of golden light flying straight at him. He knew who it was.

"This time, bird, I will finish you," he hissed loudly. He clipped the stone into the empty socket on the handle of the sword. Instantly the Sword of

Isis burst into a shining ray of golden light. It surprised the Saharadeen but he held tightly onto the handle with both hands and wielded it through the air at the oncoming bird. The seagull swerved and the blade missed. Suddenly the Sword began to shake. The seagull turned back and, with claws outstretched, dived right at the Saharadeen. It was a bold effort, but the Saharadeen, still holding tightly to the Sword, slashed out at the bird. The blade cut though its side. Blood burst out from under the seagull's wing and he fell to the ground.

Tom screamed again. "NO! – Mr Hawkins – NO!" he cried out, punching the Saharadeen's leg with his fists.

Joseph and the others heard the scream and instantly found a burst of strength within them to smash though the guards. They ran to Tom.

The Saharadeen, once again wielded the glowing sword at the comrades. They stopped short, realising what they were seeing. Their faces looked desperate and defeated at the sight before them. The seagull was lying still on the ground. Blood trickled from under him.

The Saharadeen snarled at them. "You have no chance you fools," he grinned. "Look – I have the Sword of Isis and the Stone together in my power. Your seagull friend – is dead."

They stared in disbelief at the seagull. The seagull was bleeding badly. There was no movement from him. "Captain," Joseph whispered to himself.

Tom wriggled and kicked with his legs under the boot of the Saharadeen. He screamed in desperation, trying to free himself. "Let me go!"

The Saharadeen looked at him. "Keep still boy, I will decide your fate later," he hissed.

The Saharadeen guards immediately formed a circle around the comrades who stood helpless.

"It does not matter what your Al Kadi friends are doing outside. With this one Sword I can destroy them all."

"So – you say so, do you?" came a voice from the entrance. Everyone turned. It was Bassar and the King Hafidh Al Kadi himself. Behind them, outside the tent, their army watched and waited.

"We have captured your whole army. All we have now is to rid ourselves of a snake. Surrender now and you will be spared," said the King.

The Saharadeen replied with his twisted face smiling at the Sword of Isis in his hands. "You may have captured a few men. They mean nothing to me. However, I have this and with it I have you too."

He waved the sword at them and laughed loudly. The lines on his cragged and scarred face made him look even more evil.

The King looked in horror to see the sword in the Saharadeen's hands. He saw the bright shining stone sparkling from the handle. His heart sank. He knew that with one command the Saharadeen could turn the sword on them and they would all perish.

Bassar was thinking hard how he could get to the Saharadeen and capture the sword. He stepped forward. "No, Bassar." The King spoke quietly. "Not now."

Bassar was shaking with rage. All he could think of was taking the Saharadeen.

Suddenly there was a thud as a table fell over and a huge rat ran across the floor.

Rumpitter leapt up into the air at the surprised Saharadeen and sank his sharp teeth into the Saharadeen's hand. He yelled out in pain and the sword fell from his hand onto the floor. Rumpitter kept his teeth firmly gripped into the hand. The Saharadeen screamed at his guards to do something. The sword fell close to the seagull and a trickle of his blood touched the blade. At the same time, Bassar and his men charged forward at the screaming Saharadeen and his guards. But in that same instant the seagull suddenly burst into a ball of flames, which immediately turned into a blinding, golden mist. Tom covered his eyes and rolled away as the Saharadeen lost his foothold on him.

Rays of bright light burst out of the golden glow, sending flares, like bolts of lightning, across the tent. The Saharadeen guards were struck right through with the flares of gold. As they screamed, they crumbled into dust onto the ground.

Everyone stepped back in horror and ducked for cover as the bolts of light hissed and twisted, screeching through the air all around the tent.

The comrades fell flat on their fronts to avoid being struck by the light.

The King fell to his knees at the sight before him. "Allah protect us," he said softly. Bassar was on his knees, holding his shield above his head. One flare bounced off his shield and was sent screeching across in another direction. It struck another Saharadeen guard and he crumbled into ashes onto the ground.

Tom was hiding under a round table with his hands covering his eyes.

Then something very strange happened.

He slipped his fingers away from his eyes and saw the most amazing sight.

The cloud of golden light that had consumed the seagull was changing. The bolts of flying light began to filter back into golden cloud. Within the centre of the cloud something moved. It was a dark shape flickering, moving. It seemed to be growing.

Everyone slowly uncovered their eyes and looked at the strange sight unfolding.

The Saharadeen was twisting in pain with the rat still firmly gripping his hand. He seemed powerless to shake it off and was now lying flat down on his back. It was as if something had tied him to the floor. He was suddenly helpless. He roared in anger but he could not move.

The flickering shape inside the golden cloud grew larger. At first it looked like a dark ball. Then it became slightly oval and rose up a little higher. The top of the shape was now changing. The oval appeared to have two parts, a larger shape at the bottom and a smaller shape at the top that were changing all the time.

Suddenly they could see what had transformed before their eyes.

It was the shape of a man kneeling with his head bowed down.

Gradually the figure began to move. First the head lifted up and then two arms appeared. Then they could see a man clothed in a deep red tunic with a short cut collar. His legs were covered in a light brown cloth which became trousers. He wore dark brown boots up to his knees. His belt was wide and made of brown leather with a large silver buckle. Hanging from the belt was a scabbard with no sword. The shape of his face became clearer. His hair was long to his shoulders, dark with grey streaks. The face turned towards everyone in the tent. This was a handsome face, tanned from the sun. He was sturdy looking. A small, slightly greying beard covered his upper lip and chin. His eyes were deep blue, wide and bright. He lifted slowly onto his feet until he was standing and looking at the scene before him. The golden cloud gradually cleared into nothing and, standing tall in front of everyone in the tent, was a man they instantly recognised.

Braheim was the first to speak. "Captain!" he said quietly and, on one knee, he bowed before the man in front of him.

The other comrades looked up. Joseph spoke cautiously, "Captain?" he asked.

Tom ran over to Joseph and knelt down beside him. He was stunned at what he had just witnessed.

"Are... are you Captain Hawkins?" Tom asked nervously.

The tall man smiled and in a deep, soft voice he replied. "Aye Tom, I am."

"Captain!" shouted Gordon. "It is you."

In one movement all the comrades stood up. For a second they were in disbelief.

The tall man spoke again, "It is good to see you all, men," He had a wide grin.

The comrades all spoke together. "Captain – it's the Captain. Captain Hawkins!" They all cheered.

"The curse is broken," Trouseau shouted and again the comrades cheered. "Captain Hawkins!"

Joseph and Mababe walked up to their captain. Joseph put both his large hands on Captain Hawkins's shoulders. "I cannot believe what I am seeing, but if it is you...," he paused with a lump in his throat and continued, "...I am very pleased to have you back, my friend."

"Captain?" Mababe asked. "Yes, Mababe," the Captain replied.

"It seems the evil curse is finally broken. To see you standing now, as a man, as our captain and our friend, is a sight to behold." Mababe looked at his comrades and then to Tom and then back at Captain Hawkins. "We all owe you our lives. All these many years we have mourned your parting. But the strength we have between us, kept us alive. Then this filth," he darted his eyes at the Saharadeen, "this mad scum, changed everything. What has happened here these past days is a miracle to behold." For the first time in his life, the tall, strong, dark African had a tear in his eye. "Truly a miracle," he repeated.

The Saharadeen wriggled on the ground, cursing. The comrades stood over him with their swords drawn, ready to strike him at any moment. The King and Bassar joined them.

Rumpitter darted over to the side of Captain Hawkins. He smiled down at the rat.

"You too Rumpitter. It is good to see you too." Captain Hawkins stepped forward and the golden glow completely disappeared. He bent down, picked up the Sword of Isis and held it up. "Finally we have this safely in our hands," he said, looking at the large glistening Stone. It shone brightly, sending small shots of light around Mr Hawkins's hands. The Sword glistened.

Then he looked to the Saharadeen. "Get up," he said firmly. "I have been waiting for this moment for a very long time."

The Saharadeen lifted himself onto his elbows and then onto his feet. He brushed his hands down his long black tunic in an attempt to compose himself. He was full of hate with the look of defiance across his snarling and twisted face.

"You – you are nothing without that Sword. It was I who changed you into a mere bird. I had the power." He spat on the floor. Bassar stepped forward to strike him, but he was halted by Captain Hawkins. "No Bassar, my friend – wait." He looked back at the Saharadeen.

The Saharadeen began to snigger. This became a croaky laugh and then much louder and with total arrogance he spoke to the Captain. "You are a fool. Do you think this is the end of it? You are badly mistaken!" He pointed a finger at the Captain. "You will never escape," he laughed again.

Captain Hawkins was not moved. "All this hatred you have, but yet you are a coward who makes others kill for you and your greed. Good men died to end your evil. You think you are so special but you are also nothing without this." He held the sword tightly in both hands. "Neither you nor I have the right to this sword." He held it up again for all to see and walked forward towards the King. "It belongs to you, my Lord." He bowed his head at the King and held the sword out. "Please take it."

The King held out both hands and received the sword. He bowed back to Captain Hawkins.

"By all the powers within me, I will see that this is returned to its rightful place. It will bring peace to all the lands." He smiled at the Captain, bowed again, touching his hand to his forehead and chest and said with a wide smile, "My friend."

The Saharadeen swirled around looking for an escape. He realised now that when the blood from the seagull had touched the Sword, his spell was broken and the seagull was turned back into a man. He cursed the power of the Sword of Isis. He cursed his misfortune. But yet he had a menacing sneer and an evil look in his eye. There was something he knew.

He was surrounded by the comrades, all armed and ready to strike him. His own guards were all dead, his army defeated. He was desperate, but suddenly he grabbed a sword that was lying on the floor and in the same movement hurled it at the back of Captain Hawkins. Tom shouted: "Mr Hawkins, look out!"

The Captain quickly turned to see the sword flying towards him. He ducked to one side and caught the handle of the sword in the air as it passed him. He turned and aimed it back at the Saharadeen. He stared into his evil eyes. The whole room was still as they looked on.

"There is only one way to end this." He directed his words at the Saharadeen, then walked over to Bassar and took his sword from his hand. He whirled it around in a circle. "Mmm, this is a fine sword. There is nothing magic about it. It is made of fine tempered steel and has a good balance. It is...". He took the sword that the Saharadeen had thrown at him in his other hand and whirled it around, like the first one. "... very similar to this sword."

"What are you talking about?" the Saharadeen snarled back.

"What I am talking about is very simple. You and I are just men. You had some evil power when your wife lived and you ruled thousands in your evil mines by fear and death. You had men kill for you. But without that – you were nothing. Now you are nothing. You cast me into the fire and turned me into a bird. But as you can see – now here we are. You and I and two swords. Nothing more."

He threw one of the swords at the Saharadeen, who just caught it.

"Now let us see who finally wins here. If I win, it means you are dead. If you kill me, these men will kill you anyway. So, for one final time you have the chance of some dignity. You can die knowing that for one short moment in your miserable life, you were a man."

The Saharadeen still remained defiant with an arrogant smirk across his face. But then the sudden realisation that he was doomed came over him.

Everything he dreamed of owning was gone. He had no servants to control and die for him. Suddenly he had no power. He was alone. He would not even die a martyr or as a hero.

He looked quickly to one side to find an escape route. His eyes darted around him, his mind conjuring a plan. He had no one to turn to. Now he was alone and must fight the man standing before him. Man to man, in single combat.

The comrades, the King, Bassar and the Al Kadi soldiers formed a circle around Captain Hawkins and the Saharadeen. They placed the large round Al Kadi shields in front of them to form a wall. The Saharadeen would not escape. There was a deathly hush. Even the noise from outside the tent had ceased. The battle now over, and all the Saharadeen army brought to their heels, the fighting had stopped. It seemed that the whole mass of soldiers, now gathered all around the tent, knew something was happening. The night was still.

The Saharadeen stabbed his sword into the floor and put both hands on the handle. He turned his head around the room, his evil eyes and snarled face finally focused on the Al Kadi King.

He did not speak. He just stared into the King's eyes. Then he nodded slowly, as if in a sign of acceptance to the situation he was in. The King did not move his head or show any sign of acknowledgement. There was no emotion in his eyes as he stared straight back at the Saharadeen.

Captain Hawkins stood no more than ten feet away. He held his sword down and waited.

The Saharadeen suddenly switched his gaze in the direction of Captain Hawkins. In the same instant he flicked the tip of this sword up from the floor and lunged with incredible speed. With his sword outstretched, he flew like lightning directly at the Captain. The tip of the Saharadeen's sword was suddenly inches away from the Captain's head. The Captain felt the rush of wind from the blade slip past his face as he moved his head to the right, but the blade sliced his cheek. There was an instant spurt of blood.

There was a cry from all standing around them. Bassar went to make a move, but stopped when the Captain recoiled from the hit and swung around with his back to the Saharadeen, who was now only a foot away. As the Saharadeen brought his lunging arm back with his sword, the Captain, now with his back to the Saharadeen, thrust his sword backwards. It sliced right into the Saharadeen, just above his belt. The two men stood still. The

Saharadeen slumped into the back of Captain Hawkins and, in a dying breath, he whispered: "You...will never leave the Land of Fire... as a man..."

The Captain lunged again, even harder, and it went right through the Saharadeen. It all happened in an instant. There was a deep murmur from the crowd around them. The Saharadeen was hanging by the sword that had sliced through him. He dropped his sword and his knees began to bend. He was only on his feet because the Captain had not moved. The Saharadeen's mouth opened and, in a final gasp, a deathly scream resounded all around the room. The Captain quickly withdrew his sword, turned around and, in one swoop, sliced his sword through the air.

The Saharadeen's head toppled from his shoulders onto the ground.

There was a moment of deathly silence and then the whole crowd cheered. The cheering came from not just those inside, but the whole Al Kadi army. Even most of the Saharadeen prisoners, all roared into a deafening cheer. The noise of great celebration resounded across the desert.

Lying headless on the floor at the feet of Captain Hawkins, the Saharadeen's body suddenly turned to ash and his severed head crumbled into tiny fragments. All that was left was his black and gold cape and tunic. He had finally gone.

Captain Hawkins flicked the tip of his sword under the cape and held it up high for all to see.

The whole army cheered and roared with joy. The evil reign of the Saharadeen was over.

There would be no more terror. The Saharadeen was gone for ever.

# Chapter 11 – Curse of Saharadeen

Captain Hawkins waved his sword through the air, the Saharadeen cape whirling around from the tip of the blade. The crowd roared in delight. He walked into the throng of his comrades and friends, shaking their hands and hugging his men. Then he turned towards the door. His face was bleeding badly from the cut on his cheek. Bassar suddenly took the Sword of Isis from the hands of his father and ran up to the Captain with the sword pointed at him.

"Bassar! What is this?" the King called. Joseph and the comrades all ran forward. There was silence.

"What are you doing?" Joseph shouted. Everyone was taken by surprise.

The Captain stood very still with the point of the blade at his face. Bassar looked straight into his eyes. The room was still. Bassar and the Captain stared at each other. Then Bassar smiled and touched the cut on Captain Hawkins's cheek with the blade of the Sword of Isis.

The wound immediately began to heal. The blood stopped running and the torn flesh returned to normal. Instantly it was as if nothing had ever happened. Captain Hawkins touched the side of his face and realised the Sword had completely healed his wound.

Bassar lowered the Sword and nodded his head to the Captain and smiled widely. "I think you look much better now," he laughed and everyone else burst into laughter too.

Bassar turned to his father and handed back the sword. The King smiled widely as he accepted it from his son. He then turned his head back to Captain Hawkins. "Go and show them. Tell them that it is they who changed our world for the better. And tell them that those brave men who died did not die in vain." The Captain nodded. "As you so wish, Sir," he answered and passed through the group to step outside.

With the Saharadeen's cape still attached to the tip of the sword, he held it up and waved it in the air for all to see. Thousands of soldiers burst into the most deafening cheer. They cried out in joyous laughter, waving their arms in the air. Horns sounded and the thunder of drums beating echoed all across the great desert.

Tom and the comrades ran outside to see the crowds cheering. Joseph took Tom's arm. "Tom, you and that rat of yours – truly magnificent!" He shook his head, "You are one very brave young man. We want you to know that you will always be our friend."

Tom grinned with excitement. "It's an honour to be your friend too, Joseph, but it's really Mr – sorry – Captain Hawkins, that did it," he replied. They both agreed and then laughed. Joseph rubbed his hand through Tom's hair. "You really are something, my lad," he said.

The Captain was standing on the Saharadeen's chariot waving the cape in the air. Everyone knew now that the tyranny was finally over. The riotous cheering and celebration was because in their hearts they remembered their brave brothers who died for this moment. They knew that all that was sacred, all that they dreamed of, had finally come. Peace would reign. They loved their King and their hearts were in great spirit. There would be much celebrating tonight.

Bassar ran over to join Captain Hawkins on the chariot. He put his hand on the Captain's shoulder. "My brother, how can we thank you?" At the same time he waved back to his army, punching his fist in the air. The crowd roared even more.

"On the contrary, Bassar. It is I and my comrades who should be thanking you." The two laughed together and waved back at the cheering soldiers. The Captain was astonished to see both the Saharadeen and Al Kadi soldiers standing together side by side cheering as one, as comrades.

Then Bassar called out to his troops. "The Saharadeen is dead. Long live the Al Kadi!"

The whole army roared even louder and then even louder still when they saw their great King Al Kadi emerge from the tent. They saw him standing together with the comrades and a young boy with a large rat sitting on his shoulder. The King looked down at Tom with a big smile.

"Tom, we – all of us here – owe you everything. Without you, we would not have been victorious. You and the Captain and your friends, all you have done – I cannot begin to say. But we thank you with all our hearts and love." He put his hand on Tom's shoulder and said, "Come, let us join our brothers." Tom had a wide smile on his face as he walked with the King towards the chariot to join the Captain and Bassar.

The crowd of thousands went wild with joy as the King stepped up onto the chariot.

Captain Hawkins turned his head round to see the King and Tom approaching and then looked over to his comrades all standing together cheering and laughing. It was a truly wonderful sight.

He looked up to the stars and saw a small twinkling light high above all the other stars. He smiled and took a deep breath. A sparkle of light in the sky winked like the blink of an eye. He had returned, he was a man again. He thought about all they had accomplished and thanked the stars for this victory. There was a flash of light and a shooting star flew across the night sky.

Tom was jumping up and down with great excitement. Rumpitter hung onto his shoulders with all his strength. The Captain laughed at the sight. He caught Tom's eye and motioned with his hand for Tom to join them.

Tom grinned and moved closer to the Captain. "Jump up here, Tom." The Captain took Tom's hand and helped him up onto the chariot.

The King, Bassar and Captain Hawkins looked at each other with a smile and then, all together, they lifted Tom up. Tom was slightly overwhelmed, but managed to get a foothold on the Captain's shoulders. He could see now how huge the crowd was. He waved nervously at the soldiers and they cheered again. The sound was so loud that Tom had to put his hands over his ears. Rumpitter was still hanging on. Tom heard Rumpitter's voice. *Well Tom, my lad. We did it.* Without words, Tom replied. *It's amazing Rumpitter. You're amazing, it's all just...*

*... Amazing?* Rumpitter interrupted and they said the last word together, then they laughed.

Tom ruffled his hand on Rumpitter's neck and said, without words, *I hope we can stay friends forever, Rumpitter.* He looked at the rat and Rumpitter winked an eye. *That goes without saying.* Then he rubbed his nose against Tom's cheek. "I think we can now speak normally, Tom. They seem to understand us now" Tom waved at the crowd. "Yes Rumpitter, I agree" he said and then looked down at the Captain who was smiling at Tom. He said, "Tom, you are the hero here today. Look and see how many friends you made tonight." The cheering continued.

The King looked up at Tom and then smiled at the two standing with him. They lowered Tom down and then the King turned to the crowd. Thousands of them were all holding torches, lighting the whole desert around them. Up on the hills he could see men yelling and cheering, waving their swords and lances in the air. The masses on the hills were all moving down towards the camp. It was a sight to behold.

"Allah u Akbar!" the King cried out. The crowd cheered back "And so is the King, long live the King!" they cried out again and again.

The King held up a hand to try to quieten the crowd. It took a while, but slowly the cheering faded to a gentle hum. "Quiet! The King will speak," called one of the soldiers. Everyone quietened down. There was silence. All that could be heard was the crackle of the fire torches and the gentle desert breeze catching the Al Kadi flags being held by his horsemen.

King Hafidh Al Kadi held both his arms up to the sky with his head raised upwards.

Turning to the crowd he spoke loudly for all to hear.

"We stand united. Let us never forget the men who died so that we could stand here on this land and say WE ARE BROTHERS!" The last three words caused the most deafening cheer, and the banging of swords against shields sounded like the ground was about to open up and burst wide open.

The King continued. "For too long have we endured the madness. Too long has it taken for us to conquer evil and too long has it taken us to stand side by side as brothers!"

He was now shouting against the cheering.

"Tomorrow we return to Kadistaar with our hearts lifted. Tomorrow is the dawn of our freedom and our new life. Tonight we celebrate a new beginning!"

If it were at all possible for the noise to get louder, the cheering and shouting from the thousands all around the desert camp was incredible. The ground was vibrating.

The King turned to Bassar and the Captain. "We should leave them now and let them enjoy the night." There was great pride in his face as he smiled to the comrades.

"Come." He clapped his hands.

The Saharadeen tent had been burned to the ground, his slaves set free and his gold distributed to everyone. Food and wine from the Saharadeen's personal stores were issued to all the soldiers. No one was left out.

The King's personal guard stood nearby. They were waiting with horses for the King, Bassar, Captain Hawkins and the comrades.

The King turned to the comrades. "Tonight we will dine together in my tent."

They galloped around the camp with its fires and cheering and music blasting out across the desert. Tom was sitting on the saddle in front of Captain Hawkins. Rumpitter clung for his life to the pommel. They twisted and turned along the perimeter of the camp and then up a hill. Tom could see light coming from the hill-top.

The comrades looked back down at the fantastic scene below. A bright orange and red glow lit up the desert for miles around. The sound of celebration, singing and music drifting across the dunes was astounding.

Anything that had the mark of the Saharadeen was being burned. The flames from the tents, flags and war banners burned through the night as the celebrating continued.

As they galloped up to the top of the dune, Tom saw the tents of the Al Kadi. It was a wonderful sight.

Fires burned in neat rows in the centre of the camp. The tents were all laid out in a circle around the fires. The Al Kadi flag flew from the top of the biggest tent. A bright beam of light shone through the tent walls, causing a glow around it.

As they approached, Tom sniffed the air and delighted when he smelt food being cooked on the open fires. Servants were milling around carrying trays and large pots. Arab women in brightly coloured robes with hijabs covering their heads, quickly moved into two long lines and, as the comrades rode between them, the women began to sing and chant, waving their jewel covered hands at the King and his men. King Hafidh greeted them with a huge smile and a wave.

Bassar looked back at the comrades. "Tonight we will feast and drink to our victory." He nodded in Tom's direction and smiled. "Everyone thanks you for all you have done for us. You are receiving the welcome that my people give to our warriors and heroes."

Tom was amazed. "Wow!" was all he could think of saying at that moment.

Captain Hawkins laughed and rubbed his hand through Tom's hair. "You see, Tom, I told you this would be a great adventure."

"Yes you did." Tom replied, looking closely at the man sitting in the saddle behind him. It was, after all, very odd. Tom first knew this man as a seagull and now here he was, the real Captain Hawkins. He felt an odd sadness that the bird that he had come to know and love, was no longer there, but he was now – a man. It was a strangest feeling, but Tom was happy knowing that everything had turned out well.

As they trotted along trough the Al Kadi camp, the Captain sensed what Tom was thinking. "We have much to discuss, Tom." He looked into Tom's eyes. "I know how strange all this is. Indeed it is strange for me too."

"Yes, it is strange and I feel, well, strange..." Tom was unsure what to say and the Captain smiled. "You know something, my friend? Whatever happens now will be our true story. The time we have had together here is far less than the time in your world. You do still realise that in the days you have been here, your father and his friends are still asleep on board *The Eagle*. It has been but a few seconds in their time." Tom looked oddly at the Captain. "What are you saying? Is it all over? Do I have to go home now?"

"My goodness no!" replied the Captain with a huge smile. "We still have much to do."

"We do?"

"Oh yes, Tom." The Captain gave a friendly chuckle with another smile and Tom smiled back.

The Captain looked at Tom and Rumpitter with great admiration. They were two very brave individuals and without them he would not have been able to defeat the Saharadeen, rescue his comrades and return the Sword of Isis to its rightful owner. However, he had one thing that burdened him most. Would he now, finally, be able to return to his lady, the Princess Tasia, the King's daughter? What would she be thinking? She probably thought he was dead or had run far away, never to return.

His deep thoughts troubled him and he knew that soon he must find out.

His thoughts were interrupted by Bassar who pulled his horse up beside them. "My friend..."

Captain Hawkins shook himself from his thoughts. "Bassar!"

"Take your friends to that tent there and rest. Soon we will feast with the King." He nodded towards the comrades. "No doubt you would like some time to speak with your friends?" It was more a question than a statement.

"Thank you Bassar, we are truly grateful and we will enjoy your excellent hospitality and company this night!" the Captain replied. Bassar gave a respectful bow and left them.

Joseph and Mababe were close by and heard the conversation. Trouseau was watching closely as they now drew their horses to a halt. Arab soldiers took their reins as they dismounted.

Captain Hawkins lowered Tom and Rumpitter down and dismounted. Handing his reins to an Arab guard, he walked up to his friends. He nodded with great approval and a bright smile.

"My, it is good to see you all safe," he said, looking at each one of them.

"Mon capitaine, you could not know how good it is to see you. We thought we had lost you forever." The comrades all agreed. Gordon took the Captain's hand and shook it vigorously. "Sir," he said with a lump in his throat, "we won't let you out of our sight again, Sir."

The Captain laughed and put his arms around Gordon's shoulders. "Come my friend, let us dine and rejoice!" The comrades walked into the tent, chatting and happy to see their captain back with them again.

The King had made sure they were well cared for. Their tent was laid out with fine rugs and cushions. Tables were laid with fruit, water and wine. There were large leather containers hanging from round wooden frames, filled with water for them to wash.

All around the tent there were sections, each with their own entrance to a separate room. For the first time in so long they were going to have their own rooms with soft beds of cotton cloth and cushions.

Trouseau let out a loud cry of delight when he saw his room. A pretty Arab girl passed by him and smiled, then offered him a jug of water to wash his hands. Trouseau nodded politely to her and accepted the water gratefully. The others all cheered and laughed. More Arab women brought water and cloths for the men to wash. Maris and Blake immediately ducked their heads into the large leather water containers. Braheim was next to follow. Then they were all splashing themselves in the clean water. The Captain took Tom to one of the Arabs who helped him out of his dusty tunic and gave him water to wash. Joseph smiled when he saw Tom tipping his hands into the water.

"No Tom, this is the way to wash, lad," and he threw a whole bucket of water all over him. Tom cried out as the fresh water drenched him. Everyone laughed and Tom did too. He then took a cup and filled it with water and threw it back at Joseph. This caused raucous laughter all round.

Soon they were all engaged in a water fight, throwing jugs of water at each other and laughing. Even the Arab women thought it was amusing. The Captain was taking hits from jugs of water from all directions. It was indeed a joyous moment. He called to Tom, "Tom my lad, now look what you have started!" Everyone cheered.

Rumpitter had escaped the water fight and scuttled off to find a nice soft cushion and a lump of cheese that he had taken from a plate. The pretty Arab girl screamed when she saw the huge rat nibbling away at the cheese. She threw her hands in the air and ran backwards. Trouseau grabbed her to stop her from falling over. He smiled at her. "Do not fear Madame. This is no ordinary rat. He is our friend."

The poor girl was very shaken and surprised as Trouseau lifted her back on her feet.

He held out a hand to assure her. "Please, watch me, I will show you." He went over to Rumpitter and looked at him. "You won't bite me, will you?" he asked carefully as he slowly placed his hand on the rat's back and then slowly stroked it. Rumpitter looked back at the Frenchman.

The Arab girl was still in shock.

Rumpitter said to Tom without words, *Tom, please tell him, I'm sorry, but I am absolutely starving, no time to chat and, no, I won't bite him.*

Tom burst into laughter. Trouseau looked at Tom, "What is it that makes you laugh?"

"He said he's sorry, but he's really hungry and he won't bite you because you are his friend."

Trouseau laughed and looked at the rat nibbling on the cheese. "He said that?"

The Captain replied, "He certainly did Trouseau. But you can't keep a good rat from his dinner, can you, eh?"

Everyone burst into more laughter and the Arab girl began to relax. She smiled shyly at Trouseau, who gave her a wide smile back. "He is our friend," he said to the girl with another smile. The girl bowed her head with her eyes looking at Trouseau. He bowed back.

The pleasant exchange hadn't gone unnoticed by Captain Hawkins and he smiled at the respectful contact between the Frenchman and the girl. She stepped back to carry on with her duties.

Trouseau caught the Captain's look and was slightly embarrassed. The Captain simply nodded back with a smile and a friendly wink.

The comrades began to chat over all they had been through. Captain Hawkins walked around to speak with each of his comrades.

Finally they were all washed and refreshed.

"Come friends, let us gather here for a while before the celebrating begins with our brothers outside."

The comrades sat down on the rugs and poured drinks. The Captain waited until everyone was ready and then, he too, found a seat. He looked around at his men and at Tom and Rumpitter, who were sitting together next to Joseph and Braheim.

The chatting died down and they all waited for their captain to speak.

"Friends, we have been through a great deal together. These past years have been hard for each of us." He paused for a moment to consider all that had happened between them. "When we were captured by the Saharadeen we were separated by his evil. I was, as you know, taken to his temple and thrown to the fire. By some strange magic, I was transformed into a bird. He chose to turn me into a seagull after the name of our ship, *The Glaros*. You were not aware then what had become of me. But by luck I was able to escape.

Before I met Tom and Rumpitter, our other friend here," he pointed at the rat who was still nibbling away at the cheese, "I flew back to where I had last seen the ship. By some miracle it was still where we had left it. When I jumped aboard I realised it was sailing back to where we had come from. Then I discovered that *The Glaros* had become a magical ship that could take me from this world to another. I have no idea how this happened. It took me several journeys back and forth to calculate that time in Tom's world was but a short breath in time to that in our world." He looked around at the comrades and could see they were very puzzled by all he was telling them.

"I realise, of course, none of this makes sense and even I still cannot fully understand. However, I was fortunate enough to find a splendid friend in this young lad. I soon realised that he was like us. He has the scent for adventure and is a loyal companion. When I was in Tom's world I found some good friends who have been able to help me. I finally came to accept my destiny and believed I was to stay as a bird for ever. But I knew that with the power I had been given, someday I would be able to come back for you and capture the Sword of Isis from the Saharadeen. I had revenge in my heart, indeed, but I did not know where my fate would take me." He looked at Tom with a smile. "Tom was able to help me achieve what I first believed, even with the powers I had been given, to be impossible."

He could see that the comrades were finding it all very strange to comprehend. He knew, of course, anyone would find this tale very strange and confusing. He did not think less of them for not fully understanding and decided to shorten the tale.

"It has been a long journey and many things have happened. We have lost good friends." They all nodded in respect of those who had perished and those they had been unable to save.

He raised his glass. "Let us not dwell on the past. Let us salute the true and honourable comrades we have been lucky to have known and let us salute each other for this day. This victory!"

They all raised their glasses. "To good friends and brothers," was the toast.

Tom sat patiently watching, with admiration at the comrades all chatting together and talking about their adventures. He felt proud to be amongst such honourable men. He looked down at Rumpitter who had finished his cheese and was curled up asleep on the cushion.

The friendly banter and chatting was suddenly interrupted by the Arab women who re-appeared carrying clothes. One of the women gestured to

Captain Hawkins to take the clothes she was holding. The other women offered the same to the comrades.

The Captain rolled out the clothes across the seat. He smiled when he realised what they were: ceremonial Arab tunics worn by the Al Kadi warriors. Each one of the comrades had been given the same tunics.

The comrades instantly knew that they had been given the honour of wearing the Al Kadi colours and by wearing these tunics they were now considered as Al Kadi warriors and would be held in great respect throughout the great kingdom of Kadistaar. For a moment they were speechless. Then, with pride, they dressed themselves in their new tunics. Tom was given a boy's tunic in the same colours. The white tunics carried the two crossed Swords of Isis and the crescent moon across the front. The edges, cuffs and collar were ribbed in fine gold thread. They were simple colours, but they had great meaning to anyone who had the honour of wearing them.

The head-scarf was white with a pattern of red lines and squares.

They were given shoes made of soft brown goat skin.

Braheim was eternally grateful to have been able to wash and wear the new clothes. Once he had dressed himself he paraded around the tent, looking down on his new clothes, creasing out any lines with his hands. He turned to his friends and said, "This is indeed a great honour, my friends. We will never forget this night." He waved his hands in a polite gesture to his comrades.

They saluted back to Braheim in their various ways.

A blast of horns rang out and then drums began to beat. Music started to drift across the desert night. They could sense the great excitement building outside.

Captain Hawkins walked over to Tom. He looked proudly at the young boy wearing the tunic.

"I would say that this is a night to savour for the rest of your life, Tom. This is a landmark in the history of this world. We will celebrate tonight and tomorrow you and I will make plans." He smiled at Tom. "Are you hungry?"

"Am I hungry? I could eat a horse!" They chuckled together and the Captain answered: "Well I have a feeling that won't be necessary." They laughed again together and walked towards the door of the tent. The Captain called to his friends, "Come, let us enjoy this night together."

Outside, the Al Kadi servants had prepared everything. The minute they stepped out of the tent, they were met by a thunderous cheer from the whole Al Kadi guard.

The King and Bassar stood waiting for them. "Welcome!" the King called and greeted each of the comrades with a hearty handshake. Bassar saluted them. "My father would be very honoured to have you join him to feast in his tent."

"Thank you Bassar." Captain Hawkins bowed his head to the King. "We are also honoured to be your guests," he replied.

The King gestured for them to follow.

As they walked through the camp, Al Kadi soldiers saluted them in the Arab way. Food was being passed around by women who had prepared all manner of dishes and were handing large wooden trays of food to the soldiers.

The vibrant echo of beating drums and the shrill sound of flutes and horns and the strumming of Arab string instruments carried across the desert night. Arab dancers dressed in fabulous coloured costumes whirled around the fires to the clapping of hands from all who watched.

As they continued through the crowd, soldiers bowed to their King. Calls of praise were shouted by his guards as the companions followed the great King to his tent.

Tall stakes with fire torches burned high above their heads as they entered, passing Al Kadi warriors dressed in the same colours as they. The guards bowed in respect to the comrades as they stepped into the King's tent.

Inside, the floor of the tent was covered in fabulous woven rugs of many colours and patterns. Rows of cushioned seats were placed around the tent with low tables laid with food and jugs of wine and water. Instantly Arab musicians began to play their instruments and immediately Arab women dancers appeared from the sides. They were dressed in fine coloured silk. They had head-dresses with small gold coins sewn around the edges. Their noses and belly buttons were pierced with jewels. They swayed and gyrated to the rhythm of the music. All the soldiers laughed and cheered and clapped to the beat of the drums. Tom was stunned by the amazing spectacle. The atmosphere was fantastic.

The King clapped his hands and several Arab servants came to greet the comrades and ushered them to their seats. "You sit next to me, Tom," Captain Hawkins insisted. The comrades made themselves comfortable on the soft cushions and smiled widely as they watched the dancers.

They were served flagons of wine and plates of all kinds of wonderful food. There was so much to eat. There were dates and figs, meat, couscous, vegetables and fruit and all manner of things. Braheim tucked into some small shiny round balls and Tom looked on nervously at them. "What are they?" he asked carefully. Braheim smiled at the boy. "I would ask you to try one, but I fear you may not like these, Tom."

"Oh, why?" he asked

"These are the eyes of the goat. They are a great delicacy, but you have to eat them in one go, like this," he said, slipping a whole goat's eye into his mouth and swallowing it. "Ugh, I don't think I'll have one of those," Tom replied, looking quite squeamish. Braheim and some of the others laughed.

"Here, Tom, try this." Mababe held out a fig and peeled it from its skin. Tom looked apprehensively as Mababe held it out for him to take. Mababe laughed, "You will like this, it is sweet, here, try it." Tom took the fig and popped it into his mouth and chewed. The comrades all looked on, waiting for his reaction. "Mmmm, I like this, it's lovely." Everyone laughed and Mababe put several more on Tom's plate.

The dancers were gliding around the floor and swinging their hips to the beat of the drums. They had small metal discs between their fingers and they chinked them in time with the music.

Servants carried huge trays of food around to everyone and chatted pleasantly as they moved around the seats and tables. Tom remembered he had left Rumpitter asleep in the other tent and wondered if he was all right. *He is fine, Tom,* came the words into Tom's head. He looked at the Captain, *You heard me thinking that?* Tom replied without words. *I hear everything Tom. I may have been returned as a man, but it seems I still have the power.* The Captain thought carefully about what he had just said. For a second his attention was distracted by the thought.

*Does that mean we will always be able to speak without words?* Tom asked.

*Yes, Tom, we will.* The Captain noticed the King was watching them with a smile. He smiled back and nodded. *Tom, there are only a very few of us who have this power. You and I, Rumpitter, Bazellgoose and the King.* Tom looked across the floor and saw the King smiling at them. He waved and King Hafidh Al Kadi gave a pleasant nod back at Tom.

Tom then frowned as something occurred to him. "But what about when I have to...?"

The Captain interrupted, "Go home?" he answered.

"Yes," Tom said. Now he felt sadness in his heart. The Captain put his hand on Tom's head. "We will always be able to speak, Tom, wherever we are. It is our secret code. You have the power, as do I." He smiled for a moment and then said, "But, come now, let us not speak of departing. We have a celebration to enjoy and tomorrow we can make plans. So, eat and enjoy yourself."

Tom looked into Captain Hawkins's eyes. For a second he thought he saw the crescent moon and the blink of a seagull's eye. But then it was gone. The Captain turned his head to catch the attention of one of the servants.

He took some meat from the serving plate of a young Arab girl and put it on Tom's plate. "Eat Tom, I know you are hungry." Tom gratefully took the meat and then picked up a drinking tumbler and took a large gulp. He immediately coughed and his face went bright red. The Captain and the Arab girl patted Tom on the back. "No, no Tom, don't drink that. It is strong wine. I think this is more suitable for you." The Captain handed Tom a small jug of grape juice. Tom coughed again. "Thank-you." Tom was slightly embarrassed as the Arab girl giggled when she saw him blush.

The Captain pointed to the dancers and then over to the far side of the tent. "Look there, Tom, you see, they are preparing something. I believe we will enjoy this." Tom changed his gaze from the girl over to the far side of the tent. Some men were gathering. They were swinging ropes with something tied to the end. "What are they doing?" Tom asked.

"We will see," Captain Hawkins replied and winked to the others who smiled back at the boy. The dancers were in a rhythmic trance as they swayed and vibrated to the beat of the music. Everyone was clapping and cheering. Then immediately, in time with the music and drums suddenly stopping, the dancers fell to their knees with their arms outstretched and heads bowed towards the King, who immediately rose to his feet and applauded the dancers.

"Splendid, splendid," he called and again everyone cheered the dancers as they walked backwards to the exit of the tent.

The musicians now started playing a more gentle, drifting sound and then some soldiers ran into the centre of the floor of the tent and started rolling back the huge rugs, exposing the desert sand underneath. Everyone watched with interest.

On the floor there was now a large rectangle of sand exposed. Two soldiers ran to the corners of the rectangle and placed iron fire baskets in each corner. They lit the baskets with fire torches and the flames leapt up towards the ceiling. A flap at the top of the tent was pulled open by a rope and the stars of the night in the sky could be clearly seen.

The music suddenly changed pace and this time the drummers began to beat a frantic rhythm.

Five men dressed in nothing but white cotton leggings rolled up to their knees ran into the centre. They looked tall, nimble and very strong. They stood in the centre of the rectangle with their arms folded across their chests and waited.

Bassar suddenly jumped from his seat and stepped into the centre of the rectangle. He held up his hands and the drummers instantly stopped. Everyone stopped talking and he held up his hands until the only sound was the crackling of the flames from the fire baskets. He walked towards the King and bowed. "My father, my Lord," he began.

"We have claimed the greatest victory today. The Saharadeen is finally beaten and destroyed!" Everyone cheered. Bassar held up his hands again to quieten them down. The King looked on with great interest and also with enormous pride at his son, the Prince of Kadistaar.

Bassar continued. "We have designed a special show to celebrate the fall of the Land of Fire and the rebirth of Kadistaar." Again the whole crowd cheered and applauded. This time the King stood up and calmed the crowd down to let his son continue. Bassar acknowledged his father and again continued. "This is the *Dance of Fire*. It represents the end of evil and terror in our lands. It tells the story of tyranny defeated by good. It is for the people who stand with honour and who are proud to fight for freedom – and for Kadistaar!" The thunder of feet stamping and tables being banged upon, the clapping of hands and the deafening cheers from all around the huge tent were incredible.

Bassar raised his voice above the cheering "Please, indulge me. Join with us and enjoy this journey." He turned to the five men in the centre and drew his long sword from his belt. "Begin!" he ordered.

Instantly the five men took up positions. One man stood by each fire basket and one remained in the centre of the floor. Each of them had a piece of rope, six feet long with a knotted end. The four men at the fire baskets dipped the knotted ends into the flames and immediately the ends of the ropes were in flames. The man in the centre whirled his rope around in the air, like a lasso. He twisted his body as he threw it high into the air. The rope twisted and spun as it reached the top of the tent. As it began to fall, a soldier, standing at one side, fired a flaming arrow into the air. It sliced into the knotted end of the flying rope and set it alight. The rope, now with flames leaping from the end, fell straight back down, right into the man's waiting hands. The crowd roared with delight.

Now each of the five men began to twist their flaming ropes around and around. The flames made dancing shapes that looked like curved swords as the men twisted and turned them in the air. Suddenly the four men, standing at each corner, ran towards the man in the centre. As quick as the blink of an eye they formed a pyramid. Three men on the bottom row, two now standing on their shoulders and, above them, the centre man. All the time they swirled their ropes with flames reaching high into the air. Everyone sat and watched, aghast at the tricky manoeuvre.

The three men at the bottom turned the direction they were swinging the ropes and turned them up between the legs of the two standing above them. They, in turn, did the same with their ropes and swung them up to the man on top; as they did this they caught the ropes coming up from below and swung them back down the other side of each man. Then they swung the ropes from left to right and, each man in turn, caught the rope and returned it to the next man. It was indeed a tricky and clever manoeuvre. Now the flaming ropes were swinging up and down, through their legs, around their heads and in every direction.

Then they began to throw the ropes faster and faster, until eventually all that could be seen was a tornado of fire zigzagging between and around the men. It was so fast that it really looked like the flames were burning right through their bodies. The drumming beat faster and faster to the motion of the men with the fire ropes. The flames swished through the five men, who now looked like dark shapes engulfed in flames. It seemed that it would be hopeless for them to stop without being badly burned. But it now created the effect of a golden glow. The light was so bright that some had to cover their eyes.

Tom was riveted to his seat, his mouth wide open in total amazement. He turned to look at Captain Hawkins, who was staring at the scene. The look on his face was blank and his eyes glowed from the light reflecting off the whirling flames. Tom watched his friend carefully. His stare was interrupted by another loud cheer and he turned to see Bassar walking towards the men in the ring of whirling fire. He was holding the Sword of Isis.

He shouted some words in Arabic and pointed the blade of the sword towards the scene.

Suddenly the whirling ring of flames changed direction and moved from the five men straight towards Bassar. As the burning ropes flew towards him, he threw the sword high into the air. The ropes flew directly towards the flying sword and curled around the blade. There was a blinding flash and the sword fell straight towards the ground. The tip of the blade stuck into the sand. There was a flash of light and the burning ropes completely vanished and suddenly the five men were standing in a line with their arms folded across their chests. Bassar walked towards the Sword of Isis and pulled it from the sand. He turned and held it up to the crowd. The whole tent erupted into another deafening cheer.

It was an incredible sight. The King stood to applaud and clasped both his hands together and held them up. Bassar bowed to the audience and replaced the sword back into its sheath. Then he carried it back to the King and held it out for the King to accept.

Tom quickly looked over to Captain Hawkins who, although he seemed distant, was applauding with the crowd. Everyone raised their glasses to the King. Then they saluted Bassar and Captain Hawkins, Tom and the comrades.

The King walked across the floor and shook the hands of the five men, then turned to Bassar and hugged him. The two men smiled widely at each other and laughed.

The King raised his hand and everyone quietened down.

"The Dance of Fire was indeed a sight to behold. It was a wonderful performance." He turned again to the five men and clapped his hands and everyone joined him in the applause.

"Well, my brothers, we certainly did dance with fire with the Saharadeen. For too many years, so many lands were suppressed under the terror of that man. For too many years did we have to watch our every move in the knowledge that, one day, the Saharadeen would come for us. And so he did. But we have been blessed." He turned to Captain Hawkins and bowed.

"The Land of Fire is no more. From this night on, all the lands will be known as Kadistaar!" The King continued: "We shall go home tomorrow with great pride that we have taken the fire from the heart of the devil. There will be no more terror in our world. We have restored the peace and harmony in our lands. We shall return to our homes and families, build our ships and trade again with our neighbours. Let us remember this day so that that we can tell our grandchildren that what they have is because we fought for freedom in the belief that life is good and has no room for evil. It does not matter if men choose different beliefs, because in Kadistaar we are all equal as men and women. The true faiths of all men, whatever they shall be, are with us in each of our hearts. We chose to stand together these past days in this same belief." Everyone nodded and acknowledged this by rising to their feet and saluting their King.

Joseph and the comrades all stood together with their arms around each other's shoulders. Even Trouseau and the big Braheim were embracing each other vigorously. Sam Little, Maris, Blake and Gordon were nodding in agreement to the King's words. Gordon even had a slight tear in his eye.

Tom watched the men closely and saw great emotion in them as they exchanged their mutual respect. Mababe stood tall and quiet. It was as if he were taking in every syllable, breathing every word. Joseph walked around behind Tom and put his hand on the Captain's shoulder.

"I haven't had a moment to say to you how happy I am to see you. You were missed."

Joseph gave an embarrassed cough to hide his emotion.

Captain Hawkins turned around to face Joseph and smiled. "Joseph, my dear friend, there was a time when I thought I would never see you again and my heart mourned. I too have missed you."

The two men hugged each other firmly. "For all of us, Joseph. It has been a strange and painful time. But we are here, all together and now..." The Captain paused and turned his head slightly away so Tom couldn't see his eyes. Joseph moved closer to the Captain. He seemed to be whispering something to Joseph. But Tom could hear everything. It was as clear as if they were speaking to him.

"Is everything all right, Jeremiah?"

"Aye Joseph – it is nothing. I shall be fine."

"Hmmm, I think there are things you should tell me about?" Joseph whispered.

"All in good time, Joseph, all in good time, but we must..." The Captain put a hand over his eyes.

Joseph held his head back a little to look into the Captain's eyes. He looked startled.

"My Lord, Captain, what is this?" The Captain did not reply, but Tom saw him shake his head at Joseph.

Joseph's face looked like he had seen a ghost. He noticed Tom had seen them. He quickly glanced back at the Captain and then back at Tom. He smiled at Tom, but Tom knew he was covering something. "Is everything all right?" Tom asked nervously.

"Of course lad, I think this day has been a long one." He leaned down to speak quietly in Tom's ear. "I think the Captain is tired. I shall take him to his tent to rest. You stay here with the others. Enjoy yourself!" Joseph was smiling and plucked Tom's cheek with his fingers. "You need to eat some more, my friend, eh?" Joseph nodded and looked Tom straight in the eye. "And then in the morning we will sort things out. We have much to do."

Tom nodded.

"Good, then you stay here with our friends. I will be back later." Joseph turned to the Captain who still had his back to Tom, but the Captain pushed his arm behind him to reach for Tom. His hand caught Tom's shoulder and Tom just made out the Captain's words: "See you later, Tom."

Before Tom could reply, the two men had walked away. They disappeared into the crowd and were gone.

Tom thought it was indeed very strange. Why would Captain Hawkins be like that with him?

What was happening?

He turned to look for the others who were all in a joyous mood, patting each other on the back and drinking and enjoying the dancing and music. The whole tent was filled with people celebrating. As Tom watched them, his head started to whirl and he felt dizzy with the noise and people moving all around him. He had to sit down. Suddenly he felt quite alone amongst the crowds around him. He looked at the entrance to the tent and all he could see was men laughing and talking loudly. He wanted to get away.

Suddenly he thought about his father and his friends aboard *The Eagle*. Captain Hawkins had told him that he had only been a few seconds away from them, but yet it seemed like an eternity. He wondered how he was going to get back home. When would Captain Hawkins arrange for him to make the journey back? How would it happen?

Tom decided to sneak away and find Rumpitter. He waited for the right moment and then slipped over the top of the seat onto the floor behind. He crawled along the floor until he was out of sight from the comrades. No one noticed he had gone.

Outside, the Al Kadi army was having the biggest of parties. Everyone was enjoying the night of celebration. Tom was able to walk through the crowds without anyone noticing him.

Eventually he found the tent. There was a group of guards standing around the entrance. Just in case there was a problem, he decided to find another way in and crawled under a flap which was holding the bottom of the tent wall to the ground cover and he slipped underneath and rolled inside.

No sooner had he rolled under the flap and into an outer compartment, he heard familiar voices.

"How did this happen? We thought you were free of it?" he heard Joseph saying.

"It is my fault, Joseph. I should have let the Saharadeen live."

"He would have killed you Jeremiah. You had no choice."

"I know, but he has kept his curse upon me. Joseph". The Captain paused. "Shh, someone is here."

Tom was hiding under a rug. He heard their footsteps inside the tent. They were nearby.

The footsteps were moving around him. They came nearer and Tom held his breath.

Everything went still and suddenly the carpet was pulled away from over him and, looking down at him, there was Joseph. "Tom! What are you doing here? I told you to..."

"I know you did, but I know something's wrong. I want to know what's going on," Tom demanded.

"Well, I..." Joseph was interrupted.

"It is all right, Joseph." The Captain spoke but Tom couldn't see him as Joseph's large frame was blocking his view.

Joseph nodded and then smiled at Tom. "Come lad, don't be afraid," he said, but Tom noted the seriousness in his expression. He crawled out from the rug and jumped to his feet. Joseph stepped to one side and Tom saw the Captain. He had his back to them.

"Captain?" Tom spoke but he was nervous and scared. "Why are you being like this with me? I thought we were..." The Captain interrupted, "... friends, Tom. We are, the very best of friends." Captain Hawkins turned his head around. The words were reassuring but Tom was shocked when he saw the Captain. "Oh my God!" Tom exclaimed. He saw the Captain's face and now he realised.

Captain Hawkins still had the face of a man but his eyes were those of a seagull. They were large round yellow circles edged in a thin orange line. His pupils were black circles. Then he blinked and the black circles turned into the crescent moon shape.

Tom was stunned. "Oh no – what's happening?"

"I am sorry, Tom. I didn't want you to see me like this, I didn't want... I didn't want to tell you that I am uncertain how we can get you back to Rivermouth."

"What? What do you mean? I thought..." Tom was shaking. The Captain cut him short. "Yes, Tom, I thought it would be simple. I found the way to travel from here to your world for many years. That was when I was a bird. I believed it would be a simple task to use *The Glaros* again to ship us back to *The Eagle*, to your people."

The Captain paused and shook his head. "But the Saharadeen has put a curse on me. The last words he spoke to me were that I would never leave the Land of Fire as a man. He said this to me just before I killed him. When the Sword of Isis was reunited with the stone I was returned to myself, but when I killed the Saharadeen something changed inside me. My eyes, they are changing back to those of a bird."

The Captain was clearly upset. He was finding it hard to speak clearly to Tom.

Tom shook his head in confusion. "I don't understand. Are you changing back to a seagull, or is it just your eyes that have changed?" Tom asked. "What does all this mean?"

This time Joseph spoke. "Captain, the boy is worried he will not see his home – his family. I am worried for you also, but how do you know for certain that you cannot get him back to his home?"

"I fear that because my eyes are changed, the curse of the Saharadeen has also changed things. I cannot say for certain that we will be able to return Tom home, but the final words the Saharadeen spoke to me have come true. I am not fully a man. This may also mean we do not have the power to return Tom in the way we came here. I do not know what to do."

Tom was still shaking but said, "Well, can't we try?"

Joseph added, "Yes, Captain – we should try, at least."

"I do not wish to put Tom in any danger; he has been through enough already," replied the Captain.

Then Tom had an idea and he perked up a little. "What about the sword? Now it has its full power, back with the stone replaced, wouldn't that work – somehow?"

Captain Hawkins's eyes rolled in their sockets, just like a seagull, and he stared at Joseph and Tom.

He tilted his head slightly to one side. " I do not know for certain if we can make *The Glaros* take Tom back. I believe the Saharadeen realised something that he did not tell us? It is as if he knew it would be his final blow to me, to prevent me having the powers I had before and therefore perhaps I may not be able to make *The Glaros* fly again to Tom's world. He wants me as his prisoner. He has possessed me!" He paused again and Joseph and Tom looked at each other.

Captain Hawkins continued. "I don't know if the Sword of Isis can help us, but I agree we must do something, but I am worried it will go wrong. Before – it was all so simple, but now I am worried." His strange seagull eyes looked down at Tom. "Tom I promise I will do all I can, but we must think carefully before attempting to return you. I do not want any harm to come to you – I made you a promise."

Joseph added, "We should tell the others, Captain. We should tell the King and Bassar; it could be that they can think of something."

"Aye, Joseph." The Captain nodded. He then lowered his head. There was something else. "I fear that not all is as it seems. I do not know how I am going to be able to face Tasia – like this." He spoke the last few words quietly.

Joseph suddenly realised this other predicament and raised his head to the ceiling. "I am sorry, Captain, I had not considered this either."

Tom was thinking hard. He sat down on a large cushion with his head in both hands, deep in thought.

"She was to be my wife, Joseph. How will she see me now?" said the Captain in a low voice.

As Tom sat thinking, he felt a nudge from behind him and turned quickly to see what it was.

Rumpitter had jumped up onto the cushion and nuzzled his way onto Tom's lap.

Tom spoke without words to Rumpitter. *Have you got any ideas?*

*I can only see sadness and I feel there is something standing in the way of belief. The power can only be held with belief.*

*What do you mean?*

*Believe strong enough in something and it will be as you wish. Let the dark cloud cover your heart and blind your eyes and it will destroy all you believe in.*

Captain Hawkins looked over at the boy and the rat. *You are right, Rumpitter, those are true words indeed. We MUST believe in what we started.* The Captain had heard them speak without words and replied the same way.

Tom and Rumpitter looked up and smiled at the Captain. Tom looked into Captain Hawkins's seagull eyes and he saw the crescent moon. "Those were the eyes I saw when we first met. I believed you then and I believe we will find a way!"

The Captain looked at his three friends. "Very well. In the morning we will return to Kadistaar. I admit I am nervous of meeting the Princess, but I shall have to cope with that myself. The extra time will allow me to consider our predicament. Perhaps the Sword of Isis is our answer; perhaps there is something else that I have missed."

Joseph spoke again, "We must get the comrades together and have a meeting. Many hands make light work, Captain."

"Aye Joseph that is true. Will you and Tom go and gather our comrades? Bring them back here in one hour. I need time to think. There is something I must do."

Joseph replied, "Yes Jeremiah, we'll go now."

Tom and Rumpitter stood up. "Promise me you will be all right, Captain," Tom said.

"I promise we will get through this somehow, Tom," the Captain replied. "Now, go and get the others."

Tom, with Rumpitter on his shoulder, and Joseph ran back to the King's tent. The party was going on well into the night and it was clear to see that nearly everyone had been drinking quite a lot.

All, that is, except for Mababe, Maris and Braheim, who didn't drink alcohol. But this did not stop them from enjoying themselves. The comrades were really celebrating, laughing and telling jokes. The giant Mababe was juggling daggers in the air, four at a time. His friends cheered him on with whoops and yells of encouragement.

Gordon, Sam Little and Blake were very drunk. Gordon could hardly stand. Tom raised his eyes when, finally, Gordon fell over a table and disappeared behind a wall of cushions. Two women servants went to his rescue and lifted him back onto a chair. Gordon slumped into it and fell fast asleep.

Trouseau was telling his wonderful stories to a group of Arab soldiers who were listening with great interest. Every time his glass was empty he held it out and an Arab soldier refilled it with wine. Trouseau didn't falter and just kept talking and telling his tales of his adventures with Captain Hawkins. He had drawn quite a sizeable audience.

Tom noticed that the King was not there.

Joseph shook his head. It was indeed a shame to spoil their evening, but he knew he must gather them together. He didn't know what he would do about Gordon and Blake, who had both passed out and were now sound asleep.

"I think you had better wait outside, Tom. This might take a while. Why don't you join those young men over by the fire and I'll meet you there."

Tom could see several young Arab men sitting round a fire talking and a woman was serving them plates of food.

"OK, Joseph, I'll meet you there," Tom said. He did still feel hungry and he saw Rumpitter's nose was twitching at the scent of food.

Joseph went inside the tent and Tom walked over to the camp-fire.

The young Arab men greeted Tom warmly and made a space for him to sit down. They all nodded and smiled at Tom. A woman offered a plate of goat meat, cheese and dates to Tom. He politely took the plate and handed a piece of cheese to Rumpitter. By now, most of the people had grown used to seeing Tom with his pet rat and the woman nodded with a smile when Tom gave Rumpitter the cheese. The young men all laughed and spoke in their Arabic language that Tom did not understand, but never-the-less, Tom smiled back and the atmosphere between them all was very friendly and polite.

Just a few feet away some musicians played their instruments and two Arab dancers whirled around the camp-fires to the music. Tom enjoyed watching them and, after a while, he found himself clapping his hands to the beat of the music, as all the others were doing. The woman serving the food found Tom's golden hair most fascinating and she kept running her hand over his head. All Tom could see were her bright brown eyes sparkling from the reflection of the fire. Her face was covered by her niqab, a black face veil. Tom smiled at her politely, but he was getting tired of having his hair plucked and fingered, so he decided to get up and walk around the camp. He bowed respectfully to the group and left. Rumpitter bounded along beside him.

Rumpitter spoke without words, *Well done Tom that was neatly carried out. I think you are beginning to understand their ways. They certainly like you.*

Tom giggled a little, "I just wished they would stop pulling my hair and pinching me."

Rumpitter laughed, *They have never seen anyone like you before Tom. These people don't have blond hair and they want to know where you come from. It's quite normal really. Don't let it bother you.*

"Why do some of the women cover their faces?"

"It's their way, Tom. It's symbolic in their religion. It's just the same in your world. The two worlds are very much the same. Only time has changed"

"But why, they look scary?"

"It's not scary to them. It goes back hundreds of years, Tom. It is a bit like when you go to school. You have to wear a uniform. You don't ask why, you just do it. It is right that we must respect each other's ways, don't you think?"

Tom didn't really understand, but decided it best not to pursue the question. He bent down and Rumpitter ran up his leg, jumped onto his arm and onto his shoulder.

"If we don't respect each other's ways, there will never be any peace in the world," said Rumpitter. Tom agreed with a nod.

The two walked happily through the camp, nodding and bowing to people who waved at them as they passed by.

"I suppose we had better not go too far. We'll have to get back to Mr Hawkins and the others."

"Yes, Tom. I notice you just called him Mr Hawkins," replied Rumpitter.

"Well, I don't really know what to call him now. He was Mr Hawkins when I first met him. I know he is a captain, but to me he is Mr Hawkins."

Rumpitter considered the point and then said, "Well, I suppose you can call him whatever you want. I don't think he will mind. He is very fond of you Tom. Never forget that. He will always be your friend."

"I know. I just hope he can think of a way for us to get back to Rivermouth and I hope – he will be all right," Tom said quietly.

They continued walking in silence, both considering the consequences if things took a different turn.

Suddenly Tom stopped abruptly and Rumpitter nearly fell backwards off Tom's shoulder. "Ooh, careful, Tom."

"Sssh! Look over there, under that tree." Tom bent down behind a stack of cloth bundles that were piled in neat rows next to some tethered horses.

They both peered over the top of the bundles.

On top of a small hill, standing under a tree, was Mr Hawkins. He was silhouetted by the light of the moon. At first it looked like he was alone and staring up at the stars. Then suddenly another shape appeared. At first it was a shimmering shadow, dark against the moonlight. It was hard to make it out. The shape was moving very slowly towards Mr Hawkins.

Suddenly the shape became two and then they could see that two people were standing before Mr Hawkins. At first it was hard to make out who they were, but gradually they came into vision.

The two people were King Hafidh and Bassar. The men began talking. There was some gesticulating of arms in the air from Bassar and the King put a hand on the Captain's shoulder.

They could see the three men nodding their heads in deep conversation.

"What do you think they're saying Rumpitter?" Tom whispered. Then he put his hand over his mouth. He realised that the Captain would be able to hear them speak, even if they spoke without words. Rumpitter looked at Tom. They both agreed that they shouldn't speak.

When they peered again over the pile of sacks, they saw the three men had disappeared. Tom turned and sat down with his back against the cloth bundles. He put his chin in his hands and stared at the ground. Rumpitter looked at Tom, not knowing really what to say, but then he spoke anyway. "Come Tom, let's get back to the tent. I am sure we will find a way."

Tom didn't speak; he just looked at his friend and nodded.

The two friends walked back through the camp.

Joseph had managed to get all the comrades back to the tent. He was pacing up and down outside the entrance when he saw Tom and Rumpitter approaching and then sighed with relief.

"Where have you been Tom, I was worried?"

Tom looked up at the tall man. "Have you seen Mr Hawkins since we last spoke, Joseph?"

"No Tom, but I have all our comrades inside. Some are sleeping off the wine." He indicated towards the tent with his thumb.

"Well, we have. He was talking to Bassar and the King. They were up there on that hill. But then they walked away. What do you think is going to happen now?"

Joseph could see the darkness in Tom's eyes. The uncertainty and fear in Tom's face showed so clearly. He bent down and put his hands on Tom's shoulders. "You must not fear, lad. We will get you home and everything will be all right. I give you" – he paused for a moment – "my word." He looked Tom straight in the eyes, gave a little smile and nodded.

Tom nodded back but he was still uneasy. He had truly been through the most amazing adventures and, true to Mr Hawkins's word, they had come through it all in one piece. Tom had discovered things about himself he knew he would never have known, had it not been for Mr Hawkins. However, now he knew he had to get home, but he had no idea what was going to happen.

Tom followed Joseph into the tent. The comrades were arranging their bedding to settle down for the night.

Mababe nodded with a smile to Tom, "Come, my friend, this bed is for you." He pointed at a neatly laid out corner of the tent where a low bed of cushions had been covered by a colourful patterned silk throw.

It was not until that moment, as Tom looked at the comfortable bed, that he suddenly felt extremely tired. He threw off his robe and lay down on the soft pillows. A few moments later he had drifted into a deep sleep. Rumpitter curled up into a ball at the foot of the bed and fell asleep too.

It seemed like he had only been asleep for a few minutes, when he was woken by strange sounds.

In fact Tom had been asleep for several hours, but now it was early morning and the sun was already rising over the dunes. A red glow appeared through the entrance to the tent. The rising sun cast a blanket of red light across the ground.

The comrades were packing their belongings and Tom could hear voices and carts moving around outside. He rubbed his eyes and sat up.

Trouseau was splashing water from a bowl over his face. He turned when he saw Tom stretching his arms. "Ah, bonjour mon ami. Did you sleep well?" he asked with a wide smile.

"Uh – I think so, what time is it?"

"It is time for you to get up and come with us. So, come now and wash your face."

Tom crawled out of the soft bedding and plodded across to Trouseau who poured a jug of fresh water into the bowl.

Tom splashed the cool water over his face and shook his head to wake himself up.

"Bon. Now come with me, Tom," ordered Trouseau.

Tom looked surprisingly at Trouseau and asked, "How can you be so lively so early in the morning, especially after all that wine you drank?"

Trouseau laughed, "That is simple— I am French," and at that Trouseau threw Tom's tunic at him and clapped his hands to gesture Tom outside.

The air was already very warm and the brightness of the quickly rising sun startled Tom, so he held a hand up over his eyes. As they became adjusted to the light he could see the whole camp was already almost packed and ready to march. Tents had been taken down and packed onto camels. Horses were saddled and ready to ride. Fires had been put out and sand kicked over the embers to cover any chance of relighting.

Foot soldiers were all lined up and ready to march. Some of the comrades were saddling their mounts. Joseph walked over to Tom, leading a beautiful black horse by the reins. "Good morning, Tom. I hope you slept well. Do you think you can ride this horse?" he asked, smiling.

"Er, I hope so." It was a small sturdy horse and held its head gracefully. Tom looked at it carefully. "This is an Arab horse, Tom. Bassar wanted you to have it. I think it is about the right size for you," said Joseph with a broad grin.

Tom looked at the elegant small horse. Its shining black coat and well groomed long main sparkled in the sun. He looked into the horse's black eyes and the horse snorted and nodded its head up and down. "Ah-ha, I think he likes you Tom," said Joseph, again with a smile.

"He looks a bit frisky."

"Nonsense, up you get, lad."

Tom put one foot into the leather stirrup and hauled himself up onto the saddle. The horse kicked its front hoof into the sand and snorted again. Tom gripped the reins tightly. Joseph didn't let go until he was sure Tom had control.

The Al Kadi army was almost ready to go. Lines of soldiers, carts laden with their loads, horsemen mounted, camels lined up in rows of twos were stretched back as far as Tom could see.

Tom was impressed how quickly the whole army had packed up and was ready to march. He looked around for Rumpitter. When he couldn't see him, he called for him without words.

His horse seemed to sense something and reared up. "Woah!" Tom called out and held onto the pommel of his saddle. Suddenly Rumpitter ran under the hooves of the rearing steed. He darted between its stamping legs and managed to roll away just before the front legs hammered back into the sand. There was a cloud of dust and Rumpitter scrambled away. "Rumpitter, what are you doing? You nearly had me off."

A chorus of raucous laughter from all the Arab riders around him caused some embarrassment for Tom.

Rumpitter called back, *Oh my – that was close, I will find something to climb on. How about that rock over there?* Tom saw the rock and gave a gentle nudge with his legs. The horse responded immediately. He pulled up beside the rock. Rumpitter ran to the top of the rock and then jumped onto the saddle. "Where have you been, Rumpitter? Look, the whole army is almost ready to go. I can't believe how fast they got everyone together."

Rumpitter settled himself in front of Tom on the saddle and said without words, *These people have lived for hundreds of generations this way. They are like Bedouin, masters of the desert, Tom. They know how to set up camp and then move again at a moment's notice. They know every inch of these lands and the desert is their home. It is nothing to them to be able to travel from one place to the next with all their belongings. They are truly amazing people.*

"They certainly are," Tom agreed as he looked back to see the whole army now ready to ride.

*We better get over there to the others. It looks like we are off now. Do you think you can handle this horse, Tom? He seems quite frisky.*

"I think so," said Tom hesitantly. Tom was by no means an experienced rider, but he had ridden well enough when they escaped from the Saharadeen army and somehow the sturdy Arab horse seemed happy to have Tom on its back.

Suddenly there was a loud cheer and they saw horses galloping from the back of the long column of the waiting army. It was Bassar and a few of his riders, carrying lances with the Al Kadi flag flying from their tops.

The dust rolled away from behind their horses as they galloped along the lines of the Al Kadi.

Joseph waved to Tom to get back and join them. Tom managed to get back in line just as Bassar arrived. The Prince looked approvingly at Tom on his horse. "That is a fine horse, Tom. He is my gift to you. His name is Fahd, which means panther. See, he is as black and as stealthy as the panther." Tom nodded in agreement. "He is small but very strong," Bassar continued. "He is a descendant from the King's personal stables. See – my horse is bigger, but he comes from the same line, but I like to ride a tall horse." Bassar held his head proudly as he said this. Tom nodded and said, "Thank-you Bassar, he is a beautiful horse. I shall take care of him for you." Joseph, Braheim, Trouseau and Mababe were close by and smiled as they listened to the conversation.

Bassar smiled widely showing his brilliant white teeth against his dark skinned face and said, "No Tom, HE will take care of you. Fahd is your horse. He is my gift to you." Bassar nodded in a way that invited Tom to bow to him in acceptance. Tom said again, "Thank-you, I am very honoured to have him."

Bassar nodded approvingly and spoke a word in Arabic that Tom didn't understand, but he thought it meant, "Good."

Bassar kicked his horse and it turned on the spot. He held up his hand and called out for all to hear. The words were in Arabic but it was obvious what he was saying. "Let us ride to Kadistaar!" The whole army cheered as one and shouted out together "Kadistaar!"

Suddenly there was a loud blast of horns, the ground rumbled and, in one motion, the whole Al Kadi army began to move forward.

Tom looked around him to see the vast army moving across the desert sands. The sun was beginning to reach its hottest and he pulled his head-scarf over to keep the sun from burning his face.

Joseph pulled up beside Tom. "Are you all right lad?" he enquired. Tom peered out through his scarf and nodded. "I can't see Mr Hawkins anywhere. Where is he?" Tom asked.

Joseph nodded and replied quietly, "You will see him soon enough" and then rode back a few paces to speak with Braheim, who was covered from head to foot in a white robe and a black and white Arab head-scarf. He looked quite at home on his dark stallion with his long curved sword hanging from his belt. All Tom could see of him was his deep brown eyes gleaming through a gap in his scarf.

Tom was pleased to be riding with the comrades, but he noticed some of them were not there.

Blake, Little, Maris and Gordon were nowhere to be seen. Perhaps they were at the rear of the column, he thought. He looked at Rumpitter bumping up and down on the saddle in front of him. "Rumpitter, I can't see some of our friends, only Joseph, Mababe, Trouseau and Braheim."

*I know, Tom. The others are with the Captain.* Replied Rumpitter.

"Where are they then?"

*They have gone on ahead. They will meet us later.*

"Oh, I see."

Rumpitter chose not to say any more. At least, not yet.

The night before, when all were sleeping, Captain Hawkins, after a hasty meeting with the King and Bassar on the hill-top where Tom had seen them, sneaked into the tent. He wore a long Arab robe. His head was covered by a hood. Only by his soft, deep voice did the comrades know it was him.

He woke Little, Blake, Gordon and Maris from their slumber and told them to meet him on the hill. He gave orders to Joseph to stay with the remaining comrades and look after Tom.

Bassar had arranged for horses to be saddled and ready to ride. Six of the King's men had also been made available to the Captain. They had brought provisions for their long journey and spare horses to take them back to the east coast, to the Saharadeen harbour.

It would be at least three days' ride. They had to move fast.

Although it had been kept secret, the Captain was dying from the curse of the Saharadeen. In no time at all, his body was changing fast. His eyes were weakening and his skin was cracking. He had discovered sores all over his body and face. His hands were thin and bony. His nails were turning yellow. The Saharadeen had told him he would never leave these lands as a man. At first Captain Hawkins thought he was starting to change back into a seagull, but now, it seemed, it was far worse.

The King had told Captain Hawkins at their meeting the previous night, that there was only one thing left that they could do, the only thing that might save him.

King Hafidh Al Kadi returned the Sword of Isis to the Captain and told him to take it to a secret island where, many years before, the Greek monks had rescued the mystic Sword from the raging wars in Egypt.

The secret Temple of Serapis was now situated at the top of the mountain on the small island. The island was unknown and uncharted. The monks discovered that the strange stone had miraculous powers. No one knew where the stone originated, but the monks had protected it for hundreds of years. When they saw that the King Al Kadi had brought peace to all the lands between the Egyptians and Greeks, they believed that he was surely the one who should hold the Sword of Isis as a symbol of freedom and peace for mankind.

If Captain Hawkins could return with the sword to the temple in time, the monks might be able to save him.

Because of this dreadful turn of events, the Captain had no choice but to reach the island in the hope that the monks could save him. He had promised Tom he would return him safely to his home and it would be unbearable if Tom saw him as he was now. The island was located in between two huge rocks that stood alone in the great sea of the southernmost region of the islands of Greece. The only way they could reach the island was to ride hard to the coast and then sail to the island. There was no time to lose.

That same night, King Hafidh Al Kadi had ridden with his special guard of fifty men to the city of Kadistaar.

The midday sun scorched down on the enormous caravan of the Al Kadi army as it slowly marched north to Kadistaar.

Leather bottles of water were being passed down the ranks of the soldiers and women cart drivers. Tom offered to help and rode back down the lines with Joseph and Braheim at his side.

Through the steaming hot dust he noticed the old man he had rescued with the slaves in the dungeons of the Saharadeen's castle. The man gave a wide and toothless smile when he saw the boy and held up his thin arms to greet him. Tom leaned down from his saddle and touched the old man's hand and said, "I am so pleased you are still with us; here have this water." The old man looked into Tom's eyes and said something in his native tongue and then turned and pointed behind him. It seemed that although many of the slaves had died in the battle, at least twenty of them were still alive. Tom gave a cheery wave to them and they called back waving.

"Oh, Rumpitter, they must be the bravest people I have ever met. They were so weak when we got them out of that place and still they wanted to fight. Look at them, they're still hanging on."

"They are indeed Tom. I am sure the King will reward them when we get to the city". To tom's surprise Rumpitter spoke normally to him.

Tom looked down at his friend and asked, "What's the city like?"

"Well, it's not like any other city. It has great walls that defend it from the desert in the south and a large port that opens out to the north. The Kadistaanians have been peaceful traders to the countries of all the northern and western empires for hundreds of years. They only needed to defend themselves from the Saharadeen, but now, with the Saharadeen gone, that will change. There are great fields of crops and wonderful forests surrounding the city on two sides. A beautiful river runs right through the fields to the great sea. Do you know, Tom, every single Kadistaanian has their own home and has an important part to play in the way things are in Kadistaar? There are no people without anything to do. They do not consider their responsibilities as work. They look at it as essential to life and strongly believe that everyone should work for each other. The great King started this many years ago and it has made Kadistaar a wonderful place to live. No one goes hungry, there is no crime and everyone is treated well."

"That sounds almost too good to be true," Tom said quietly and then asked: "So how many times have you been to Kadistaar?"

"Oh, only twice. Both times with Captain Hawkins."

"Then how many times has he been there?"

Rumpitter looked at Tom carefully before answering "Well, he did live there for quite a while, but that was a long, long time ago."

"I do know about Princess Tasia, you know, Rumpitter. Do you think she will be waiting for him? I bet she will be pleased to see him, now that he isn't a seagu..." Rumpitter interrupted abruptly, "..Tom, enough questions for now, my lad. It is very hot and this fur coat of mine hates the heat. Do you mind pouring a little water over me?"

The quick change in the conversation worked and Tom was delighted to cool his friend down with a sprinkling of water, at which Rumpitter responded, "Oh, oh, yes that is just heavenly. Thank-you, thank-you."

Joseph rode over to Tom, "Careful with the water lad, we have to spare it. I am told we will reach an oasis this evening, where we will be able to replenish our water and rest. Bassar tells me that the oasis is guarded by a tribe of desert people, loyal only to the Al Kadi."

"How far is Kadistaar?" asked Tom, looking forward to seeing if he could see beyond the front of the lines of the army. The dust clouded his vision and the shimmering heat from the desert floor cast an almost blinding light, so he gave up and covered his face with his head-scarf.

Braheim drew up beside Joseph. "It is a good two days from here if we keep a steady pace.

There are a few tricky places along the way. These could slow us down, but Bassar's scouts will keep ahead and let us know what is in front."

Tom looked at the companions and asked, "Have you all been to Kadistaar before?"

Joseph and Braheim looked at each other and Joseph replied, "Aye, lad, we have."

Tom sensed a strange, cautious tone in the men, but he was uncertain about it and therefore chose not to pursue it.

Rumpitter sensed Tom's thoughts and quietly said, "We'll keep riding as fast as we can until the sun goes down. Then we will speed up. We should reach the first camp in good time for you to eat and sleep. We have a long way to go Tom, so be patient and stay steady."

Tom nodded back but said nothing.

The day was long and the trek across the soft golden sands of the great desert was slow. The horses found the soft sand harder going than the camels, but they moved on with great determination. The sun blazed down and the heat seared through their white tunics. The women, driving the water wagons, kept offering water from the leather flagons. Tom noted their hardiness and how they shouted words of encouragement to the men on foot. It was interesting to see how everyone supported each other. The entire army moved as one.

When someone fell, they were picked up and laid in a cart to rest. The carts had white cloth tent covers to protect them from the blistering sun.

Far to the left, high on a hill-top, walking slowly across the sand, was a rider on a camel silhouetted by the large fireball of the sun. Tom peered through his face-scarf when he noticed the rider. "Who's that up there?" he asked Rumpitter.

"He is a scout for the Bedouin. He has been following us for three hours. When we are near their camp, he will disappear."

"Why?"

"He will ride fast to his camp to inform his chiefs that we are coming. He can also see far away from both sides of this valley. If any danger is likely to come our way, he will see it first and warn us."

"Wow," said Tom almost to himself and then, "Is any danger likely to come our way?"

"I hope not."

Several uneventful but tiring hours passed by as the Al Kadi maintained a steady pace through the desert sands. Rumpitter remained attached to the pommel of Tom's saddle and seemed to be in a distant world of his own. But Tom was too weary to talk. They just trudged along with all the others.

Suddenly a voice called out from the high dunes. It startled everyone as they turned to look up at him. The camel rider was waving a red flag and shouting something. Instantly, a team of Arab riders broke away from the front ranks and galloped back to where the comrades were following.

Words were exchanged quickly between the soldiers and Braheim who, in turn, relayed the instructions to the others. As Tom shook from his weary daze, he saw the whole Al Kadi army were forming a massive circle. Orders were shouted out and there was a sudden seriousness about them.

Braheim grabbed Tom's reins and pulled him towards his horse. Mababe and Trouseau galloped over and joined them. Out of nowhere a strong wind picked up and dust began to fly everywhere. Riders began to struggle to hold their horses from stampeding.

Bassar was shouting commands and waved his hand to the camel rider on the hill. More words were exchanged.

"What is it? What's happening?" Tom asked.

He saw everyone dismounting their horses and camels and pulling their beasts down onto the ground.

"Get down off your horse Tom, follow us now. Watch how it is done. Watch the others," Braheim called.

Tom watched the Arab riders dismount and pull their animals onto the ground to lie down.

The wind was really blowing hard and sand and grit blew and twisted in the air.

Rumpitter jumped down off the horse and called up to Tom. "Hurry Tom, do it now!"

Tom dismounted his horse and gave a gentle tug on his reins. It was as if the horse knew exactly what to do and immediately lay down on the ground.

"Get in close to your horse, Tom," Rumpitter shouted against the deafening wind.

Tom crawled up close to his horse and curled in between its legs. "What's going on?" Tom asked again. Everything had suddenly changed so quickly.

"Sandstorm coming! Stay close into your horse. Cover his head and keep your face covered. Keep your eyes shut."

Everyone was now lying on the ground, either under their animals or under the carts. A huge circle had been formed to keep everyone together. Tom threw part of his tunic over his horse's head. Then he tucked in tightly to the horse's belly.

The ground began to tremble violently. A low rumbling sound came from over the top of them and then, within seconds, the storm of blasting sand and dust blew across the desert and over the whole army. The sky went black with dust and the sun disappeared.

Stones and grit pelted them. The flying sand felt like hot embers as it roared over them. It all happened so fast. Amidst the deafening roar of the sandstorm, horses and camels could be heard crying out. It was as if they were miles away in the distance.

Tom's horse twitched as the sand blew over them, but it never moved or made a sound. Tom had both hands firmly gripped on the bridle and hugged his horse tightly as the ground under them shook and twisted. Rumpitter was tightly curled up under Tom's arms.

In moments they were in total darkness and Tom had the feeling of being heavily weighed down. He realised that they were completely covered by sand and grit which had been churned up from the ground by the storm.

The howling wind and the rumble of the ground moving underneath suddenly stopped. Everything went quiet. Just the gentle rush of sand breezing above them was the only sound.

No one moved.

After a short while, Tom heard a snorting sound and suddenly felt himself being dragged through the sand.

His hands were still tightly gripped to the reins. He felt a tugging motion and then found himself being lifted upwards. The next thing he heard was a gentle snort from the horse and then he saw daylight. His horse had pulled them out of the sand and was standing upright looking down at the boy and the rat. Both were completely covered in sand and dust. The horse then gave a mighty shake and dust flew off its back. It stamped its hooves into the ground and snorted again with a vigorous shaking of its head. Tom was completely dazed as he looked up at the horse and then all around him. Rumpitter scuttled out of the sand and shook himself. "Ugh, I have sand everywhere," he complained.

Tom brushed the sand out of his hair and was pleased to see people crawling out from under their horses and camels and shaking the sand from themselves and then each other. Soldiers called out to each other and the large circle of people gradually revealed itself from the ground.

They all helped to pull each other out of the sand. Some were buried deep and it took some fast digging to get them out before they suffocated from the hot dusty sand. People choked and coughed as they slowly got back onto their feet. After a short while, it appeared that no one was hurt.

A voice called out in Arabic from up on the hill and, this time, the lone camel rider waved a white flag.

Joseph and the others walked over to Tom and patted him down. They offered him a drink of water. Tom poured some into a leather cup and offered it to his horse. The horse gratefully lapped up the water. Tom stroked the horse's neck and wiped the dust from its eyes. "Thanks Fahd, you are a good horse." The horse simply nodded its head up and down and grunted, then stamped a front hoof at the sand.

In a fairly short time the whole army had regained position in ranks, ready to continue the march.

Orders were given as men rounded up the camels, carts and horses and re-joined the lines.

Three horses galloped towards the comrades. It was Bassar and his personal guard.

Bassar looked at his friends with a smile. "I am pleased you are well. These sandstorms can be very dangerous." He pointed up to the scout on the camel up on the hill. "We have good men like him to keep us informed of these dangers. He will be rewarded for his awareness."

"Aye, Bassar, it is well he has a sharp eye," Joseph replied. Bassar nodded in response and then said, "So, shall we continue our journey, my friends?" He looked at Tom who, feeling quite bedraggled after the shock of the sandstorm, just nodded.

Bassar said nothing more. He turned his head and called out to his men in Arabic and, once again, the army began to move forward.

Tom and Rumpitter mounted Fahd and rode forward. The comrades kept a close distance behind them.

For five more hours the Al Kadi army rode across the vast desert in silence. Finally, as the sun gradually began to set and fall behind the dunes, the air became cooler. The sunset over the western hills cast a deep red and orange blanket across the sands. It was a fantastic sight. The riders watched the huge red ball of the sun slowly fall behind the hills and within a few minutes they were in darkness, save the fantastic spread of stars covering the whole desert sky.

As Tom rode forward with his head gazing up into the star lit sky, he wondered about Mr Hawkins. He saw a shooting star and wanted to make a wish.

Rumpitter sensed what was going through Tom's mind as he watched him staring up at the stars.

"Don't worry Tom, we will see the Captain again soon. Now come on, pay attention, I think we are nearing the camp."

Tom lowered his eye to look around, "What makes you think we're near the camp? I can't see anything. It feels like we have been riding for days."

Rumpitter stood up, his hind legs on the saddle, and twitched his nose in the night air. "I can smell it."

"What can you smell?" Tom asked again. "I can smell the camp, it is very near. You just wait and see." And with that Rumpitter sat down and peered between Fahd's ears. Tom thought Rumpitter was saying something to the horse and then Fahd nodded his head up and down vigorously and gave another snort.

"Yes, that confirms it. Your horse agrees with me. We are near the camp," Rumpitter said with some satisfaction and then sat back down on the saddle. Tom smiled at the rat and then looked to see Fahd had turned his head to look at him. He shook his head in bewilderment, but also with affection at the two animals. *It's all a dream, I'm sure it is* he thought to himself.

*No Tom, it is not a dream. This is really happening and, remember, we can still speak without words when we need to and I can hear your thoughts.*

Tom was amazed and replied, *Do you think Mr Hawkins can hear my thoughts? Because if he can, he will know that I am thinking about him and want to see him back with us soon.*

Rumpitter chose his words carefully. *I am sure the Captain can hear your thoughts Tom. It is just that he is very busy at the moment and has a very important thing to do. I am sure all will be well soon.*

Tom didn't reply and as he began to think about what Rumpitter had said, there was a shout from the front of the line of the Al Kadi horsemen. Suddenly a bolt of fire shot over their heads.

"What was that?" Tom asked. Then there was more shouting from behind. The bolt of fire was from an arrow. It landed in the ground, still alight. One of the Al Kadi archers pulled it from the ground and set it into his own bow. He aimed it into the sky and released the string. The arrow flew high into the night sky and over the shadow of the peak of the dunes.

After a few moments there was a chorus of shouting voices from high up on the dune. The comrades looked up and suddenly the hill-top was lined with dark shapes holding fire torches.

It soon became clear that these were Arab riders. Their dark shapes danced like ghosts against the dark backdrop of the night sky and the flickering flames from their torches.

The Al Kadi army came to an abrupt halt. A group of Al Kadi horsemen broke away from the ranks and galloped up to the foot of the dunes. One of them shouted something and waved the Al Kadi flag which was tied to the tip of a spear. More words were exchanged from the top of the dune and suddenly sand began to roll down the hill as the Arab riders descended towards the Al Kadi horsemen. Tom saw Bassar gallop over to join his men. Then the entire ranks of the Al Kadis turned to face the descending shapes. There was a deathly silence as the riders came closer. The torches cast shadows that danced down the slopes of the dunes as the riders approached. It was an eerie sight.

Finally the riders reached the bottom of the dune. There were at least a hundred of them, Tom thought. He whispered to Braheim, "Who are they?"

"These men are the Shebah. They are the fiercest of all the Bedouin tribes in the desert. They have been known to strike out a whole army without even being seen. We can be thankful that they are friends with the Al Kadi."

One of the Shebah warriors walked his horse forward to meet Bassar.

The Bedouin riders' faces were completely covered by their black head-dresses; they wore long, black robes with black cloth turbans wrapped over their heads. Tom noticed their long curved swords hanging from their belts. The remaining Bedouin warriors sat very still and tall on their horses. Their fire torches cast dancing shadows across the ground.

They watched on quietly as the two leaders greeted each other and a few words were exchanged. The Bedouin chief bowed his head to Bassar and then held up his torch and waved it in the air. He called out a few words in a deep throaty voice and his riders turned and rode towards the front of the Al Kadi army with Bassar at the front, now joined by the Arab chief.

Braheim nudged Tom, "We now go to the Shebah camp." Tom noticed how nervous Braheim was looking.

They moved on in silence following the Bedouin tribesmen. After a while they passed through a gorge that ran between two high rock walls. As Tom looked up he could see hundreds more Bedouin all along the tops of the gorge. Their dark shapes were silhouetted by the starry night sky and the flames from their torches.

Finally they passed through a wider gorge which opened out into a ridge overlooking a valley. Down in the valley they saw a massive camp with fires lit all around and tents spread across the whole area. The trail leading down to the camp was lined on both sides with Bedouin tribesmen who watched in silence as the Al Kadi passed down the trail.

No one spoke and the only sounds to be heard were from the shuffle and thud of horses' hooves and the grunt from the camels and the clatter of carts as they made their way into the camp.

As they neared the perimeter of the camp, they could see the Bedouin people more clearly. They were clothed in flowing dark robes with head-dresses covering most of their faces. The women's faces were completely covered except for their eyes. The men had long curved swords hanging from their belts and round leather shields strapped to their backs. Horses were tethered in pens, and corrals made from sticks and wooden stakes housed goats and sheep. The baying of animals all around the camp and the smell of wood fires and cooking filled the night air.

In the centre of the camp was a cleared area where four larger tents were erected. Guards stood still by the entrance to each tent.

The chief of the riders, who had met the army at the pass, turned his horse around and halted the visiting army. Bassar rode together with the chief to one of the large tents. Tom saw them dismount and walk inside. A few seconds later Bassar appeared at the entrance and called to one of his guards. A few words were exchanged and then the guard rode back to the ranks.

He called out for everyone to dismount.

Tom and the comrades dismounted and waited. Tom was standing by his horse with Rumpitter still sitting on the saddle. Braheim had already dismounted and was casting a wary eye around the camp. He kept his face covered and his eyes moved everywhere.

Joseph walked over to him and put a hand on his shoulder. "Fear not comrade, you are with friends. We will be with you all the time."

Tom heard Joseph and asked, "What's the matter with Braheim, Joseph?"

Joseph leaned down close to Tom's ear and whispered. "Braheim comes from a different Arab tribe. Many years ago his tribe fought with these people in a bloody war. It would not be good for them to know who he is."

"Oh, right, well we better keep him out of their sight hadn't we?" Tom replied, looking at Braheim.

"Indeed lad, we shall." Joseph looked at Braheim and although he couldn't see his face, he chuckled at Tom's remark. "Innocence is a fine thing, Braheim, remember that." Braheim just nodded.

Rumpitter had jumped onto Tom's shoulder and was sniffing the air, taking in all the smells and activity around them. Then he poked his nose into Tom's cheek. "I think I shall make myself scarce for a while Tom. I am not sure if these people will appreciate me so readily."

"Where are you going Rumpitter?" Tom replied, as he watched the rat hop down onto the ground.

"I won't be far away, I promise. Call me if you need me," Rumpitter replied and then scampered off into the night. Tom saw him disappear behind the horses and then he was gone.

The comrades took their horses to a tethering post of ropes that ran between lines of wooden stakes. Some of the Shebah people came over to them and gave the horses water from a well situated under a cluster of palm trees. They helped take the saddles and bridles off their backs. The comrades thanked them with a nod and a wave.

They watched Bassar slip back inside the largest tent.

The comrades walked closer to the tent.

"What's going to happen now?" Tom asked.

"We wait and see," Joseph replied. No sooner had he said that, Bassar reappeared and walked over to them.

"These people will take care of our needs and feed us. Provision will be made for the army to be given rest and food. You will all come with me." He clapped his hands together as if it were an order and turned towards the tent again.

Two Arab guards stood perfectly still outside the entrance. Their eyes were fixed on the comrades as they entered. These people were not to be reckoned with, Tom thought.

Inside, the floor was covered in woven coloured rugs, and torches lit the sides of the vast room. The light from the torches flickered over the roof of the tent and lit up the entire space inside. To one side, cushions were placed around a low wooden table. Food and jugs of water were placed on it. Some Arab women stood by. Tom noticed how their faces were covered by veils.

At the head of the room was a large raised area, also covered in rugs and cushions. Sitting in the centre was a very large Arab. His face was almost ebony black, his eyes were deep brown. He had a thick jawline which sported a trim, pointed black beard. He had jewel studded rings on almost every finger. His long gown was black and red with silver edges around the cuffs and rims. In his waist belt he had a dagger with jewels studded into the handle which sparkled under the flickering light of the torches.

Sitting next to him were five younger Arab men, all wearing traditional Bedouin robes, but not quite as ornate as the large Arab in the centre. He was quite clearly a man of great importance.

The large Arab gestured to the comrades to walk over and sit before him. Each of the comrades sat on a large cushion in front of the Arabs, who watched inquisitively as the comrades approached them and sat down. Bassar stood next to them and spoke a few words to the six men sitting before them. When he finished speaking he bowed to the large Arab in the middle. He then turned to the comrades. "My friends, may I introduce you to the great and wise Al Jadda." He gestured with his hand to the large Arab.

"He is leader of the Shebah. He is friend of the Al Kadi and welcomes us to his camp. He wishes you to eat with him and his sons."

The comrades sat silently and looked at each other for something to say. Joseph nodded to the chief and said, "We thank you for your hospitality and accept your kind offer of food and refreshment. We would also be grateful for somewhere to sleep."

The chief didn't understand Joseph and turned to Bassar with a questioning look. Bassar translated Joseph's words to the chief. When he had finished, Al Jadda nodded and smiled displaying his bright white teeth and three large gold fillings. He clapped his hands and the women brought across the trays of food and water.

Al Jadda spoke again in his native tongue to Bassar and then gestured to his sons, all sitting obediently around him. He then pointed at Tom and spoke to him in Arabic. He pointed a large, jewel-studded finger at Tom as he spoke to him. Tom was not sure how to respond and felt awkward. He looked to Bassar for support. Bassar had an amused look on his face and gently laughed. "The chief has heard of you, Tom. He is curious about where you come from. He also said that if he had a son like you he would be proud. He knows you confronted his enemy, the Saharadeen. The chief also knows Captain Hawkins and has learned of his friendship with you." This is why you have been summoned to eat with him. You have all been welcomed as warriors and friends of the Shebah tribe. This is a great honour for you to be able to sit here with Al Jadda." Bassar then sat down with the comrades and picked up a piece of meat and some bread. He was about to put it in his mouth when the chief suddenly stood up. It was now that the comrades could see how large this man was. He spoke again to Bassar and gestured towards Tom.

Bassar put the food back down and said, "Al Jadda wishes you to sit next to him." Bassar nodded to Tom to join the chief. Tom stood up but didn't move. He was nervous. Bassar ushered Tom again with his hand. "Go and sit with him," he said, nudging his head towards the chief.

Tom looked at the comrades for some support. "It is all right Tom, we are here. You have nothing to fear. The chief just wishes you to sit with him and his sons."

Bassar spoke again to Al Jadda. Suddenly the large Arab roared into laughter. He said some more words, this time to his sons. They all immediately began to laugh. The chief explained his laughter to Bassar, who then turned to the comrades and Tom, smiled again and said, "The chief does not mean to startle you Tom. He has heard great things about you from my father. He knows you are not from this world and is interested in you. As long as you are his guest he simply wishes the young warrior to sit and eat with him. It is a simple friendly gesture, nothing more."

Tom smiled and nodded to the chief. He walked over and sat down beside Al Jadda, who patted Tom on the head and laughed again. Then he clapped his hands and instantly several women ran into the tent with more food and drink. Two men ran in and sat down cross legged in the middle of the tent and began to play some stringed instruments. Three women, dressed in fabulous ornate costumes of red and gold with small silver discs studded all over their gowns, and waving bright orange veils, glided into the room and began to dance to the Arab music.

Tom watched carefully, studying the Arab men. Al Jadda was indeed a very large man and he felt dwarfed by his presence, sitting beside him. He watched the five sons as they ate their food with their hands. They all stared back at Tom with great interest and chatted amongst themselves, nodding towards Tom as they spoke to each other. It was obvious they were talking about him. Tom cast an eye over to the comrades and watched them eating as the Arabs did, so he picked up a piece of meat and some bread and began to eat. It was delicious and suddenly he was scoffing into everything on the tray. Al Jadda watched the boy and laughed and nodded with delight as he saw Tom diving into his food.

The musicians played on and everyone ate and drank their fill.

Bassar moved nearer to Al Jadda and they began to talk. The conversation seemed intense and both of them appeared oblivious to the entertainment or anyone else in the tent.

# Chapter 12 – Mysticonissi

The ship emerged through an early morning mist. A lone and faceless figure in a dark and hooded robe stood at the upturned prow as the vessel cut between the rocky pitons that sprouted from the ocean.

A blue-grey haze shimmered across the water as the oars dipped and lifted, pulling the ship through the water, bringing the vessel towards the shore. A ghostly shoreline emerged through patches of mist. Tall grey cliffs and jagged rock formations appeared before them. The oars were lifted out of the water as the helmsman brought the ship gracefully alongside a short quay built of flattened grey stone. Standing along the wall a small group of monks waited for the ship to dock. They were clothed in long dark robes, their heads covered by hoods. Their faces were sullen and pale. A crewman threw a rope line to one of the monks who tied it around a thick wooden stump. Another line was cast ashore to the stern.

Two crewmen jumped ashore. One of them, a tall Egyptian in a dark flowing robe, spoke quietly to one of the monks. He then turned to the Master, who had now moved from the bow to the beam of the vessel where a ladder had been placed. The man moved with great difficulty but was just able, with help from Gordon and Sam Little, to slowly lift his leg over the side of the ship and then the other. He stumbled as he tried to put a foot on the next step and two men ran to the foot of the ladder. Blake climbed up a few rungs and held his hand up to offer support and helped him climb down.

The man nodded his thanks and in a soft croaky voice he whispered, "Take this." He pulled the sword from under his tunic and passed it down to Blake, whose face showed great concern for the man on the ladder. "Let me help you, Captain," Blake said softly. He took the sword and slung the leather strap over his shoulder so he could have both hands free to help him.

Captain Hawkins grunted in pain as he lowered his foot to the next rung and then again as he slowly descended. Gordon and Little leaned over the rail and stretched down from the topside of the ship to be ready to grab his arms, should he stumble again.

The Egyptian tapped Blake on his shoulder as the Captain finally made it to the stone quay. "I can carry him," he whispered and Blake stood back.

As he reached the quay, Captain Hawkins almost fell, but the tall Egyptian grabbed him just in time. "Permit me, Sir," the Egyptian quietly said.

The Captain grimaced with the pain he was suffering and nodded his acceptance for the assistance. The Egyptian carefully lifted the frail man over his shoulder, turned and nodded to the monks. "Take us now," he said sternly. One of the monks gave the sign of the cross, nodded and gestured for them to follow him. All the monks turned, and in silence they began to climb a narrow stairway up the side of the cliff.

It was quickly agreed that Blake, Little and Gordon would follow. Maris and the other Arab crew would remain with the ship.

It had been a long and arduous journey from the Al Kadi camp, across the desert to the Saharadeen harbour. The heat and dust from the desert had worn the men down. They had to kill one of the horses along the way as it had broken a leg. The journey took them three days. They travelled almost without stopping, resting only for short intervals before continuing. They rode day and night. Captain Hawkins was deteriorating rapidly from the curse of the Saharadeen. The once strong and enigmatic adventurer and worldly sea captain had become a crippled old man. His eyes had turned yellow, like those of a bird, his skin was cracked and drying, like old parchment. Every muscle in his body ached and his bones creaked with every move he made. He could hardly speak, save a few hoarse grunts and whispers. His devoted comrades cared for him as they rode through the scorching heat of the desert. The Captain could no longer ride his horse and was towed on a stretcher made of large branches and palm leaves gathered from the desert.

On the second day, they came to a well. Together with a few of his most loyal soldiers, the King had sent his own loyal and trusty physician, a tall and wise Egyptian called Rashidi.

At the well, Rashidi peeled off the muslin bandages and washed the wounds and scars from the cracked skin which riddled the Captain's body. The physician had his own special ointments, which stung when applied to the wounds. The Captain screamed with the terrible pain he was in and from the biting sting from the orange ointment. "I am sorry for your pain, Captain, but this will help you until we reach our destination. I am doing everything I can for you Sir, please understand this." Rashidi said and shook his head in frustration, wishing he could heal the man properly.

Captain Hawkins nodded, biting his sore lips when the ointment was applied. He knew Rashidi was doing his best and he squeezed his hands tightly around Rashidi's arm when the pain came again and again. He could not help but scream out when the pain became unbearable. His cries echoed out across the desert.

Gordon knelt down beside his captain and then turned to Blake. "Why can we not use the sword? It saved me from certain death."

Blake replied, "Aye, it is a strange thing. I cannot understand it either."

Rashidi took Blake and Gordon to one side. "The curse of Saharadeen is taking the Captain. The power of the sword has been destroyed by the curse. There is only one hope and that is why we must take the Captain with the Sword of Isis back to where it came from. The monks on Mysticonissi are the only ones who can help him now. If they can restore the power of the sword it will only be because they can reverse the curse. This can be possible, but it can also have the worst effect. We must try to keep the Captain confident in his belief in surviving. This in itself will be the strength he will need when the monks take him."

Maris spoke carefully, "How do you mean – when the monks take him?"

"You will see soon enough," Rashidi replied.

Blake and Gordon looked at each other with deep sadness. They knew there was nothing they or anyone could do for their captain now. It was going to be in the hands of the monks.

Sam Little was listening to the conversation and came over to speak. "This Mysticonissi, how far is it?" he asked.

"It is two – maybe three days' sail from the Saharadeen harbour. I have been there only once. It is not an easy place to find and it can be treacherous. The ocean can be dangerous as we approach. This is why no one knows of its existence. No ships have ever found it, because it is hidden amongst tall rocks that rise from the ocean. There is always a strange mist that surrounds the rocks and many ships have perished when they have been too close." Rashidi replied quietly so as not to let Captain Hawkins hear him.

"So how can we get there without perishing like others have before?" Sam asked. His comrades all nodded at his question. They had been on many expeditions with Captain Hawkins in the past, but then the Captain made all the decisions.

"I know the way there from the coast and so do those men over there." Rashidi pointed to the group of Arabs who were resting by their horses. "The coast is another day's ride from here. These men are from the King's own ship from Kadistaar. They are very experienced sailors and they have been to Mysticonissi and know of the dangers, but they also know the only way in."

Gordon nodded. "It is good we have these men with us. We would be helpless without them. We are grateful to the King for sending them with us and, Rashidi, we are grateful to you too. We know you are doing everything you can for the Captain." The comrades all nodded in agreement, to show their gratitude.

"We will rest for one hour and then we must continue." Rashidi bowed as he replied and then went back to tend to Captain Hawkins. The others rested by the well and filled their leather water containers for the journey forward.

The following night they finally arrived at the Saharadeen harbour. It was deserted. The mud built huts that once housed the Saharadeen workers were empty. One of the Saharadeen ships was tied alongside the pier.

"Thank the stars for that," whispered Blake.

"Mmm," Sam Little replied. "But look, she is not a big ship."

"She looks sturdy enough to me and besides, if she has been equipped for these waters, then she will work well for us," said Maris.

The comrades and the Arabs rode as fast as they dared with the Captain down the trail to the deserted harbour. The comrades remembered well the horrors that met them last time they tried to flee from the Land of Fire.

Rashidi told them to take care as they approached down the path into the port. The trail was rocky and any sudden movement would cause more pain to the Captain.

They arrived at the pier and stood silently looking up at the Arab boat. She was indeed so different to the type of vessel they knew, but they could see she looked sturdy. The sail was folded on the cross boom. The mast looked strong and was rigged well. It had ports along the hull to take the long oars used to row the ship in and out of harbours and anchorages.

Blake was the first to board and quickly ran around the ship checking the rigging. Sam Little went through a door under the bridge where the helm was. A few minutes later he reappeared. "It seems everything is fine below. It all seems satisfactory. The Captain can use the bed in the Master's cabin. He will be comfortable there."

Rashidi, Gordon and three of the Arab sailors helped to bring Captain Hawkins on deck, carrying the stretcher. The Captain lifted his head slowly and in a husky voice he thanked them.

"The sea air will be good for you, Sir," Gordon said, trying to put on a smile.

"Is she a fine ship? I would like to see her," the Captain asked as his eyes looked out from the bandages around his face.

"She seems fine enough, Captain. We will take you to your cabin; you will feel better after some rest," Rashidi insisted.

"In the morning, then," he croaked. "Yes Sir, in the morning." Rashidi nodded to the others to carry the stretcher straight to the Master's cabin. He would then apply the ointments and change the bandages. He turned to Maris, "Check for provisions, we will need everything available to us. You should check the buildings ashore for anything that we might be able to take with us."

Maris and Blake immediately ran across the wooden pier and into the huts.

After a short while they returned with news that they had found three barrels of water that had obviously been stored in a cellar to keep cool. They also found dried breads wrapped in cloth and boxes of rice and flour.

Gordon found an armoury with swords and shields, axes and long spears and also bows with arrows. He picked a selection of swords and shields and as many bows and quivers of arrows he could carry. "I hope we won't need these," he said to his friends.

"I hope so too," replied Sam Little.

They unsaddled their horses and led them into a corral. They found hay and poured water into a trough for them. "We won't be needing the horses. I hope someone will find them before it's too late," Blake said. The comrades were grateful to their horses for taking them safely across the desert, but now they must leave them and put to sea.

The Arab sailors immediately set about preparing the ship to set sail. The comrades went below to tell Rashidi that they were ready to go.

Blake sat down by the Captain and leant over to speak in his ear. "Captain, Sir. We are ready to sail. Permission to leave port Sir?"

Rashidi smiled at Blake's thoughtful gesture to his captain. Captain Hawkins lifted his head to reply. He tried to smile but it was painful enough just to lift his head, so he just nodded and softly said, "Carry on Mr Blake, you have my full permission."

Blake tipped his forehead with his hand "Aye-aye Sir." Blake nodded to Rashidi and left the room.

They cast off and dipped the oars on the port side. The Arabs expertly back-rowed to bring the bow away from the pier. As the bow slowly slipped to port, the triangular sail was lowered. It caught just enough breeze to turn the ship away from the pier and out to the estuary of the bay. After a short while the wind filled the sail. The rope sheets were drawn back around the wooden cleats to take the strain. The Arab sailors manned the rig with great skill and Blake thought to himself how wise the King was to have offered his own men to sail with them, knowing that they had the experience in sailing the Arab boats.

There was no moon and they sailed in darkness all through the night. They navigated by the stars and the Arab captain and his crew explained to the comrades which of the stars were their marks of direction. Blake recalled how Captain Hawkins could steer his ship with the stars at night. Although Joseph was the best man the Captain could have on his ship, Blake realised that Joseph would be of better use where he was, looking after Tom. Although the Saharadeen had been beaten, there could still be dangers in the desert before they arrived at Kadistaar.

The Captain had promised to return Tom to his home and he could not bear to let him down.

It was unforeseen that the Saharadeen would turn his own destruction into a curse that would break the power of the Sword of Isis. Captain Hawkins was distraught with the thought he may now not be able to get Tom back to his own world and his family. The only thing that mattered now was to find a way to turn the curse around, but Captain Hawkins did not know what fate awaited him. The journey to Mysticonissi was the only thing left and even this was uncertain.

Rashidi carried the Captain up the narrow stone steps which wove their way up the steep cliffs. They climbed higher and higher. The monks led the way until they were hundreds of feet above the sea. Nearing the top, the wind became stronger and whistled around them. Gordon stumbled on a slippery step and then tripped forward. One leg went over the side and sent rocks spinning down into the blackness and the sea far below. Blake grabbed Gordon's arm just in time and managed to pull him back onto his feet and then pinned him against the damp cliff wall. Gordon panted, his chest heaving from the shock. Neither of them spoke but Gordon nodded his appreciation to Blake. The sound of the wind howling around the cliffs was deafening.

The monks climbed up the steps easily. It was as if, Blake thought, they were floating rather than walking.

Finally they all passed through the small stone archway. More monks were waiting there with torches. They did not speak, but lowered their heads as the comrades entered and then turned to walk in front.

Rashidi had to bend down and carry the Captain under the low arch.

The sound of their feet echoed loudly as they walked along the slippery stone floor.

Ahead there was a glimmer of light and Rashidi was grateful that the ceiling of the passage was becoming higher. He had carried Captain Hawkins a considerable way up hundreds of steps and then along, what seemed to be, an endless passage with barely enough height to stand.

The monk who was leading the way turned to them and held up his hand. His pale face looked ghostly in the flickering light of his torch. He did not speak but pointed to Rashidi to follow him. He then nodded at one of the other monks, who bowed and held out an arm which pointed to another passage. It was clear they wanted Rashidi to proceed ahead and the others to go another way.

Blake spoke out. "Wait!" his voice echoed all around. "Sssh!" responded one of the monks who then nodded his head from left to right. "You shall not speak in this place." The dull tone of his voice came from under the monk's hooded head, but his face was unseen.

Blake was adamant. "We stay with the Captain," he insisted.

There was a long pause and the monks turned to each other. Finally the leading monk tapped the end of his torch pole on the floor and nodded to the others. The second monk waved them on.

They entered into a larger chamber. This was a round room, about sixty feet in diameter with high, stone-grey walls. There were no windows but there was an opening at the very centre of the domed ceiling which was almost a hundred feet high.

Around the room were twelve wooden seats with high arched backs covered in ornate carvings. On the head of each of the wooden seats was an upturned gold crescent moon. Painted around the walls were hieroglyphs and strange signs and symbols.

In the centre of the room was a raised stone platform covered in a black cloth. The top of the cloth displayed the golden image of a crescent moon. Standing on top of the platform was a bowl made of bronze. Symbols of crescent moons were engraved around the side of the bowl.

Blake and the comrades stood very still as they took in the scene before them. It was indeed a strange place.

Rashidi carried Captain Hawkins towards the monk who had led them into the room.

He bowed to the monk and spoke slowly and softly.

"You know me and you know from where we come. I am aware the message was sent to you from our King with whom you share great wisdom and knowledge. My King has asked me to tell you that he is, and will for ever be, in your debt. His honour to the Sword of Isis has been fulfilled by him as he has promised. Evil has been ended and we seek new life and peace in our lands. He returns the Sword of Isis to you and the Captain, who you know well. Great harm has been done to this man who vowed to defeat the evil one who sought to destroy all. As you know, he was cursed once and turned into a bird, but by the powers he was given, he was able to rise again. He has been taken from us by the evil one who he killed. We ask you, as you are the only ones who can help us, to save him and, in return, we give you the Sword of Isis." Rashidi turned to Blake and held out his hand.

Blake pulled the sword from its sheath. For a moment he held it in both hands and stared at the stone that was set into the handle. It did not glow. His eyes moved along the blade and looked at the engravings. Then he looked at the walls around him. They were the same as the engravings and symbols on the sword.

He choked the words out. "Th-the stone does not shine." Then he handed the sword to the monk. Suddenly sections of the wall around them moved and from behind hidden spaces, more monks appeared. There was a murmur and a low muffled tone of voices sounded around the room. The monk held the sword and, with a cold and pale sullen face, he stared at Rashidi and then at the comrades. Then he looked towards the monks standing around the walls of the room. He nodded to them and instantly they all moved in one motion. Each monk sat in one of the twelve seats surrounding the room. Three monks were still standing. One of them took up the bronze bowl and ushered Rashidi to move towards the platform. He gestured to Rashidi to lay the Captain on the platform.

The Captain moaned as he was lowered down. Rashidi shook his head in frustration. He did not want to cause the Captain any more pain.

The Captain lay still on the platform but his eyes moved, taking in the scene around him.

The head monk stared down at the ageing and decaying man on the stone platform. His pale face was sullen and expressionless. Then he raised his head to look at Rashidi and the others and spoke in a deep monotone voice. "I am Herallinos. I know this man who lies before me." The monk shook his head in sadness as he looked down at Captain Hawkins. "It saddens us to see the sword returned to us in this way." He stared into Rashidi's eyes and then spoke. "Many years ago we offered the Sword of Isis to a man who we entrusted to keep and use it wisely. The sword is a symbol of peace, freedom and liberty, never to be used in anger but only to defend the good from evil. The sacred secret of the Sword of Isis is thousands of years old. It comes from before the tenth dynasty of the Pharaohs. Our ancient order in this temple has been devoted to protecting the secrets since the time of the destruction of the original Temple of Serapis. The great King of the Al Kadi was given this sword with our trust that he would protect the world from evil. The King had our blessing to pass on the sword to this man who lays before us. He was a good man and we know of his efforts to slay the evil one."

He lowered his head to look at Captain Hawkins and then continued. "The great powers that the sword and the stone hold and the secrets that come from within should never have been taken by one so evil." He shook his head slowly and his eyes moved to each of the comrades.

"You come to us with great expectations. For centuries people have searched for the Sword of Isis and wished for the powers and the knowledge of the Golden Secret of Isis, and for centuries we have protected it from falling into evil hands. What has been done may not be able to be reversed."

There was a murmur and Blake stepped forward. His expression spoke volumes. "What do you mean? Are you saying you cannot help? We MUST save the Captain. The sword was supposed to have protected him. We have nowhere else to go. No-one, except you, can help him." Blake was almost in tears and the others ran forward and pleaded. Rashidi was struck with silence; words failed him and he shook his head in desperation.

Herallinos held up his hand. "Wait! Be silent!" His rough voice cut through all the shouting and protesting and the comrades immediately fell quiet. He gently placed both his hands on the Captain's forehead and stared into his eyes. Quietly he spoke. "You know what must be done?"

Captain Hawkins managed to move his head in acknowledgement and his eyes closed. In a weak and croaky voice he replied, "Yes."

The monk looked back at the comrades and with a heavy sigh he continued, "You do not understand what has happened here. Great harm has been done. The power of Isis has been passed into the underworld. We now must call upon the powers of Osiris, the love of Isis."

Blake spoke out. "What? Who the hell is Osiris?"

Herallinos glared back at Blake. "He was once a great Pharaoh who brought knowledge and civilization to the people of his lands. The great Osiris was the symbol of the forces of nature, the teacher of humanity and now is the Lord of the afterlife. His teachings and powers were carried through the dynasties across the Empires. He was killed by his evil brother and so became the ruler of the afterlife. It is only he who can save this man and bring the powers of the stone and sword back from the underworld – but this is no simple task. There are dangers that await us."

The comrades were stunned and stood in silence, until Gordon stepped forward. "What nonsense is this? The Captain needs medicine and treatment. You have Rashidi here, who is the King's physician. You can use him to help you. Don't talk to us about Pharaohs and the underworld. Help us!"

Again the monk glared at Gordon and the twelve monks sitting in the tall chairs around the room all stood and turned to the comrades. They did not speak, but it was clear that Gordon had angered them.

Herallinos drew the Sword of Isis and raised it over his head. He towered over Captain Hawkins who lay helpless on the stone platform. The immediate reaction from the comrades was to defend their captain. They drew their swords and moved to cover the Captain. Blake was poised, ready to strike the monk with his sword.

Rashidi stepped forward, "NO!" he screamed. "Stand back, comrades. This is not what you think." He turned to Herallinos. "Please forgive my friends. They do not understand your ways. The Captain is their friend, he is their leader. They only wish for you to help him."

The tall monk held the Sword of Isis in both hands above the Captain. Slowly he lowered the sword and then placed it beside the Captain on the stone platform. Then he folded his arms with his hands concealed inside the sleeves of his gown. He turned to the other monks and nodded his head slowly. The twelve monks walked closer to the platform and formed a circle around the comrades. The other three stood by the entrance of the room.

"Please withdraw your weapons," Herallinos said, again in his monotone voice. "I understand your intensions and I have more to tell you."

The comrades looked at each other and then Rashidi nodded to the comrades. "Replace your swords – no harm will be done. We must listen to him and hear what he has to say."

The comrades agreed and withdrew.

The monk spoke again, "You must not interfere with our methods. My brothers and I will do what we can. You must leave us to do our work." He looked at Rashidi, "You. Please ask your friends to leave us. You will stay." He pointed to one of the monks and spoke to him in strange words, which sounded like ancient Greek. The monk who had been spoken to bowed to Herallinos and stepped towards the comrades. He did not speak, but held out a hand, pointing to the door where the other monks waited. The comrades were still for a moment and looked at their captain. Blake turned to Herallinos. "We are afraid – we are afraid to leave him alone."

Very slowly Captain Hawkins turned his head towards them. He tried to sit up, but his body was too weak now. Gordon held one of the Captain's hands and Blake and Little stood close to them. "Listen to me – my friends," he said slowly, almost in a whisper. "Wh- whatever – happens to me – is now in the hands of – these people. I have no choice." He found the words hard to speak and his cracked lips made it hard for him to move his mouth. "I must believe in them. Believe in what – they say." He closed his eyes in pain and moved his head towards the monk standing over him. "Can you really help me?" he croaked.

The monk leaned closer to the Captain and spoke quietly. "If you believe – then we may find the way." He looked up again at the comrades. "Your concerns and your love of your captain are touching. I have made arrangements for the assistance of two others who have been sent for. Your friend the physician will remain here. You three will return to your ship. You will be sent for in time. What we do here is our way. It is the only way if we are to restore the powers from the dead and return this man to life. He is, at this time, awaiting the afterlife." He looked at the Captain and sighed, "You know this, do you not, Captain?" Captain Hawkins nodded.

Meanwhile, back at the Shebah camp, the deep conversation between Bassar and Al Jadda had not gone unnoticed by Joseph. Bassar caught Joseph's stare from the corner of his eye and, for a second, he gave an expressionless look back at Joseph, then he nodded with a very slight smile. Then he turned back to Al Jadda. They spoke again for a few minutes until they were interrupted by a commotion at the entrance to the tent. A Bedouin guard entered the room. He was followed by an Al Kadi soldier, tired and covered in dust. His face was black from the sun.

The guard greeted Al Jadda: "As Salam Alaikum," he said, and bowed.

"Wa Alaikum Salam," Al Jadda replied. The guard then turned to Bassar and greeted him the same way and then said: "Your officer has news Sir."

"Then let him speak," Bassar replied and was now standing. "Come, brother, what news do you have at this late hour?"

The soldier was panting from his long ride and thankful that he had finally reached his destination. He bowed and greeted Bassar. "My Lord – I have news from the King. I must speak with you in private."

Bassar looked oddly at the soldier and then his face changed to that of concern. "We are amongst friends, soldier; whatever you have to say can be said here."

The soldier looked worried and then his eyes seemed to scan the room. He finally fixed his eyes on Tom, who was standing between Braheim and Joseph.

The soldier shook his head and looked back at Bassar. His look said enough for Bassar to realise that the man needed to speak in privacy. Bassar nodded and said, "Very well, come with me." He turned to the comrades and to Al Jadda and his sons. "Please forgive this interruption. It seems I must speak with this man alone." He bowed to Al Jadda and left through a flap in the side of the tent. The Al Kadi soldier bowed to all and followed Bassar.

A faint mutter of voices could be heard from outside but no one could make out what was being said. A moment later Bassar re-entered the tent. His face showed great concern.

He spoke a few brief words to Al Jadda who listened intently, nodding as Bassar spoke.

As soon as Bassar finished, Al Jadda clapped his hands and instantly the musicians and dancers, who had already stopped performing, immediately left the tent. Al Jadda turned to his sons. They all stood and bowed to the comrades in the Arab way. They too, left the tent.

Bassar approached the comrades.

"My friends..." The expression on his face was serious. "I must tell you that we have to change our plan. We will meet my father and my sister, Princess Tasia. But not in Kadistaar."

Tom was delighted at the thought of meeting the Princess. Captain Hawkins had mentioned her often and Tom knew of their deep love for each other.

Joseph smiled widely and replied, "Well, that is good news! We haven't seen the Princess for..." Bassar interrupted Joseph. "No, I am sorry, you do not understand – I must finish."

"Go on," Joseph replied. The others stood by, slightly confused as to what was happening.

Bassar looked at Tom and shook his head slowly. His dark expression was concerning to the comrades.

"The Captain – he has arrived at a secret place in the great sea of islands..." Bassar was about to continue when Tom stepped forward. "What? We're supposed to meet in Kadistaar! I don't understand."

Joseph put his hand on Tom's shoulder, "All right lad. Let Bassar finish."

Bassar knew this was going to be a difficult conversation. He had hoped that it could have been avoided but he had also anticipated the dire situation that Captain Hawkins was in. During the meal he had discussed with Al Jadda what alternative plans should be made if things took a turn for the worse. It seemed they had.

Al Jadda had agreed to offer his assistance with transportation, men and provisions to take Tom and the comrades to the coast instead of riding to Kadistaar.

The Shebah camp was closer to the small fishing port along the coast where they could sail from to catch up with the Captain, if they needed to. Now, it seemed, they must.

Kadistaar was another day's ride away and it would be too far to go if they had to change their plan. Indeed, Bassar was right. The plan was changing now.

He had not considered that his sister, Princess Tasia, would be required to join them. Bassar had prayed that Captain Hawkins would recover and they could meet together properly in Kadistaar.

The Al Kadi family had even discussed plans for the wedding between Princess Tasia and the Captain, but Bassar, after the meeting in the desert with his father and Captain Hawkins, had not been convinced that things would go well. He could see the Captain was deteriorating fast and was scared to say anything to his sister until he was certain the Captain was going to recover. The disappointment his sister would endure would be too painful for her.

The Princess was already aware that her love, Captain Hawkins, had returned and she was beside herself with joy that he was coming back for her. She had smiled for the first time in so many years. Her father had told her that the Captain, after his long journey, had returned. She learned of the victory in the battle in the desert and that Captain Hawkins had finally destroyed the Saharadeen. Two days ago she was the happiest woman in the world and life was coming back to her. She had learned of Captain Hawkins's journey to another world and that he had escaped as a bird. She also heard about the brave young boy who had helped him return. Although it was such the strangest thing and there were so many unanswered questions, she was finally happy again and her heart beat for her love of the man she would marry.

Bassar looked solemn when he turned to Tom. He had to let the boy know that all was not well. There was no other way to say this, but to tell the truth. The boy was needed now, more than ever. Bassar took a deep breath and then continued.

"Captain Hawkins is now at the temple of the secret island of Mysticonissi. He took himself there with some of your comrades. My father provided his best seamen to sail them to the island. He sent his personal physician to go with him. We have received word from the monks of Mysticonissi, who are the only people who understand the secrets and powers of the Sword of Isis. The Captain is now in the hands of the Serapian monks. His condition has worsened and we fear he is dying." The comrades stood speechless, shaking their heads in disbelief.

"They have called for my sister, Princess Tasia, to sail to the island. They believe she must be with the Captain to assist them in their work. They must reverse the evil curse of the Saharadeen." He paused for a moment as Joseph wanted to speak.

"Bassar, we were all aware of the Captain's sudden change but we did not realise it was so bad. What are his chances?" Joseph looked pale with worry and Tom fell into a seat. He put his head in his hands.

"They are not good. He becomes weaker every day," Bassar replied in a low melancholy tone.

Braheim sat down beside Tom and put his arm around the boy. But he too was speechless. Trouseau wanted to say something but Bassar held his hand up, "Please, my friend, let me finish, this is very hard for me too." Trouseau just nodded. His eyes began to well up and he lowered his head to look at the floor. His arms hung limp by his sides.

Bassar went on: "The Captain has been cursed. His body has weakened and he is beyond the help of any physician. The monks have the knowledge of the power of Isis, which has been also cursed." Bassar tried to clear his throat with a cough. "The power of the Sword and the Stone of Isis, we are told, has been delivered into the underworld. The Saharadeen's last promise to the Captain has come true. He told the Captain, just before he died, that the Captain would never leave this world as a man. The power, it seems, has gone and the Captain appears to be dying with it."

Tom burst into tears, "NO! – please no!" he cried with his face in his hands.

Braheim's face was pale with shock and as he stood up his legs went weak. He looked up at the ceiling and tears ran down his cheeks. Then he turned to Bassar. "Then we must all go to the Captain. We must help the monks with whatever they need. If there is any chance of saving the Captain, we must do what they wish. We will take the Princess. I have heard of this island, Mysticonissi. But I have heard it is a perilous place to find at sea."

Bassar responded to Braheim. "The island is a difficult place to approach as there are great rocks which rise from the sea and many other rocks around them. There is only one way into the small bay where a ship can go. My father has been there. He and his captain will show us the way."

Mababe had been standing in silence as he listened to Bassar relay the situation. "What about the boy?" He pointed at Tom. "Who will look after him while we sail to this place?"

Bassar replied. "The monks have called for us to take him. It is he and my sister they have need of."

Tom looked up. His eyes were red with crying and tears streaked down his face. "I want to see Mr Hawkins. Why have these monks asked for me anyway?"

"I do not understand their ways, Tom," Bassar replied, "but as Braheim has correctly said, we must do as they wish. These monks are very wise." Bassar paused and then knelt down beside Tom and held the boy's arms in both hands and looked straight into his eyes. "Tom, I must tell you this. Please listen carefully." Tom stared back with his red and swollen eyes and nodded with a sniff. Bassar was about to continue when there was a scratching sound from behind the cushions where Tom was sitting, and suddenly Rumpitter hopped out from behind and leapt onto Tom's lap.

Al Jadda looked in amazement and went to draw his dagger to strike the rat. "No!" called Mababe, "the rat is with the boy – they are friends." Mababe held out his huge hands to make Al Jadda withdraw his dagger. "It is all right," he continued and nodded to Al Jadda to step back.

Tom looked down at Rumpitter and the rat looked deep into Tom's eyes. *Can you hear me Tom?* Rumpitter spoke without words. Tom nodded and replied, *Yes.*

Bassar looked strangely at Tom for a second, but Tom was looking at the rat.

*Then don't you see, Tom? If you can hear me and I can hear you, the power still lives.*

Tom's eyes widened as he took in what Rumpitter said. He looked up at Bassar and the others all standing around him. "Yes, yes, that's it!" he exclaimed. "The power is not gone. Rumpitter and I can still speak, don't you see?" Tom looked at all the men who were completely bewildered.

"What are you talking about Tom?" Joseph asked.

Bassar grabbed Tom's arms again and said, "I am not sure what you are saying, but you must let me finish. This is important."

"Yes?" Tom replied.

"The Captain is in a very bad way. He is dying. If the monks cannot save him he will go very fast and then... we do not have the way to get you home."

Tom sat still with Bassar's words sinking in fast. The reality hit him quickly and he looked at Rumpitter, who just stared back at Tom with his sparkly bright eyes and nodded. *You can hear me Tom, I can hear you. We can speak without words. The power still lives in us and I believe if we can get to the Captain fast enough, we can still save him.*

Tom didn't need any more convincing and looked back at Bassar and then turned to the comrades. "We must go to the Captain now!"

Bassar nodded back to Tom, "Yes, Tom we will." He tried to give the boy a smile but then stood up to address the comrades and Al Jadda.

"The Princess will arrive at Kartusa on the north coast, one day's ride from here. Al Jadda has provided for our journey. He bowed to Al Jadda and with his hand on his heart said, "We thank you, my brother." Al Jadda waved his hand down from his head to his chest and bowed. He spoke in Arabic to Bassar. "It is but a small thing that I do. I wish I could help more."

Joseph put his hand on Bassar's arm. "We must go now – there is no more time for talking." He looked at Tom and the rat. "I have a feeling there is something we can do, or should I say, that HE can do to save the Captain." Joseph nodded in Tom's direction. Bassar replied, "There is obviously something strange about this. The boy knows something. I do not understand myself, but you are right. We shall go now."

The comrades collected their belongings and Braheim turned to Tom who was now standing up with Rumpitter on his shoulder. "Tom, we have a long journey. We go now – come."

Their mounts were ready and waiting for them. Al Jadda had also provided a cart with four fast horses and two of his men to drive the cart.

Bassar was brought a large black eagle by one of his men. He wore a long leather glove on which the eagle sat motionless. He stared into the eyes of the huge bird of prey and whispered something. Then he stroked its head and tied something to one of its legs. "Take this and fly like the wind, my friend," he whispered. Then he held up his gloved hand and the bird lifted into the air and disappeared into the night.

The whole Al Kadi army and the Shebah tribesmen stood up to greet Bassar and Al Jadda.

Fire torches lit the camp and lined the path out into the desert.

Although Tom was very tired he insisted he wanted to ride with the others. Braheim told him that he should rest through the night. He could ride at daylight when they would need to ride fast to meet the Princess and the ship that was waiting to take them to Mysticonissi. Reluctantly Tom agreed and climbed into the cart. Immediately they moved out of the camp in a cloud of dust and the thunder of hooves.

Tom lay on a bundle of soft sacks covered with a rug. Through an opening in the cloth roof, he looked up into the warm night sky and watched thousands of stars flicker past as the cart rattled along. He could sense riders on horses to either side of the cart and heard the cart driver cracking a whip in the air and the thud of hooves thunder across the dry desert floor.

Rumpitter sat at the rear of the cart looking over the wooden flap into the night. A dark cloud of desert sand blew a trail of dust behind the cart as it raced along.

The motion of the cart, as it lolled and rucked from one side to the other, gradually caused Tom to drop his head and nod. He tried to fight it and open his eyes, but finally he couldn't keep them open any longer and he nodded off.

Rumpitter turned around to see his friend fast asleep and sighed. *Sleep well, Tom, you will need all the rest you can get* he thought to himself.

The riders charged on tirelessly through the night with their dark shapes bent forward in their saddles. They did not speak and the only sound to be heard was the thud of galloping horses and the rattle of the cart's wheels on the hard desert floor.

In the early hours of the morning fishermen tended their nets and prepared their small wooden boats. On the small quayside a few Arab men stood around a fire. Some camels stood in a group under a palm tree. Small mud huts were scattered around the perimeter of the small fishing port.

A larger sailing ship called *Galênê* sat alongside the quay with its crew silently standing on deck, looking over the rails to the hills beyond the village. A lantern glowed at the stern of the ship casting a gentle orange beam of light along the decks.

Suddenly the quietness of the night was broken. A voice called down from the top of the mast to the men on deck. The Arab watching from the mast now pointed to the hills. Other Arabs ran to the sides of the ship and those standing around the fire also turned to look. In the distance they saw the dark shape of riders flowing over the crest of the hill. They were galloping at great speed towards the port. The approaching riders became clearer and they could see the staff carriers holding the Al Kadi flag which flowed in the air as they raced into Kartusa.

Urgent words were called out and quickly the men on deck rushed to open the side of the ship to lower the wooden boarding plank. An Arab in a long white robe, and a turban wrapped high around his head, shouted some orders and the Arabs standing by the fire quickly picked up their swords and leather helmets. They formed a line from the quay to the boarding plank. Immediately there was a sense of excitement and urgency.

Others lit more torches around the harbour and ran to the entrance of the port. They formed a line along either side of the street. The small group of fishermen stood in silence by their nets and looked to see the group of riders moving closer.

More orders were called out and men rushed through an arched wooden door onto the deck. They instantly formed a line in the centre of the ship. These men wore the uniform of the Al Kadi guard and were armed with swords and bows, their round shields strapped to their backs.

The Arab in the white robe and turban stepped down the gang-plank and began walking quickly along the line of men holding torches to the end of the street that led out into the desert and the oncoming riders. When he reached the end of the street, he stood still and waited. Then, when he could see more clearly who was approaching, his eyes opened wide and he whispered something to himself, but it was just loud enough for the others to hear. He said: "Princess Tasia – Al Kadi..." His mouth fell open. He dropped to his knees and his head touched the floor. All the other Arabs passed the words along the line, all the way back to the soldiers waiting on the deck of the ship – "Tasia!" Everyone fell to their knees.

Finally the riders pulled up in front of the Arab who was on his knees. The horses snorted and panted from exhaustion. King Hafidh Al Kadi looked down at the man on his knees before him and then dismounted. He touched the man on his head and spoke to him quietly. The Arab rose to his feet and bowed. The King turned around and immediately the group of horses moved aside to let a tall white horse pass through them. Mounted on the white horse, wearing a long bronze-coloured robe and head-scarf, was the most praised and loved woman in all the lands.

She dismounted and stood beside the King. She stepped up to the Arab and bowed to him. He had tears running down his face. She touched the side of his face and gently wiped a tear with her finger and smiled to him. Her piercing green eyes and perfectly smooth, light tanned skin shone beneath her dark auburn hair, which fell down her shoulders as she removed her head-scarf. There was a gentle murmur of awe as the Arabs saw their beloved Princess for the first time in so many years. To them, she symbolised life itself.

Princess Tasia looked at the men before her and nodded in a way that showed her thanks and her respect for them. The King passed the reins of his horse to one of his men and then took his daughter's arm. "Come, my dear," he said simply and together they walked through the line of torch holders. As they walked along the line of men towards the quay, everyone bowed.

The King's riders dismounted when they were almost at the ship. They followed closely behind their King and the Princess, but there was no need to protect them. They were in no danger here.

The Princess saw the fishermen who were kneeling and looking up at her in awe as she approached. She stopped and walked over to them and, one by one, she took their hands in hers. She nodded and smiled to them. Then she turned to one of her guards and nodded. The guard knew exactly what to do and walked to the leather bags hanging from the saddle of his horse. He produced some small cloth pouches and handed them to the Princess. She gave each of the fishermen one pouch of silver coin. They bowed and held their hands together in thanks. Their baskets of fish were taken aboard. She thanked them and continued towards the *Galênê* where her father waited.

No one spoke, but everyone wanted to cheer aloud. Their Princess had returned to them. However, everyone knew that, had this been in different circumstances, it would have been a celebration. They knew why the Princess and the King had arrived here to the small fishing port in secret, in the darkness.

Bassar and the comrades galloped on through the night. As the sun began to rise and a red glow rose above the desert, Bassar, still riding at a full gallop, turned in his saddle and nodded to Joseph. In turn, Joseph nodded back to his comrades and instantly Braheim and Trouseau fell back behind the cart, where Mababe was riding at the rear. Still riding at a fast pace, Trouseau took one foot out of his stirrup and leapt onto the cart. He slipped under the cloth roof and jumped inside. Braheim brought Tom's horse up to the wooden flap at the back of the cart. They were still riding fast.

Trouseau saw the young boy asleep and nudged him. "Tom, Tom, wake up," he called.

Tom was drowsy as he rolled his head round to see Trouseau standing over him. "Come, wake up. It is time." Rumpitter jumped onto Tom's chest. *Tom, it's time to go* he said without words.

The cart rattled and slammed from side to side as Tom pulled himself up onto his knees.

He looked out of the rear of the cart and saw Braheim on his horse. He held the reins of Tom's horse, Fahd, galloping along beside. Tom turned to Trouseau, "What's happening?" he said sleepily.

"Do you think you can jump on your horse from here?" Trouseau shouted over the din of the rattling cart and pointed to the wooden flap which had been lowered and was protruding from behind the now open end of the cart.

"What?" Tom asked, slightly in shock.

"We cannot stop. We have no time. You have to jump to your horse from here. Braheim will pull your horse up as close as he can. He will take your hand and help you. I will help from here. Be careful!" Trouseau was shouting loudly over the clatter of the cart thundering along the rough ground beneath.

"I-I think so."

"Good, then go!"

Tom crawled to the rear of the cart and saw the dusty trail of sand billowing up from behind and then looked at Braheim and Fahd. Rumpitter ran up to the opening and looked at the horse. *Oh dear, this could be tricky* he said to himself and then looked into Fahd's eyes. The horse immediately seemed to sense the situation and charged further forward towards the opening of the cart and stuck his head over the wooden flap. Braheim suddenly lost hold of the reins and tried to get closer, but the horse had bolted forward on its own.

*NOW, Tom!* Rumpitter shouted without words. Tom threw his arms around Fahd's neck and pulled himself out of the cart, with one leg over the horse's neck. He clung on tightly, and, for a moment, it looked as though he might slide round and fall. But Fahd quickly pulled his head back and Tom managed to grab the pommel of the saddle and hung on tightly. Rumpitter leapt out from the back of the cart onto the saddle too, clinging on with his teeth and claws. Tom finally hooked both feet into his stirrups and took up the reins.

Fahd pulled to the left and charged away from the cart. Braheim galloped alongside Tom with a look of amazement on his face. He rode closer to the cart, now with the reins of Trouseau's horse. Trouseau jumped into his saddle from the moving cart.

Mababe quickly galloped up beside Tom to check he was safe. He nodded back to the others and shook his head with a broad smile. "That was good!" he shouted.

The companions and Tom galloped ahead as the cart turned away and disappeared behind them in a cloud of dust.

Joseph and Bassar smiled to each other as Tom, Trouseau, Braheim and Mababe drew up beside them. Without a second wasted, the comrades raced on together across the desert with the rising sun now peering over the hills to the east.

They rode at a full gallop without stopping. Al Jadda and his men looked at the boy and his comrades with great respect. On and on they rode, relentlessly.

After a while they started to climb a hill. They finally came to a trail at the crest. Down in the distance they saw the coastline and the deep blue haze of the sea. For the first time they slowed their pace very slightly. Al Jadda came up closer to Bassar's horse and called across, speaking in Arabic. Bassar leaned over to shake Al Jadda's hand. They exchanged a few short words. Then Al Jadda shouted over to the comrades: "Go in peace my friends!" The comrades nodded their thanks for his help and waved to Al Jadda and the other Arab riders, who waved back. Then Al Jadda and his men slowly pulled their horses to a halt, leaving Bassar and the comrades to charge ahead. They stood in line along the hill crest and watched the comrades charge down the trail towards Kartusa. Tom looked behind him and saw the figures of Al Jadda and his men slowly fade into dark dots on the horizon.

The look-out called to his chief and more shouting rang out around Kartusa.

Immediately the Arab crew on the *Galênê* began to prepare the sails. No time would be wasted. As soon as Bassar arrived, they would set sail.

Men ran to the quay to take the ropes. They stood by to await their instructions. Six horsemen galloped up the trail to meet the riders charging down the hill.

The King walked quickly to the rail when he saw them coming. He spoke to one of his men who immediately ran below decks. A moment later the Princess appeared. The sun was now lighting up the sky. The morning light illuminated the beautiful figure of the Princess as she walked quickly across the deck to her father's side. Her soft skin and perfectly formed lips and the lines of her face looked radiant as she walked over to join her father. She grabbed his arm tightly. He could sense her excitement and, yet also, her anxiety. It was with mixed feelings that she waited nervously for the riders to approach them.

"The boy comes?" she asked in a quiet voice. "He is here," the King replied and looked down at his daughter sensing the apprehension in her voice.

Tasia smiled as she recognised her brother's robes flowing in the wind as he galloped into the village. Still she held tightly onto her father's arm. She was intrigued by the tales she had learned of the strange young boy from another world. She knew of the Captain's love for the boy and now, for the first time, she would meet him.

Bassar and the comrades finally arrived at the top of the track into Kartusa and, for the first time, they slowed their horses to a trot. The horses snorted and grunted from exhaustion. Their riders were covered in dust. Bassar swept the sweat from his brow and lowered the scarf covering his face. He turned in his saddle to the comrades. "We have arrived – follow me," he said. Then he gave his horse a gentle nudge and cantered forward.

The soldiers lining the road into the village stood in silence. As Bassar rode through the street, each soldier bowed his head.

Finally they arrived at the ship. Bassar immediately dismounted and walked quickly to the gang-plank.

Tom peered through his head-scarf to see the crew standing by the rails of the ship. They were peering down at them. Then he saw the King standing by the rail. Standing next to the King was the most beautiful woman Tom had ever seen. He noticed how she stared back at him. He noticed her bright green eyes. They seemed be to staring right through him. Tom removed the scarf from his face and tossed it over his shoulder. He looked at Rumpitter who was sitting on his other shoulder. *Is that the Princess?* He said without words. *Yes, Tom – that is her* replied Rumpitter. Then Tom saw the Princess give a slight smile and she bowed her head very slightly.

Joseph tapped Tom on the shoulder. "Come on lad," he said quietly and took the reins of Tom's horse. "Down you get." Tom lifted a leg over the saddle and jumped down onto the quay.

The comrades all dismounted and, together with Tom, they climbed the gang-plank and boarded the *Galênê*.

Bassar greeted his father with an embrace. "You have done well to get here so fast," the King said.

"We did not rest, Father. It was a hard ride. Al Jadda was most helpful," Bassar replied and then turned to the Princess. "My sister," he said simply and embraced her. He noticed his sister could not keep her eyes from the boy. She was still looking at Tom over Bassar's shoulder. He smiled with a gentle nod and whispered in her ear. "He is a fine boy. I now can see why the Captain cares for him." He pulled away and kissed his sister on the cheek. Then he turned to the comrades and beckoned them over to him.

Joseph walked quickly up to the King. He bowed and then he turned to Princess Tasia with a wide smile. "It is so good to see you again, Tasia." He felt slightly awkward and went to take her hand, but the Princess threw her arms around Joseph and said, "It has been too long, Joseph – I have prayed for so long that I would see you all again. I wish this could be in happier times."

Joseph nodded. "We all pray for the best." With tears in her eyes, she pulled her head back a little to look at the large man standing before her. "I know you have been through so much – but I see you are still the strong, brave Joseph." She kissed him on the cheek and then moved quickly to greet the others.

One by one the comrades greeted her. The feeling of great mutual respect and fondness was apparent. These men were the Captain's closest friends. She knew of their undying loyalty for their captain and she loved them for it.

At last she came to the small figure standing between Trouseau and Braheim and looked down upon him with a smile. Her piercing eyes met again with Tom's and he stood speechless in front of her.

Princess Tasia bent down slightly and held out her hand. Tom thought she was going to shake his hand and held his out in front. But the Princess moved her hand to his left shoulder where Rumpitter was sitting. She stroked Rumpitter on the head. "Rumpitter, you are the bravest rat in all the lands. I am so pleased to see you too," she said in a soft, warm voice. Rumpitter lifted himself up onto his hind legs and twitched his nose and ears.

Tom giggled when he saw Rumpitter swooning at being stroked by the Princess.

Tasia turned her eyes to Tom. "He is a very brave rat, don't you think, Tom?" she asked. Tom almost melted at the sound of her velvet voice.

"Y-yes, he is," Tom replied nervously.

"And they tell me that you are the bravest of all."

Tom was so embarrassed; he didn't know where to look. Tasia touched the sides of Tom's face and swept the curls of his hair away from his eyes. "I have heard so many fine things about you. I feel I have known you for ever. I hope you and I will be good friends." She spoke quietly, but to Tom it sounded like a chorus of angels. Her soft touch and warm smile captured him and he suddenly understood why so many people loved her. He imagined the Captain standing next to her – the two of them, majestic and tall and wonderful.

"I-I'm sure we will be," Tom replied nervously, and then asked, "Can I call you Tasia?"

The Princess gave a little chuckle, "Of course you can, Tom." Then she took his hand and turned to her father.

The King was pleased to see that she had acquainted herself well with the boy. He spoke to the comrades. "It is good to see you all again. I pray we are on time." Then he clapped his hands and immediately the crewmen ran to the rigging. Orders were called out by the *Galênê*'s captain. Bassar went over to him and put his hand on his shoulder. "You have done well, Sadi. Thank-you for your help."

"I have done nothing, my Prince," Captain Sadi replied. He bowed and then walked away to prepare the ship for departure.

The comrades helped the crew release the shore lines and set the sail. Bassar walked over to Joseph. "The winds are with us this morning. Let us pray for a safe journey and that we are not too late." Bassar's face showed great concern. Everyone had been wondering if they would make it to the island in time. They prayed that the Captain was still alive.

The Princess led Tom across the deck and up onto the higher level where the helmsman and Captain Sadi waited. Bassar, the King and the comrades joined them.

They watched the ropes being hauled aboard from the quay and then the large sail started to roll down. Long poles were brought out from the sides of the ship to push her hull away from the quay. The gentle breeze picked up and filled the top half of the great sail. The helmsman and Captain Sadi pulled the huge wooden tiller over to starboard and very slowly the *Galêné* began to pull away from the quay. Soldiers lined the shore and watched in silence as the large wooden ship began to slip away in the breeze. The rest of the sail was dropped and the wind filled it.

The crew pulled the thick ropes that set the sail. The wooden cleats creaked under the strain of the ropes which were tightly tied around them. The sun had risen over the hills behind Kartusa and cast a bright beam of light across the bay as they sailed out into the great sea.

Tom and the Princess were standing together at the stern of the ship and watched Kartusa slowly shrink into the distance. Rumpitter sat on the ship's rail and watched the Princess and the boy.

Tasia was looking at Tom. There were so many questions she wanted to ask him, but she knew they must wait. She wanted to know this young boy, to understand more about where he came from and why her love, the Captain, had found his way to the boy's world and how they became friends. So many questions whirled around in her head. She had been told that only she and the boy could save Captain Hawkins, but she had no idea how.

"They tell me you are a man of the sea yourself, Tom," Tasia said, breaking the silence.

Tom looked up at her and shook his head, "Well – not really, not yet. My father is – but one day I will be – when I'm older."

Princess Tasia put her hand gently on Tom's head and said, "You must believe in your dreams, follow your heart and, in time, you will find your true path."

Tom cleared his throat and said, "Mr Hawkins has a dream. His dream – is to be with you."

The Princess lowered her head and then looked back at Tom. There was great sadness in her eyes and her voice seemed to tremble slightly. "This too, is my dream. To be with him." A tear appeared in her eye and she wiped it away with a finger.

"We will get to him in time, won't we?" Tom said finally.

Tasia was unable to speak now and simply nodded. She turned to Rumpitter, who hopped over to Tom and said, without words, *Er – are you hungry, Tom?*

Tom held out his arm for Rumpitter to run along it and jump onto his shoulder. *Yes, I am a bit* Tom replied without words.

*Good, well why don't we go and see if they have a cook on this boat?* Rumpitter looked at the Princess and she gave a little smile. She took Tom's hand and led him down to the lower deck and through the arched door.

The *Galênê* sailed with ease as the wind stiffened in their favour. The sun cast a yellow glow across the sea.

Herallinos looked out of the small stone window from the tower. The morning light over the ocean cast a dim shadow across the pale skin of his bony face. The darkness in his eyes showed the years of waiting – waiting for the darkness to become light.

Rashidi appeared between the two stone pillars in the centre of the hall and looked at the thin, hooded figure standing at the window. He coughed slightly to make the monk aware of his presence and then asked: "Do you really believe you can save him?"

The monk did not reply. He did not even turn to Rashidi. He just stood still in the darkness, looking out to the sea.

The comrades on Mysticonissi had returned to the ship. They sat around in silence, unable to eat or rest. They were powerless to do anything for their captain. All they could do now was wait.

Gordon sat on the cross beam at the top of the mast, looking out to sea. Beyond the ragged rocks that surrounded the island, there was nothing but the ocean and the sky. He watched for hours, but there was nothing.

As the sun had reached its highest point, a bright golden light flashed in the sky. Suddenly, from out of the glow of the sun, he saw a dark shape. At first he thought it was his eyes and he rubbed them to look up again. The dark shape became larger and it seemed to be flickering –then it grew bigger. He heard something. It was a high pitched, shrill sound. It seemed to come from the shape in the sky, which was moving closer. Gordon shook his head again to try to focus better. Then he saw – it was a large bird. Its wings were tipped upwards at their ends. Its head was large with a curved beak. The black eagle now swooped directly over the small harbour towards the ship.

"In the sky!" Gordon shouted down to the men on deck. They all immediately looked up to see a black eagle soaring over them. It screeched as it passed over and then turned upwards towards the tower at the top of the cliff.

Herallinos leaned out of the window and held out his arm. "Finally," he whispered to himself.

The eagle hovered in the air by the window and then settled on the monk's arm.

"You have done well, my friend," the monk whispered to the large bird. The eagle let out another screech.

Herallinos stepped back from the window with the large eagle on his arm and turned to Rashidi, who had been sitting on the floor, patiently waiting. "They are coming?" Rashidi asked in a quiet voice. Herallinos nodded and said, "Soon." He took a small piece of parchment which had been tied to the eagle's leg and opened it.

Then he nodded to one of the monks standing nearby, who took the eagle from Herallinos and left the room.

"Tell me, what do you know of this boy?" Herallinos asked.

"He comes from another world. It is a land far from here."

Herallinos thought for a moment and looked at Rashidi. The monk's face was expressionless.

"He may never see his world again." Rashidi frowned and simply shook his head and sighed.

The wind picked up and Captain Sadi had ordered the crew to reduce sail as the ship crashed through the waves. The helmsman worked hard to hold a true course.

"How long until we see the island?" Braheim asked Bassar. "Sadi says it will be night before we can tell. The wind is strengthening. As long as it comes from the south, we will make good time."

The sky had turned grey and dark clouds had covered the sun. The comrades watched the dark clouds slowly fill the sky. Then there was a loud crack in the air and a bolt of lightning streaked out across the ocean. Joseph called over to his friends. "I think we have a storm coming."

"I think you are right, we had better make everything secure," Mababe replied, and went with Trouseau to help the crew fasten down hatches and secure the rigging.

The ship lifted out of one wave and crashed down through another. Hour after hour they ploughed through the waves and rolled from side to side.

Bassar and Joseph were hanging onto the rails and Bassar shouted to be heard against the wind, to Joseph, "The *Galênê* – she is a strong ship, but she does not live up to her name."

"Oh and what is that?" Joseph shouted back.

"*Galênê* – it is a Greek word, meaning *Calm Seas.*" Joseph raised his eyes and shook his head. Then he called back, "Well – she seems to be holding up."

Just then a wave crashed over the rail, soaking the two men.

Tom had fallen asleep in the main cabin. Princess Tasia sat beside him.

She noticed her father watching them. He had been sitting in a chair, studying the map which had been rolled out on a wooden table. A wave smashed against the window behind him and then rolled away behind the stern of the ship in a mass of green froth.

"I feel your heavy heart, my daughter." Tasia just nodded to her father.

"You know this is the right thing to do?" the King said. Again Tasia just nodded. A small tear rolled down her cheek and she looked down at the boy asleep on the bed beside her.

"He is so young. Jeremiah would not wish him any harm – he loves this boy, like he is his own," Tasia finally said.

"And we will do all in our power to protect him," replied the King and then shook his head, "but I fear we are against a foe far greater than we have faced before."

Tasia stared at her father. "He would die for this boy. I would die too if it were to save him."

The King stared at his daughter with deep sadness, but said nothing.

Another large wave caught the bow of the ship and, as the hull crashed back into the sea, it woke Tom.

"What's happening?" he called, as he rolled off the bed onto the floor. Another wave hit the side of the hull and the ship leaned heavily to one side. Tom slid across the floor. Princess Tasia managed to hold onto a post which supported the ceiling of the cabin. The King held tight onto the table, which had been secured to the floor. He turned towards the door.

"Stay here, both of you. You will be safe here," the King said and staggered against the rolling deck to the door. They heard the crashing waves and thunder as he opened the door and stepped on deck. The door slammed shut.

Tom lifted himself up and grabbed onto a shelf by the window. He could see the dark sky and the cracks of lightning streak across the sea. The waves rolled past, thrashing into the ship. Everything creaked and groaned. It was as if the ship was calling out in pain for the wind to cease.

Rumpitter was sent scrambling on all legs across the deck and fell into a heap at the far end of the cabin.

"I hope this ship is strong enough," Tom called over to Tasia, and then he asked, "Are you all right?"

Tasia was still clinging to the post and replied, "Thank-you, Tom – I am fine."

The crew on deck fought to keep the ship's head up. Now there were two men at a time holding onto the large tiller, keeping the ship on course. When a large wave came, they ran to one side and then to the other, pulling the tiller with all their strength as they rolled up huge waves and then crashed down the other side. It seemed as though it was never ending, but the ship seemed to take the punishment and defiantly pushed on across the vast ocean.

Finally the rain came. It fell out of the skies like a monsoon. Everyone was soaked through to the skin, but still the ship ploughed on regardless of whatever the weather threw at it.

Captain Sadi stood by his men and proudly watched them manning the ship through the terrible weather.

Eventually, by late afternoon, the wind began to decrease, but the rain was relentless. The thunder and lightning ceased, leaving the dark rain clouds to release a torrent upon the ship. It stayed that way long into the night, until finally, hours later, the rain stopped.

During the passage, no one had eaten, but now the cook, a very large round Arab called Mahmoud, rang the chimes to call everyone on deck.

Bassar shouted down from the top level at the stern of the ship. "Mahmoud, I am pleased to see you are still with us. The men are hungry." Mahmoud smiled with a wide grin, showing how few teeth he had left in his mouth. He bowed to Bassar and replied, "There is plenty for all, my Lord," and continued ringing his chimes until all the crew were on deck.

Tasia, Tom and the King joined them.

Rumpitter scurried away to find a place to eat a piece of meat he had got from Mahmoud a short while before he came on deck to announce to all that dinner was served.

A long table was set out along the centre of the deck and the whole crew, including the King, Bassar and Princess Tasia, all sat there together. The helmsman and Captain Sadi remained on duty to sail the ship. They would eat later, and Mahmoud made certain there was plenty left for them.

Tom was famished. The King looked at the boy devouring the food on his plate and nodded to Bassar and Tasia. "It is good to see the boy has such an appetite."

Bassar nodded back and then noticed his sister was not eating. His eyes caught hers and he nodded to her plate. "Please, sister, eat," he gestured again at her food, "You will need strength."

The King leaned over to his daughter and whispered in her ear, "Listen to your brother, he is right. You must be strong. For whatever has to be done will require your strength and courage."

Tasia looked at her father and then at her plate. She picked up a small piece of fish and put it in her mouth. Tom had been watching them. He smiled awkwardly when Tasia caught his stare.

"It's very good food – my compliments to the chef," Tom said cheerily to Mahmoud as he walked past carrying a wooden bowl of warm baked dough balls. He placed one on Tom's plate and smiled at the boy, nodding in appreciation that the boy was enjoying his cooking. Tom dipped the bread into the fish sauce on his plate and popped it into his mouth. "Delicious!" he called out with his mouth full of food. It caused everyone to chuckle and even Tasia managed a smile. She had instantly warmed to the boy and had wished that they could have met in happier circumstances.

There was no moon as the ship sailed gently onwards. Now the bad weather had cleared, it had turned into a quiet peaceful night, but it was dark with just a few stars to light the sky.

Mahmoud had been grateful for the help he had received from the men as they helped to clear the table and thanked him for the food.

Tom watched with interest as the King chatted with the men. He thought how strange it was, and yet it seemed quite normal, that the King had sat at the table with the crew as if he were one of them. Tom also realised that he too had felt quite relaxed in the company of such impressive people. He never thought, in his wildest dreams, that he would become the friend of someone so important. He thought about Mr Hawkins and where his journey was leading. He thought about what he had seen and experienced during the days he had been in this strange land. Where was he going now? What was to become of him, the comrades and Mr Hawkins?

His mind drifted away – far back to his home. What would it be like if a King visited Rivermouth? How would it be? Would the King expect everyone to bow to him and look up to him in awe, or would he be happy to sit at the table of a normal family and chat and share their food? How would his mother receive a King? It just wouldn't be so simple in his world.

He was leaning over the rail of the ship, staring out to sea, when a voice called his name. He shook his head from his day dreaming and turned round. Joseph was standing behind him. "Tom, I have been calling you. Did you not hear me?" Joseph had a deep but gentle voice. He stood still for a moment and then walked closer to Tom.

"Sorry Joseph, I was just – looking." Joseph walked over to stand beside Tom and leant over the rail. For a moment he didn't speak, he just stared out across the dark sea. Then he turned his head up to the sky. "Not so many stars up there this night, Tom. Those clouds still linger up there – could be a long night."

Tom didn't reply, he just looked up at the tall man standing next to him.

"Reckon a good night's sleep will do you well, my boy." Then Joseph looked down and smiled. He put his hand on Tom's head and said in a soft voice, "You should get some sleep, lad."

Tom nodded and the two of them walked across the deck and through the door into the Captain's quarters. Joseph led Tom to a small room which had a wooden bunk with a thick woollen cloth thrown over it. "In you get lad. I'll wake you when we are there."

Tom didn't say anything. He just nodded to Joseph, took off his robes and lay down on the small bunk.

As Joseph closed the door behind him, he heard a small voice say, "Good night Joseph."

Mababe was standing outside when Joseph appeared. He had a smile on his face.

"It seems we have all taken kindly to the boy, my friend," said Mababe, who was also smiling.

"Aye, he is a fine lad," replied Joseph.

The two men walked together to the bow of the ship.

Mababe shook his head and looked up at the night sky. "I fear great danger for the boy. They say that these monks work in strange ways. I do not trust this. What do you know of this place, Mysticonissi?"

"It is a small island hidden inside a group of large and dangerous rocks. Few men know there is even an island there. It is uncharted and a hazardous place to take a ship. Many have perished who have been unfortunate to have sailed too close to the rocks. Only a few people know the way in."

Joseph leaned out over the bow to see the waves washing past the hull. Small dots of phosphorous flickered like fireflies across the top of the water. He rubbed his thick stubbled chin with his hand. He turned his head round to look aft and saw Captain Sadi at the helm with one of his crew. "That man there knows the way through the rocks. The King did well to afford us the help of the Egyptian. We should be safe enough – as long as the weather holds."

Joseph turned back to face out to sea again and, in a low voice, he said, "I too have worries for the boy. I hope we are doing the right thing."

Mababe nodded and replied, "What choice do we have? We must try to save the Captain – and pray to the Gods that the boy will survive this too."

As the sun rose up from the east, it cast a golden light across the sea. The wind was gentle and the *Galênê* sailed quietly onwards.

Captain Sadi was standing at the stern with his helmsman when Bassar climbed up the stairs to the higher level to join them.

"At last a fine morning," said Bassar as he scanned his eyes across the ocean.

Captain Sadi bowed and greeted Bassar in the Arab way. "All is well for the moment, my Lord, but we must wait until we approach the rocks of Mysticonissi. Then we will have the mist and then we will see what welcomes us." Sadi nodded his head towards the bow of the ship as he spoke.

"You have done this before, Sadi. You can do it again. We all have faith in your skill and judgment and, with Allah's will, we shall arrive on time."

Captain Sadi nodded again, "With Allah's will, yes. May he guide us safely." Captain Sadi raised his hands to the sky and then crossed himself.

All day, the crew kept themselves busy and they sailed onwards. They all knew in their hearts that their destination was a strange place of unknown dangers.

Mysticonissi, the secret island, waited for them.

Joseph climbed down the stairs to find Trouseau and Braheim sitting on wooden barrels playing a dice game. Mababe was leaning against a wooden beam, watching them.

They all looked up as Joseph bent down to step through the low doorway and entered the small cabin. Hessian sacks of grain and spices and woven rope bags holding large glass containers of water swung from hooks attached to the low ceiling. Wooden crates were stacked all around the sides of the cabin. It was cramped and there was an odour of salty dampness in the air.

Joseph nodded to his comrades as he entered and sat down on one of the crates.

Whatever conversation the men had had before Joseph entered the room, immediately stopped. The three comrades waited for Joseph to speak.

Joseph cleared his throat before he spoke. "Friends, it will not be long before we find the island." He paused with a deep breath before continuing. "We have been through many things together and for many years. We have stayed strong together and we have stood by Captain Hawkins's side for as long as I can remember." He raised his head to the ceiling and pointed with his finger. "Up there is a young boy who we have come to like very much. No matter how strange we feel about all that has happened, that boy saved our captain and brought him back to us. I do not, and I think I will never, understand anything about what has happened these past days, but we have an obligation to watch out for the boy and to save our captain." The comrades all nodded and muttered sounds of agreement. "Bassar has told me that the monks have called for the Princess and the boy because they believe they can help them to save the Captain. I do not understand these things, but we have no choice but to follow this path and let the monks do their work."

Trouseau spoke first. "I cannot believe that Bassar would allow his sister to come to any harm – so it must be that these monks know what they are doing."

"I agree," said Braheim, "the King would not sacrifice his beloved daughter. He knows of these monks and their powers – and so I have faith that all will be well." Braheim crossed his forehead and chest with his hand. "I pray to Allah that he will watch over them."

Joseph nodded as his friends spoke their piece, and then replied, "We will stand by our friends – my brothers." he placed one hand down on the wooden table with the dice. The comrades put their hands on top of his and they held their hands firmly together.

"Together as always – and for ever," they all said.

The hours passed by slowly, but as the sun began to dim into a purple evening sky, a voice suddenly shouted down from the mast top. Everyone stopped whatever they were doing and ran up on deck to see what the shouting was about. One of Captain Sadi's crewmen had been keeping watch from the top of the mast. He was pointing straight ahead as he shouted.

Captain Sadi ran forward to the bow of the ship. He was followed by Bassar and Joseph. "There's mist ahead," Sadi said quietly. "We must now take great care – there will soon be rocks everywhere." He turned his head up towards the man on the mast and shouted back some orders. "Keep your eyes wide open and tell me everything you see," he shouted.

Then Sadi ordered the sail to be lowered and the oarsmen to get ready. "We cannot sail through the mist," he said to Bassar. "We must have everyone on deck and I will need men to handle the poles." He pointed at the long wooden poles lying against the railings down each side of the ship.

Joseph called over to Mababe, Braheim and Trouseau. "We will help you Captain; we know what to do with these," he said, and took up one of the long poles. Bassar called to some of his men and they too each grabbed a pole. Then they stood along the sides of the ship and waited. The King was up on the higher level with the helmsman. Tasia and Tom were with him. The large sail had been rolled in and tied safe. Captain Sadi then took over the helm and called out to the crew: "Oars ready!"

In just a few moments they had drifted into the thick mist. The oarsmen pulled together and the ship moved forward through the mist. Visibility was now just a few feet. Every now and then a pocket of mist cleared and then closed in again. The dark blue sea had now turned grey. The sun had disappeared. Suddenly, just as a pocket of mist cleared, a tall dark shape loomed out of the sea – the first rock. Waves were breaking against it, causing the sea to become confused. Suddenly, just a few yards ahead of the rock, they saw another, much bigger, and there were other smaller rocks around it. The sea was breaking heavily against the black rocky formations that rose out of the sea like giant monsters.

Captain Sadi carefully steered the *Galênê* past the tall rock, which was dangerously close to them. As they passed it, the sea began to roll the ship slightly from side to side and the oarsmen worked hard to keep a straight course. "Poles ready!" shouted Sadi and immediately everyone with the wooden poles hung them over the sides. A wave came at them from the second rock as they rolled close by. A small rock appeared just a few feet off the side of the ship and Joseph thrust his pole out, catching the end of the pole on the rock and he pushed heavily. One of the others saw what he was doing and lunged his pole at the rock. The two men pushed away. Then two others did the same with their poles, pushing the ship away from the rock. It was just enough to prevent the hull from slicing into the jagged edges of the rock and it helped the oarsmen as they heaved hard to steer the ship away. They just slipped past the rock, missing it by inches.

Joseph wiped his brow. "That was close," he said to Bassar.

"I think that is just the start of it," Bassar said with a look of concern in his face, as he peered over the sides of the ship into the grey mist.

"Look there!" shouted Trouseau and everyone rushed to the rails as another massive rock appeared directly ahead of them. "Everyone to the rails!" shouted Captain Sadi as he heaved on the tiller to turn the ship. All the poles went out in readiness to push the ship away from the rock. The waves rolled under the hull of the ship, thrusting it forward.

The oarsmen pulled with all their might. Captain Sadi pulled the tiller all the way over to the port side and the oarsmen heaved again. They caught another wave which picked the ship up on its crest and suddenly they were surfing straight towards the huge rock.

Bassar called up to the Captain, "Sadi! – the rock!" Sadi maintained all his effort to guide the ship away. With the help of his crewmen, they pulled the tiller as far over as it would go. The wave suddenly veered away and, with just a few inches to spare, the ship surged past the rock. The oarsmen gave a final heave and they rolled again to the right. Finally, the huge rock was astern of them. Everyone gave a sigh of relief.

Almost immediately, the rock disappeared into the mist and the air began to clear ahead of them. The sea calmed down. Then the look-out called down from the mast.

Ahead of them was the dark island of Mysticonissi. Its high, grey cliff tops disappeared into the clouds which hung like a dark veil over the island.

Everyone looked ahead to see the grey, rocky island looming nearer as the oarsmen rowed on.

Mababe was standing at the bow with Joseph and Bassar. "It is no surprise that this island is unknown. Who would wish to come here?"

The island looked barren, grey and eerie. It was an uninviting place indeed.

Bassar walked back to the stern to thank Sadi for getting them through safely. "You have done well, Sadi. We thank you."

Sadi wiped his forehead and looked up at the sky. He said nothing, but just touched his forehead with his fingers and raised his hand upwards, in thanks to his God.

The ship drew closer to the island and then they saw the other ship lying alongside the small quay.

Joseph smiled when he saw the ship. "We have arrived," he said to his friends.

Trouseau jumped up onto the side rail to get a better look. "I can see people aboard her – wait, I can see Gordon, and, yes – also I see the others. They are all here!" Trouseau smiled down at his friends.

Captain Sadi called out orders to his crew and the *Galênê* slowly turned into the tiny bay.

One of the Arab crewmen threw a rope, with a weight attached to one end, into the water and called out the depth to his captain as they approached.

Large hessian sacks were hung over one side and mooring ropes were tied to the wooden cleats.

"Prepare to come by," shouted Sadi. The oars on the shore side were pulled back on board and the oarsmen on the outside pulled their oars backwards to stop the ship and ease it slowly alongside. Sadi nodded in approval of his men and their skill in bringing his ship safely into the small harbour.

The comrades saw their friends waiting to greet them and take their lines.

Joseph noticed the look on Blake's face and then turned to see Sam Little and Gordon and Maris. Not one of them was cheering or looking happy. Indeed, they looked very serious.

Braheim turned to his friends who were standing beside him. "Things are not good here – see, our friends do not look happy; something is wrong."

The King came up on deck with Princess Tasia. She ran to the sides of the ship with Tom. They saw the other comrades waiting for them. Tasia glanced to the quay and noticed the monks. They looked pale and sullen with expressionless faces. Their hoods covered their eyes. There was a sense of depression – no one smiled. The grey walls of the cliffs looked uninviting and the dampness in the air sent a cold feeling through her. She shivered and put her arms around Tom as the *Galênê* docked alongside. Rumpitter jumped up onto the rail next to Tom and sniffed the damp air.

"It doesn't seem very nice here," Tom said quietly and Rumpitter turned around to look at him. "Let us hope we won't have to stay here too long."

Tasia turned to her father, "We must hurry, Father. We must get to him quickly." The King nodded and summoned Captain Sadi. The Captain walked over to them quickly.

"Thank-you Sadi, you will be well rewarded for your services." Captain Sadi bowed and thanked his King. "Now we must hurry to do what must be done," the King continued.

Sadi nodded and signalled for the crew to drop the gang-plank over the side onto the deck of the other ship. This was immediately carried out. Joseph greeted Blake, Little, Gordon and Maris and all the comrades shook hands and exchanged greetings, but it was a solemn moment. They all knew this was a desperate situation. There was no time for pleasantries.

Blake spoke to the comrades who had just arrived. "We must hurry, the monks will take you to the chamber where the Captain is waiting – he is not well." He looked at Princess Tasia and bowed respectfully. She bowed in return. "Hello, Blake – I wish it was in better times," she said. "That we can all agree on, Princess," he sighed and then saw Tom. "Hello Tom, I am pleased to see you. I expect you have been told that the monks need you to assist them? For the sake of the Captain?"

Tom nodded and looked nervously around him and then at Tasia.

"What do they want me to do?"

Joseph put his hand on the boy's shoulder and looked at Tasia. "We do not know what they want of you and Tasia, but if you can help the Captain, we will all be in your debt."

Three monks walked down the quay to approach the comrades. One of them spoke.

"This is the boy?" he asked. Tasia nodded "And I am Princess Tasia."

"I know who you are. It is good that you came." He bowed to the Princess and gestured with his arm towards the stone steps. "Please – come with us."

The King and Bassar approached the monk. King Hafidh spoke. "You know who I am?"

"I do." The monk bowed respectfully to the King and Hafidh continued: "Good. My son and I shall come with them." The monk paused for a moment and turned to the other monks standing behind him. One of them nodded. Then the monk turned back to the King. "Very well. You will follow us please." Joseph and the comrades walked up to follow, but the monk held up his hand to them. "No, you must stay," said the monk sternly. "The hell we will!" Joseph replied angrily and took two long steps forward. The monk held his hand out and Joseph saw his reddened eyes, staring through his white, pale face. There was no emotion in the monk's face as he hissed the words out. "If you wish to save your captain, you must trust us. Every moment you delay us, his death grows nearer." Joseph stopped and swallowed hard. Never, in his life before, had he been so intimidated and so helpless. He stared back into the lifeless red eyes of the monk, in defiance at first, and then he took a deep breath and nodded. "Very well – but if he dies, so do you and your sorcerous friends." The monk did not react; he just lowered his hand from Joseph's chest, turned around and walked towards the steps that led to the temple. The others followed.

Bassar quickly turned to Joseph and said, "Do not fear, my friend, I will be watching them. The monks mean no harm. They live in ancient ways."

"I am only doing this because you and the King trust them. The Captain came here of his own will and therefore he must know of their ways. We will be close by. Call for us if you need us – immediately, you hear?"

Bassar nodded and then quickly joined the others who waited at the steps. As he approached the first step, and was about to climb up, he turned again to look at the comrades. He knew, in his heart, how much they loved their captain and he prayed they would not be let down by the trust they had bestowed in him.

The group climbed to the top of the steps and arrived at the small entrance. Quickly the door opened and another monk led them into the passage.

Tom looked around for Rumpitter, but couldn't find him. He called him without words. *Rumpitter, where are you? Please don't get lost – where are you?* For a second there was no reply and then he heard, *Don't worry, Tom, I am close by. Go with them, I will be near you.*

Tom looked up at Tasia, "It's a bit dark in here and it's a bit strange too," he said nervously. Tasia just squeezed his hand, but Tom saw the anxiety in her face as she hurried them along the passage, keeping up with the monk who was leading the way. The others followed quickly behind.

At last they came to the large wooden doors. The leading monk rapped twice and they creaked open. Two monks pulled the doors apart so they could enter.

Inside, the large round room was lit by candles and shadows danced from the flickering lights.

Tasia suddenly let out a loud yell and ran across the room. She saw, in the centre of the room, the stone platform and a body lying on top. Next to him lay the Sword of Isis. Standing beside the stone was the old monk Herallinos and, with him, Rashidi, the physician.

Tom ran across to join Tasia and looked in horror as he saw the degrading state of his friend lying on the stone. Tom was speechless and then tears ran down his cheeks.

Tasia screamed in despair when she saw, for the first time in so long, the desperate sight of Captain Hawkins.

He lay still, as if he were dead. His body had faded away to almost a skeleton. The skin on his hands had darkened and looked like wrinkled parchment. His eyes were closed and his beard and hair had turned grey. He looked as if he had been dug from an ancient tomb.

Tasia was beside herself and cried in agony and fell to her knees. Bassar and the King ran to her and helped her onto her feet. Bassar turned to Herallinos, his face pale with worry. "Are we too late?"

Tom screamed out, "NO! – MR HAWKINS! Please – please don't die! No, no." Rashidi tried to calm the boy. "Please, we must try, at least. We need your help!" he pleaded.

But Tom was staring at the limp body lying on the stone. His whole body was shaking. Then he threw himself past Rashidi and leapt up onto the stone. He pulled the cloth scarf away from the Captain's face and cried out again when he saw the full extent of the horror. "No, no!" he continued crying.

Herallinos went to pull Tom away, but Tom repelled the monk with his arm, "No," he shouted, "Mr Hawkins – come back!"

Tasia threw herself over the body, her tears rolled down her face and one tear fell from her lips onto the Captain's cracked mouth.

Rashidi and Herallinos tried to pull Tom away. "Please – we understand your pain, I am sorry," Rashidi said.

Tom looked defiantly at the monk, "You – you said you needed us –you must bring him back!" he screamed. Tom, in his rage, accidentally grabbed the Sword by the blade and it sliced through his hand. His blood dripped over the sides of the stone platform.

Herallinos suddenly moved closer; his eyes opened wide when he saw the blood. He shouted something to another monk, who quickly took a bronze bowl and, as Tom's blood dripped over the side of the stone, it fell into the bowl.

The King and Bassar tried to console Tasia, but she was in a trance of total desperation.

Tom winced with the pain from his cut hand and dropped the Sword. It fell on the Captain.

Herallinos then took the bowl to the Captain's mouth. A drop of Tasia's tears fell into the bowl with Tom's blood.

"Get him away now!" Herallinos ordered. Two monks climbed up to take Tom down from the stone platform. He tried to tug himself free from them, but they grabbed his arms and pulled him away from the body. Blood was dripping from Tom's hand. Herallinos grabbed Tom's blooded hand, pulled the cloth away from the Captain's face and placed the bleeding hand on the Captain's forehead. The blood dripped freely over the cracked skin and down his face.

Suddenly Herallinos raised the bowl in the air and began to mutter strange words. The other monks formed a circle around the body and began chanting. The sound of the monks chanting echoed around the room. Tom stopped struggling and threw his arms around Tasia. They both stood helpless as they watched the monks chanting and swaying. Then they heard a sound. It seemed to come from the body. Tom quickly turned to look at the Captain. Suddenly the Captain's body began to twitch and shake. "What's happening?" Tom called out, but the monks couldn't hear him. Each of them was in a deep trance. Herallinos still held the bowl above his head and waved it from side to side. Strange words were coming from his mouth and echoed loudly around the room.

Then came the sound again. A loud groan came from the Captain and his lips moved. Tom went to move closer, but Rashidi grabbed his arm. "No, Tom – please wait,"

he shouted above the voices of the monks' chanting.

The Captain's eyes suddenly rolled opened and Tasia gasped in horror. They were each bright yellow with a black circle in the centre. Everyone stepped back in shock. Tom froze, he couldn't speak, he couldn't move.

The blood on the Captain's head rolled down the sides of his face and into his mouth. Suddenly, as if from some deep cavern far away, they heard a dreadful sound, it was like a roaring monster but it seemed to come from far away in the distance. The Captain's body began to shake violently.

Herallinos continued his chanting. The King and Bassar pulled Tom and Tasia away from the stone platform. Tom noticed then that Tasia, her father and brother had fallen to their knees with their heads touching the floor, as if in prayer.

The strange words from Herallinos echoed loudly all around the room and the monks began to sway even more frantically and their chanting grew louder. Then the room began to shake and the candles that were burning all around the room started to flicker wildly as a strange breeze started to blow through the windows high above them.

Tom stood still against the stone wall, his eyes were wide open. He was oblivious to the blood dripping from his wounded hand. Strangely, the pain had gone but now he couldn't move.

A terrible scream came from the Captain and a bright golden light burst from his mouth and whirled into the air. With it came a terrible screeching sound.

Herallinos stopped chanting and moved closer to the body lying helplessly on the stone. The other monks continued their frenzied chanting in strange voices that sounded like the screams of dying men, and the noise of their high screeching tones filled the room. Herallinos tipped the bowl over the Captain's lips and poured its contents into his mouth.

Then he picked up the Sword of Isis and climbed up onto the stone. He stood with one foot each side of the Captain. Then he began to speak again in strange words. Now he spat the words out. His voice was dark and the words croaked from his mouth in a deathly tone.

Rashidi suddenly ran forward. He held out his arms and fell to his knees. He started to shout in words similar to those of Herallinos. Tom was stunned and still he could not move. Tasia raised her head and began to rock her body back and forward. The strange words now came from her mouth also, but to Tom it seemed as though she had been possessed by something. She was rocking wildly back and forth in her trance.

Herallinos looked down at the shaking body beneath him. Still speaking in the strange tongue, he suddenly lifted up the sword and held it in both hands with the tip of the blade pointing down at Captain Hawkins. The Captain's bird-like eyes stared up at the monk.

Tom wanted to move, but his whole body was rigid; he couldn't move and he shook violently from inside, with his eyes wide and wild. It was as if he had been paralysed. He fought to break the hold as he watched, in horror, Herallinos with the Sword poised above the Captain. He was going to plunge it down into the Captain.

Tom had to break free, he had to move. In his head he tried to concentrate – make his mind work – think hard – break free; what was this hold over him? Then he worked his mind. *Mr Hawkins, don't let them kill you.* Then again he thought *Rumpitter!* and again *Help us!*

His body shook and juddered. His mind was trying to break out. He was trying to shout, "Free me!"

With the sword held over the body, Herallinos suddenly screamed out the most dreadful noise, a sound that no human could have made. The sword came down towards the Captain.

"NO!" Tom yelled. He suddenly snapped from his frozen state and screamed aloud. Bassar, the King and Tasia woke from their state and saw Tom run across the room. Tasia screamed at Herallinos as the sword came down.

A bright golden swirling light shot around the room, bringing with it a weird screeching sound.

The blade was plunging straight at the Captain's heart.

Mababe suddenly opened his eyes and jumped to his feet. Joseph heard it too, then Trouseau, Maris, Blake – all of them. They all heard the screams and ran to look up at the tower. The Arabs ran to the sides of their ships and stared up to the high cliffs above them. They could see the grey walls of the temple and then a glow of golden light flashing through small openings.

They heard the screams echoing through the sky around the temple and then a loud roar that shook the mountain. The sound carried out over the cliffs and then they saw the golden light swirling around the turrets.

Mababe drew his sword. "What is this evil?"

Joseph stood up and immediately started walking down the gang-plank. He called back to the others. "I do not know, but we will not wait around here. Come on men, we are not standing by any longer."

The comrades ran to the steps and immediately began the long climb up the cliff.

Captain Hawkins's eyes stared wildly. They were like those of a seagull – they stared upwards at the sword coming down towards him. Suddenly his arms moved and his hands lifted. A terrible roar, like the sound of a lion, came from his mouth. The blade fell towards him and suddenly, out of the air, a small, dark shape flew through the golden swirling light, straight towards the Captain and landed on his chest. As the blade came down, it thrust straight through the dark shape and into the heart of Captain Hawkins.

Herallinos immediately released his grip from the handle of the Sword of Isis and slumped backwards, his arms flopped down by his sides and his body fell limp. His knees collapsed and he fell onto the stone platform beside Captain Hawkins.

Tasia screamed out and Tom rushed towards the body. The screeching noise echoed all around them.

Rashidi was in a trance; his eyes were wide open, staring upwards. Tom ran around Rashidi and, as he approached the stone platform, the roar sounded again. It came from the Captain whose hands were gripping around the blade of the Sword. The golden swirling lights were flying everywhere and the sound of dark, strange voices filled the room.

Herallinos was kneeling beside the Captain as Tom came close. He turned his head towards Tom and opened his mouth. His blood red eyes caught Tom's bewildered look and then he spoke in a strange voice. It stunned Tom and he took a step back. He recognised the voice. "What? It can't be! No!"

Tom quickly turned to see the Captain's head was lifting from the stone slab. He was pulling the sword out of himself. As he did this, Tom suddenly saw Rumpitter lying across the Captain's chest. The sword had gone straight through him into the Captain's heart. Bravely, he had tried to save Captain Hawkins, but the sword had penetrated right through him and into the Captain. Tom was beside himself. "Rumpitter – no, no!" he screamed. He was suddenly taken even more aback when the Captain lifted himself up and pulled the sword out from his own chest. Rumpitter rolled over like a limp rag onto the stone top.

Herallinos growled the words, "You- you and him" he sneered down at the captain, "You thought you had killed me, but you were wrong." He pointed a crooked finger towards Tom and, in a terrible, deep croaking voice, he hissed the next words, "You young fool – stay where you are." Tom was completely stunned and very scared. Now, standing over the Captain, Herallinos spoke with the voice of the Saharadeen.

The King, Bassar and Tasia drew back in horror, but then Bassar pulled his sword from his belt. The other monks were still in a trance and the screeching still echoed all around them.

Herallinos stood tall and upright on the stone platform and turned his head around the room to see all those around him. His eyes were evil and menacing. Rashidi crawled away on his hands and knees as a bolt of fire flew over his head. The flame just missed him. He rolled over and quickly managed to grab Tom and pull him away from the stone.

At that moment the large wooden doors swung wide open and the comrades charged in, each of them with their swords drawn.

Rashidi called out, "The Saharadeen has returned from the underworld, keep back!"

The golden, swirling lights shot, like fire flashes, all around the room. Then there was another roar. The sound came again from the Captain, who was now on his knees. He held the Sword of Isis in both hands. Herallinos turned to look at the Captain. To everyone's astonishment he was beginning to change back from the wrinkled, dying wreck of a man, to himself. "Captain!" Tom yelled at the top of his voice and Tasia screamed as she saw Herallinos standing over him.

Joseph and the others made to rush forward, but Herallinos turned his hand towards them. A flash of light flew out from his hands and a ball of fire exploded in the air. The comrades all fell back. Everything was happening so quickly. Tom was trembling with fear, but somehow he found the strength to think hard and, without words, he said to the Captain, *Get him, Mr Hawkins, it's not Herallinos – it's the SAHARADEEN!*

Suddenly Captain Hawkins shook his head, as if he had just woken from a dream. He pushed down on the sword to lift himself up onto his feet. His torn and blooded robe fell to the ground. His face was bloodied, his skin had turned back to normal, but his eyes were still those of a seagull. He stared at the Saharadeen. Rashidi suddenly called out, "Only you – Captain. Only you can destroy him – with the sword!"

Tom stared at the sword and thought hard. He felt a strange force inside him. It was telling him to concentrate. "Think, think hard," he whispered to himself, and then, without words to the Captain, *Use the Sword, Mr Hawkins, the Sword!*

The Captain suddenly lifted the sword high above him and instantly the Stone in the handle of the sword began to flicker. Tom saw it and shouted, "Yes! That's it!"

Rashidi tried to keep Tom close, but Tom managed to pull himself free and charged over to the stone platform. Joseph screamed at him, "NO, Tom, stay back!" Tom didn't hear him and as he neared the stone, Herallinos saw him and waved his hand at him. A fire bolt caught Tom and knocked him over. He tumbled across the stone floor. Tasia ran to Tom, but Herallinos screamed at her. The tone of his voice was terrifying. Herallinos had been possessed by the Saharadeen. "Stand still or you will die!" Tasia looked over at Tom who lay still on the floor. "Tom!" she called. There was no answer.

Captain Hawkins suddenly swung the sword down, but Herallinos lifted into the air. He laughed and his evil laughter rang out all around. The roof shook and mortar began to fall from the ceiling.

The Captain was weak on his feet, but his eyes were wide open and his gaze was fixed on Herallinos.

Thunderbolts of flames whirled around the room. Everyone fell to the ground as the bolts of flames bounced off the walls and exploded.

Tasia threw herself over Tom as a fire bolt screeched past them. The Captain saw her and, for a second, he was transfixed. He looked at Tasia lying over the boy. Then a bolt of fire struck him and threw him across the stone platform onto the floor. The comrades tried to assist, but more fire bolts flew at them from the hands of Herallinos. Then, three of the monks were struck and died instantly. Herallinos was sending fire bolts all around the room. One flew straight at Mababe, but he managed to hold up his shield just in time and it bounced away and struck one of the of chairs, sending it bursting into flames. The golden crescent moon on the top of the chair fell to the floor.

Weird and dreadful sounds came out of Herallinos's mouth. Then he screamed out, "I will take you with me to the underworld. I am all powerful, I am King, I am..." The Captain suddenly screamed back at him, but it was not the true voice of Captain Hawkins, but some deep other voice. Tasia looked at him in terror.

"No – Saharadeen – I am King!" said the Captain as he thrust the Sword of Isis downwards and it caught Herallinos on his shoulder. Another terrible scream rang out. The comrades fell to the floor as the fire bolts whirled around once more. Then they heard the sounds of many strange voices. The confusion was so intense they were completely stunned and helpless.

Herallinos flinched from the strike of the sword, but then turned again to face the Captain. His twisted face glared and then he struck again with more fire bolts. The Captain leapt from side to side to escape the onslaught. Herallinos held both his arms upwards. He was shouting more strange words. He turned his head upwards to the ceiling. This gave the Captain a split second to react and he hurled the sword at Herallinos and it struck him directly in the heart.

There was violent explosion and a thunderous sound. Stones fell from the walls and the temple rocked. The floor began to move and the ceiling cracked. Lumps of stone fell down onto the floor. The pillars moved and began to topple. The whole temple was crumbling from the terrible thunder.

Suddenly everything stopped.

The bolts of fire vanished. Herallinos stood bolt upright. Everyone watched in horror. Then, slowly, Herallinos lowered his head to see that the sword had gone right through him and out of his back. He dropped to his knees. The Captain walked towards Herallinos and lowered his head. The stone in the sword was now glowing brightly.

Tasia felt Tom move under her. She slowly lifted up Tom's head. She was relieved to see his eyes opening. He blinked and then smiled. "It's over, isn't it?" he said.

Tasia kissed him on his forehead and turned to see Captain Hawkins standing over Herallinos. The Captain was fully restored as a man, but his head hung low. Rashidi rushed to the stone platform and took Herallinos's hand. The monk very slightly turned his head to Rashidi and nodded. Then he looked up at the Captain. "You -you have finally taken him from life – now he is gone. You should have used the Sword of Isis when you thought you had defeated him in the desert – then I..." Herallinos groaned and took a slow, deep breath. "Then I..." His head slumped forward and his body fell limply to the ground. The remaining monks immediately rushed forward. The King and Bassar walked towards the Captain, who was now kneeling beside Herallinos. With his fingers he closed the monk's eyes. Slowly he stood up and pulled the sword from the body. The other monks formed a circle around Herallinos and carried him to the stone platform, then lay him down, covered his head, knelt beside the stone and began to pray. The Captain laid the sword beside him and bowed to the body of the brave monk who had sacrificed his soul to save them. Captain Hawkins suddenly began to sway. Tasia and Tom caught him before he fell. Tasia held him in her arms. He dropped to his knees and the Princess dropped down beside him. Tom stepped back to leave them together. Tears streamed down his face. She placed her soft hand on the Captain's face and kissed him on his lips. The Captain looked up and she smiled to see his deep blue eyes looking back at her. They held each other tightly.

Tom walked across to the stone platform and saw Rumpitter's body lying there. He was covered in blood. Tom was sobbing as he stroked Rumpitter. He cried and thumped his fist on the stone, "Why – why Rumpitter?" As his hand hit the stone, he suddenly looked at the Sword and then at the blood from the wound in Rumpitter's side. He caught one of his tears as it fell down his cheeks and tipped it onto Rumpitter's wound and then placed the blade of the sword over Rumpitter. Nothing happened and he burst into tears again with his head in his hands. Suddenly he heard a voice from behind. "Tom, Tom." He lifted his head and saw the Captain standing over him. He placed a hand on Tom's shoulder. "No need for crying, Tom – look!" Captain Hawkins nodded his head towards the stone top and Tom turned around. He couldn't believe his eyes. Rumpitter was sitting up, twitching his nose towards him. Tom was overjoyed. "Rumpitter, you're alive!" he shouted.

Then he laughed aloud as he saw the rat wiping his eyes with his paw. "You're alive!" he rejoiced again. He lifted Rumpitter up and hugged him. "Ooh, be careful, Tom – not too tight, please. Oh, really," said Rumpitter.

The comrades were all standing around the boy. They cheered with delight to see Captain Hawkins had come back to them. They laughed at Tom cuddling the rat and they all threw their arms around each other in joy. Tasia held her Captain tightly and adoringly. For the first time in so many years, they were reunited. Captain Hawkins was so very happy and the Princess was able to laugh again. The moment they had waited so long for, had come.

The Captain looked into Tasia's green eyes and said, "My love, I knew we would be together – it was just a matter of time." He kissed her lips and she threw her arms around him.

Joseph and the comrades, each in turn, greeted their friend, their Captain, with the warmest embrace. Joseph was delighted when he shook his old friend's hand. "I hope you are not planning any more mad tricks now, Jeremiah. I don't think I could take the stress Captain," he laughed.

Captain Hawkins took Joseph's hand and holding it tightly turned to his comrades. He smiled and said, "I promise – no more tricks." Everyone laughed. The King held the Captain by both his arms. For a short moment he said nothing, but just stared into the Captain's eyes. Everyone looked on in silence. Then he hugged the Captain and said, "I cannot find the words to say how special this moment is. For the first time in so long, I see my daughter smile, I see men standing together who I thought I may never see again." He turned to Tom, adding, "And I see a young boy who comes from another world, but who will always be a part of ours – and will always be our friend." He stepped aside and bowed to Tom, who didn't know what to reply to such comments. Everyone cheered Tom and patted him on the back. Tom grinned at Rumpitter and then threw his arms around Captain Hawkins. "I'm so pleased you came back, Mr Hawkins."

The Captain looked down at Tom and said, "I owe everything to you, Tom. Thank-you."

Rashidi was looking on from the side, with a wide smile on his face. The King and Bassar looked appreciatively at the Egyptian and nodded to him. Rashidi bowed back to them.

Captain Hawkins went over to the body of Herallinos and knelt down beside him and the other dead monks.

The comrades realised that Herallinos had allowed himself to be possessed by the evil spirit of the Saharadeen, who had been sent to the underworld, leaving behind his evil curse. Herallinos knew the only way to heal the Captain was to bring the Saharadeen back from the underworld and for the Captain to slay him with the Sword of Isis. This way the Saharadeen would be banished for ever and the secret power of Isis would be returned to the Sword.

Joseph looked puzzled as he watched the Captain kneel beside the dead body of the monk who had sacrificed his life for the Captain's.

"I do not understand," he said, shaking his head quietly to Bassar. Then Rashidi came over to them. "Master, if I may explain?"

"Please do," Joseph replied. Everyone listened as the Egyptian began to unravel the complicated course of events.

He explained: "Herallinos knew that the Saharadeen had been slain, but unfortunately the Captain had used just a normal sword. This meant that the Sahaadeen was not completely dead. When he went into the underworld he still possessed his secret powers. Herallinos told me that the only way the Captain could be freed from his journey into the afterlife, would be to bring back the Saharadeen and kill him with the Sword of Isis. Only then would he be completely destroyed."

The physician continued: "Herallinos called on the great lord of the afterlife, Osiris, who loved the Goddess Isis. Together they were all powerful and vowed to save life from evil. Their love was bonded by the blood of lions, the courage of youth, the sacrifice of true friendship and the tears of love. This is why Herallinos needed the boy and the Princess." Rashidi paused for a minute and then continued. "I am not certain he accounted for an animal, such as a rat. I wonder if he thought the boy would be the ultimate sacrifice." Everyone turned to look at Tom, who stood motionless.

"However it seems that Herallinos knew of Tom's undoubted loyalty to the captain but to sacrifice the young boy to save the Captain was not the objective. I believe Herallinos realised this at the end". Rashidi turned to the body of Herallinos lying on the stone platform. "Therefore he made the ultimate sacrifice – not only to save the Captain, but for all and for the Sword of Isis and its secrets. He knew the sword must, at any cost, be kept from the hands of the Saharadeen who could have caused untold evil from the darkness beyond." Rashidi shook his head sadly, "I do not know if Herallinos knew he would die, but it was a risk he knew he must take. He was indeed a man of great courage." They all turned to look at Herallinos and the monks who stood next to the body.

Rashidi continued, "Herallinos made the ultimate sacrifice for he believed it was the only way. He believed in all things that are good and that all evil must be destroyed. He devoted his life to his God and to peace in all mankind. We salute Herallinos and pray that his spirit is free and at peace".

The comrades bowed their heads to the dead monk and then to the others. There was a moment of silence as they all thought of the words that Rashidi had delivered.

King Hafidh walked towards the stone and lifted up the Sword of Isis.

He turned to the monks and asked, "Who will now be your master?" The monks looked at each other. For a moment there was no answer, until they all turned to one who was standing slightly behind the others. His face was covered by his hood. He stood still with his arms folded in the sleeves of his gown. Suddenly all the monks bowed to him and stepped back for him to walk forward.

The monk walked calmly towards the King and lowered his head. "I am the one." His words were softly spoken. There was an air of serenity in the tone of his voice. The room was quiet. No one spoke or moved.

"Then to whom do I offer this Sword?" the King asked.

The monk bowed. "I am Christos," he replied. The monk lowered his hood and revealed his face. He was young and, unlike the other monks, he wore his hair long. In his blue eyes there was wisdom, and there was a sense of great strength and knowledge in his demeanour.

Christos smiled in a calm way that caused the King to feel strangely humbled in his presence. Everyone watched on in silence as the young monk stepped towards them.

The other monks went down on their knees with their hands together as in prayer.

Christos turned to Captain Hawkins and Princess Tasia and smiled. "Your lives together will give hope and joy to many. May you live long and in peace." The Captain bowed in thanks to the monk and said, "We owe so much. We will strive to make our world a good place – and for all." The monk nodded with a smile. "I believe you will," he replied and was about to turn away when the Captain stopped him.

"I have one further quest that must be fulfilled," he said. The Captain looked at Tom. "He must return to his..." The monk instantly interrupted the Captain. "I know of your quest, Captain Hawkins, and, indeed, you have a great task ahead of you." Christos looked carefully at the boy and then back at Captain Hawkins. "All that you have been blessed with is still with you. This gift has been given to you. Use the powers well and for none other than good – for the sake of all."

The Captain was about to say something when Tom stepped forward, "Um – excuse me, but I found this." Tom held out the gold crescent moon that had broken from one of the chairs and fallen on the floor.

The young monk looked at Tom very carefully for a short while, then he smiled and held out his hand. Suddenly, the golden moon lifted from Tom's hand and drifted through the air. It landed in the monk's hand. Tom and the others were amazed. "Wow!" said Tom, who was totally impressed by the monk's magic. "That's a great trick – how did you do that?" Tom asked with eyes wide open.

As Christos held the golden moon in his outstretched hands towards Tom, a screen of golden light glowed all around him and up towards the skylight in the dome of the ceiling. Suddenly there was a brilliant flash of light and then the golden glow disappeared. But the gold crescent moon had shrunk to half its size.

The monk stared into Tom's eyes.

"This is not magic – it is no trick. But it is for you. Please take it." The monk offered the small crescent moon to Tom.

"For me – why?"

"This is the moon that connects all worlds, the planets and stars and the past and future. Take this so that it may pass from this world to the next."

"But I don't understand," Tom said as the monk placed the small golden moon in his hand.

Christos smiled and said, "There is nothing to understand. It is for all that has passed and that is still to come. You will see."

"Thank-you – I will keep it safe for ever," Tom said, still unsure of what the monk really meant.

The Captain asked, "You mention the task ahead of us. We have to return Tom to his home. When will I know that the time is right to go?"

The monk nodded, as if he were considering the question carefully, but then he smiled again.

"The moon fell from the twelfth seat of the sacred circle of Serapis. It represents the twelfth sequence of the cycle of our moon. You will make your journey on the twelfth sequence."

The King now asked, "How will we know when the twelfth sequence falls?"

Tom was listening carefully and nodding to the questions being asked of the monk.

"Today shall be the first sequence of the cycle. Therefore you should journey on the twelfth day from this day." He looked at the boy. "I wish you well in your life ahead."

Tom looked up at the monk and swallowed the lump in his throat. He looked at his wounded hand and could not believe his eyes – the cut was completely healed, not even a scar.

The Captain looked at Tom and hoped that all would be well. They now must plan a difficult journey for him.

The monk turned to the King and held out both his hands. The King handed the Sword of Isis to Christos and bowed again. "I return this sword to you, as was my word. It has served its purpose well, but now it belongs with you to keep safe for all time and so that no evil will find its way again to the power it holds." The King stepped back and looked at the sword. It had meant so much and had such powers. He knew that it must be returned to the monks from whence it first came. The secret would stay with the monks for all time.

Christos held the sword for a moment and saw the stone shining brightly. He nodded to the King and turned to face all the comrades. He said simply, "This sword –it is not *what* it is, it is *why* it was given. It is nothing and yet it is everything. It is, therefore, what it represents – no more, no less." He bowed again to the comrades, turned and walked away with some of the other monks and disappeared through a door.

Tom scratched his head trying to understand what Christos had meant. It was beyond him, but he looked at the small golden crescent moon and wondered.

Four monks remained in the room.

One of them walked up to the King. "We will take our brothers now. You may leave. Our work is done here. We wish you a safe journey home."

Tom held the gold moon tightly in his hands and said, "I'm sorry about Herallinos – he was very brave."

The monk turned his head to one side and bowed.

The King bowed and gave his thanks.

In the early hours of the next day, the two ships sailed safely away from Mysticonissi.

They sailed in convoy. Captain Hawkins, with Princess Tasia and the comrades, took command of the small ship they had arrived in and the King and Bassar, with their men, sailed on the *Galênê*.

On that first evening, Tom gazed out across the blue sea and watched the *Galênê* sailing close beside them. It looked magnificent with the evening light shining on the triangular sail, casting an orange glow around the boat. He watched the King walking along the deck. He seemed to have a smile on his face. All was finally at peace.

He looked back at Captain Hawkins and Princess Tasia standing together at the stern of their ship. As the sun finally went down in the west, the evening sky began to sparkle with millions of stars twinkling above them. For the first time in many days, the moon was high in the sky and cast a soft, silvery glow across the ocean. It was a beautiful evening.

As Tom saw the couple standing together, in each other's arms, he saw a flash of light, like a shooting star, fly from the moon straight towards them. He was about to call out to them, but the Captain turned around and smiled. There was a blink of golden light from his eye.

Tom just smiled back.

After three uneventful days at sea, they finally sighted land. In the distance was the coast of Kadistaar and, beyond the shore, they could see the great city.

Tom was so excited to see land and all the small boats sailing out to greet them.

Rumpitter hopped up onto the rails. He said, without words to Tom and Captain Hawkins, *Oh my, what a wonderful sight. There was a moment when I thought we wouldn't...* The Captain interrupted and said, *Rumpitter, my dear friend, it was written that we would return here one day.* Tom heard the conversation and grinned. *I don't think I want to go through all that again."* The Captain laughed. *No fear of that, Tom.*

Tasia took the Captain's arm and hugged him. Rumpitter and Tom looked at each other and knew it was a good time to slip away and leave them.

Hundreds of small boats sailed out to circle the two big ships. The people on board the boats waved and cheered at the safe return of their King and Prince Bassar. They rejoiced even more when they saw Princess Tasia, who they had not seen in so many years. They also heard of the brave Captain Hawkins and his comrades and cheered up at them when they were spotted standing on the deck.

The sun was shining down, the sea was calm and blue and it was a welcome and happy return.

Eventually the two ships reached the entrance to the harbour of Kadistaar. Their sails were dropped and the oarsmen pulled the ships into the harbour.

As they docked alongside the harbour wall, horse riders from the King's personal guard were waiting to meet them on the quay.

The leader of the horsemen galloped along the harbour wall. When he saw the King, he saluted and called across to him, "As Salam Alaikum", and the King returned the greeting. "Wa Alaikum Salam".

"Everything is ready, my King – the city awaits your return." The guard turned with a wide smile across his face to the Princess and again bowed his head. "My Princess, we are so very pleased you are home again. So many people will be happy to see you here."

"Thank-you Ali, I cannot wait to see our home too." Tasia's face was alight with joy and she looked at the man standing beside her with a huge smile.

The rider greeted Captain Hawkins. "Sir, Captain, I am your servant. My country owes you so much. You will find many happy people waiting to see you in Kadistaar."

Captain Hawkins thanked the horseman and smiled at Tom and the comrades who were all grouped beside them.

Bassar greeted the riders and told them to bring horses.

No sooner had the ships tied their ropes to the quay, horses were led up to the foot of the gangways.

There was great commotion as a massive crowd formed along the harbour wall. Arab women began wailing in high pitched sounds and men waved and cheered.

As the King stepped down from his ship, the noise of cheering from the crowd was deafening.

He waved to his people. The welcome reception was incredible.

The King turned to the comrades. "This is truly a happy day," he said with outstretched arms and a wide grin.

The horses were lined up for the comrades to mount. One of the Arab soldiers pushed through the line of horses with Fahd, Tom's horse. The small horse stamped his hooves into the ground and neighed and snorted, bobbing his head up and down excitedly.

"Fahd!" Tom called out, and the small Arab horse leapt, with both front hooves, into the air. The handler held on tightly to the reins as Fahd stamped forward to greet Tom.

Bassar laughed. "I think he is very pleased to see you, Tom," he said.

Tom walked towards Fahd and the horse settled down and nuzzled his head into Tom's side.

Tom put both arms around Fahd's neck and hugged him. "Hello, Fahd," Tom said affectionately.

The horse gave a happy, satisfied snort as Tom hugged him.

The comrades all smiled to see the happy reunion.

Bassar and the King climbed onto their horses and the crowd roared with delight and then, when Tasia and Captain Hawkins mounted their horses, the crowd went wild with excitement.

As soon as everyone was ready, the soldiers called the crowds to move aside. As they passed through the streets Tom noticed how the rows of white houses were neatly arranged. The city was perfectly laid out with wide streets and row after row of whitewashed walls of houses in different shapes and sizes. Lush bushes with bright red and pink and yellow flowers were in abundance, growing up the sides of houses and along the tree-lined streets. Palm trees and wonderful fruit trees grew everywhere. Tom noted how well-kept everything was and how well dressed the people were. The wide array of coloured costumes was fantastic.

Then the sound of horns and drums started. People danced in the streets. Some jumped up onto rooftops to see them ride past and threw flowers down on them. It was a joyous occasion. Rumpitter had taken up his usual place sitting on the pommel of Tom's saddle and people laughed and cheered to see the young boy and the rat riding along.

Joseph and the comrades were waving back at the crowds and shaking hands with people as they rode through the streets. Trouseau was cheering back to people and, being the usual showman that he was, stood up on his saddle and bowed and waved. This caused even more excitement and cheering. The comrades all laughed as they watched Trouseau showing off.

Children ran along the streets and screamed with delight when they came alongside Princess Tasia's horse. She bent down to shake their hands and touch them. The children went wild with excitement to see their beloved Princess had returned.

Trumpets blew and people cheered as they followed the party all the way to the great palace.

The palace gates were open and the Al Kadi guards allowed the people into the grounds. They charged through in hoards.

The beautiful building was set amongst hundreds of tall palm trees and surrounded by beautiful grass lawns and by colourful plants. There were fantastic ponds with fountains and desert flowers growing around them. Tall marble columns were set along the pathway up to the main building, which was built in a sand-coloured stone. The roof was an enormous golden dome. Set onto the top of the dome was a giant golden crescent moon.

Finally they arrived at the palace. The King turned his horse around to greet the huge crowd that followed them through the gates and into the grounds. He waved to the crowds and they cheered back at him. Then the King addressed his people.

"Thank-you, people of Kadistaar, for your warm welcome. It pleases me to be able to tell you, this..." He paused for a moment and then continued, "All people of these lands are as one. There will be no more wars, no one will be hungry. No one will suffer. Our children will know no fear. We will live in peace together. The Saharadeen is gone – for ever!"

At this the crowd went mad with excitement. The cheering and screams of delight could be heard all across Kadistaar.

Then the King signalled to Captain Hawkins and Tasia to join him by his side. Again the crowd went wild. Tasia waved and cheered back. Tom and the comrades watched with pride as Captain Hawkins waved back at the thousands who had come to greet them.

The King called out to his people again. "Tonight we celebrate! We shall celebrate the victory and the future. Kadistaar is free and together we shall build a new world."

Again the crowds of thousands cheered.

All through the night, the city of Kadistaar was alive with celebration. People danced in the streets, musicians played and children joined in and laughed together.

The comrades were taken into the palace where they were given fresh clothes to wear and rooms to rest and wash. Everywhere was beautifully decorated.

A huge feast was prepared in the courtyards of the palace for the people of Kadistaar.

Captain Hawkins and Tasia took Tom to a room with a balcony that overlooked the palace grounds. From there, he could see far across the city. To one side he saw endless acres of date trees and fields of crops of all kinds. To the other side he saw the vast desert.

In the distance was the sea.

A large bed was prepared for Tom and, neatly placed on top, were the clothes that he had originally arrived in. Princess Tasia had arranged for them to be collected. She knew that if Tom was going to return to his own world, he would need his own clothes. They had been mended, washed and pressed. The Captain noticed Tom looking at them, and then he saw sadness in his face. He walked over and put his hand on Tom's shoulder. "Are you all right, Tom?" he asked.

Tom just nodded. "Tasia had your clothes mended and made ready for you," said the Captain quietly.

Then he saw a tear in Tom's eye. "Thanks," Tom said quietly.

He turned to Captain Hawkins and looked up at the tall man – the man who he first knew as a seagull and who had changed his life and taken him on the most amazing adventure.

He studied Captain Hawkins carefully. He was a tall, strong man with a rugged, but handsome, face. His tanned skin and brown shoulder-length hair gave him the character of a sailor, but yet there was something else about him that he hadn't noticed, until now. He looked ageless, if that was possible. And there was something else, too. He reminded Tom of his own father. The Captain's hair was not as grey and was longer. But his thin beard was similar – *perhaps that was it* Tom thought, and then he shook himself to speak. "I know I must go home, but I'm going to miss..."

"Shush now, Tom," Captain Hawkins interrupted, "let us not talk off such things, eh?"

Just then Tasia came into the room from the balcony.

She sat next to Tom on the bed and ran her hands over his clothes. She noticed how different they were to the clothes worn in Kadistaar, but then, of course, the boy came from another world, completely different to hers.

She kissed Tom on his cheek and it made him blush. Then he threw his arms around her and she held him tight and looked up at Captain Hawkins. She noticed the sadness in his eyes.

Captain Hawkins nodded and held back his emotions. "Tom, we have to make plans for your return. In the morning you and I will go down to the harbour. Rumpitter will go with you."

Tom pulled himself away from Tasia and looked up at the Captain.

"How will I get home?" he asked, holding back a tear.

"Why, *The Glaros*, of course. The same way you got here." The Captain paused for a moment and then said, "As much as we would love you to stay – your family will be waiting for you." The Captain now sat down on the other side of Tom and put his arm around him.

Tom said, "The last time I saw my father and the others they had fallen asleep on *The Eagle*." He suddenly jumped up. "Oh my God, I have been away for ages, they'll be searching for me. They'll think I'm dead!"

Captain Hawkins smiled and, in a reassuring way, said, "No, no Tom. You have forgotten. Remember what I told you about the times – the difference between our worlds? Yes, you have been here for days, but in your world, where your father is, it has been but a few seconds. They are still asleep."

"What? Oh, oh yes. Let me think. How many days have I been away?" Tom was trying hard to work it out.

"Tom, you need not worry. One day in this world is but a blink of an eye in yours. In your time – your world – you have been gone for just a few seconds." Captain Hawkins stood up and started to think to himself.

"Let me see. We must be at the cross point on the twelfth sequence of the moon. We have passed four already," he said, thinking out loud, and then he walked out onto the balcony, talking away to himself. The sun was going down and the purple-red sunset appeared over the desert.

Tasia joined the Captain on the balcony. In the distance they could hear the sounds of people celebrating. "Do you think all will be well, Jeremiah?" she asked.

Captain Hawkins turned to her and nodded, "It will be well – as long as we get there on time."

"When you came back, you were..."

"Yes, I know – I was a bird. But I still have the powers. I know I do. The monk told me so. I just cannot feel anything right now.". He leaned over the balustrades and gazed into the distance. "I feel strangely uneasy about it. The time was perfect when I met Tom and the crescent moon was in the right sequence. I made it work – just right." He paused in thought and then said, "As long as we set off at exactly the right time, it will work – it must."

"When will you go?"

"Tomorrow – we will set sail in the afternoon. It will take us two days to reach *The Glaros*. This time we will arrive from a different location. But I still do not know if I can do it. The monk, Christos, told me I still have the power – but where is it? I feel nothing."

"I shall come with you," Tasia said adamantly, looking into his eyes. The Captain's eyes seemed distant. "No, my love – I have to do this alone." He held her arm tightly and then kissed her on the forehead.

Tasia gazed into the Captain's eyes. "I could not bear to lose you again, my love."

In the great hall, a huge feast was prepared and servants happily went about their business of serving everyone. The comrades joined in and chatted with all the other guests. Heads of tribes gathered from all parts of Kadistaar. Al Jadda and his sons were delighted to see the comrades all safe and well. It was a wonderful reunion of people from all corners of the lands.

At last, there came the sound of trumpets and the large doors swung open. Several soldiers in magnificent robes entered the great hall. Through the doors, the King appeared, accompanied by his wife, Queen Dorothea radiant and beautiful, dressed in a long white and gold robe, with a jewel-covered gold head-dress. She was the daughter of a highly respected Greek King. She had fallen in love with King Hafidh when they were children and they had been together ever since. Many spoke of her Goddess-like appearance and the people respected her as the woman who helped to bring peace to the lands of the east. By marrying King Hafidh Al Kadi, the lands from east and west had formed a strong bond of friendship.

Everyone cheered as they entered.

Queen Dorothea waved to the guests. The comrades bowed to her as she approached them. She didn't speak, but her smile was enchantingly captivating. She was delighted to see them all again.

Then there was another blast from the trumpets and Prince Bassar entered. Closely behind him came Captain Hawkins with Princess Tasia on his arm. Everyone cheered and applauded them.

Earlier, before the guests were called to the great hall, Braheim and Joseph had visited Tom in his room. They laughed to see three young servant girls trying to dress him in a long white Arab robe. The girls giggled when they tried to get Tom into the regalia, but Tom was all arms and legs. He was so embarrassed.

Braheim told the girls that he would assist the boy. He thanked them for their efforts and the girls left the room.

Then the rest of the comrades came into Tom's room. They too had all dressed in fantastic traditional festive regalia.

"You see, Tom, it is not just you who must dress for the occasion," said Trouseau, who tugged and pulled his tunic to try to make it fit properly.

When the comrades all looked at each other, with the exception of Maris and Braheim, they laughed.

"These are the traditional robes to wear in the court of the King. It is nothing to laugh at," Braheim said.

"Aye, Braheim, my friend, but you and Maris are used to such things. We are not. But I must admit, one does feel strangely civilised in this attire – don't you think so, men?" he said to the comrades.

"Oh, yes, Joseph, completely civilised," answered Gordon, and then Sam Little said, "It is the least we can do for such generous hospitality, I say."

The comrades all agreed that to wear such noble clothes in the house of the King of Kadistaar was absolutely the right thing to do.

Then they all patted each other on the back and laughed. Tom enjoyed being with these courageous and most excellent men and had a very wide smile on his face as he looked at them all chatting and laughing together. Then he thought how much he was going to miss them. He knew, after tonight, he would never see them again.

Joseph sensed Tom's thoughts and discretely coughed loudly. The others all realised exactly why and stopped talking. They all turned towards Tom.

Mababe, the giant African warrior, stepped towards Tom and put his hands on the boy's shoulders. Tom looked up at the huge man. Mababe's deep brown eyes smiled kindly at him.

Mababe, being a man of few words, did not need to speak, but Tom could read his thoughts.

One by one the comrades stepped over to Tom and embraced him as a friend. Joseph was the last to do so and then he spoke for all of them.

"Tom, lad." He cleared his throat. "Ehem, I – we all want you to know that we feel greatly honoured to know you. We will always think of you as one of us – our friend, our comrade." Joseph looked around at the others. They all nodded in agreement.

"It has indeed been a very strange time for all of us and many unexplained things have happened. To be honest, I will never fully understand any of it." Then he smiled, "Why, it has been quite some adventure – don't you think?"

"Yes Joseph, it certainly has," Tom replied with a wide smile.

Joseph nodded and put his hand on Tom's shoulder. "Wherever you are, whatever you are doing, in whatever world you may live – always remember us and look upon us as your brothers. We will never forget you. Why, we can be your other family, Tom. You can see us as your other family in another world, eh?" Joseph was still smiling when Tom looked at all the men standing around him. Tom had a large lump in his throat and was trying very hard to hold back a tear.

"I could never forget you all and I will miss you very much. Thanks for being my friends."

They all shook Tom's hands and then started chatting together about all the things that had happened.

They could now look back on all the events that had taken place. There had been many dangerous and worrying moments, but now it was over. For a while they talked and laughed and joked about everything and it made Tom feel better.

What an adventure it had been indeed.

The great hall of the palace of the King and Queen of Kadistaar was huge. The high walls were covered in brightly coloured frescoes and wall paintings of the desert and Arab life. There were wonderful statues of past rulers, prophets and writers and scholars. Large coloured woven carpets and rugs hung from gold rails around the walls. Tall sculpted marble pillars lined each side of the hall. The ceiling was a painted blue sky with white clouds that seemed to move slowly, as if they were being carried by the breeze. In the centre of the ceiling was the gold crescent moon with stars scattered around it. Tom was convinced he saw the stars sparkle.

The marble-tiled floor was also covered with enormous woven rugs of many colours.

In the centre of the room was a long ebony black table with a hundred chairs set all around. The table was lavishly dressed with white and gold linen tablecloths and gold plates and goblets.

The servants brought huge trays of food into the hall.

The King gestured to the guests to sit wherever they wished.

Everyone chatted and laughed and enjoyed the wonderful food cooked by the King's chefs.

Speeches and toasts were made and everyone laughed at the jokes and stories told around the table.

Tom looked around the room, watching everyone talking and enjoying the festive occasion.

He knew this would be his last evening with these incredible people. He saw Trouseau chatting happily with Rashidi, the physician, and Braheim and Maris deep in conversation with one of the King's seniors. Sam Little and Gordon were picking their way through the food as if it was the last meal they would ever have. Gordon sat smiling at everyone. He seemed to be far away in a day dream.

Captain Hawkins caught Tom's eye from the other end of the table. He winked at Tom and, just for a split second, Tom saw a flash of light sparkle from the Captain's eye. Tom smiled and then heard the Captain's voice. *Can you hear me Tom?'* he asked without words. Tom replied *Yes, I can.*

*Good – I know what you are thinking, Tom. Enjoy this evening and tomorrow we must travel. Do not worry – all will be well.*

*I just wish I wasn't going* replied Tom. *I don't know what I will do when I get back. I'm not going to see you again, am I?*

There was a pause and Tom looked down the table. Captain Hawkins was suddenly staring at him with wide eyes. His stare was quite odd, as if he had seen a ghost.

*Mr Hawkins, are you all right?* Tom asked without words. *Mr Hawkins?* he repeated.

*Tom – oh my Lord. It has come to me.*

*What has – are you all right?*

Captain Hawkins was still staring; his stare was very intense, as if he had suddenly realised something. He called over to Tom. "Quick Tom – we have to go now. I have made a big mistake." Suddenly Captain Hawkins jumped out of his chair. He took Tasia by the arm and led her to one side of the hall. Tom saw them speaking quickly together. The King and Bassar noticed them talking and Bassar left the table and went over to them. "My friend, are you well, you seem troubled?" Bassar asked and looked over his shoulder to see his father watching them.

"Bassar, I have made a mistake. I have to take Tom now. I can only sail to the crossing place on the twelfth sequence. I have to find the navigator stars and be in exactly the right place on time."

Bassar nodded his head, trying to take in what the Captain was saying. "But you have at least six days – there is no hurry, surely?"

"Yes, we must hurry. I had not considered the winds. At this time of the season the winds are slight. If we don't go now, we may not make the crossing point in time. It could take us days to get there. I need to be under the stars to navigate the line to the crossing point. Then *The Glaros* will do the rest. This is what happened before. I cannot risk it any other way."

Bassar's expression suddenly changed. He realised what the Captain had said was true.

"Then we must make haste," he said quickly and turned to his father and nodded to him.

Captain Hawkins looked over to find Tom still staring across the room at him. Without words, he said, *Tom, you will have to come with me. We must go now!*

Tom was stunned by the sudden reality of what was happening. He was really leaving and it was now. Tom jumped out of his chair and walked quickly to join the Captain.

Joseph and the comrades noticed what was happening and looked to each other to make a move.

Joseph was the first to leave his seat and joined them. "Jeremiah, what is happening?"

"Joseph, I am afraid I must take Tom now. I am sorry for this sudden change. I miscalculated the sailing time and I fear we may be too late."

Joseph looked at the boy and back at the Captain. "Then we shall go now. We will go with you."

"No Joseph, I have to do this alone, but thank-you."

"Captain, please. You will need all the help you can get and we are with you on this. We will help you sail to *The Glaros* and see Tom safely home. It is the least we can do."

Tasia held Captain Hawkins by the arm and said, "Let them go with you, my love – you may need them and they want to help."

After a short pause, the Captain finally said, "Very well, Joseph. Thank-you my friend."

There was no time to lose.

Horses were brought immediately to the courtyard of the palace. The comrades and Bassar said their farewells to everyone, then mounted their horses and galloped off ahead into the night, towards the harbour.

Tom looked around him to see, for the very last time, the wonderful palace of Kadistaar.

Princess Tasia threw her arms around Tom and then she gave him a cloth bag.

She hung the strap of the bag over his head so that it hung around him. She adjusted the strap so he would not lose it.

"Tom, you will need this. Inside are your clothes," she said. Tom saw a tear in her eye. "Thank-you Tasia, I wish I could stay." Tasia hugged him tightly and kissed him on the side of his face.

"One day, Tom, we shall see each other again. But for now, I shall pray for your safe journey home." Then she kissed him again. "Now go, my little Prince and God go with you."

Captain Hawkins came over to them with two horses. "I am sorry, we must leave now," He held the Princess in his arms and spoke quietly to her. "I will see he gets home and I promise you I will return, my love." The Princess held her Captain tightly and said, "I shall wait for you – please take care and come back to me. I do not want to lose you again." She kissed him goodbye.

Tom turned to see the King standing before him. He leant down and took Tom's hand.

"Look after yourself. We have everything to thank you for and we will always honour your name in these lands, Tom." The King smiled and then said, "Go with your heart and your strength – back to your world. Take with you all that you have learned and never forget. You will never be forgotten here." The King, putting a hand on Tom's head, closed his eyes. It was as if he was saying a prayer. Then he took his hand away and stood up. The Queen came over and smiled. She took Tom's hand and kissed him on the cheek. "Go in peace and be safe," she said very softly.

Al Jadda and his sons also came to say farewell. Tom thanked Al Jadda for his help in the desert.

Captain Hawkins came over with Fahd.

"Tom, think you can ride him one more time?" Tom smiled to see his horse. "You bet I can!" he replied and everyone laughed. It was really more that they laughed to hold back their emotions. The departure of the boy was never going to be easy for anyone.

"Up you get then Tom," the Captain said and Tom climbed up into the saddle and took the reins.

They were about to set off when Tom called out, "Wait!" Everyone turned round.

"What is it Tom?" Captain Hawkins asked

"Rumpitter, where's Rumpitter?" Tom said, looking all around him.

Suddenly a voice came into his head, *Tom, I am coming – just get going!* Tom smiled when he heard the voice and he saw that Captain Hawkins had heard it too. "You see, Tom," he said, "I told you all would be well." The Captain turned in his saddle to see Princess Tasia with her mother and father standing on the steps of the palace. He gave a little wave and bowed to the King and Queen. Tasia held up her hand and blew a kiss. Rashidi appeared on the steps waving his arms in the air. They all carried on waving until the Captain and Tom had disappeared into the night.

They charged through the winding streets of Kadistaar and out onto the road to the coast.

Soon they arrived at the harbour. The King's ship, *Galênê*, lay alongside the long stone wall. The two soldiers from the King's guard who accompanied Captain Hawkins and Tom, took the reins of their horses. Tom dismounted and gave Fahd a farewell hug. The horse neighed and snorted, stamping his front hooves on the ground. "Goodbye, Fahd. I will miss you too," Tom said quietly into the horse's ear. The horse nodded his head up and down and turned his head to look at Tom. His eyes looked sad and Tom gave him another big hug. Then, with a tear in his eye, Tom pulled himself away and ran up the gang-plank with Captain Hawkins.

The comrades were standing along the sides of the ship.

"Everything is ready. Sails ready to drop and lines ready to let go. We will help to row her off," said Joseph.

Bassar came up to the Captain and embraced him. "This is where I must leave you, my brother.

"I will pray for your safe journey and speedy return." Then he gave a wide smile and nodded in the direction of the palace. "My sister awaits you."

"Thank-you, my friend. Look after her for me. I will return to Kadistaar as soon as I know Tom is safely returned to his people."

Bassar shook Tom's hand. "It has been a pleasure to know you – young one. I hope you will think of us occasionally." Then he smiled and nodded his head in the direction of Fahd. "I will look after your horse – just in case you should decide to come and see us again, yes?"

Tom smiled up at Bassar and said, "Yes, thank-you Bassar. That would be very nice. I hope I will."

"Good – then it is done." Bassar clapped his hands firmly on Tom's shoulders and said goodbye.

No sooner had Bassar left the ship, the gang-plank was hauled aboard and the shorelines released. The comrades took the oars and rowed the ship away from the harbour wall.

A single light glowed from a lamp at the stern as she slowly slipped her mooring and sailed through the still waters of the harbour towards the open sea.

Tom looked back at the harbour and saw Bassar galloping along the beach on his beautiful black stallion. He was holding the flag of Kadistaar. He charged towards the rocks at the end of the estuary. The comrades watched him reach the point at the end of the bay. His horse reared up on its hind legs. Bassar called out some words in Arabic. It was very faint with his voice being carried in the wind. "What's he saying, Braheim?" Tom asked.

Braheim smiled at Tom and replied, "He says, go in peace – Kadistaar will always be your friend, Tom Parker."

Tom smiled and waved. The *Galênê* sailed out of the estuary, round the point and then Bassar and Kadistaar were gone.

Captain Hawkins took the helm and steered the ship into the great sea. The stars lit the sky like diamonds against a backdrop of dark silk. Their reflections sparkled on the surface of the water. It was a still and peaceful night. *Too still* thought Captain Hawkins.

Tom stood next to the Captain and watched with a heavy heart as the lights of Kadistaar slowly disappeared behind them. He wondered if he would ever see the beautiful city again.

# Chapter 13 – Flight of The Glaros

A sudden sound caused Tom to turn quickly. His heart lifted when he saw Rumpitter hop onto the rail bedside him.

*Hello Tom. Well it seems our journey has begun quicker than we thought* Rumpitter said without words. Tom was delighted to see the rat looking up at him with his sparkling brown eyes.

"Captain Hawkins said we had to leave because there won't be much wind. I think he's worried we won't make it in time," Tom replied.

"Yes, that is correct".

"But what will happen if we don't get where we have to be, on time?"

"Well – let us see what the good Captain can come up with, shall we?" Rumpitter replied, and then he said, "Knowing Captain Hawkins, he will have something up his sleeve. Why don't you get some rest. It could be a long night." Rumpitter jumped down from the rail and started towards the companionway. Tom followed him down the stairs. He found a cabin and fell into a bed. In no time at all he was asleep. Rumpitter stayed with him for a while curled up at the end of the bed,.

The comrades rowed the ship relentlessly until they were completely exhausted. For so few men to row such a heavy ship was very hard and they were making little progress.

At last, after some considerable time, a slight breeze filled the sail and suddenly they were sailing. "Thank the Lord for that!" Gordon said, flopping onto his side. Blake and Little also let go of their oars and fell back in exhaustion with sweat running down their faces. Although it was slow going, the small Arab ship was finally moving with some wind in her sails.

Mababe took a bucket of water and threw it over the men to cool them down. It was very welcome.

Captain Hawkins ran down the steps to the rowing deck. "You have done well, men – thank-you. Take a well-earned rest now. You will find plenty of water and food. The King has provisioned well for us. We will not go hungry or thirsty on this voyage."

Joseph stood up and stretched his aching back. He walked over to the Captain. "How long will it take to reach our destination, Jeremiah?" he asked.

"I have calculated three days to reach *The Glaros*. Then we will have one clear day." He gestured for Joseph to walk away with him to one side. He needed to speak in private.

"Yes Jeremiah, what is it?" Joseph asked.

"While Tom is sleeping, I wanted to talk to you." He paused and then looked into Joseph's eyes.

"I am worried, Joseph. The last time I did this, I was a seagull with the powers of the Stone of Isis. I was able to do many things at that time. I am not certain that I still have these powers and I cannot guarantee that I will be able to take Tom across to the other side. To his world. If I do, I can't be sure if I will be able to return." He took Joseph by both arms and spoke quietly and in a serious tone, "Joseph, you and the comrades will only come with us as far as *The Glaros* and then I will take Tom across alone."

"What are you saying Jeremiah?"

"I am saying that I do not know what will happen. All I know is that we must return Tom to his people – before it is too late." The Captain stepped away and stared out to sea. "Out there, Joseph, is a strange place where I once discovered that I could cross into the other world. The first time I did it, I did not realise what would become of me. After all, I was a seagull. I was the victim of an evil curse, but I had been given such strange and mystic powers, I could do many things. I knew I would not grow old. In my heart, I knew that.

How do I know now that, as a man, I can achieve the same journey – to go there and return as I am? How do I know that I can get Tom back to his people and return to where we came from? The monk told me that I have the power, but I do not feel anything. It is not like before – it feels different."

Joseph studied the Captain for a moment and then replied: "I do not understand about strange powers, but I do know one thing. That wise monk, Christos, at Mysticonissi, told you that you have what is needed. So, you must search inside yourself for the answer. Whatever happens, my friend – we are with you and we will help you do whatever must be done."

The Captain looked at his friend and nodded. He knew that somehow he must find the way.

The two men stared out across the ocean for a while until Joseph said, "I think you need some time to yourself, my friend. Think hard on this and find a way." He patted the Captain on the shoulder and walked away.

All through the night, Captain Hawkins stared out to sea, alone and in deep thought.

In the early hours, while all were sleeping, the Captain stood alone at the helm looking out across the starry sky. The sea was so calm and the gentle breeze barely moved the ship through the water.

Captain Hawkins paced up and down along the deck. *Think hard, why can't I feel anything?* he thought to himself. He tied a rope around the wooden tiller to keep the ship on course and then started pacing back and forth, asking himself over and over again, *There must be something – where is it?*

*You are not thinking logically,* came a voice in his head.

It startled him and he turned around to look down the deck. No one was there. He shook his head. *It must be my imagination.*

*Yes – you have it Captain – use your imagination,* It was the voice again. This time Captain Hawkins grabbed the lamp from the hook behind the helm and held it up to shine a light down the deck. "Who goes there?" he said nervously, looking into the darkness.

*It is me Captain* said the voice. The Captain held the lamp a little further forward and then he saw Rumpitter sitting on a wooden box.

"Rumpitter – it's you!"

"Yes, Captain – I heard your thoughts. If you don't mind me saying, I don't think you are thinking this through properly."

"What, what do you mean?"

Rumpitter jumped off the box and hopped onto the rail next to Captain Hawkins. He took a big breath and said, "Excuse me for being so blunt, but you seem to have forgotten something."

"You think? How so?"

"Well, in the past, when you have wanted to make something happen – you just thought it and it happened. Use your imagination – that's what you always told me."

"Easy for you to say that, Rumpitter, but I can't remember how to."

Rumpitter interrupted, "Yes you can!" He stood up on his hind legs and whispered into the Captain's ear.

Captain Hawkins pulled his head away and stepped back. "I – I can't do that!" he said out loud.

"Shush," said Rumpitter, "you will wake everyone up. Now come on, pull yourself together, you know it is the only way." Then Rumpitter shook his head from side to side. "I can't believe I am saying this to you, of all people."

Captain Hawkins stepped back to the far side of the deck and turned to look across the sea and then up at the stars. His eyes searched through the night sky. Rumpitter sat on the rail and his little brown sparkling eyes stared hard at the Captain.

Captain Hawkins gripped his hands tightly on the railing as he looked up to the stars.

For a moment all was still. Suddenly he began to shiver. His hands shook and then his legs wobbled. Up amongst the stars, a bright light flashed across the sky. A crescent moon appeared, beaming down a ray of light. It shot directly towards the Captain.

There was another bright flash and Captain Hawkins let out a dull grunting sound. Rumpitter tipped his head to hear what was happening. He couldn't see the Captain's face. "Captain?" he asked curiously.

Captain Hawkins suddenly turned round to face Rumpitter and the rat jumped back, nearly falling off the rail into the sea. He managed to grab the rail just in time and scrambled back on top.

"Oh my – I think you have done it, Captain."

Captain Hawkins stared across the deck at Rumpitter. His eyes had turned golden with a black circle in the centre. In the middle was a small crescent moon. His eyes blinked and a golden light sparkled out from them.

For a moment the Captain seemed to be staring into space, but then he began to shake again. He crouched down on his knees. There was a flash of golden light and, to Rumpitter's utmost surprise, standing before him was a large seagull.

For a moment the bird seemed to wobble a little. It looked very unstable sitting on the rail. Rumpitter quickly jumped up.

*Oh no you don't*, Rumpitter said without words and, with his nose, he pushed the seagull onto the deck. *Not until you find your wings, Mr Hawkins.*

The seagull wobbled around and then tried to flap its wings. Then it fell over.

*Come on – you will have to do better than this* said Rumpitter. *Think hard, use your imagination.*

The seagull floundered around on the deck and twisted its neck from side to side.

"Ugh, ouch, ow! It's easy for you to say, Rumpitter," the seagull replied. He looked at the rat sitting on the deck in front of him.

"Did it hurt?" Rumpitter asked as he prodded the bird with his nose to stop it falling over again.

"Ouch There's no need to be so rough, Rumpitter."

"Sorry. I am trying to help. How do you feel?"

The seagull shook its head, "I don't know really. It doesn't hurt so much, but it feels, well, –cramped."

"You will get used to that I suppose. You have done it before. Do you think you can fly?"

"Give me a moment, it is not so simple," said the seagull, now standing a little straighter.

"Mmmm, well, take a breath, count to ten and try," Rumpitter said and then stepped back.

The seagull sighed and then lifted one of his wings and flapped.

"That is not going to do it. You'll have to try harder than that," Rumpitter insisted.

"Rumpitter, you are intolerable sometimes," said the seagull and then he lifted the other wing.

"That is as may be, but you have to try harder – you always say practice makes perfect. So now, come on, up you get – and do it!" said Rumpitter with an air of authority.

The seagull gave a moan and stood up on both legs. "I will try," he said reluctantly.

He lifted both his wings and flapped them. He jumped up and then fell back down.

"Come on – that was a good start," said Rumpitter, moving back a little further.

"I AM trying," the seagull said defiantly.

He lifted both wings again and, this time, gave a hefty flap up and down. He rose up off the deck and flapped his wings again.

"Yes, yes, that's it, good," encouraged Rumpitter.

The bird lifted up about four feet and then gave another flap. He was in the air, but as he raised his wings again he came crashing back down onto the hard deck.

"Ouch!" he cried. "I cannot believe this is so difficult," he said, straightening his neck from the rough landing.

"Then do it again. You need to get the rhythm right – up and down, up and down," Rumpitter insisted. "This time really believe you can do it. Now come on, before you wake up the whole ship."

Mr Hawkins looked up at the mast. He wondered if he would be able to get as high as that.

He jumped up, raised his wings together and gave a final flap. Suddenly he was airborne. He flapped again and rose up a little higher.

"Yes, yes," said Rumpitter excitedly. "Go for it."

Mr Hawkins kept up the rhythm with his wings, trying to get them working together. He hovered for a moment and then raised his neck and lifted both wings. The air caught underneath and, amazingly, he was in the air. "I can do it Rumpitter, I'm flying, look." Suddenly the breeze caught him and he was whisked to one side, then turned upside down. He flew straight into some rigging. He tried to lift his wings to get away but became entangled in the ropes. Rumpitter covered his eyes with a paw. The seagull crashed back down to the deck with a mighty thump.

Rumpitter hopped over to him. "Oh dear, are you all right?" he whispered.

The seagull ended up in a heap with his wings over his head. There was a grunt and a moan and a cloud of bright golden light appeared. Rumpitter, dazzled, cowered back and then saw Captain Hawkins had returned – as a man. He was curled up in ball, not moving.

Rumpitter nuzzled him with his nose. "Captain?" he said quietly.

Another moan and suddenly the man moved an arm, and then one leg moved from under him.

"Ugh – ouch." Captain Hawkins moaned and pulled himself onto his knees. He held his head in his hands. "That was not very good, was it?" he said painfully.

"No, not really." Rumpitter was relieved that the Captain was alright.

The Captain gave Rumpitter a hard look.

"Well, I suppose it wasn't a bad first attempt. You will need a little more practice before we try anything else."

Captain Hawkins sat on the deck looking at the rat. Now, fully restored as a man, he wiped his brow and rubbed his bruised arm. He sighed, "I hope I can do this Rumpitter – I have to."

Rumpitter suddenly looked up, his nose twitched and then he whispered, "Someone is coming, quick." He scampered away into the shadows.

Braheim appeared on the steps leading up to the helm deck and saw Captain Hawkins leaning on the tiller with his head held down. He was wiping his eyes. He looked oddly at the Captain. "I thought I heard something fall – is everything well, Captain?" he asked.

"Yes, Braheim, all is well thank-you, I dropped the marlin pin. I am sorry if I woke you."

Braheim saw the wooden pin used for securing ropes through the wooden cleats. He picked it up and put it back in its rightful place. He looked at the Captain again curiously. "Captain, maybe you should rest. I can take over here if you wish."

The Captain did not know if his eyes had returned to normal and held his scarf over them, pretending to wipe the salt from his face.

*Rumpitter?* he called without words.

*You are fine, Captain. Get some rest* came the silent reply.

Captain Hawkins removed the scarf and smiled at Braheim. "All is well my friend. If you wish to take the helm for a spell, I would be most grateful. Maybe a short nap would do me good," he replied heartily.

Braheim gave a wide smile, now he could see all was well.

The morning came with a ray of sunshine through the cabin window. The gentle rocking motion of the ship caused the sunlight to flicker across Tom's face. He blinked when the sun shone across his eyes. He pulled himself out of bed and walked across to the window. The sea was as flat as glass. There was not a single cloud in the sky. He could hear the sails flapping and the ropes tugging in their wooden cleats. The ship was almost at a standstill. Then he heard footsteps above him. He wiped his eyes, put on his shoes and went up on deck.

The comrades were all peering out across the flat sea. Captain Hawkins was pacing around by the helm. Joseph was leaning on the tiller looking up at the sails.

"I think we should get the oars out, Jeremiah," said Joseph, shaking his head.

"We have to do something, Joseph, or we will flounder like this all day."

"Aye, Captain. I will get the men into action," Joseph replied and called down to the deck below.

"Men, break out the oars and let's get this ship moving," he yelled. The comrades dashed down to the rowing deck and broke out the oars. In no time at all, there was a series of clumping sounds and then several splashes as the large wooden oars were pushed through the rowing ports and dipped into the sea.

With only a few men, they knew well that it was going to be tough going to move such a vessel through the sea with just the oars, but the comrades pulled the long oars through the water and slowly the ship moved along. But it was very slow.

The Captain admired his comrades for their effort, but he knew it would not be nearly enough. They needed more speed. Much more speed.

He watched in frustration as the sails flapped on the booms. He could hear the grunts and strains from the comrades as they tried to move the ship. It was hopeless.

He thought hard, *What shall I do? I need a miracle. We have lost a day already. There must be something.*

From somewhere in the distance, he heard a sound. Then it went. He tried to listen again, but there was nothing. He shook his head from the thought and went below to take an oar alongside the comrades.

Tom saw the comrades heaving on the oars and decided to try and help. He took hold of an oar and tried to pull on it. It was too heavy and he was unable to keep in time with the men.

"Thank-you Tom, but even we cannot pull this ship. We are too few," said Joseph.

The Captain threw down his oar. "You are right, Joseph. Give it up, men. It is hopeless to think we can row like this all day. Take a rest."

The comrades looked at the Captain and saw the frustration he was suffering. They wanted to help, but there was nothing they could do.

"Captain, the wind will come soon, I am certain," said Trouseau, trying to cheer things up.

The Captain nodded and smiled at his friend and went back up on deck. The comrades looked at each other and felt sad that they could not do any more.

Captain Hawkins stood at the foot of the mast and gazed up at the lookout post, high up at the top of the mast. He put one foot into the rope ladder and began to climb to the top. When he reached the lookout platform he stepped on and looked down at the deck below. He could see Tom standing at the helm looking up at him. Tom waved and he waved back. The comrades were chatting amongst themselves and Braheim had the tiller, trying to keep a course as they floundered on the calm sea. The sun beat down on them and the day grew hotter and hotter.

Captain Hawkins scanned his eyes all around. The sea was as flat as mercury. There was nothing in sight – not a single cloud, not a single thing, just miles and miles of flat, blue sea.

*There must be something I can do* he thought, *but what?* He thought and thought as he gazed across the ocean.

His thoughts were suddenly shaken when he heard a faint voice calling. "Captain, Captain." He looked around and cast his eyes down to the deck below.

He saw the comrades all running to the stern of the ship. Tom was waving up at him with both arms in the air. "Captain Hawkins!" Tom shouted.

"Yes Tom, what is it?" he called back.

Tom waved his arms franticly. Then the Captain saw him pointing behind them. He looked back across the sea and his eyes opened wide in astonishment.

A large black cloud was moving towards them. It seemed to be changing in shape. The black cloud was lifting up and then down towards the sea.

*What kind of cloud is that?* The Captain wondered to himself. It grew larger as it came closer. Then he saw something. He immediately called down to the men on deck. "Everyone – hold on – NOW!" He saw the comrades run to the centre of the ship. He looked back again. The black shape was now much closer, moving towards them very quickly.

Suddenly a strong gust of wind came at them from nowhere. It filled the sails and the ship started to move through the water. The black shape was causing the wind to blow from behind them. The bows of the ship lifted up and then crashed down into the sea. Captain Hawkins looked again, focusing his eyes on the large black shape. It was almost upon them. The ship began to roll from side to side and the wind pushed the *Galêne* through the water.

Quickly the Captain looked down on the deck and saw everyone below rushing to hold onto something. He saw Braheim and Blake had taken hold of the tiller as the ship picked up speed. The sail was so stretched it was in danger of being ripped to pieces.

*The wind will blow us to shreds* he thought. *What is this?*

Then the Captain's eyes opened wide – as he saw what was coming.

"NO, I don't believe it!" he cried out to himself and then realised he didn't have time to climb down to the deck. Hastily he grabbed the mast and put both legs against the rail of the watch tower and braced himself. "I don't believe it," he said again.

He spoke without words, *Rumpitter – do you hear me?*

*Yes Captain, I do.*

*Have you seen what is coming our way?*

*Yes, I wondered when you would come up with something.*

*I didn't call him* the Captain replied.

There was no answer from Rumpitter.

*Rumpitter, do you hear me? It was you, was it not? You called him.*

There was still no answer.

*Rumpitter?*

Captain Hawkins looked up to see the huge dark shape flying over the ship. It completely shadowed them from the sun. There was a deathly loud shriek. The ship rolled violently to one side as a massive wave caught them full in the beam. Everyone held their ears from the painful noise and then dropped to the deck as the ship crashed into another wave. The mast creaked under the strain. The sail started to stretch with the pressure. Ropes were straining towards breaking point. The ship hammered into the waves. They had no control of the *Galênê*. At any minute she would roll right over.

Everyone gasped when they saw the giant eagle, Kharamun, soar over the ship. It caused another whirl of wind and suddenly the ship was surfing on the top of a wave at a terrifying speed. Everyone held onto whatever they could. Tom was lashed to the rail with a rope and Rumpitter held onto the rope with his front legs as his back legs and tail stretched backwards through the air. "Oh no, perhaps this wasn't such a good idea!" he shouted.

"Rumpitter! What have you done?" demanded Captain Hawkins.

The Captain twisted round on the lookout platform to see where the eagle now was.

"Oh no!" he shouted. The giant bird circled round and turned back towards the ship.

Captain Hawkins thought hard. He gritted his teeth and turned to face the giant Kharamun as he turned in the sky and began to descend. "No – he'll rip us to pieces. Kharamun!" he screamed, "No – not like this!" Suddenly the Captain began to shake. His eyes turned golden. They became seagull eyes, glaring at the approaching eagle, flashing a beam of golden light. The giant bird was within a few feet of the mast top when it suddenly lifted into the air and rose high up over the ship.

The comrades looked up in horror as the huge dark shadow soared above them. The eagle could destroy the ship in one strike. But somehow, suddenly, it changed course and turned away.

They looked up to the mast top. The Captain was no longer there.

Joseph called up to the lookout, "Captain?" There was no answer.

"Where is he?" Tom called, straining his eyes against the sun to find the Captain.

Everyone looked up into the sky to see Kharamun circling high above them. His huge shape was like a giant black cloud in the sky.

Then they saw the strangest thing. Flying around the head of the enormous eagle was a small white bird. It was circling and then darting up and down.

Rumpitter stared up into the sky. *Yes, I knew he could do it!* he said to himself with a wry smile.

The *Galênê* rolled to one side and then righted itself. The comrades rolled, head over heels, across the deck, scrambling to hold onto anything they could.

"What in the Lord's name is happening?" shouted Joseph as he slid across the deck and thumped into the mast.

Tom looked up into the sky. He saw the giant eagle and the small white bird, circling above.

"Rumpitter, is that who I think it is?"

"Yes it is Tom. The Captain has found himself again."

"What? That's Captain Hawkins?"

The ship began to steady itself, as the sea calmed down and the wind dropped. Tom ran to the stern of the ship and stared into the sky.

"How – how did he do that? He, he's a seagull again?"

"It was just a matter of time, Tom. He needed something to happen to find his powers. He needed a little coaxing."

"I don't understand – how?" Tom was confused.

"He nearly did it last night, but made a bit of a mess of it. So I decided to lend a hand. I must admit, I didn't expect things to go quite so mad," Rumpitter replied.

Tom turned around to see the comrades all staring at him with mouths wide open.

Joseph ran up onto the helm deck. He shook his head in disbelief. "Tell me this is not happening, Tom," he said, still staring up at the eagle circling in the sky. All the comrades ran to join them.

Tom was also in shock and shook his head in disbelief. He didn't know what to say, but then he heard a familiar voice. *Tom, do not be afraid. I have found the power again. I am able to transform from myself to a seagull. Everything has come back to me. Kharamun can help us. Tell everyone to make themselves secure. We are going for a ride!* Captain Hawkins's voice was a welcome sound to Tom's ears, but he was still in shock. "I don't understand," he said out loud.

*I can explain Tom, but we must do this. Tell the comrades now and let us get the Galênê moving. I will tell Kharamun to keep behind this time. He gets a little excited sometimes. I need to keep him well behind the ship so he doesn't cause any more damage. He will give us the wind we need to make it to The Glaros on time.*

Tom stood still for a moment in disbelief, staring up at the eagle and the seagull. *Amazing!* he said to himself, and then turned to face the comrades. "Quick, we have to secure everything down. Find something to hold onto. I think it's going to get a little hairy!"

Braheim grabbed Tom by the arm. "What are you saying Tom, what is happening?"

Trouseau asked, "Is that...?" Tom cut in, "Yes, Trouseau, that's Captain Hawkins, but don't worry, he'll come back." Tom turned around to look for Rumpitter.

The comrades were stunned and in shock. "This cannot be," said Blake, totally confused.

Maris put his face in his hands and stared into the sky. "I do not understand, how can he be?"

"We must do what Tom says. There will be time for questions later. I think I understand what is happening now," said Joseph and then he looked at Tom. "You are the voice between the Captain and us. Tell us what to do, lad."

"Mr Hawkins wants you to prepare for the ride of your life. Kharamun is going to make this ship sail faster than you ever thought possible. That's what's happening and we had better find somewhere safe to be when it gets going." Tom started searching for Rumpitter and for something to hold onto.

"Rumpitter, where are you?" he called, running all the way up to the bows of the ship calling for the rat.

He heard the voice again. *Tom, there is no time now. I am sure Rumpitter is safely hidden somewhere.* Then they both heard another voice. *I am down below in the cabin, don't worry about me, I am fine. I just don't like being up there when things start to happen.*

Tom giggled when he heard Rumpitter's voice, but he was actually very excited about what was to come.

Captain Hawkins spoke: *All right now Tom, I cannot hold Kharamun back any longer. He is getting quite impatient. Tie yourself to something and hold on tight. We don't want to lose you now.*

Tom quickly found a rope that was tied to the wooden hand-rail in front of the mast. Then he tied the other end around his waist. He looked back to see that all the comrades were also tied down.

Joseph held up his hand to signal that they were ready.

Tom saw the seagull hovering above him and he waved. The seagull did a quick swoop over the ship and along the deck. He could see everyone was secure.

*Here we go, Tom – hold on!* he said and in no time at all there was a huge gust of wind from behind the ship. Tom stretched his head round to see what was happening and then saw the giant eagle lift his enormous wings in the air and then fan them downwards. This was followed by another gust of wind and then a wave built up from beneath the sea. It was at least thirty feet high and started rolling towards the *Galênê*.

"Oh my God!" Tom shouted. The huge wave rolled towards them and the wind grew stronger and stronger.

Kharamun lifted up again and then came down with an almighty whoosh. The wave caught the stern of the ship and the wind blew straight into the sail. Suddenly the *Galênê* thrust forward at such a speed that the comrades were all thrown backwards. They hung on for their lives as the wave rolled under the ship. Then they were surfing at an incredible speed. The bows lifted right out of the sea and the mast bent forwards with the strength of the wind.

The ship flew through the air with its keel barely touching the water. Everything shook and parts of the rigging flew into the air. Ropes came loose and disappeared overboard. Two wooden barrels that had not been tied down rolled along the deck, right past the comrades, and bounced into the air and then flew over the sides. One of the barrels almost knocked Mababe out. He ducked just in time as it disappeared into the sea.

The *Galênê* flew forward like a rocket. Tom was unable to move. He was completely pinned down. All he could see was the sea and white foam from the top of the wave rushing past him at an amazing speed.

Then another wave rolled into them and again the ship ploughed forward. The vessel was shaking so much Tom thought it would break into pieces at any minute. Suddenly there was a loud bang and the sail ripped straight down the middle. It blew right up into the air and disappeared. But the ship continued surfing on the huge wave.

On and on they smashed through the sea. Parts of the ship, ripped from their fixings, started to fall away.

Tom wanted to shout out but he couldn't open his mouth. The force of the wind was so strong, he couldn't even think. He shut his eyes as they were filling with moisture. Then he heard a faint sound. *Not long now, Tom. We are almost there.* The voice sounded amazingly cheerful.

*I hope so, Mr Hawkins, or this ship is going to fall to bits* he replied without words.

Tom tried to see where they were going, but the water in his eyes began to sting. He couldn't move his hand to wipe them.

The frantic movement seemed to last for ages, until finally the bows dipped and the keel began to sit back in the water.

The explosion of white foam bursting across the waves gradually dispersed and Tom could see blue water again. It was moving past them but not nearly at the speed it had been. Now he was able to move his hand and wipe the water from his eyes He was soaked to the skin from the spray. He smiled when he saw that all the comrades were safe, although they looked somewhat bedraggled.

"That was fantastic!" Tom exclaimed.

*Pleased you enjoyed the ride, Tom. Look, there is the island ahead of us.*

Tom looked up to see Captain Hawkins flying above the ship.

Then he saw, high up in the sky, the dark shape of Kharamun gliding through the clear blue sky with his enormous wings outstretched.

*Wow – he's fabulous* Tom said to himself.

Tom untied the rope and staggered to find his feet. The ship was still moving along at quite a speed, but the wind had died away and the sea was calm again.

The comrades picked themselves up and started lashing down ropes and rigging that had come adrift from their fixings.

Mr Hawkins swooped down from the sky and landed on the deck by the helm. Braheim and Blake were exhausted from steering the ship and flopped down on the deck.

Mababe and Joseph took over the helm. Everyone was shaken.

"That was quite some ride. I think it will be a week before I find my legs," said Trouseau as he sat down and leant against the rail, wiping his brow.

Tom arrived to join them. "Is everyone all right?" he asked.

"Aye, lad. We are fine. You are soaked through – look at you." Joseph smiled and then said, "Well the Captain has done it again. Look ahead, there is the bay and I can see *The Glaros.*

Tom jumped up onto a seat to get a better look. "We made it!" he said.

"Yes Tom, we certainly did," Came a soft voice from behind. Tom turned around and there standing before him was Captain Hawkins. "Captain!" Tom called. "You're back!"

Everyone turned around and saw their captain had returned as a man again.

They were stunned and speechless.

"Well, men. It seems I have found the answer to fast sailing." the Captain said in a hearty voice.

Tom stood in awe. Then Joseph smiled. "It seems we shall just have to get used to this new captain. Half man, half seagull? I cannot pretend that we understand, Captain, but, at least we have you back with us and you look well enough to me." Joseph pointed to the island ahead and changed the subject. "Course to the island, Captain?"

"Yes please, Joseph. We should be able to drift right into the bay. Steer straight ahead and prepare the anchor. We will drop it in the middle of the bay. Take the small gap to starboard of the reef. It is just wide enough for us to pass through."

"Aye aye, Captain," said Joseph, still smiling. He nodded to Mababe. "May as well get this ship back in order then. We will have to repair the sails and the rig. Get the anchor ready, lads."

The comrades decided Joseph was right. There was no point in any more questions. The Captain had indeed become an unusual man, with the strangest magic. But that, they agreed, was how it was. They all nodded and went about preparing the *Galênê* to anchor in the bay.

Tom walked over to Captain Hawkins. "How did you know you could do this? Do you feel anything like, well, does it hurt when you...?"

Captain Hawkins looked down at Tom and winked. "You mean when I change from me to a bird? Well, you can thank Rumpitter for it," he said with a smile. "No, it doesn't hurt and I found it quite easy – eventually. I know it is a strange thing. I do, however, feel much easier about getting you home now."

"That was an amazing ride. I thought we were going to take off," Tom said, looking back at the ship. "At least it's still afloat."

"Yes, Kharamun can get a little carried away sometimes, but he was very useful wasn't he?" the Captain replied, looking up in the sky. The giant eagle made a wide turn and soared higher in the air and glided away into the distance.

Soon they approached the narrow gap of the beautiful lagoon. The *Galênê* slipped past the reef and floated gently right into the middle of the bay. Tom rushed across the deck to see this wonderful place he remembered from when they had first arrived. Up in the sky, the Navigator stars flickered like small candle lights.

"It's amazing!" Tom said with a bright smile.

He felt something tap his leg and looked down. Rumpitter was looking quite queasy and a little wobbly on his legs.

"Are you all right, Rumpitter? Look, we are in Heaven's Bay, where we first arrived. It's amazing," Tom said again. Rumpitter jumped up onto the rail. He was still very unstable and nearly fell right over, but Tom caught him. "I really don't like boats," said Rumpitter, shaking his head. Tom laughed and then replied, "You may have a bit of explaining to do." Tom indicated with his thumb towards the Captain. "He knows you called Kharamun. You know he nearly destroyed the whole ship?"

"Mmm, yes, I know. I forgot how excited he gets. But it worked Tom. Last night the Captain tried to make the change. Then he tried to fly – nearly finished himself. Had it not been for me and..." Rumpitter was interrupted. "Aha, there you are," said the Captain, as he walked over to join them at the rail.

"Well, Rumpitter. What shall I say to you?" said the Captain, looking down at the rat.

Rumpitter looked up in a nonchalant way and replied, "Well, how about – thank-you?"

The Captain laughed and patted Rumpitter on the head. "You are a good friend, Rumpitter, and yes, I do thank you for your much needed assistance, last evening. I am not sure I would be feeling so confident today about getting Tom home, without that little push, eh?"

"Well, I am glad you appreciate it. Kharamun is not an easy chap to get hold of. He's quite unpredictable at times."

"You can say that again."

"He's quite unpredict..."

"Yes, all right Rumpitter – very good." The Captain smiled. Tom giggled. It was indeed a happy day after all.

They heard a loud splash and the rope of the heavy anchor rolling through the runners on the bow. "Ah, they have the anchor down. Excellent!" said the Captain and walked off to see the comrades.

"Lower the long-boat," shouted Joseph, and Maris and Braheim swung the pulleys and ropes which held the long-boat over the side of the *Galênê*.

Trouseau climbed into the boat and they lowered him into the water. The aqua blue of the lagoon was as clear as glass and Tom could see hundreds of coloured fish swimming under the boat. He could even see the white sandy bottom. It was the most beautiful bay he had ever seen. Something inside him told him he just had to do it. He took off his tunic, head-dress and shoes, climbed up onto the rail and dived over the side.

As he hit the surface, Tom felt the cool freshness of the water pouring over his hot body. It was a wonderful feeling. He felt the burning heat from the sun sizzling from his skin.

He rolled around and came face to face with a shoal of inquisitive fish circling around him. He couldn't believe his eyes at the sight of so many different types of fish. The colours and shapes were fantastic. His head reared out from the surface and he swung his hair around, shaking away the salty water. He had a wide grin on his face and then laughed when he saw all the comrades looking down at him from the ship.

Captain Hawkins called out, "How does that feel, Tom?"

"It's fantastic!" Tom called back, "Why don't you come in?"

Suddenly there was a big splash and Joseph hit the water like a huge rock. He popped out of the water like an arrow. "Oh yes!" he called and then splashed Tom, who splashed Joseph back. The two laughed at each other.

"He is a true boy, that one, look how he laughs with Joseph," said Mababe.

Braheim said, "Captain, do you mind if I...?"

"Be my guest," replied Captain Hawkins. Braheim did not waste a moment. He stripped off his robes and plunged into the cool water. Then, without any hesitation, Maris, Blake, Gordon and Sam Little leapt over the side too.

Captain Hawkins laughed when he saw them all splashing each other and laughing. It was indeed a happy sight. Trouseau rowed back after making sure the anchor was holding well. He tied the long-boat to the ship and then stripped off his clothes and did a back flip into the water.

Joseph laughed when he saw Trouseau appear from the surface. "Always the showman, Trouseau," he laughed.

"Tom, catch this," called Captain Hawkins and he threw a ball made of rope into the air and the comrades all swam to catch it.

Mababe was the first to reach the ball. He threw it up into the air and Tom caught it.

"To me, Tom," shouted Blake and then Braheim called out, "No, to me, Tom." Tom threw it up and everyone splashed through the water to grab it. In no time at all, the comrades were having a great game in the water and the Captain leant over the rails watching them with a big smile.

"I do think, sometimes, humans are quite mad," said Rumpitter, as he trotted along the rail to join the Captain.

"Yes, Rumpitter, we most certainly are," the Captain replied and stroked Rumpitter across his head.

"It is good to see Tom laughing and enjoying himself. This is his last day here – tomorrow we leave," said Captain Hawkins. He looked down at Rumpitter and then said, "Is everything ready?"

Rumpitter looked back at Captain Hawkins and said, "We are as ready as we will ever be."

"Very well," replied the Captain and then he said, "I never thanked you properly for all you have done. I could not have achieved any of this without you – I owe you much, my little friend." He stroked Rumpitter and smiled.

Rumpitter replied, "You are most welcome Captain. But we are not there yet."

The Captain pursed his lips and nodded. Then he turned back to watch the comrades enjoying a hearty game with the rope ball. After all they had been through, they deserved this moment of fun.

He walked to the prow of the ship and looked over at *The Glaros*. He could see that all was well. The golden figurehead of the seagull gleamed in the sunlight. Her masts were well rigged and she looked ready to sail. He turned his head to the sky and saw the navigator stars. It never ceased to amaze him how they shone in the day and also at night. He studied them for a while and considered how he would use them to find the crossing point where the crescent moon would be waiting to send them back into another world.

He took in a deep breath and then gave a little sigh. He knew that tomorrow was going to be the final test. Even though he could feel his magical powers had returned to him and that he was miraculously able to change himself from man to a seagull, would these miracles work well enough for him to transport Tom back to his people? And if they did get there, would he be able to return himself back to Kadistaar, to Princess Tasia.

He turned around and saw Rumpitter staring at him with his bright brown eyes.

*One more time, Captain, just to convince yourself* Rumpitter said without words.

Captain Hawkins gazed into Rumpitter's eyes and then nodded.

Suddenly there was a flash of gold light and, in the blink of an eye. a seagull was perched on the bow of the ship.

The seagull twisted his neck and blinked. "It is definitely getting easier, Rumpitter," said the seagull. Then he lifted up and into the air. Rumpitter looked up at the seagull gliding high above the mast. Then he watched him turn and fly towards *The Glaros.*

Rumpitter hopped across the deck, jumped up onto the rail and looked across the bay. He studied the comrades splashing around in the water, shouting and laughing, throwing the rope ball to each other. None of them had noticed the seagull aboard *The Glaros.*

Later that day, after their swim, the comrades washed with fresh water from the water barrels and changed their clothes. Braheim and Maris went to the galley to prepare a hearty meal.

"Tonight, my brothers, we shall dine beneath the stars for Tom's farewell," Braheim announced and everyone cheered.

Tom went into the Captain's cabin and found the bag that Tasia had given him. He pulled out his own clothes and looked at them. He realised he would need to wear these to return to his father and friends on board *The Eagle.* The Arab clothes would look most odd in Rivermouth. He giggled at the thought of what people would say if they saw him walking along in the Arab tunic, head-dress and scarf.

As he took the clothes out, something fell out of the bag. He looked down on the floor and saw the small crescent moon that Christos, the monk, had given him. But now it was connected to a thin gold chain. He studied it carefully. It was a simple gold moon just two inches long, but then he noticed some tiny markings had been engraved along one edge. He looked closer and ran a finger over the engravings. They looked like Arabic symbols, or perhaps ancient Greek, but he wasn't certain. He would ask Captain Hawkins.

He pulled the chain around his neck and clipped the hook. The small golden crescent moon hung nicely on him. "Thank-you Tasia," he whispered to himself.

He pulled on his trousers and shirt, slipped on his shoes and went up on deck.

That night, the comrades enjoyed a sumptuous meal. Food was laid out on a long table on the deck. It was a warm evening and the stars sparkled like diamonds, lighting the sky like the lights on a Christmas tree.

"Ah, Tom – welcome. Come and join us," Joseph said and pulled out a wooden seat for Tom to sit. They all noticed Tom was wearing his own clothes and, although they tried to act cheerfully, they all felt a great sadness inside. This was the last supper together. Tomorrow the boy would leave them.

Tom sensed the sad feeling amongst the comrades and it made him feel the same way. Everyone sat down. Braheim and Maris started serving plates around the table and Gordon poured the wine.

Tom looked at the empty seat at the end of the table. "Where's Captain Hawkins?" he asked.

"I am sure he will be here soon, Tom," said Joseph and no sooner had he said it, the Captain arrived. He had returned as a man and Rumpitter was sitting on his shoulder.

"Good evening gentlemen!" said Captain Hawkins in a cheerful tone. "My, this looks like a feast for a king!" he said, pulling the seat out and sitting down. "My compliments to Braheim and Maris for this most excellent table of food." The Captain raised his glass. "A toast!" he said.

Everyone raised their glasses and waited for the Captain to speak.

"To us and all those we care for," Captain Hawkins called. Everyone repeated the toast.

Captain Hawkins looked round the table at the comrades. "It has been an eventful time together, these past days." Everyone nodded, including Rumpitter, still sitting on the Captain's shoulder.

"I know how strange and difficult it has been for you. So many unexplainable things have happened. For myself – I have now to try to understand what has become of me and try to live in a way that no one would ever conceive. For you – all I can say is that without your friendship, your loyalty and courage, not only would I have not survived but Kadistaar would have been lost. But to see tyranny and terror stamped out by those who see the truth and have love in their hearts is a wonderful thing. I pray the world shall never have to face such evil again." Everyone nodded and murmured in agreement.

"I thank you for believing in me and for accepting things as they have become." He took a sip from his glass and continued, "What a journey we have had. Indeed it has been quite an adventure, eh Tom?" He looked at Tom with a big smile.

"Yes – it most certainly was!" Tom replied. Everyone nodded and chuckled. Joseph was sitting next to Tom and patted him on the back. "Couldn't have done it without the boy, Captain," said Joseph.

Captain Hawkins nodded to Tom, "I was just coming to that," he said and again raised his glass.

"Gentlemen – I wish to make a toast to our new comrade – to Tom Parker, a true warrior and adventurer and a true friend." Everyone cheered heartily at the toast. "To Tom!" they all cheered.

Tom smiled at everyone and thanked them. Then his eyes began to well up and his lips tightened together. He tried very hard not to cry. He heard Rumpitter speak without words.

*Chin up, Tom – this could just be the beginning.*

Tom looked at Rumpitter questioningly and then turned to everyone around the table.

"I, um – I would just like to say thank you for everything, for..." Suddenly he was stuck for words. He held back his emotions and shook his head. "I'm sorry, I don't have the words to say what I wanted to say."

The Captain saw how difficult this was for the boy and jumped in. "It is all right, Tom – none of us have words to describe how we really feel tonight." He rubbed his hand across Tom's golden hair. "It is all right, lad – we understand." Then he quickly turned to Trouseau.

"Trouseau, why don't you tell us one of your adventures?" Everyone agreed and cheered for Trouseau to speak.

"It would be my pleasure," Trouseau said with a wide smile. He cleared his throat and then began.

"Let me think – ah oui – I have it," he said and winked at Tom, who returned a wide smile.

"Some time ago, I was invited to the palace of the King of France..." He was about to continue when the comrades all laughed and cheered. "I think this is going to be a good tale, Trouseau," said Captain Hawkins. He raised his glass at the Frenchman. Whether his stories were true or made up, no one ever really knew. Trouseau always had a way of telling his tales so that they just had to be believed. But the comrades loved his stories just the same.

Trouseau continued. He told a fantastic story in the most dramatic way, occasionally standing up on his seat and walking around the table. There were many jokes and anecdotes.

Trouseau, the entertainer, was in his element!

Eventually the story ended and everyone cheered and raised their glasses to the little man with the big heart. It was a happy end to the evening.

The comrades ate and drank and laughed and sang all through the night.

Tom could take no more and finally fell asleep at the table. Captain Hawkins lifted him up and took him below to the cabin. Rumpitter agreed to stay with him. The Captain quietly walked back on deck to join the comrades.

The next morning came quickly. The comrades were waiting by the ladder to the long-boat.

There was an air of sadness as Tom walked with Captain Hawkins to join them.

One by one, and with heavy hearts, the comrades shook Tom's hand, each of them nodding, but saying nothing. There no words to say. They all knew how they felt about Tom's departure.

Captain Hawkins threw over the rope ladder and gestured for Tom to climb down.

Tom climbed over the rail and, just before going down, he looked back at the comrades.

"I shall never forget you," he said in a soft voice. He lowered himself down the ladder and into the longboat.

Captain Hawkins said farewell to the comrades and joined Tom in the boat. Rumpitter jumped up onto the Captain's shoulder just as he was climbing over the rail.

Joseph was already waiting in the long-boat. He cast the rope back to Blake, set the oars and began to row towards *The Glaros*.

The boat looked magnificent as she rested on her anchor. The golden figurehead of a large sea bird with its wings stretched back along the hull, sparkled in the sunlight. Along the top rail of the hull were the twelve shields, six on each side, and all in different colours. Each had a gold crescent moon painted in the centre. Tom noticed how the two masts had been converted with their triangular sail rig and looked with interest at the angled booms that would hoist the large sails. *The Glaros*, unlike other ships of Kadistaar, had a large wheel for the helm. She was the most unusual looking ship, but nevertheless was beautifully rigged and prepared.

As Joseph rowed them closer to *The Glaros*, Tom looked back and watched the comrades for the last time. Each of them stood in silence along the sides of the *Galênê*.

Trouseau ran forward to the bow and was standing on the wooden bowsprit. He saw Gordon climb the rope ladder to the top of the mast. The comrades stood in silence and watched them rowing away.

Finally they reached *The Glaros*. "Up you get, Tom," said the Captain quietly. Then he turned to Joseph. "Thank-you, my friend," he said simply. The two shook hands and the Captain climbed up to join Tom.

Joseph rowed out a short way from *The Glaros* and then stopped. He just sat in the boat and looked back at the ship.

Captain Hawkins walked to the bow and cast away the rope connected to the anchor. Tom looked over the rail to see the rope sliding away and finally splash into the water.

"Come up here, Tom, and watch what happens," called Captain Hawkins. Tom ran back to the helm and stood next to the Captain.

Captain Hawkins looked down at Tom and smiled. "Are you ready, Tom?" he asked.

"Yes – I think so," Tom replied.

"Good, then prepare for the ride of your life."

Rumpitter hopped onto the thick wooden rail in front and grabbed onto a rope.

"If I were you, Tom, I would hold onto something," he said. So Tom took hold of the rail and looked up at the Captain. "I'm ready now," he said with anticipation.

Captain Hawkins held up his arms and pointed to the sails. Suddenly they dropped and immediately billowed out as if they were filled with wind and then *The Glaros* began to move slowly through the water.

Tom couldn't understand how they were moving when he couldn't feel any wind. It was as if the sails were being filled by some magical power of their own.

"How can they do that?" Tom said, looking up at the sails.

"It's magical, isn't it Tom?" replied the Captain.

"It certainly is!" Tom said.

Gradually *The Glaros* began to move faster. As they sailed parallel to the *Galênê*, Rumpitter said, "Look there, Tom."

Tom looked across. All in the same motion, the comrades raised their right arms up towards the sky. Then he saw the Captain return the gesture.

"They are saluting us Tom," said Rumpitter.

Tom ran over to the rail and held up his right hand. "Goodbye!" he shouted.

*The Glaros* picked up speed and headed out of the beautiful bay and into the ocean, beyond the reef. Tom stood at the stern to watch the comrades until they finally faded into the distance and then disappeared from sight. He sighed and returned to stand next to Captain Hawkins at the wheel. He looked up at the Captain, who just stared ahead.

"Are you all right?" Tom asked and put his hand on Captain Hawkins's arm. The Captain looked down at Tom and smiled, "Aye, lad, I am fine. Thank-you."

Tom put his hand inside his shirt and pulled out the small golden crescent moon. He studied it and then asked, "Do you know what these markings are, here?" He pointed at the engraved signs on the moon.

"Yes I do, Tom."

"Well, what do they mean?"

"It is not what they mean, Tom, it is what it says."

Tom looked curious and inquisitive.

"It says, *HE WHO SEES THE TRUTH SHALL SEE HIS DESTINY AND THE WORLDS SHALL UNITE*. It is written in ancient Greek. You must never lose it, Tom. You must keep it for ever. One day you will know why."

Tom was puzzled, but, as he had realised many times before, there was so much about Captain Hawkins and the things he said, that Tom often found it better to think first before asking further.

"Do you think that monk, Christos, knows our destiny?"

"Yes, Tom. I most definitely do."

Tom thought a little and then said, "Wow!"

Rumpitter looked at the two and, just for a moment, Tom thought he was smiling.

Tom decided to change the subject. "How long until we get to – well, you know?"

Captain Hawkins put his arm around Tom's shoulder. "Not long, lad, not long."

*The Glaros* sailed past the reef and into the sea. Tom looked up and saw the stars. No one would ever believe him if he told them he had seen stars in the daytime.

"Are they the navigator stars? he asked, stretching his neck up at the sky.

"Yes they are – without them, we would never find the crossing point of the two moons. Watch them carefully Tom, soon you will see something most unusual."

"Two moons?"

"Yes, the stars will line up and we shall follow their course. *The Glaros* will take over and we need do no more. At the end of the line of navigator stars are the two moons –the one from this world and the one from yours. When they are in line, we dive."

"Dive?"

Rumpitter joined in the conversation. "Yes, Tom, we dive and that is the bit I hate!"

Captain Hawkins said, "Tom, surely you recall when you first came here on *The Glaros?*"

"Well, yes – it all seems so long ago." Then he thought about it. "Yes, I remember we were tied to the mast and we went through a storm and crashed down from the sky."

"Exactly Tom. As I said, I hate that bit," Rumpitter remarked and shook his head.

Tom looked up at Captain Hawkins again. "Is it safe – will it work?"

Still with his arm around Tom, Captain Hawkins hugged him a little tighter and said, "Let us hope so Tom. It worked before, so it should work again.".

Tom was uneasy about this and felt, for the first time in ages that this was all very odd and that he would wake up and realise it was all a dream.

He saw Rumpitter staring at him and said, "It isn't, is it?"

*No Tom, it is no dream. It is all very real* Rumpitter said without words.

Suddenly Captain Hawkins took his arms away from Tom and pointed up at the stars.

"Indeed, this is no dream, Look up there."

Up in the sky, the strangest thing began to unfold before their eyes. The navigator stars began to move. They were forming a long line of stars, one in front of the other. Far away in the distance they saw a black dot. "The stars are pointing the way Tom. We are almost there. Get ready!"

Tom began to feel a little scared and stared up at the strange stars, which were moving quickly. They flashed like comets through the sky and each one of them burst into a bright golden light as it fell in line with the one in front. "Wow, they're amazing!" Tom said with his eyes wide open.

He looked at Captain Hawkins. "Is this it?" he asked and then gasped when the Captain looked back at him. His eyes had turned gold. "Oh my God!" Tom exclaimed. "This is it, isn't it?"

Without words Captain Hawkins said, *Hold on both of you – we are about to take off.*

No sooner had he said it, *The Glaros* began to shake and suddenly there was a loud crash from the sea underneath them and the ship lifted and then crashed back down.

Tom braced himself and grabbed onto the rope handle. Captain Hawkins let go of the wheel and held up his arms. "What are you doing?"

Tom shouted. "Don't let go, you'll fall!" The wind began to whistle around them and *The Glaros* picked up more speed.

Rumpitter gritted his teeth and held on as tight as he could. "Ooooh, here we go again," he said.

Tom held on tightly but kept his eyes on Captain Hawkins. Suddenly there was another crash and a huge gust of wind. The sails blew out with a bang. The ship began to creek and then lifted right out of the water. They ascended upwards towards the navigator stars.

*Hold on, Tom. Whatever you do DON'T LET GO! The Glaros will take over now. Just HOLD ON!* Captain Hawkins said without words. There was a bright flash of gold light and he vanished. "MR HAWKINS!" Tom called.

He looked around but the Captain had gone. "Where are you?" he called again. *The Glaros* continued rising up into the sky. They were now a hundred feet up in the air.

"Don't worry, Tom, just keep holding on," Rumpitter said.

"I'm not letting go, Rumpitter. Where's Captain Hawkins?"

A voice came from somewhere: *It is all right, Tom, I am with you. Just do as Rumpitter says.*

*The Glaros* roared upwards and upwards at an incredible speed and the navigator stars grew bigger and bigger. The sky began to turn yellow and when Tom tried to look down over the ship's side, all he could see was a cloud of golden dust. There was no sea below them.

Way ahead, in the distance, a black dot grew larger. Then there was a bright flash from the centre of the black dot. *The Glaros* raced through the sky. The black dot was now a large dark spinning circle. Tom clung tightly to the rope. He stared ahead as they raced towards the centre of the black spinning circle.

Suddenly flashes of gold light burst around them. They were now amongst the navigator stars.

The noise of the wind roaring around them and the bursts of exploding stars was deafening.

Rumpitter shouted out, "There it is – he's done it!"

"What, Rumpitter – what is it?" Tom shouted back nervously.

"The crescent moon. He's found it!"

Tom stared ahead as they sped through the sky. Then he saw it. Right in the centre of the black circle in the sky was a large gold crescent moon. They were heading straight for it.

The golden figurehead on the bow of *The Glaros* was aiming directly towards the centre of the black shape and the crescent moon. *The Glaros* shook and rattled. Then lightning flashed from both sides and crashes of thunder roared out of the black circle. "Rumpitter, I'm scared," Tom shouted.

*Just hold on, Tom, it won't be long now* a voice said.

In seconds they were suddenly in total darkness. The stars had disappeared and it was pitch black. The golden crescent moon was directly in front of them.

*The Glaros* slowed down and levelled itself. Then, out of the blackness, a white shape flashed past them. It circled, turned and then came straight towards them.

Tom ducked as it flew over his head. Then – he saw it. The large seagull landed on the rail in front of Tom and Rumpitter.

"Mr Hawkins!" he exclaimed.

"Hello Tom, I'm back," said the seagull.

Tom's face lit up with delight. "Amazing!" was all Tom could say.

Captain Hawkins hopped onto the large wheel. "In a few moments we will be in line with the two moons. Now, you must listen carefully. The next part is the most dangerous. We will descend very quickly. All being well, we will head straight for the sea below. Then you will see *The Eagle* where your father and friends are. I hope they have not woken up."

"What will happen then," Tom asked and then said, "Why is it suddenly so dark? I can't see a thing."

"We are between two worlds. This is the crossing place. You might consider it as an empty space in the middle of a bridge."

Tom looked around. It was so black. There was nothing but darkness all around them. The golden crescent moon hung in the blackness but did not cast any glow.

"Now, listen to me, Tom. When *The Glaros* hits the sea, you must be ready to jump off at exactly the time I tell you. You cannot fail to jump when I say. Do you understand?"

"Yes, I do," Tom replied. Then he looked at Rumpitter. "What about you Rumpitter, how will you...?"

"I will do exactly the same as you Tom. I just hope the good Captain can get close enough to *The Eagle* for us to make the jump."

Tom looked at the seagull "Can you do this Mr Hawkins? It sounds very difficult."

"Err, well, I will just have to do my best. I did it before, when we picked you up. I see no reason why it cannot be done the other way round too."

*The Glaros* drifted gently through the blackness, gliding slowly towards the golden moon.

"Tom," said Mr Hawkins, "we can only do this once. There will be no time for long goodbyes. You must jump the very moment I tell you."

Tom looked at his friend. "It's all very strange, but I will do what you say. But – what will you do, where will you go?"

Mr Hawkins stretched his neck, gave it a little shake and then flapped his wings.

"I must stay with *The Glaros*, Tom. I cannot come with you," he said in a very sad tone.

Tom's eyes began to well up. "Will I see you again?"

"Tom, you will..." He was about to say something else when suddenly he stopped.

"Dear Lord, it is there already!" said Mr Hawkins excitedly and then hopped into the air.

Tom ran over to the rail and peered into the black abyss. "What's there, Mr Hawkins?" he called.

"Look down there, Tom. It is your moon. We are almost in line. You must get ready NOW!"

Instantly *The Glaros* lurched forward. The ship began to creak and moan again and suddenly a chilly wind came from nowhere. The golden figurehead bowed downwards.

"Get back here, Tom," Rumpitter shouted "And HOLD ON!"

"Yes Tom, this is it. Whatever you do, my dear friend, do not let go," said Mr Hawkins, who suddenly took off back into the air.

The bow of *The Glaros* bent lower and Tom almost fell out of the ship into the sky. He managed to grab the rope handle just in time before the ship thrust forward.

Then they saw the small moon below them. The golden crescent moon was now right above them. Tom looked back to see it begin to glow. He looked downwards as *The Glaros* fell though the sky and saw the other moon directly in line with them. They were heading straight for it.

"We'll crash!" Tom shouted. "We're heading straight for it."

A voice came to him. *It is not as it seems, Tom. Remember: He who sees the truth will see his destiny and the worlds shall unite.*

*The Glaros* was falling at an enormous speed through the sky. The darkness was becoming lighter and lighter by the second. The moon below them grew bigger and bigger. Tom was sure they would crash. He was scared and shut his eyes. "Rumpitter, I don't like this!" he shouted.

"That makes two of us. Just hold on!"

They fell down and down. Tom's legs were flying through the air behind him as he clung, with all his strength, to the rope handle. His knuckles went white, his hair raked back and the skin on his face was dented by the force of the air blowing through him.

Suddenly they were in the midst of a bright golden cloud. They continued falling downwards. Tom shut his eyes. The light was too bright. Then there was a loud bang and thunder boomed all around them. The wind whistled through Tom's ears and he screamed out. But his scream was drowned by the noise of the bangs and thunderous crashes around them.

Tom heard a voice. *Get ready Tom. Open your eyes and be ready.* It was Mr Hawkins. Tom opened his eyes and saw the sea moving towards them at an incredible speed. He looked around but couldn't see Mr Hawkins anywhere. He saw Rumpitter holding on with all his might. Rumpitter was still screaming. Then Tom yelled out, "It's there! I can see them. It's *The Eagle.*"

"Ya-hoooo," Tom cried out. "We're heading right for it. It's amazing!" he shouted with great excitement.

Rumpitter opened his eyes and saw *The Eagle* coming closer and closer. "Oh no. We're too close; we're going to crash into her. Captain!"

There was no answer "Captain!" Rumpitter called again.

*The Glaros* was falling out of the sky like a meteor. *The Eagle* was directly below. Tom could now see the crew on deck. They seemed to be lying down. He frowned as he tried to find his father. They were falling so fast he couldn't see. Suddenly there was a huge crash and the sea was all over them. Then they were under the sea and then they were blasted up into the air and *The Glaros* was flying across the surface of the water. Tom heard a voice, *Now Tom, NOW. GO NOW!* It was Mr Hawkins's voice but Tom couldn't see him anywhere. "Mr Hawkins, where are you?" Tom called as he ran to the rails.

"Come on Tom, come on – hurry, there is no time," Rumpitter called. Tom saw Rumpitter leap into the air as he raced to the side of *The Glaros*. They had come right alongside *The Eagle* but *The Glaros* was moving so fast. Tom tried to jump from the bow but he was too late. *RUN, TOM – JUMP!* Came a voice. Panic struck Tom as he charged along the deck. *The Eagle* was moving away so quickly. *The Glaros* was going to pass it before he could make the jump.

He climbed onto the rail and saw *The Eagle* slipping away. Its bows appeared before him.

*GO TOM, GO NOW!* Came the voice again. Tom leapt into the air with his arms outstretched.

*The Glaros* flew past and a huge wave crashed into the bows of *The Eagle*. The ship rose up on the wave and crashed back down into the sea. Tom was hanging onto the bowsprit right on the end of *The Eagle's* prow. He swung his leg over the wooden pole of the bowsprit and turned just in time to see *The Glaros* plunge down into the sea, right in front of *The Eagle*. A huge wave smashed over the bows. It threw Tom into the air and he crashed onto the deck and rolled over on his back. All he saw was the sky moving up and down.

He rolled onto his front and saw the tail of a rat slip by.

"What in God's name was that?" someone said.

Tom looked up. There was a blurred figure standing in front of him. Tom rubbed the salt from his eyes and then he screamed out, "Jacob!"

"Good Lord, lad – what happened to you?" Jacob pulled Tom up onto his feet. Then he looked forward. "Where in God's name did that wave come from?"

"Tom!" a familiar voice called. Tom turned around. "Dad!" he shouted and ran straight towards his father and threw his arms around him. "Tom, are you all right? You're soaked to the skin?"

Suddenly all the crew of *The Eagle* were running along the deck.

Bernard was rubbing his sore head. The crew were shaking their heads. "What happened?" they were all asking each other. "It was a freak wave," Matt Flynn said. Jacob Morgan rubbed his head. "Something hit me. It feels like I was knocked out or something." Tom looked at all the crew and smiled. He was back.

Jack Parker stopped and turned. He looked around *The Eagle*. His mouth hung wide open.

"What on earth...?" he said with a bewildered look. Everyone stopped chatting and looked around. They were surrounded in a golden mist. The sea was suddenly dead calm.

"What is this? Where the hell did this fog come from?" Jacob said and walked back along the deck. "We are completely becalmed." He held out his hand to feel the damp mist, but it was strange. There was no dampness. In fact the air was particularly dry. "What is this?" he said again.

Jack Parker looked down at Tom. "How did you get so wet Tom?" he asked.

Tom shook his clothes. At first he couldn't think of an answer. "I- er, well, I was standing at the bow when the wave came over the top. It got me full on," Tom replied.

Jack scratched his head, "That's odd, I could swear you were standing with me at the helm."

"Oh – I was, but then – when the wave came, I ran forward." Tom knew it was not true but what else could he say?

Jack Parker didn't consider the matter further, but shook his head. He couldn't remember.

Was the wave so big it knocked them all over? What happened? Where did it come from?

Tom bit his lip and hoped his answer had done the trick. It was all a whirl and his head began to spin. He looked all around and all he could see was the gold mist drifting lifelessly in the air around them.

Jacob called out to his crew. "Better get the sails down, lads. I'll fire her up."

Henry Higgins and Flynn called out instructions to get the sails in and the rig tied down.

Tom saw his father and smiled. *Thank-you, Mr Hawkins, for keeping him safe* he said to himself.